007

"CASINO ROYALE"
"CASINO ROYALE"
Chapter Headings
Chapter 1 : The Secret Agent
Chapter 2 : Dossier for M.
Chapter 3 : Number 007
Chapter 8 : Pink Lights and Champagne
Chapter 9 : The Game is Baccarat
Chapter 10 : The High Table
Chapter 11 : Moment of Truth
Chapter 14 : "La Vie en Rose?"
LIVE AND LET DIE
by Ian Fleming.
From CURTIS BROWN, Ltd.
6 HENRIETTA STREET, COVENT GARDEN,
LONDON
LIVE & LET DIE - typescript
THE MOONRAKER
By
IAN FLEMING
GOLDFINGER
by Ian Fleming
author of Casino Royale, Dr No, etc.
Goldfinger, the man who loved gold, said, "Mr Bond, it was a most evil day for you when you first crossed my path. If you had then found an oracle to consult, the oracle would have said to you "Mr Bond, keep away from Mr Auric Goldfinger. He is a most powerful man. If Mr Goldfinger wished to crush you, he would only have to turn over in his sleep to do so".
With the lazy precision of Fate, this, Ian Fleming's longest narrative of secret service adventure, brings James Bond to grips with the most powerful criminal the world has ever known - Goldfinger, the man who had planned the "Crime de la Crime".
Le Chiffre, Mr Big, Sir Hugo Drax, Jack Spang, Rosa Klebb, Doctor No - and now, the seventh adversary, a Goliath of crime - GOLDFINGER!
15s. net
March 23
DOCTOR NO
by
IAN FLEMING.
2 Vols
THE ROUGH
WITH THE SMOOTH.
Five secret exploits
of
James Bond
by
IAN FLEMING.
THE SPY
WHO
LOVED ME
by
IAN FLEMING
(With VIVIENNE MICHEL)
BOOKS
From JONATHAN CAPE LIMITED
THIRTY BEDFORD SQUARE LONDON WC1
DUPLICATE COPY
NOT TO BE USED FOR SETTING
WITH CARE
ON HER MAJESTY'S SECRET SERVICE
FILE No.
NAME
ADDRESS
DATE
G.W. Copy
THE MAN WITH THE GOLDEN GUN
by
IAN FLEMING

JAMES BOND

The Man and His World

The Official Companion to Ian Fleming's Creation

Henry Chancellor

John Murray

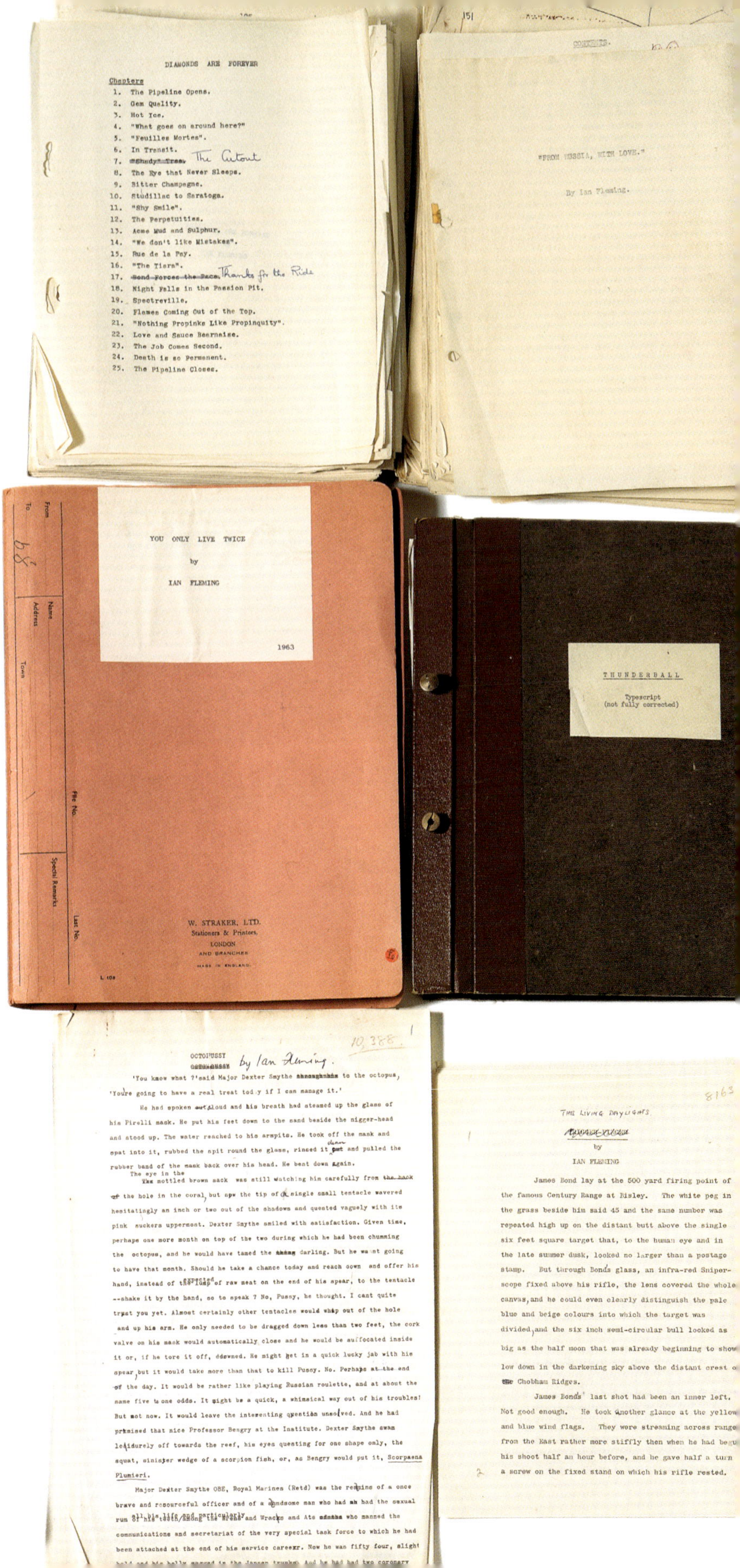

First published in Great Britain in 2005 by John Murray (Publishers)
A division of Hodder Headline

1

A CIP catalogue record for this title is available from the British Library

Hardback ISBN 0 7195 6815 3
Trade paperback ISBN 0 7195 6860 9

Book design by Craig Burgess
Original photography by Derek Askem
A full list of illustration credits and copyright holders is
given on pages 242–4

Printed and bound by L.E.G.O. SpA, Vicenza, Italy

Hodder Headline policy is to use papers that are natural, renewable and recyclable products and made from wood grown in sustainable forests. The logging and manufacturing processes are expected to conform to the environmental regulations of the country of origin.

John Murray (Publishers)
338 Euston Road
London NW1 3BH

CONTENTS

SIT DOWN, MISTER FLEMING

'Everything I write has a precedent in truth.'

One of the most surprising facts in the short life of Ian Fleming is that he created James Bond at all. The best-known secret agent of the twentieth century, who ranks alongside Sherlock Holmes as a globally recognized fictional character, was dreamed up not by a secret agent, nor even by a man of action, but by a forty-three-year-old journalist with a well-stocked mind and a riotous imagination, trying to take his mind off his imminent wedding.

On 17 February 1952 Fleming sat down at his desk at Goldeneye, his house in Jamaica, and gazed out at the unbroken Caribbean Sea. He had already swum out to the reef that morning, as was his habit, before breakfasting on his usual scrambled eggs and Blue Mountain coffee. Somewhere out in the garden, Ann Rothermere, his wife-to-be, was painting a watercolour of flowers. The sounds of the waves and the birds filtered up into the room. After putting a fresh sheet of paper in the roller of the battered Royal portable in front of him, with six fingers he typed out the words 'Scent and smoke and sweat hit the taste buds with an acid thwack at three o'clock in the morning.' This became 'Scent and smoke can suddenly combine together and hit the tastebuds with an acid shock at three o'clock in the morning.' Then finally he got the opening line right: 'The scent and smoke and sweat of a casino are nauseating at three in the morning.'

Suddenly he was off, writing in a fast, uninhibited way so that by lunch he had already typed out 2,000 words. These had been pulled straight from his memory and his imagination: he had no notes, no plan of where he was going. At around five, after a siesta, Fleming returned to what he had written and reread it, making a few minor corrections before stowing the manuscript in the bottom left-hand drawer of his desk. Then, as the sun began to set, he went out on to the terrace to have a drink.

The following day he did exactly the same thing, and he stuck to this iron regime until on 18 March he hammered out the final bitter sentence, 'The bitch is dead now,' and the book was finished. It was a thriller named *Casino Royale*, and its hero was called James Bond.

Having finished the 60,000-word manuscript, Fleming put it in his briefcase, with the vague intention that when he returned to work in London he would tinker with it further. On his way home he stopped in New York and asked an old girlfriend, Clare Blanchard, to read it. 'You can't publish this,' she said. 'It will be a millstone around your neck. Or if you must publish it for heaven's sake do it under another name.'

Fleming was not at all sure about what he had written. He remained so diffident about his 'thriller thing' that it was months before he eventually let his friend the poet William Plomer read it, and then only on the understanding that he should not mention it to anyone. Fleming claimed he had just dashed it off using 'half his brain', and that it was really a 'dreadful oafish opus'. Of course Plomer ignored the protestations, and finding that he liked it he showed the manuscript to the veteran publisher Jonathan Cape. Cape was not convinced, and he agreed to publish the book only because Ian was the younger brother of Peter Fleming, the distinguished travel writer and journalist, and Peter had also put in a good word. 'He's got to do much better if he's going to get anywhere near Peter's standard,' Cape said.

Even before he began writing books, Fleming visited as many exotic places round the world in the course of his work as did his creation, James Bond. This is a passport photograph taken in the 1950s.

The rest, as they say, is history. For the next dozen years Fleming would repeat the pattern of writing a new James Bond novel between January and March at Goldeneye. In time he became surer of what he wrote, but he still dismissed the James Bond books as the 'pillow book fantasies of an adolescent mind' that in no way qualified as literature. James Bond and his adventures gradually captured the imagination of Britain, and then, through the endorsement of President Kennedy, the United States, and by the time of Fleming's death in 1964 the Bond books had sold over 40 million copies worldwide. Secret agent 007 would also become the hero of one of the most successful movie franchises since the Second World War, now grossing over a billion dollars a film. All this from an idea that Fleming apparently plucked out of thin air that balmy February morning in Jamaica, and dashed off with only half his brain.

The truth, of course, is quite different. Behind the amateur jokiness lay a steely resolve that was considered a Fleming family trait. Fleming had been thinking about writing a book since the 1930s, but just hadn't had the confidence and the threat of marriage to spur him into action. While he may have been genuinely unsure of the quality of what he had written, he was in no doubt why he had written it – and it was not just to while away the tropical mornings in Jamaica; Fleming wrote to make money. Even before *Casino Royale* was published, he bought up a dormant company, Glidrose, into which he would plough the profits he fully expected to make from his first book. Success was something that the Fleming family did well; failure was not.

Ian Fleming may have been very practical about writing James Bond, but at heart he was a romantic. He wrote so fast and with such apparent ease because he was tapping directly into a deep wellspring of his own imagination, which he laced with an unusual blend of sex, travel, culinary detail and fine living that perfectly encapsulated the aspirations of the age, and was absolutely an expression of Fleming himself. He may have dismissed his creation as idle fantasy, but he was entirely serious about the world he had created. There are barely any jokes in the James Bond novels, and there is little irony or satire either. Ian Fleming could not put any clear water between himself and his fiction because he was living his work as he wrote it: he was transforming the commonplace and unexciting into a glamorized version of life as he would have liked it to be. To discover the origins of James Bond one has to begin by exploring the deep streams that fed the well of Fleming's imagination, and his own complicated personality.

Ian Fleming went to a psychiatrist twice in his life, and on both occasions he found the experience unhelpful. Had he persevered, the shrink might have had an interesting time trying to make sense of a man so full of

contradictions. On the one hand he was a melancholic loner who did not understand people, yet on the other he needed male company and was intolerant of melancholy in others. He loved women, but often treated them brutally. He disliked intellectuals, but craved literary recognition. He was both introvert and extrovert, and tried to arrange his life to indulge both. After his death at the relatively early age of fifty-six from a lifetime's heavy smoking and drinking, many of his friends attempted to make sense of his confusing personality in quasi-psychological terms: it was all to do with his mother, who never really let go of him, or it was all about trying to compete with his older brother, who was brilliant and successful, or it was about never quite forgiving his long-dead father for having left him. Whatever the textbook interpretation of the paradoxes at the heart of Ian Fleming's character, in the invented world of James Bond Fleming did manage to achieve the order and symmetry that were lacking in his own. And, having invented such a vivid world for his alter ego, 007, it was a short step to imagine that he had as good as been there himself. This desire to escape had been present from the start.

Eve Fleming and her four sons. Ian, the second, is on the left. Widowed during the First World War, when the boys were still small children, Eve was a dominant influence in their lives.

Ian Lancaster Fleming was born on 28 May 1908, the second son of Valentine and Eve Fleming. Valentine was an honourable, moneyed young Conservative MP, whose wife, Eve, was a striking bohemian beauty. Eve's sparkling eyes, red cheeks and penchant for wide-brimmed hats did much to ameliorate the domineering, autocratic personality which cast a long shadow over Ian's life. The Flemings were a glamorous couple, and enjoyed all the outward trappings of wealth and success that one associates with the long, hazy summer of the Edwardian era. They lived at Braziers Park, a large Gothic house near Ipsden in Oxfordshire, where Valentine kept his own pack of beagles, or when in London at Pitt House, a white Georgian house on the edge of Hampstead Heath.

The Flemings had the appearance of landed wealth that stretched back generations, but in fact their privileged lives were all down to the acute financial acumen of Robert Fleming, Ian's grandfather. Robert Fleming was one of those late Victorians who made a vast amount of money in a very short space of time. He had started with nothing, growing up in considerable poverty on the Liff Road, a slum in Dundee, as one of seven children, five of whom died in childhood. Deciding not to follow his father on to the factory floor, Robert left school at thirteen and was taken on as a clerk by Baxters, the established Dundee jute barons. He soon proved himself to be a remarkably shrewd young man, and at twenty-seven he set up the Scottish American Investment Trust, a pioneering fund that invested in the American railroad boom and guaranteed a 6 per cent return. This was an enticing prospect – the risk was low, and the return was double that offered by the London Stock Exchange – and the fund's immediate popularity set Robert Fleming on his way. By 1900 he had become the doyen of what are now known as unit trust managers, and one of the richest men in London.

In spite of his wealth, Robert remained at heart an austere, tough Taysider. Famously, he never took a taxi in his life, and he would not have enjoyed the trappings of English high society had he not married a socially ambitious woman, Kate Hindmarsh. Kate was every bit as steely as her husband, and she saw to it that they lived in some style in a large house in Grosvenor Square and sent both their sons to Eton and Oxford. The Flemings also bought a 2,000-acre estate in Nettlebed, Oxfordshire, tearing down the modestly sized William and Mary country house that came with the estate to erect a forty-four-bedroomed faux Gothic monstrosity, complete with an eleven-ton fireplace shipped in from Carrara and the largest conservatory in south Oxfordshire. 'Let the deed shaw', the family motto, was carved next to the front door.

Peter (left) *and Ian* (right) *playing in the sand next to a traditional 'bathing machine' on a family holiday. It was while building a sandcastle on Bude beach, in Cornwall, that Ian first met his lifelong friend Ivar Bryce.*

Robert Fleming made a great impression on young Ian. Both he and his brothers inherited some of the old man's puritanical austerity, and as a boy Ian was well aware that his family's great wealth was only one generation deep. Money, and the lack of it, would become one of his lifelong preoccupations, and wealth as a mask for villainy became one of the features of his fiction.

In his immediate family, the greatest influence on Ian's early years was his brother Peter. Barely a year younger, Ian would be destined to shadow Peter throughout his schooldays, first at prep school and then at Eton. Their mutual competitiveness increased when Peter, who had started out as a sensitive and somewhat sickly child, blossomed into the kind of model pupil that schoolmasters dream about. He was extremely clever, sensible beyond his years, and – worse – a natural leader. While at Eton, Peter won the Loder prize, the Spanish prize and the King's French prize, and became Captain of the Oppidans (top scholar) in 1927. This unbridled success continued at Christ Church, Oxford, where he edited *Isis* and achieved an effortless first in English. As a contemporary remarked, if any young man of his generation was 'destined to select the felicitous adjective' it was Peter Fleming.

As the second son, Ian was in the unenviable position of always being compared to his older, more brilliant, brother, and it is hardly surprising that when his younger brothers Richard and then Michael joined them Ian assumed the role of joker in the pack. He was always the tall, naughty one; he had little option to be anything else. It was this quartet of 'strong, handsome black-haired, blue-eyed boys' that Ivar Bryce, a lifelong friend of Ian, first met digging a sand fortress on Bude beach in 1917. 'The leaders were Ian and Peter, and I gladly carried out their exact and exacting orders. They were natural leaders of men both of them, as later history was to prove, and it speaks well for them all that there was room for Peter and Ian in the same platoon.'

Peter (left) *and Ian* (right) *in the rose garden at Braziers Park.*

At that time the eldest three were at Durnford School, just outside Swanage, a Spartan place run by a parent-friendly dictator named Tom Pellatt, who presided over a regime of bad food and physical activity. There were earth closets, obligatory cold dips before breakfast, and punishments in abundance. Ian told a girlfriend that he had been beaten soon after he arrived. 'Why?' he had asked. 'Because you've arrived!' came the reply. The food was uniformly dreadful. Ian once found a rabbit's head floating in his stew, and it was experiences like this that, according to Peter, forged Ian's very conservative taste in food. For the rest of his life Ian Fleming liked nothing better than scrambled eggs ('Scrambled eggs never let you down,' as he famously opined), sausages or a bit of fish. Nothing that would impress the adventurous gourmet that James Bond became; nothing that might have a rabbit's head in it. While Ian was at Durnford one boy even died: he had caught a cold, and the matron refused to take notice of it. 'Dear Mum,' wrote Ian, 'My coff has gone to whoping coff now, please don't tell Mister Pellat, cause just this morning he said that nun of us had got coffs. I am afraid that I do not like school very much.'

The Fleming boys stuck together in the face of the brutalities of school life, and soon Ian discovered ways in which to escape this hostile world. Every Sunday evening the whole school would gather in the hall to hear Elinor Pellatt, the headmaster's wife, read out an adventure story. *The Prisoner of Zenda*, *Bulldog Drummond* and *The Devil Doctor* (featuring Dr Fu Manchu) were all read aloud, and Ian was captivated. Over thirty years later, discernible features of these classic tales would appear in the world of James Bond. Ian's other form of escape was of a very different kind. During afternoons in the summer term, boys would snake down to Dancing Ledge, a lip of rock at the base of the cliffs that jutted out into the sea. Here there were ammonites to collect and rock pools teeming with minute life, and Tom Pellatt had dynamited a sea-water pool for the boys to swim in. Ian's lifelong curiosity with the marine world was born on these warm summer afternoons.

While at Durnford the Fleming boys suffered a setback that would affect their entire lives. Valentine Fleming, who had gaily ridden off to war in 1914 with the Oxfordshire Hussars, endured three years on the Western Front before he was killed by a shell as he crawled out of his trench in the early hours of Sunday 20 May 1917. Val, as he was known, was by all accounts a hero, brave in battle and adored by his men, and if his letters home from the trenches are anything to go by he was particularly fond of his second son. Ian, who was not quite nine, was deeply affected, and though he never spoke of his father in later life, he kept a signed copy of Winston Churchill's moving obituary of his fellow officer and friend framed on his bedroom wall. Val's death changed the family dynamic immediately and for ever. The day after the news arrived, his mother drew ten-year-old Peter to one side. 'You must be very good and brave, Peter, because now you must take your father's place,' she told him. Peter never forgot these words, and assumed a marked sense of responsibility for the family that would continue throughout his life. Ian ascribed the start of his hero-worship of his older brother as dating from around this time.

Valentine Fleming, in a photograph taken while he was at Eton.

Apart from these long-lasting complications, it was Val's will that had a more immediate effect. Pitt House and most of his possessions had already been given to Eve, his thirty-two-year-old wife, before he left for the trenches in 1914. His estate, however, valued at over £265,000 (approximately £8 million in 2005 terms), was left in trust to his children. Eve was entitled to draw an income of £3,000 a year (£90,000 in 2005 terms) from this so long as she did not remarry. This was a common sort of will at the time, aimed at preventing money passing out of the family in the event of the remarriage of a war widow. It was therefore not intended to be a punitive will, but in reality it became one, as throughout her long life Ian's mother never had a significant incentive to remarry. This meant that her sons were always dependent on her for funds, and Eve, who was highly critical, protective and ambitious for all of them, used this financial power to attempt to control their lives. When Ian became engaged to the daughter of a Swiss businessman in 1931, Eve decided that she was not good enough for him and threatened to cut off his allowance. She also cut off Peter's funds when he began to write books, relenting only when he became famous and popular. Mrs Val, as she was known, was determined that all her children should be successful or she would have nothing to do with them. During school holidays she made all four boys end their nightly prayers 'Make me more like Mokie' (their pet name for Val – from Smokey, for his habitual pipe smoking), and on occasions she even invoked his spirit when she wanted them to do something they did not. It was a maddening relationship for Ian, who spent so much of his early life being a failure, and yet was unable to escape from her controlling influence because of the financial ties that bound them together. Mrs Val, intriguingly, was also known as 'Mie', or M for short.

Ian followed Peter to Eton in 1921, and continued to play his role as the black sheep of the family. His housemaster, Sam Slater (described in the official history of Eton as a sadist), chose not to understand Ian but to discipline him. While Peter's star blazed even brighter, Ian decided to opt out of the competition altogether, invariably committing some misdemeanour or other for which Slater administered the appropriate punishment. These forbidden adventures, in which Ivar Bryce was often an eager accomplice (Bryce had a motorbike secretly garaged in Windsor), provided Ian with the inspiration for the early love life of Vivienne Michel in *The Spy Who Loved Me*. Her seduction on the floor of a box in Windsor's Royalty Kinema commemorates precisely where he first made love to a girl.

The Fleming boys grow up. Clockwise from upper left *Michael, Richard, Ian and Peter.*

Apart from such exciting diversions, it is difficult to know whether Ian enjoyed Eton or not. The only area in which he really excelled was on the athletics field, where in 1925 he outran, out-jumped and out-threw everyone else to become the Victor Ludorum, or school sports champion. Then, setting a remarkable record, he won the prize again the following year. This was a great achievement, though at the time a somewhat hollow crown, as athletics champions did not enjoy quite the same prestige as members of the cricket eleven. Nonetheless, Victor Ludorum was something of Ian's own, and he remained justly proud of it. In the cover blurb for *Casino Royale* he wrote, 'Like his brother Peter – a more famous author – he was educated at Eton, where he was Victor Ludorum two years in succession, a distinction only once equalled – presumably by another second son trying to compensate for a brilliant elder brother.'

The strangest story of Ian's days at Eton emerged courtesy of his friend the writer Paul Gallico. When the two men returned to the school thirty years later, they revisited Ian's room. 'I hated every minute of it here,' he told Gallico, who recalled that 'At one point I thought he was going to be sick.' Fleming then told him a story about how he was once due to be birched for some misdemeanour and to run in a steeplechase at the same time, twelve noon. Ian had asked for his punishment to be brought forward by quarter of an hour, so he eventually ran the race with 'his shanks and running shorts stained with his own gore'. This brutal story was confirmed by Ian's brother, Richard, and according to Gallico it left Ian with a lifelong interest in torture and 'an implacable distaste for Eton'. When Gallico came to describe the event in his 1961 introduction to *Gilt-Edged Bonds*, a compendium of three Bond novels, Ian crossed out the reference to torture and changed 'implacable distaste' to 'mysterious affection'. 'So much for torture,' he added. His change of heart expressed his continuing confusion about the place.

The Eton army cadet corps. Ian Lancaster Fleming is seated second from the right.

After school, which he left a term early to avoid the embarrassment of being expelled, Ian found himself at Sandhurst Military Academy. Mrs Val, seeing that her second son was not academic but a fine sportsman, had decided that a good Scottish regiment was the right place for him, and in September 1926 Gentleman Cadet Ian Lancaster Fleming found himself standing alongside the rest of the new recruits to 20 Platoon No. 5 Company on the windswept parade ground. Tall and strong, Ian certainly looked like a soldier, but he had never been enthusiastic about taking orders, or in this case being bawled at by a collection of hard-nosed sergeant majors intent on dragooning him into a fighting machine. From dawn to dusk cadets were kept on the move, running or even bicycling between activities to keep to their schedule, often wearing several layers of clothes that they would strip off as the activity required. There was a 10 p.m. curfew, and, predictably, Gentleman Cadet Fleming was constantly being caught climbing back over the barracks wall and gated. 'He could do really well if only he would realize that as he is at Sandhurst he might just as well make the best of what is to him a bad job and settle down,' wrote Major the Lord Ailwyn at the end of his second term. Plenty of unconventional soldiers had made the best of a bad job at Sandhurst; even Field Marshal Montgomery had once set fire to a cadet in his dormitory. In the event, however, Ian never did knuckle down.

Ian in his teenage years.

During his many escapades outside the barracks he had fallen in love for the first time, with Peggy Barnard, the attractive daughter of an army colonel. On the Sandhurst annual sports day Peggy came down with Mrs Val to watch Ian run the 120-yard hurdles, which he won in 16.5 seconds, but the celebrations afterwards were interrupted by another young man, who had arrived to take Peggy off to an Oxford commemoration ball. Ian had forgotten about this long-standing arrangement, and it riled him. If Peggy went to the ball, Ian threatened, he would go to London and 'find myself a tart'. Peggy apologetically went her way and, in a fit of pique, Ian went his. He drove up to London, to the 43 Club in Soho, and found a girl, and several days later he was horrified to discover that she had left him with a dose of the clap.

At first Mrs Val decided Ian should drop a term to recover from this antisocial disease, but in the ensuing rows and bitter recriminations between mother and defiant son it became obvious to both that Ian would never make a soldier. In August 1927 he resigned from Sandhurst, having failed to pass out. In later years Ian Fleming never told his friends that he had left both Eton and Sandhurst early, and the family always maintained that it was because he had hurt his back. Somehow the pain of failure that was, he wrote, 'so much worse than the pleasure of success' remained a raw scar that needed hiding from the world.

Though his army career had ended, Mrs Val had not finished with him yet. She decided that Ian should become a diplomat and therefore needed to pass the Foreign Office exams, which required more academic training. Once again Ian followed in Peter's footsteps, this time to Kitzbühel, a sleepy market town in the Austrian Tyrol, where he was sent to learn French and German in the care of Ernan and Phyllis Forbes Dennis. This excursion might have been just one more undistinguished phase in the early life of Ian Fleming had it not been for this eccentric English couple who achieved what no one else had yet managed: they encouraged Ian just to be himself, to read, and, more importantly, to write.

It was not an auspicious start. When he first turned up at the Tennerhof, the Forbes Dennises' large wooden chalet on the lower slopes of the mountain, Ian let it be known that he was in disgrace. To Ralph Arnold, a fellow pupil who would also go on to become a writer, Ian portrayed himself as a romantic exile who had just had some dark quarrel with his family and had been banished from the military academy. He seemed to be rather enjoying the role. To Ernan Forbes Dennis Ian was a typically bad-mannered Etonian, and showed every sign of having been spoiled as a child. Forbes Dennis imagined that the saintly Valentine was probably responsible, having naturally tried to counterbalance his wife's devotion to her brilliant but fragile elder son.

Up in the mountains and far away from the reach of his family, the Forbes Dennises set about encouraging their headstrong young charge, and for the rest of his life Ian would remain touchingly grateful for their efforts. 'Without their careful praise,' he wrote much later, 'heaven knows where I should be.' Fleming studied German and French all day, and found he was capable in both. The evenings were more interesting, as it was then that Phyllis would appear. Phyllis Bottome (her pen name) was an extraordinary woman. Much of her life had been spent in a TB sanatorium, but what she lacked in experience of life she more than made up for with her vivid imagination. She used this to great effect every morning, in bed, where she sat furiously writing romantic thrillers. Each evening she would appear at the dinner table, her dark eyes and hollow cheeks half hidden beneath a cloud of prematurely white hair, her expression that of a melancholy eagle. Then Phyllis would spin long yarns about the grotesque deeds of imaginary characters, and challenge the boys at the Tennerhof to do the same. Ian soon discovered that he had a talent for this, and invented an endless story about one Graf Schlick, a count who lived in the castle at the end of the valley, whom Ian had committing a series of Gothic crimes and misdemeanours. At the end of one tale Schlick is seduced by what he thinks is a ghost, but turns out to be the beautiful lady of the house, who has been locked away in the attic as a leper. Schlick's death is swift and agonizing. Ian remembered his macabre story and years later retold it at a Caribbean dinner party to amuse Princess Margaret. No one laughed.

Ian Fleming always generously credited Phyllis Bottome for having encouraged him to become a writer, and his first short stories date from around this time. One of these, 'A Poor Man Escapes', written in 1927, tells the story of Henrik, a starving beggar who watches helplessly as his wife dies, then staggers out into the frozen streets of Vienna in search of a meal. He pawns a bundle of her possessions, but hesitates over a small bottle marked 'Poison'. 'It was a dark red colour – what a lovely pink smudge it would make if he threw it hard into the snow and it broke.' Henrik thinks better of it, and slips the bottle into his pocket instead. Soon he finds his way into a stylish Viennese café, where he hides behind a newspaper and proceeds to gorge himself on cake and coffee and vermouth. As the heat of the restaurant melts his shivering core, Henrik slips into a dream. He is flying through a magical landscape. 'Everything was rose-coloured and gold. He was floating through an infinite sunset across green hills towards a distant range of mountains. If only he could get there. He strove to reach them, when suddenly the sunset collapsed beneath him and he fell – thump-thump-thump.' He wakes to find the waiter hitting him on the back. Henrik has been discovered, and the waiter calls the police to throw the beggar out. Just as the officer arrives and stamps the snow off his boots, Henrik pulls the poison bottle from his pocket and takes a swig. At that moment he enters the landscape of his dream and reaches the sunset, and then he dies.

Among Ian Fleming's earliest trips abroad were his visits to Kitzbühel in the Austrian Tyrol. Here he mastered skiing, and, with his newly acquired German, courted a number of attractive young Viennese girls. Fleming is on the right in local dress; the woman in the centre is Lisl Popper. She remained a friend for many years, and Lisl is the name given to a girl in the short story 'Risico.'

On the surface this short story bears no relation to what Ian would eventually write, but there are some odd parallels. Henrik, like Bond, is an outsider, and he too dreams of finding a peace and perfection that are not possible in this world. Also, the opulence of the café and the greedy descriptions of the food are an aperitif to the locations and feasts that Fleming's secret agent would enjoy some twenty-five years later. Ian would often sit in a café or restaurant alone with a book, watching, dreaming, imagining. It is perfectly possible that he saw a poor man in one of the great Viennese cafés he visited from Kitzbühel, and concocted this short story around him.

Fleming looked back at Kitzbühel as 'that golden time when the sun always shone', and it was to provide him with a wealth of memories that would end up in James Bond novels. For instance, Ian very quickly learned to ski – 'like a ghost' thought some, 'like a typical Englishman' thought others, but either way with great enthusiasm. Once he deliberately set off down a slope that had been closed off for fear of an avalanche. As the wall of snow cracked behind him, he was thrilled to find himself pursued and then overtaken by the deluge, and this experience was to inspire a famous scene in *On Her Majesty's Secret Service*. A more serious brush with death occurred one evening as he returned to Kitzbühel from Munich in 'Zoroastra', his trusty Morris Tourer. As Ian approached the little railway line from Munich to Kufstein, he failed to see the small train approaching the crossing ahead. He was travelling much too fast to stop, and before he had time to react he collided with the front of the engine and was dragged fifty yards down the track. Miraculously, Ian walked away shaken but unhurt, though his little car was beyond repair. This near-miss left him with a permanent association between danger and light railways, and he used them as plot devices in both *Diamonds are Forever* and the final scene in *The Man with the Golden Gun*.

Ian's restless desire to turn every picnic into a pursuit and every potentially dull situation into something fantastic made him a popular member of the Forbes Dennises' little school. There was an air of danger about him, enhanced by his piratical broken nose – a souvenir from the playing fields of Eton – and he found many local girls more than willing to indulge in the kind of uncomplicated liaisons he enjoyed. 'Technique in bed is important,' he scribbled in a notebook, 'but alone,' he added somewhat churlishly, 'it is the scornful coupling that makes the affairs of Austrians and Anglo-Saxons so fragmentary and in the end so distasteful.'

After a year at Kitzbühel, Ian had developed a good command of French and German and a taste for literature, and he went on to spend two more years abroad, first in Munich and then at the University of Geneva. In Munich he continued where he had left off: he read avidly and pursued girls ruthlessly – while doing his best to ignore the rise of Nazism in that city. Switzerland was more interesting – though not for its cultivated innocence, as he wrote almost thirty years later in his travel book *Thrilling Cities*. 'Soothed by the clonking of cowbells, besieged by advertisements for dairy products and chocolate, and with cuckoo clocks tick-tacking in every other shop window, the visitor to Switzerland almost feels as if he had arrived in some gigantic nursery.' Fleming was far more intrigued by the dark secrets that he imagined lurked behind the bland façades of the banks in Calvin's 'God-fearing city'. Here it was not hard for Ian to play the flashy eccentric Englishman, which he did to the hilt, tearing around the town in his sleek black two-seater Buick, 'half Faust–half Byron', charming and appalling the solid burghers of Geneva in equal measure. He also kept up his hearty mountain pursuits. In *From*

Russia with Love James Bond looks out of his aeroplane window at the Alps far below and sees himself again 'a young man in his teens, with the leading end of the rope round his waist, bracing himself against the top of a rock-chimney on the Aiguilles Rouges as his two companions from the University of Geneva inched up the smooth rock towards him'. This is a fair description of Ian Fleming at the time.

While at Geneva University, twenty-one-year-old Fleming fell in love for the second time in his life. Monique Panchaud de Bottomes was an attractive dark-haired businessman's daughter from Vich, just inland from Lake Geneva, and during an idyllic summer spent swimming in the lakes and walking in the mountains Ian became closer to Monique than to any other girl he had ever met. By the autumn of 1931 they were engaged, but two events conspired to prevent this union from going any further. In September of that year Ian returned to London to sit the Foreign Office exams, alongside the usual crop of bright young students from Oxford and Cambridge. A month later he discovered he had come twenty-fifth out of sixty-two candidates, which was good enough to pass, but not good enough to be offered a job. In that particular year that honour was awarded only to the top six students. Against such stiff competition Ian might have regarded his pass as an adequate attempt, but he was acutely aware that he had once again disappointed his ambitious mother. In later life he would maintain that he had actually come seventh, and that that year the Foreign Service had decided to take only the top five candidates. As with Eton and Sandhurst, cruel Fate, as he would have it, had played her part once again.

Ian became engaged to Monique Panchaud de Bottomes (above). *This did not please his mother, and the relationship did not endure. Her name, however, lives on: Bond's mother is called Monique Delacroix.*

The result of this latest hiccup was that Ian returned to London without an income and moved in with his mother. Mrs Val, in her search to find the reason for Ian's latest failure, decided that his infatuation with Monique was partly to blame and thereafter began a campaign to break up their relationship. But Ian persisted. Two years later, according to another of Ian's girlfriends, Mrs Val presented him with a choice: either call off his engagement to Monique or lose his allowance. He decided that the money mattered more than the girl.

Meanwhile Ian needed a job. Mrs Val forced him to write a begging letter to Sir Roderick Jones, the head of the Reuters news agency. Jones knew Fleming to be the right sort of chap, with the right sort of background, from the right sort of family, and he was prepared to overlook the Foreign Office failure and give the young man a chance. So on Monday 19 October 1931, less than a month after his exam, Ian found himself sitting in Reuters' Carmelite Street office as an apprentice journalist. Here his life as a writer really began. 'At Reuters I learned to write fast and, above all, to be accurate,' he said. 'Because in Reuters if you weren't accurate you were fired and that was the end of that.' And he was lucky enough to be given some dream assignments.

Nine months into the job, Ian was sent off to cover the Alpine motor trials, an international competition that took place over 1,580 miles of twisting mountain roads. Ian would not only cover the event, but actually take part in it, as the navigator for the British rally driver Donald Healey, competing in his $4^1/_2$-litre Invicta. Amateur car racing in those days was a glamorous business, and would often make the front pages as cars and their drivers were fast becoming symbols of national pride. It was also extremely dangerous: the cars were as fast as their brakes were crude, and fatalities among drivers and spectators were common. Each night a dusty parade of Bugattis, Lancias, Mercedes-Benz and Bentleys would take place outside a glamorous hotel where drivers from across Europe would dress for dinner and discuss the day's race. Ian was thrilled to be part of this world, and the combination of fast cars and fine living would find many echoes in the fictional world of James Bond.

Another adventurous assignment for Fleming was one of his own making. In March 1933 he heard from an old school friend, in confidence, that six British engineers working for the Metropolitan-Vickers electrical company had been arrested in the Soviet Union and charged with espionage. Fleming quietly wrote up the story, which went on to make headlines around the world and almost prompted a trade embargo between Britain and the Soviet Union. Reuters already had a bureau chief in Moscow, a young American named Robin Kinkead, but Ian's monocled editor, Bernard Rickattson-Hatt, decided that 'first-class' coverage was needed, and to ensure that Reuters got it he sent Ian, 'one of our ablest young men', to help. So it was that Fleming flew to Berlin and from there proceeded by train to Moscow with a sleeping carriage all to himself. This was a highly unusual journey to make at that time: few foreigners ever visited Stalin's capital. Ian found it brutal and rather appealing; he was charmed by the endless shuffling queues and the oily vodka. Equally intriguing was the trial itself. This was a Stalinist showpiece in which the Russian accomplices had to grovel and plead for their lives before the inscrutable military judge Vassili Ulrich, dubbed 'the Russian Judge Jeffreys', who remained half-hidden by a pile of papers and barely whispered into his microphone. The prosecutor, Andrei Vyshinsky, was a cantankerous brick-shaped man who roundly denounced the West and its villainy, much to the approval of the 400-strong 'audience' of citizens.

As the events unfolded, Fleming took great pleasure in competing with the other international journalists to get his copy home first. Though he was certainly the most inexperienced among them, he developed an ingenious system of throwing his scribbled bulletins out of the window of the courthouse to a boy waiting down below, who ran them over to the cable office where they were sent to Reuters before the other journalists had even left the courtroom. When the final verdicts were delivered, however, Ian's system failed him. Loudspeakers around the building boomed out the breaking news and another correspondent waiting to be connected for a telephone call simply heard the announcement and passed it on. Rickattson-Hatt fumed and spat, but Ian was able to see the funny side of this particular failure.

His final act in Moscow was to request an interview with Joseph Stalin himself. To his utter amazement, he actually received a signed reply stating that the great leader was too busy. Stalin's letter was not the only colourful trophy Ian took home from Moscow: the other was an enormous tapeworm, christened 'the Loch Ness Monster', that he had swallowed in some bad Beluga.

A facsimile of Stalin's signed letter declining Fleming's request for an interview. Ian had made the request on his trip to Moscow in 1933, and he was both flattered and astonished to receive a reply.

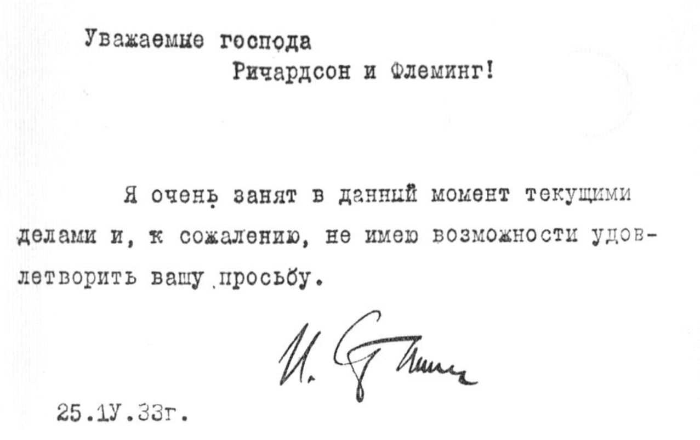
Уважаемые господа
Ричардсон и Флеминг!

Я очень занят в данный момент текущими делами и, к сожалению, не имею возможности удовлетворить вашу просьбу.

25.1У.33г.

During this trip Ian Fleming proved that he had the abilities required to be a journalist. He had an eye for the main chance and a love of facts, and his prose, though purple, was highly readable. 'Tonight,' he wrote in his bedroom on the sixth floor of the National Hotel, 'thousands of enemies of the Soviet State are skulking in cellars, gnashing their teeth.' When Kinkead pointed out that very few Moscow houses had cellars, Fleming replied breezily, 'My dear fellow, don't let's worry too much about that. It's the sense of the thing that matters, and evil-doers always gnash their teeth and skulk in cellars.'

Having finally found a job suited to his talents, Fleming's next career move seemed perverse. He had been offered a job in the Shanghai bureau of Reuters, a glamorous posting that a twenty-five-year-old with a love of the exotic might have been expected to relish. While he was mulling over this enticing job offer Fleming was sent to Berlin, and as he lined up potential interviews with Goebbels – and possibly even Hitler himself – he came to the surprising decision to leave Reuters for good. He had been offered a lucrative job in the City, and he decided to take it. 'It's a beastly idea giving up all the fun of life for money,' Ian wrote to his boss Rickatson-Hatt, 'but I hope to make a packet and then get out and come back into journalism at the other end. Anyway the decision had to be made and I was pretty well pushed into it from all sides. I was assured it was "the right thing to do" for the sake of the family – so there it is.'

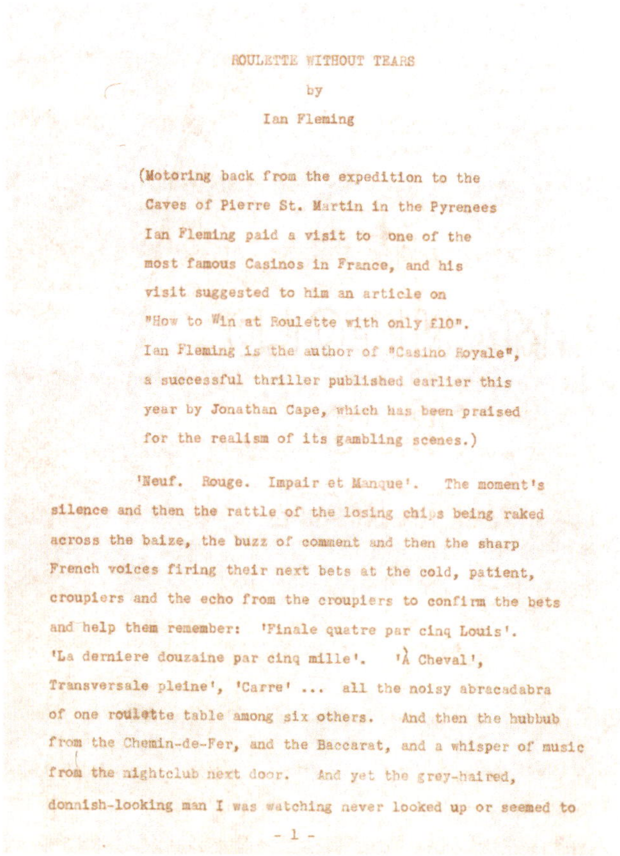

ROULETTE WITHOUT TEARS

by

Ian Fleming

(Motoring back from the expedition to the Caves of Pierre St. Martin in the Pyrenees Ian Fleming paid a visit to one of the most famous Casinos in France, and his visit suggested to him an article on "How to Win at Roulette with only £10". Ian Fleming is the author of "Casino Royale", a successful thriller published earlier this year by Jonathan Cape, which has been praised for the realism of its gambling scenes.)

'Neuf. Rouge. Impair et Manque'. The moment's silence and then the rattle of the losing chips being raked across the baize, the buzz of comment and then the sharp French voices firing their next bets at the cold, patient, croupiers and the echo from the croupiers to confirm the bets and help them remember: 'Finale quatre par cinq Louis'. 'La derniere douzaine par cinq mille'. 'À Cheval', Transversale pleine', 'Carre' ... all the noisy abracadabra of one roulette table among six others. And then the hubbub from the Chemin-de-Fer, and the Baccarat, and a whisper of music from the nightclub next door. And yet the grey-haired, donnish-looking man I was watching never looked up or seemed to

- 1 -

The young Fleming gained considerable experience of the gaming tables. Following the success of Casino Royale, *his journalism on Bond-related themes was much in demand. This 1958 manuscript – typed on the reverse of Congress of the United States stationery – is filed together with a 'carte d'admission' to the casino in Pau, France (see page 24).*

Reuters was fun, but a change had overtaken the Fleming family to shift the dynamic once again, and it was now quite possible that Ian could no longer rely on his mother's allowance to supplement his Reuters pay. Robert Fleming, the eighty-eight-year-old scion of the dynasty, had died at Black Mount, his beloved Argyllshire deer forest. His vast legacy of £3 million (£90 million in 2005 terms) had been left to his wife, Kate, and, when she died, to their surviving son, Philip, Ian's uncle. No provision had been made for Valentine's children. Old Robert, his former financial acumen now dimmed by age, clearly believed that through Val's estate these boys were now taken care of, but this logic depended upon Eve marrying another man. Ian's mother was now having an affair with the painter Augustus John, but as John was 'the most renowned Lothario of his generation' she was increasingly unlikely to marry and forfeit her own sizeable income of £3,000 a year from Val's trust fund. Somehow the Fleming millions seemed destined to sidestep Ian and his brothers, and the onus now was on all of them to stand on their own two feet. The youngest two, Michael and Richard, had already joined the family bank and were solvent. Peter, whose star had blazed so brightly during his early years, had also tried banking but he had found the City and its denizens utterly boring, and he was now carving out a successful career as a travel writer. His first book, *Brazilian Adventure*, had been published to great acclaim, and he was in the Far East at work on his second. Only Ian remained dependent on his mother, and a City job would offer him, if nothing else, enough money to step outside her orbit at last.

Given his acute interest in wealth and the world of the very rich, it was ironic that Ian soon discovered he was not much good at accumulating money. After a couple of years he changed jobs from banking to stockbroking, and became a partner at Rowe & Pitman, but he never really got to grips with the financial markets. According to one friend, he was 'the world's worst stockbroker'. His problem was he couldn't take the work all that seriously. The mid 1930s were a slack time for stockbrokers generally, and a large part of Ian's job was to take prospective clients out to a good lunch where, over the lobster or tournedos, he expanded on his investment strategies, making them sound convincing even if he had not quite grasped all the minutiae himself. Afterwards he would show his guest around the client investment section, and that was about it. Lancy Hugh Smith, the senior partner of Rowe & Pitman, was well aware that Ian was a decided amateur, but he regarded him as a good company asset because he had the right name – which counted for something in the City in those days – and because he was a young man who had been outside the cage: he had been to Moscow. He also recognized that Ian had a talent for ingratiating himself with older men, who were invariably delighted by this zestful young dining companion who never bothered to toady to them. It was a skill Ian would soon put to good use.

While his career drifted, Ian was able to follow his other passions. These, in no particular order, were girls, good food, golf, and now, with his new found wealth, gambling. His many girlfriends of this time included a collection of rich married women whom he saw more or less regularly and a succession of well-bred, free-spirited young things he had charmed at cocktail parties. When

One of Fleming's greatest pleasures was playing golf. He played off a handicap of nine (as does James Bond). He took part in this 1957 tournament, and recounted the experience in an article entitled 'Nightmare among the Mighty' for the Sunday Times*.*

bored, he cast his net further afield, and once enjoyed a brief but exciting romance with a nightclub dancer – a 'bubble girl' – named Storm. According to a close family friend, Lady Mary Clive, 'he looked on women as a schoolboy does – as remote mysterious beings. He could never hope to understand them, but, if he was lucky, he felt he might occasionally shoot one down.' Ian's ruthless bed hopping gained him a terrible reputation, and he remained far too nonconformist for society hostesses to adopt him as an eligible young man, despite his sleek looks and his money. He was adored by women, and fascinated by sex, but adoration bored him, and sex was, for Ian, just sex. 'For Ian,' said a girlfriend, 'women were like fishcakes. Mind you he was very fond of fishcakes, but he never pretended there was any mystique about eating them.'

Memories of Ian's philandering certainly inspired many of James Bond's sexual conquests, but, unlike his alter ego, Fleming was never able to let go entirely. He wanted women that he could turn 'on and off like a light switch', but life was not that simple. As he once wrote in one of his notebooks about a man who obsessively moves from woman to woman, 'what happens is that, as with drugs, he needs a stronger shot each time, and women are just women. The consumption of one woman is the consumption of all. You can't double the dose.' A few of these girls recognized the cause of his obsessive behaviour. 'The trouble with Ian is that he gets off with women because he cannot get on with them,' said the writer Rosamond Lehmann, who was more perceptive than most. And at the back of his mind there was a certain puritanical streak that disapproved of his endless philandering.

In 1937 Ian found a setting to complement his new role as a cultivated man of the world. Number 22b Ebury Street had been a Baptist chapel before Oswald Mosley, the leader of the British Union of Fascists, had turned it into a home, and it was to here that Ian, aged twenty-nine, finally escaped from his mother's house in

Ian Fleming's first London home of his own, in Ebury Street, combined a colourful history with an atmosphere worthy of a Bond villain. This is the typescript for an article written about Jamaica for Horizon.

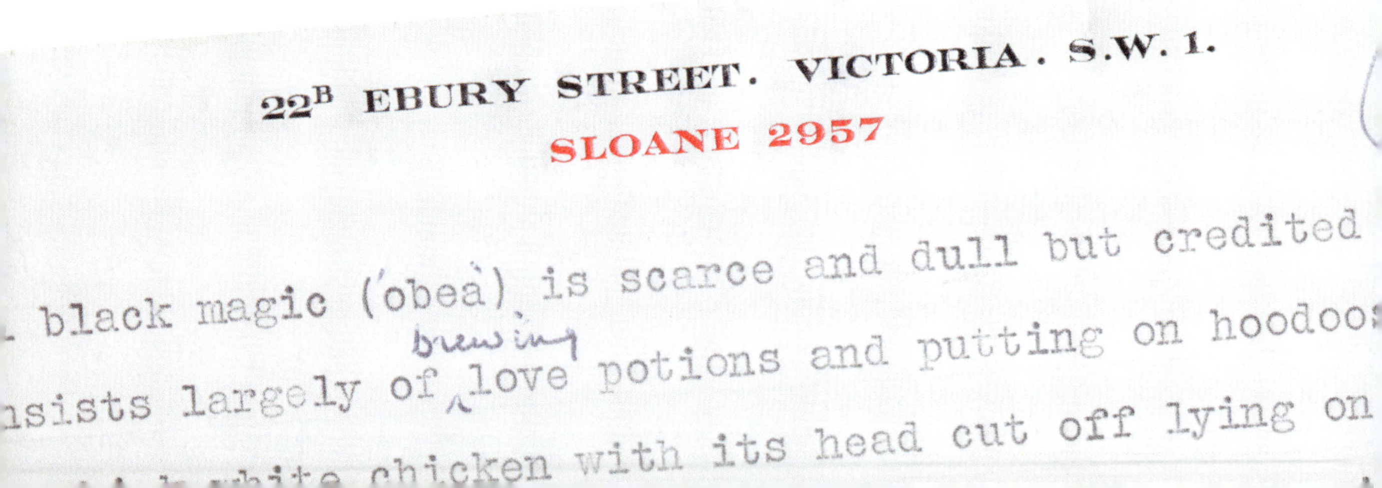
22B EBURY STREET. VICTORIA. S.W. 1.
SLOANE 2957

black magic (obea) is scarce and dull but credited
nsists largely of brewing love potions and putting on hoodoo
chicken with its head cut off lying on

Chelsea. The interior of the chapel remained largely intact, and it had no windows. Ian placed dark-blue glass in the skylight and a lavatory where the altar had been. He made the dingy interior even darker by painting the walls dark grey, and complemented them with some uncomfortable black furniture. In the bookcases flanking the walls were volumes of Thomas Mann and French erotica, alongside first editions of works that were 'milestones of human progress'. Beside *The Origin of Species* were works on miners' lamps and making plastic, all of which had been chosen by Percy Muir, a bookseller Ian had first befriended in Kitzbühel. Fleming had provided Muir with funds and the freedom to choose any book, however technical, that 'made things happen'. Ian liked the idea that these obscure tomes might one day prove a sound investment (as indeed they did). The first editions certainly looked impressive: Ian kept them in black cases lined up on the shelves rather like racks of ammunition boxes, their bulky black forms completing the odd Berlin Jewish (as he called it) decor that he had created at Ebury Street.

Gambling remained a fascination throughout Fleming's life, though his own bids were cautious. Sometimes recreation and work would coincide, as shown by this photograph taken in Monte Carlo during research for his collection of travel writing, Thrilling Cities.

In this gloomy sepulchre the main exhibit was, of course, Ian himself. Girlfriends recalled visiting Ebury Street to find him stretched out on the black sofa in his dark-blue suit, invariably reading or gazing into space with the melancholy expression of a fallen angel – an elegant, bored animal, waiting to ravish or be ravished. There would be a fire blazing in the grate, even in midsummer, and invariably 'The Skaters' Waltz' on the gramophone. They would sit down on the little internal balcony and eat kedgeree by candlelight, washed down with either whisky or champagne. And then coffee, and then bed. Ian had a love of gadgets, and he had installed a hatch so that the serving girl he employed didn't have to come into the room. He also had a tip-up soap dispenser in the bathroom, of the type usually seen in hotels. When he moved it was with the speed of a lizard, dashing up to get a book or change the record. Women noticed that despite his Don Juan reputation there was something curiously feminine about him, which only added to the intriguingly heady cocktail he had created. During these years Ian was the orchid and Ebury Street was his orchid house; it was all a stranger, camper version of the bachelor life he would eventually give James Bond.

Now that he was in the City, Ian appeared to have given up all ambition of writing. As Peter's fame as a travel writer burned ever brighter, Ian did not bother to compete. 'My brother Peter's the writer in the family,' he told a friend, 'and he's really terribly good at it.' 'The better Peter was,' noted one friend, 'the badder Ian became.' He was far more interested in material things, and the crowd with whom he now mixed were of a similar disposition. Weekends were spent playing golf at the

CASINO ROYALE

1953

First line

The scent and smoke and sweat of a casino are nauseating at three in the morning.

Story

James Bond, the best card player in the British secret service, arrives at Royale-les-Eaux to take on a French union boss at cards. Le Chiffre is actually a Russian agent of SMERSH who has misappropriated their funds, and Bond must bankrupt him to bring him into disrepute. He is aided in this by Vesper Lynd, a beautiful girl from the French station; René Mathis, of the Deuxième Bureau (the French secret service); and Felix Leiter, from the CIA. Bond takes on Le Chiffre in a high-stakes game of baccarat, which he loses, whereupon he is bailed out by Leiter (as Marshall Aid) and succeeds in bankrupting Le Chiffre. The villain then kidnaps Vesper. Bond gives chase, but he too is captured and is then savagely tortured by Le Chiffre, who thrashes his testicles with a carpet-beater while Bond is strapped to a bottomless chair. 007 is saved from death by a SMERSH assassin who shoots the villain but refrains from killing Bond, slashing his hand with a **Щ** (for щпцон – 'spy'). Having his life saved by the enemy confuses 007, and while he lies in bed recovering from his wounds he wonders whether he is on the right side. He then seduces Vesper, and even contemplates marriage, only to discover that she is a double agent working for the Russians. Vesper reveals all to Bond in a passionate suicide note, having realized that the Russians are moving in on her. She has taken an overdose.

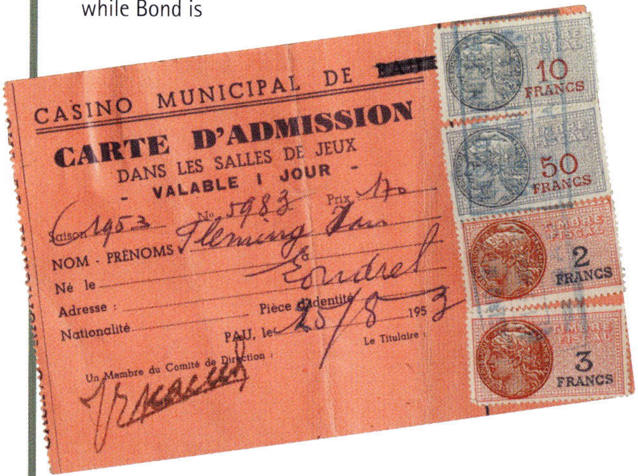
CASINO MUNICIPAL DE [redacted]
CARTE D'ADMISSION
DANS LES SALLES DE JEUX
- VALABLE 1 JOUR -
Saison 1953 No 5983 Prix 170
NOM · PRENOMS Fleming Ian
Né le
Adresse : Londres
Nationalité
Pièce d'identité
PAU, le 25/8 1953
Le Titulaire
Un Membre du Comité de Direction :
TIMBRE FISCAL 10 FRANCS
TIMBRE FISCAL 50 FRANCS
TIMBRE FISCAL 2 FRANCS
TIMBRE FISCAL 3 FRANCS

Last lines

'This is 007 speaking. This is an open line. It's an emergency. Can you hear me? Pass this on at once. 3030 was a double, working for Redland.

'Yes, dammit, I said "was". The bitch is dead now.'

Inspirations

In his usual airy tone Fleming claimed that 'there are three strong incidents in the book which carry it along and they are all based on fact. I extracted them from my wartime memories of the Naval Intelligence Division of the Admiralty, dolled them up, attached a hero, a villain and a heroine, and there was the book.'

The first of these incidents is the assassination attempt on Bond as he is walking down a tree-lined street in Royale-les-Eaux. Two Bulgarians step out of the shadows carrying two identical cameras slung over their shoulders. One is coloured red, and is a bomb; the other is blue, and is a smokescreen. The idea is to throw the bomb and then set off the smokescreen, enabling the assassins to get away, but the Bulgarians – who have been hired by SMERSH – mistrust their equipment. They

Fleming himself designed the layout for his first book's jacket, published in Britain by Jonathan Cape. The story is set not in Monte Carlo (right, in a picture collected for Thrilling Cities*), but in the fictional northern-French resort of Royale-les-Eaux – not unlike Fleming's pre-war haunt of Le Touquet.*

decide to set off the smoke first, then the bomb. Unfortunately for them, both cameras are bombs, and there is nothing left of them but a hole in the ground. According to Fleming, this was identical to the method used by a real Bulgarian in his attempt to kill the Nazi spymaster Franz von Papen during the war. But, like Bond, both he and his wife were protected from the blast by a tree.

The second incident is based on a trip that Fleming and Admiral Godfrey made to Lisbon en route to America in 1941. This neutral city was crawling with spies and agents of all countries, and Ian suggested a trip to the casino at Estoril, where, according to him, they encountered some German secret agents at the high table playing *chemin de fer.* With £50 in his pocket, Ian took on the chief German agent, but after three *suivis* he had lost it all. 'A humiliating experience,' he wrote, 'which added to the sinews of war of the German Secret Service and reduced me sharply in my chief's estimation.' Unfortunately Fleming's account of this incident was largely fantasy. According to Godfrey, they did go to a casino, but only played a group of Portuguese businessmen – and lost. Afterwards Ian had said, 'What if those men had been German secret service agents, and suppose we had cleaned them out of their money; now that would have been exciting.'

Even though Ian's story wasn't true, he did know men who gambled against the Germans. The Yugoslav agent Dusko Popov, who pretended to be a German double agent in New York, was one, and Ralph Izzard, one of Ian's Naval Intelligence colleagues, was another. Izzard had played against a group of expat Nazis while en route to South America, and he remembered that Ian was fascinated by his story.

The most harrowing torture ever inflicted upon Bond was also inspired by a real incident. He claimed that the thrashing of the naked genitals while strapped to a bottomless chair was a 'greatly watered-down version of one of those French-Moroccan tortures known as *passer à la mandoline*.' This procedure, actually practised on British agents captured during the war, involved the scrotum being sliced in two with the steel string of a mandolin.

What the readers said

'I have to admit, when reading *Casino Royale* on loan from the library bus, that I had to skip a paragraph or two of the torture, it came *so* close!'

'I cannot recall being so delighted with a secret agent story, such evil, elegance and terror'

'On page 126 you quote the French imperative "*allez*" but what Frenchman would ever use it?'

What the critics said

'Exciting and extremely civilised' – *Times Literary Supplement*

'Supersonic' – John Buchan, *The Listener*

'The ethical code is that of Bulldog Drummond, spiced, not altogether convincingly, with scenes of brutality and strong sexual interest' – *Punch*

'Mr Fleming should cut down on the physical violence in his next novel' – *Western Mail*

'Ian Fleming has discovered the secret of the narrative art . . . which is to work up to a climax unrevealed at the end of each chapter. Thus the reader has to go on reading' – John Betjeman, *Daily Telegraph*

'Fleming keeps his incidents and characters spinning through their paces like juggling balls. As for Bond, he might be Marlowe's younger brother except that he never takes coffee as a bracer, just one large Martini laced with vodka' – *Time Magazine*

Royal St George's club in Kent, or gambling at Le Touquet, or taking over the Granville Hotel in Ramsgate. To his companions Ian remained a mystery. He would invite friends to dinner and then not turn up himself. 'Oh, don't be so soft,' he would say the next day, when they asked where he had been. He had simply met a girl and decided to go somewhere else, and this was typical of his restless energy, his relentless pursuit of the next amusement, whatever it might be.

Ian would probably have remained in this easy undemanding world, with a career that only half engaged his mind and a lifestyle entirely built around his own pleasure, had it not been for the Second World War. The war might be said to have saved Ian Fleming. From the outset he walked into a job at the Naval Intelligence Department that was tailor-made for him, and was to provide much material for the James Bond books. Throughout the 1930s Ian seems to have been on the fringes of intelligence while he whiled away his City life. It is highly likely that on his return from Moscow in 1933 he, like many other travellers, was unofficially debriefed by the secret service, and thereafter he used his regular skiing and climbing trips to Kitzbühel to supply unsolicited reports about Austria and Germany to the Foreign Office. These amateurish efforts were not appreciated: Major-General Noel Mason-Macfarlane, the defence attaché in Berlin between 1937 and 1939, considered his bulletins 'gullible and of poor and imbalanced judgment', and added that he was no fan of Fleming himself.

If Ian wanted to be a real spy then he could have had no better model than Conrad O'Brien-ffrench, a dashing figure he met while skiing at Kitzbühel in 1935. O'Brien-ffrench was posing as a tour guide, but in reality was monitoring the German troop build-up in Bavaria on behalf of the mysterious Z Organization, a semi-autonomous intelligence ring that worked alongside the secret service. Ian was intrigued by this Buchanish character and his shadowy network, and in the spring of 1939 he seems to have been given his own chance as an unofficial observer. Ian was engaged by *The Times* to return to Moscow and report on a government trade mission led by the Secretary for Overseas Trade, Robert Hudson. The only other journalist present was Sefton Delmer of the *Daily Express*, who was convinced that Ian was involved in some shady business at the behest of the Foreign Office: whenever the Russians looked at him he suddenly started typing. As an old Moscow hand, Ian booked a suite at the National Hotel, where he had stayed six years earlier, and here he met an attractive 'Odessa Jewess', whom he promptly seduced. Fitzroy Maclean, a young diplomat, remembered bursting into Ian's room with a dinner invitation from Hudson to find Ian and the girl in a compromising position. He returned to Hudson and apologized, reporting that Ian could not come as he was 'very, very busy'. It was only later that Ian discovered that the Russians had specially arranged for the girl to keep an eye on him.

Ian's report for *The Times* included a few 'cautionary notes' about the value of the Russians as allies. He expressed his admiration for their army – 'these tough grey-faced little men (the average height of the army is 5'5")' – and an exasperation at their administration – 'a Sargasso sea of all the red tape in the world'. He concluded that Russia would be an extremely treacherous ally who would 'not hesitate to stab us in the back the moment it suited her'. This hyperbole was hardly the dry, factual language of an intelligence report, and if the language was at all similar in his unsolicited reports on Germany this probably explains why his efforts in this field were not appreciated. But it did prove that, in spite of the materialist cocoon which he had spun for himself in the City, Ian had lost neither his natural ability with words, nor his imagination.

It seems that Ian's long-standing interest in intelligence helped him secure his wartime job. On 24 May 1939 he was invited to the Carlton Grill to have lunch with two admirals. This was remarkable in itself, and Ian did not know that one of them, the clear-eyed, irascible John Godfrey, had just been appointed Director of Naval Intelligence (DNI) and was looking for a capable young man to act as his assistant. During lunch Ian showed all his abilities in charming older men, and he impressed enough to ensure that several months later he became Lieutenant Ian Fleming in the Royal Naval Volunteer Reserve – the RNVR, or 'Wavy Navy' as it was known. While Ian had never been aboard a warship, and had no wish to, his new boss, John Godfrey, was anything but a 'Strand Sailor'. A hard taskmaster who was not afraid of making enemies, Godfrey had just been plucked from the bridge of HMS *Repulse* to add some steel and vigour to a department that between the wars had become something of a graveyard for deadbeat officers on their last outing before retirement. Godfrey never made any secret of being a sailor first and foremost, and he was never completely at home in the world of intelligence, nor in the ants' nest of Whitehall. Ian, to his immense satisfaction,

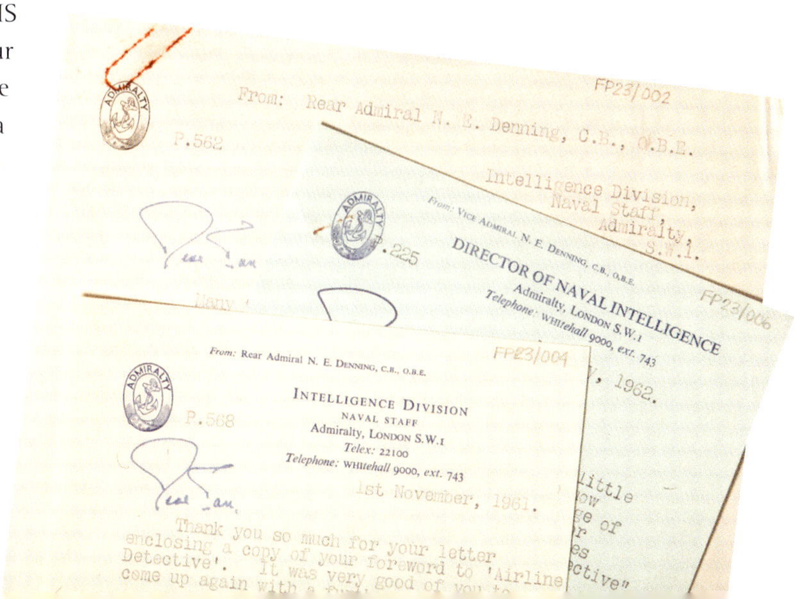

Fleming remained in touch with his former wartime colleagues at the Department of Naval Intelligence during his later years as a novelist. His files include correspondence with Admiral Norman Denning, who became a post-war director of the DNI.

found that he was, and it was quite obvious to many people who worked with Godfrey and his brusque, imaginative PA that in reality their roles were reversed. 'Ian should have been DNI and I his naval adviser,' Godfrey later confessed in his unpublished memoirs, which according to those who knew the admiral was the highest praise possible.

The full story of Ian Fleming at the Department of Naval Intelligence could alone be the subject of a small book, and it has been well documented by his two biographers John Pearson and Andrew Lycett. Broadly speaking, from his desk just outside the green-baize door to the DNI's office in Room 39 of the Admiralty, Ian was responsible for realizing much of the planning and imaginative thinking that came out of that department during the war. He was given remarkable powers by Admiral Godfrey, who was able, like Ian himself, to delegate effectively, and so his role was far more than that of a straightforward assistant. He would liaise on Godfrey's behalf with the Secret Intelligence Service, the Political Warfare Executive (charged with spreading rumour and propaganda in enemy countries), the Special Operations Executive (sabotage and subversion in enemy countries), the Joint Intelligence Committee and the press, as well as writing daily situation reports and fielding endless requests for information from the Prime Minister, Winston Churchill, himself. 'He was primarily a man of action and initiation,' wrote Godfrey, 'and a supremely good staff officer, but his great ability did not extend to human relations or understanding of humanities. He had plenty of ideas and was anxious to carry them out but was not interested in, and would prefer to ignore, the extent of the logistic background inseparable to all projects. In this respect he resembled Mr Churchill.'

One of the few existing wartime photographs of Fleming. He is standing in front of the fireplace in Room 39, wearing the uniform of an RNVR commander.

In the early days of the war, Room 39 resembled 'something like an Arab bank'. The desks were tightly packed together, and staff squeezed through this way and that carrying memos and fielding telephone calls to the constant clatter of typewriters. At his desk by the window outside his master's door, Ian sat in a cloud of cigarette smoke slightly removed from it all, dealing with his own never-ending pile of paperwork. As Godfrey's eyes and ears, he enjoyed a power quite out of proportion to his lowly rank, and clearly some of the Admirals of the Fleet resented this. It is notable that neither

Fleming nor Godfrey received any decorations for their work when the war was over, which was unusual enough to be remarked upon at the time. Certainly Godfrey was quixotic in his approach to intelligence, but he never lost the faith of his personal assistant. 'He is a real war winner,' wrote Fleming to a colleague, 'though many people don't realize it and are put off by his whimsy. He has the character and mind of a bohemian mathematician. At least so I have decided after discarding many other descriptions.'

Ian Fleming's job changed somewhat when John Godfrey was unceremoniously sacked from his post in the autumn of 1942, and thereafter became admiral of the Royal Indian Navy. Why Godfrey was removed has never been recorded, but his replacement, Admiral Rushbrooke, was a far less prickly character who had less need for Ian's particular political skills. With his spiritual master gone, Ian's power was gradually eroded. Nevertheless, as PA to the Director of Naval Intelligence, Ian had found the best job of his life, and his enthusiasm for it led him to arrive at his desk at 6 a.m., which he had never done before, and would never manage again.

One of the reasons for Ian's devotion to intelligence was finding himself in a world whose business was as exciting as any spy fiction. Naval Intelligence was a global, round-the-clock agency where anything and everything was considered. Months after he arrived at Room 39 the department produced a report into various *ruses de guerre*. Their list of inspired suggestions included schemes to lure U-boats and German warships towards false shipwrecks surrounded by mines, and spreading the (serious) rumour that turtles had been sighted around the British Isles. A torpedo nose, someone noted, bore a striking resemblance to the head of a turtle; when a curious enemy vessel pulled alongside the 'turtle', the torpedo could then be detonated. There was also the 'not very nice' suggestion number 28: 'The following is contained in a book by Basil Thompson: a corpse dressed as an airman, with dispatches in his pockets, could be dropped on the coast, supposedly from a parachute that had failed.' This was the germ of the idea behind one of the famous stories of deception in the Second World War, 'the man who never was', devised by Ewen Montagu, also in Naval Intelligence. This operation, in which Ian assisted, involved floating a corpse with a briefcase containing misleading intelligence documents off a submarine near the Spanish coast. Turtle heads, torpedoes and dead bodies – it was Ian's daydream world made real.

Ian also acted as a conduit for any bright ideas that 'civilians in uniform' might have, and one of the first to walk into Room 39 was

Merlin Minshall, an independent-minded adventurer who had recently sailed through the canals of Europe in an old Dutch ketch. He suggested using the Danube as a means to defeat the Germans. Ian was intrigued, and several months later dispatched Minshall to neutral Belgrade to assist the tough British agent Michael Mason in chartering six cement barges to sail up the river to the Iron Gates, the narrow passage between Romania and Yugoslavia. Once there, the plan was to scuttle the barges and make the river unnavigable, so disrupting Germany's transport system. In the event the local Nazis caught wind of what was happening and intercepted the barges 100 miles short of their destination, whereupon both agents escaped, Minshall in a high-speed air–sea–rescue launch. The Germans were furious that the British were using a neutral country in their attempt to block the Danube, and so was the Foreign Office. Ian brazened out the storm, and continued to throw out ideas that in the words of a colleague 'were plain crazy.' But there was always an element of possibility within the fantasy that meant that his schemes could not be dismissed out of hand immediately.

Courier's Passport.

THIS PASSPORT IS ONLY GOOD FOR THE JOURNEY SPECIFIED AND MUST BE GIVEN UP WITH THE DESPATCHES.

Valid for a journey to Gibraltar and return to Madrid. 16 February 1941.

No 777

Renewed and valid for a journey to London via Lisbon 26 February 1941.

By His Britannic Majesty's Minister at Madrid.

Le Soussigné Ministre de S.M. Britannique à Madrid

These are to request and require, in the Name of His Majesty, all those whom it may concern to allow

prie et requiert au nom de Sa Majesté tous ceux à qui il appartiendra de laisser passer librement

Mr. Ian Lancaster Fleming

charged with Despatches to pass freely without let or hindrance and to afford him every assistance and protection of which he may stand in need.

chargé de Dépêches et de lui accorder en toute occasion l'aide et la protection dont il pourra avoir besoin.

Given at Madrid the sixteenth day of February 194[illegible].

One of Ian's wartime missions was to Tangier. This is the February 1941 document that allowed him passage to Gibraltar from Madrid, returning to London via Lisbon.

One idea was for him to be marooned on an island off Heligoland with an observer to watch the shipping lanes outside Kiel; another was to set up an observation post just outside Dieppe harbour by sinking a great lump of concrete into the English Channel with men hidden inside it. Both of these were rejected, but they were not as outlandish as they might seem: elsewhere in the Admiralty there were plans afoot to create an unsinkable airstrip out of straw and ice that would be floated out into the mid-Atlantic and used as an air base to protect the convoys. 'What nonsense they were,' wrote Fleming many years later, 'those romantic Red Indian day dreams so many of us indulged in at the beginning of the war.' Nevertheless, the Red Indians sustained Ian's powerful imagination, and the more he immersed himself in the planning of these operations the more he vicariously shared in the adventure of actually taking part.

On two occasions during the war Ian did get closer to the action. The first was during the battle for France in 1940, when he was sent to maintain contact with Admiral Jean Darlan, the head of the French navy, whom the British were very concerned would not come over to their side. The French army had already capitulated, but the navy – then the fourth largest in the world – was modern and well equipped and under the patriotic Darlan (whose great grandfather had been killed at Trafalgar) was reluctant to retreat to the safety of the English ports, the home of the old enemy. Ian was unable to keep up with the Admiral, who fled south as the German army swept down through France, and by the time he reached Bordeaux he gave up the chase and was asked to assist in the chaotic evacuation at the harbour instead. Thousands of refugees were crowding the quayside clamouring to get on board the ships out in the roadsteads about to sail for England. Ian strode calmly into the centre of the maelstrom, immaculate in his blue naval uniform, and under the eyes of curious German bombers took it upon himself to direct the embarkation. He saw to it that the first to board was a large consignment of Rolls-Royce aircraft engines, followed by an orderly parade of well-heeled British expatriates sweating in their furs and jewels; Fleming allowed them only two suitcases each. Just as the last boatload was about to cast off, a blast of klaxons heralded the arrival of King Zog of Albania and his royal motorcade. The convoy came to an untidy halt on the quayside, whereupon the King, his court and his crown jewels all demanded safe passage: Fleming saw to it that they too were safely stowed aboard. As darkness fell, all that remained was a long line of abandoned Bentleys and Rolls-Royces.

Fleming stayed on, waiting to sail with the British ambassador, and it was to him that he voiced another characteristically bright idea about how to placate the intractable Admiral Darlan. 'Why doesn't His Majesty's government', Ian suggested, 'offer Admiral Darlan the Isle of Wight for the duration of the war, and make it French territory under the French flag for the entire period?' This idea might have been considered, albeit briefly, by Admiral Godfrey in the Department of Naval Intelligence, but in the realpolitik of war there was no place for Ian's fantasy. Barely two weeks later Darlan's continued resistance provoked the British to bombard the French fleet at Mers el Kebir, and in a mere five minutes they destroyed seven ships and claimed 1,250 lives. In one brutal stroke Admiral Darlan's power had been cut from beneath him. 'From that moment,' wrote Fleming, 'I thought I had better stick to my duties as a Lieutenant RNVR, and leave the conduct of the war to older and conceivably wiser heads.'

Admiral Godfrey was generally reluctant to allow his gifted PA out of Room 39 'for a bit of fresh air'; Ian simply knew too much to risk his falling into enemy hands. But in August 1942 he was allowed another opportunity to get closer to the action, in his role as an observer on a commando raid on Dieppe. Operation Jubilee, in which 6,000 Canadian and British commandos attempted to storm the beach at dawn, was intended as a dry run for D-Day. Ian was there to witness a small group of commandos under his control go ashore and grab any German naval intelligence material they could lay their hands on. He had been forbidden to accompany them, and remained on HMS *Hunt* 800 yards offshore to watch the battle. This appeared to begin well, but then almost everything that could go wrong did, and the raiders found themselves and their landing craft pinned down on the narrow shingle beneath the withering fire of German positions built into the cliffs. Ian later wrote an account of this raid, in which he took care to describe all the sensations of that fascinating, bloody scene. He was particularly struck by the orchestra of sounds made by the different types of guns – 'the hasty bark of the pom poms, the whiplash crack of the naval 4 inch and the unnerving, deliberate "knock knock knock" of the German anti-tank guns. The noise seemed so unhurried and deliberate that it cut through the permanent welter of sounds with a disturbing authority.' In among the din and smoke, Ian was intrigued to see a gaggle of geese flying lazily through the battle, utterly unconcerned, and a sailor sitting on an ammunition box equally oblivious to the shells falling around him. He was reading a book entitled *A Fortnight's Folly*. At one point Ian's destroyer was hit by a shell that killed one man and injured four others, and soon a steady stream of wounded were being brought on board. It was clear that Ian's special commandos, who were aboard a gunboat waiting to go ashore, were never going to make landfall. Then 'The Government exhortation, "Is Your Journey Really Necessary?" came to my mind,' he wrote, 'heavily underlined by the shells from the shore batteries that came zipping through the rigging.'

By the end of the day almost 3,000 Allied troops had been captured or lost their lives on the beach, and this event undoubtedly had an effect on him. Fleming may have wanted desperately to go ashore, but from the deck of HMS *Hunt* Ian saw for himself that the reality of battle was neither romantic nor fun. His sister-in-law, the actress Celia Johnson (the future star of *Brief Encounter* and other films, who had married Peter Fleming in 1935), saw him a few days later, and he told her he had just been at Dieppe. 'It must have been hair-raising and awful and wonderful and fearful as anything could be,' she wrote. 'Even Ian, who in Fleming fashion understates nicely, seemed not exactly staggered but as if he had his breath taken away once or twice.'

The small number of commandos who failed to get ashore at Dieppe were part of a new unit Ian had just formed known as 30 AU. This was, in effect, the private army of the Naval Intelligence Department, and Ian had taken the idea from the activities of Otto Skorzeny, a bullish German stormtrooper who had led a similar unit of armed looters who had snatched codes, maps and equipment during the German invasion of Crete in May 1941. Skorzeny and his men had obviously known what they were looking for, and Ian wanted his own 'Red Indians', as he called them, to match the Germans' success. These men were seconded from other commando units and given special training in safe-cracking, lock-picking and unarmed combat at the various training schools used by the Special Operations Executive. The unit, initially only thirty strong, was Ian's direct responsibility, and he would plan its raids in meticulous detail, even memorizing the aerial photographs himself. 'I was astonished', remarked Dunstan Curtis, an officer in 30 AU who led a raid in North Africa, 'at how much he knew about Algiers, how extremely detailed his intelligence was . . . and he often become so excited about the job it was as if he was coming with us.' Of course desk-bound Ian never did, but he came to know many of the buccaneering characters in his private army, and these 'tough commando types', as he later referred to them, provided him with some of the inspiration for James Bond.

The formation of 30 AU had taken a sustained campaign of politicking on Ian's part, and once it was established he struggled long and hard to keep it under his control before it was finally prised away from him on D-Day. According to Edward Merrett, the man who sat opposite him in Room 39, Ian's direction of his 'Red Indians' was as close as he ever came to the activities of James Bond. 'He was a pen-pusher like all of us. Of course he knew everything that was going on, but he never seemed to show any real inclination to take part in it. If he was secretly longing for action I never saw any sign of it. In short, Ian's war had plenty of sweat and toil and tears but no real blood.'

When not planning these raids, Ian was involved in a range of different projects that kept him busy and interested. Together with Donald McLachlan, he set up unit 17 Z, which used a 'black-propaganda' radio station, Atlantiksender, based at Woburn Abbey, to broadcast realistic-sounding rumours to U-boat crews out in the mid-Atlantic. On occasion he would sit down at the microphone himself and harangue any listening German sailor about how much German prisoners of war were earning working in America. Another favourite project of his was Operation Goldeneye. This was a sophisticated plan to maintain communication with Gibraltar and conduct a campaign of sabotage if the Germans tried to invade Spain. The detailed planning for this provided him with another excuse to avoid the humdrum life in Room 39, and it took him off to Madrid, Gibraltar and Tangier at regular intervals. He also made a number of trips across the Atlantic, first to meet the British intelligence chief in North America, 'Little Bill' Stephenson, and then 'Big Bill' Donovan, the man who became one of the founding fathers of the CIA.

Fleming's correspondence with Peter Smithers provides a fascinating insight into the wartime activities of both men. Smithers, who was recruited to the DNI by Fleming, joined the SIS in France.

When Ian first met Donovan, 'Big Bill' was canvassing ideas about what sort of intelligence agency the United States would need after the war, and Ian was quick to offer suggestions. According to Ivar Bryce, these were so detailed that Ian was coerced into setting them down on paper, and spent two days locked in a room at work on 'a document of some seventy pages covering every aspect of a giant secret intelligence and secret operational organization'. This memorandum, dated 27 June 1942, survives in the Office of Strategic Services records, and Donovan undoubtedly read it before submitting his own report to President Roosevelt. Most of Ian's thoughts were either too unrealistic or too obvious to merit inclusion, though there were some typical Fleming touches: he proposed that Donovan 'should make an example of someone at an early date for indiscretion, and continue to act ruthlessly where lack of security is concerned'. While Ian cannot not claim the credit for having written the original charter for the CIA (as he later mischievously suggested), Donovan did consider his contribution useful enough to be rewarded with the present of a .38 Colt revolver inscribed 'For Special Services'. Ian dined out on this story thereafter, and he could not help hinting that the weapon was given in recognition of some more shadowy deed.

It was on another of his transatlantic trips that Ian may – or may not – have had his most Bond-like experience of the war. While attending the Quebec conference in August 1943 (at which Churchill and Roosevelt discussed future Allied strategy) Ian apparently paid a visit to Camp X, the secret training school at Oshawa, on Lake Ontario, that was being used to teach recruits the dark arts of clandestine warfare. According to Bill Stephenson, Ian enrolled on one of the two-week courses, and proved a model pupil. His height and strength ensured he did well at self-defence and unarmed combat, and on the firing range he blasted away using a Sten gun 'with extraordinary relish'. He received top marks for a particularly hazardous underwater exercise, where pupils were challenged to swim out to an old tanker moored in the lake and attach a limpet mine to the hull without being detected. This adventure was remarkably similar to James Bond's nocturnal mission to place a mine on

Personal

INTELLIGENCE DIVISION,
NAVAL STAFF,
ADMIRALTY, S.W.1.

EHALL 9000.
ENSION 743.

11th March, 1941.

My dear Peter,

Your various excellent letters have reached me on my re-urn from a slight excursion abroad, which was enormous fun, ut about which I shall have to tell you later.

Incidentally, I met the American whom we both like o much, who used to work with Bill, and he told me that he had een you.

I am sorry your career in Washington has been rather hequered, and it is infuriating that things have not gone more moothly, in spite of the very categorical signals which D.N.I. as made; I will try and have another sent when a suitable pportunity arises, but I think it would be as well to let atters take their course for the time being, particularly as he situation seems to be getting easier.

At the same time you might tell the Naval Attache that ou have heard from me, and that D.N.I. is rather chafing at he bit at not having yet received answers to the questionnaire hich was sent out with you. This is not true, but might have ome effect, and I know that your Section here are concerned hat the exchange of intelligence with your colleagues is so ar pretty well a one-way traffic.

Things are very much the same here, and the Town is not uch draughtier than when you left it, although I expect it will ecome so before the end of the year.

Our little operation with the uniforms has not yet come ff, but I think you may find that they have been baptised by the ime I see you again. We have played various other practical jokes along the same lines, but details of these must wait for he time being. The opponents with whom you used to concern ourself particularly are still as bone-headed and giving good alue.

Very little news of Bill, whom I only see from time to ime, and I fear that he is rather a fish out of water in London. t would not surprise me if his sphere of work were changed uring the coming months, and I will at any rate mention your uggestion that he might be valuable in America, but he is not an asy man to fit in, and his expense sheet would look worse in ollars than it did in francs.

I should not worry too much about the dullness of your work or the time being, as you may find yourself required for something ore exciting if America decides to get more than her ankles wet n this war.

In the meantime try and avoid, above all things, queering our pitch with the Naval Attache and his staff, and curb your ostalgie de la boue.

Let me have some more letters now that you have learned o type.

Yours ever

IF

t P.H.B. Otway-Smithers,
R.N.V.R.

given two clues on his conduct, (1) that he suffers l-health, and (2) that his lack of an educational F.O. List) renders him particularly sensitive to of Magdalen bucks and the scintillating candelabra otables which appear to be gathered in your capital. ay be a great deal in this analysis and I leave it ogical acumen to pierce the straw thatch of this son

I am sure you have no intention of taking the ilitary colleague, which would be no help to any-y to assist matters at all.

been away for six weeks on a millionaire's ruise, the high point of which was the Mena I enjoyed the luxury of fried eggs, orange juice, Pyramids. I unfortunately missed Teheran and ed bronchitis which I thoroughly enjoyed. I am f using up rapidly the sunshine and vitamins which n a week or so I shall be once again in the sub-h is my normal lot. Otherwise there have been no gh I hope for some to help me through this year.

as your post-war aspirations are concerned I cannot use of Commons, at any rate until we have settled sonable line of statecraft. Bill D. is very your services, and since he will be back at the old Germans are defeated I am sure you would like to ces at his disposal. Please let me know on this

s delighted to get your letter of the 13th which nearly as long as I should have liked it and certainly full good meat.

I got back here about 10 days ago after various ad-ures of which I will tell you one day, and I am at the moment ining at the leash to go and catch a few sturgeon in the h but this has not come through from there yet.

All you say sounds very sensible but I have certain s about your mixing yourself up in the C.S.As. I think you d keep as far away from them as possible, myself, or we shall nto trouble with D.N.I. Ottawa. However, I expect you have ed all the pros and cons.

I am delighted to hear that you have bought a motor-car hope it will be still intact if and when I visit you again. k often with nostalgia of my life at Castle Smithers and ularly of one weekend which I hope will not have the results you anticipate in your last paragraph. As you say, corres-e through your safe hand has not been very considerable so t you have drawn your own conclusions.

I am quite certain that you are right in what you say xchange of intelligence in the Far East. I thought all

Secret & Personal

Tel: Whitehall 9000
Ext. 991

Intelligence Division,
Naval Staff,
Admiralty, S.W.1.

13th October, 1941.

ear *Peter*,

I am afraid I have been very remiss in not answering our excellent letter of 31st August before, but I have recently ad to take on a whole lot of new work which has taken my mind ight off the United States for the time being.

I won't bother you by going back over old ground such the visit of McCollum and Chappell. Suffice to say that the sit went off extremely well and I saw that they were given all e small attentions on which you have always been asking for ciprocity from the Navy Department. They were certainly eatly impressed, but I question whether they will be able to do y much propaganda in the O.N.I. which I feel will never change spots to any great extent during this war.

I took the opportunity of reading extracts of your letter D.N.I. and he was pleased and in many cases amused. At the e time I have a feeling that he was inclined to think that you le about a bit too much in other people's puddles and are to stir up ~~those~~ false hares (this metaphor appears to have a little mixed but I dare say hares sometimes do get into les!) I have explained to him on many occasions that this ency of yours very often has excellent results, and that you a most valuable antidote to stagnancy wherever you may be inted. I think what put the whole thing into his mind inally was your blitz visit to Ireland where I believe he you went beyond your brief. In this I am certain he is r but I am afraid that is not a vice of his which can be ssed.

Anyway, to cut a long story short, endeavour to move in the jungle, avoiding the corns of its many denizens, ering the while the famous Japanese proverb "The dragon in w waters becomes the prey of shrimps". Here again I am not hether dragons and shrimps are found in jungles, but you now what I mean.

Your news about Castle Smithers, the car, etc. gave me e attack of nostalgia and you can imagine how often I ish to be there rather than here. When I tell you that oy Hotel are now mixing Martinis out of bath-tub gin and you will know that we are rapidly progressing back to ife and the transitional period is distasteful. However, moved to the Athenaeum Court, which is a hideous block of Piccadilly, and I flit uneasily from one to another of restaurants in the evening. Josef is still able to cks out of straw but he is correspondingly expensive and I also have a car now whose motive power is a mixture petrol, water and moth-balls which make the petrol last

Boegner, as I wrote to you before, is a most able man and an acquaintance of mine. I knew his brother very well and I have the greatest admiration for the family. I am sure you will find him extremely useful, and I personally wish that he had been given a position on de Gaulle's Council, though I suppose

Lieut. P. Otway-Smithers, R.N.V.R.

this ..

P.S. If there is any way me Chesterfield cigarettes, please do so to any amount. I will repay

F

P.P.S. Please pass on enclosed.

the hull of Mr Big's vessel in *Live and Let Die*, the second James Bond adventure, written in 1953.

Having completed these physical challenges, Fleming then faced two sterner tests. Would-be agents had to somehow infiltrate themselves into the main Toronto power station, which had already been alerted that they would be coming. Fleming was sensible enough to play to his strengths: he adopted his best Etonian manner, simply rang up the station claiming to be a visiting expert from London, and arranged a formal tour. His ruse succeeded. But it was the final test that, according to Stephenson, proved to be the most interesting. The students were told that an enemy spy was holed up in a room downtown, and that he was

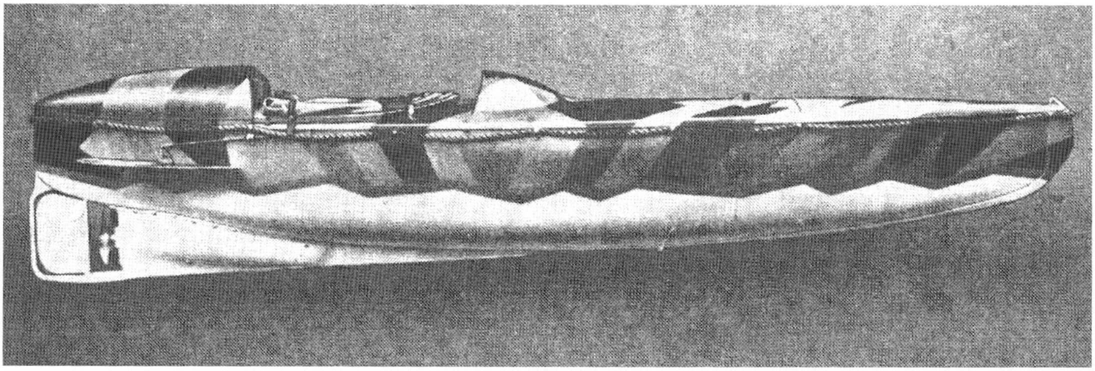

The top-secret Descriptive Catalogue of Special Devices and Supplies issued by the War Office for SOE includes gadgets like exploding briefcases and cigarettes, limpet mines (opposite) *and camouflaged submersibles* (above). *These are the sorts of inventions that would have inspired Q Branch.*

to be disposed of. Armed with a revolver, each pupil was sent to the address to attempt to kill him. According to Stephenson, this man was actually a camp instructor who was confident of using a series of clever feints to dodge any bullet fired at him. When Fleming arrived at the address, he spent a long time out in the corridor, deliberating, and then he left without ever opening the door. Ian claimed afterwards that 'he could never kill a man that way'. He had failed the ultimate test, and Stephenson said this is why he would never have made a decent field agent. Ian simply could not kill in cold blood.

If it is true, then this is a tantalizing story about the man who created James Bond, the ultimate secret agent of the twentieth century, the fictional character with a licence to kill. If Fleming had been to Camp X, then surely his experiences there are the source for all Bond's methods of killing and spycraft. The story also fuels the myth, which Fleming was careful never to entirely deny, that in some way he *was* James Bond and knew all about this world through personal experience. Once Fleming had become a successful writer, journalists were sent out to Goldeneye to meet the 'real' James Bond, and when pressing him on the similarities between himself and 007 they interpreted Fleming's careful demurring as an admission. He was invariably photographed gun in hand, with *film-noir* lighting raking his craggy features and a cigarette burning between his fingers. And the story did Bill Stephenson no harm either. As neighbours in the Caribbean after the war the two men often got together and swapped colourful tales, some of which Stephenson unwisely included in his autobiography, *A Man Called Intrepid*. Unfortunately, by committing some of these half-truths and fabrications to print, Stephenson served only to undermine his own real achievements.

Regrettably for Bond fans, however, the whole story of Ian Fleming attending a course at Camp X was almost certainly an invention. David Stafford, who has written the history of Camp X, can find no evidence of Fleming ever enrolling as a pupil there; nor has he uncovered any underwater limpet-mine missions or attempts to kill foreign agents. No one who taught there remembers either Ian Fleming or any of the courses Stephenson described. That is not to say that Fleming never went there: he may well have visited Oshawa while attending the Quebec conference in 1943. He certainly knew all about it through Stephenson and his friend Ivar Bryce, who was working for British intelligence in America and who recruited South American agents to put through the school. But in truth Camp X could have taught Ian nothing about clandestine warfare that he had not found out already through his commandos in 30 AU and through his brother Peter, who was well acquainted with irregular warfare. Camp X is yet another Fleming myth that, courtesy of Bill Stephenson, seems to have grown in the telling.

Despite the frustrating lack of evidence about Fleming and Camp X, the claim that he was unable to kill is probably true. Peter Smithers, a colleague of Ian's in the Naval Intelligence Department, believed that Fleming's basically aggressive nature was repressed by a desire for authority. During the war Ian plumped for power over danger, despite the fact that in principle he craved adventure and excitement. And there is other anecdotal testimony to his essentially passive nature. Fleming's friend Ernie Cuneo, a fast-talking New York attorney, once challenged him to a mock fistfight. Cuneo noticed that, despite standing a clear head and shoulders taller than him, Fleming had no idea how to square up as a boxer; no one had ever taught him how to. Another friend remembered a drunk hitting Ian over the head with a chair that sent him crashing to the floor. Fleming just lay there, trembling. When asked why he didn't retaliate, Ian replied, 'If I did, I would have killed him.' The truth was that, unlike James Bond, Fleming was not by nature a violent man.

By the time of the Normandy landings in June 1944 Ian's real men of action, his 'Red Indians', numbered 150 strong. It was in these final stages of the war that 30 AU would make made its greatest contribution to the war effort. As Germany retreated, top-secret devices were left hidden in farms and factories across France, and there was a scramble among the Allies to capture these curiosities first. Ian fired off orders sending his unit in all directions looking for anything and everything useful. Particularly keen for his men to get there in the most dramatic form possible, he was insistent that a company of 30 AU should parachute into the Bois de Boulogne ahead of the Allied advance on Paris. When this idea was mooted by higher authorities, he suggested his men drop directly on to the German naval headquarters at Kiel. Ralph Izzard, Fleming's friend, remembers that when Ian asked for volunteers for this suicidal mission 'everyone took two sharp steps backwards.'

Yet 30 AU did succeed. Its war booty was impressive, and on paper sounds like the list of props from a James Bond novel. It captured a beautiful female French professor who specialized in making liquid nitrogen, a two-man submarine that was picked up on a road outside Paris, a one-man submarine washed up on the beach at Ostend (with its decomposing crew still inside, one with his dead eye pressed to the periscope), and an acoustic homing torpedo hidden inside a mushroom farm in Houilles. The greatest prize was stumbled upon in Tambach castle, an Alpine redoubt that contained the entire German naval archives dating back to 1870. This treasure trove was guarded by an elderly German admiral and his two assistants, and Ian spent the last few months of the war trying to organize the archives' safe transfer to London and deciding what to do with the three admirals. According to one source, he became convinced that, if left alive, these men would only start scheming for the next war. After all, it had happened in 1919, and Ian firmly believed it would happen again. He told the young officer in charge that the three old men should be eliminated. When the subaltern refused to murder prisoners of war, Fleming relented and admitted with some unease that there were plans to bring them to England. His last signal to his unit was 'Find immediately the twelve top naval commanders and make each one write ten thousand words on why Germany lost the war at sea.'

The most significant event for Ian during the last year of the war had nothing to do with the crushing of Germany, as it concerned his own future. In the autumn of 1944 he was sent to Jamaica to attend a conference on the U-boat threat in the Caribbean, and he travelled down from Washington with his old school friend Ivar Bryce. The pair spent three long days sweating in the ballroom of the Myrtle Bank Hotel, Kingston, before managing to escape on the last evening and pay a visit to Bryce's tumbledown house in the hills. They arrived unannounced, and found the house shuttered up and dark, with no one at home but the ancient and slightly deaf housekeeper, who stumbled around after them in a mild panic. With nothing but a bottle of grenadine syrup to drink, the two friends sat out on the veranda, watching the lightning breaking over the distant purple hills. The soft, warm melancholy of the place made a profound impression on Ian. By the following morning he had made up his mind that this was his idea of paradise, and he wanted a tropical hideaway of his own. A few months later, with Ivar's help, he found what he was looking for: an old donkey racetrack east of Oracabessa on the north shore of the island. There were no roads between the field and the sea, and it had a cliff that gave way to a small, secluded beach.

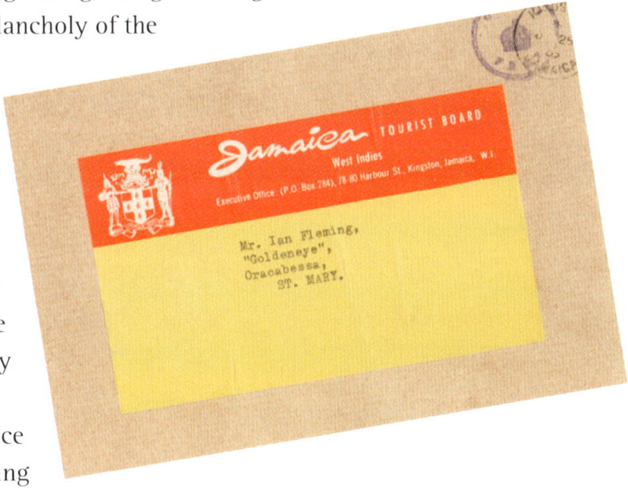

Back in Room 39, Ian whiled away his office hours doodling designs on Admiralty blotting paper for the house he would build there, and when he had finished he christened it Goldeneye, the mysterious name that he had used for one of his wartime schemes. The name was also a reference to Carson McCullers's novel *Reflections in a Golden Eye*, which he was reading at the time, and to Oracabessa, which means 'Head of Gold'. Most apposite of all, on the property there were the remains of an old Spanish tomb on which was inscribed a golden eye in a golden head. The name was entirely appropriate for what he had in mind. Here he would live, work, and create a legend for the house that would far outstrip 'any of the great houses that had stood there so long and achieved nothing'.

When Ian Fleming finally left His Majesty's Service, on 10 November

1945, he had spent six and a half years at the Admiralty, had reached the rank of commander, and was due fifty-six days' leave. Despite all the frustrations of his unusual job, he had found the combination of power, intrigue and travel particularly suited to his own complex personality. He had, albeit at one remove, experienced much that would later end up in James Bond novels – experiences without which the world of 007 would not have been born. He had the raw material and, according to his friend Robert Harling, he now had the ambition as well. Harling remembers eating Spam rations with Ian as they sat beside their jeep in northern France in July 1944. It was a beautiful afternoon, and the conversation swung towards what they planned to do once the war was over. When Harling had finished, Ian said simply, 'I am going to write the spy story to end all spy stories.' He had no commitments, enough money, and Goldeneye would become the perfect bolt-hole in which to write it. All the signs were that this was precisely what he meant to do as soon as peace returned.

But, as ever with Ian Fleming, his fate took a rather different turn. Ignoring all the raw material still fresh in his memory, Ian turned his back on the notion of a romantic, impecunious life as a freelance writer in the Caribbean and accepted the post of foreign news manager of the Kemsley newspaper group. Bond, and Goldeneye, would have to wait a further seven years before Ian finally let down the jalousies on the outside world and hammered out the first words of *Casino Royale.*

The opening lines of Casino Royale *mark the birth of a character whose exploits have captivated readers for over half a century. This is a carbon copy of the first page of the published manuscript.*

CHAPTER 1

The scent and smoke and sweat of a casino combine together and hit the taste-buds with an acid shock at three in the morning. Then the soul-erosion produced by high gambling - a compost of gree and fear and nervous tension - becomes suddenly unbearable and the senses awake and revolt at the smell of it all.

James Bond caught this smell through his concentration and

Fleming discovered Jamaica's north shore in the last year of the Second World War, and it was here that he chose to build his house, Goldeneye. All the Bond books were written from here, where Fleming spent two months every winter. As his fame as the author of the James Bond novels spread, Fleming was featured 'at home' in Jamaica in a number of publications. He gave this picture, which shows the view from Goldeneye, to the Jamaican Tourist Board.

LIVE AND LET DIE

1954

Original title
The Undertaker's Wind

First line

There are moments of great luxury in the life of a secret agent.

Story

James Bond, now fully recovered from his lashing by Le Chiffre, is sent to Harlem to investigate Mr Big, a voodoo baron and unlikely SMERSH agent, whom M suspects is behind a smuggling operation that is funding Soviet agents in America. Seventeenth-century gold coins have been turning up in Harlem and Florida, and M believes that these are part of a larger hoard buried in Jamaica by the Welsh pirate Sir Henry Morgan. Bond goes up to Harlem with CIA agent Felix Leiter, only to be captured by Mr Big on arrival and quizzed by his mind-reading girlfriend, Solitaire. Bond senses she is a trapped bird trying to escape. He rescues her, and together with Leiter they flee to Florida, where a nocturnal visit to a warehouse confirms the treasure is being smuggled in under the sand at the bottom of fish tanks. Bond follows the trail to Jamaica alone (Leiter has had his leg and arm bitten off by a shark in the warehouse, and Solitaire has been recaptured). There he completes a dangerous underwater swim to Mr Big's island, and manages to plant a limpet mine on Big's boat before being discovered. He is then captured, lectured, and bound to Solitaire behind Big's boat. The pair are about to be fatally dragged over a shallow coral reef when Bond's limpet mine explodes. Big is then devoured by a shark; Bond is granted 'passionate leave' with Solitaire.

Last lines

There was open sensuality in Solitaire's eyes as she looked up at him. She smiled innocently.
'What about my back?' she said.

Inspirations

Ian Fleming had made many trips to New York: first during the war as assistant to Admiral Godfrey, then afterwards as a journalist. His guide on these trips was often Ernie Cuneo, a short, wide, fast-talking attorney, who really opened Ian's eyes to America. Cuneo arranged for him to spend a night in the Upper West Side with a couple of local detectives as they patrolled the dance clubs of Harlem. Here his imagination was ignited by meeting a local crime boss and discovering the scale of drug trafficking in the city. This inspired him to create Mr Big, who was not a mafioso in the Al Capone mode but black and hugely powerful. That he was a SMERSH agent as well chimed with a contemporary conspiracy theory alive in America (which at the time was in the grip of McCarthyism) that the National Association for the Advancement of Colored People was sponsored by the Soviet Union.

Fleming then took the same journey as later did Bond, from New York to Florida by train. The Silver Phantom, a great serpent of chrome and aluminium, carried him south to St Petersburg, on the Gulf of Mexico, which became the model for the town of awful oldsters avoiding death in the sun. When Fleming reached Jamaica he pitched in all the local colour he could think of, and he took Carbitta island, off Port Maria, as the model for Mr Big's treasure hideaway. Here Henry Morgan had careened his ships and, it was rumoured, buried the vast amount of Spanish gold he had ransacked from the city of Panama in 1687. Nothing has ever been found.

Voodoo plays a large part in the book (Mr Big is supposed to be a zombie – you can't kill him because he is already dead), and Fleming had more than a passing interest in this subject. One night after his car had broken down in Jamaica he was forced to walk three miles back to his home in the dark. On the way he unexpectedly came across a voodoo wedding, and it captivated him. Most of the Haitian voodoo he draws upon in this book is from his friend Patrick Leigh Fermor's *The Traveller's Tree*, from which he quotes at considerable length at the beginning.

The vivid description of Bond's epic underwater swim through the reefs out to Mr Big's boat was almost certainly inspired by Ian's first scuba experience with Jacques Cousteau in 1953:

> I put on 30 lb of equipment and went over the side, and looked down into the limitless grey depths and tried to remember to breathe quietly through the aqualung. I swam slowly down and drifted with my arms round the broad tubes of the suction pump. It rattled and shook against me with the upward jet of stones and broken pottery. I looked up at the distant hull of the ship and at the idle screw. The surface of the sea was like a sheet of mercury illuminated in one spot, like a star sapphire, the sun.

To this Ian added the real-life wartime adventures of the Gamma Group, crack Italian frogmen who sank over 54,000 tons of shipping in Gibraltar with limpet mines they attached using mini-submarines.

What the readers said

'I have not read a thriller with such enjoyment since Bulldog Drummond at the age of 14!'

'Won't you admit to being a little bit doughty in permitting the Hotel St Regis to serve butterscotch sauce? With Liebfraumilch? Butterscotch is for bobby soxers!'

What the critics said

'How wincingly well Mr Fleming writes' – *Sunday Times*

'Tense; ice-cold, sophisticated; Peter Cheyney for the carriage trade' – *Evening Standard*

'Contains passages which for sheer excitement have not been surpassed by any modern writer of this kind' – *Times Literary Supplement*

'His story moves swiftly and he writes with obvious enjoyment. Altogether a thriller *de luxe*' – *Birmingham Post*

What Fleming said

In a letter to Winston Churchill, sending him a copy of the book: 'It is an unashamed thriller and its only merit is that it makes no demands on the mind of the reader.'

As with Casino Royale, *Jonathan Cape's hardback cover design for Fleming's second novel featured the title lettering prominently. The Pan Books 1957 mass-market paperback cover art by Sam 'Peff' Peffer (which replaced a version showing a representation of the Bond character's face by Josh Kirby) is suitably epic.*

THE SLOW BIRTH OF BOND

Models and Ideas

When Ian Fleming strode up the steps of Kemsley House on Gray's Inn Road on his first day as the foreign news manager of the Kemsley newspaper group, he gave every appearance of a man on his way to the top. It was 1946, and he was thirty-eight, well connected, self-assured and accustomed to power. His newly-created job was as head of the Mercury News Service, a kind of in-house news agency dedicated to gathering foreign stories that Ian would circulate through Kemsley's thirty regional and national publications – ranging from the barely literate *Empire News* to the *Sunday Times*. This paid him a generous £5,000 a year, plus expenses, and the unheard-of bonus of two months' annual paid holiday that he would spend at his new house in Jamaica. Ian had considerable charm and panache – which was just as well, since this lofty appointment inevitably caused some resentment among the old hands in the newsroom. But he paid little attention to that. On the face of it Ian had found another perfect job, and he would stick at it for the next fourteen years, long after his initial enthusiasm for the newspaper world had soured. Also, in Goldeneye, he had a daydream hideaway, the perfect retreat in which to write his 'spy story to end all spy stories'. Why then did it take seven years to get started?

Despite all his arrogance and apparent self-assurance, inside the hurricane room of Ian Fleming's mind there was still a knot of self-doubt. Ian had not put his name to any published piece of writing since his trip to Moscow in 1933, and in the intellectual world he was still Peter Fleming's younger brother. Before the war, Peter's books had made him a household name, and it was much easier not to bother to compete. Now, with his exciting years in the Admiralty behind him, Ian knew that there was no point returning to the City and resuming his career as 'the world's worst stockbroker.' He wanted to write; but first he had to find his voice.

Ian was not an intellectual, and intellectuals for the most part intimidated him; but he admired writers. At Kitzbühel he had read Thomas Mann's *The Magic Mountain* in German, and he was still able to recite passages of this favourite book off by heart. His youthful enthusiasm had also brought him into contact with William Plomer, a gay poet and novelist to whom Ian had sent a fan letter in 1926 after reading his novel *Turbott Wolfe*. This proved the catalyst for a lifelong friendship, as Plomer – a diffident, uncompetitive man, who stood outside the London literary cliques – proved the perfect foil for Fleming's own complex soul. In time Plomer would go on to edit all of the James Bond books, and he was responsible for some of the best-known quirks of 007's character. Through Plomer Ian met T. S. Eliot and Paul Gallico, and even became an unlikely companion of Edith Sitwell, with whom he discussed a joint book on the mystic philosopher Paracelsus. This lofty ambition never came to anything, but Ian – charming and immaculate as ever in his dark-blue suit – managed to ingratiate himself with this extraordinary grande dame, who invariably dressed like a Tudor king.

Ian enjoyed these dalliances in the literary world, but in the immediate post-war years he was under no illusions about joining its highbrow ranks. For a start he was extremely diffident about his writing abilities, and it is interesting that in all his time at Kemsley newspapers he never wrote a single leader or foreign news report. He was not a man who could ever pretend to be interested in something, and foreign politics bored him as much as the domestic variety. What did interest him was escape, and this became the subject of an article published in Cyril Connolly's highly-regarded literary magazine *Horizon* in 1947. It was couched as a letter to a young man thinking of moving to Jamaica. 'My dear John,' he begins. 'You are one of the million or more English citizens who intend to seek

Fleming's career at the Sunday Times *covered a variety of roles, including those of foreign news manager and 'Atticus' columnist. Throughout the 1960s he continued to contribute pieces on a wide range of subjects.*

fortune and freedom abroad and I would like to encourage you because I don't believe we can go on indefinitely feeding 48 million people on borrowed money.' Ian then takes up the position of an insider well informed on his adopted paradise, explaining the delights of 'cold distilled coffee' (simply reheated, but in his schoolboyish enthusiasm it became something far more complex) and black crabs, 'which', he writes, 'are a great delicacy and they are eaten highly spiced. Every now and then they march inland in herds (like lemmings in reverse) and if your house is in the way they march through it or over it and if your body in your bed is in the way, they march over that too, and your face.' To those who knew him, in this article Fleming had simply reproduced his own speech rhythms on the page. 'I can assure you', he drawled, 'that sun and calm blue seas and brassy heat can be more wearing and exasperating than the grey but ever-changing porridge in which you live and make sweet moan.' This is precisely the knowing, unorthodox guidebook style that would become so familiar in the Bond books.

Writing about Jamaica might have been fun, but at this stage it was only a diversion. Money was important, and anyway, Ian liked the routine of office life. He sat in his tiny office in the Kemsley building on Gray's Inn Road in front of a map of the world that twinkled with little lights denoting the location of his eighty-odd foreign correspondents. He would hire them, cajole them and direct them, and in return they would send in their stories – 'intelligence', as he liked to call it. Fleming was, in fact, behaving like the head of some secret intelligence service, halfway between John Godfrey and M. And this was not so far from the truth; Kemsley correspondents were often from a secret service background, and continued to spy while working for Ian. For a man so deeply involved in the wartime intelligence world, it is not surprising that Fleming found it hard to let go. And all the while he kept daydreaming about his spy story to end all spy stories.

Occasionally these dreams broke the surface. In 1947, during an evening at the 36 Club, a dining society for former members of Naval Intelligence, a friend asked what kind of man he would employ as a secret agent. Ian immediately sketched out a profile of a ruthless, tough character, patriotic and promiscuous enough not to get entangled in relationships. He was reasonably affluent, and a loner. This figure reappeared again in 1950, in an article Fleming wrote for *The Kemsley Manual of Journalism*, where he described the ideal foreign correspondent, who was at ease with ambassadors and 'the most wastrelly spiv ... physically strong and not addicted to drink ... with a knowledge of shorthand and able to drive a car'.

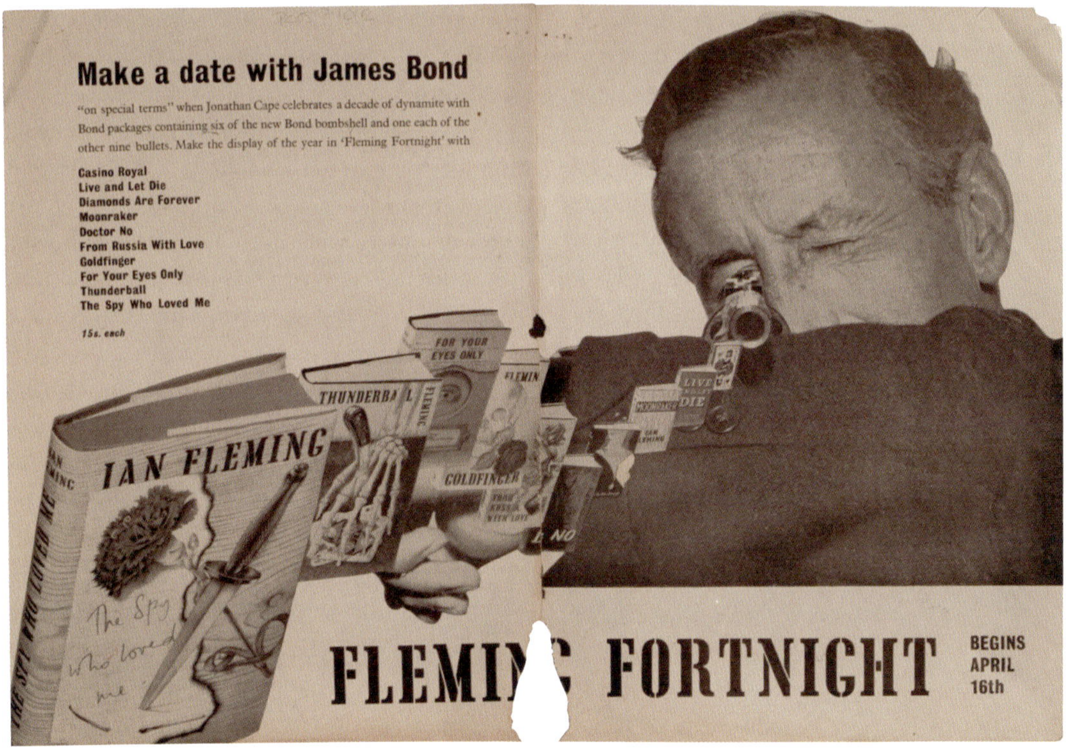

The Bond books presented an unprecedented marketing opportunity for their publishers, with collectable editions of the Jonathan Cape hardbacks remaining available in Britain long after Pan had issued the novels in paperback.

As well as dreaming about his ideal secret agent, Ian was also thinking of plots. One friend, the critic Peter Quennell, remembered Ian recounting a story as they shared a lift back to London after a country weekend. It was a tale of unmotivated murder; there was a body, but no weapon. The investigating detective was asked to dinner by the suspects and served a leg of mutton; it turned out that this leg, when frozen, had been the murder weapon. Ian never found a use for this ingenious device, and eventually he magnanimously suggested it to his friend Roald Dahl, who rewrote the story as 'Lamb to the Slaughter', published in 1953.

Ian's ambition to write nothing less than 'the spy story to end all spy stories' meant that whatever he wrote would have to stand comparison with the tales of his youth. He was a connoisseur of the genre, and had grown up on now almost-forgotten authors such as Dornford Yates, L. Phillips Oppenheim and William Le Queux. The best of them was John Buchan, who created the classic Edwardian secret agent Sandy Arbuthnot and also Richard Hannay, the hero of *The Thirty-Nine Steps*, *Greenmantle* and *Mr Standfast*. Buchan's heroes were tough and tweedy to their core, always at their best out in open country, on the move, with an assassin on their tail. Their adventures provided the inspiration to a generation of young men who went off to spy for their country in 1940.

'I spent a large portion of World War Two working for SOE,' wrote Richard Usborne, whose classic study of the genre, *Clubland Heroes*, was written in the same year as *Casino Royale*. 'Practically every officer I met in that concern, at home or abroad, was, like me, imagining himself as Hannay or Sandy Arbuthnot.' Hannay was a particularly unusual hero in that he was a man of action who was also a doubter. He would constantly chide himself for being chicken-hearted, and on occasion even ran away to save his own skin. This shortcoming – and it is a shortcoming in a hero of this kind of thriller fiction – was something that appealed to Fleming: one of the great surprises in store for anyone reading the James Bond novels for the first time is how vulnerable agent 007 appears compared to the all-conquering action hero he has become on screen.

Appealing as he was, neither Richard Hannay nor any other muddy-booted hero would have done for Ian Fleming, whose idea of hell was the annual Fleming family pilgrimage to Scotland to shoot grouse. Another fictional model was Somerset Maugham's *Ashenden* – a series of lightly fictionalized short stories about Maugham's own days as a spy in the First World War – which Fleming had been addicted to when young. Ashenden, the spy, is an ambivalent, world-weary figure who takes delight in double-crossing his opposite numbers, but likens himself to a doctor faced with a terminally ill patient: he wants to change everything, but he knows that in reality there is little that can be done – human nature has set country against country, spy against spy. *Ashenden*, published in 1928, is often cited as the beginning of modern spy fiction, and it influenced Graham Greene and Raymond Chandler among others. It is nothing like the Bond stories, although Maugham's R, the cynical and devious boss of the secret service, bears more than a passing resemblance to M, Fleming's equivalent.

Somerset Maugham proved to be far more influential on Fleming as a man than as a writer; they met soon after Ian married Ann Rothermere in 1953. By then Maugham was the grand old man of English letters, and the richest writer in the world, enjoying a life of well-ordered luxury at the Villa Mauresque on the Côte d'Azur. Ian envied the elegance of the writer's life: here was a man who on the dot of twelve every morning put down his fountain pen and dived into his beautiful swimming pool, who dressed for dinner each evening, who had first editions in his bookcases and Picassos on his walls. Somerset Maugham was a serious author who had made it – a man Ian could aspire to emulate. Ian never succeeded in drawing out Maugham on his own spying past, but it did not matter, as Maugham immediately joined Ian's pantheon of father-figure heroes, and once Ian had found his own literary feet he made several attempts to ape the master. 'We are the only two writers', he wrote to Maugham later, 'who write about what people are really interested in: cards, money, gold and things like that.'

At the other end of the scale from Somerset Maugham – and possibly beyond its outer limits – was Sapper's Bulldog Drummond, who first appeared in 1921. Many critics identified this big-hearted, ugly ox of a man as the true literary father of James Bond, which was a trifle unfair, as 'Sapper' (Lieutenant Colonel H. C. McNeile) was a far inferior writer to Fleming and had no pretensions to literature whatsoever. Nevertheless, there are some similarities between 007 and folk hero Drummond, who today offends political correctness on almost every level. Bulldog lives at the glamorous address of 60A Half Moon Street, Mayfair – tel. Mayfair 1234 – and when not huntin', shootin', fishin' or chasin' topping girls around town he is rough-housing villains with his team of beer-drinking amateur sportsmen. These villains are always foreigners – usually dagos, wops or, worse, Russian Jews – controlled by some demon king who is ensconced in the Ritz or a large country 'grange'. Bald as eggs, and sometimes disguised as clergymen, these *über*-villains are out to undermine jolly old England. They organize strikes and pray for a Communist revolution – crimes for which they must be roundly punished. Drummond finds his way into their moated lair, disguised as a 'typical Negro' or a 'typical plumber', and at the right moment he goes berserk. As he is a former public-schools heavyweight boxing finalist, the crunch of bones and the animal yelp of the foreigner are inevitable. 'We merely anticipate the law,' Bulldog tells two grovelling Jews before flogging them within an inch of their lives with a cat-o'-nine-tails. Most of these enemies end up dead, but occasionally one is let off with a caution – like the Pole who is found lashed to the railings of Whitehall 'with one half of his beard and hair shaved off, and the motto "Portrait of a Bolshevist" painted on his forehead'. Curiously, Bulldog never gets punished by the authorities for this antisocial behaviour.

William Somerset Maugham (1874–1965) was one of the most successful British writers of the twentieth century. Fleming was a great admirer, both of his writing – which included Ashenden, *a highly influential collection of spy stories – and of his commercial success.*

Drummond has a considerable number of skills for an amateur agent. He is a big man, but he has an uncanny ability to move silently in the dark, a technique he learned from the Dutch trapper van Dyck. And he is handy with the revolver too, having killed countless men during his nocturnal wanderings into no man's land during the First World War. On the whole he doesn't approve of shooting unarmed men, preferring instead to finish them off using the ju-jitsu grip that Olaki 'the Jap' taught him, which can kill a man in a second. It usually does. After all this excitement Bulldog then returns to his set in Mayfair for copious amounts of beer with Algy, Ted, Toby and the rest of the chaps, and then out to a nightclub with the gels who – inevitably – are a breed of superfit, superwhite fillies. Bulldog tends to judge these creatures as any horseman would – by their feet. One topping young thing, Phyllis, Bulldog takes to be his bride, and from then on, in book after book, the silly goose finds herself kidnapped, trussed up in a chair, or pursued around her home by a cross-eyed hunchback with a cylinder of poison gas. Bulldog always rides to the rescue, and more often than not Phyllis rides to his too – on one occasion smashing a spanner down on an assailant's head to kill him.

Bulldog Drummond is by and large a cheerful bruiser, uncomplicated by doubt and not particularly bright. He has a decent respect for the working classes, having witnessed their hearts-of-oak courage in the trenches, and as long as they wash regularly and love England he has no problem with them. What he dislikes is 'the type which Woodbines its fingers to a brilliant orange; the type that screams insults at a football referee on Saturday afternoon', those dissenting characters who call Drummond 'Pansy-face' instead of 'Guv'nor'. These deviants inevitably come a cropper with Bulldog Drummond. His greatest foe is Carl Peterson, a mortal enemy of the British Empire, who, unlike him, is fiendishly clever, a master of disguise, a mass murderer and, what's more, a West End clubman. Sapper was so smitten with this great villain that it takes three books for Drummond to finally kill him off, and even then we never really know what Carl Peterson looks like or who he is. Irma Peterson, his loyal wife and accomplice in crime, escapes and, one assumes, remains at large to this day.

Bulldog Drummond held a special place in the Fleming family. Not only were his adventures read out loud to the boys when they were growing up at school, but Peter Fleming actually played Drummond in a production of one of his adventures staged at the Electric Theatre, Newport Pagnell, while a student at Oxford. Peter developed a Drummondesque way of speaking that became a kind of in-joke among his friends and family. 'Pipes drawing well,' he would say after breakfast, 'a move was made to the gunroom' – which meant, 'Let's get up now.' 'Pity,' he would say with maximum understatement after some calamity, or '*Exactly*' when he meant 'Shut up'. When Ian went to visit Peter after the war at Nettlebed, his Oxfordshire estate, the two brothers would invariably revert to this kind of knockabout public-school badinage.

Peter Fleming had, in his own way, a considerable part to play in the birth of James Bond. Ian was an incorrigible hero-worshipper, and his elder brother was a natural hero. Peter was handsome and clever, and his swashbuckling travel books had made him a household name. In *Brazilian Adventure* (1933) he described wading through swamps in the Amazonian jungle on the trail of a lost explorer, Colonel Fawcett, who, it was rumoured, had found Eldorado but had been eaten by cannibals on the way back. Then for *One's Company* (1934) he had travelled as special correspondent for *The Times* from Russia to China through the little-visited land of Manchuria. After that he wrote *News from Tartary* (1936), his account of an extraordinary 2,000-mile journey on horseback from Beijing to Kashmir in the company of an intrepid Swiss female explorer, crossing the bitter Taklamakan desert and the high passes of the Karakorams. These adventures were described with an acid wit and a vivid style that had ensured his place in the pantheon of great travel writers.

Peter Fleming, Ian's older brother, was a highly successful travel writer in the 1930s. After the war, he wrote works of history about the countries through which he had travelled.

Though Peter never saw front line action during the war (nor for that matter did James Bond), he had a similar kind of gypsy experience of it all. After he had been reported dead in Norway, having flown there on a reconnaissance mission, he set about defending the south coast of England with Mad Mike Calvert (later of jungle and SAS fame) against an imminent German invasion. He and his men dug a series of well-disguised burrows across southern England, where they lived and planned a clandestine nocturnal war against the German forces that they imagined would soon be encircling London. By October 1940 there were 3,000 of these troglodyte soldiers, and one of their largest hideouts was positively Bond-like: it was an enormous badger sett hundreds of years old whose tunnels extended deep into the hillside. The entrance was disguised as a tree stump, and opened on a hinge. Once the threat of invasion passed, Peter was sent to Greece on an SOE mission to hold the Monastir Gap, a narrow pass on the Greek–Yugoslav border that was about to be overwhelmed by German paratroopers. In his retreat he narrowly escaped death when the small fishing vessel he had commandeered was attacked and sunk by German fighters. Thereafter he spent three years in Delhi, organizing a campaign of strategic deception against the Japanese. This involved selling them forgeries of plans through Chinese intermediaries, and on one occasion planting 'General Wavell's briefcase' in the boot of a jeep which he then crashed in the jungle ahead of the Japanese advance in Burma. He hoped that this bundle of well-executed forgeries would persuade Japanese intelligence that the British Commander-in-Chief himself had been involved in this accident, and that, according to the documents in his briefcase, he had far more troops under his command than they had previously supposed. Peter never managed to find out if the ruse had worked.

Fleming always said that he had appropriated the name 'James Bond' from the author of this guide, a copy of which was on his bookshelf at Goldeneye. He was delighted to meet the original James Bond in 1962.

Peter, like Ian, was an escapist. After the war he surprised many of his friends by proving that he had no conventional ambition at all: he rejected the career path that would have led him to edit *The Times*, he had no desire to stand as a Member of Parliament for Henley, as his father had done, and he even rejected the road that could easily have taken him to the head of MI5. Instead, he decided to pick up the threads of his writing career and manage the Nettlebed estate, whose 2,000 acres in Oxfordshire had been passed to him from his grandfather via his uncle. The role of literary squire was one to which he was entirely suited. Whereas Ian had told a friend that after the war he wanted to write 'the spy story to end all spy stories', Peter, when asked about his post-war plans, replied that he wanted to 'shoot and shoot and shoot and shoot'. He may have been joking, but he did accomplish this aim, and much of what we know of his life comes from his game book. He liked nothing better than setting off by himself, with a shotgun, to the remotest corners of the forest or the highest peaks on the family's Scottish estate, sometimes covering forty miles in what he would call his *stravaig*, a Gaelic word meaning wanderings. At Nettlebed he would often go after birds on an old bombing range that was full of shell holes and thickets, and there was something Bond-like about Peter's relentless solitary pursuit of a quarry. Unlike Ian, and therefore unlike Bond, Peter was immune to comfort and had absolutely no sense of taste – a legacy from a childhood illness – which resulted in him being able to eat yak, beetles and other exotica without flinching. A friend once saw him putting pepper on his peaches.

Alongside all that shooting Peter Fleming did keep writing – first a novel titled *The Sett*, which he abandoned after 30,000 words (interestingly it had a character named Miss Moneypenny), and then *The Sixth Column*, which was published in 1951. He dedicated this to Ian, and in it he unwittingly provided yet another fictional model for his younger brother to follow. *The Sixth Column* was a satire set in Britain some time in the future, when the Soviets had hatched a plot to make Britain a satellite state by turning everyone into small-minded bureaucrats. This scheme was known as Plan D. The novel, a Buchanish satire on contemporary Britain, was politely received and not particularly good, though it did contain an intriguing character. Archie Strume was a successful writer of thrillers that mixed violence with 'curious events which had far-reaching international implications'. His protagonist was Colonel Hackforth, who combined 'the sober, clear-eyed resource of Captain Hornblower with the urbane, faintly swashbuckling sangfroid of Raffles and Rupert of Hentzau' (the hero of *The Prisoner of Zenda*). Hackforth had a brusque relationship with authority – he was always demanding to speak to the Home Secretary, in person – and he played for high stakes, invariably attempting to save the Houses of Parliament or Hong Kong from imminent peril. This combination struck a chord with the public, and Peter Fleming described why:

> He [Strume] wrote for an Age of Little Men. A few years earlier the British had emerged with the status of heroes from a long and bitter war in which, but for their stubbornness and daring, the greater part of mankind would have lost their liberties. For longer, and against greater odds than any of their allies, the British had ranged the skies, the oceans and the continents to challenge the King's enemies, and at home they had stood up to dangers and deprivations which had made their endurance a byword among nations.

But something had happened to this once great nation. When they disarmed they became as meek as mice; they became bureaucratic and risk-averse, and they accepted their 'mousehood' gladly. The brusque Colonel Hackforth was a welcome 'antidote to the restrictions and frustrations of life in England at that time'. He was a different kind of fictional hero – a respite from the 'pseudo-American toughness which the writers of thrillers had come, at this period, to regard as a more or less obligatory part of their heroes' make-up, [which] was not wholly to the British taste'.

In *The Sixth Column* Peter Fleming was shining a light on the contemporary landscape of thrillers and unwittingly showing his brother the way. Peter really did believe that post-war Britain was experiencing an Age of Little Men, that the wartime heroes had turned into mice, and that the country was now floundering in a bureaucratic soup. Had Colonel Hackforth existed as the fictional hero of a real thriller, he would, in Peter's estimation, have enormous appeal. This cowed nation was ready for a clear-eyed, urbane and faintly swashbuckling character, and willing to share in his curious adventures. Ian may or may not have shared Peter's view about the state of modern Britain, but *The Sixth Column* certainly proved to be a catalyst of sorts: six months later Ian Fleming sat down to write a serious spy thriller, *Casino Royale*, whose hero was also urbane, clear-eyed and faintly swashbuckling.

Fleming's design for the cover of Casino Royale. *The book launched one of the world's best-known fictional heroes – a character for which many have laid claim to being the inspiration.*

Alongside Peter Fleming there is an ever-growing parade of men who claim to be, directly or indirectly, the inspiration for James Bond. A justification for their assertions came from Fleming himself, who once told an interviewer, 'James Bond came out of thin air really . . . he was a compound of all the secret agents and commando types that I met during the Second World War when I was Personal Assistant to the Director of Naval Intelligence. The thing was my job got me right to the heart of things . . . and it was all the things that I heard and learned about secret operations that finally led me to write about them in a disguised way and with James Bond as the central character.'

Merlin Minshall, the colourful explorer Fleming used to attempt to block the Danube, was the first to suggest that he was the model; then came Patrick Dalzel-Job, a commando who rescued 4,000 civilians almost single-handedly in Norway, and who claimed Fleming had told him he was the model. Then there was Michael Mason, the tough boxing champion who also worked for Fleming behind enemy lines. Sir Fitzroy Maclean is another candidate who is persistently mentioned, though he himself never claimed that he was Bond, despite his adventures behind enemy lines in the Balkans, which were as heroic and dangerous as anything 007 accomplished. Other secret-agent candidates are men like Conrad O'Brien-ffrench, the glamorous skiing spymaster whom Fleming met before the war, Biffy Dunderdale, a dapper naval intelligence officer, who drove around Paris in a bulletproof Rolls-Royce, and Dusko Popov, the promiscuous star double agent. Even Ian Fleming's closer friends in 30 AU – Ralph Izzard, Sir Peter Smithers and Robert Harling – can claim to have had some part in it all, having carried out Ian's clandestine missions. The list of models for James Bond is endless, and the search for a single suspect fruitless: there were more heroes in that particular generation than you could shake a stick at. After the war a rash of memoirs flooded the bookshops describing all manner of derring-do; there were the escape stories (*The Wooden Horse*, *The Colditz Story*, *The White Rabbit*), the raiders (*The Cockleshell Heroes*, *The Greatest Raid of All*), the specialists in irregular warfare (*Ill Met by Moonlight*, *Popski's Private Army*), the SOE agents working with the French resistance (*Duel of Wits*, *Odette*), and the airmen (*The Dambusters*, *The Last Enemy*). Heroes were everywhere, and James Bond might have been any one of them.

Noël Coward (1899–1973) was a playwright, actor, singer, songwriter and society figure. A tax exile from Britain after the war, he was one of the Flemings' expatriate friends in Jamaica.

The reason why he wasn't exactly any of them is because so much of James Bond was Ian Fleming himself. Ian was never able to write about anything he did not know, or any place he had not been. James Bond had been around a long time – as long, in fact, as Ian Fleming had been dreaming himself into fantasy situations. When he finally emerged on paper, 007 was a toughened-up younger-brother version of Ian himself: more straightforward, less interesting, the kind of young hothead Ian might have been had he not valued power above adventure. He was a man who actually stole code books, gambled with Nazis, and attached limpet mines in nocturnal underwater raids, instead of dreaming about it all in Technicolor behind his desk in the Admiralty. Why did it take Ian seven years to bring him to life? For the most part it was lack of confidence. When Ian Fleming wrote *Casino Royale* he did not intend to become a full-time writer; it was only after meeting Somerset Maugham that that career became attractive. It has also been suggested that the defections of Guy Burgess and Donald Maclean in May 1951 may have been the spur, as they demonstrated the moral ambiguities of the Cold War that Ian reflected in *Casino Royale*. Certainly the first book is unique in that it is the only instance where Bond expresses any doubts about being on the right side. But if Ian was really interested in the grey realities of spying he would have continued to explore them. He did not. More prosaic and equally likely was that he was fed up with being badgered by his neighbour Noël Coward to 'write his bloody book'. So he just sat down and he did.

MOONRAKER

1955

Original titles include **Mondays are Hell, Wide of the Mark, Out of the Clear Sky, The Inhuman Element**

First line

The two thirty-eights roared simultaneously.

Story

Unlike the previous two novels, *Moonraker* is set entirely in England. James Bond, still sunburnt from his 'passionate leave' with Solitaire, is asked by M to solve a problem. Sir Hugo Drax, a highly successful stockbroker and national hero, whose £10 million rocket the Moonraker he has offered to donate to the defence of Britain, has been discovered to cheat at cards. Bond is asked to expose his system, which he does in a 62-page sequence set at Blades club. Bond is then sent down to Kent to investigate the Moonraker rocket himself, taking the place of another agent who has just disappeared. Drax has built a launch site in the cliffs overlooking the sea, from where he will send the rocket on its first test flight. A key member of his rocket team is Gala Brand, an undercover policewoman, whose job is to plot the rocket's co-ordinates. Bond notices that all the workers at the plant – including their odious leader, Krebs – are German, and have moustaches and shaven heads. Soon Drax attempts to kill him and Gala by causing a cliff to collapse on top of them as they walk on the beach below. When that fails, Drax traps them inside the launch pad and, having tied them up, reveals that he is a German SMERSH agent and that the Moonraker is targeted on central London. Miraculously, Bond and Gala manage to reset the rocket's co-ordinates just before the launch, and then escape the engine blast by hiding in a ventilation tunnel. After a brief flight the Moonraker lands harmlessly in the sea – coincidentally, on top of the submarine that is ferrying Drax and his faithful countrymen back to Russia. Bond fully expects his just deserts from Gala, but much to his surprise she rejects him, as she's just about to marry someone else. The end is as sad as it is unexpected.

Last lines

'Well, goodbye, Gala'. He held out his hand.

'Goodbye James.'

He touched her for the last time and they turned away from each other and walked off into their different lives.

Inspirations

The story of the Moonraker rocket targeting London and Bond's attempts to stop it was originally conceived for a film. 'The reason why it breaks so badly in half as a book', Fleming explained to Joyce Briggs, Rank's script editor at Pinewood, 'is because I had to more or less graft the first half of the book on to my film idea in order to bring it up to the necessary length.' Ian's film idea had been about a German V-2 rocket, which he updated to an early intercontinental nuclear weapon – an extremely topical subject, as both the Americans and the Russians were rushing to develop this new technology. As he was not an expert in this field, Ian went to great lengths to make sure his Moonraker rocket was correct, writing to Arthur C. Clarke and the British Interplanetary Society to check his facts about range and accuracy.

On to the unfamiliar Ian grafted on something that to him was almost second nature. For a man who spent every week of his London life at one of his clubs, it was inevitable that clubland and club life would make an entrance in James Bond. Blades is a mixture of White's and the Portland Club, which were (and still are) different kinds of exclusive gentlemen's club in London. White's was where Ian met his old intelligence pals, diplomats and suchlike; he went to the Portland Club to play serious bridge. Bridge was first played in England at the Portland in 1826, and the club is still considered to be the custodian of the game. Its rules of 1916 state that membership should be restricted to men over forty and earning 'not less than £10,000 a year'. Members are expected to be good bridge players, which Ian was, but, unlike Bond, he was a very cautious gambler. He spent a considerable amount of time working out the crucial bridge hand, and spent a full 18 pages describing it. The bridge scene in Blades is really Fleming's homage to this world.

As an inveterate player, Fleming was also fascinated by the idea of cheating at cards. The most famous incident of this crime, known as the Tranby Croft case, took place in the 1890s, and still reverberated around clubland in the 1950s. It was named after the house in which it had occurred, where William Gordon Cummings – 'possibly the handsomest man in London and certainly the rudest' – was discovered cheating at baccarat by surreptitiously adding to his stake when the odds were in his favour. This in itself was enough to guarantee Cummings ostracism from clubland, but what made the scandal worse was that his friend Edward, Prince of Wales, was also at the table. The newspapers eventually found out, and a high-profile trial followed in which the Prince of Wales was somehow implicated in the scandal. In 1953 Fleming met a woman who had been present at Tranby Croft that night, and he quizzed her so persistently about the affair that she burst into tears.

Drax's launch site, at St Margaret's Bay, Kent, was a place Ian knew intimately; this was his bolthole from London, and each Friday afternoon and Monday morning he would make the journey with metronomic regularity. Such was his passion for detail that he even asked his stepson to double-check the times of the various journeys in the book so that they were correct. On one of these Bond finds himself behind a juggernaut that sheds its cargo at the top of a hill – an idea that had been knocking around ever since Fleming's pre-war days in Kitzbühel and was perhaps one of his recurring driver's nightmares. The car chase through Kent is now an enjoyable period piece.

What the readers said

'As you appear to be a perfectionist, whether it is wine, cars, gambling, food etc., it might interest you to know that the most exclusive watch in the world is the Audemars-Piquet'

'I should like to point out a small mistake; a creature like Krebs would not dream of addressing his superior as "*mein Kapitan*" . . . *Kapitan* is strictly a navy term, meaning the captain of a ship'

'I do like your heroines – they can stand a bit of rough treatment and yet are very far from unfeminine'

What the critics said

'"Astonish me!" the addict may challenge; Mr Fleming can knock him sideways' – *The Scotsman*

'It's all utterly disgraceful and highly enjoyable' – *The Spectator*

'Mr Fleming is splendid, he stops at nothing' – *New Statesman*

'Two-fisted espionage by the author of *Casino Royale*' – *San Jose Mercury*

'Bridge at high stakes, food at fancy prices . . . and well-developed secretaries further the rapid approach to climax . . . E. Phillips Oppenheim never handled things better' – Lockhart Amerman, *Pittsburgh Press*

Like Live and Let Die, Moonraker *had cover artwork directed by Fleming but executed by Kenneth Lewis. High-tech weaponry (like Drax's rocket) and communications devices were hot topics in the 1950s and '60s; Lockheed advertised the Agena* (right) *as 'America's most versatile satellite'.*

A MAN IN HIS TIME

The Life of a Fictional Character

'He was good-looking in a dark, rather cruel way'.
From Russia with Love

At the end of the penultimate James Bond novel, *You Only Live Twice*, 007 is living the simple life of an awabi fisherman on the island of Kuro in southern Japan. His mind is empty, his broken body tended by the beautiful Kissy Suzuki, who protects him from the suspicious outside world. The world's most famous secret agent has become one Taro Todoroki, who each day rows Kissy and her cormorant David (named after David Niven) out to the reefs where Kissy dives naked for awabi shells. This is no ploy to ensnare a villain: Bond has total amnesia. In his waking hours he believes that their little stone and wood house and the endless horizon of sea are the limits of his world. Only at night, in dreams, is he haunted by the faces and big cities of his previous life. Kissy is very protective of him: she never allows Bond to walk over to the other side of the island to see the smouldering remains of Ernst Blofeld's castle, which Bond single-handedly destroyed, and lost his memory in the process. Bond is missing, presumed dead. It is this loss that prompts M, his curmudgeonly old boss, to write 007's obituary in *The Times*. For the first time since he stepped on to the world stage in 1953 the early life of James Bond was revealed.

11th December, 1962

Dear Mr. Paul,

As Mr. Fleming is away from London I sent him your letter and here now is his description of James Bond:

Height:	6 ft 1 in.
Build:	Slim hips, broad shoulders
Eyes:	Steely blue-grey
Hair:	Black, with comma over right forehead
Weight:	12 stone 8 lb.
Age:	Middle thirties
Features:	Determined chin, rather cruel mouth. Scar down right cheek from cheekbone. Cleanshaven
Apparel:	Wears two-button single-breasted suit in dark blue tropical worsted. Black leather belt. White Sea Island cotton shirt, sleeveless. Black casual shoes, square toed Thin black knitted silk tie, no pin Dark blue socks, cotton lisle. No handkerchief in breast pocket Wears Rolex Oyster Perpetual watch

I hope this information is sufficient for your purpose.

Yours sincerely,

Secretary to Ian Fleming

Mr. Arthur Paul,
Art Director,
PLAYBOY,
232, East Ohio,
Chicago 11, Illinois.

OBITUARY

James Bond was born of a Scottish father, Andrew Bond of Glencoe, and a Swiss mother, Monique Delacroix, from the Canton de Vaud. His father being a foreign representative of the Vickers armaments firm, his early education, from which he inherited a first-class command of French and German, was entirely abroad. When he was eleven years of age, both his parents were killed in a climbing accident in the Aiguilles Rouges above Chamonix, and the youth came under the guardianship of an aunt, since deceased, Miss Charmian Bond, and went to live with her at the quaintly-named hamlet of Pett Bottom near Canterbury in Kent. There, in a small cottage hard by the attractive Duck Inn, his aunt, who must have been a most erudite and accomplished lady, completed his education for an English public school, and, at the age of twelve or thereabouts, he passed satisfactorily into Eton, for which college he had been entered at birth by his father. It must be admitted that his career at Eton was brief and undistinguished and, after only two halves, as a result, it pains me to record, of some alleged trouble with one of the boys' maids, his aunt was requested to remove him. She managed to obtain his transfer to Fettes, his father's old school. Here the atmosphere was somewhat Calvinistic, and both academic and athletic standards were rigorous. Nevertheless, though inclined to be solitary by nature, he established some firm friendships among the traditionally famous athletic circles at the school. By the time he left, at the early age of seventeen, he had twice fought for the school as a light-weight and had, in addition, founded the first serious judo class at a British public school. By now it was 1941 and, by claiming an age of nineteen and with the help of an old Vickers colleague of his father, he entered a branch of what was subsequently to become the Ministry of Defence. To serve the confidential nature of his duties, he was accorded the rank of lieutenant in the Special Branch of the RNVR, and it is a measure of the satisfaction his services gave to his superiors that he ended the war with the rank of Commander. It was about this time that the writer became associated with certain aspects of the Ministry's work, and it was with much gratification that I accepted Commander Bond's post-war application to continue working for the Ministry in which, at the time of his lamented disappearance, he had risen to the rank of Principal Officer in the Civil Service.

Right from the beginning Fleming set out to write about a man who was only a silhouette. 'The paradox is that I quite deliberately made him rather anonymous,' he told Ken Purdy, a journalist who interviewed him in 1964. 'This was to enable the reader to identify with him. People have only to put their own clothes on Bond and build him into whatever sort of person they admire. If you read my books you'll find that I don't actually describe him at all.' But as the series continued Fleming threw in

Opposite and above
While James Bond quickly became 'known' to millions, it was only after a number of his adventures had appeared in print that his vital statistics could be confirmed.

tantalizing details about Bond's past life, loves, abilities. ('Didn't know you could ski,' says M with mild curiosity in *On Her Majesty's Secret Service.*) It is only at 007's supposed death, after twelve years of adventures, that Fleming finally reveals the origins of Bond and in doing so answers many of the questions that his fans had been pressing for. What is striking is how similar the past life of James Bond is to that of his creator, though in certain crucial respects the two men are fundamentally different.

The dates for Bond's acquisition of his classic 4½-litre Bentley may not quite add up, but there is no doubting the model. In 1962 Fleming even posed for photographers with a similar car.

It is no surprise that Bond turns out to have been a public-school boy – an Etonian, even, however briefly. And it is equally no surprise that Bond was a rebel. Fleming was as class-conscious as anyone in 1950s Britain, and he was extremely careful not to present Bond as an upper-class thug or a booby. Bond is not a snob about people (though he is a snob about things – a crucial difference). In fact when Bond is offered a knighthood, at the end of *The Man with the Golden Gun*, he turns it down as an encumbrance. He does not want to lose his anonymity. Fettes, being Scottish, stood outside the snobbery associated with the major English public schools, yet it said just enough about wealth and a good sporty background to vouchsafe Bond's entry to the club. And Bond's solitary nature sat well in this background. In fact he was always aware that there was something 'alien and un-English about himself' – his Swiss mother, perhaps. His enthusiasm for judo was another mark of a loner – exotic individual combat, not a team sport.

In addition to a predilection for fighting and a weakness for girls, there are glimpses of Bond's past scattered in no particular order across the books. As he sits on the beach at Royale-les-Eaux facing the setting sun, 007 is caught up in a childhood reverie 'of the velvet feel of the hot powder sand, and the painful grit of wet sand between young toes when the time came for him to put his socks and shoes on, of the precious little pile of sea-shells and interesting wrack on the sill of his bedroom window ("No, we'll have to leave that behind, darling. It'll dirty up your trunk!")'. Bond lights a cigarette and shrinks back from these memories of 'the Cadbury milk-chocolate Flakes and the fizzy lemonade'. When Ian Fleming began writing the first James Bond novel in 1952, he had no idea that he would still be writing 'his autobiography', as he teasingly referred to the Bond books, ten years later. 007 was around for so long that Fleming had to tinker with the dates to keep his age – late thirties – the same throughout the series. If Bond was born in 1924 – as M claims in 1963 – then the sketchy details of his pre-war life described in previous novels are particularly interesting. For instance, in the first book, *Casino Royale*, Bond buys his 4½-litre Bentley when it is 'almost new in 1933', which according to M's obituary, written ten years after *Casino Royale*, would make him about nine. Then in 1939 he succeeds at 'bowling out' the Romanian gambling team in Monte Carlo to the tune of a million francs, which he is obliged to turn in to the Section, which is a shame, as the fifteen-year-old Bond would have found ample opportunities to spend it – perhaps in Paris, which he visited later that year. 'He had done what Harry's [Bar] advertisement in the *Continental Daily Mail* had told him to do and he said to his taxi driver, "Sank Roo Doe Noo." That had started one of the memorable evenings of his life, culminating in the loss, almost simultaneous, of his virginity and his notecase.'

Harry's Bar in Paris was already a legendary watering hole by the time Bond had reached his adolescence. Could it have been here that he first sampled the martini with which his name would become synonymous?

Once Bond leaves school his career follows much the same trajectory as his creator's. He attends the University of Geneva, like Fleming; he learns to ski in Kitzbühel, like Fleming, where he is taught by Hannes Oberhauser (who ends up murdered in *Octopussy*). Here Bond is awarded the Golden K, which presumably means he is very good – or at least good enough to out-ski the avalanche that pursues him in *On Her Majesty's Secret Service*. For both Bond and Fleming, these pre-war alpine holidays were some of the happiest days of their lives.

Having joined the RNVR in 1941 (Fleming signed up in 1939, at the outbreak of war), Bond finds his life taking a different and more mysterious course. He is variously mentioned as being in America, Jamaica, Hong Kong (where he acquires a liking for pyjama coats), and, in 1944, in the Ardennes, firing a bazooka. What, it may be asked, was an RNVR doing in a forest firing a bazooka? The answer, one assumes, is that James Bond had very little to do with the navy at all: it was a convenient front. Bond was secret service from the start – with SOE, as an intelligence commando in 30AU, or with some other shady organization – and this is why he is awarded his 00 status, his licence to kill, for two jobs he executes during the war, both of which are described in *Casino Royale*.

The first involves the assassination of a Japanese cipher expert, who is holed up on the thirty-sixth floor of the RCA building at the Rockefeller Center, New York, busy cracking British codes. Bond and his fellow marksman stake him out from the fortieth floor of a skyscraper opposite, and when the code-breaker eventually looks out of the window Bond's colleague shoots first, making a hole in the toughened glass, and a split second later Bond's bullet passes through the hole and into the gaping mouth of the Japanese. This assassination was wishful thinking on Fleming's part, and would have provoked a wry smile from intelligence insiders, as the Rockefeller Center was the New York address of the real British intelligence during the war, and on the floor below was the Japanese consular office where a cipher expert was indeed transmitting coded signals back to Tokyo. Fleming was on hand when British agents burgled this office and microfilmed the code books, and this adventure became the inspiration for Bond's first mission. For his second assignment James Bond has to eliminate a Norwegian who has turned double agent and betrayed two British agents. He flies to Stockholm and kills the man in his bedroom with a knife. It was, according to Bond, not so pretty: 'He just didn't die very quickly.'

With his licence to kill, Bond decides to stay on in the service after the war. One presumes that the life suits him. 'It's not difficult to get a Double O number if you're prepared to kill people,' he explains. 'It's a confusing business but if it's one's profession, one does what one's told.' But the role of government assassin sometimes depresses him. At the beginning of *Goldfinger* Bond is found mooching about the departure lounge of Miami airport, having just killed a Mexican with a single hand chop to the Adam's apple. With two double bourbons inside him, he gazes out at the evening sky and stews:

> It had been kill or get killed. Anyway, people were killing other people all the time, all over the world. People were using their motor cars to kill with. They were carrying infectious diseases around, blowing microbes in other people's faces, leaving

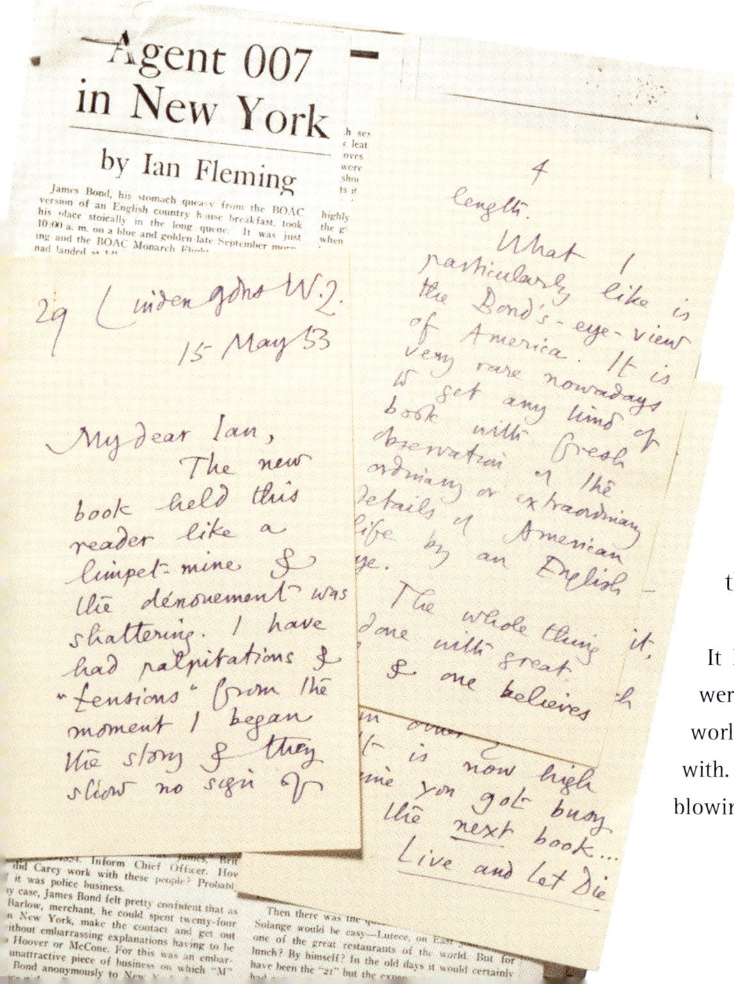

Agent 007 in New York

by Ian Fleming

James Bond, his stomach queasy from the BOAC version of an English country house breakfast, took his place stoically in the long queue. It was just 10:00 a.m. on a blue and golden late September morning and the BOAC Monarch ...

29 Linden Gdns W.2.
15 May 53

My dear Ian,
The new book held this reader like a limpet-mine & the dénouement was shattering. I have had palpitations & "tensions" from the moment I began the story & they show no sign of

4
length.
What I particularly like is the Bond's-eye-view of America. It is very rare nowadays to get any kind of book with fresh observation of the ordinary or extraordinary details of American life by an English eye.
The whole thing is done with great ... & one believes ...
It is now high time you got busy [on] the next book...
Live and Let Die

007 cut his teeth on a wartime mission in New York, detailed in this short story – which was serialized in the New York Herald Tribune. *In his editorial letter about* Live and Let Die *Fleming's editor, William Plomer, was especially excited by Fleming's ability to evoke the atmosphere of the United States.*

> gas-jets turned on in kitchens, pumping out carbon monoxide in closed garages . . . Was there any person in the world who wasn't somehow, perhaps only statistically, involved in killing his neighbour?

For the record, the James Bond of the books (in total contrast to the Bond of the films) not only does not enjoy killing people, he does not actually kill that many of them. Over the course of fourteen books he accounts for a mere thirty-eight deaths, plus one shared with a shark. In addition to this there are seventy-odd others when nuclear installations blow up or cars tumble down mountainsides, but none of these fatalities is by Bond's own hand.

James Bond's moments of doubt and regret – 'the deathwatch beetle of the soul' – afflict him with a regularity that is just enough to keep him human, but his true nature is revealed when he falls asleep: 'With the warmth and humour of his eyes extinguished, his features relapsed into a taciturn mask, ironical, brutal and cold.' It is a quality recognized by his friends, and admired by his enemies. In *From Russia with Love*, a group of shaven-headed Russian generals pore over a photograph of Bond with a magnifying glass. They see:

> a dark, clean-cut face, with a three-inch scar showing whitely down the sunburned skin of the right cheek. The eyes were wide and level under straight, rather long black brows. The hair was black, parted on the left, and carelessly brushed so that a thick black comma fell down over the right eyebrow. The longish nose ran down to a short upper lip below which was a wide and finely drawn but cruel mouth. The line of the jaw was straight and firm. A section of dark suit, white shirt and black knitted tie completed the picture.
>
> General G. held the photograph out at arm's length. Decision, authority, ruthlessness – these qualities he could see . . . 'He looks like a nasty customer,' he said grimly.

Bond may have looked the nasty type, but he is in essence a 1950s off-the-shelf attractive man. Contemporary Bond fans would have had no trouble imagining what he looked like, as James Bond was everywhere. Advertisements for suits, whisky, cars, cigarettes all showed a tall, dark man with comic-book good looks, whose muscular frame looked good in a single-breasted suit. In films this type was Gregory Peck, Cary Grant, Gary Cooper – a type of male omnipresent before the 1960s introduction of the skinny rock star. The artless Tatiana Romanova in *From Russia with Love* is the first to make the comparison. '"You are

LICENSED TO KILL
007's victims include

The Robber
Mr Big
Jack and Seraffimo Spang
Wint and Kidd
Red Grant
Dr No
Oddjob
Auric Goldfinger
Aristotle Kristatos
Emilio Largo
Sluggsy and Horror
Ernst Stavro Blofeld
Francisco Scaramanga

very handsome," she said. She searched for a comparison that would give him pleasure. "You are like an American film star." She was startled by his reaction. "For God's sake! That's the worst insult you can pay a man!"'

What Ian Fleming added to this standard saturnine male was a dangerous coldness (note the scars – this man likes fighting) and a solitary, enigmatic nature. Kingsley Amis, writing in the early 1960s, identified Bond as the natural successor to Heathcliff and Mr Rochester – a kind of Byronic hero who is out of sorts with the world. 'Mr Fleming', he wrote, 'has brought off the unlikely feat of enclosing this wildly romantic, almost narcissistic and (one would have thought) hopelessly out-of-date persona inside the shellac of a secret agent, and so making it plausible, mentally actable and, to all appearance, contemporary.' It is unlikely that Fleming was consciously thinking of Byron when he wrote James Bond, as that dark broodiness was Fleming's own. He too was tall and saturnine, with a 'slightly cruel mouth' and a long broken nose.

To Fleming, and to his readers, James Bond was a real person living in the modern world. The details of his life appear only sporadically in the books, but they proved vitally important in grounding him in his time, which made his extraordinary and often implausible adventures seem possible. In the fourth book, *From Russia with Love*, we are given a small glimpse of Bond's domestic routine, and discover that 007 lives in Chelsea.

Bond's cigarette lighter was a Ronson – a black-oxidized model. The company's contemporary advertising happens to portray the dark, handsome man, successful with the ladies, who became ubiquitous in films and promotions in the 1950s.

The blubbery arms of the soft life had Bond round the neck and they were slowly strangling him. He was a man of war and when, for a long period, there was no war, his spirit went into a decline.

In his particular line of business, peace had reigned for nearly a year. And peace was killing him.

At 7.30 on the morning of Thursday, August 12th, Bond awoke in his comfortable flat in the plane-tree'd square off the King's Road and was disgusted to find that he was thoroughly bored with the prospect of the day

> ahead. Just as, in at least one religion, *accidie* is the first of the cardinal sins, so boredom, and particularly the incredible circumstance of waking up bored, was the only vice Bond utterly condemned.
>
> Bond reached out and gave two rings on the bell to show May, his treasured Scottish housekeeper, that he was ready for breakfast. Then he abruptly flung the single sheet off his naked body and swung his feet to the floor.
>
> There was only one way to deal with boredom – kick oneself out of it. Bond went down on his hands and did twenty slow press-ups, lingering over each one so that his muscles had no rest. When his arms could stand the pain no longer, he rolled over on his back and, with his hands at his sides, did the straight leg-lift until his stomach muscles screamed. He got to his feet and, after touching his toes twenty times, went over to arm and chest exercises combined with deep breathing until he was dizzy.

The date – 12 August (a significant day in the Fleming calendar – the birthday of Fleming's son, Caspar, and the day on which Fleming himself died in 1964) – was one Ian had long associated with boredom, as it was the start of the grouse shooting season. From an early age he had travelled with his brothers to Scotland to indulge in this sport, but he never enjoyed it or claimed that he was any good at it. So, as the rest of his family set off on their annual pilgrimage north, Ian stayed behind and worked, played golf, or found some excuse to take a holiday abroad.

It is not known whether Ian Fleming exercised each morning *à la* Bond. When in Jamaica he usually swam, and as a young man he had been very fit, climbing mountains before breakfast. Now, at the onset of middle age (when he wrote these lines), he must have envied Bond his fitness – which, from the effort involved, was a hard-earned affair. Fleming once challenged his friend Ivar Bryce to a $5,000 wager, paid to whoever succeeded in reducing his waist size from 38 to 32 inches in six months. When the time came, both men were disappointed to discover that the other had managed it. Bond was always a younger and fitter man than his creator, but, whatever his physical achievements on the floor of his bedroom before breakfast, 007's fitness, like Fleming's, was blunted by his ration of 60 cigarettes a day.

Chelsea was a smart address, though not extravagant. Fleming had lived there before the war, in his mother's house in Cheyne Walk. Chelsea placed Bond almost as precisely as his school had done: it said money, but not too much of it, as in the 1950s the King's Road still retained some of the rougher bohemian character it had before it became the haunt of pop stars and designers during the 1960s. Bond could afford to live there because he was paid £1,500 a year – the salary of a principal officer in the Civil Service – and he had another thousand free of tax of his own. When he was on a job Bond could spend as much as he liked, and frequently did, provoking bouts of self-loathing at his own excess (presumably his ancient Scottish puritanical genes coming to the fore). The rest of the time his £2,000 net was enough to leave him comfortably off. In fact his salary was far higher than a real secret agent's. In 1955 a fireman earned approximately £475 per year, a miner £690. And a spy? Perhaps £1,200.

Fleming did not know precisely, but he knew Bond was better paid than he should be. The higher income glamorized 007, and allowed him his little luxuries. Sometimes, however, the Fleming fantasy pay scale runs too far out of kilter: M, a retired admiral and head of MI6, is paid £6,500 – yet somehow he is also a member of Blades, a club whose entry is confined to gentlemen who can show £100,000 in cash or securities. There is never any explanation of how M has squirrelled away this considerable sum of money.

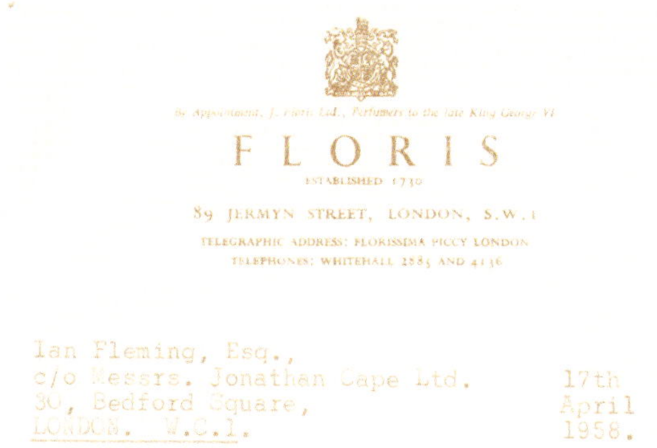
By Appointment, J. Floris Ltd., Perfumers to the late King George VI
FLORIS
ESTABLISHED 1730
89 JERMYN STREET, LONDON, S.W.1
TELEGRAPHIC ADDRESS: FLORISSIMA PICCY LONDON
TELEPHONES: WHITEHALL 2885 AND 4136

Ian Fleming, Esq.,
c/o Messrs. Jonathan Cape Ltd.
30, Bedford Square,
LONDON. W.C.1.

17th April 1958.

Fleming's correspondence with many of the makers of the products he featured in his novels was considerable, as was his correspondence with fans about the brands he had name-checked. Messrs Floris of St James's were so grateful for their mention in Dr No *that they sent Fleming a bottle of Lime Bath Essence.*

Having done his exercises, 007 steps sweating and panting into the shower. James Bond is a great showerer, at times indulging himself four times a day, first with a cold one, then a hot one. He washes his hair with Pinaud Elixir, 'that prince among shampoos', is partial to a particularly delicious-smelling soap, Guerlain's Fleurs des Alpes, and shaves with a Hoffritz razor he picked up in a drugstore in New York. In all of these ablutions he follows Fleming, who was an early devotee of the shower, and whose great complaint about English women was that they washed in their own dirty bathwater. Unlike Fleming, Bond does not use Trumper's hair oil to keep his hair neat; 007 has nothing more than a brush, and generally fails in his attempts to control the unruly 'black question mark' of hair that bobs above his eyebrow.

Having completed this ritual, James Bond dresses in his standard dark-blue Sea Island cotton shirt and navy-blue tropical worsted trousers. 'He always wore dark blues and blacks and whites, the colours that betray an underlying melancholy,' wrote Fleming in his notebook. He might have been referring to himself, as Fleming cared little for fashion, preferring understatement before anything too flashy, and regularly wearing his own dark-blue suits until they were threadbare. He liked spotted bow ties, loosely tied – 'like Churchill' – whereas Bond prefers black-silk knitted ties, which were considered an extravagance at the time. Fleming never wore shoes with laces, and always wore short-sleeved shirts, because he couldn't stand dirty cuffs, buttons or studs. Friends remarked how odd it was to see such a well-dressed man wearing a suit without any shirtsleeves visible underneath. Bond shared these sartorial foibles, unusual in an otherwise conventional, conservative dresser. When colour did enter the wardrobe it was with wild abandon. In Jamaica, Bond shares his creator's taste for bright, bold beach shirts made by Antonio's in Falmouth. These were knocked up from remnants of cloth imported for the African trade; they were cheap and exclusive – both of which appealed to Ian.

James Bond is undoubtedly well turned out, and though he rarely goes shopping, he shows enough awareness of clothes on girls and villains to judge them as expressions of personality. When Goldfinger turns up to play golf dressed from head to toe in rust-coloured tweed, Bond can't fail to notice. 'It was as if Goldfinger had gone to his tailor and said "Dress me for golf – you know, like they wear in Scotland." Social errors made no impression on Bond, and for the matter of that he rarely noticed them. With Goldfinger it was different.' Occasionally Fleming also indulged in clothes reading. 'You should distrust people who tie their ties with a windsor knot,' he records in a notebook. 'It is a mark of vanity, egocentricity and a pawky mind.' He gives these thoughts to James Bond when sizing up Red Grant, the SMERSH assassin in *From Russia with Love*.

2nd April, 1963

The Editor,
The Sunday Times,
Thomson House,
Gray's Inn Road,
London, W.C.1.

Sir,

I am being deluged with enquiries as to why James Bond should dress his hair with pink tooth-powder. This misunderstanding arisés from Mr. Raymond Mortimer's most generous review of my opus-cula in which the late Mr. Trumper's "Eucryl" appears instead of his "Eucris". (In fact Bond uses nothing on his hair and the Eucris featured only in M. Draco's spare-room bathroom.) And your rendering of Bond's "Attenhofer Flex" ski-bindings as "Attenborough Fox" in Mr. Mortimer's most kindly reference to my efforts to achieve accuracy has resulted in one scornful winter sportsman suggesting I take a refresher course at Zermatt.

Could it be, Sir, that a sub-cell of SPECTRE is building up in your literary department?

Yours faithfully,

Ian Fleming

For the most part, Fleming is a stickler for accuracy, though on occasion there seems to be a gleeful delight in confusion that might arise.

Having sweated out his ennui, Bond slips into some black leather sandals, walks through into the long big-windowed sitting room of his flat, and sits down to his favourite meal of the day – breakfast (for more information on that turn immediately to the chapter on 'The Right Way to Eat'). Then, having thumbed through *The Times* – 'the only paper Bond ever read' – he generally goes straight out to work. We are told he has a sitting room lined with books, and a little Empire desk where he sits to study technical manuals, but this must be a rare occurrence as Bond

5th June, 1958.

I have just got back from abroad to find your sapient rebuke of 007's time-keeping equipment.

I have discussed this with him and he points out that the Rolex Oyster Perpetual weighs about six ounces and would appreciably slow up the use of his left hand in combat. His practice, in fact, is to use fairly cheap, expendable wrist watches on expanding metal bracelets which can be slipped forward over the thumb and used in the form of a knuckle-duster, either on the outside or the inside of the hand.

In passing on his comments to you, I would add that James Bond has trained himself to tell the time by the sun in either hemisphere within a few minutes.

Thank you, nevertheless, for raising the point and 007 wishes to assure you that when an appropriate time-piece is invented he will wear it.

B.W. Goodden, Esq.,
10, Old Broad Street,
London, E.C.2.

Bond's Rolex Oyster Perpetual is mentioned in a number of the stories. Fleming was able to respond nimbly to an eagle-eyed reader's criticism regarding its use in the field.

hardly reads, and in fact he is not a cultured man at all. The only books that are mentioned in Bond novels are plugs for Fleming's friends and admirers. We are told he has read John F. Kennedy's *Profiles of Courage*, some Raymond Chandler, some thrillers by Eric Ambler, and Patrick Leigh Fermor's *The Traveller's Tree*, but his greatest treasures are *Hogan on Golf* and *Scarne on Cards*, a manual that explains cheating and how to do it.

When it comes to art, Bond has no interest whatsoever. When Honeychile Rider appears on the beach naked except for a leather belt and a hunting knife strapped to her thigh, Bond compares her to Botticelli's *Birth of Venus*, and that is the last we ever hear about it. Fleming also preferred nature to art, and his only recorded visit to an art gallery was in Chicago, where he declared that the Impressionist masterpieces on show 'had no goddam right to be there'. He mischievously suggested that art galleries should provide roller skates at the entrance for punters in a hurry.

Given that Fleming tried hard not to make Bond too 'interesting', the enduring fascination with 007 as a man always puzzled him. 'The odd thing about Bond', he told the journalist Ken Purdy in 1964, 'is that I didn't think of him as a "character" at all. I didn't intend that he would have any characteristics at all – except be a blunt instrument in the hands of the British Government. He's a cipher, in fact. What's happened over the years is that he has become a "character" largely exaggerated in the public mind . . . He's a man of action primarily, and he's not a person of much social attractiveness. But then I never intended him to be a particularly likeable person, which makes me wonder a bit about the real motives behind the people who treat him like a cult.'

One reason why James Bond remains fascinating to so many people is because he is a fantasy character who is accessible. He is a good shot – the best in the service – but he is not as good as the instructor. He is also a natural sportsman, plays golf off a handicap of nine (as did Fleming), can swim two miles without tiring, and can throw knives with precision and drive extremely fast, but this does not make him a superman. All Bond's skills are acquired rather than innate. He has been well trained, and this sets him apart from the fictional secret agent characters of the previous generation – men like Bulldog Drummond, Richard Hannay and Lord Peter Wimsey, whose adventures Fleming had read at school. Bond is, above all things, a professional, whereas these men were all amateurs who lived off private incomes and whose exploits were often a diversion from their normal lives. The fact that Bond does what he does *for a living* makes him more dangerous, as if he might actually enjoy being tortured and killing people. This implication is what disturbed the critics and thrilled the public.

It takes Bond less than ten minutes to drive his Bentley with its Amherst Villiers supercharger from Chelsea to the secret service headquarters – a tall, grey building overlooking Regent's Park. This is a fictional building, though during the war the service was housed in the similarly nondescript Broadway Buildings, by St James's Park tube station, which Fleming certainly visited. Once he has arrived at 'Universal Export', the service's cover name, Bond goes straight up to the eighth floor, where he shares an office with 008 and 0011. As both of these agents are always off prosecuting their business around the world, Bond has ample opportunities to flirt with their shared secretary, Loelia Ponsonby: '"Morning, Lil," he said. The careful warmth of her smile dropped about ten degrees. "Give me that coat," she said. "It stinks of cordite. And don't call me Lil. You know I hate it." Bond took off his coat and handed it to her. "Anyone who gets christened Loelia Ponsonby ought to get used to pet names."' And so it goes on.

Once installed in his office, Bond ploughs his way through secret files and cipher decrypts on obscure subjects such as 'The Inspectoscope – a machine for the detection of contraband,' or 'Philopon – A Japanese murder-drug'. While reading these reports, Bond smokes compulsively, always reaching into his gunmetal cigarette box and lighting up with his

The great traveller Patrick Leigh Fermor's first book was written in part at Goldeneye – where he broke an underwater spear gun. Bond reads its passages on voodoo culture in Live and Let Die.

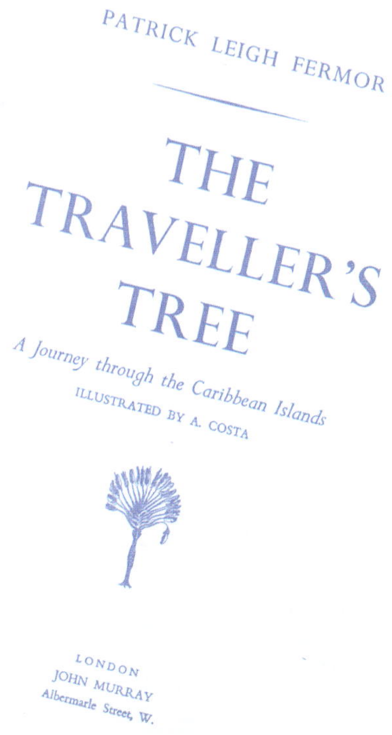

black-oxidized Ronson lighter. He inhales ostentatiously, sucking down each lungful and then blowing the smoke out through his teeth with a 'luxurious hiss'. Bond was once asked why he smoked so heavily, and he could only offer the rather lame excuse that 'I don't know what to do with my hands.' The fact is that Bond enjoys smoking as much as Fleming did. Fleming began smoking bespoke cigarettes made for him by Morlands of Grosvenor Street in the 1930s at the suggestion of his bookselling friend Percy Muir, who did the same. He stipulated a particular mixture of Turkish and Balkan tobacco, containing a higher than average tar content, and when the war came Fleming added three gold bands to the filter, mirroring the three stripes on the sleeve of his commander's uniform. Bond shares this affectation, and generally burns through sixty of these 'Morland Specials' a day – rising to seventy on one occasion after a long sweaty night at the casino – which makes it a very expensive habit. His tobacco intake today seems either heroic or foolhardy, and received a similar response even in the 1950s, when smoking was far more common. Fleming acknowledges this, and when Bond has to accomplish some physical feat such as the long underwater swim in *Live and Let Die* he makes sure 007 cuts down to about twenty a day, and feels a lot better for it. But once the mission is complete, the villain destroyed and the girl saved, Bond invariably reverts to the old routine. He knows it is bad for him, but what's the point in trying to give up if he could be killed on his next mission? As Fleming said of himself, having tried and failed to cut down from his own sixty-a-day habit, 'I will not waste my life trying to prolong it. I will use my time.'

Morland continued to make up Fleming's order of between three and four hundred bespoke cigarettes a week right up until his death in 1964. Unlike many other firms whose brand names were mentioned in the Bond books, Morland never acknowledged the enormous service Fleming had done them; nor did they offer him unlimited supplies of his favourite cigarette. Fleming remained unrepentant. 'When I make him smoke certain cigarettes,' he told an interviewer, 'it's because I do so myself. I know what these things taste like, and I have no shame in giving them free advertising.'

Occasionally M puts 007 on night duty, which Bond is surprised to find he quite enjoys. Aside from admiring the professionalism of the secret service – where the wires hum twenty-four hours a day with reports from agents around the world – these night hours give Bond a chance to work on his book, *Stay Alive!*, a technical handbook on secrets of unarmed combat that he hopes will become the service standard. Without such meagre entertainments a grinding sense of ennui suffuses

Fleming was rarely photographed without a cigarette in his hand. He smoked Morlands, and his consumption of them was almost as prodigious as Bond's.

Bond's soul. He stares out of the window at the windy park below, complains about the British weather, and drinks far more than he should. Between jobs, and therefore between books, Bond is a caged tiger, bored, indolent, and thoroughly fed up. 'It was only two or three times a year that an assignment came along requiring his particular abilities,' wrote Fleming in *Moonraker*. 'For the rest of the year he had the duties of an easy-going civil servant – elastic office hours from around ten to six; lunch, generally in the canteen; evenings spent playing cards in the company of a few close friends, or at Crockford's; or making love, with rather cold passion, to one of three similarly disposed married women; weekends playing golf for high stakes at one of the clubs near London.'

This weekly routine may well have been an accurate description of Fleming's life (if his favourite restaurant, Scott's, were substituted for the canteen), but it does not ring true for Bond. Bond is not a relaxed and clubbable fellow; he does not have male friends, and this is the only mention of any in the whole series. Even Bill Tanner, Chief of Staff and the man Bond likes most in the secret service, is never really fleshed out. Every male character in the James Bond novels with the exception of M (who essentially plays the role of father figure), and the villains (who are also father figures – gone mad) is somehow inferior to the hero. James

'Universal Export',
Regent's Park, NW1
Bond's secret service
headquarters was
situated near here
Pitt House, No
Avenue, Hamp
The Fleming far
home in Londo
Harley Street, W1
Bond fails to find
succour here after his
wife's death
John Bell & Croyden,
Wigmore Street, W1
Bond's pharmacist
Sotheby'
New Bond Street, W
The auction hous
that features i
'Property of a Lad
27 Green Street, W1
Ian Fleming's
birthplace
Morland & Co.,
Grosvenor Street, W1
Bond's and Fleming's
tobacconist
Hyde Park
Bond drives to work
through the park – and
SMERSH conducted a
hit here, according to
Casino Royale
Soviet Embassy,
Kensington Palace
Gardens, W8
Blades, Park Place, SW1
On the site of the real-life Pratt's
Club, M's gentlemen's bolthole
The Dorchester, Park Lane, W1
A favourite Fleming haunt. Bond loses at
cards in a flat near here in Thunderball
The Ritz, Piccadilly, W1
Bond stays here
St James's Street
Another gentle
club frequen
Fleming, and a
inspiration for
Curzon Street, W1
The headquarters of
MI5, and location of
Geo. F. Trumper, who
provide grooming
products for Bond
Natural History Museum,
Cromwell Road, SW7
Bond draws on the
museum's know-how for his
adventure in Live and Let Die
16 Victoria
Square, SW1
Ian and Ann's
London home
Sloane Square, SW1
Scene of a notable
distraction for Bond
on his way to work in
Moonraker
Eaton Terrace Mews, SW1
Fleming's girlfriend Muriel
was killed by a bomb in her
flat here in March 1944
London Airport and Eton
Fleming's and Bond's
school
Old Church Street, SW3
Location of Vivienne
Michel's flat
Ebury Street, SW1
Fleming's home
before the war,
and Hugo Drax's
London hideaway
King's Road, SW3
Bond's flat is in a
converted
Regency house
near here
Eve Fleming's home,
Cheyne Walk, SW3
Fleming also lived
nearby when he first
married Ann

JAMES BOND'S LONDON

Bond is best at a kind of male relationship that does not reveal too much of himself, one that is based on mutual purpose. When he talks shop with Quarrel, the Cayman Islander in *Dr No*, their conversation is 'that of a Scots laird with his head stalker; the authority was unspoken and there was no room for servility'. This is a key characteristic: it reveals that Bond is a natural aristocrat. This is also the case with Felix Leiter, the CIA man with whom Bond shares many adventures: Bond is just somehow always 'playing for higher stakes'. Fleming also had that air of effortless authority, which to some came across as arrogance. For Bond this quality separates him from his contemporaries and adds to the enigma. No woman ever held this man, remarks Vivienne Michel perceptively. No man really understands him either. Bond sits alone, enduring the long months reading ciphers all day, knowing that sooner or later the red telephone on his desk will give a soft, peremptory burr. '007? Can you come up?'

This is usually at the start of the novel. Bond walks down the thick carpet to M's office. After some brief repartee with Miss Moneypenny, the boss's secretary, Bond knocks on the door. '"Yes?" said the cold voice that Bond loved and obeyed.' Bond enters; M gives him his brief, and the secret agent is once more unleashed on the trail of some dangerous megalomaniac.

For anyone familiar with James Bond from the films, the most striking difference between the super-hero of the screen and his original incarnation is that in the books 007 is a serious character. One of the best-known 'charms' of the screen James Bond is his dry and rather obvious wit. The one-liners, so memorably associated with the movies, are conspicuously lacking from the novels, where from the outset Bond appears to have no sense of humour. He is a hard, blunt instrument, and everything about him is serious; he doesn't even attempt to crack a joke until *Goldfinger*, the seventh novel, in which he playfully orders Oddjob around: 'Quick march! Chop chop! Don't stand there looking

JAMES BOND'S 'FAVOURITES'

Favourite country: England (closely followed by Jamaica)

Least favourite country: Korea

Favourite river: Loire

Favourite cuisine: English, at its best

Favourite restaurant in France: the modest-looking place opposite the train station in Etaples run by Monsieur Bécaud. Bond eats turbot *poché*, sauce mousseline, and half a roast partridge

Favourite foods: anything gourmet; also Eggs Benedict, stone crabs, caviar, lobster and partridge

Favourite fish: sole meunière

Least favourite fish: all members of the ray family

Favourite drinks: vodka martini, bourbon and branchwater

Favourite shampoo: Pinaud's Elixir

Favourite soap: Guerlain's Fleur des Alpes

Favourite perfume: Ode by Guerlain

Favourite cigarettes: Morland Specials

Favourite car: customized Bentley

Favourite gadget: knives hidden in his shoes

Favourite book: *Hogan on Golf*

Favourite colour: dark blue

inscrutable.' This may sound lame, and it is, as Bond is not a joker. When the critics complained that Bond was too serious, Fleming was in no doubt that he had to be, as he firmly believed that irony and satire were not appropriate weapons for the thriller writer. But the seriousness did change after the first film, *Dr No*, came out in 1962. Richard Maibaum's script injected many of the quips that would become such a standard ingredient of the films, and this affected *You Only Live Twice*, the book which followed that film. In it James Bond does seem to have become more relaxed – more like his film persona, and less like Ian Fleming.

One element of the novels almost ignored by the films is Bond's vulnerability. We assume that Bond is brave, resourceful and tough, which is why he is a secret agent. But he also shivers with fear, faints with pain, and occasionally even weeps. He is aware that these are weaknesses that might one day get him killed, but he cannot help his nature. For instance, in *From Russia with Love* Bond flies over the Gulf of Corinth en route to Istanbul, and his plane encounters a storm. The turbulence is terrifying:

> There came a blinding flash of blue and white light and a crash as if an anti-aircraft shell had hit them . . . Bond smelt the smell of danger . . . In the centre of Bond was a hurricane-room, the kind of citadel found in old-fashioned houses in the tropics . . . Now he retired to this citadel, closed his mind to the hell of noise and violent movement, and focused on a single stitch in the back of the seat in front of him, waiting with slackened nerves for whatever fate had decided for BEA Flight No 130.

Fleming experienced this terror himself, recorded it in his notebook, and used it here.

The original James Bond is a man who struggles to be tough, and his body bears all the marks of his trade. When he strides down the beach he looks as if he has been in the wars, the scars from various knife fights standing out pale against his bronzed skin. And as the series goes on, Bond becomes more preoccupied with how many more head-stampings and testicle-beatings he can take. He knows that his licence to kill will be revoked when he reaches the age of forty-five, which is always just around the corner, and then he will either have to leave the service or put up with a desk job, to which he is patently unsuited. His future is never resolved, but Bond feels the threat of accidie, the torpor of the soft life, almost as keenly as the threat of a violent and painful death that lurks at the end of every assignment. 'Those whom the Gods wish to destroy, they

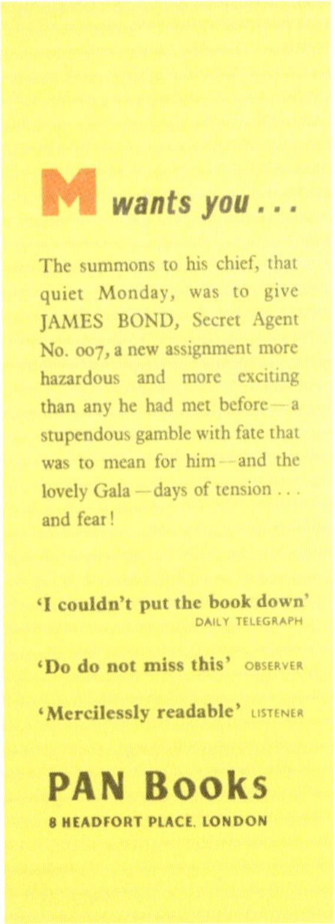

M wants you . . .

The summons to his chief, that quiet Monday, was to give JAMES BOND, Secret Agent No. 007, a new assignment more hazardous and more exciting than any he had met before—a stupendous gamble with fate that was to mean for him—and the lovely Gala—days of tension . . . and fear!

'I couldn't put the book down' DAILY TELEGRAPH

'Do do not miss this' OBSERVER

'Mercilessly readable' LISTENER

PAN Books
8 HEADFORT PLACE, LONDON

There is something of a courtly ritual to the process of Bond receiving a new assignment from M. The scene became a hallmark of most of the stories – and is here used to promote Moonraker *on the back of the Pan jacket.*

first make bored,' says 007. The fear of such a fate probably accounts for some of his vices.

At the beginning of *Thunderball* (1961) Bond is in such a bad way that M sends him to a health farm to purge the poisons in his system. M has just been there and eaten a lot of yoghurt and uncooked vegetables, and he insists that 007 does the same. Bond's medical report demands it. 'When not engaged upon strenuous duty,' it reads,

> the officer's daily consumption of alcohol is in the region of half a bottle of spirits of between sixty and seventy proof. On examination, there continues to be little definite sign of deterioration. The tongue is furred. The blood pressure a little raised at 160/90. The liver is not palpable. On the other hand, when pressed, the officer admits to frequent occipital headaches and there is a spasm in the trapezius muscles and so-called 'fibrostis' nodules can be felt. I believe these symptoms are due to the officer's mode of life. He is not responsive to the suggestion that over-indulgence is no remedy for the tensions inherent in his professional calling and can only result in the creation of a toxic state which could finally have the effect of reducing his fitness as an officer. I recommend that No 007 should take it easy for two to three weeks on a more abstemious regime.

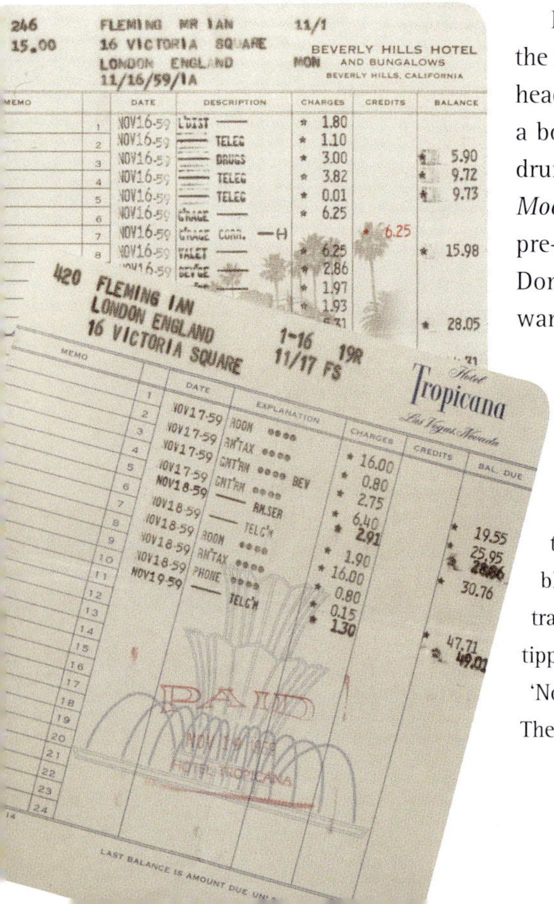

Fleming's itemized hotel bills provide the same sort of intriguing glimpses of life away from home as his descriptions of Bond's travelling habits.

Half a bottle of spirits a day was not considered excessive at the time, and even M is forced to admit that Bond does have 'a head like a rock'. This enables him to drink a lot more than half a bottle of spirits when working, but he rarely appears to get drunk. For instance, before taking on Drax at bridge in *Moonraker*, Bond consumes a vodka martini, then a carafe of pre-war Wolfschmidt vodka from Riga, then a bottle of 1946 Dom Perignon champagne. This is fine, but because Bond wants to keep his wits about him in the ensuing card game he adds his own ingredient.

> Bond took the envelope that was handed to him and slit it open. He took out a thin paper packet and carefully opened it under the level of the table. It contained a white powder. He took a silver fruit knife off the table and dipped the tip of the blade into the packet so that about half its contents were transferred to the knife. He reached for his glass of champagne and tipped the powder into it.
>
> 'Now what?' said M with a trace of impatience.
>
> There was no hint of apology in Bond's face. It wasn't M who was

going to have to do the work that evening . . . 'Benzedrine,' he said. 'I rang up my secretary before dinner and asked her to wangle some out of the surgery at Headquarters . . .' He stirred the champagne with a scrap of toast so that the white powder whirled among the bubbles. Then he drank the mixture down with one long swallow. 'It doesn't taste,' said Bond, 'and the champagne is quite excellent.'

Benzedrine, or racemic amphetamine sulphate, was prescribed as a stimulant and an antidepressant. During the war it was given to commandos on nocturnal raids, and Fleming occasionally took it himself through an inhaler. Benzedrine also formed an essential part of the evading packs issued to Allied aircrew on bombing missions over Germany, concealed in the hollowed-out heels of their flying boots. During the 1950s the drug was common enough for Anthony Eden, the prime minister, to declare during the Suez crisis that he 'lived off Benzedrine'. Bond does not live off it, but he is partial to some stimulation if he has to stay awake all night to swim across Shark Bay (*Live and Let Die*) or dispose of two very nasty hoodlums (*The Spy Who Loved Me*). In this instance (*Moonraker*) Bond overdoes it. He wants to appear drunk to trick Drax into betting unwisely on his hand, so Bond consumes a large brandy followed by another whole bottle of champagne on top of what he has already had, and pays for it in the morning. 'Champagne and Benzedrine! Never again.'

Another of Bond's vices is his fondness for gambling and card games. During the 1950s gambling was illegal in England except in private members' clubs, so the fact that 007 both liked it and was good at it (he was the best gambler in the service) lent him a rarefied glamour beyond his status and allowed readers a glimpse into a world they had heard about only in the gossip columns. To a public used to austerity, rationing and the bomb-smashed cities of the post-war years, there was something thrillingly decadent about the antics of the super-rich in the gambling towns of Europe, which seemed to have bypassed the war and its aftermath altogether. A certain Lord Brougham and Vaux, who had inherited a fortune of £500,000, had managed to gamble his entire fortune away; on one occasion he even bet £10,000 on the turn of a single card at Monte Carlo. When his creditors finally caught up with him, even the few chickens running around his estate were seized as assets.

Bond enjoys the understated drama of the casino, the dry riffle of cards and the quiet figures round the green tables. He likes being an actor and a spectator, engaging in 'other men's dramas and decisions, until it came to his own turn to say that vital "yes" or "no", generally on a fifty-fifty chance.' Most of all he likes the fact that gambling is one's own fault. Cards have no memory; it is all a matter of luck. And it comes as no surprise that 'Bond saw luck as a woman, to be softly wooed or brutally ravaged, never pandered to or pursued. But he was honest enough to admit that he had never yet been made to suffer by cards or by women.'

Bond may be lucky, but he also has a slow pulse and a sanguine temperament, and his cold, silent face is seemingly unfazed by the massive sums on the table. In *Moonraker*, M takes him into Blades to work out how Sir Hugo Drax cheats at bridge. (It turns out to be 'a shiner', a highly polished silver cigarette case that reflects the value of the card before the dealer puts it down on the table.) Once Bond realizes

HOW TO GAMBLE SENSIBLY

First you must get a strong grip on yourself and defeat the inner voice. You can't beat Aristotle, but you might - just might - trick the old boy. You can control the psychology that is working against you.

Decide the maximum amount you will lose and stick to it! If you violate this rule, nothing can help you except Fort Knox. It's better to divide your amount by days so that you can't lose your maximum for the whole visit, the first day and have to wrestle psychology for the rest of your visit.

Now, here's the hard part, decide the maximum you will win and stick to it; this prevents your becoming a jazzy chass*. If you follow these two rules, you're well on your way to having fun without pain.

When you're ready to play, watch the game for a while. Games run hot and cold-- that is, for short stretches the house will win or lose fairly steadily (naturally winning more than they lose) -- try to sit in a game on a "cold" dealer or croupier, when he turns "hot" go to another table.

Your wins and losses will follow unpredictable cycles. Do not double when you lose -- double when you win. Your possibility of winning twice in a row is greater than winning after a loss.

Set a maximum you will lose on each table. When you lose it, go to another table. If you get ahead, put aside some pre-decided portion of your winnings, and if you get down to that, quit the table and go to another. This process will limit your loss on each table and, if you hit a streak of luck, will let you get away from the table ahead of the game (maybe,perhaps, could be, could not be).

Above all else, if you catch yourself making a bet and thinking of the things you could buy with the amount of the bet, QUIT! Never let the amount you are betting become large enough to be important to you!

Nothing or no one can give you a system for winning; but if you follow these simple rules you can control your losses and enjoy your visit.

*GLOSSARY

CINCH: Gambling as viewed by the owner of any gambling device.

CON: To persuade forcibly and against good judgment.

TOUT: Noun. Person who gives gambling advice in return for money or bet placed in his name. Verb To Tout: to pursuade by questionable but exciting logic.

SHILL: Employee of house who poses as customer to keep table from emptying.

JAZZY CHASS: A term of contempt describing a winner who is trying to get rich. ~~Recognizable by a glazed look in the eyes and typified by heave and ostentatious betting and/or spending.~~

PIGEON: A term of contempt used to describe a loser who is trying to get even by increasing his bets (Example: Starting with a $25 bet and doubling to get even, 6 losses will put you $1575.00 in the hole - 10 losses $25,575.00).

PIT BOSS: Foreman of dealers; can be observed lurking in background smiling.

This was written during a trip to Las Vegas that features in Thrilling Cities. *It is advice that Bond tended to follow, avoiding the pitfalls succumbed to by some of the great gamblers of his age.*

what Drax is up to he explains the situation to M, whereupon he is given licence to beat him by cheating himself. He pockets the pack that has been cut to him and, under the cover of a handkerchief, substitutes a stacked pack containing the 'famous Culbertson hand' hidden in his pocket. Drax falls for the trap, and walks out £16,500 poorer (almost £190,000 in 2005 terms). If this seems a bit unreasonable, it is justified by M's assumption that cheating at cards 'in so-called Society, [is] about the only crime that can still finish you, whoever you are'. Drax had to be taught a lesson, and Fleming – the clubman who played bridge several nights a week – took this very seriously. 'Card cheats still have to resign from their clubs and suffer social ostracism,' he wrote in an article about gambling, 'and there is not a woman who reads this who would not tremble at the idea of a husband or brother being caught in the act.'

Though Fleming was a gambler, he was an unexpectedly cautious one. Before the war he would spend weekends with a crowd of well-heeled friends gambling at Deauville and Le Touquet, whose casinos were run by a group of financiers and shipowners known as the Greek Syndicate. Their representative at the tables was a small, ice-cold gambler named Nicki Zographos, who used to run the bank. Zographos was thought to be one of the greatest gamblers of all time, and shortly before Fleming died he began a short story in which James Bond actually meets this legend. '"Now, Mr Bond." Zographos laid a hand on Bond's sleeve and quickly withdrew it because he knew Englishmen, just as he knew the characteristics of every race, every race with money, in the world. "There are two gamblers . . . the bookmaker and the punter. The casino and, if you like" – Mr Zographos's smile was sly with the shared secret and proud with the right word – "the suckers."' Ian Fleming once scribbled down his own rules about how not to be a sucker, which he titled 'How to Gamble Sensibly', made while on a visit to Las Vegas. His maxims could be those of 007.

Apart from drinking, smoking and gambling, there is another crucial aspect to Bond's character, and that is his irrepressible interest in women. This is something his boss, the crotchety old bachelor M, can never understand. 'Doesn't do to get mixed up with neurotic women in this business,' he tells Bond in *From Russia with Love*. 'They hang on your gun-arm, if you know what I mean.' Bond does know what he means. He recognizes it is a weakness himself, but he can't deny his essentially lustful, chivalrous nature. He is drawn to sweep up girls 'like a prince in fairytales' and then take them to bed. Bond's ideal type remains the same: 'Gold hair. Grey eyes. A sinful mouth. Perfect figure. And of course she's got to be witty and poised and know how to dress and play cards and so forth. The usual things.' He forgot to add the ability to make a perfect Béarnaise sauce, another of 007's particular requirements.

If Bond has a problem with women it is when he has to work with them. 'Women were for recreation,' wrote Fleming in *Casino Royale*. 'On a job, they got in the way and fogged things up with sex and hurt feelings and all the emotional baggage they carried around. One had to look out for them and take care of them.' Bond resents all this. Fleming later explains why:

> With most women his manner was a mixture of taciturnity and passion. The lengthy approaches to a seduction bored him almost as much as the subsequent mess of disentanglement. He found something grisly in the inevitability of the pattern of each affair. The conventional parabola – sentiment, the touch of the hand, the kiss, the passionate kiss, the feel of the body, the climax in the bed, then more bed, then less bed, then the boredom, the tears, and the final bitterness was to him shameful and hypocritical. Even more he shunned the *mise en scène* for each of these acts in the play – the meeting at a party, the restaurant, the taxi, his flat, her flat, then the week-end by the sea, then the flats again, then the furtive alibis and the angry farewell on some doorstep in the rain.

The precise mapping-out of the affair must have been very familiar to Fleming, who tapped out these words, aged forty-three, on the brink of marriage, looking back on the many affairs and brief liaisons he had enjoyed during his bachelor days in Ebury Street. According to an old girlfriend, when Ian was about to end one of his dalliances he would give the girl a copy of *Toi et Moi*, a series of vivid French poems about an affair, ending in an angry farewell on a rain drenched doorstep. The girl in the poem does not have an umbrella, so – unlike in Bond's affairs – she comes back in again. They sit in his flat, waiting for the rain to stop, he in his solitude, she in her ennui.

Critics often disapproved of 007's sexual exploits, but when counted up they don't sound that bad. In every trip abroad Bond collects one girlfriend, and in only two books, *Thunderball* and *Goldfinger*, does he have two women. That amounts to not more than fourteen overall, between 1953 and 1964. Of these he drops only five between one novel and the next, and all of them live abroad. For a man like Bond that sounds almost moderate, particularly compared to his on-screen persona. In the first twenty Bond films there are fifty-eight Bond girls, and Bond makes love seventy-nine times. He had intended to marry Vesper Lynd, the first Bond girl, until she committed suicide (and each year

Bond, ever the sentimental hero, lays flowers on her grave), and ten books later he finally decides to marry Tracy di Vicenzo, to whom, interestingly, we are first introduced while she is also attempting to commit suicide.

In the intervening novels Bond is often voicing misgivings about marriage that were entirely Fleming's own. For a start, Bond cannot marry anyone because he is married already – 'To a man. Name begins with M. I'd have to divorce him before I tried to marry a woman. And I'm not sure I'd want that.' Also, 007 loathes the idea of domesticity. 'She'd get me handing round the canapés in an L-shaped drawing room. And there'd be all those ghastly, "Yes you did, No I didn't" rows that seem to go with marriage. It wouldn't last. I'd get claustrophobia and run out on her. Get myself sent to Japan or somewhere.' Bond never finds out if he would run out on his wife, because, only hours after he marries Tracy, Blofeld cruelly guns her down. In the next book, *You Only Live Twice*, Bond does indeed get sent to Japan, finds amnesiac solace in the arms of Kissy Suzuki, and leaves her without realizing she is pregnant with his child. Somewhere on the small island of Kuro is the only known descendant of 007, born in 1963.

Peff's artwork for Pan's edition of For Your Eyes Only *focuses on the classic Bond girl's deadly allure.*

As the novels go on James Bond becomes less grumpy about women, except when they are behind the wheel of a car. 'In general Bond regarded them as a mild hazard and he always gave them plenty of road and was ready for the unpredictable. Four women in a car he regarded as the highest danger potential, and two women nearly as lethal.' Far better they stay off the road altogether, or drive alone, very fast, like Tracy di Vicenzo in her Lancia Flaminia Zagato Spyder: 'If there was one thing that set James Bond really moving in life, with the exception of gunplay, it was being passed at speed by a pretty girl.' As the 'sexy boom' of Tracy's twin exhausts echoes off into the distance, Bond's animal instinct compels him to give chase.

The same is true with lesbians. Pussy Galore, the gay gangstress who was raped by her uncle at the age of twelve, leaps into bed with Bond the moment they are alone together. He 'felt the sexual challenge all beautiful lesbians have for men', whereas she had 'never met a man before' – apparently. One beautiful lesbian who remains immune to Bond's charms is Tilly Masterton, the attractively boyish girl in *Goldfinger*, and she is one of the few women ever to deliver Bond a rebuff. This prompts 007 to reveal his reactionary views on homosexuality in general:

> Tilly Masterton was one of those girls whose hormones had got mixed up. He knew the type well and thought they and their male counterparts were a direct consequence of giving votes to women and 'sex equality'. As a result of fifty years of emancipation, feminine qualities were dying out or being transferred to the males. Pansies of both sexes were everywhere, not yet completely homosexual, but confused, not knowing what they were. The result was a herd of unhappy sexual misfits – barren and full of frustrations, the women wanting to dominate and the men to be nannied. He was sorry for them, but he had no time for them.

Fleming's own early conquests of women encountered in hotel lobbies were legendary among his friends. He kept this Monte Carlo brochure in his files; the hospitality industry did not shy away from associating itself with glamour, luxury and feminine allure.

It is hardly surprising for such a conservative, heterosexual soul as Bond to hold the views of a large proportion of the male population of the time. Homosexuality became legal in Britain only in 1967, and it was something that Fleming himself was undecided about. On the one hand, as the clubman who played bridge and went round the links at Royal St George's golf club at the weekends, Ian entirely agreed with Bond; on the other hand, some of his closest friends were gay, notably Noël Coward and William Plomer. And Fleming himself didn't necessarily conform to the heterosexual stereotype of the time. For instance, he liked scented soaps, used a lot of lip salve (which several friends did not know wasn't lipstick), and often had alarming tantrums. Noël Coward said he treated Ian as he would 'a highly strung beautiful woman', and Fleming loved him for it.

Bond's relentless chasing of girls, disapproval of homosexuals, and love of clubland, gambling, golf and old cars make it difficult to think of him as a modern man in any form. 'I wouldn't say he is particularly *typical* of our times, although he is *of* the times. I think he's sort of an amalgam of romantic tough guys, dressed up in twentieth-century clothes, using twentieth-century language,' Fleming once told an interviewer, aware that 007's odd blend of old-fashioned patriot, censorious clubman and gambling epicure was rapidly becoming less fashionable in the 1950s and early '60s. Yet underneath this fictional agent whom Fleming tried so hard to set in his own time was a much older heroic character. 'Bond is really a latter-day Saint George,' he teased. 'He does kill wicked dragons after all.' This, surely, is the heart of James Bond's appeal.

SOME OF THE MAJOR CONQUESTS OF IAN FLEMING'S JAMES BOND

Vesper Lynd
Solitaire
Tiffany Case
Tatiana Romanova
Honeychile Rider
Jill Masterton
Pussy Galore
Patricia Fearing
Domino Vitali
Vivienne Michel
Tracy di Vicenzo
Kissy Suzuki
Mary Goodnight
Solange

1956

First line

With its two fighting claws held forward like a wrestler's arms the big *pandinus* scorpion emerged with a dry rustle from the finger-sized hole under the rock.

Story

Bond is sent off to investigate a diamond-smuggling pipeline, which begins in French Guinea and ends in Las Vegas. His cover is as a diamond smuggler and this leads him first to Tiffany Case, a fast-talking American blonde, and then to her employers, Jack and Seraffimo Spang, twin brothers who run the 'Spangled Mob' and control both ends of the pipeline. Bond follows their trail to Saratoga Springs, where they are attempting to win a horse race with the help of a crooked jockey, and from there on to Las Vegas. Here Bond's cover is exposed, and he is kidnapped by Seraffimo and locked up in 'Spectreville', a ghost town outside Las Vegas that Spang is turning into a Wild West resort. Here Bond is savagely trampled on by Wint and Kidd, two hoods in football boots, who leave him for dead. When he comes around he manages to escape with Tiffany on a small locomotive, only to be pursued by Seraffimo in The Cannonball, his own Wild West train. Bond manages to send this, and Spang, crashing into a disused mine shaft. Believing they are safe, Bond and Tiffany then return to London on board the *Queen Elizabeth*, unaware that Wint and Kidd are watching. The two hoods then capture Tiffany, but Bond rescues her by bursting through the window of her cabin on a rope and killing both her captors. At the very end, the story returns full circle to French Guinea, where a helicopter arrives to pick up diamonds smuggled by a miner. Bond shoots this down with a Bofors artillery piece, killing the pilot, who is none other than Jack Spang.

Last lines

For Bond it was just the end of another adventure. Another adventure for which a wry phrase of Tiffany Case might be the epitaph. He could see the passionate, ironical mouth saying the words:
'It reads better than it lives.'

Inspirations

Ian first read a story about illicit diamonds leaving Sierra Leone in the *Sunday Times* in 1954. It intrigued him, and through some old school friends he found an entrée into the closed world of diamond trading. Here he met Sir Percy Sillitoe, the former head of MI5, who was now working for De Beers investigating the illegal diamond trade, and a diamond broker named Harry Abrahams, who gave him information and, most thrilling of all, a diamond. The subject stayed with Fleming, and several years later he wrote a factual book, *The Diamond Smugglers* (1957), about a real-life diamond spy, John Collard, who was trying to police this trade in Africa.

In August 1954 Ian Fleming travelled with Ernie Cuneo to Saratoga Springs, a small, sleepy spa town in upstate New York, which for one month of the year – August – goes 'hog wild'. 'It's probably the smartest race-meeting in America,' he wrote in *Diamonds are Forever*, 'and the place crawls with Vanderbilts and Whitneys.' This is exactly what Ian had found. He was not the slightest bit interested in horses but, like James Bond, 'he rather liked the life that went with them'. He was also interested in racetrack swindles, and had recently written an article about a Romanian jockey scandal in his Atticus column. While at Saratoga Springs Ian also sampled a mud treatment, and by accident rather than design he found himself in a very run-down establishment where he was locked in a vat of brown mud alongside a collection of gangsters and bent jockeys similarly encased. This provided the inspiration for the famous scene at the Acme Mud and Sulphur Baths.

Later Ian went on to Las Vegas with Ernie in tow. This provided more inspiration, and a chance to take on the strip. Together they bet a dollar apiece on a game of blackjack, and as soon as they were a dollar up they moved on to the next casino. By 4 a.m. the two friends, now rather the worse for wear, were telling anyone who would listen that they had taken on every casino in Las Vegas and won.

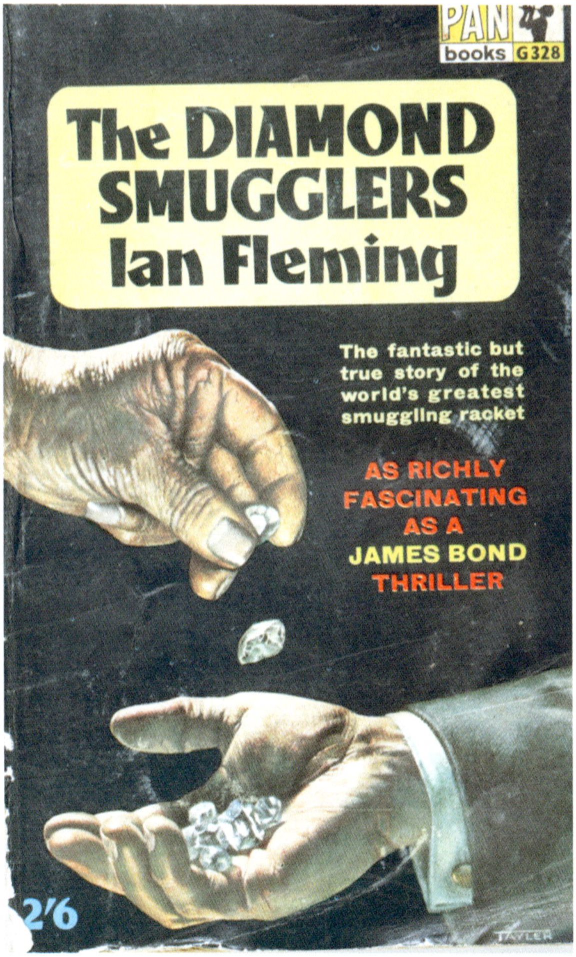

What the readers said

'I have never yet seen a mobile Bofors gun where a corporal, or any other rank, could turn the elevating and traversing cranks at the same time'

'An extract from *Diamonds are Forever* was read out at a recent meeting of the co-ordinating committee of Shannon Airport. The shops are my responsibility, and I was astonished to learn that you considered the goods on offer to be "junk"'
From John Ryan, Commercial Division, Shannon Airport

'You know my weakness for girls in bondage, and after the original way in which you handled it in previous books, I was disappointed not to find any this time'

'Dear Mr Fleming, I love your books and I adore perfume, but I think I must complain. Vent Vert does not come from Dior – it is from Pierre Balmain!'
Fleming's reply: 'Alas, attributing Vent Vert to Dior was nearly as bad as when in one of my books I made Bond eat asparagus with sauce Béarnaise instead of mousseline . . . If I go on like this I shall one day find myself giving my heroine green hair.'

What the critics said

'Exciting, but still only a shadow of *Casino Royale*' – *The Tablet*

'His hero, James Bond, fulfils every male fantasy known to me' – *The Spectator*

'Mr James Bond, that oh-so-superior British agent, does nothing really fantastic this time though I was glad to see him manning a Bofors gun at the end. Thrillers rarely go in for the use of the cannon' – *News Chronicle*

Cape's hardback jacket was designed by Pat Marriott. The Diamond Smugglers *– a non-fiction account of the illicit gem trade in West Africa – was first published the following year. It attracted almost as much publicity as a Bond novel.*

THE RIGHT WAY TO EAT...

The Right Way to Drink

From a brochure in Fleming's collection. Monaco was one of the few places in the world that could provide the escapist opulence that became a hallmark of the Bond novels. 007 would be no stranger to a table such as this.

'You must forgive me,' he said. 'I take a ridiculous pleasure in what I eat and drink. It comes partly from being a bachelor, but mostly from a habit of taking a lot of trouble over details.' So says James Bond to his beautiful companion Vesper Lynd in *Casino Royale*, moments after he had very precisely ordered a mouth-watering meal. He goes on: 'It's very pernickety and old-maidish really, but then when I'm working I generally have to eat my meals alone and it makes them more interesting when one takes trouble.' Bond begins this particular culinary odyssey with caviar and plenty of toast (one can *never* get enough toast), followed by a very small tournedos, underdone, with Béarnaise sauce and a *cœur d'artichaut*. Then, while Vesper tucks into her favourite strawberries and cream, Bond will have half an avocado pear and a little French dressing. To accompany this first 'millionaire's' meal, Bond chooses champagne, a Taittinger '45, which the sommelier agrees is good, but, if he may suggest, 'the Blanc de Brut 1943 of the same marque is without equal.' Bond acquiesces. '"That is not a well-known brand . . . but it is probably the finest champagne in the world." He grinned suddenly at the touch of pretension in his remark.'

So this is what it is all about. When it comes to restaurants, food and drink, Bond knows best, and this amuses him because he is actually an impostor in the world of fine living. James Bond is an expense-account gourmet. His connoisseurship of fine food and fine wines is entirely courtesy of the secret service, whose deep pockets have provided him with tastes far beyond the reach of his own salary. Fleming somewhat unconvincingly claimed that Bond was not a gourmet by nature: when he was at home in England he made do with simple fare – grilled sole, scrambled eggs, cold meat and potato salad, that sort of thing. Frankly, this sounds unlikely in a man who takes such care over what he orders and then consumes it with such relish. In the numerous dining scenes the conversation more or less grinds to a halt when the dishes arrive, and doesn't resume until the coffee and cigarettes. 007 is far too busy savouring his food to make idle chit chat.

What kind of food does James Bond eat? With one notable exception, it is always the best local fare on offer. 'What I endeavour to aim at is a certain disciplined exoticism,' wrote Fleming, and to that end he collected menus from his own peregrinations around the world to delight the well-travelled tastebuds of 007. His eye was always drawn to the curious and unusual, such as this meal he copied down on the back of a postcard in the Seychelles:

Cordonnier ze smeitana (Polish)
Consommé Bourgeois (Seychelles)
Escalope of Pork with Bilambee and Aubergine
Dodine de Canard (French)
Senegalese rice with green turtle (West African)
Baked Pawpaw

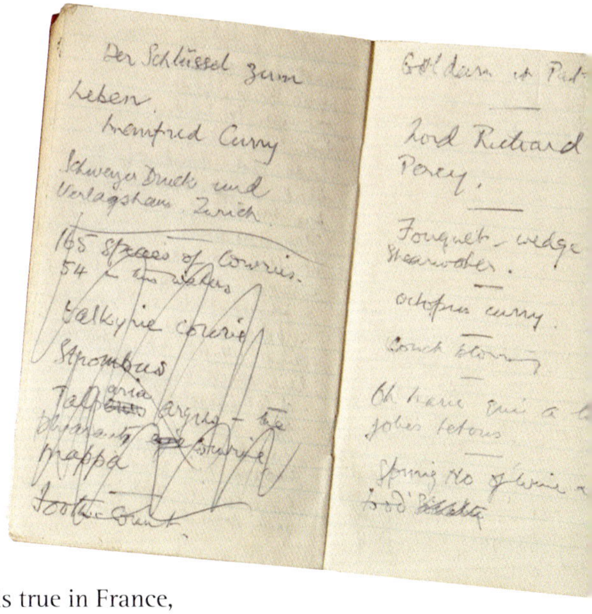

Fleming's notebooks are filled with stream-of-consciousness jottings, names, places and phrases. They show a particular fascination with exotic food.

Fleming's careful culinary tourism ensured that Bond rarely puts a foot wrong. In Istanbul 007 sits down on his balcony overlooking the Topkapi Palace and orders in French what he already knew would be the best breakfast on offer in Turkey: 'He was not disappointed. The yoghurt, in a blue china bowl, was deep yellow and with the consistency of thick cream. The green figs, ready peeled, were bursting with ripeness, and the Turkish coffee was jet black and with the burned taste that showed it had been freshly ground.' The same is true in France, where Bond's mastery of local fare is ludicrously precise. 'Please buy us lunch,' he barks at Tilly Masterton. '"Anything you like for yourself. For me, six inches of Lyon sausage, a loaf of bread, and half a litre of Mâcon with the cork pulled." Their eyes met and exchanged a flurry of masculine/feminine master/slave signals. The girl took the money. "Thank you. I'll get the same things for myself."'

On Fleming's travels for the Sunday Times *he was usually given red carpet treatment. This was an invitation to lunch when he was in the Far East to research* Thrilling Cities.

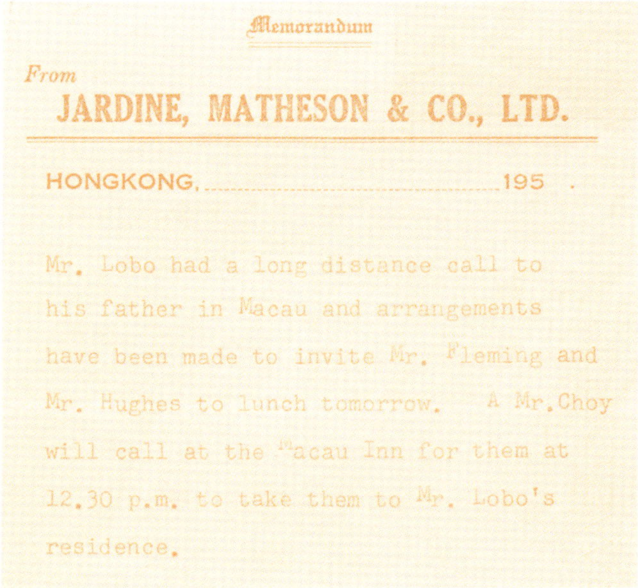
Memorandum

From

JARDINE, MATHESON & CO., LTD.

HONGKONG, ... 195 .

Mr. Lobo had a long distance call to his father in Macau and arrangements have been made to invite Mr. Fleming and Mr. Hughes to lunch tomorrow. A Mr. Choy will call at the Macau Inn for them at 12.30 p.m. to take them to Mr. Lobo's residence.

Occasionally Bond fails to order 'the best': in Istanbul he chooses a conservative grilled-sardine starter followed by doner kebab, which is good, but the tourist menu, and not nearly as interesting as Darko Kerim's strips of raw fish followed by a kind of steak-tartare beef burger and lettuce. In Japan Bond lets himself be guided by Tiger Tanaka, the head of the Japanese secret service, and is just coming to grips with using chopsticks to eat a lobster when the crustacean decides enough is enough and totters off across the table. '"Good God, Tiger!" Bond said aghast. "The damn thing's alive!"'

For Fleming, the reason why he wrote so greedily about food was clear. He was in the business of writing thrillers, and it was the job of the thriller writer to stimulate the reader's senses rather than his mind, and that included exciting the taste buds. He could not understand why fictional English heroes routinely live off a such a banal diet. 'Banality is the enemy of the English fiction writer,' he thundered, and the acme of banality was tea. A girl from the secret-service canteen once makes the mistake of bringing Bond a cuppa while he is on night duty. 'Bond looked at her severely. "I don't drink tea. I hate it. It's mud. Moreover it's one of the main reasons for the downfall of the British Empire. Be a good girl and make me some coffee."' No tea then, or for that matter anything else predictable.

Fleming was often accused by critics of having his hero eat meals that were well beyond the means of most of his readers, which was true, but, he argued:

James Bond very specifically favours certain brands of marmalade and jam – most of which are still made today. He called on William Plomer and other knowledgeable friends to help with these choices.

> Leaving out the economic factor, that is, the actual price of the food, it is surely more stimulating to the reader's senses if, instead of writing 'He made a hurried meal of the Plat du Jour – excellent cottage pie and vegetables, followed by home made trifle' (I think this is a fair English menu without burlesque) you write 'Being instinctively mistrustful of all Plats du Jour, he ordered four fried eggs cooked on both sides, hot buttered toast and a large

> black cup of coffee.' No difference in prices here, but the following points should be noted: firstly, we all prefer breakfast foods to the sort of food one usually gets at luncheon and dinner; secondly, this is an independent character who knows what he wants and gets it; thirdly, four fried eggs has the sound of a real man's meal and, in our imagination, a large cup of black coffee sits well on our tastebuds after the rich buttery sound of the fried eggs and the hot buttery toast.

James Bond never eats four fried eggs in this fashion, but he does have something of an obsession with breakfast food, which is his and Fleming's favourite meal of the day. In *From Russia with Love* Bond sits down in his flat to eat eggs from French Maran hens (boiled for three and a third minutes) which he eats off Minton china. This is followed by toast with either Frank Cooper's Vintage Oxford Marmalade, Tiptree 'Little Scarlet' strawberry jam or Norwegian Heather Honey from Fortnum & Mason. The coffee, brewed in an American Chemex, was from De Bry in New Oxford Street. If this sounds extraordinarily fastidious and more than a little old-maidish, then it was, as all these details were provided by William Plomer, Fleming's bookish, gay editor, who was always on hand to suggest the precise make of jam or type of hen if Fleming needed it. In the manuscripts of the books these details were routinely left blank and were filled in only once Ian had canvassed around for some expert opinions on the precise brand and vintage.

Regarding eggs, Ian Fleming would eat them for breakfast and then at all other mealtimes as well – and in the best restaurants in town if he felt like it. He took a kind of perverse pleasure in going to Lutèce on 42nd Street, one of the most expensive restaurants in New York, where he would order scrambled eggs followed by strawberries, which the patron took as one more example of English

Bond's housekeeper, May Maxwell, is supposedly responsible for this recipe. It was also Fleming's preferred way of preparing scrambled eggs.

SCRAMBLED EGGS

by

IAN FLEMING

For 4 as a main dish:

12 eggs
Salt & Pepper
5 - 6 oz of butter

Break the eggs into a bowl, beat thoroughly with a fork and season well.

In a small copper (or heavy bottomed)saucepan) melt 4 oz of the butter. When melted pour in the eggs and cook over a very low heat, whisking continuously with a small egg whisk.

While the eggs are still slightly more moist than you would wish for eating, remove pan from heat, add rest of butter and continue whisking for half a minute.

P.S. I think you sometimes add cream instead of the last piece of butter. G.

eccentricity. 'Scrambled eggs and coffee never let you down,' he once famously remarked, though occasionally they let James Bond down. In the original typescript of *Live and Let Die*, James Bond consumed scrambled eggs so often that a perceptive proof-reader at Fleming's publishers, Jonathan Cape, suggested that this rigid pattern of life would surely be a security risk. If Bond were being followed, his tail would only have to go into restaurants and say, 'Was there a man here eating scrambled eggs?' to know whether he was on the right track or not. As a result, Fleming went back and obligingly changed all the menus.

Fleming may have seen it as his duty to stimulate the reader's taste buds, but his concern with food was particularly apposite to the time. It is difficult to fully appreciate the utter drabness of post-war British cuisine. Rationing had been in place ever since 1940, restricting essentials such as milk, eggs and meat, and these privations continued long after the war had ended. To many, this enforced austerity seemed a hard price to pay for victory, but in March 1953 egg rationing finally ceased. Coincidentally, this was the same month that *Casino Royale* was first published. Over the course of the next year sugar, butter, cheese, beef and bacon followed suit, making 1954 a year of culinary liberation for the British people. For the first time since the war they could eat whatever they liked, which added particular interest to the descriptions of James Bond tucking into his caviar and tournedos. Bond's first dessert,

Bond wasn't loyal to any particular champagne marque. Besides Pol Roger and Krug, the stories feature Taittinger, Veuve Clicquot and Dom Pérignon, among others. Even Babycham makes an appearance in On Her Majesty's Secret Service.

half an avocado pear, would have seemed highly exotic at a time when avocados were seldom imported into Britain and many people had never even seen a banana.

Perhaps the most mouthwatering feast in the entire James Bond series occurs near the beginning of *Goldfinger*. At Bill's on the Beach, in Miami, Bond sits down to fresh stone crabs, a dish he had never tried before, washed down with a pint of pink champagne served in a silver tankard. His companion is a corpulent American businessman named Du Pont, who has chosen this particular local delicacy.

> With ceremony, a wide silver dish of crabs, big ones, their shells and claws broken, was placed in the middle of the table. A silver sauceboat brimming with melted butter and a long rack of toast was put beside each of their plates. The tankards of champagne frothed pink. Finally, with an oily smirk, the head waiter came behind their chairs and, in turn, tied round their necks long white silken bibs that reached down to the lap.
>
> Bond was reminded of Charles Laughton playing Henry VIII, but neither Mr Du Pont nor the neighbouring diners seemed surprised at the hoggish display. Mr Du Pont, with a gleeful 'Every man for himself', raked several hunks of crab on to his plate, doused them liberally in melted butter and dug in. Bond followed suit, and proceeded to eat, or rather devour, the most delicious meal he had had in his life.
>
> The meat of the stone crabs was the tenderest, sweetest shellfish he had ever tasted. It was perfectly set off by the dry toast and the slightly burned taste of the melted butter. The champagne seemed to have the faintest scent of strawberries. It was ice cold. After each helping of crab, the champagne cleaned the palate for the next. They ate steadily and with absorption and hardly exchanged a word until the dish was cleared.
>
> With a slight belch, Mr Du Pont for the last time wiped butter off his chin with his silken bib and sat back. His face was flushed. He looked proudly at Bond. He said reverently, 'Mr Bond, I doubt if anywhere in the world a man has eaten as good a dinner as that tonight. What do you say?'

Bond never ate at this particular Hungarian restaurant in Vienna, but Fleming kept its modest wine list among his travel memorabilia. He was never as much of an oenophile as Bond.

UNGARISCHES RESTAURANT
„Csárdásfürstin"
WIEN I, SCHWARZENBERGSTR. 2 / TEL. 52 92 46

Flaschenweine:

Wines in bottles — Des vins en bouteilles — Vini in bottiglia — Red and white wines from Austrian vineyards Des vins rouges ou blancs de l'Autriche — Vino rosso austriaco, Vino bianco austriaco

Ungarische Weine

per Flasche Schilling

Tokayi Aszú (Dessert)	38.—
Tokayi Szamorodni (Edes)	52.—
Orig. ung. Badacsonyi	48.—

Rotweine

Ruster Stierblut	38.—
Beaujolais - Supérieur Orig. franz. Rotwein	60.—
Châteauneuf-du-Pape Bouchard Ainé & Fils, Orig. franz. Rotwein	105.—

Weißweine

Riesling - Muskat - Ottonel	38.—
Grinzinger Steinwein (Rieslingtraube)	40.—
Dürnsteiner Katzensprung (Grüner Veltliner, Spätlese) Winzergenossenschaft Wachau	48.—
Loibner Kaiserwein, Rheinriesling Dinstlgut — Loiben	48.—
Gumpoldskirchner, Spätrot-Rotgipfler Eigengewächs: Ökonomierat R. Rasser	48.—
Roter Veltliner, Spätlese	50.—
Steiner Hund (Rotgipfler) Wachauer Weingut: Dr. Rebiczek-Rosar	60.—
Rheinriesling, Krems-Wachtberg Weingut R. Kutschera & Söhne	60.—
Dürnsteiner Himmelstiege Grüner Veltliner, Auslese. Kontrolliert und prämiiert von der Winzergen.	70.—

Even Bond is momentarily revolted by his gluttony, but he admits that 'He had made his wish and the wish had not only been granted, it had been stuffed down his throat.'

Fleming had first eaten fresh stone crabs at Joe's Stone Crab on Miami Beach with his friend Ivar Bryce, and they remained one of his own favourite dishes, though he never made any pretence to being a card-carrying gourmet. In New York 007 sits down to room service in the St Regis Hotel that consists of 'soft-shell crabs with tartare sauce, flat beef Hamburgers, medium-rare, from the charcoal grill, french-fried potatoes, broccoli, mixed salad with thousand-island dressing, ice-cream with melted butterscotch and as good a Liebfraumilch as you can get in America.' Ian Fleming's own tastes were rather different. Dismissing all the famous eateries in Manhattan, he sauntered off to his 'favourite restaurant in America', the crypt-like oyster bar at Grand Central Terminal. Here very old gloomy-faced Croats in white hats would deftly prepare oyster soup for each customer in a steamer, stirring in the oysters, cream, paprika and Worcestershire sauce and allowing it to simmer. Then the broth would be decanted into the customer's bowl and served up with crackers and an ice-cold bottle of Miller's High Life, which Fleming christened 'the champagne of beers'. This was simple fare for serious soup-eaters, and Ian adored it.

When in New York, Miller High Life was Fleming's preferred tipple. It was rather more affordable than the parade of high-end drinks his characters enjoy.

Given his own granite tastes, Ian's friends were often baffled by how he was able to produce so many sensual descriptions of food in his fiction. 'One of the things that still makes me laugh whenever I read Ian's books is the contrast between the standard of living of dear old Bond and the sort of thing Ian used to put up with at Goldeneye,' said Noël Coward. 'When Bond drinks his wine it has to be properly chambré, the tournedos slightly underdone, and so forth.' At Goldeneye 'the food was so abominable that I used to cross myself before eating it. Stewed guavas and coconut cream, salt fish and ackee fruit, I mean, it tasted like armpits! And all the time there was old Ian smacking his lips for more and you are tormented by the thought of all those exquisite meals in the books.' Fleming tolerated all this as it was 'local fare' made by his faithful housekeeper, Violet, and he was determined to enjoy whatever came out of her kitchen, be it goat's head soup or goat fish curry. 'Above all,' he had once written of Jamaica, 'if the settler or visitor is to be happy, he must really *embrace* the tropics.' Goldeneye, and Violet's cooking, were always an adventure.

When in London, and not enjoying his trusty scrambled eggs, Fleming would take himself off to Boodle's or Scott's with a book and eat oysters and fried fillets of sole washed down with half a bottle of Chablis. Fleming may have aspired to be Bond in many aspects of his fiction, but in reality he was far closer to M, as this is exactly the sort of solitary fare that M eats every lunchtime at Blades. But even M shows the occasional flash of idiosyncrasy: he has a weakness for old-fashioned marrowbones, scooping the marrow out with a spoon. Fleming would never have eaten anything as canine as that.

If scrambled eggs and stone crabs were about all that Fleming had in common with Bond at the table, when it came to alcohol the two men were more or less in accord. 'Basically, he's a hard liquor man,' admitted Fleming. Martinis are Bond's drink, made, if possible, with Russian or Polish vodka as Ian liked them. If there was no vodka, English gin would do, but, as Fleming explained in an article for the benefit of American tourists visiting London,

> It is extremely difficult to get a good Martini anywhere in England . . . The way I get one in a pub is to walk calmly and confidently up to the counter and, speaking very distinctly, ask the man or girl behind it to put plenty of ice in the shaker (they nearly all have a shaker), pour in six gins and one dry vermouth (enunciate 'dry' carefully) and shake until I tell them to stop. You then point to a suitably large glass and ask them to pour the mixture in. Your behaviour will create a certain amount of astonishment, not unmixed with fear, but you will have achieved a very large and fairly good Martini, equal in size to about three New York Martinis, and it will cost you about $1.25.

Opposite, top
On a trip to Los Angeles in 1960, Fleming kept careful ratings of his favourite dining experiences. This range of cuisines would also have greeted 007 on his arrival in the City of Angels – and would have come as a revelation to many of his British readers.

This kind of barmanship is a favourite habit of James Bond, who, with his CIA companion Felix Leiter by his side, is often found nursing several of these very large, potent cocktails and casting an expert eye on the bar, the barman and the drinkers. Neither man suffered fools in this department, as is evident the first time they sit down together in *Casino Royale*. Here Bond lays his serious drinker credentials on the line:

> He looked carefully at the barman.
> 'A dry martini', he said. 'One. In a deep champagne goblet.'
> *'Oui, monsieur.'*
> 'Just a moment. Three measures of Gordon's, one of vodka, half a measure of Kina Lillet. Shake it very well until it's ice-cold, then add a large thin slice of lemon peel. Got it?'
> 'Certainly monsieur.' The barman seemed pleased with the idea.
> 'Gosh, that's certainly a drink,' said Leiter.

It certainly was, as Kina Lillet was an obscure wine aperitif strongly flavoured with the bitter taste of quinine, which would have given this particular martini a very harsh, unpleasant taste. One assumes Fleming knew this, but it is possible he just liked the name and may never have tasted James Bond's invention. Bond called it a 'Vesper', after Vesper Lynd, his beautiful secret-service companion. Fleming had named her after another cocktail, a particular rum punch he had drunk in Jamaica.

If martini is not available, James Bond generally drinks half-pints of bourbon, with plenty of ice, or whisky sodas. Fleming had been converted to bourbon in the early 1950s, when his doctor insisted that he cut down on his habit of drinking up to a bottle of gin a day, and he particularly liked an unusual brand named Old Grand-Dad. This, he had been reliably informed, was best mixed with 'branchwater' – simply still water, but supposedly taken from somewhere close to the source. This conceit amused both Fleming and Bond, and 'branchwater' also mystified most American barmen. While writing his novels in Jamaica, Ian Fleming liked to drink in what he called the American style – that is to say, he would drink nothing at breakfast or lunch, but towards sundown vodka martinis, 'very brown' whisky sodas, and half-pints of bourbon

007 is for ever linked to the martini – preferably made with Wolfschmidt Polish vodka and/or Beefeater or Gordon's gin. Less well known is his partiality for bourbon – Jack Daniels and, Fleming's own favourite, Old Grand-Dad.

would appear. These would continue in a steady succession, so that by dinner Fleming and his guests had drunk a considerable amount, yet when he sat down to dinner he drank only water and very occasionally beer or wine. After dinner he would usually pick up where he had left off, and the following morning wake up to a hangover. It is no wonder that the pick-me-up breakfast of scrambled eggs and coffee was Ian's favourite meal of the day.

When Bond left the safety of hard liquor and drank wine, Fleming found himself in an altogether more testing arena. 'He's not a wine snob,' Fleming once said. 'He very seldom drinks wine, just an occasional glass of champagne.' Nevertheless, this being 007, the champagne has to be the best. Despite being on the wine committee of the Portland Club, Fleming was no wine snob either: wine just did not interest him, and so as ever he asked his connoisseur friends to guide him. But even they occasionally got it wrong. When Goldfinger served up shrimp curry and a Piesporter Goldtröpfchen '53 an irate reader wrote to Fleming to tell him this wine was a Moselle, not a hock as described. Then, in *On Her Majesty's Secret Service*, Bond ordered a half-bottle of Pol Roger, which, as Fleming's friend the writer Patrick Leigh Fermor pointed out, was the only champagne *not* produced in half-bottles. These maddening mistakes aside, Bond's choice of wine was usually impeccable, and Fleming succeeded in convincing most of his readers that 007 really knew what he was talking about, even if his creator had never tasted any of it. Ian's own favourite was a harsh, cheap Algerian red he nicknamed 'The Infuriator'. This would never have done for the finicky Mr Bond, so, as with most of his own unpretentious tastes, he gave it to M to drink instead.

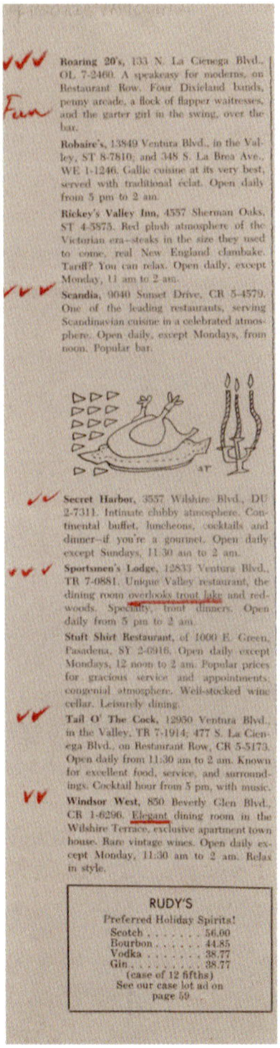
Fun

Roaring 20's, 133 N. La Cienega Blvd., OL 7-2460. A speakeasy for moderns, on Restaurant Row. Four Dixieland bands, penny arcade, a flock of flapper waitresses, and the garter girl in the swing, over the bar.

Robaire's, 13849 Ventura Blvd., in the Valley, ST 8-7810; and 348 S. La Brea Ave., WE 1-1246. Gallic cuisine at its very best, served with traditional éclat. Open daily from 5 pm to 2 am.

Rickey's Valley Inn, 4557 Sherman Oaks, ST 4-5875. Red plush atmosphere of the Victorian era–steaks in the size they used to come, real New England clambake. Tariff? You can relax. Open daily, except Monday, 11 am to 2 am.

Scandia, 9040 Sunset Drive, CR 5-4579. One of the leading restaurants, serving Scandinavian cuisine in a celebrated atmosphere. Open daily, except Mondays, from noon. Popular bar.

Secret Harbor, 3557 Wilshire Blvd., DU 2-7311. Intimate clubby atmosphere. Continental buffet, luncheons, cocktails and dinner–if you're a gourmet. Open daily except Sundays, 11:30 am to 2 am.

Sportsmen's Lodge, 12833 Ventura Blvd., TR 7-0881. Unique Valley restaurant, the dining room overlooks trout lake and redwoods. Specialty, trout dinners. Open daily from 5 pm to 2 am.

Stuft Shirt Restaurant, of 1000 E. Green, Pasadena, SY 2-6916. Open daily except Mondays, 12 noon to 2 am. Popular prices for gracious service and appointments, congenial atmosphere. Well-stocked wine cellar. Leisurely dining.

Tail O' The Cock, 12950 Ventura Blvd., in the Valley, TR 7-1914; 477 S. La Cienega Blvd., on Restaurant Row, CR 5-5173. Open daily from 11:30 am to 2 am. Known for excellent food, service, and surroundings. Cocktail hour from 5 pm, with music.

Windsor West, 850 Beverly Glen Blvd., CR 1-6296. Elegant dining room in the Wilshire Terrace, exclusive apartment town house. Rare vintage wines. Open daily except Monday, 11:30 am to 2 am. Relax in style.

RUDY'S
Preferred Holiday Spirits!
Scotch 56.00
Bourbon 44.85
Vodka 38.77
Gin 38.77
(case of 12 fifths)
See our case lot ad on page 59

1957

First line

The naked man who lay splayed out on his face beside the swimming pool might have been dead.

Story

The first 119 pages of this novel are all about a SMERSH plan to assassinate Bond 'with ignominy' as revenge for all the setbacks the organization has suffered in the past. Rosa Klebb, a SMERSH colonel, appoints its top executioner for the job, a massive ex-IRA man named Red Grant. The idea is to lure Bond out to Istanbul on the pretence that a beautiful Russian cipher expert called Tatiana Romanova is ready to defect to the West on account of having seen his picture in a KGB file and fallen in love with him. This flimsy bait is made irresistible by the promise that when she meets him she will hand over the coveted Spektor coding machine. Bond suspects a trap, but he travels to Istanbul anyway, and places his life in the hands of Darko Kerim, a redoubtable Turk who controls the local British spy network. After surviving several attempts on his life, Bond finds Tatiana naked in his hotel bed. She insists on escaping the following day aboard the Orient Express, which they catch with Darko Kerim in tow. Three Russian assassins are watching; Kerim deals with two of them, before dying in a struggle with the third. Bond thinks Kerim's death has ended the plot until he meets an odd English agent in the south of France, Captain Nash, a.k.a. Red Grant. Grant drugs Tatiana and then attempts to murder Bond with a gun disguised as a book. He fails, and in a titanic struggle Bond manages to kill him. Bond then escapes from the train with Tatiana and delivers the Spektor machine to Paris, where he locates Rosa Klebb herself. First she attempts to blow him up, then she attacks him with poisoned knitting needles, but René Mathis of the Deuxième Bureau arrives just in time to overpower her. In Fleming's first draft he had written a love scene between Bond and Tatiana, but in the final version he has Klebb lashing out at Bond with her shiny buttoned boot. The toe conceals a poison-tipped steel knife, and Bond's fate hangs in the balance.

Last lines (the death of James Bond?)

Desperately he focused Mathis.
'I shan't need a girl, René,' he said thickly.
Now he had to gasp for breath. Again his hand moved up towards his cold face. He had the impression of Mathis starting towards him.
Bond felt his knees begin to buckle.
He said, or thought he said, 'I've already got the loveliest . . .'
Bond pivoted slowly on his heel and crashed headlong to the wine-red floor.

Inspirations

In February 1950 Eugene Karp, a naval attaché at the American embassy in Bucharest, attempted to escape from Romania after being tipped off that he was about to be arrested for espionage. He had with him Soviet intelligence papers about a blown US spy network behind the Iron Curtain, incriminating him and many other agents. Boarding the Orient Express at Budapest, he bought a ticket for Paris, unaware that Soviet assassins were already on the train. Soon afterwards the conductor was found drugged, and Karp's body was later recovered from a railway tunnel south of Salzburg.

The death of Karp was an inspiration for this story, as was Fleming's trip to Istanbul in 1956 to cover an Interpol conference. His guide to that city was Nazim Kalkavan (who became Darko Kerim), and Ian was so taken with this larger-than-life character that he copied down great chunks of his conversation, which he later reproduced verbatim. Istanbul was an important spy centre at the time, as it was widely feared that the Russians had plans to march through Turkey into Kurdistan and then on into Iraq, to take possession of the vast oil reserves. Like Bond, Fleming took the Orient Express from Istanbul back to Paris, having long wanted to travel on 'the most glamorous train in the world'. The reality, somewhat predictably, turned out to be rather monotonous.

The idea of using the Orient Express may well have come from Ludovic A. Forbes from Staffordshire, one of Fleming's most vociferous fans, who wrote to him after each book with reams of suggestions. Forbes had been reading thrillers since 1897, and in 1955 he badgered Fleming to write a thriller set on that train. Also, he suggested, 'Get James really worked up over an Italian beauty, a Contessa.' Fleming was always grateful for his readers' suggestions, and may well have taken this one to heart. Not only did Bond take the Orient Express, but he later ended up marrying Tracy di Vicenzo, an Italian contessa.

Not surprisingly, the Cold War looms large in this novel, and Fleming went to his usual lengths to make sure everything seemed real. The precise details about SMERSH and its headquarters came from Colonel Tokaty-Tokaev, a defector, and Red Grant's book gun was inspired by the Russian assassin Nikolai Khokhlov's cigarette case, which fired poison-coated bullets. The encoder machine entrusted to Tatiana was not a Cold War invention but a version of Enigma, the German device whose code book Fleming had come up with his own plans to steal during the war.

What the readers said

'Sir, no one could ever believe in a character who has his eggs boiled for three and a third minutes and reads only *The Times*. Give him some vices at least, even if it is only reading the *Daily Mirror*'

'Being a Scot, I retain a certain disapproval of authors and books as works of the devil, but I really cannot let you go about killing my favourite Secret Service man like that'

'He's not really dead, is he? You simply cannot do this to us! How on earth are you going to write your next book without him?'

'Do you really think British Intelligence has sunk so low? And if so, why publish it abroad to warn our enemies?'

What the critics said

'If a psychiatrist and a thoroughly efficient copywriter got together to produce a fictional character who would be the mid-twentieth century subconscious male ambition, the result would inevitably be James Bond' – *Sunday Times*

'Ian Fleming is in a class by himself' – *Oxford Mail*

'Mr Fleming is intensely observant, acutely literate and can turn a cliché into a silk purse with astute alchemy' – James Sandoe, *New York Herald Tribune*

What Fleming said

'Personally I think *From Russia with Love* was, in many respects, my best book, but the great thing is that each one of the books seems to have been a favourite with one or other section of the public and none has yet been completely damned.'

The Jonathan Cape edition was the first Fleming book to feature the distinctive artwork of Richard Chopping. Turkey was a country that sat on one of the Cold War's fault lines, and, as Fleming's notes show, was fertile ground for the kinds of intrigue that so appealed to both himself and Bond.

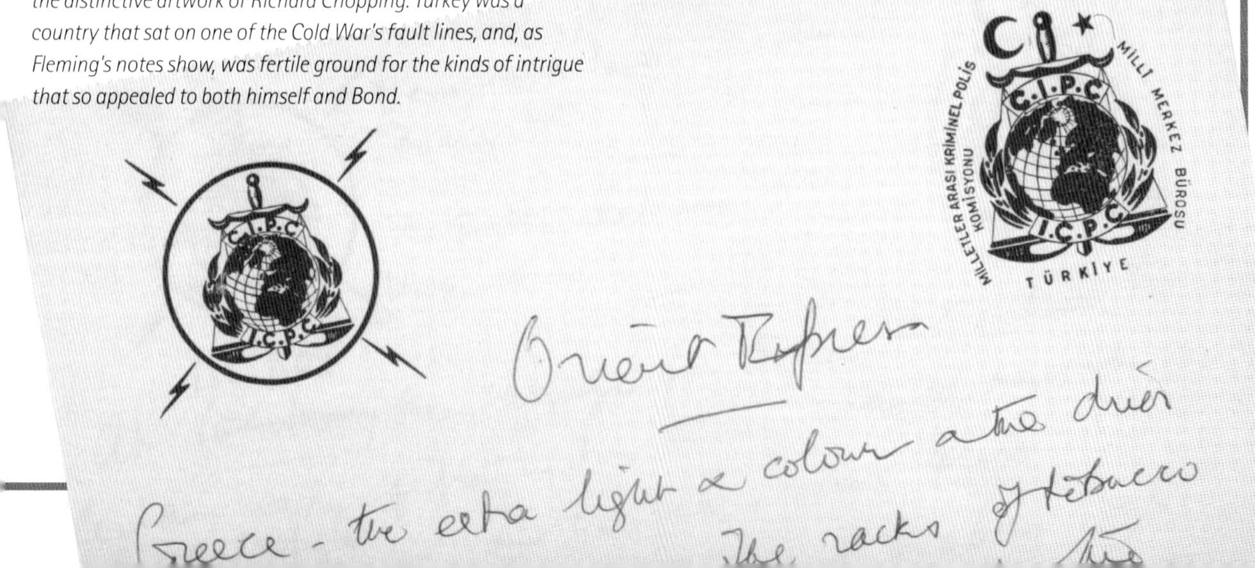

CHRONOLOGY OF JAMES BOND'S ADVENTURES

The dates below are drawn from when events might actually have happened, not when the stories were first published. For instance, Fleming conceived *Casino Royale* to have happened in 1951, but wrote it in January 1952 and it was published in March 1953. Not all Bondologists agree that this is the way to date 007, however, as in some years more than one Bond novel appears to take place. There is also the problem of the short stories: were these supposed to happen when the[y] were written, or at other times? Bond's dates a[re] discussed at length in *Annotations and Chronologies f[or] Ian Fleming's Bond Stories* by John Griswold. Flemin[g] was always vague about dates, but as long as reade[rs] were given some indication that one adventure followe[d] another, he was satisfied.

1920? Born of a Swiss mother, Monique Delacroix, and a Scottish father, Andrew Bond of Glencoe (M's obituary states 1924, which Bondologists believe to be a blind; 1921 also suggested).

EARLY 1930s Parents killed in a climbing accident in the Alps. Aged 11 goes to live with his aunt, Charmian Bond. At 13 sent to Eton; expelled after two terms and transfers to Fettes.

LATE 1930s Loses his virginity in Paris. Attends University of Geneva. Taught to ski by Hannes Oberhauser of Kitzbühel.

1937–41 Aged 17 (depending on year of birth), claims he's 19 and enters the RNVR as a Lieutenant, then the secret service.

1939 Takes a million francs off the Romanian gambling team in Monte Carlo.

1941–4 Assassinates a Japanese codebreaker in the Rockefeller Center, New York. Knifes a Norwegian double agent in Stockholm. Awarded his 00 'licence to kill' status. Travels around the world; America and Jamaica mentioned.

1944 Sees action in the Ardennes forest.

1945 In Hong Kong. Ends war as Commander RNVR. Decides to stay on in the '00' section, retaining his licence to kill.

1945–51 Sent on two or three missions per year, rising to the rank of Principal Officer.

1951 Takes on Le Chiffre at cards in Royale-les-Eaux. Bond's life is saved by a Russian assassin. *Casino Royale*

1952 Sent to America to expose M[r] Big's smuggling racket. Bond follow[s] the trail to Jamaica. Awarded CMG despite 'an impetuous strain in his nature' and granted leave with Solitaire. *Live and Let Die*

1953 Asked by M to expose Hugo Drax as a card cheat. Pursues Drax to Kent where he is about to launch the Moonraker rocket. *Moonraker*

1954 On his return from two weeks' holiday, Bond follows a diamond-smuggling pipeline from French Guinea to Las Vegas. *Diamonds are Forever* (Bondologists claim this adventure occurs directly after *Moonraker*, the previous year.)

1955 Sent to Istanbul to pick up Tatiana Romanova and the SPECTRE coding machine, and returns on the Venice Simplon-Orient-Express where he is almost killed by Red Grant. In Paris he finds the SMERSH chief Rosa Klebb, who poisons him. *From Russia with Love* (Bondologists claim this also happens a year earlier.)

1956 After recovery and a dressing-down, he is given a new gun (Walther PPK), and sent to investigate the death of an agent in Jamaica, which leads him to Dr Julius No's tropical hell, Crab Key. *Dr No*

1957 Sent to kill a Mexican heroin smuggler in Miami, where he encounters Goldfinger cheating at cards. Investigates and works undercover in Goldfinger's smuggling operation, thwarting his plan to rob Fort Knox. *Goldfinger*

1957/8 Five short missions as described in *For Your Eyes Only*:

OCTOBER 1957 Pursues a narcotics ring in Rome, which leads him to Venice. 'Risico'

APRIL 1958 Sent to the Seychelles to observe the Communist threat to the British fleet; takes a trip with Milton Krest to a remote atoll in search of a rare fish. 'The Hildebrand Rarity'

MAY 1958 On his way back from a failed mission in Austria, Bond assists Station F in uncovering a nest of Soviet assassins ambushing dispatch riders in St Germain forest near Paris. 'From A View To A Kill'

OCTOBER 1958 As a personal favour to M, Bond goes to Vermont to kill a gang of hoods. 'For Your Eyes Only'

WINTER 1958 A short mission to Nassau to sabotage Castro's gun-smuggling operation; he is told a long anecdote by the Governor. 'Quantum of Solace'

1959 Drinking, smoking and gambling far too much. Sent to a health farm, where he is almost killed, then to the Bahamas, where he encounters Largo – a member of Blofeld's SPECTRE – who has stolen two nuclear warheads. *Thunderball*
In October travels to West Berlin to assassinate an assassin – a golden-haired Russian cellist. 'The Living Daylights'

1960 On the trail of other members of SPECTRE. One lead takes him past Dreamy Pines Motor Court in upstate New York, where he finds Vivienne Michel engaged in a desperate battle with two minor villains. *The Spy Who Loved Me*
Bond asks to be sent to Jamaica to find Dexter Smythe, an ex-Commando who murdered Hannes Oberhauser. 'Octopussy'

1961 A short mission to New York to warn an agent that her boyfriend is a member of the KGB. '007 in New York'
In June Bond bids against the head of the KGB in London at Sotheby's auction house. 'Property of a Lady'
Still on a fruitless search for Blofeld and about to hand in his resignation when Tracy di Vicenzo's father gives him a promising lead. Bond discovers Blofeld's alpine lair, which he destroys, but once again his quarry eludes him. Marries Tracy in Munich on New Year's Day; hours later she is assassinated by Blofeld. *On Her Majesty's Secret Service*

1962 A grieving shadow of his former self; he bungles two missions and is nearly killed. M revokes Bond's '00' licence and sends him to Japan, which unexpectedly gives him a chance to get even with Blofeld. *You Only Live Twice*

1963 The epic fight with Blofeld leaves him without a memory. Now Taro Todoroki, a fisherman, Bond lives on the island of Kuro with Kissy Suzuki, until the word 'Vladivostock' jogs his memory. Travels to Russia, is brainwashed, then returns to London and attempts to kill M. He fails and is given one chance at redemption: to assassinate Francisco Scaramanga in Jamaica. Succeeds, but declines knighthood. *The Man with the Golden Gun*

FAIRY TALES FOR GROWN-UPS

'Personally I am sufficiently in love with the myth to write basically incredible stories with a straight face.'
Ian Fleming, interviewed at the BBC

'Fairy tales for grown-ups' is how Ian Fleming in a frivolous moment once described his books. James Bond was St George, the defender of the British government (and the free world), who fights the dragon, named Goldfinger or Blofeld or Dr No, and – having slain him – then beds the girl. Perched on top of this mythical story was all the worldly know-how of cars, gadgets, food and gambling that Fleming corralled from his own experience. The Italian writer and critic Umberto Eco once famously broke down the mythic fairy tale that is the backbone of many of the Bond books into a series of nine moves:

1. M calls Bond up to his office, explains the problem, and hands Bond the file – usually marked For Your Eyes Only.
2. The villain makes a move and confronts or is revealed to Bond.
3. Bond moves and checks the villain, or the villain checks Bond.
4. The Bond girl moves and shows herself.
5. Bond takes the girl (he possesses her or begins her seduction).
6. The villain captures Bond (with or without the girl, or at different moments).
7. The villain tortures Bond (with or without the girl).
8. Bond beats the villain (he kills him, or kills his representative, or assists in their killing).
9. Bond convalesces and enjoys the girl, whom he then loses.

Ian Fleming came up with this more or less standard thriller plot from the outset in *Casino Royale*, and used more or less the same template thereafter. That the pattern is broadly familiar only adds to the books'

When Fleming went to the Seychelles in 1958 to research an article called 'Treasure Hunt in Eden', James Bond was already seen as his alter ego by some in even the highest places – as this anonymous note shows.

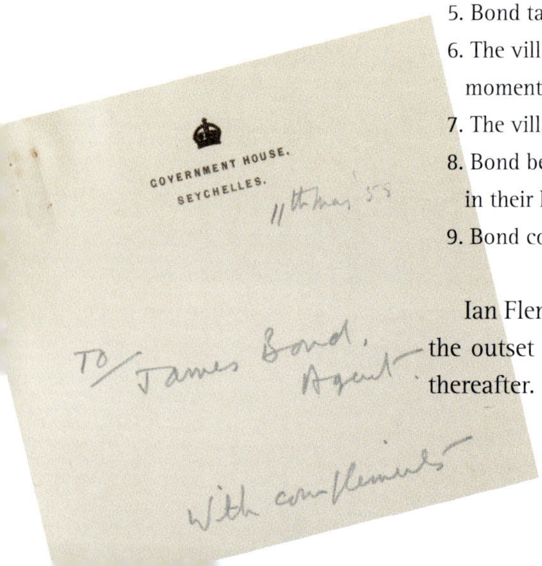
GOVERNMENT HOUSE, SEYCHELLES.

11th May 58

To/ James Bond, Agent.

With compliments

appeal, though Fleming went to great pains to make sure that his readers didn't notice this familiarity too much by setting a breakneck pace. 'Each chapter is a wave to be jumped as we race with exhilaration behind the hero like a water-skier behind a fast motor boat,' he once wrote. 'There is only one recipe for a best seller and it is a very simple one. You have to get the reader to turn the page . . . Nothing must be allowed to interfere with this essential dynamic of the thriller.' But in Fleming's case he discovered that there was another essential rule, which was to stick to the Bond template. In *The Spy Who Loved Me*, which departs from the norm by telling the story from the Bond girl's perspective, 007's entrance is delayed until chapter 10. Chapter 10! This was far more than his fans and critics could bear, and such was the hostility towards his experiment that a chastened Fleming never tinkered with the recipe again.

Having established his basic structure, Fleming was constantly on the lookout for plot lines to make each new adventure seem different from the last. The James Bond novels were all written at Goldeneye between January and March, while Ian was on his annual visit, and were published in the spring of the following year. Fleming kept up this rhythm for fourteen years, so at any time during that period he had at least three books on his mind. For instance, in January 1956 he went off to Goldeneye to write *From Russia with Love*. When he came back to England in March, he publicized *Diamonds are Forever*, the novel he had written on his previous visit to Jamaica, and then, while not attending his newspaper job, he corrected the proofs of *From Russia with Love* and set about trying to find a plot for his next novel, *Dr No*, which he would have to write on his next visit to Goldeneye. The speed of production ensured that the James Bond series quickly developed into a long-running saga, in which each new book picked up where the last one left off, and Fleming occasionally felt obliged to tie up some of the loose ends of the previous adventure (particularly what happens to the girls) before sending Bond off on his next assignment.

Ian wrote 'chiefly for pleasure, and then money' – in that order – but given the treadmill he had constructed for himself it is hardly surprising that he regularly complained to his friends of the difficulties of coming up with yet another Bond story, and that he sometimes felt thoroughly fed up with that 'cardboard booby'. He even toyed with killing off 007 at the end of *From Russia with Love*, but such was the indignation of the affronted fans that in *Dr No* (which he had written anyway) he brought Bond back from his near death experience.

As a writer who always feared that his well of inspiration was about to run dry, Ian constantly sieved his busy London life for any nugget that

PEOPLE & THINGS

By ATTICUS

Raised Eyebrows Dept.

Faces and Fortunes

Anatomy of Smiles

FACES AND FORTUNES

Scorched Air Policy

I Kid You Not!

"The Man From Surrey"

The Sunday Times *'Atticus' column allowed Ian to show his fascination with interesting facts.*

caught his eye. He was still at the *Sunday Times*, no longer as foreign news manager (Ian's Mercury News Service was considered an expensive luxury and wound up), but from November 1953 as 'Atticus', the prestigious columnist who wrote about 'People'. On taking up this mantle Fleming immediately changed the title to 'People and Things', in recognition, perhaps, that he was an unconventional choice for a gossip columnist. He had no interest in London tittle-tattle, and not much in people in general. His friend Cyril Connolly hazarded that the column should be renamed 'Attila' to match Fleming's antisocial stance – a suggestion the new Atticus thought witty enough to print. When writing about 'People' Fleming managed to include some tidbits of London gossip overheard at his wife's dinner parties, which he squeezed in among more interesting intelligence gossip – also overheard, at his club – and shameless plugs for his heroes such as Jacques Cousteau, who, 'unhonoured and scantily sung, has put man back under the sea where he came from'.

When writing about 'Things' Fleming was on surer ground, and he trumpeted any curious gadget that had caught his eye – the Victorian 'mob pistol', for example, a vicious-looking weapon that could fire four bullets simultaneously in different directions, and the bizarre 'anti-garotte collar', a steel neck brace patented in 1856 to protect ladies when walking through the park late at night. He also wrote about giant solar panels that had been invented to boil eggs and melt steel bars, the eye of a giant squid that was found in the belly of a whale, and a plan to drain the Mediterranean. In July 1955 he penned a couple of paragraphs about l'Isle du Levant, a small island that was both a nudist colony and a French weapons-testing site. He proposed to his fellow writer Eric Ambler that the island should be turned into a spy colony. Naked girls, spies and nuclear weapons – all the elements of his forthcoming book *Dr No* contained in a short article about a real place.

Fleming's three years as Atticus certainly provided him with a cornucopia of odd facts and ephemera that in one way or another informed the Bond novels. 'I *do* take a lot of my plots from life,' he said. 'They are certainly bizarre, but they are also made up of real things. Espionage is like an iceberg. So much more is hidden beneath the waves. The trouble is, espionage always goes one better than a plot I can think of myself.'

Fleming was a great hoarder. Wherever he went he kept articles, notes, menus, brochures and even bus tickets. All of these served as a springboard for his imagination.

Apart from his Atticus column, Ian Fleming wrote a number of other articles on subjects that captured his romantic imagination. Foremost among these was treasure hunting, which had been an obsession since childhood. 'There comes a time in every rightly constructed boy's life

when he has a raging desire to go somewhere and dig for buried treasure,' he wrote, quoting Mark Twain, and to that end he went to Creake Abbey, Norfolk, with a team of mine detectors, and also travelled to the Seychelles to report on the search for a lost hoard of pirate gold. He found nothing; but treasure in its various forms is a part of several James Bond plots. He also wrote a series of articles about his ever-increasing interest in the underwater world: he dived with Jacques Cousteau, and described the odd sensation of being mistaken for a shark by a Remora fish, which attempted to attach itself to his body in the hope of scavenging a meal. He also accompanied an expedition exploring the vast prehistoric caverns of Pierre Saint Martin, in the Pyrenees, and went to meet an eccentric French inventor who had built a flying saucer and was extracting gold from seawater. Seen through the prism of his imagination, these adventures became far more exciting than the humdrum reality he encountered: Ian didn't dwell on the hours Cousteau spent washing through brown encrusted lumps dredged up from the ocean floor, nor the long march up to the entrance to the cave with the speleologists, and the even longer time spent sitting in the baking sun awaiting their return. According to Noël Coward, this was exactly how Ian saw the world; essentially a dull place that his imagination polished up into something sparkling and fantastic. So Las Vegas, a very respectable town according to Coward – 'a bit like Cheltenham' in fact – became a dangerous gambling town smelling only of gasoline and greed.

Given his interest in facts and his magpie curiosity about other people's trades, one might expect Fleming to have filled shelves full of notebooks with potential material for future James Bond books. In fact the very opposite is true. Though Ian was very diligent about collecting his facts for journalism – he usually scribbled them into small, pocket-sized notebooks – most of his Bond notes are now contained in a foolscap file of loose leaves of paper and a single brown A4 'Eduserve' notebook, which he kept for ten years. This Bible was broken down into categories such as Plots, Titles, Names, Places and Restaurants, People and Murder, Advertising, and so on. Fleming would generally add to these notes in July or the end of December each year, and then take the notebook with him to Goldeneye. Each time he used a title or a snappy phrase he would cross it out. Fleming was inspired to keep such a book by Scott Fitzgerald,

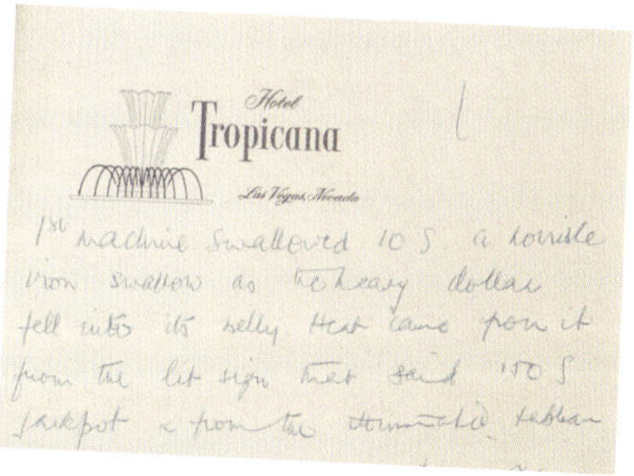

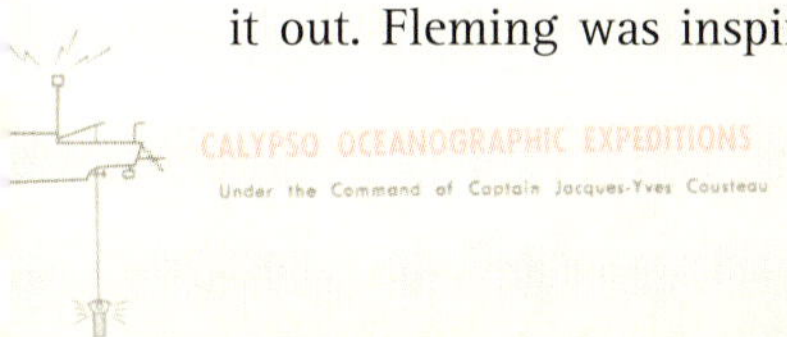

whose own collected notebooks, published as *The Crack-Up*, Ian possessed and even borrowed from himself. Much of Fleming's Bond Bible is filled with 'Smart Chat' either overheard or copied out from other authors: 'his gun shouted its single word and the angry blue full stop was put at the end of the man's life'; 'If you don't like my peaches, why do you shake my tree?'; '"Don't think so hard," she said. "It will keep all the blood in your head – not where it's supposed to be for making love"'; 'His name's Twombly. He's known as Twembly Twombly because he's so nervous'; 'They freshened up the place with some neon and some girls.'

A few of the notebooks and folders in which Fleming collected his clippings and research material. Some of the notes include phrases and names that found their way into the James Bond books.

In among all the clever phrases are a considerable number of obscure plot devices that Fleming thought of using but never did. 'Make use of the high tides in the Bay of Fundy,' he wrote on 31 December 1958; 'Bond feigns deafness and, in order to prove that he is deaf, the gangsters make him walk in front of an oncoming train'; 'Bond, as a double agent, has to shoot his own assistant to keep his cover.' None of these ideas ever made it into a James Bond story, whereas one of the briefest of notes from that year did. 'Biological warfare. Atom watchers on the Jungfrau and a skiing sequence' became, in 1962, *On Her Majesty's Secret Service*.

Of all the different elements in his books, it was invariably the plot that gave Fleming the most trouble. Once he had thought of a plot he would jealously guard it, and on occasion he would reuse stories that he had dreamed up for other purposes. In 1958 Ian was commissioned by CBS television to write thirteen episodes for a potential James Bond television series, and almost all of their plots were concocted from books he had already written or were used in others that he would write in the near future.

Once he had found his idea, Fleming was always being encouraged by his friends to rein in his more fantastic flights of fancy. 'For God's sake, don't go so far!' Noël Coward would tell him. 'Don't make them too absurd. Don't overdo it.' By and large his readers agreed, particularly after *Dr No*, whose subterranean 'mink-lined prison' offended those who liked the documentary elements of Bond. But Fleming always argued that truth was on his side, that fact was always stranger than fiction. 'My plots are fantastic,' he wrote in 1963, 'while being often based on truth. They go wildly beyond the probable but not, I think, beyond the possible. Every now and then there will be a story in the newspapers that lifts a corner of the veil from Secret Service work. A tunnel from West to East Berlin so that our Secret Service can tap the Russian telephone system, Crabb's frogman exploit to examine the hull of a Soviet cruiser; the Russian spy Khokhlov with his cigarette case that fired dum-dum bullets ... this is all true Secret Service history that is yet in the higher realm of fantasy, and James Bond's ventures into this realm are perfectly legitimate.'

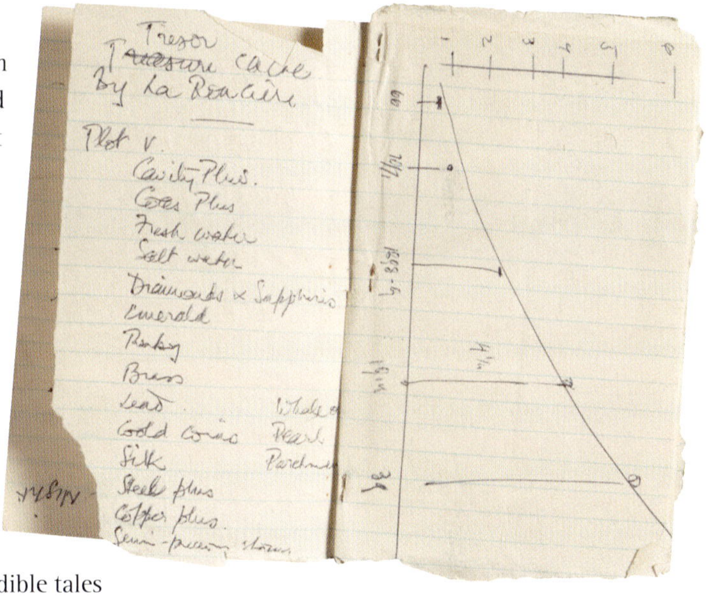

If James Bond was a fantasy, then Fleming made sure it was a well-researched one. He considered that one of the great failings of the contemporary British thriller, apart from the predictability of the plot – about a private eye and a millionaire's nymphomaniac daughter – and the setting – beginning in drab Soho and ending in drab Tangier – was that the story was 'badly documented, illiterate, but worse', he thundered, 'naive'. Fleming set his own sights far higher. He wanted his fiction to be escapist, glamorous and fantastic, but he realized early on that the only way to anchor James Bond's incredible tales was to fill them with as much verisimilitude as possible, by including plenty of places and things that were real. 'I see no point in changing the name of the Dorchester to the Porchester,' he wrote, 'or a Rolls-Royce to an Hirondelle.' And whatever he described – be it rockets, heraldry or gold smuggling – he first wrote to experts, then spoke to manufacturers, and read the relevant books. All of this assembled research sat on his desk at Goldeneye as he wrote each novel. Then, when he returned to London three months later, the new manuscript was sent to William Plomer at Jonathan Cape to be edited, then to his brother Peter, who signed himself 'Dr Knittpick', and finally Fleming himself corrected the galley proofs. Even more detailed research happened at this stage, but it did not prevent a small army of friendly fans writing in to point out that Vent Vert is made by Balmain and not Dior, that the Orient Express has vacuum and not hydraulic brakes, and that mousseline sauce, not Béarnaise, accompanies asparagus. Fleming took all this advice with

Over
William Plomer was Fleming's diligent editor for all of the James Bond books. In Ian's files for each one, there is always a handwritten note from Plomer enthusing about the plot and characters in question. This prepares the ground for extensive copy-editors' queries that follow. It was a highly successful editorial partnership.

PLOMER

not at all "as from"
30 Bedford Square
WC1

18 June 1957

My dear Ian,

I've greatly enjoyed octor No — and so will, I hope, illions of other readers. A od brisk start, tension well aintained, Caribbean local olour most acceptable, wishful-otic element, "physical exertion, ystery, & a ruthless enemy" all ll up to standard — and fresh. short, congratulations. I think y favourite moment is when No taps his contact-lenses h his steel claws. (I've been actising with my Biro on my ctacles, but it doesn't ring ue.) All the detail is immensely

(3)

Some general observations

1. Would it be a good idea to include a map of Crab Key? Yes?

2. Spelling of Honeychile: I don't see why it should be like that. If there is to be an apostrophe surely it ought to come after the l, i.e. Honeychil'. But that looks awkward. Suggest you drop the apostrophe, or spell it Honeychild.

I don't like "dam'", which you use. I have put "damned" in pencil. Or "damn" would do. "The damn thing," "damned old women" — yes, but not, please, "dam'." It seems pointless.

PLOMER

Sunday 1st July. 56

My dear Ian,

I've just finished From R, with L, & hasten to say that I've greatly enjoyed it & all your skilful inventiveness. V.g. beginning, & Red Grant & Rosa Klebb are outstanding in your lengthening gallery of monsters. I thought the planning in Moscow more thorough than suspenseful, but with a nicely knowledgeable air. All the Istanbul part & return journey the greatest fun. A fight "to the death" between two naked gipsy girls very Ianesque: I felt a mixture of relief & disappointment that it wasn't quite to the death. The periscope a great lark, but not madly credible. Excellent use made of Orient Express, & I particularly like the conclusion, with its to-be-continued-in-our-next air.. A master-stroke to leave Bond

"J'aime les sensations fortes" would make just the right epigraph to your collected works!

I thought the mouth of Marilyn Monroe (confirm spelling) business v.g. & v. cinematic.

2

not cock-a-hoop but wounded & unconscious — & the reader in suspense. I thought Tatiana very well & quickly trained, & was struck by ~~the~~ the contrast between her early nervousness & diffidence and her self-possession when on the job.

I have gone through the typescript with a fine-toothed lea pencil & corrected or queried a good many points of spelling, punctuation, mis-typing, &c., An I enclose a list of details, so of which may be helpful.

This letter comes
From William,
With Congratulat

also with thanks for the pleasure of reading the story & all best wishes for its success. Klebb is in the basket, & I hope Success is in the bag!

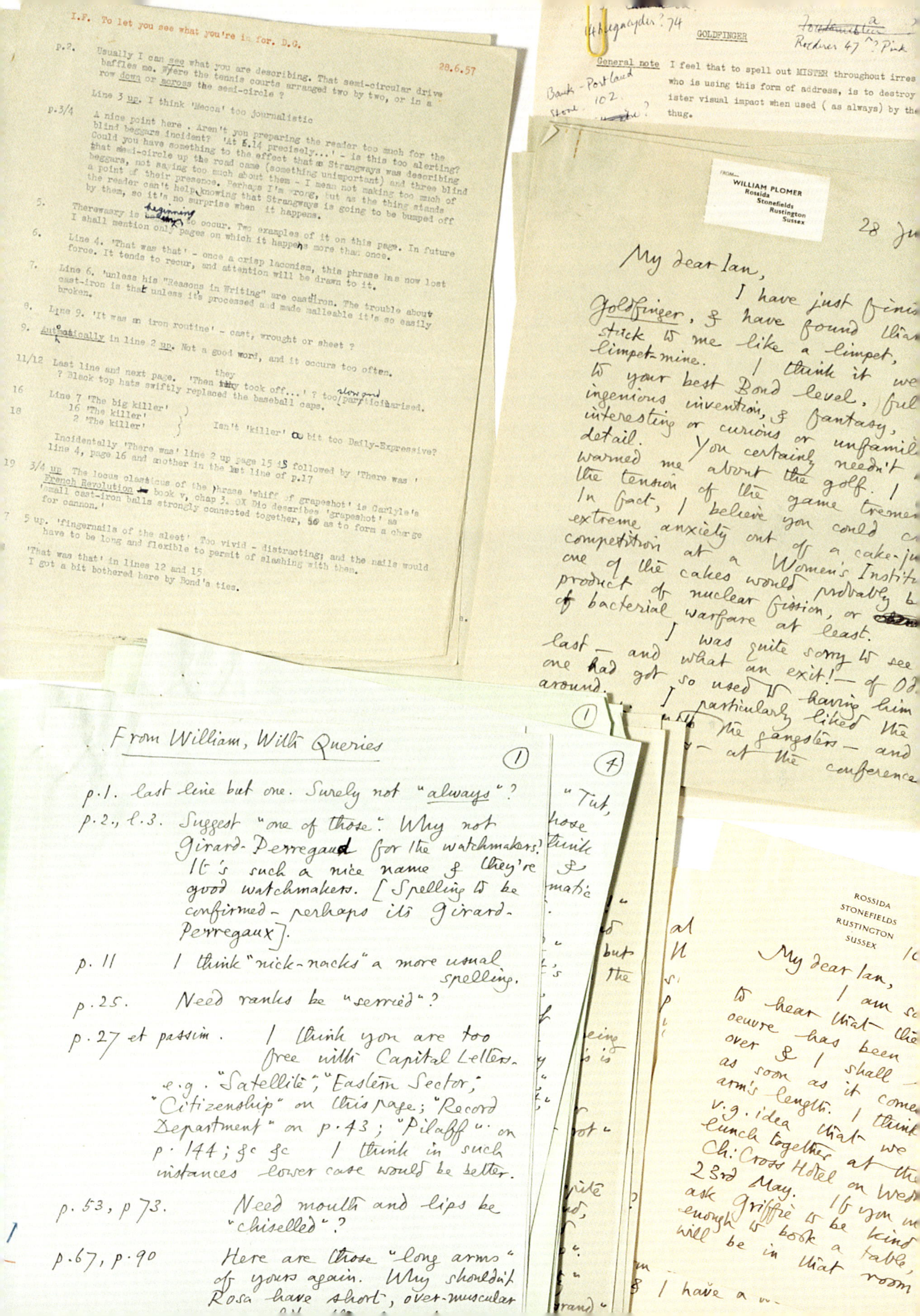

I.F. To let you see what you're in for. D.G.

28.6.57

p.2. Usually I can see what you are describing. That semi-circular drive baffles me. Where the tennis courts arranged two by two, or in a row down or across the semi-circle ?

Line 3 up. I think 'Mecca' too journalistic

p.3/4 A nice point here . Aren't you preparing the reader too much for the blind beggars incident? 'At 6.14 precisely...' - is this too alerting? Could you have something to the effect that Strangways was describing that semi-circle up the road came (something unimportant) and three blind beggars, not saying too much about them - I mean not making too much of a point of their presence. Perhaps I'm wrong, but as the thing stands the reader can't help knowing that Strangways is going to be bumped off by them, so it's no surprise when it happens.

5. Thereaxxy is beginning to occur. Two examples of it on this page. In future I shall mention only pages on which it happens more than once.

6. Line 4. 'That was that' - once a crisp laconism, this phrase has now lost force. It tends to recur, and attention will be drawn to it.

7. Line 6. 'unless his "Reasons in Writing" are cast-iron. The trouble about cast-iron is that unless it's processed and made malleable it's so easily broken.

8. Line 9. 'It was an iron routine' - cast, wrought or sheet ?

9. Automatically in line 2 up. Not a good word, and it occurs too often.

11/12 Last line and next page. 'Then they took off...' ? too slow and particularised. ? Black top hats swiftly replaced the baseball caps.

16 Line 7 'The big killer'

18 16 'The killer'
2 'The killer' Isn't 'killer' a bit too Daily-Expressive?

Incidentally 'There was' line 2 up page 15 is followed by 'There was ' line 4, page 16 and another in the last line of p.17

19 3/4 up The locus classicus of the phrase 'whiff of grapeshot' is Carlyle's French Revolution book v, chap 3. OX Dic describes 'grapeshot' as 'small cast-iron balls strongly connected together, so as to form a charge for cannon.'

7 5 up. 'fingernails of the sleet' Too vivid - distracting; and the nails would have to be long and flexible to permit of slashing with them.

'That was that' in lines 12 and 15

I got a bit bothered here by Bond's ties.

GOLDFINGER

General note I feel that to spell out MISTER throughout irres who is using this form of address, is to destroy ister visual impact when used (as always) by the thug.

FROM— WILLIAM PLOMER Rossida Stonefields Rustington Sussex

28 Ju

My dear Ian,

I have just finis *Goldfinger*, & have found that stick to me like a limpet, limpet-mine. I think it we to your best Bond level, ful ingenious invention, & fantasy, interesting or curious or unfamil detail. You certainly needn't warned me about the golf. I the tension of the game treme In fact, I believe you could extreme anxiety out of a cake-ju competition at a Women's Institu one of the cakes would probably b product of nuclear fission, or of bacterial warfare at least.

I was quite sorry to see last — and what an exit! — of Od one had got so used to having him around.

I particularly liked the with the gangsters — and at the conference

From William, With Queries

1

p.1. last line but one. Surely not "always"?

p.2., l.3. Suggest "one of those". Why not Girard-Perregaud for the watchmakers? It's such a nice name & they're good watchmakers. [Spelling to be confirmed – perhaps it's Girard-Perregaux].

p.11 I think "nick-nacks" a more usual spelling.

p.25. Need ranks be "serried"?

p.27 et passim. I think you are too free with Capital Letters. e.g. "Satellite", "Eastern Sector," "Citizenship" on this page; "Record Department" on p.43; "Pilaff" on p.144; &c &c I think in such instances lower case would be better.

p.53, p73. Need mouth and lips be "chiselled"?

p.67, p.90 Here are those "long arms" of yours again. Why shouldn't Rosa have short, over-muscular

ROSSIDA STONEFIELDS RUSTINGTON SUSSEX

My dear Ian,

I am s to hear that the oeuvre has been over & I shall as soon as it come arm's length. I think v.g. idea that we lunch together at the Ch: Cross Hotel on Wed 23rd May. If you ask Griffie to be kind enough to book a table, will be in that room

& I have a

surprisingly good humour, promising to correct the mistake in the next edition, or to do better next time. He positively enjoyed hearing what his readers thought about it all.

The most remarkable aspect of Fleming's method of writing is that he would literally sit down one morning and just begin. He treated it like a sprint, a mental version of all those athletics competitions he had won at school: the gun went and he was off, at a gallop. Certainly he knew what he was going to write, and he had done his research, but there were no sketches for characters, no lists of scenes, outlines, or aborted attempts at chapters – none that have survived, at any rate. Also, the story that Fleming produced in his first draft was more often than not almost identical to what was finally published. With the notable exception of *Casino Royale*, the original manuscripts that he banged out with six fingers on his Royale portable are not heavily annotated or rewritten; there are no instances of chapters being rearranged, and hardly any large chunks taken out. When Fleming's blue Biro scrawl appears it is usually to change the adjectives, substituting 'The voice was warm, comforting' with 'The voice was velvet, dangerous'. He wrote 2,000 words a day, between 9.30 a.m and 12.30 p.m, and he claimed he never reread anything he had written. 'Once you look at the book,' he noted, 'you are lost. How could you have written such drivel? How could you have used "trouble" six times on one page? And so forth. If you interrupt the writing of fast narrative with too much introspection and self-criticism, you will be lucky to write 500 words a day and you will be disgusted with them into the bargain.'

For such a bravura performance, the writing must have come easily. Also the character of James Bond himself, a man so in tune with Fleming's own complex imagination

The Flemings' London home at 16 Victoria Square was where Ann liked to entertain and Ian began to enjoy his success as a bestselling author. Filed away with some jottings on Victoria Square stationery are these typed notes of various Bondian snippets and phrases.

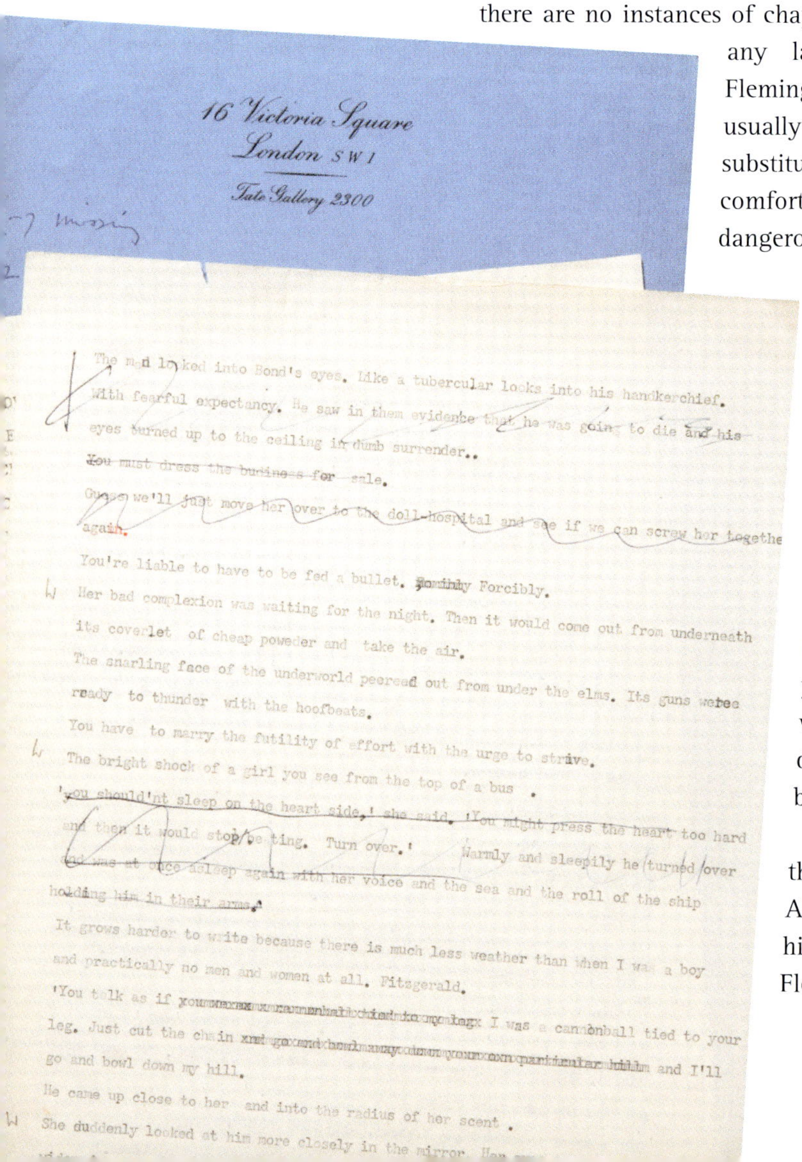
16 Victoria Square
London S W 1
Tate Gallery 2300

The man looked into Bond's eyes. Like a tubercular looks into his handkerchief. With fearful expectancy. He saw in them evidence that he was going to die and his eyes turned up to the ceiling in dumb surrender..

~~You must dress the business for sale.~~

~~Guess we'll just move her over to the doll-hospital and see if we can screw her together again.~~

You're liable to have to be fed a bullet. Forcibly.

Her bad complexion was waiting for the night. Then it would come out from underneath its coverlet of cheap poweder and take the air.

The snarling face of the underworld peered out from under the elms. Its guns were ready to thunder with the hoofbeats.

You have to marry the futility of effort with the urge to strive.

The bright shock of a girl you see from the top of a bus .

~~'You should'nt sleep on the heart side,' she said. 'You might press the heart too hard and then it would stop beating. Turn over.'~~ Warmly and sleepily he turned over ~~and was at once asleep again with her voice and the sea and the roll of the ship holding him in their arms.~~

It grows harder to write because there is much less weather than when I was a boy and practically no men and women at all. Fitzgerald.

'You talk as if I was a cannonball tied to your leg. Just cut the chain and I'll go and bowl down my hill.

He came up close to her and into the radius of her scent .

She suddenly looked at him more closely in the mirror. Her

and sophisticated intelligence, was almost second nature to him. Fleming's method certainly ensured that the pace was fast, but it is also to blame for the novels' failings. In the less successful stories Fleming simply runs out of energy, usually somewhere in the third quarter, before the final denouement, and then the narrative begins to falter. This lack of pace is always rectified by the end, but if Fleming can ever be accused of being boring (a sin, in his book) it is where his novels run out of steam.

Ian Fleming made no great claims for his work as literature. He saw himself as neither an author nor an artist; he was a thriller writer, nothing more. 'I am not an angry young, or even middle-aged man,' he wrote in an article in 1962. 'I am not "involved". My books are not "engaged". I have no message for suffering humanity and, though I was bullied at school and lost my virginity like so many of us used to do in the old days, I have never been tempted to foist these and other harrowing personal experiences on the public . . . [the books] are written for warm-blooded heterosexuals in railways, airplanes or beds.'

This kind of simple-man approach was so far from the truth that one critic pithily remarked, 'No one knows better how to write himself up by writing himself down.' It was obvious that Fleming cared very deeply about his prose, regardless of his subject. 'I have certainly got vivid powers of imagination,' he admitted, 'but I don't think there is anything very odd about that. We are all fed fairy stories and adventure stories and ghost stories for the first twenty years of our lives, and the only difference between me and perhaps you is that my imagination earns me money.' He just happened to take a few exciting incidents, inspired by a newspaper article, a conversation or an obscure wartime memory, added his hero, his heroine and a nasty villain, and the story told itself. What he did not mention was all the style that he brought to it all, and the endlessly intriguing nature of his alter ego, James Bond.

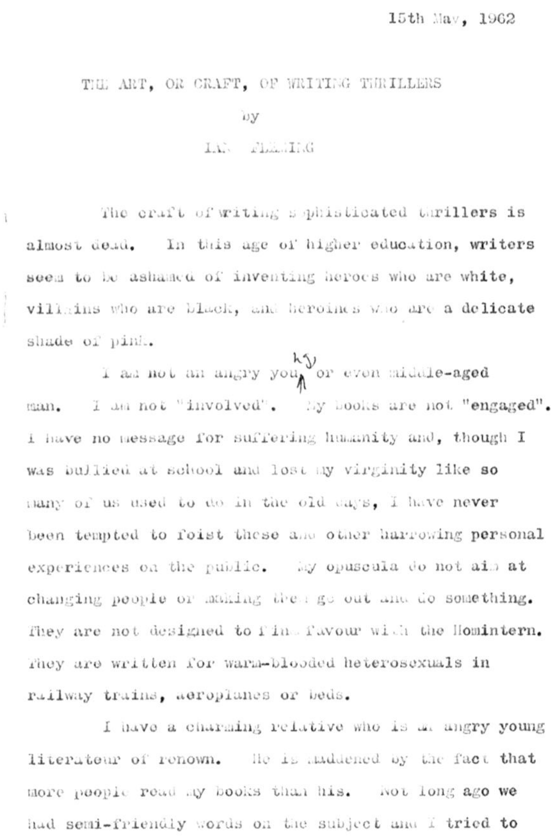
15th May, 1962

THE ART, OR CRAFT, OF WRITING THRILLERS
by
IAN FLEMING

The craft of writing sophisticated thrillers is almost dead. In this age of higher education, writers seem to be ashamed of inventing heroes who are white, villains who are black, and heroines who are a delicate shade of pink.

I am not an angry young or even middle-aged man. I am not "involved". My books are not "engaged". I have no message for suffering humanity and, though I was bullied at school and lost my virginity like so many of us used to do in the old days, I have never been tempted to foist these and other harrowing personal experiences on the public. My opuscula do not aim at changing people or making them go out and do something. They are not designed to find favour with the Homintern. They are written for warm-blooded heterosexuals in railway trains, aeroplanes or beds.

I have a charming relative who is an angry young litterateur of renown. He is maddened by the fact that more people read my books than his. Not long ago we had semi-friendly words on the subject and I tried to

By 1962 Fleming had spent ten years perfecting his craft and was more than qualified to title this article 'How to Write a Thriller'. He later delivered a lecture on the subject at Harrod's department store.

1957

Original title
The Wound Man

First line

Punctually at six o'clock the sun set with a last yellow flash behind the Blue Mountains, a wave of violet shadow poured down Richmond Road, and the crickets and tree frogs in the fine gardens began to zing and tinkle.

Story

After a compelling opening sequence, in which Strangways, the head of the Jamaican station, is murdered, Bond enters the story having returned from an extended leave to recover from the effects of his poisoning at the end of *From Russia with Love*. Immediately he is grilled by M about his failure to kill Rosa Klebb (his Beretta had jammed, so Bond is now issued with a Walther PPK) and he is given a dead-end assignment to find out why Strangways was killed. This takes Bond to Jamaica and to Strangways's last case, investigating Crab Key, a private island owed by a mysterious Chinaman, Dr Julius No, who has made millions out of exporting guano and whose men are known to be very hostile to intruders.

With Quarrel, his faithful Cayman Islander (introduced in *Live and Let Die*), at his side, James Bond makes an illicit trip to Crab Key and there meets Honeychile Rider, a beautiful, feral white Jamaican collecting shells on the beach. They are soon spotted by Dr No's men, hunted through the swamps, and finally cornered by a 'dragon' – an amphibious flame-throwing jeep. Quarrel is incinerated; Bond and Honeychile are captured and brought into No's 'mink-lined prison', a kind of hotel-cum-hospital built inside the mountain. They are then drugged, and when they come round are given dinner by No, a huge worm-like man with steel claws instead of hands. No explains that he has developed a radio beam to deflect the missiles being tested by the US Air Force on nearby Turks Island, and using this device he intends to hold the West to ransom. Bond has been spared for the sole purpose of undergoing a hideous obstacle course that No has devised to examine the human limits of pain. This involves an electrified grille, a heated tunnel, a cage of tarantulas, and finally a duel with a giant squid. Bond survives it all, and manages to kill No by dropping an enormous bucket of guano on his head. He frees Honeychile, and she sails him back to the safety of Jamaica. The story ends at her dilapidated family home, where she gives Bond dinner.

Last lines

The girl let go his hand and climbed into the sleeping-bag. She looked up at him. She said, practically, 'I bought this today. It's a double one. It cost a lot of money. Take off those clothes and come in. You promised. You owe me slave time.'
'But . . .'
'Do as you're told.'

Inspirations

In March 1957 Ian accompanied Ivar Bryce to Great Inagua, the southernmost island in the Bahamas, on an expedition to count the flamingos nesting there. Inagua was barely 100 square miles, and most of it was inaccessible mangrove swamps and salt flats that supported a small village, Matthew Town. Apart from panning salt, the locals eked out a living collecting guano – cormorant dung that was used as a potent natural fertilizer. Ian was intrigued by this harsh tropical place that was home to thousands of flamingos, egrets, roseate spoonbills and many other wading birds. He also enjoyed riding about on the salt producers' swamp vehicle, which, according to Bryce, was 'a kind of Land Rover mounted with huge wheels, giant tyres that supported the strange vehicle on the surface'. This was to inspire Dr No's 'dragon'.

The story was based on a treatment for a TV film that Ian had written a year earlier at the behest of Henry Morgenthau III, a budding Hollywood producer, who wanted to turn James Bond into a screen character. Nothing came of Morgenthau's efforts, and Ian (who by this stage claimed that his muse had deserted him) was loath to throw any good Bond ideas away.

Dr No himself owes much to literary precedents, particularly to Sax Rohmer's evil Dr Fu Manchu, who Ian admitted was his inspiration. But his extraordinary lair, built inside the guano-spattered mountain and extending beneath the sea, is a triumph of Fleming's own riotous imagination. Ian had a particular interest in the mysterious places that mountains concealed, and in August 1953 he accompanied an expedition to the Pyrenees, where speleologists descended almost 2,000 feet into a vast system of caves to chart the course of an underground river. This was highly dangerous work, and all that Fleming saw of it was the gaping hole of the cave mouth; nevertheless, it captured his imagination. *Dr No* is the most fantastical of the early novels, and its visual nature ensured that it was the first book to be made into a film, in 1962.

What the readers said

'I do think you should keep Bond away from the West Indies, especially where they have Black Emperors, voodoo and all that. Straight secret service stuff is best'

'*Dr No* is thrilling enough, but one reads it, as it were, with tongue in cheek'

'I just don't believe in Dr No; he seems a puppet to put Bond through the hoops – or rather the obstacle course'
Fleming's reply: 'As a matter of fact, I entirely agree with you. Dr No was very cardboardy and need not have been . . . The trouble is that it is much more fun to think up fantastic situations and mix Bond up in them.'

What the critics said

'I have just finished what is, without doubt, the nastiest book I have ever read . . . Sex, sadism and snobbery' – Paul Johnson, *New Statesman*

'A less accomplished writer, lacking Mr Fleming's quick, descriptive gifts and his power of making his characters talk in such a lucid and natural style, would never have got away with this story' – *Times Literary Supplement*

'With his forked tongue sticking right through his cheek, he remains maniacally readable' – *Observer*

Pat Marriott was responsible for the extraordinarily intense cover of Cape's Dr No. *Macmillan's jacket in America took a similarly dark, but more figurative, approach.*

WHAT'S IN A NAME?

'Fine Lingam'
Anagram of 'Ian Fleming', courtesy of Ivar Bryce

One of Fleming's greatest pleasures in his stints at the typewriter hammering out his daily quota of Bond was dreaming up names for characters. As he would have it, his method was very ad hoc; when stuck for the name of an Italian-American gangster, he would shout down to Ann, who would be pottering somewhere in the garden, and ask her for a suggestion. If it was good he would use it; if not he would think of people he was at school with and simply change their names around. This method ensured that many of the names he came up with were effectively private jokes between himself and the original bearers. So in *Live and Let Die* James Bond and Solitaire take the cover names of Mr and Mrs Bryce on their train journey down to Florida. The Bryces were great friends of Ian's, as was Ernie Cuneo, who became Ernie Cureo, the big-hearted, short-lived Las Vegas taxi driver in *Diamonds are Forever*. Geoffrey Boothroyd, the handgun enthusiast who wrote to Fleming in 1956 complaining about Bond's trusty Beretta ('Ladies' gun, sir'), gave his name to Major Boothroyd, the secret-service armourer who equips Bond with the more powerful Walther PPK 7.65 mm at the beginning of *Dr No*.

Occasionally this jokiness landed Ian in hot water. In *Diamonds are Forever* he wrote of his villain, 'Kidd's a pretty boy. His friends call him "Boofy". Probably shacks up with Wint. Some of these homos make the worst killers. Kidd's got white hair although he's only thirty. That's one of the reasons they like to work in hoods.' 'Boofy' Gore, later 8th Earl of Arran, was a school friend of Ian's and related to Ann by marriage, and as soon as he heard about his name being used he was enraged. 'Boofy' had strong views on the proposed relaxation of the laws against homosexuality. He was absolutely unable to understand why Ian had chosen his name for such a character. It took some time for Ian to smooth his ruffled feathers.

Fleming always maintained that James Bond was named after the American ornithologist who had written the *Field Guide to the Birds of the West Indies* that sat on the shelf beside his desk at Goldeneye. 'I wanted the simplest, dullest, plainest-sounding name I could find,' he said; James Bond was much better than something more interesting like 'Peregrine Maltravers'. 'Exotic things would happen to and around him but he would be a neutral figure – an anonymous blunt instrument wielded by a Government Department.' This is the official line, but since Fleming's death beady-eyed readers have pointed out that the name James Bond has yet another, little known, literary precedent. James Bond is the main character in a short story by Agatha Christie, 'The Rajah's Emerald', published as part of the collection *The Listerdale Mystery* in 1934. But Christie's James Bond bears little relation to Fleming's hero: he is an unimpressive young man, never without a copy of *Do you want your salary increased by £300 per annum?*, a little yellow book that he hopes will one day help him cultivate a dynamic personality.

James Bond may have been ploddingly christened, but this was a singular attribute in the exotic world that Fleming created around him. Besides drawing on his old friends and enemies from school, Fleming had an unerring ear for the unusual and copied down the names of cafés, cleaning products and Jamaicans mentioned in the *Daily Gleaner* (his favourite newspaper) with a view to future use in Bond. 'Old Shatterhand' was a curiously-named café that Fleming had seen in Hamburg in 1959; he used the name for Blofeld's cover in *You Only Live Twice*. Other names in his notebook included Betty Freshette, Manny the Girl, Pearl Dazzle, Tost (he's also known as Tostoff), Viscount Recluver, Pelikan Strat, Doctor Thong, Slappy Hapgood and Peter Bull the villain. '"Miss Moneypenny,"' scribbled Fleming on a scrap of paper, '"Would you give me a name for 007? He should have rank and sound fairly important." There was a pause.

"Would Major Patrick Blaize do, sir?"'

Sable Basilisk *On Her Majesty's Secret Service*
Originally named Rouge Dragon – the real title of Ian's heraldic researcher Robin de la Lanne Mirlees. Fleming changed the name to Sable Basilisk – a play on the fact that Mirlees had a flat in Basil Street, and that a basilisk is a type of lizard or dragon. Mirlees's ancestry could be traced back to one of the oldest families in Spain – the Peyrigne de la Lannes – whose members were generally born without earlobes, a characteristic borrowed for Blofeld in *On Her Majesty's Secret Service*.

Blanche *Dr No*
An old guano tanker, named after Blanche Blackwell, Ian's neighbour – and later lover – in Jamaica. Blanche was also the mother of Chris Blackwell, the founder of Island Records (and later the owner of Goldeneye).

Alfred Blacking *Goldfinger*
The golf professional at Royal St George's, Sandwich, was called Alfred Whiting.

Charmian Bond *You Only Live Twice*
Charmian was the name of Fleming's first cousin, with whom he used to play as a child and who married his brother Richard. Charmian's sister was known as 'Pet', and Charmian Bond lives at 'Pett Bottom'.

Hilary Bray *On Her Majesty's Secret Service*
The name Bond takes as his cover while ostensibly working for the College of Arms is that of an old-Etonian friend with whom Fleming had worked at Rowe & Pitman.

Bryce *Thunderball*
Largo rents his luxury beachside villa from an Englishman named after Fleming's great friend Ivar Bryce, who had a Bahamian beachside pleasure palace named Xanadu.

Monique Delacroix *You Only Live Twice*
Bond's mother, named after Monique Panchaud de Bottomes, the girl Ian was engaged to in the early 1930s. Delacroix was a play on Ste Croix Rose, Fleming's mother's maiden name.

Tony Hugill *The Man with the Golden Gun*
A sugar planter, 'he was in Naval Intelligence during the war, sort of Commando job, so he knows the score.' The real-life Tony Hugill was a member of Ian's 30 AU unit, who went on to manage Tate & Lyle sugar plantations in the West Indies.

Marc-Ange Draco *On Her Majesty's Secret Service*
Father of Tracy di Vicenzo and major crime operative. 'El Draco' was the nickname Spaniards gave to Sir Francis Drake, the English privateer and scourge of the Spanish Main.

Harling *Thunderball*, *The Spy Who Loved Me*
Commissioner of Police in the Bahamas, named after Robert Harling, a wartime friend who became editor of *House and Garden* magazine. He also gave his name to the printer who made the most out of 'the old-fashioned typefaces that were all our steam-age jobbing printers had in stock' in *The Spy Who Loved Me*.

Homer *Goldfinger*
The device used by Bond to track Goldfinger's Rolls-Royce across France. Also the code name of a Soviet radio signal, and the word used by MI5 for the Soviet spy identified inside the British embassy in Washington, 1944–5.

May Maxwell
Bond's Scottish housekeeper. Named after Ivar Bryce's housekeeper, an owlish little lady from near Dundee (like the Flemings), who looked after Ian at the Bryces' house on 74th Street in New York.

Octopussy 'Octopussy'
The coracle that Blanche Blackwell gave to Ian as a present for letting her stay at Goldeneye.

Pett Bottom *You Only Live Twice*
A real place where Bond goes to live with his aunt after the death of his parents. Young Bond lives opposite the Duck Inn, where Fleming went to eat steak and kidney pie after a round of golf at Sandwich.

Shrublands *Thunderball*
The name of Ann's friend Peter Quennell's parents' house, which became the fictional name of Enton Hall Health Farm.

Duff Sutherland *Moonraker*
A 'scruffy-looking chap', and the best bridge player at Blades. Named after a friend of Ian's.

Superintendent Ronnie Vallance *Moonraker*
'Ronnie' from Sir Ronald Howe, the assistant commissioner at Scotland Yard, with whom Fleming travelled to an Interpol conference in Istanbul; 'Vallance' from Vallance Lodge, the name of Ian's accountants.

VILLAINS

‘Bad men are as rare as good men.’

‘“Everyone’s looking for a father figure,” said Bond.’
Ian Fleming’s notebook

‘Where Bond goes, trouble is a fellow-traveller’

Daily Express

Meet JAMES BOND,
Britain’s key Secret Service agent against the dreaded Soviet murder organization SMERSH. Bond lives dangerously—he expects to kill or be killed; he’s no stranger to torture.

Meet MR BIG,
a huge American Negro—master criminal, head of a Voodoo cult, high in the SMERSH guild of terror.

Meet SOLITAIRE,
an exotic Creole beauty. Was she a helpless bait in the trap for James Bond, or was she herself the trap?

Alongside his plots, the other aspect of the James Bond books that taxed Fleming’s fertile imagination was the creation of a decent villain. He knew from his years as a thriller reader that the villain of the piece has to be as interesting, if not more so, than the hero, and that heroes are judged by the calibre of their adversaries. ‘It is so difficult’, he wrote to his editor William Plomer, ‘to make these villains frighten, like Fu Manchu and the other classical *Schweinerei*, but one is ashamed to over-write them though that is probably what the public would like.’ Sapper, the creator of Bulldog Drummond, the Bondian hero of a previous generation, understood this conundrum exactly. At the end of *The Final Count*, the last Bulldog Drummond adventure, Bulldog finally gets to grips with his great enemy, Carl Peterson – but the author explicitly avoids describing what makes this master criminal tick. ‘For a full five seconds did he stand there before the end came. And in that five seconds the mask slipped from his face, and he stood revealed for what he was. And of that revelation no man can write.’

This sense of other-wordly, indescribable power is what Fleming is striving for, and his best villains are megalomaniacs whose schemes of nothing less than world domination make them worthy opponents for Bond. They are all extraordinary: Mr Big is ‘probably the most powerful negro criminal in the world’, Dr No ‘one of the most remarkable men in the world’, Goldfinger ‘the richest man in England’, who is planning ‘one of the biggest conspiracies of all time’ in order to become ‘the richest man in the world’. Ernst Stavro Blofeld is already ‘the biggest crook in the world’, whose devious plans are ‘on a scale of a Caligula, of a Nero, of a Hitler, of any of the great enemies of mankind’.

These *über*-villains are accorded every symbol of power that Fleming could think of, the first and most obvious of which is their age. Fleming revered older men, often becoming unaccountably obsequious and fawning towards them, and in his mind age was always associated with wisdom and power. The ghost of Valentine Fleming, officer, gentleman and hero of the trenches, loomed large in Ian's life, and father-worship was something he knew all about. It is no accident that the two weakest books, *The Spy Who Loved Me* and *The Man with the Golden Gun*, lack the presence of an older, super-intelligent villain. 'I have one of the greatest brains in the world, Mister Bond,' explains James Bond's arch-foe, Ernst Blofeld. He's not joking.

Unlike Bond girls, who by and large are variations upon a type, Bond villains come from the fringes of human physiognomy. They are either tall – well over six foot – or short and squat – about five foot four or less. Almost always heavy (Le Chiffre weighs in at eighteen stone, Blofeld at twenty), they are men at the top of their profession and move with the economy of a big fish. 'The sweat was running down either side of the banker's beaky nose,' Fleming writes of Le Chiffre. 'His thick tongue came out slyly and licked a drop out of the corner of his red gash of a mouth. He looked at Bond's cards, and then at his own, and then back at Bond's.' If they have hair at all, then it is often red. The tall men (Hugo Drax, Red Grant, Goldfinger) are uncomfortable in their red skin; they tend to sweat a lot. Some (Le Chiffre, Blofeld) have eyes whose pupils are entirely surrounded by white, like a doll, or Mussolini. Behind these eyes, and the eyes of every Bond villain, is the tell-tale 'glint of red', a lick of flame that is the only outward sign of the raging bushfire of malevolence driving them on. To Hugo Drax, the villain of *Moonraker* and perhaps the most believable of all these extraordinary creations, Fleming adds another visual clue to his megalomaniac tendencies: Drax has pronounced diastema of the centrals – in other words, a large gap between his front teeth. This has been caused by sucking his thumb as a child, and was identified by the psychiatrist E. B. Strauss as a symptom of galloping paranoia, jealousy and persecution. Strauss had lent Ian his book *Men of Genius*, which explained this theory.

LE CHIFFRE
Casino Royale
The name means 'The Number' or 'The Cipher'. His doll-like eyes, his 'dear boy' expression, and his sadism are those of Aleister Crowley, the great Satanist.

MR BIG
Live and Let Die
When Fleming's American editor asked him to change the name of this villain, Ian leaped to his defence. 'Nicknames', he wrote, 'have an uncanny habit of "exposing" the owner. Therefore "Mr Big" conveys a certain personality. This personality does not accord with the "educated carefully spoken man with philosophical ideas"'.

Not only are Bond villains brilliantly devious and physically revolting, they are sexually unpleasant as well. Le Chiffre, whose fleshy body is entirely covered in hair (Bond winces at the thought), is a self-flagellant. Goldfinger likes his girls painted from head to toe in gold, so that once a month he can make love to the precious metal. Dr No is part man, part enormous grey worm, with hard eyes that enable him to swim underwater with his eyes open (a distinct advantage in Fleming's book) and a pair of great crushing metal hands. The most hideous of all is Rosa Klebb, the vituperative Russian colonel, who squeezes her toadlike form into a diaphanous orange nightie in an attempt to seduce the beautiful Tatiana Romanova. The scene is nasty to the point of being pornographic. All this unpleasantness only aids Bond's cause, because a great villain requires a great hero to bring him to heel.

HUGO DRAX

Moonraker

'Drax Hall' was a Great House on the north coast of Jamaica. Also, Fleming was at school with the future Admiral Sir Reginald Plunkett-Ernle-Erle-Drax, who led the last pre-war mission to Moscow in 1939.

Only two sub-villains – Emilio Largo, the conspicuously handsome Italian of *Thunderball*, and Red Grant, the IRA turned SMERSH hit man – stand out among this collection as good-looking, but even then they are somehow repulsive. At the beginning of *From Russia with Love*, Grant – handsome in a butcher's-boyish way – is lying naked beside the pool being massaged with rose-scented olive oil by a half-naked girl. As she kneads his bulging muscles we expect sex, and sex is often what occurs when the girl is similarly attendant on athletes and footballers. But with Red Grant it is somehow different. The girl feels no desire for this magnificent male specimen, only an instinctive animal fear: she knows he is a killer.

KREBS

Moonraker

Inspired by Lieutenant General Hans Krebs, the last head of the German General Staff to be appointed by Hitler. The name was also in the news while Ian was gathering his material for Moonraker*: in 1953 the German émigré scientist Sir Hans Krebs won the Nobel prize for medicine.*

Power then, both sexual and physical, is a key ingredient of the Bond villains. In some ways they are all errant father figures who, having captured their wayward son, James Bond, then bring him to heel and invite him into the comfort of their book-lined lair. This study or dining room – at once an intimidating place for 007, as he doesn't read much at all – might be inside a mountain or, in Dr No's case, under the sea. The older man attempts to maintain a veneer of civility, but he invariably struggles because he is boiling with anger at Bond's antics, as are the rest of his men. By way of explaining the coming punishment, he then proceeds to lecture Bond about something the secret agent cannot hope to understand (accidie, criminal genius, power) before thrashing him to within an inch of his life. Bond has heard this before; many times, in fact. His response is nearly always the same. 'I suppose you know you're both as mad as hatters,' he tells Blofeld and Irma Bunt, as he drops his lighted cigarette on the carpet and leaves it to smoulder. Blofeld ignores this adolescent gesture. 'So was Fredrick the Great, so was Nietzsche, so was Van Gogh. We are in good, in illustrious company, Mister Bond. On the other hand, what are you? You are a common thug, a blunt instrument wielded by dolts in high places.' This was exactly how Fleming, in his darker moments, used to describe Bond himself. In the face of pure evil, Bond seems nothing more than an efficient policeman.

This scene, the lecture followed by a beating, was a fanciful version of a scenario that Ian Fleming was all too familiar with. As a persistently naughty schoolboy, time and again he was summoned to his housemaster's study to be punished. At Eton the senior boys were also permitted to thrash their fags in this way, so young Fleming (tall for his age, insolent, rebellious) was inevitably also beaten by his elders – boys who wielded powers of command, reproof and corporal punishment over him. In the 1920s, Fleming's day, the public-school system condoned this system of junior justice, which was vacuum-sealed from state law, and the only scrap of comfort for younger boys was the knowledge that one day they too would become prefects and be able to dish out such punishment themselves. This system might also explain the vast popularity of the schoolboy's hero Bulldog Drummond, a man who when not being thrashed himself went out and thrashed rotters and foreigners for the good of England. His world of bruising rough justice, for which he was personally unaccountable, was one they could easily identify with.

In Fleming's adult version, the fact that the older men administering the punishment are physically monstrous makes them even more frightening. Bond is like a child in their hands, and we gasp at his audacity when he insults them. It is like being rude to a grown up. '"My dear boy," Le Chiffre spoke like a father, "the game of Red Indians is over, quite over. You have stumbled by mischance into a game for grown-ups and you have already found it

ERNST STAVRO BLOFELD

Thunderball, On Her Majesty's Secret Service, You Only Live Twice

Tom Blofeld was a Norfolk farmer, chairman of the Country Gentlemen's Association, and a fellow member of Boodle's. He had also been a contemporary of Fleming's at Eton. His son is the cricket commentator Henry Blofeld. Incidentally, the fictional Ernst Blofeld shares the same date of birth as Ian Fleming, 28 May 1908.

JACK AND SERAFFIMO SPANG

Diamonds are Forever

Ian noted down this uncommon German surname on a trip to America. In Old German it means 'maker of shoe buckles.'

a painful experience. You are not equipped, my dear boy, to play games with adults and it was very foolish of your nanny in London to have sent you out here with your spade and bucket. Very foolish indeed and most unfortunate for you."' The carpet-beater quivers for a moment, and then the dear boy – naked and strapped down – receives another smack through the open seat of the chair. It is all Bond can do to stop himself falling helplessly in love with his tormentor in the inevitable 'sexual twilight' that Bond's friends who had been captured and similarly tortured by the Gestapo had warned him about.

ROSA KLEBB

From Russia with Love

Хлеб – *pronounced 'khleb' – is Russian for 'bread'. The fictional character had two real-life counterparts: Madame Rybkin, a Russian colonel in the MVD, whom Ian had written about in his Atticus column – he believed her to be the most powerful woman in espionage – and Major Tamara Nicolayeva Ivanova, another powerful, nervous spinster high up in Soviet intelligence.*

It seems that Fleming had been thinking about the all-powerful archetypal villain for a long time. According to his friend Lady Mary Clive, Ian always looked particularly sinister as he sat in the sepulchral gloom of his dark chapel in Ebury Street before the war, inhaling Benzedrine. When she pointed this out he replied, 'When I write my book I'm going to have a villain who sits alone in a room just like me, and he'll live off a diet of Benzedrine and women and be hairless and quite horrible to look at.' Fleming knew that in reality most real villains were quite ordinary-looking, normal men, but he could not resist giving them an enormous bulbous head or some other unusual physical feature. Fleming recorded suitable repulsive characteristics wherever he encountered them. In a notebook he took to the Seychelles in 1957 he diligently scribbled down the various names of trees, carnivorous plants and exotic menus. Then suddenly the tropical mood is shattered by an alarming description of halitosis:

> After school and war and other uncivilized experiences B [Bond] was used to bad smells but there was one he could not stand – bad breath and particularly the bad breath of a rich man. There was something particularly horrible about such effluvia insinuating from a polite mouth in a polished face – 'And what's your particular line of country eh Bond?'
>
> 'Oh Desk Job.'
>
> 'You got good muscles for a desk man. Lacrosse? I used to play a lot of lacrosse. Figure skating, I like those ice sports. Ever done the Cresta?'
>
> Bond nodded and imperceptibly turned upwind.

One likely real-life model for a villain was Aleister Crowley, who inspired Le Chiffre, the Benzedrine-sniffing fish of *Casino Royale*.

Crowley (1875–1947) – the 'Great Beast', as he was nicknamed by his own mother – was the arch-Satanist of England, and had written many books on black magic and devil worship. He presided over extraordinary orgies at his studio in Fulham, and in 1920 he founded an experimental Thelemic community in Sicily whose only rule was 'do what you like'. Here Crowley attempted to summon demons and suggested self-improvement through mystic buggery. All this provoked derision in the press, and by 1939 Crowley was regarded as a national joke – 'a fat jolly man with hypnotic eyes (with the whites surrounding the pupils) and pointed ears . . . the archetype of Lucifer, or the magician', according to his biographer. A heroin addict, he now lived quietly near Torquay peddling patriotic poetry in support of the war effort. In the summer of 1940 the Great Beast was approached by Louis de Wohl, a Hungarian astrologer serving in the British army and attached to the Department for Psychological Warfare. The purpose of his visit is not entirely clear, but one of the results was 'Operation Mistletoe', a bizarre occult ritual held in Ashdown Forest that, according to Aleister's son, Amado Crowley, Ian Fleming had attended. The idea, apparently, was to telepathically contact certain leading Nazis who had been members of the Order of the Golden Dawn, an organization to which Aleister Crowley had once belonged before being expelled for 'extreme practices'. It was also hoped that this complex ritual, involving a dummy in Nazi uniform being placed on a throne, would also influence Rudolf Hess, a known occultist and Hitler's deputy. Ian's involvement in this crazy-sounding scheme might explain why, once Hess had crash-landed in Scotland on his misguided one-man peace mission, he suggested to Admiral Godfrey that Crowley was just the man to interpret the German's cabalistic ravings. Crowley even offered his services to the Director of Naval Intelligence personally. 'If it is true', he wrote, 'that Herr Hess is much influenced by Astrology and Magick, my services might be of use to the Department in case he should not be willing to do as you so wish.'

The idea of Satan's high priest doing his bit for the war effort caused considerable mirth in Room

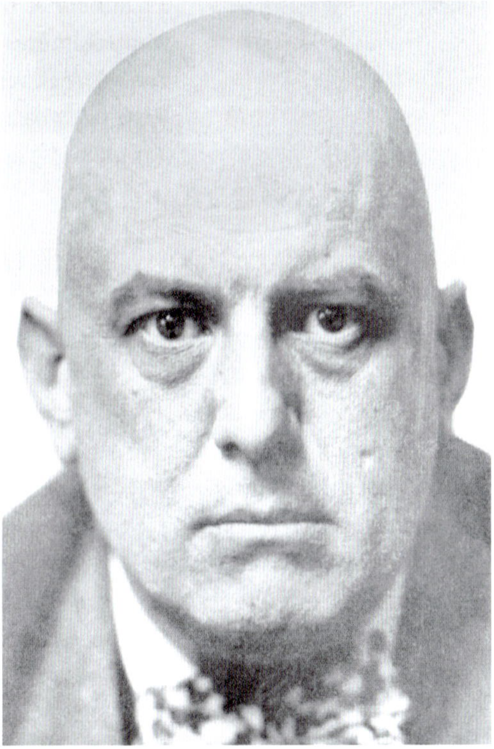

Aleister Crowley was the self-appointed representative of Satan on earth. It is no accident that his features lend him the appearance of the quintessential Bond villain: he was still notorious when Fleming was writing Casino Royale.

RED GRANT

From Russia with Love

This was the name of a Jamaican river guide whom Ian knew. 'A cheerful, voluble giant of villainous aspect', he commanded rafting trips down the Rio Grande and made Fleming's favourite black crab stew.

39, and his offer was never taken up. But Ian filed away the image of this great necromancer for future use, as he knew a good villain when he saw one. And there was another aspect of Crowley that chimed with Fleming's idea of evil. Fleming was interested in sadomasochistic pornography, and in his youth he would enjoy his girlfriends' shocked reactions when he showed them his collection of French books on the subject. Also, there is much evidence to suggest that he occasionally enjoyed the same kind of pleasures with his wife. In Crowley's writings (which the young Fleming – fascinated by sex and interested in books – would have found hard to ignore) the Great Beast preached a gospel of guilt-free sex, attainable only through total humiliation and the complete destruction of the personality. This meant reciprocal punishment. But Crowley soon discovered that he liked to humiliate others far more than he enjoyed the whippings himself. He beat his male lovers, he beat his female lovers, he beat his wife, and he beat the guides and porters on his expeditions, not for sexual pleasure but for the pure enjoyment of inflicting pain itself. This sadism infused his writings, and inevitably influenced Ian Fleming: when Le Chiffre goes to work on Bond's testicles with a carpet-beater and a carving knife, the sinister figure of Aleister Crowley is there lurking in the background.

DR NO
Dr No

An odd choice that was the villain's own. 'I changed my name to Julius No – the Julius after my father and the No for my rejection of him and of all authority.' 'I've always been inclined to say no,' wrote Fleming in his notebook. 'It's a shorter word than yes. And it commits you less' (though Caractacus Potts gives the children exactly the opposite advice in Fleming's Chitty Chitty Bang Bang).

Sadism is common to all the Bond villains, as by and large they are all interested in the limits of human endurance. The greatest enemy for all of them (and incidentally for Bond himself) is 'accidie' – boredom. Fleming knew this feeling, and the dark shadow of melancholy that attended it, because he may well have suffered from depression himself. Boredom could waste a life, so endeavour must be celebrated and measured. The creative villains (Dr No, Goldfinger, Blofeld) have built assault courses or machines designed to explore the limits of pain, and James Bond – like some lunatic test pilot – has to endure and overcome these infernal contraptions. Circular saws, cages of tarantulas, and tubes of boiling mud are all employed at one point or another, and Fleming was always robust in their defence. 'You have only to read about the many tortures used in the war by the Germans which were practised on several of our agents to realize that mine is mild stuff compared with that,' he once said. 'People tend to hide from the truth.'

It is sometimes difficult to remember that, though synonymous with the coming affluence of the 1950s and '60s, the James Bond series began less than ten years after the end of the Second World War. 007's first readers were fully aware of the horrors of Nazi concentration camps, the sadistic pseudo-scientific experiments on children, the forced starvation in Stalin's gulags, and the horrendous tortures endured by prisoners of war at the hands of the Japanese. This catalogue of violent deeds from a very recent past was far worse than anything meted out by a fantastic villain to James Bond, and Fleming wanted to be true to the violence of his age. 'The kind of thing which happened to Bulldog Drummond just won't do any more,' he told an interviewer. 'He used to get a bang on the head with a wooden stick, but that's not life!'

The proximity of the Second World War also accounts for the provenance of the Bond villains, who are all foreign, and more often than not German. Hugo Drax, Auric Goldfinger, Ernst Blofeld – even Milton Krest, the brash American, was in fact 'a Prussian. So that was it! The old Hun again. Always at your feet or at your throat.' During the 1950s former Gestapo and SS men were still the official bogeymen of the world, and there was considerable public speculation that certain prominent Nazis – perhaps those responsible for some of the worst war crimes – had quietly returned to civilian life without having been brought to justice.

AURIC GOLDFINGER

Goldfinger

John Blackwell, a golfing friend of Ian's, knew Erno Goldfinger, the British modernist architect, who was married to his cousin. Blackwell did not like Goldfinger, or his brutalist buildings. Ian latched on to the name, though he never met the man. He had considered 'Goldfinkle', and Cyril Connolly had lewdly suggested 'Goldprick', but Ian had rejected both. Coincidentally, Fleming's Goldfinger and the real Mr Goldfinger had many striking similarities.

Bond's opponents are often power-crazed; many harnessed nuclear technology, in its infancy in the 1950s, in their ambition to master the world. This grainy clipping shows a German nuclear research establishment.

The fledgling science of plastic surgery that fascinated Fleming (it was how Hugo Drax obtained a new identity) was thought to be the method by which these men had disappeared into obscurity. Men like Le Chiffre, in fact, whose name – 'The Number' – refers to his lack of any family history. He was found wandering about Dachau displaced persons camp in 1945, apparently suffering from total amnesia and paralysis of the vocal cords.

VON HAMMERSTEIN

'For Your Eyes Only'

Borrowed from the steely General Baron Kurt von Hammerstein (1878–1943), a former chief of the German army, who had attempted to block Hitler's rise to power.

By the standards of most Englishmen, and unlike James Bond, Fleming was a Teutonophile. He spoke German, had spent a happy year at Munich University, and loved Hamburg. But even he could never disguise his deep-seated reservations about one particular aspect of the German race. 'I left Berlin without regret,' he wrote in his travel book, *Thrilling Cities*. 'From this grim capital went forth the orders that in 1917 killed my father and in 1940 my youngest brother. In contra-distinction to Hamburg and to so many other German towns, it is only in Berlin and in the smoking cities of the Ruhr that I think I see, against my will, the sinister side of the German nation. In these two regions I smell the tension and the hysteria that breeds the things we have suffered from Germany in two great wars and that, twice in my lifetime, have got my country to her knees.'

If the war provided Fleming with a colourful backstory for his German villains, he was equally conscientious with his Russians. Colonel Rosa Klebb, the head of SMERSH, apparently won her spurs during the Spanish Civil War, where she was both the lover and the killer of the POUM leader Andrés Nin. This sounds like a clever detail, and it is, as in June 1937 Nin – a popular Trotskyite leader – disappeared, presumably murdered by Stalin's secret agents. Fleming simply took this famous unsolved crime and attributed it to his fictional colonel, who might plausibly have done it.

ARISTOTLE KRISTATOS

'Risico'

Fleming met Aristotle Onassis, the Greek shipping magnate, with a view to writing a film about the Monte Carlo casino in which Onassis was the principal stakeholder. The name 'Christatos' originally appeared in a notebook.

Having given his villains a credible backstory, Fleming then went to great lengths to give them a plausible apparatus of power. In the first eight novels the villains are controlled by SMERSH, part of the Soviet global intelligence network, whose name meant 'Death to Spies' (see 'Stranger Than Fiction: The Real Cold War' for more detail). These men are often criminal masterminds who have clandestine organizations of their own, just like those spy chiefs whom Fleming and

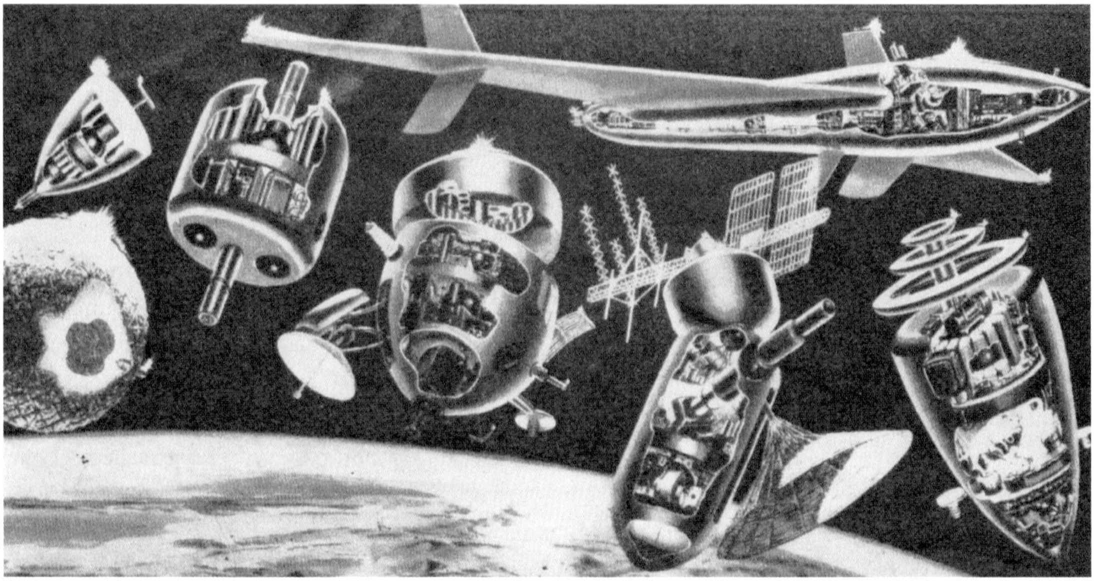

his colleagues at the Department of Naval Intelligence tried to outwit during the war. The great German spy net was run by a man whom Fleming had a particular interest in, Admiral Wilhelm Canaris. Canaris was an intriguing character: a short, half-Greek German who had once been the lover of Mata Hari, and had spied for his country since 1915. After helping Hitler gain power in 1933, Canaris requested and was given the job of Chief of Intelligence, a position he had coveted all his life. From this bastion he watched with fascination and then ill-concealed horror as the Nazis purged the country. Somehow he escaped the noose until July 1944, when he was arrested after the failure of the Stauffenberg plot to kill Hitler. By this time Canaris had set up a vast network of Nazi spies, based on the model of the British secret service. Canaris was a man who frequently spoke in riddles, but at certain times during the war he seemed to want to negotiate with British Naval Intelligence, if his overtures to Don Gomez-Beare, the British naval attaché in Madrid (and great friend of Fleming's), are to be believed. According to Fleming's DNI colleague Donald McCormick, Fleming often toyed with the idea of kidnapping Canaris on one of his visits to Algeciras, where he would secretly meet Gomez-Beare and other agents.

This selection of cross-sections of satellites and other spacecraft features in a clipping collected by Fleming. This is precisely the sort of technology that would appeal to the Bond villain, and the later Bond films developed this further.

Another inspirational German spymaster was Franz von Papen – the German ambassador in Ankara, Turkey – who had also played the spy game all his life. During the Second World War 'the Old Fox' controlled a web of Nazi agents that stretched from the Black Sea to the Indian

Ocean, and extended the length of North Africa, from Cairo to Morocco. It was his attempted assassination by the Soviets, on 13 March 1942, that Fleming stole as an idea for *Casino Royale*. As von Papen strolled down the Boulevard Atatürk in the morning sunshine, an agent leaped out of the shadows and threw a bomb at him. Von Papen had cheated death many times before, and once again he was fortunate: a tree saved him and his wife from the blast. The assassin – believed at the time to be Kurdish, but actually a Bulgarian – was blown to bits. Von Papen had many glamorous girls in his spy corps, including the beautiful honeytrap known to British agents as 'Tinkety Tony', who lived at the fashionable St Georges Hotel in Aleppo. Here she sought out French and British officers dining alone in the restaurant and charmed their secrets out of them. Another of von Papen's adventuresses was the colourful Baroness Lydia von Stahl, who had previously been a member of the Switz Gang in 1936.

Fleming once interviewed the French inventor Henri Coanda, a scientist who had successfully designed and built a flying saucer, called a 'lenticular aerodyne' (above). It was powered by achieving a vacuum around the edge of the wing – seen opposite from above.

The Switz Gang were one of the most remarkable mercenary spy syndicates of the twentieth century, and were undoubtedly at the back of Fleming's mind when dreaming up SPECTRE, his own freelance crime syndicate, which replaced the Soviet SMERSH in 1959. Unlike Fleming's invention, the Switz Gang did not attempt global domination, although they did sell state secrets to the Germans, the Russians, the French, the Poles and the Yugoslavs, and their methods were straight out of the pages of spy fiction. The Switz Gang's mastermind was one Rashevsky, a top Russian agent who sank unlimited Soviet funds into the group's ventures, and, like Blofeld at the end of *Thunderball*, when the rest of the gang members were rounded up he alone escaped. Other members included Gordon Switz, a former US air-force officer, a certain Madame Davidovici, and a Romanian dentist, who supplied the gang's couriers with hollow gold teeth in which copies of secret documents written on rice paper were concealed. Beneath this executive was another tier that included an international financier, an explosives expert, and a biologist at a university in Paris; some of these individuals even formed a small orchestra that toured European capitals

EMILIO LARGO
Thunderball

A Roman who was the 'epitome of a gentleman crook', Largo took his name from Key Largo, south of Miami. Fleming often flew over the archipelago en route to Nassau to visit Ivar Bryce, and on his trips to Jamaica.

carrying contraband inside the instruments. As the Switz Gang were paid by all their clients and owed their allegiance to no one, it was only their own farcical attempts to double-cross the French and the Soviets that finally exposed them.

Fleming's own mercenary gang went beyond intelligence. SPECTRE – which stands for Special Executive for Counter-Intelligence, Terrorism, Revenge and Extortion – was a twenty-strong council of wolves led by Ernst Stavro Blofeld, whom 007 takes on in *Thunderball*, *On Her Majesty's Secret Service* and finally *You Only Live Twice*. In this novel Blofeld first appears as Dr Shatterhand, stomping about his sulphurous garden of death dressed as a Valkyrie, complete with winged helmet and chain mail. Above him looms the equally menacing castle of black granite and gold that he has recently acquired. It is a theatrical indulgence, made possible by Blofeld's seemingly limitless wealth – a characteristic shared by the majority of Bond villains. With the exception of Rosa Klebb, a few American hoods and Scaramanga (the man with the golden gun – a mere pistoleer with three nipples), Bond villains are all extraordinarily rich. Usually they start out with nothing, and while SMERSH might bolster up their organizations, they are all effectively successful self-made men, in business on their own account.

SLUGGSY AND HORROR

The Spy Who Loved Me

These two cartoon mobsters are straight from the pages of American pulp fiction. 'Sluggsy' Morant is very short, very white, and completely bald. 'Horror' Horowitz is tall and reptilian, with black eyes and lips like an unstitched wound. Both names are from Fleming's Bond bible.

Wealth had always been something of an obsession for Ian Fleming. He admired buccaneering newspaper proprietors, oil magnates and vulgar financiers not because of who they were but because they had made it. His own grandfather Robert Fleming had been born in a slum in Dundee but had become a multimillionaire. Ian shared this strong entrepreneurial streak (which for him was more romantic than practical) and he had an innate fear of poverty, both of which dictated the course of his entire life. He had forsaken journalism for the City to make money; he had shunned writing freelance for a managerial job at the *Sunday Times* to make money; and, most successfully, he wrote James Bond for

money. He was fascinated by great wealth and high living, and he had an entry into this world through his oldest friend, Ivar Bryce.

'Burglar' Bryce (as he was known) was a good-looking Aztec god with sensuous lips and a suave manner. Ian had bunked off school with him to meet girls and ride motorbikes, and Bryce continued to play Ian's accomplice in many escapades during the 1930s and beyond. As the scion of an Anglo-Peruvian family who had made their fortune trading guano, a highly prized phosphate-rich fertilizer, Ivar led the life of a leisured sybarite, basking in a lazy, moneyed world, and always at Ian's beck and call for some adventure or other. In 1950 he married Jo Huntington, the second-richest woman in America, and suddenly he was catapulted into the league of the super-rich, as his new wife had inherited the A&P supermarket fortune – worth $350 million dollars. She lived off the considerable interest of $15 million a year less tax (approximately $200 million a year in 2005 terms).

IRMA BUNT

On Her Majesty's Secret Service

Irma was also the name of the wife of Carl Peterson, Bulldog Drummond's great foe.

Ian was fascinated by the denizens of this rare world and their eccentricities. 'He's so rich,' he scribbled in a notebook, 'he doesn't have to wear glasses when he's driving his car. The windscreen is ground to his prescription.' Ian also liked the look of a particular Rolls-Royce that had an interior 'entirely covered in hand-stitched lizard skin'. This is the kind of car a Bond villain would be driving. In this company, Ian recognized that his old friend Ivar's happy sybaritic state was almost unique. 'Most very rich people', he wrote in his notebook, 'are in search of identity. They want to be known as something else besides rich. They are happy to spend a lot of money only on identity – to become a racehorse owner, a picture owner, a philanthropist. X was one of those rare rich people who knew who he was and didn't want to become someone else.' The Bryces bred horses (a pastime which in those days was not the preserve only of wealthy Arabs and American syndicates) and spent the rest of their time in the pursuit of pleasure, flitting between their string of fully-staffed houses around the world accompanied by a coterie of hangers-on. At Nassau in the Bahamas they had a sumptuous villa named Xanadu, which gave on to a long crescent of private beach with a sculpted sphinx standing guard at each end. The sand alone had cost $1,000 a foot. In Vermont their home was Black Hollow Farm, an estate

FRANCISCO 'PISTOLS' SCARAMANGA

The Man with the Golden Gun

The three-nippled pistol man was named after another boy with whom Fleming was at school.

encompassing forests and mountains; in Jamaica it was Bellevue, one of the great houses on the island. In Europe the Bryces were regulars at Schloss Mittersill, a sporting club that had become the playground for the super-rich in the Austrian Alps. In England they lived at Moyns Park, a Tudor mansion in Essex, where Ivar had grown up. Moyns was equipped with four butlers and a valet, an intercom system connecting the rooms, and a vast kitchen that provided the kind of dream breakfasts that Ian adored. All of these houses inspired the villains' lairs in the James Bond books, and many contained such 'Bondian' trappings of wealth as private cinemas, indoor jacuzzis, and servants in livery.

Ian envied Ivar his lifestyle, but he could never luxuriate in it as his friend did. His own restless nature wouldn't let him, and there was something in his Scottish puritanical soul that mildly disapproved of this world entirely devoid of work. Instead, Ian merely appropriated the trappings of Ivar's life for his villains, and then invested them with the same nervous energy and drive he admired in other successful men – the same energy that he had mustered to write James Bond. He became so successful that in the last two years of his life he was able to buy a large house of his own, Sevenhampton Place in Oxfordshire, which Ann set about restoring to its former greatness. He had joined the club of the super-rich through his own endeavours, but by the time he had he was too ill to enjoy it. The pressure of attempting to keep up with his alter ego, James Bond, had literally destroyed him.

MILTON KREST

'The Hildebrand Rarity'

'Milton' was the code name of a Greek sea captain who made countless passages through the German-held Dodecanese during the Second World War, ferrying British soldiers and agents. He was awarded a DSO for his bravery and became an honorary OBE. Krest was a brand of tonic and ginger beer from Mozambique that Ian drank during his trip to the Seychelles in 1958.

II. CAUSES DE DÉCÈS

II. CAUSES OF DEATH

1. TAUX ANNUELS DE MORTALITÉ PAR 100 000 PERSONNES, 1955-1957

1. YEARLY MORTALITY RATES PER 100 000 POPULATION, 1955-1957

Pays — Country	1955	1956	1957	1955	1956	1957	1955	1956	1957
	1. Accidents dus à des véhicules automobiles 1. Motor vehicle accidents (BE47)			2. Tous autres accidents 2. All other accidents (BE48)			3. Suicide et blessure faite à soi-même 3. Suicide and self-inflicted injury (BE49)		
— AFRICA									
Mauritius	10.2	13.7	12.8	21.5	22.0	17.5	9.1	6.7	6.0
Africaine — Union of South Africa:									
n blanche — White population	18.4	20.1	24.0	27.7	31.8	27.7	11.3	11.1	11.5
n asiatique — Asiatic population	16.8	15.0	18.1	24.4	23.3	25.5	12.4	8.3	10.0
n de couleur — Coloured population	20.4	18.6	21.8	40.2	40.1	42.0	2.3	3.0	2.8
E — AMERICA									

1959

Original title
The Richest Man in the World

First line

James Bond, with two double bourbons inside him, sat in the final departure lounge of Miami Airport and thought about life and death.

Story

This is the longest and densest of all the Bond novels. Weighing in at over 311 pages, it is broken into three sections: 'Happenstance', 'Coincidence' and 'Enemy Action.' In the first part Bond is sent to investigate the richest man in England, Auric Goldfinger, whom the Bank of England suspects of smuggling gold out of the country. Bond has already met Goldfinger in Miami, and, having discovered that he cheats at cards, 007 humiliates him by exposing his system and stealing his girlfriend, Jill Masterton. Bond then learns all about gold and suggests to M that somehow he should meet Goldfinger again and become employed by him.

Part two begins with an eighteen-hole game of golf between Goldfinger and Bond, in which 007 cheats and eventually wins. He is then invited to dinner at Goldfinger's mansion, which is staffed entirely by Koreans (including 'Oddjob') and contains a secret smelting works. Bond is immediately suspicious, and follows Goldfinger's Rolls-Royce across France to Switzerland, where he discovers that Goldfinger's car is actually made of gold, which is how he smuggles the metal out of the country. Along the way Bond realizes that Goldfinger is working for SMERSH, and that he is not the only one pursuing the villain. Tilly Masterton is also tailing Goldfinger (though she does not care to admit it), and this is confirmed when Bond encounters her in the grounds of Goldfinger's villa with a sniper rifle. She is about to kill him in revenge for her sister, Jill Masterton, whose liaison with Bond so displeased Goldfinger that he had her suffocated by covering her from head to foot in gold paint. Oddjob then discovers Bond and Tilly, and they are brought before Goldfinger.

Part three begins with Bond being led off to the Pressure Room. Just as he is about to be sliced in half by a circular saw, Goldfinger changes his mind. Instead of killing 007, Goldfinger decides that he would be better off if Bond and Tilly were working for him on 'Operation Grandslam,' his bold attempt to steal $15 billion worth of gold bullion from Fort Knox. His plan is to doctor the town's water supply, drugging the 20,000-strong garrison, whereupon he will blow open the vaults and take what he wants. Assisting him in this enterprise are the biggest criminal gangs in America, including Pussy Galore and The Cement Mixers, a tough lesbian outfit from Harlem. Luckily Bond has managed to get a message to Felix Leiter about the forthcoming debacle, and Leiter arranges for all the soldiers and civilians in the town to appear to be dead. Once Goldfinger and his team have reached Fort Knox, the 'dead' soldiers spring back to life and a fierce gun battle ensues. Goldfinger escapes, Tilly Masterton does not, and Bond is kidnapped. He finds himself sitting next to Oddjob on Goldfinger's stolen plane, bound for Russia. Pussy Galore is also on board, and eager to help Bond escape. Using the knife concealed in the heel of his shoe, 007 smashes the window, immediately depressurizing the cabin and sucking Oddjob out into the blue. As the plane plummets, Bond and Goldfinger grapple and Bond finally strangles him. The plane then slams into the sea, and Pussy and Bond are picked up by a nearby weather station.

Last lines

She looked into the fiercely slitted grey eyes. 'When's it going to start?'

Bond's right hand came slowly up the firm, muscled thighs, over the flat soft plain of the stomach to the right breast. Its point was hard with desire. He said softly, 'Now.' His mouth came ruthlessly down on hers.

Inspirations

Fleming had originally conceived the scene involving Bond's card game with Goldfinger, set at the Hotel Fontainebleau, Miami, as a separate short story, and the same is true of the scene where Bond smashes the aeroplane window and Oddjob is sucked out of it. An American passenger flying over the Lebanon had suffered the same terrible fate several years earlier, and Fleming, as a frequent flyer in the early days of international travel, was understandably concerned about such accidents. References to metal fatigue and pressurization pepper his notebooks.

Alongside this particular fear of flying, Fleming managed to weave in his love of golf, which he played almost every weekend of the year. Like the bridge game in *Moonraker*, the vast golf scene, encompassing three chapters, was Ian's homage to a particular place and a game he loved. The Royal St George's Club at Sandwich provided the inspiration, and Bond's weakness – a flat swing 'like a housemaid sweeping the floor' – was exactly Ian's own.

It has been suggested that Auric Goldfinger was based on Erno Goldfinger, the modernist British architect. Fleming never met the real Goldfinger, but he certainly knew of him through a mutual friend, and there were some similarities. Both Erno and the fictional Auric were Jews who had come to Britain in the 1930s, and both men had vast egos. Whereas Auric was in love with gold, and this coloured his entire vision of the world, Erno Goldfinger was similarly obsessed with reinforced concrete. But physically they could not have been more different: Erno Goldfinger was six foot five and a non-smoker, whereas Auric was squat, heavy, and smoked compulsively. A far more likely suspect was the American gold tycoon Charles W. Engelhard Jr., a great bear of a man who had set up the company Precious Metals Development to export solid gold pulpit tops, dishes and baubles to the Far East, where they were melted down into bullion. Engelhard travelled the world in his $1 million Convair 440 airplane, and Fleming had actually met him in 1949 when Engelhard's company was incorporated by Robert Fleming and Co.

What the readers said

'Although no psycho-pathologist, I think it is slightly naughty of you to change a criminal lesbian into a clinging honey-bun (to be bottled by Bond) in the last chapter'

'Of course, you cannot tee the wrong ball up if the ball itself conforms with the rules of golf. I consider Goldfinger won the last round, under the strictest rules of golf'

What the critics said

'The things that make Bond attractive: the sex, the sadism, the vulgarity of money for its own sake, the cult of power, the lack of standards' – *Evening Standard*

'Gilt-edged Bond' – *Sunday Times*

'Only Fleming could have got away with it . . . outrageously improbable, wickedly funny, wildly exciting' – *Manchester Evening News*

Fleming was fascinated by gold. He had a gold typewriter (that he didn't use), collected gold cobbs and reals, and even had a gold top made for his Bic biro. He once paid a visit to a French scientist who was patenting a method of extracting gold from sea water. During the 1950s gold was second only to heroin as the most smuggled commodity in the world. A considerable proportion of that illicit bullion went to India, where importing it was illegal and its value was seven times that in London. In 1955 1,364 kilos of gold were seized at various Indian ports – a fraction of the total quantity believed to be entering the country at that time. Goldfinger melts his down to form airline seats; real methods included secreting it inside tins of condensed milk, or as parts for movie projectors. Best of all, gold nuggets shaped like pigeons' eggs were carried internally. Couriers used this method – and others – to hump an estimated 50 tons of gold around the globe each year.

Goldfinger *saw a return to the stencil-style lettering and Richard Chopping illustration for the Cape jacket. Goldfinger's round of golf with Bond forms a significant part of the book – a testament to Fleming's passion for the game and his eye for detail.*

The woman portrayed on the Cape Diamonds are Forever *jacket represents the epitome of the girls whom Bond was drawn to.*

Fleming's own life, and were made perfect through the prism of his imagination. Bond girls are not 1950s girls: they don't wear pedal-pushers, sing along to Elvis Presley on transistor radios and talk about fashion. Even Vivienne Michel, the Canadian Bond girl who narrates *The Spy Who Loved Me*, is not particularly 'with it': she likes fishing and camping, 'fights like an elk' and listens to the Inkspots. Her sexual odyssey through 1950s London is effectively Fleming's, and she is even seduced at the back of the Windsor Royalty Kinema, the scene of his own deflowering thirty years earlier. These girls are like James Bond himself: they are in their time, but not of it.

When these beautiful creatures have their clothes on, they generally wear well-cut shirts and pleated skirts: understated, expensive items that have been made to measure, not bought off the shelf. 'They all dress like Lesbians,' said Ann, waspishly. Evening wear is equally timeless. 'Her dress was of black velvet, simple yet with the touch of splendour that only half a dozen *couturiers* in the world can achieve. There was a thin necklace of diamonds at her throat and a diamond clip in the low vee which just exposed the jutting swell of her breasts.' This is Vesper Lynd at the casino, but it could be any number of Bond girls. What makes them 'modern' is that they are prepared to go to bed with the handsome, dangerous James Bond, if only for one night. This so easily could be a writer's wishful thinking, but for Fleming it was a reality, as many of his conquests amounted to precisely that.

'I think seduction has now replaced courtship,' Fleming once told an interviewer, 'the direct approach to sex has become the norm.' The direct approach was the one he himself always favoured. From the 1920s onward there are countless stories of him entering a party and walking straight up to the prettiest girl there, and ten minutes later asking her to go to bed with him. If she agreed they left immediately; if not, and Fleming was dispatched with some withering putdown, he was not the slightest bit offended – he merely retreated and went off to seek a

SOLITAIRE (A.K.A. SIMONE LATRELLE)

Live and Let Die

Named after the Jamaican solitaire bird. A white Caribbean brought up on voodoo and one of the most beautiful women Bond has ever seen, Solitaire is 'born to command', and literally puts a spell on him. He rescues her from Mr Big.

more favourable quarry. He would chase women whom he spotted walking through hotel lobbies, sitting in airplanes or trains, or, *à la* Bond, driving fast cars. When he was young, this behaviour earned Fleming a certain notoriety, though it did not prevent a succession of girls from falling hopelessly in love with him. He had looks, charm (when it suited) and effortless Etonian superiority, and he cultivated a sense of mystery about himself. Almost without exception, he treated all his girlfriends appallingly: he did not want their love, he only wanted sex. The few long-term relationships he forged during this time were with various married women, and these continued throughout his entire life. These women understood the limits of Ian's requirements, and were happy that their relationship should remain physical, and nothing more.

One girl who lasted longer than most was Muriel Wright, whom Ian met in Kitzbühel in 1935. 'Mu' was twenty-six – a pretty, vivacious country girl from a wealthy family, who loved nothing better than the outdoor life. She was one of the best female polo players in Britain, she skied with brilliant abandon – far better than Ian did – and she was one of the first women from the upper echelons of society to model bikinis. One of Ian's friends declared Muriel to be 'a girl in 10,000', and Ian was frankly dazzled. What's more, she adored him, would do anything to please him, even to the extent of carrying both his and her own golf

GALA BRAND

Moonraker

Named Galatea after her father's ship, which in turn was named after the beautiful sea nymph of Greek mythology. Had Bond known his etymology he might have picked up a clue to her nature from her name, which means 'she who is milk white.' Bond finds this beautiful 38–26–38 policewoman to be 'reserved, efficient, loyal, virginal – a professional.'

The girls that Bond conquers so effortlessly were always found at the world's best resorts, as seen in this early-1960s promotion for Monte Carlo.

Ian first met Muriel Wright in Kitzbühel. The tragedy of her death during the war had a lasting effect on his life and work.

clubs around Huntercombe whenever they played together. 'Honeytop', as Ian liked to call her because of her shock of frizzy golden hair, was an archetypal Bond girl, but she had fallen in love with a man who could not commit to her, or anyone else. Ian was also put off by the fact that, for all her charms, Mu was not very bright. Nevertheless, he enjoyed many holidays in Kitzbühel with her at his side, and had no qualms about endlessly stringing her along, treating her like a 'cowering slave' according to one of his friends. Muriel's family soon realized what was going on, and one morning her older brother, Fitzherbert, appeared on Ian's doorstep with a horsewhip in his hand, intent on giving him a thrashing. Ian had already received advance intelligence of 'Fitz's' intentions and had made sure he was not at home.

TIFFANY CASE

Diamonds Are Forever

A wordplay on the packaging of the famous New York jeweller. An all-American hellcat, she is the tough-talking daughter of a San Francisco madam. Eventually she goes soft on Bond, but laughs at his definition of an ideal woman as 'somebody who can make sauce Béarnaise as well as love.' 'Holy mackerel!' she snorts. 'Just any old dumb hag who can cook and lie on her back?'

This on-and-off relationship continued at Ian's convenience into wartime, when Fleming managed to secure Mu a job as a motorcycle dispatch rider at the Admiralty. Her tasks included picking up his weekly delivery of Morland Specials from Grosvenor Street, and it was after collecting one of these orders in March 1944 that tragedy struck. Muriel returned to her flat in Eaton Terrace Mews, and later that night German bombers appeared over London. A bomb fell on the house opposite, sending a piece of masonry cannoning in through Muriel's open window, striking her on the head as she slept. She was killed instantly. As her only known contact, Ian was summoned from his bridge table at the Dorchester to identify Muriel's body, still wearing her nightdress. This was his first – and only – experience of death at first hand, and the experience haunted him for the rest of his life. For months afterwards he was consumed with guilt at how badly he had treated Muriel; he refused to go to restaurants they had visited together, and wore her bracelet on his key ring. Friends were surprised at how much Ian the old clubman had melted over the death of a girl he had so taken for granted. 'She was too good for me,' he told a friend, 'too good to be true.' Fleming atoned for his callousness in his fiction. In *Casino Royale*, written eight years later, James Bond comes into Vesper's room to find her stone-cold body in bed. 'She was asleep. She must be. Her eyes were closed. There was no change in the dear face. She was just as she would look and yet, and yet she was so still, no movement, no pulse, no breath. That was it. There was no breath . . . Bond rose to his feet and shook himself . . . He walked blindly

TATIANA ROMANOVA

From Russia with Love

'Romanov' is the name of the Russian royal family. This patriotic Russian agent is a Greta Garbo lookalike, and sexier than her predecessors. Bond has wild sex with her. Her mission is to lure him to his death on the Orient Express, and she almost succeeds.

Ian and Ann at home in Victoria Square. By this stage their marriage had become strained.

away without a backward glance.' Eleven years later, in *You Only Live Twice*, the penultimate novel, Fleming appropriates the method of Muriel's death for James Bond, who is struck by a glancing blow to his temple as he clings desperately to the mooring rope of a helium balloon. He decides to die. 'What was it all about? Bond didn't know or care. The pain in his head was his whole universe. Punctured by a bullet, the balloon was fast losing height. Below, the softly swelling sea offered a bed. Bond let go with hands and feet and plummeted down towards peace, towards the rippling feathers of some childhood dream of softness and escape from pain.'

HONEYCHILE RIDER

Dr No

'Honeychile' was the nickname of socialite Patricia Wilder, a former showgirl, who had married Prince Alex Hohenlohe, the co-owner of Schloss Mittersill, the exclusive alpine club that Fleming patronized. 'Honeychile' was also a Creole term of endearment that Ian particularly liked. A wild Caribbean child of nature, Honey is perhaps the most beguiling of all the Bond girls.

After the war, according to one girlfriend, the thirty-eight-year-old Fleming's attitude to women changed. Perhaps Muriel's death had affected him, for he emerged from six years at the Admiralty a more compassionate man than the brittle, arrogant creature who had entered it in 1939. He had got tired of 'chasing virgins in the back of taxis', and by now had embarked on a grown-up affair with Ann Rothermere, who was married to his friend Esmond Rothermere, the proprietor of the *Daily Mail*. Typically, Ian – who was not himself a jealous man – did not regard having an affair with his friend's wife as unreasonable behaviour. Ann was an intelligent, blue-blooded Englishwoman, handsome rather than sexy, whom he eventually married in 1953. She had a son a year later, and thereafter Ian continued ploughing the same furrow as before, seeing his long-time girlfriends and occasionally meeting new ones, though in this he was becoming less successful, as middle age and a steady diet of nicotine and alcohol softened his once angular, saturnine looks. He was still handsome, in an 'old shoe kind of way', but aware that his attractions were fading. 'One of the moments of great truth is when you see your hung-over face in a muddy, badly-lit mirror,' he wrote gloomily in a notebook. Elsewhere he wrote, 'You can have love for nothing up to the age of forty. After that you have to tell a story to get it. And it's the story that hurts.' A year

'Proud', 'jutting' breasts are to the fore in Peff's art for Pan's first edition of Goldfinger.

before he died he was positively acidic: 'The older women are best,' he quipped, 'because they always think they may be doing it for the last time.' But Fleming had not always been so misogynistic. 'There must be gaucherie – the human factor,' he wrote in 1955. 'In love and perhaps only in love, the amateur is greater than the professional.' Many of the Bond girls have this quality that so appeals to Bond. But it is not sexual innocence; none of these women is a virgin. 'Innocence', wrote Fleming in another notebook, 'is appealing but it isn't interesting. It belongs to flowers, and vegetables and tadpoles only. The guilty are interesting because they have lived in the world we know, which is a guilty place full of guilty people. The only interest of innocent people is that they are about to become guilty as one must with age.'

PUSSY GALORE

Goldfinger

Ian borrowed this name from Mrs 'Pussy' Deakin, formerly Livia Stela, an SOE agent who had married the academic William Deakin. Both were friends of Ann's. Graham Payn, Noël Coward's partner, claimed that Ian had based Pussy Galore on Blanche Blackwell.

The type of women to whom Ian was most attracted, and those whom his wife was most intimidated by, were not the thrusting blonde nymphettes of his books but thirty-something, dark, sharp, intelligent women. Lisl Popper, an early girlfriend in Kitzbühel, was one; Monique Panchaud de Bottomes, to whom Ian was engaged in the early 1930s, was another. Blanche Blackwell, an attractive neighbour in Jamaica, with whom he had a long affectionate affair towards the end of his life, was also out of this mould, as indeed was his mother, Eve. It is interesting that none of these women ever became the prototype for a Bond girl, and nor did Ann. Only the glacial Vesper Lynd, the double agent in *Casino Royale*, bore any physical resemblance to her; in general they were all far younger, far more exotic creatures.

It is no secret that Ian found his marriage difficult. In Ann Rothermere he had married a woman his equal in intellect and somewhat beyond him in class (her grandfather was the eleventh Earl of Wemyss – and status mattered to Ann) as well as being just as self-centred and needy as himself. She loved being at the heart of a vortex of London intelligentsia, and had an 'almost Proustian' appreciation of the English class system, with all its levels, half-levels and quarter-levels in between. For his part, Ian could not be bothered

JILL AND TILLY MASTERTON

Goldfinger

'Masterton' was a play on Sir John Masterman, the MI5 agent and Oxford academic who ran a highly successful double-cross system during the Second World War. Jill and Tilly are sisters; Jill is a classic English beauty who is suffocated by being covered in gold paint, and 'mannish and open-air' Tilly is a lesbian who has eyes only for Pussy Galore. Fleming particularly liked the name Tilly: Tilly Soames was Bond's secretary in the aborted television series, and Tilly Chagrin was another invention that Fleming recorded in his notebook.

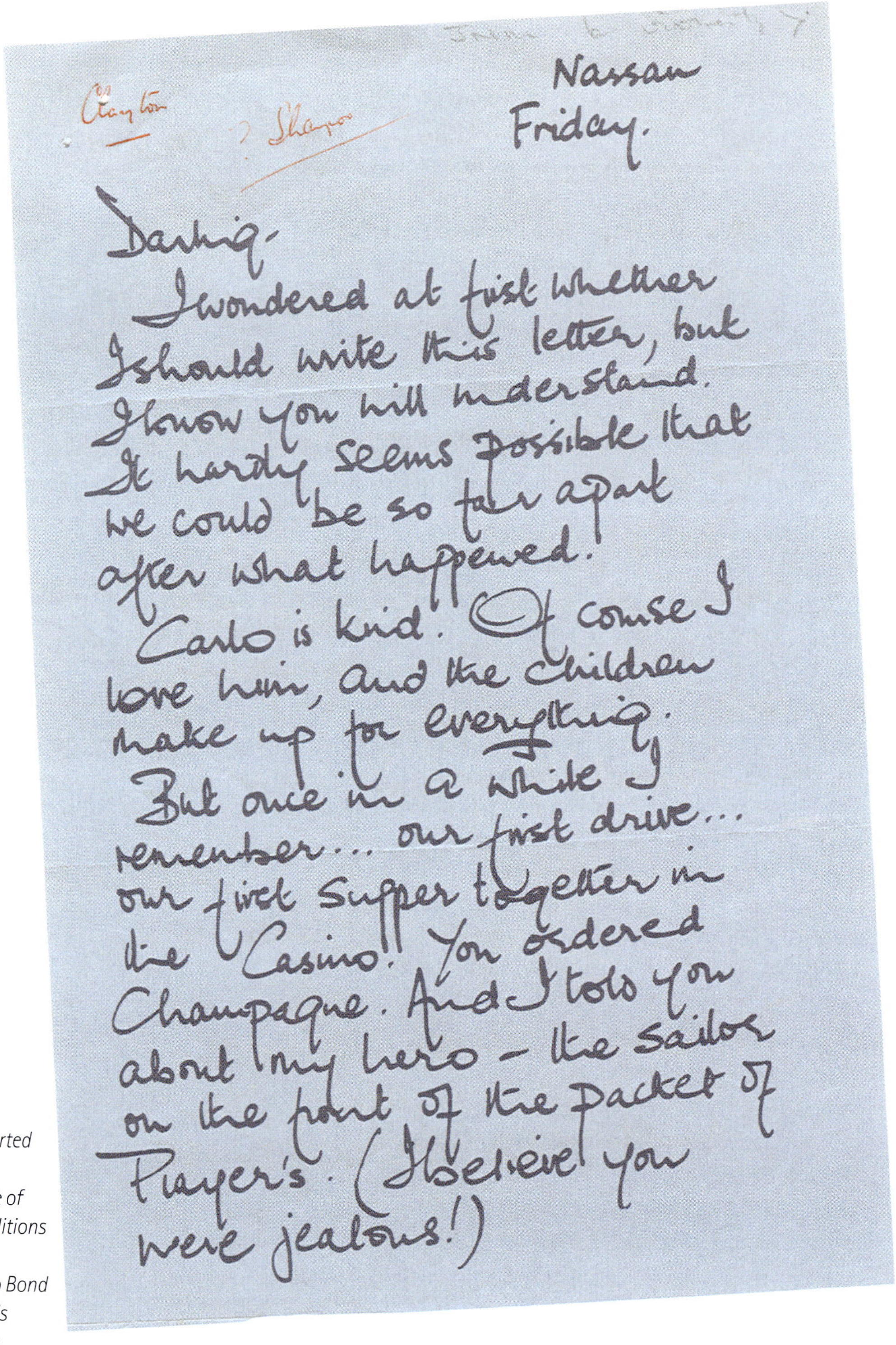

Nassau
Friday.

Darling -
I wondered at first whether
I should write this letter, but
I know you will understand.
It hardly seems possible that
we could be so far apart
after what happened.
Carlo is kind. Of course I
love him, and the children
make up for everything.
But once in a while I
remember... our first drive...
our first supper together in
the Casino! You ordered
Champagne. And I told you
about my hero - the sailor
on the front of the packet of
Player's. (I believe you
were jealous!)

In this letter, inserted as promotional material into one of the paperback editions of Thunderball, *Domino writes to Bond with an offer he is unlikely to refuse.*

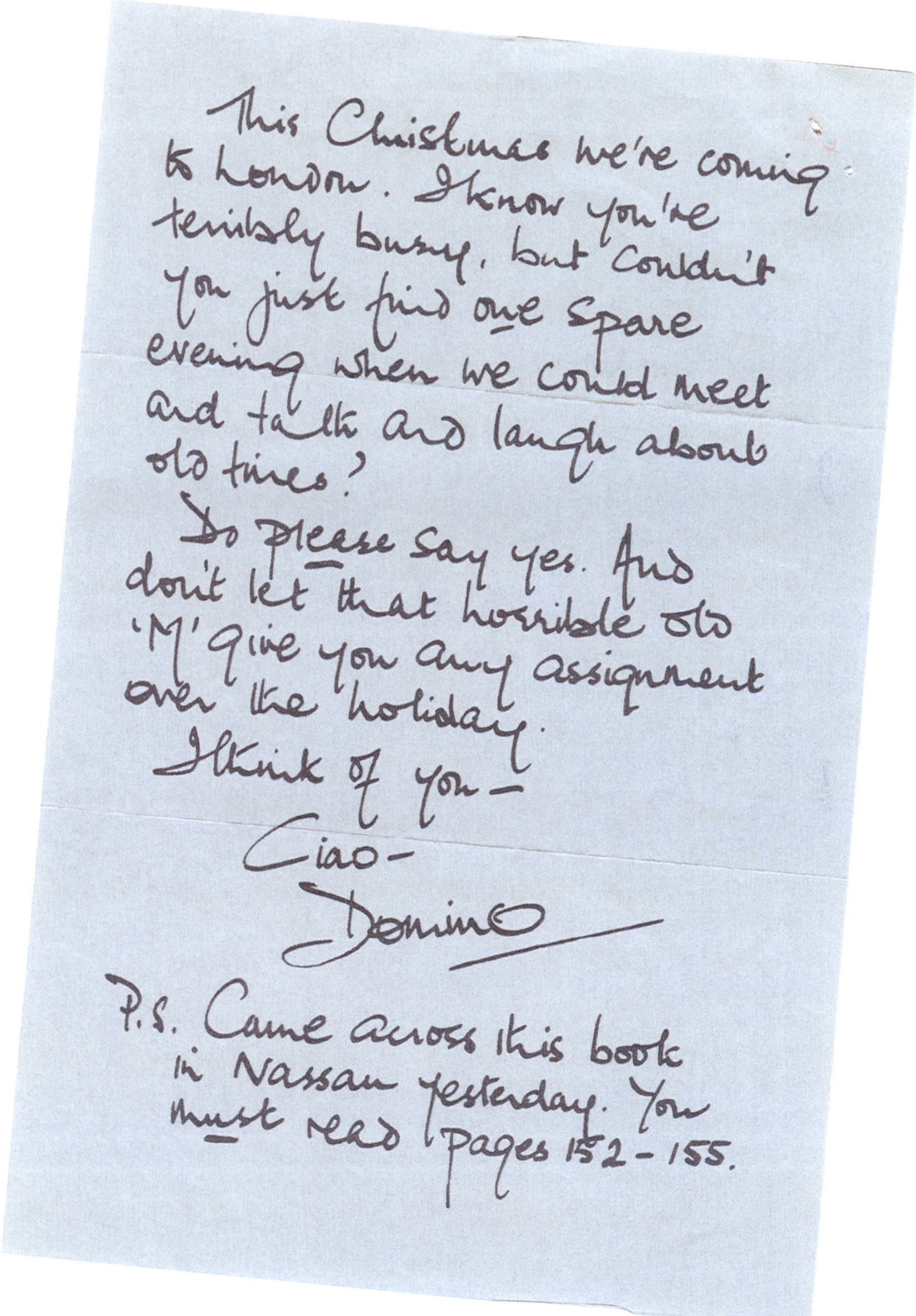

This Christmas we're coming to London. I know you're terribly busy, but couldn't you just find one spare evening when we could meet and talk and laugh about old times?

Do please say yes. And don't let that horrible old 'M' give you any assignment over the holiday.

I think of you –

Ciao –

Domino

P.S. Came across this book in Nassau yesterday. You must read pages 152–155.

For Pan's Moonraker, *Peff's heroine looks suitably doe-eyed, comforted by Bond while Drax's rocket is launched in the background.*

with gossip, or with the intellectuals and politicians who buzzed around his wife, and he sat somewhat detached throughout the frequent dinner parties she hosted for them at their house in Victoria Square. Some of his old friends – Noël Coward, for instance – couldn't understand why Ian, aged forty-three, had bothered to get married at all, so profoundly was his character unsuited to compromise and sharing. The truth was that Ann was pregnant, and Ian, though he could not be described as a 'gentleman' in any traditional sense, felt himself duty-bound to marry her. 'We are, of course, totally unsuited,' he wrote to Hugo Charteris, Ann's brother, in a peculiarly prescient letter just before they tied the knot in Jamaica. 'Both Gemini. I'm a non-communicator, a symmetrist of bilious and melancholy temperament, only interested in tomorrow. Ann is a sanguine anarchist/traditionalist. So china will fly and there will be rage and tears. But I think we are both optimistic, and I shall never hurt her except with a slipper.' Ian's optimism lasted about two years; thereafter the honeymoon was over and the Flemings' marriage deteriorated into an increasingly loveless and

JUDY HAVELOCK

For Your Eyes Only

A havelock is a light-coloured cover for an army cap with a flap hanging down at the back that protects the neck from the sun. Ian makes a little etymological joke about this in the last line of the story: Judy Havelock marches up through the woods behind Bond, and 'as she walked she pulled the tired bits of golden-rod out of her hair and undid a ribbon and let the pale gold hair fall down to her shoulders.'

abrasive relationship that continued its tragic downward spiral until Ian's early death aged fifty-six. To counter his increasing unhappiness Fleming found solace in his clubs and on the golf course, and poured his energy into his writing, whereas Ann found stimulation in her literary salon, and love in the arms of the leader of the Labour Party, Hugh Gaitskell. Ian could hardly take Ann to task over this long affair, and to his credit, he didn't.

It was while he was locked into this tempestuous relationship that Ian Fleming wrote all his James Bond novels. At first critics were polite about the girls and the sex, but as the decade wore on and the austerity of the immediate post-war years made way for the new 'age of affluence' Ian was accused of tapping into the degenerate Zeitgeist of the 1950s. According to some, the new prosperity had created a morally vacuous society akin to the last days of Rome. The 1960s is always thought of as the age of permissiveness, but the seeds of this licence were sown a decade earlier, when sex became more prominently used in advertising, films became more 'daring', and novels became ever 'franker.' Sex was, in fact, something of a national preoccupation; in 1959 the 'Public Morality Council' led a campaign against the rise of strip clubs in London, of which there were now two hundred, 'outstripping Paris'. All these establishments were restricted to members only, and some had as many as 50,000 on their books – 'male solitaries in raincoats and spectacles seeking nourishment for their sad and obscure preoccupations', according to the Public Morality Council. This was not entirely true: one was a policeman, investigating allegations of flagellation, simulated sex and masturbation, who went to a performance of 'Bonnie Belle the Ding Dong Girl' no fewer than five times to check that the act was obscene. He decided that it was. 'But', he added, 'I must say it was done in an artistic way.'

Two self-appointed guardians of national standards, the critics Paul Johnson and Bernard Bergonzi, accused Ian Fleming's James Bond of setting a thoroughly modern, thoroughly bad example with girls who really should know better. If this was so, and Fleming was promoting a new degenerate society, then it was entirely accidental, as in truth

DOMINO VITALI

Thunderball

In Italian, 'Domino' is short for 'Dominetta' – 'Little Dominator.' Described in an early film script of Thunderball as 'a fiery young sex-animal', her first love was the sailor on the packets of Player's cigarettes; he saw her through Cheltenham Ladies' College. Like Solitaire, she is named after a Caribbean bird (the Domino, or Maryland Yellow-Throat) described in Field Guide of the Birds of the West Indies, *by James Bond.*

A Thrilling Cities *trip to Hamburg in 1960 yielded research material that would have entertained Bond as much as his creator.*

HAMBURG: MORE RATHER JAMES BOND ADVENTURES BY IAN FLEMING

Das müßte verboten werden ist die Ansicht einiger Spiesser über unsere Darbietungen. Wir aber meinen, daß jeder erwachsene Mensch sich ansehen kann, was ihm gefällt. Wer unser Programm zu gewagt findet, kann ja wegbleiben !!! Wer jedoch was erleben will, geht immer in den

EROTIC FILM-NIGHT-CLUB

NUR Gr. Freiheit 39 I. Etage

Eintritt und Garderobe frei, kein Tanz. Garantiert keine Pausen!

doubt that other people knew what was going on: friends of Ann would often joke that she was always 'black and blue' from Ian's beatings.

LISL BAUM
'Risico'

A Viennese call-girl – blonde, plump and fun. 'Lieber Mr Bond,' she croons, 'all men are pigs.'

There are hints of similar shenanigans in the James Bond books too, though nothing is ever followed through, in print at least. Whenever Bond threatens to spank a girl, it provokes either a sweet smile or no response whatsoever. In 'For Your Eyes Only', Judy Havelock insists on shooting the villain, von Hammerstein, from 100 yards with a mere bow and arrow. Bond is exasperated 'All right then. But I can tell you that if we get out of this you're going to get such a spanking you won't be able to sit down for a week.' Judy is absolutely unconcerned. In *Dr No* Honeychile Rider flirts artlessly with Bond as she cavorts naked inside Dr No's mink-lined prison. 'For a moment they looked at each other, their eyes bright with desire. She was breathing fast, her lips parted so that he could see the glint of teeth. He said unsteadily, "Honey, get into that bath before I spank you."' Honey merely smiles sweetly. James Bond even threatens to assault Britain's last line of defence, the redoubtable Miss Moneypenny, when she teases him about being sent to a health farm at the beginning of *Thunderball*. 'Any more ticking-off from you and when I get out of this place I'll give you such a spanking you'll have to do your typing off a block of Dunlopillo'. Miss Moneypenny is amused. 'I don't think you'll be able to do much spanking after living on nuts and lemon juice for two weeks, James.'

MARY GOODNIGHT
The Man with the Golden Gun

Ian's secretary at the Sunday Times *was named Una Trueblood; Mary Goodnight was a similar interesting elision. She first appears in* On Her Majesty's Secret Service *as a 37–22–35 honey with blue-black hair and blue eyes who is being pursued by 006, a former Commando. In this final story Mary has transferred to the Jamaica station, her hair is golden and Bond has her all to himself.*

Spanking in jest is fine, but when serious sadomasochism occurs it turns Bond's stomach. Milton Krest, the obnoxious millionaire in 'The Hildebrand Rarity', punishes his beautiful trophy wife with a hideous three-foot whip made from the barbed tail of a stingray. 'We call it my "Corrector",' boasts Krest. 'The Arabs use them on their wives.' This is unacceptable behaviour in Bond's book, not only because it is illegal, but because he suspects the pleasure gained from the Corrector is not mutual. 'This was a girl who lived in fear. Perhaps she also lived in loathing.' In Bond's world, and Fleming's, the whip must always be accompanied by the kiss. 'Some women respond to the whip and some to the kiss,' he wrote in a notebook. 'Most of them like a mixture of both but none answer to the mind alone, to the intellectual demand, unless they are a man dressed as a woman.' And there are certainly none of those in James Bond.

MARY ANN RUSSELL

'From a View to a Kill'

With 'everything that belonged in Bond's fantasy' – tall, blonde and velvet-skinned – she drives like a maniac in her battered black Peugeot 403. A secret-service agent, she is cynical about playing 'Red Indians' with the Russians. Shoots straight enough to save Bond's life.

LIZ KREST

'The Hildebrand Rarity'

A model-turned-slave for Milton Krest, 'she still moved her beautiful body with the unselfconsciousness of someone who is used to going about with nothing, or practically nothing, on.' A child of nature, she eventually kills her husband with a rare fish, but never beds Bond.

These beauties are part of a selection of pin-ups collected by Fleming on a trip to Hong Kong. 007 too is not immune to the charms of the East.

FOR YOUR EYES ONLY

FIVE SECRET OCCASIONS IN THE LIFE OF JAMES BOND

1960

An anthology of five short stories

FROM A VIEW TO A KILL

Original title **The Rough with the Smooth**

First line

The eyes behind the wide black rubber goggles were as cold as flint.

Story

This story begins with the assassination of a military dispatch rider, carried out by a band of Russian agents living secretly in the forest near Saint-Germain. Bond hunts around for clues, eventually hiding in a tree above a large clearing in the forest, where he witnesses the Russians coming out of their underground lair with a motorbike. He then dresses himself as another dispatch rider and, having enticed the Russian assassin to pursue him, he throws his motorbike into a skid and shoots him dead. A gun battle follows in the forest clearing, and Bond's life is saved by Mary Ann Russell, the girl from Station F (the French SIS station).

Last lines

Bond took the girl by the arm. He said: 'Come over here. I want to show you a bird's nest.'
'Is that an order?'
'Yes.'

Inspirations

Fleming had originally dreamed up a wartime version of this story to provide the background to Hugo Drax, the villain of *Moonraker*. In it Drax played the part of a motorbike assassin who, on crashing his bike, is taken to an American field hospital which is then hit by a bomb. This leaves Drax faceless, and in the confusion that follows he is presumed to be British and is given plastic surgery and a new identity. Fleming used this story for one of the TV episodes in the aborted James Bond series written in 1958.

The Russians' underground hideout may well have been inspired by his brother Peter's troglodyte soldiers, who had dug a clandestine network of holes from which they would attack the Germans in the event of an invasion in 1940. A more contemporary inspiration (if Fleming knew about it) may have been the observation posts used by the SAS to spy on Soviet troops in East Germany during the Cold War, which were similar to what Fleming described here.

What the readers said

'Brilliant opening – excellent Bond's eye view of Paris (long overdue) – and a nice plain name for the girl for a change!'

FOR YOUR EYES ONLY

Original title **Man's Work**

First line

The most beautiful bird in Jamaica, and some say the most beautiful bird in the world, is the streamer-tail or doctor humming-bird.

Story

This short story is in effect a compressed Bond novel, and its premise features M at his most unspeakable. Two elderly friends of M's, the Havelocks, have been murdered because they refused to sell their beautiful Jamaican house to a crook named von Hammerstein. M tells Bond about the case, hoping that his favourite agent will assassinate the villains for him. No orders are ever given, but Bond puts aside his reservations and agrees to act as a personal hit man for M. He follows the trail deep into the forest in Vermont, to a cabin beside a lake where von Hammerstein and his crew are hiding. As the hoods frolic on the lawn, Bond lines up his shot, only to be interrupted by a girl with a bow and arrow. This is Judy Havelock, the murdered couple's daughter, who has tracked Bond to the killers' lair, where she is bent on taking revenge herself. She insists on shooting von Hammerstein herself, and her arrow enters the back of his neck at the precise moment he dives into the lake. This triggers a fierce gun battle in which Bond accounts for the remaining villains.

Last lines

She fell in behind and followed him, and as she walked she pulled the tired bits of golden-rod out of her hair and undid a ribbon and let the pale gold hair fall down to her shoulders.

Inspirations

Again, this story was originally conceived as an episode in the 007 TV series. It was to be episode three, 'Rough Justice', and was set in the forests of Vermont, near Ivar Bryce's Black Hollow Farm, where Ian had spent several summer holidays.

QUANTUM OF SOLACE

First published in *Modern Woman* magazine in November 1959.

First line

James Bond said: 'I've always thought that if I ever married I would marry an air hostess.'

Story

This is an anomaly in Fleming's work, as it is not a secret-service story but an anecdote about love and society. James Bond has been sent to the Caribbean to blow up a ship running guns to Castro's Cuban rebels (whose cause, incidentally, he supports), and while in Nassau he attends the obligatory dinner party at the governor's residence. Once the other guests have departed, the governor attempts to fill the uneasy silence by picking up on Bond's opening remark, and launches into a story about Philip Masters, a contemporary of his who married an air hostess named Rhoda Llewellyn. Rhoda was happy at first, but soon embarked on a very public affair with the dashing young son of a wealthy family. Masters couldn't take the humiliation, and eventually a friend took pity on him and he was transferred to Washington for a six-month project. On his return everything had changed. Rhoda's affair was over, and Masters treated her with icy reserve, even dividing their tiny house in half so that they could coexist without ever seeing each other. Eventually Masters left, and Rhoda – shunned from society and destitute – wound up as a telephonist in a Jamaican hotel. Several years later she met a Canadian millionaire and married him, and then the governor reveals that James Bond had sat next to her that very evening. Bond is stunned: suddenly the violence of his calling seems hollow and cheap compared to this tale of emotional turmoil.

Last lines

He reflected on the conference he would be having in the morning with the coastguards and the FBI in Miami. The prospect, which had previously interested, even excited him, was now edged with boredom and futility.

Inspirations

This story was directly inspired by Blanche Blackwell, a neighbour and lover of Ian's in Jamaica, who had told him about a real-life police inspector to whom this had happened. Ian gave her a slim Cartier wristwatch in return.

'Quantum of Solace' is also Fleming's homage to Somerset Maugham, who made this kind of anecdotal tale his own. His *Ashenden* series of short stories, so admired by Ian Fleming, contained the story 'His Excellency', which has parallels with 'Quantum of Solace'. In it, the British ambassador tells Ashenden (the secret agent) how he had mistakenly renounced his love for a promiscuous but vital acrobat to marry a more acceptable woman from the right class. The Ambassador for ever regretted his decision, though he went on to have a distinguished but dull career as a result. W. H. Auden regarded this tale of duty over passion as Maugham's finest short story (Ian's own favourite was 'The Hiccup'), and 'Quantum of Solace' is undoubtedly an attempt to follow in the master's footsteps. It was also an opportunity to step off the tracks of the standard Bond tale that by now was beginning to bore Fleming.

The 'quantum of solace' is itself a numerical scale that the governor has invented to measure the amount of humanity and comfort required for love to flourish. When the needle on the scale registers zero, then there can be no love. This was a direct reference to Ian and Ann's failing marriage, a sad fact that made the story so poignant to its writer.

RISICO

First line

In this pizniss is much risico.

Story

If 'Quantum of Solace' is an anecdote expanded, 'Risico' is a full-size Bond adventure squeezed into the tiny box of a short story. Bond is sent to Italy to break up a drug-smuggling operation, and his contact is one Kristatos, a spy-cum-double agent. Kristatos informs him that the man behind the operation is Enrico Colombo, and events appear to bear that out as Bond is pursued around the Lido in Venice and eventually captured by the short, squat Italian and taken on board his ship, the *Colombina*. While Bond prepares to escape, Colombo tells him that it is Kristatos who is running the smuggling operation and, what's more, he is backed by the Russians. To prove it, the following morning the crew of the *Colombina* surprise the smugglers loading what appear to be rolls of newsprint from a warehouse on to a ship at a private wharf. Colombo's crew attack, and in the gun battle that follows Kristatos appears – only to be accounted for by Bond. The drugs are hidden in the newsprint.

Last lines

Bond picked the thing up. It was a key with a heavy metal tag attached. The metal tag was inscribed Albergo Danielli. Room 68.

Inspirations

This was another story that Fleming lifted directly from his aborted James Bond TV series. The local colour was gleaned from a trip to Venice with Ann in the spring of 1958, during which Ian sat in cafés drinking Campari and daydreaming while his wife visited the churches and galleries. The well-written pursuit scene along the Lido beach was inspired by Ian's excursion there, following in the footsteps of his hero Thomas Mann, who had used the same beach in *Death in Venice*.

Enrico Colombo is another larger-than-life, salt-of-the-earth character in the Darko Kerim mould, although he also owes something to Lucky Luciano, the Mafia chief who had infiltrated the teamsters' and dockers' unions on behalf of the FBI during the war. Luciano's efforts had prevented the sabotage of the Atlantic convoys, which were of particular interest to Ian in the Department of Naval Intelligence. In 1958 Fleming arranged for his friend Raymond Chandler to interview Luciano for the *Sunday Times*.

Fleming's editor William Plomer wrote:

'I loved Venice, but perhaps this is a little too close to a standard Bond adventure and not quite rich enough in those sardonic little inventions you use so well.'

The Jonathan Cape cover features an eye peering through a keyhole in a door marked with Fleming's name. The five stories allow the reader a broader view of Bond's world.

THE HILDEBRAND RARITY

First line

The stingray was about six feet from wing tip to wing tip, and perhaps ten feet long from the blunt wedge of its nose to the end of its deadly tail.

Story

This is another non-secret-service story, but is set in familiar territory – involving a millionaire, a yacht, a girl and a fish. James Bond has been given a week's leave in the Seychelles before he returns to London, and he decides to accompany his friend Fidele Barbey on a trip to a remote atoll in search of a rare fish named the Hildebrand Rarity. They are the guests of Milton Krest, a brash American millionaire, who is cruising through the islands collecting rare animals and plants for his bogus Krest Foundation, a tax-dodge charity. The most interesting object in his collection is his beautiful, helpless English trophy wife, named Liz. Liz appeals to the St George in James Bond – particularly after Krest boasts that he whips her with the 'Corrector', a lash made from the barbed tail of a stingray. It is all Bond can do to keep himself from punching the sadist, who nettles him further by pouring poison into the reef, killing countless innocent creatures in his pursuit of the elusive fish. In the end Liz takes matters into her own hands, and as the drunken Krest rolls in his hammock she removes the Hildebrand Rarity from its specimen jar and rams it down his throat. Bond discovers the body, which he tactfully rolls overboard. Neither Liz, Barbey nor Bond mentions what has happened, and, as they return to the inevitable speculation about the fate of Krest, Bond is both intrigued and somewhat awed by Liz's composure.

Last lines

There had been something about that particular way of killing a man . . .

But the beautiful, candid eyes did not flicker. She looked up into Fidele Barbey's face and said, easily, charmingly: 'That won't be a problem. I've decided to give it to the British Museum.'

James Bond noticed that the sweat dew had now gathered at her temples. But, after all, it was a desperately hot evening . . . The thud of the engines stopped and the anchor chain roared down into the quiet bay.

Inspirations

Fleming visited the Seychelles in spring 1958 in search of treasure. He didn't find any, but that trip, as well as his daily underwater forays on the reef at Goldeneye, inspired this story. Here his ecological awareness of marine life is very much to the fore, and Fleming writes with particular anger about Krest's destruction of the entire reef by dropping a vat of curare poison into it. He had witnessed scientists using this method to collect specimens at Pedro Cays, two small islands off the south-east coast of Jamaica, when he and Blanche Blackwell visited them in 1958.

The Hildebrand Rarity itself.

What the readers said

'"Whack-o!" seems the best comment. I found Liz a little underdone at first, but she certainly redeemed herself in the end'

What the critics said of the collection

'The stories give you the feeling that Bond's author may be approaching one of those signposts in his career and thinking about taking the straighter path' – *Queen*

'I thought it better than the novels . . . but fancy James Bond not knowing that while pheasants are hung, human beings are hanged!' – *Guardian*

'Each new Bond adventure has been less probable and more preposterous than the last, and now our hero seems to have lost, as well as any claims to plausibility, the know-how, the know-who, know-what and sheer zing that used to carry the unlikely plots along. Perhaps all that mattress pounding is taking it out of poor Bond' – Christopher Pym, *Spectator*

BOYS' TOYS

Gadgets, Cars and Guns

'It is the gimmicks in my books, rather than the more or less straightforward plots, that stay in people's minds.'
Letter to reader

Fleming had long been a collector and admirer of inventions, and the 1950s and '60s were an age of the gadget. After the austerity of the immediate post-war years, the 1950s saw the mass production of many of the machines we now take for granted. For instance, when *Casino Royale* was published in 1953, 8 per cent of households had a fridge and television was a rarity (there was only one channel). By 1962, when *The Spy Who Loved Me* appeared, 33 per cent of households had a fridge and 75 per cent possessed a television. Suddenly, affluent American culture – long familiar from films – was in the home, as were other interesting novelties such as vacuum cleaners, stereophonic televisions, electric irons and washing machines. The proliferation of these gadgets was made possible by the increase in wages, which rose a staggering 130 per cent between 1955 and 1969, while the cost of food and clothing actually fell, thanks to mass production.

For a man who gave every appearance of being an old-fashioned, bridge-playing clubman, Ian Fleming was an unlikely enthusiast for the gizmos of the modern age. As an early adopter of newfangled devices, Ian made sure that he knew not only how things worked but also what was the best of the breed. He was one of the first subscribers to *Which?* magazine, launched by the Consumers' Association in 1957. Despite his enthusiasm for inventions, certain devices never

Ronson's 'Penciliter' would no doubt have amused Q Branch. The model bears more than a passing resemblance to the Bond type – although his shirt, unlike Bond's, has long sleeves.

failed to get his dander up; he had a deep personal loathing for the blaring transistor radio and its moon-eyed owner: 'He is sounding the modern leper's bell,' he wrote. 'Keep away from me, I am the world's chaos and malaise.'

Unlike any thriller writer before him, Fleming was acutely aware of the new value of these mundane objects of desire, and the technical detail that he wove into his books about gadgets, cars and boats was like the blurb in a 1950s brochure about some clever-sounding contraption. Some of what he described was science fiction, improbable but not impossible; the majority was real technology that already existed. This imaginative use of information, which Kingsley Amis christened the 'Fleming Effect', is present in all James Bond novels, though nowhere does it loom larger than in *Thunderball*. Here is a description of the villain Largo's yacht.

> The motor yacht, *Disco Volante*, was a hydrofoil craft, built for Largo with SPECTRE funds by the Italian constructors, Leopoldo Rodrigues, of Messina, the only firm in the world to have successfully adapted the Shertel-Sachsenberg system to commercial use. With a hull of aluminium and magnesium alloy, two Daimler-Benz four-stroke diesels supercharged by twin Brown-Boveri turbo superchargers, the *Disco Volante* could move her 100 tons at around fifty knots, with a cruising range at that speed of around four hundred miles. She had cost £200,000.

Fleming was fascinated by the status symbols of the super-rich. He used a 50-ton Chris-Craft yacht as a getaway vehicle in For Your Eyes Only.

This kind of detail does not further the plot, and the Shertel-Sachsenberg system is never mentioned again, but it is helpful because when Emilio Largo then pulls two stolen nuclear warheads out of an underwater trap door on the *Disco Volante*, all we know about this supercharged yacht makes us believe that this unlikely scenario might just be true. 'I take very great pains over the technical and geographical background to James Bond's adventures,' Fleming once wrote, 'and during and after the writing of each book I consult innumerable authorities in order to give solidity and integrity to his exploits. Without this solid springboard, there would perhaps be justification for the frequent criticisms that James Bond's adventures are fantastic, though I maintain that such criticism comes from people who simply do not read newspapers or who have not taken note of the great underwater iceberg that is Secret Service warfare.'

The great iceberg of secret-service warfare, presented in the Bond books as something on which Fleming had the inside track (partly true, mainly not), comprised a mixture of real Cold War spycraft and his own imagination. In his notebooks Fleming jotted down numerous devices that he might have been able to use: 'radio strapped to leg with aerial concealed up the back. A switch in the trouser pocket switches it off and on'; 'fit camera with flashlight into headlights of car'; 'cigarette impregnated with mustard gas would cause the smoker to die of septic pneumonia'. These kinds of gadget, which have become familiar to the point of self-parody in the films, actually have a very minor role in the books; there isn't even a character called Q.

An innocent-looking attaché case could in the hands of Q Branch secrete all manner of gadgets for 007 to use in the field. Bond's case is from Swaine & Adeney.

'Q branch', however, was a part of the real secret service that Fleming reproduced in the books. The name had come from the First World War, when warships disguised as freighters and unarmed trawlers were referred to as 'Q' ships, and the letter had stuck. By 1940 Q branch was an obscure part of the Ministry of Supply, and Ian first discovered its existence when he hatched an ambitious plan to steal a Kriegsmarine Enigma code book. His idea hinged upon a British crew flying and then ditching a Heinkel 110 bomber into the sea in the hope of being picked up by a German ship, which the plucky young airmen would then commandeer and sail back to a British port. As all German ships carried the vital code book, Fleming considered that this was the best method of obtaining it.

This plan went some distance: Charles Fraser-Smith, one of the Q-branch boffins, went to great lengths to provide Fleming with six correct Luftwaffe uniforms, and he was also responsible for providing a captured Heinkel 100 bomber. In the event Operation Ruthless, as it was known, was cancelled, but Fleming kept in contact with Q branch. He was particularly intrigued by a hollowed-out golf ball in which Fraser-Smith had hidden a compass to be sent to prisoners of war, and appropriated this device for transferring uncut diamonds in *Diamonds are Forever*.

Apart from these escape aids, Q branch also provided SOE agents with all kinds of gadgets for clandestine use with the French resistance. It created exploding rats (booby traps), hollowed-out keys concealing microprints, miniature radio sets, and the famous 'L' pill, an optional extra to be used only as a release from unbearable torture. The pill, which contained potassium cyanide, had an insoluble coating so that if it was held in the mouth and then swallowed it passed through the body harmlessly. But if crushed between the teeth death was almost instantaneous.

Q branch provides 007 with an L pill concealed in the special attaché case it issues in *From Russia with Love*. This is the boffins' greatest contribution to the novels, and as a box of gadgets it is certainly handy. The carefully-tooled Swaine & Adeney interior has been ripped out to pack in fifty rounds of ammunition and a brace of flat throwing knives 'built by Wilkinsons, the sword makers', slotted into the sides, and a tube of Palmolive shaving cream conceals the silencer for Bond's Beretta. The L pill, which 007 flushes straight down the lavatory, is hidden in the handle. As in the films, the literary James Bond does not really see the point of using too many gadgets in the field; he even mildly disapproves of them – an indication that deep down, beneath his cruel professional veneer, he shares the sensibilities of an older generation of spies who believed in level playing fields and all that. Nevertheless, he has to keep up with the opposition, who are usually far better equipped. In *From Russia with Love* Red Grant has a gun disguised as a book, and his boss, Rosa Klebb, goes one better: she has a gun disguised as a telephone, and a dainty pair of boots fitted with extrudable poisoned blades. Blofeld has at various times an electric chair, an electrical 'machine' and even a volcanic geyser at his disposal. Mr Big has a desk that fires bullets, Goldfinger a circular steel saw to slice the spreadeagled Bond in half. For 007, simple is best, and invariably the most useful tools of his trade, apart from his gun, are his shoes, the heels of which conceal knives that save his life on more than one occasion.

This catalogue of devilish clever devices, occasionally employed by Bond but more often wielded against him, helped to make the fantasy world of 007 seem as modern as possible. In fact this stuff is absolutely the stock in trade of spy fiction. William Le Queux, E. Phillips Oppenheim and countless *Boy's Own Paper* stories that Fleming had read at school were peppered with cunning gadgets designed to conceal or maim: they were what readers of this genre expected. Spies of this older generation were routinely poisoned by pins stuck into towels, killed by 'a most deadly and diabolical contrivance' – the exploding cigar – or poisoned

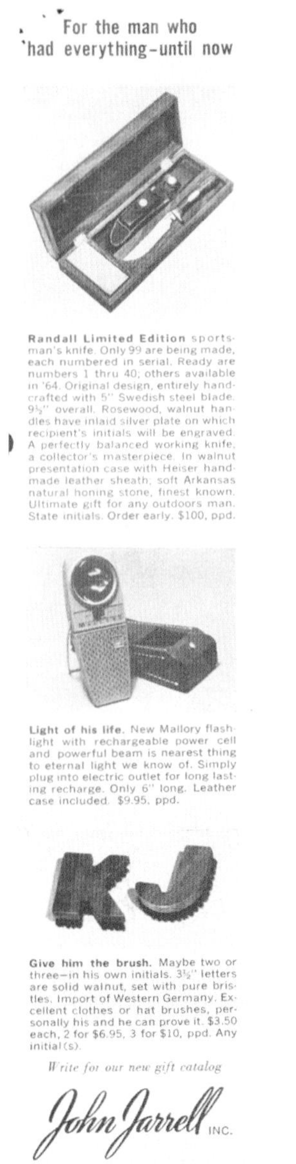

Men's magazines of the 1950s and '60s are crammed full of 'executive' luxury goods, high-end cigarettes and spirits, and gadgets 'for the man who has everything.' Fleming loved gadgets himself, and made sure his alter ego was equipped with only the best.

by lethal gases. To disguise their identity they routinely wore false eyebrows, and they wrote their letters in invisible ink, before rolling them up into small metal tubes which they concealed, either by inserting them into themselves or, as a last resort, into their pet dog. James Bond's gadgets are really Fleming's attempt to update this aspect of the thriller genre to the 1950s, in the knowledge that the bizarre realities of the Cold War actually underwrote many of his fantastical machines.

The same sense of updating the genre is also true of James Bond's cars. No one in a James Bond novel simply gets into 'a car': it is always a vehicle of a specific make, model and colour. Just as in the previous generation of spy stories written by John Buchan and others a destroyer is not just 'a destroyer', it is always a 'Zulu Class destroyer', or a 'Mark III destroyer', so Fleming is also specific. In fact his enthusiasm for motoring was as fundamental as his interest in gambling, golf and fish. The car, for Fleming, defined the character. James Bond starts off with a battleship-grey 1933 4½-litre Bentley convertible fitted with an Amherst Villiers supercharger – a technical detail that characteristically had a personal significance: Amherst Villiers was a friend of Ian's and later in life even painted his portrait. Bond had chosen this particular Bentley for its 'imposing, even brutal appearance' and of course its 'particularly fine deep exhaust note'. For Ian, the sound of a car was almost as important as its appearance. He even named Chitty Chitty Bang Bang – the fantasy car of his children's story – after the sound it made. James Bond keeps his car serviced with 'jealous care', and it is always capable of ninety miles an hour, with thirty held in reserve – in theory at least. This Bentley, driven with great dash by Bond, was considered a museum piece even when it first appeared in 1953, and it was also the stock in trade of the secret agent, as Bulldog Drummond had one. It lasts only three novels: Bond almost writes it off in *Casino Royale*, doesn't drive it at all in *Live and Let*

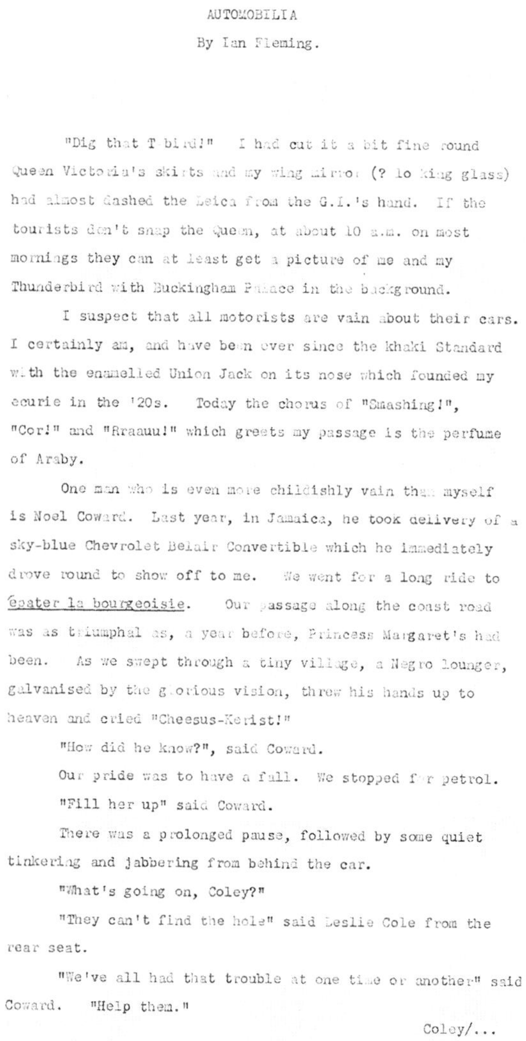

AUTOMOBILIA

By Ian Fleming.

"Dig that T-bird!" I had cut it a bit fine round Queen Victoria's skirts and my wing mirror (? looking glass) had almost dashed the Leica from the G.I.'s hand. If the tourists don't snap the Queen, at about 10 a.m. on most mornings they can at least get a picture of me and my Thunderbird with Buckingham Palace in the background.

I suspect that all motorists are vain about their cars. I certainly am, and have been ever since the khaki Standard with the enamelled Union Jack on its nose which founded my ecurie in the '20s. Today the chorus of "Smashing!", "Cor!" and "Rraauu!" which greets my passage is the perfume of Araby.

One man who is even more childishly vain than myself is Noel Coward. Last year, in Jamaica, he took delivery of a sky-blue Chevrolet Belair Convertible which he immediately drove round to show off to me. We went for a long ride to épater la bourgeoisie. Our passage along the coast road was as triumphal as, a year before, Princess Margaret's had been. As we swept through a tiny village, a Negro lounger, galvanised by the glorious vision, threw his hands up to heaven and cried "Cheesus-Kerist!"

"How did he know?", said Coward.

Our pride was to have a fall. We stopped for petrol.

"Fill her up" said Coward.

There was a prolonged pause, followed by some quiet tinkering and jabbering from behind the car.

"What's going on, Coley?"

"They can't find the hole" said Leslie Cole from the rear seat.

"We've all had that trouble at one time or another" said Coward. "Help them."

Coley/...

Cars were an obsession for both Fleming and Bond, even if their personal tastes diverged. This 1958 article for The Spectator *is in typically escapist vein – though it does draw on a world of which Fleming himself was a part.*

Die, and in *Moonraker* has to concede second best to Hugo Drax's modern, fast Mercedes 300 S. Bentleys 'used to be good in the old days', says Drax. 'Now they're only built for going to the theatre.' Bond may not agree, but with his windshield screwed flat down on to the bonnet and his supercharger screaming he can barely keep up with Drax's steady 110 m.p.h., and even then he is passed by an Alfa-Romeo supercharged straight-eight. A few pages later Bond collides with some fourteen tons of newsprint bouncing down the hill towards him, and the trusty old Bentley is written off for good.

James Bond drives several cars during the course of Fleming's stories; the Aston Martin DB III becomes his vehicle of choice only in Goldfinger. *The* Goldfinger *files contain a copy of the model's 1957* Autocar *road test.*

For the rest of the novels, when not driving the odd Thunderbird convertible or Sunbeam Alpine abroad, Bond is behind the wheel of 'the most selfish car in England', a second-hand Mark II Continental Bentley. Its previous owner had abandoned it after wrapping it around a telegraph pole. Not content with a standard car, 007 has it fitted with a Mark IV engine with 9.5 compression, to which he adds an 'Arnott supercharger controlled by a magnetic clutch' (more 'Fleming Effect'). Then the body is sawn off and replaced with a convertible hood and two bucket seats, upholstered in black morocco. This bastardized Bentley is not pretty, and Bond adds extra menace by having it painted in rough battleship grey and fitted with twin two-inch exhausts that growl and thunder like a Gatling gun. He calls it 'The Locomotive', and it goes like a bird and a bomb.

Fleming assigned some very sexy models to the Bond girls. Tilly's Triumph TR3 in Goldfinger *is no exception.*

All this mechanical detail suggests that Ian Fleming was an expert who knew what he was talking about. This is partly true (gimlet-eyed fans noted that Mark II was a misprint; Bond's Bentley must be a Mark VI Continental with a Mark VI engine), but in cars, as in all things, Fleming was a great delegator. Aubrey Forshaw, the head of Pan Books, was a car enthusiast who, unlike Fleming, also knew what went on under the bonnet, and he was tasked to find out how to make Bond's Bentley go faster. This he dutifully did, with the help of a Rolls-Royce technical expert. 'You may rest assured', he wrote, 'that Bond is driving a Feasible Proposition. There have been stranger marques.' Ian simply copied the details into his books.

If Bond's customized monster is an expression of his character, then the other cars driven in James Bond novels are, to the enthusiast, equally revealing. Domino Vitali, the Italian hothead of *Thunderball*, drives her sporty little sapphire-blue MG with the aggressive expertise of a rally driver. Tracy di Vicenzo, another girl racer, cheekily cuts Bond up in her low white two-seater Lancia Flaminia Zagato Spyder. James Bond is aroused, not only by the 'sexy boom' of the twin exhaust, but by the engineering too: 'he enviously watched the way her de Dion axle married her rear wheels to the rough going [cobblestones], while his own live axle hopped and skittered as he wrenched at the wheel.' The beautiful, glacial Tilly Masterton of *Goldfinger* drives a dove-grey Triumph TR3 convertible; is this perhaps a veiled clue to her sexuality? Is it a little mannish for a lady?

For the villains, Fleming chose his cars with equal care. It was appropriate that Hugo Drax, the clever German, should have an advanced Mercedes 300 S – 'the sports model with a disappearing hood', whose wide door closes 'with the rich double click of a Fabergé box'. There is, reflects Bond, something 'ruthless and majestic' about these cars. Goldfinger drives a 1925 solid-gold Rolls-Royce Silver Ghost – 'so ugly twenty years ago, so strangely beautiful today' – that fits with his suitably ostentatious obsession. And then there is Blofeld in his harsh red Maserati – fast, sporty, the perfect cover for an assassin.

The most famous Bond car of all, the Aston Martin DB III that Bond drives in *Goldfinger*, seems to have been inspired by a reader's letter. When the early books were published, various readers complained to Fleming that the Bentley was becoming too recherché. 'Have the decency to fix him up with a proper bit of machinery,' wrote one, a member of the Aston Martin Owners Club. 'The DB III coupé is capable of a fair rate of knots and presumably could be fixed up for a bit of high-powered snogging.' Fleming, always attentive to his readers' concerns, obviously agreed, and in *Goldfinger* Bond chooses the Aston Martin from the secret-service car pool. More appropriate than the Jaguar 3.4, he decides, for his cover as an adventurous young man with a taste for the fast things in life. This Aston also happens to be his favourite colour, battleship grey, and includes a few Q-branch gizmos: a switch that alters the type and colour of the lights (useful for night pursuits), reinforced bumpers fore and aft should he need to ram, and a long-barrelled Colt .45 in a trick compartment under the driver's seat. Most important of all, it is also kitted out with a radio that receives a signal from a 'Homer' device which will enable Bond to keep track of Goldfinger's Rolls-Royce as it crosses France. All useful, practical stuff, and considerably less equipment than the DB III has in the 1964 *Goldfinger* film, whose Q modifications include a bulletproof rear windshield, tyre shredders, an ejector seat, oil sprays and a pair of rockets. Almost forty years later the on-screen James Bond is *still* driving his beloved Aston Martin (surely one of the most lucrative franchises ever created: how Jaguar must be kicking themselves that Bond never plumped for the 3.4!), he is still kitted out with gizmos by Q branch, and, as a measure of how far the films have moved away from Fleming's original conception of gadgetry, in *Die Another Day* (2002) Q's

Goldfinger's Rolls-Royce was something of a customized hybrid. Fleming's files include a souvenir programme for the Rolls-Royce Silver Ghost Jubilee Rally 1907–1957, from which this image of a pre-war model is taken (above). *But he also kept contemporaneous advertising for 'the gentleman's carriage par excellence'* (below).

Aston Martin actually becomes invisible. Ian's adage that the fantasy is 'not impossible but improbable' has been left far behind.

As a car enthusiast himself, Fleming had driven just about everything from a khaki Morris Oxford – named Zoroastra – to a 16/80 open Lagonda, taking in a succession of little Renaults, a 2.4-litre Riley and a pre-war Hillman Minx along the way. After a bad experience with a Daimler Convertible and a small windfall from the sale of the film rights to *Casino Royale* in 1955, Ian decided to buy himself a selfish present. That summer he went to stay with Ivar Bryce at Black Hollow Farm in Vermont, and there he met William Woodward Jr., a wealthy young socialite who drove an unusual American car called a Studillac, which was a Studebaker equipped with a powerful Cadillac engine. The speed and comfort of it impressed Ian, and he shamelessly appropriated this car in *Diamonds are Forever*:

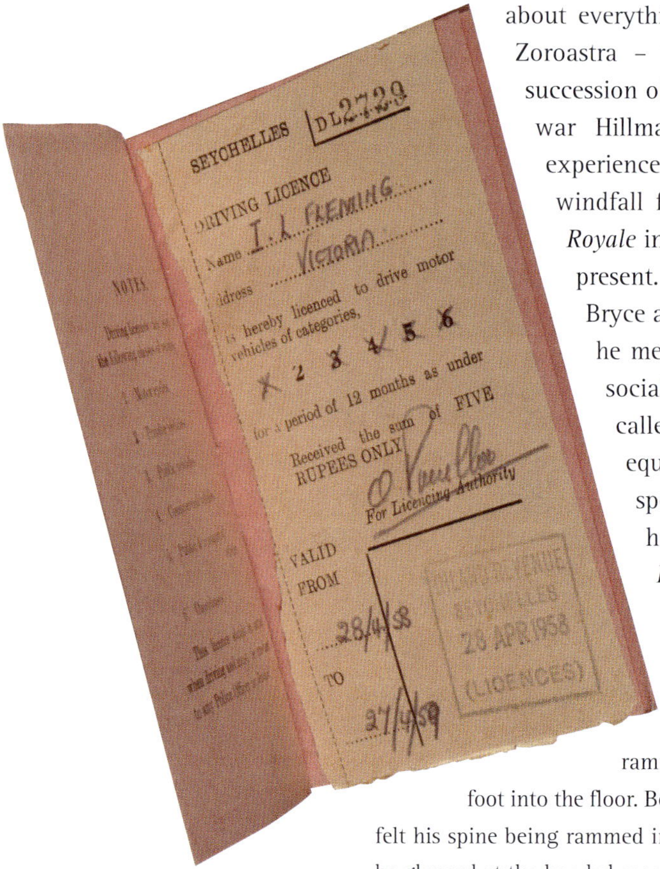
SEYCHELLES DL 2729
DRIVING LICENCE
Name I. L. FLEMING
Address VICTORIA
is hereby licenced to drive motor vehicles of categories,
X 2 3 4 5 6
for a period of 12 months as under
Received the sum of FIVE RUPEES ONLY
For Licencing Authority
VALID FROM 28/4/58 TO 27/4/59
SEYCHELLES 28 APR 1958 (LICENCES)

Wherever Fleming travelled, he liked to be able to drive. This is his local licence for the Seychelles, which he visited in search of pirate treasure for the Sunday Times *in 1958.*

> There was a straight stretch of empty road in front of them. Leiter gave a brief glance in his driving mirror and suddenly rammed the gear lever into second and thrust his foot into the floor. Bond's head jerked back on his shoulders, and he felt his spine being rammed into the back of the bucket seat. Incredulously, he glanced at the hooded speedometer. Eighty. With a clang Leiter's hook hit the gear lever into top. The car went on gathering speed. Ninety, ninety-five, six, seven . . .

The roomy, powerful Studillac confirmed Ian's long-held admiration for big American cars. When he saw a Thunderbird parked on a London street later that year he fell in love with this 'magnificent creature' and bought one for himself. 'The beauty of its line and the drama of its snarling mouth and the giant flaring nostril of its air intake,' he gasped. He also liked the fact that, unlike most post-war British cars he had driven, everything worked. 'True it isn't a precision instrument like English sports cars,' he wrote, 'but I count that a virtue. The mechanical margin of error in its construction is wider.' Fleming went on to drive his black Thunderbird almost 50,000 miles without having so much as to change a spark plug, and the engine, 'a huge adapted low-revving

Mercury V-8 of 5 litre capacity', never gave the impression of stress or strain. Bond's admiration for his own customized Bentley is similar; he also likes being able to start it cold every day of the year, and enjoys the lazy, grunting power of the engine. Fleming drove his Thunderbird for four years before exchanging it for a more powerful four-door version, to which he fitted all mod cons except, strangely, power steering. Ann had never liked Ian's favourite toy: she regarded the Thunderbird as being 'above our price bracket and below our age range', and the experience of travelling in it induced an odd ailment she could only describe as 'Thunderbird neck'.

Fleming finally wrote off his beloved T-bird in 1961. He ploughed into the back of an ice-cream van, with Ann and his small son, Caspar, on board. This accident only confirmed his long-held fears about the ever-increasing dangers of travelling on English roads: in 1952 he had written 'An Open Letter to the Transport Minister', printed in the *Daily Graphic*, exhorting Alan Lennox-Boyd to make road signs more strident and vulgar in an attempt to persuade 'the road hog in his juggernaut' and the 'motorcyclist trying to break the sound barrier that he is aiming a loaded gun from the moment he leaves the garage'. At that time there were 4,000 casualties from road accidents each week, and in Ian's view this figure alone justified exchanging 'Blanktown welcomes careful drivers' to a more tasteless 'Look First. Live Longer', or the mawkish 'Death is so Permanent'. Fleming's fears were fully justified, as these statistics continued to keep pace with the rapid rise of the car. When *Casino Royale* was published in 1953, there were just under 3 million cars on British roads; by the time of *The Man with the Golden Gun* in 1965, that figure had tripled to over 9 million. Most of these roads were still narrow, often uncambered, and there were no motorways except the first modest stretch of the M1 that had opened in November 1959. And millions of new drivers set out driving cars that were – by today's standards – primitive. Most had heavy steering, rudimentary brakes, short windscreen wipers, and weak headlights; and these shortcomings were aggravated by a lack of seat belts and by windscreens that shattered on impact. All of this contributed to the huge rise in accidents, traffic jams and general concern about the motor car.

This contemporary background is worth bearing in mind when considering the way James Bond drives in the novels. He effortlessly cruises along at 90 m.p.h., his mind barely engaged on the road ahead. He is without a seat belt and, in the case of his first Bentley, often without a windscreen, as it lay flat down on the bonnet. Bond is probably driving at twice the speed of everyone else, which may account for his fits of road rage aimed at various Ford Populars, family saloons and anyone else who gets in his way. 'He changed down and contemptuously slammed the DB III past on the inside. Silly bastard!' This kind of road-hoggery certainly amazed his readers, who found Bond's driving 'fabulously exciting' and his night pursuit of Drax, at 110 m.p.h., at night, without lights, 'frankly incredible'. Fleming's Thunderbird was certainly capable of this turn of speed, but he never pushed it, claiming that even his big, safe American car did not have the brakes for 'dangerous driving'. On the whole he preferred to do his motoring on the comparatively empty roads of France, as did Bond. Here death was equally permanent, but slightly more avoidable.

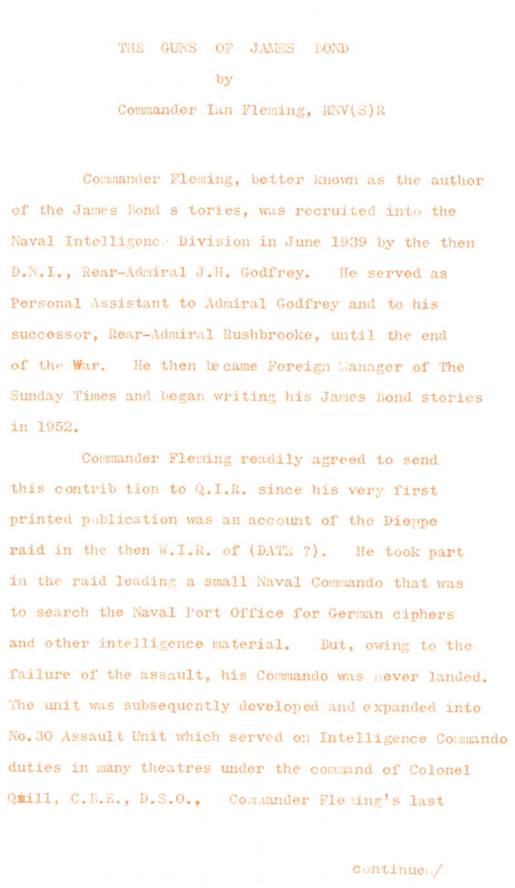

THE GUNS OF JAMES BOND

by

Commander Ian Fleming, RNV(S)R

Commander Fleming, better known as the author of the James Bond s tories, was recruited into the Naval Intelligence Division in June 1939 by the then D.N.I., Rear-Admiral J.H. Godfrey. He served as Personal Assistant to Admiral Godfrey and to his successor, Rear-Admiral Rushbrooke, until the end of the War. He then became Foreign Manager of The Sunday Times and began writing his James Bond stories in 1952.

Commander Fleming readily agreed to send this contrib tion to Q.I.R. since his very first printed publication was an account of the Dieppe raid in the then W.I.R. of (DATE ?). He took part in the raid leading a small Naval Commando that was to search the Naval Port Office for German ciphers and other intelligence material. But, owing to the failure of the assault, his Commando was never landed. The unit was subsequently developed and expanded into No.30 Assault Unit which served on Intelligence Commando duties in many theatres under the command of Colonel Quill, C.B.E., D.S.O., Commander Fleming's last

continued/

This 1961 article allowed fact and fiction to mingle.

Aside from the gadgets and cars, the last coveted object of desire synonymous with James Bond is his gun. There was no room for fantasy here, and this was another subject where one particular reader had a profound influence on James Bond's choice of weapon. In May 1956, soon after *Diamonds are Forever* was published, Fleming received an unusual fan letter from Geoffrey Boothroyd, a thirty-one-year-old Bond enthusiast. Boothroyd was a firearms expert, whose collection of forty-five weapons included everything from a Lee Enfield .303 rifle to a Ruger super Blackhawk .44 Magnum, the most powerful handgun in the world. His pastimes included extinguishing the candles on a Christmas cake using a pistol and blanks. Boothroyd declared that he 'loved Bond' but took exception to 'his deplorable taste in firearms', and in particular Bond's beloved .25 Beretta with a skeleton grip. 'This sort of gun',

Boothroyd went on, warming to his theme, 'is really a ladies' gun, and not a really nice lady at that.' Far better, he suggested, was the Smith & Wesson .38 Centennial Airweight, a 'real manstopper weighing only 17 ounces loaded. The gun is hammerless so that it can be drawn without catching in the clothing and has an overall length of 6 inches.' And the perfect holster for this deadly little weapon would be the Mississippi-made 'Lightning' Berns-Martin Triple Draw holster, which holds the gun in place by means of a spring, and could be concealed in the waistbelt. Having made these helpful suggestions, Geoffrey Boothroyd then set out how Bond should draw this weapon correctly, assuming he is right-handed:

1. Ready position. Note that the gun is not noticeable.
2. First movement. Weight moves to left foot. Hand draws back coat and sweeps forward to catch butt of pistol. Finger outside holster.
3. Gun comes out of holster through the split front.
4. In business. This draw can be done in 3/5ths of a second, and with practice and lots of it you could hit a figure at 20 feet in that time.

This onslaught of technical information and expert know-how overwhelmed Fleming. Apart from possessing a Colt .38 Police Positive, he really knew nothing much about handguns at all. He fired off an

Together with his long correspondence with Geoffrey Boothroyd on gun matters, Fleming's files also contain letters about weaponry to and from other interested readers. One, Mr Graham Woodward, was so kind as to send in a series of drawings to aid Fleming's research, complete with notes on salient characteristics of the guns.

enthusiastic reply to Boothroyd's 'splendid' letter, guessing correctly that the writer was a bona-fide expert and telling him that 'his colleague James Bond' had agreed to give a fair trial to the holster, but that he was rather concerned about losing his trusty Beretta, placing his accuracy with it above its failings as a stopping weapon. However, Fleming hinted darkly, M might force Bond to make the change, and he would also advise Bond to carry a .357 Magnum in his car for longer-range work. In the same letter Fleming then asked what the Russian agents of SMERSH might use, and in return for all this invaluable information Fleming offered Boothroyd the carrot of being put forward as a technical adviser on any film of James Bond that might be made in the future.

Boothroyd's voluminous reply about Russian weaponry included the suggestion of a Walther PPK 7.65mm for Bond. This was not the most accurate of weapons – it was well beaten in trials by the Japanese Nambu and the Russian Tokarev – but it was more powerful than Bond's Beretta and had the advantage of firing .32 calibre ammunition readily available all over the world. Silencing it, however, would be a problem. Boothroyd pointed out, knowingly, that silencers are more often found in fiction than in real life: 'so few people are familiar with what a gun sounds like that I would have little hesitation in firing one in any well-constructed building.' Fleming responded in kind. 'The trouble is that there are often occasions when they are essential to Bond's work . . . our Secret Services developed some very good ones during the war, in which the bullet passed through rubber baffles. I have tried a Sten Gun silenced with one of these and all one could hear was the click of machinery.' In the event Fleming did choose the Walther PPK, and, as it was too late for his next book, *From Russia with Love*, he managed to weave the change of weapon into the beginning of the following novel, *Dr No*. Geoffrey Boothroyd was rewarded for his interest by becoming 'Major Boothroyd', the secret-service armourer, to whom M gives a ringing introduction: 'You may not know it, 007, but Major Boothroyd's the greatest small-arms expert in the world.'

Despite all this expert advice, when *Dr No* was published Fleming was dismayed to discover that more of 'the dreadful technical errors that dog each of my books here again crept in.' Another expert wrote a sharp letter to Boothroyd, stating that the Berns-Martin holster can carry only a revolver, not a Walther PPK automatic. Yet another expert complained that Major Boothroyd sends Bond off to tackle Dr No with a Smith & Wesson .38 Centennial Airweight for long-range work, which the real Boothroyd had originally recommended only for short-range work. Bond should have had the larger S&W .357 Magnum – also Boothroyd's original suggestion, which Fleming had overlooked. 'Quite honestly,' said Fleming, 'the whole question of expertise in these matters bores me'. He was relieved to send on the hundreds of letters from the 'weapons maniacs – and they ARE maniacs' direct to Geoffrey Boothroyd. The upshot of all this correspondence was that Fleming and Boothroyd became friends, and Boothroyd even lent him his own S&W Centennial Airweight with a sawn-off barrel and cut-away trigger guard for Fleming to have copied for the cover of *From Russia with Love*. Geoffrey Boothroyd went on to lecture on the 007 fan club circuit and, as Fleming had originally promised, he became the technical consultant on *From Russia with Love*, the second Bond film, made in 1963.

Advised by Boothroyd and other specialists, Fleming was keen to ensure that details of the guns he featured were accurate.

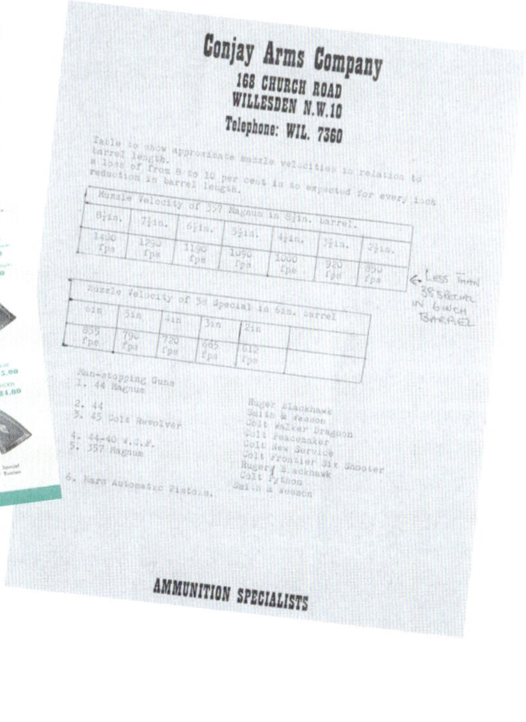

Conjay Arms Company
168 CHURCH ROAD
WILLESDEN N.W.10
Telephone: WIL. 7360

Table to show approximate muzzle velocities in relation to barrel length.
a loss of from 8 to 10 per cent is to expected for every inch reduction in barrel length.

Muzzle Velocity of 357 Magnum in 8½in. barrel.						
8½in.	7½in.	6½in.	5½in.	4½in.	3½in.	2½in.
1400 fps	1290 fps	1190 fps	1090 fps	1000 fps	920 fps	850 fps

← LESS THAN 38 SPECIAL IN 6 INCH BARREL

Muzzle Velocity of 38 Special in 6in. barrel					
6in	5in	4in	3in	2in	
855 fps	790 fps	720 fps	665 fps	612 fps	

Man-stopping Guns
1. 44 Magnum
2. 44 — Ruger Blackhawk, Smith & Wesson
3. 45 Colt Revolver — Colt Walker Dragoon, Colt Peacemaker, Colt New Service, Colt Frontier Six Shooter
4. 44-40 W.C.F. — Ruger Blackhawk
5. 357 Magnum — Colt Python, Smith & Wesson
6. Mars Automatic Pistols.

AMMUNITION SPECIALISTS

THUNDERBALL 1961

The title was taken from the expression used by US soldiers witnessing an atomic test to describe the mushroom cloud.

First line

It was one of those days when it seemed to James Bond that all life, as someone put it, was nothing but a heap of six to four against.

Story

Thunderball opens with a hangover. Bond, who has been idly gambling and drinking far too much, is sent off to Shrublands, a health farm, to purge his system for two weeks. At first he bridles against the yoghurt-and-soup regime, then he discovers it actually improves his spirit. But his recovery is marred by a certain Count Lippe, who attempts to kill him on a traction machine, and Bond returns the compliment by turning up the Italian's heat box to 180°F. These childish pranks are a prelude to the main story, in which a NATO bomber with two atomic warheads on board is stolen and ditched in the Bahamas. The bombs are taken off and hidden under a remote atoll by Emilio Largo, a member of the international criminal organization SPECTRE, led by Ernst Blofeld. Blofeld then warns the British and US governments that he has the weapons, and demands £100 million not to set them off. Bond is reluctantly sent down to the Bahamas to investigate, convinced he is far away from the real action, but once he meets Domino Vitali and her then boyfriend, Emilio Largo, he becomes suspicious of Largo's huge treasure-hunting yacht, the *Disco Volante*. Bond makes a nocturnal reconnaissance of this vessel, and finds an underwater trapdoor large enough to launch a mini-submarine. Then, with Felix Leiter, Bond discovers the crashed NATO bomber, complete with the body of its Italian pilot, Domino's brother. As Blofeld's deadline approaches, the *Disco* sets off at high speed to recover the warheads, tracked by Bond aboard a US Polaris submarine. Once the *Disco* drops anchor, 007 leads a team of marine commandos to intercept Largo and his mini-subs, and a violent underwater battle begins involving CO2 guns, harpoons and sharks. Just as Bond is about to be killed by Largo, Domino appears and skewers Largo with her spear gun. Bond, half dead, is pulled from the water. The warheads are retrieved, and Bond enjoys his rewards with Domino, who has been tortured by Largo for her treachery.

Last lines

The girl watched the dark, rather cruel face for a moment. Then she gave a small sigh, pulled the pillow to the edge of the bed so that it was just above him, laid her head down so that she could see him whenever she wanted to, and closed her eyes.

Inspirations

The Shrublands section was inspired by Fleming's 1955 visit to Enton Hall for a 'hydro', an attempt to cut down his alcohol and nicotine consumption. Bond's medical record, read out by M at the beginning of the book, is a slightly modified version of Ian's own.

Much of *Thunderball* takes place underwater. Once again Ian drew upon real wartime exploits for these action sequences: for instance, he knew that both the Nazis and the Soviets hid weapons in underwater caches during the war, and that some of these arms had never been recovered. Also, he was inspired by the exciting exploits of the Italian Gamma Group frogmen, who, 'in the greatest piece of effrontery of the underwater war', cut a trapdoor beneath the waterline of a rusting hulk in Algeciras harbour which they used as a secret base to raid British shipping. Ian may have known that MI6 also kept a number of their 'X'-craft midget submarines in Stokes Bay, Gosport, and one of these was nearly used by Buster Crabb in his infamous dive to inspect the Russian battle ship *Ordzhonikidze* in 1956. Crabb's exploit certainly inspired Bond's own nocturnal inspection of the *Disco Volante*.

What the critics said

'*Thunderball* is the best written since *Diamonds are Forever*, four books back. It has pace and humour and style. The sex is the old mixture of astuteness and silliness. The violence is not so unrelenting as usual: an improvement, I think' – *Financial Times*

'A sensational imagination, but informed by style, zest and – above all – knowledge' – *Sunday Times*

'Hey! – that man is taking off his clothes again. So is the girl . . . Can't anybody *stop* this? Unfortunately not. Not this side of the bestseller lists. I don't envy Mr Bond's wealthy creator, Ian Fleming. I wish I could pity him' – *Daily Herald*

'The fact that he has made such a dull book out of such a good idea leaves me in no doubt that Bond must go' – *Time and Tide*

Richard Chopping's Thunderball *cover for Cape featured a skeleton's hand grasping an ace of spades and a queen of diamonds – pinned to a table with a knife. The story's gripping underwater battles are terrific set pieces – rather more energetic than the scene depicted in one of a series of cartoons that Fleming kept from the Seychelles visit of 1958.*

more than a fetid mangrove swamp, reeking of sulphurous marsh gas, and Ian filled a small blue notebook with succinct impressions of this tropical hell:

Sulphur Dioxide – nasty gas
mosquitos in May & Oct kill donkeys
Orange pink crochet
Eat tiny clams
2ft deep lake

Chuckling honk
6ft wing span. 6ft long beak to toes
golden eyes
Shocking pink horizon
pulled by warden for 4 miles
Aubros 25,000 pairs, now 10 left
Largest colony in the world.
Like coming down to a full cocktail party

'Adventure in the Sun' was a 1956 article on the Caribbean for the Sunday Times, *but the title could have described a number of the Bond plots. Fleming's fact-checking for his work was extensive, and this ephemera gathered in Las Vegas provided useful background for* Diamonds are Forever (opposite).

These short, precise sensations, pressed extremely hard in pencil on to Fleming's knee, provided the inspiration for Crab Key, Dr No's guano-spattered refuge, which became one of the most memorable of all Bond locations. Wherever Fleming went he would usually come back with little jewels such as these.

To this meticulously realized travel fantasy Fleming adds another attractive ingredient: good weather. 'I think you will find that the sun is always shining in my books,' he wrote in 1962. 'This, so to speak, "pleasures" the reader and takes him out of his dull surroundings into a warmer, more colourful, more luxurious world. In a fashion, which I suppose nowadays would be described as "subliminal", this predisposes him favourably towards the book.' With the exception of *Moonraker*, which is set entirely in England, the good weather of James Bond's destination is always in strong contrast to the weather in London. At the start of a novel Bond is often found staring out of his seventh-floor window at the windy park below. If it is not unpleasantly sticky (rare in England, admittedly), then it is all gunmetal grey and cold. The weather at the beginning of *Dr No* is particularly atrocious. 'March came in like a rattlesnake . . . Hail and icy sleet, with a Force 8 gale behind them, lashed at the city and went on lashing as the people streamed miserably to work, their legs whipped by the wet hems of their mackintoshes and their faces blotching with the cold.' Fleming probably took perverse pleasure in tapping out these lines at his desk at Goldeneye, describing the scene from which he had absconded himself. He hated winter in England; he craved sunlight, and he was acutely aware of the balming effect upon an Englishman's soul of an unbroken stretch of blue sky.

Fleming had another reason for making Bond travel so much. Ever since he was made foreign news manager of the Kemsley newspaper group in 1946, he had been crusading for foreign news stories to be included in British newspapers. In his 1950 article for *The Kemsley Manual of Journalism* he acknowledged how difficult it was to get insular Englishmen to appreciate the world beyond their shores. 'The Englishman's knowledge of geography has always been hazy,' he wrote, 'and he dislikes having to remember the difference between Bucharest and Budapest. He is not interested in even the simplest political facts about those countries which are not at war with him.' Ian also had a bee in his bonnet about where his countrymen went on holiday: 'English people should become empire-minded for their holidays,' he declared. He spent most of his own holidays in Jamaica, and decided that the rest of the population should follow his lead. The Bond books were, in their way, also seeking to broaden the horizons of the insular British, as Fleming not only provided a lot of advice about wine and food, but also delivered something of a geography lesson, if only to follow the story. *Diamonds are Forever* begins under a bush beside a scrubby road in French Guinea, then proceeds at breakneck pace to Hatton Garden in London, New York, Saratoga, Las Vegas, Spectreville, Los Angeles, New York again, and the Atlantic, before finishing close to the bush where it all started in French Guinea.

Initially, Fleming did not realize that his vivid descriptions of exotic locations provided the reader with the literary equivalent of going on holiday. When *Moonraker*, his third novel, came out in 1955, Fleming received a number of letters from disappointed readers complaining that Kent, even on the most glorious English summer's day, did not compare with the tropical heat of the Caribbean. 'We want taking out of ourselves,' declared one old couple, who read Bond novels to each other aloud, 'not sitting on the beach in Dover.' As with many other parts of the James Bond recipe, Fleming discovered what

he had to keep in only when he dared to leave it out, and in every story thereafter 007 escapes from England's shores.

Bond's preferred method of travel to these warmer climes is by air. 'He liked flying almost sensually,' wrote Fleming in his notebook. 'There was plenty of action, but without responsibility. Plenty of rest, plenty of tranquillity and always the flirtation with the death wish that was inside him.' And there was also the flirtation with the air hostess. 'I've always thought that if I ever married I would marry an air hostess,' declares Bond at the beginning of the short story 'The Quantum of Solace', 'always tucking you up and bringing you drinks and hot meals and asking if you had everything you wanted.' But for Bond there were limits to this relationship: 'Trouble is hostesses, like geishas, want to give pleasure. To refuse is to give pain. Bond said to the one blue eye that seduced him while the right hand brushed aside the pretty cascade of tumbling blonde hair, "I'm sorry I can't play. I've got to work when we get there."'

Alongside the luxurious pampering, Fleming loved the 'hysteria' of speed that came with air travel. The 1950s was the decade in which this exciting new mode of transport really took off, and the aeroplanes that Bond flies about the world in were far more glamorous and interesting than their modern equivalents. The Boeing Stratocruiser, a direct descendant of the B-29 Superfortress bomber, had two decks, a bar and sleeping berths, and carried only 100 passengers. Travelling in one was expensive and arduous, as the flight times were lengthy. When Fleming took a BOAC Comet to Hong Kong he stopped at Zurich, Beirut, Bahrain, New Delhi, and Bangkok, covering the 7,000 miles in twenty-six hours. Today it takes under eleven. Even the standard trip from London to New York took eleven hours – via Shannon Airport, where dinner was served. Fleming actually disapproved of getting there any faster: when a new direct route opened in 1961 he didn't like the fact that he wouldn't be able to get out, eat in the restaurant, and riffle through the 'junk' in the duty-free shop. 'Gander, Reykjavik and Shannon are the great waiting rooms of the West,' he recorded in his notebook, 'as are Hong Kong and Manus in the East. Transients are uninterested in the hinterland behind these waiting rooms. Only in their lavatories and their custom-free goods. The people who work there know

Air travel features in James Bond's adventures. He usually flies with the longhaul British national airline of the time, BOAC.

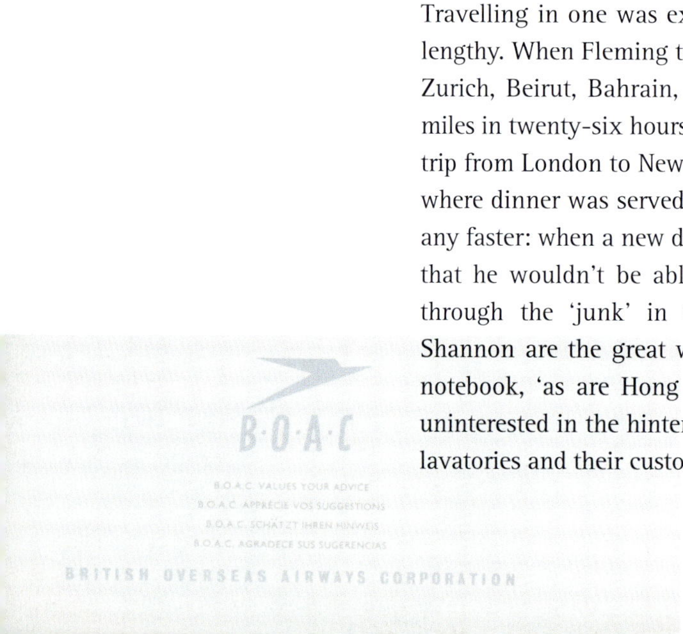

it, and they are no more interested in the passengers than a banana seller on a refrigeration ship is interested in an individual banana.'

James Bond may be an experienced traveller, but there are large parts of the world to which he never ventures. If he flies, then in general it is west to America and then on to Jamaica or the Bahamas. This was Fleming's own familiar stamping ground, and the scene of nine out of 12 novels. Bond flies east on only three occasions: first to Turkey in *From Russia with Love*, then to the Seychelles in 'The Hildebrand Rarity', and finally to Japan in the penultimate novel, *You Only Live Twice*. Fleming himself had visited all these countries, which might suggest that he stuck rigidly to his axiom of never writing about somewhere he hadn't been himself. In fact he was oddly selective about where he sent his secret agent. James Bond never disappears into the souks of North Africa, or gets lost in the deserts of the Middle East, or goes diving in Australia; whereas Ian had done all these things.

The omission of North Africa is particularly curious, as it might have been a fertile area for Bond. Tangier had been a major spy capital during the war, when Fleming had visited it, and he returned there in April 1957 to meet John Collard, the real-life diamond spy who provided him with material for his factual book *The Diamond Smugglers*. Though Fleming came to admire Collard, whom he regarded as a kind of 'reluctant hero, like all Britain's best secret agents', he had little enthusiasm for Tangier itself. 'The paint is peeling off the town and the streets are running with spit and pee and worse,' he complained, 'and its inhabitants, the Arabs, are filthy people and hate all Europeans.' He took a similar view of Beirut, where he stayed with his friend the SIS agent Nick Elliott in 1960. At the time Beirut was the smuggling

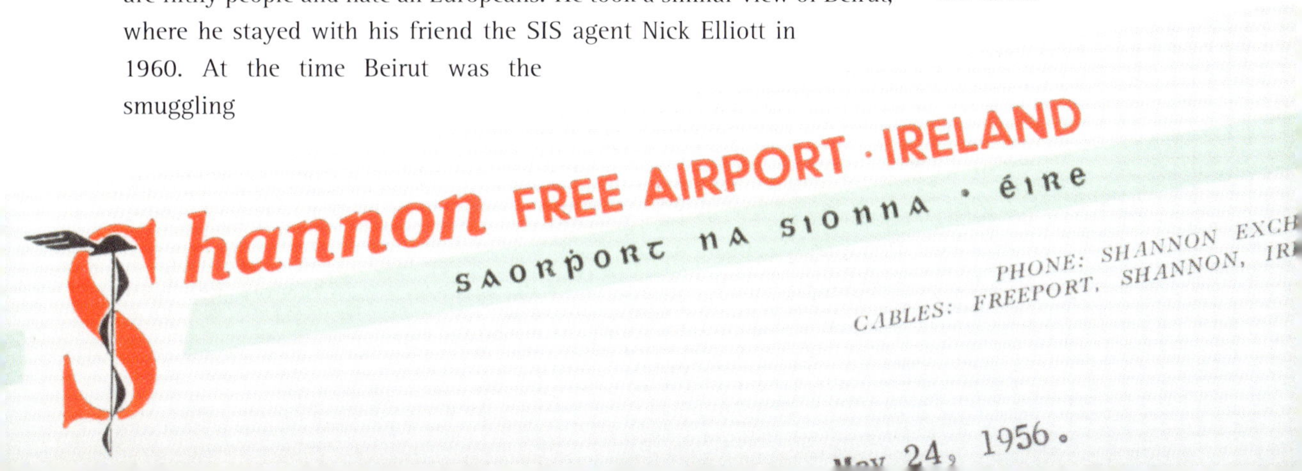

One memorable reader's letter came from an official at Shannon Airport, complaining at the dismissal of its shops in Diamonds are Forever. *He suggested that Fleming must have had very little time actually to inspect all the goods on offer there – though he acknowledges Ian's appreciation of their Irish coffee.*

Monte Carlo – 'a sunny place for shady people' according to Somerset Maugham – sees the kidnapping of gangster Magnus Blomberg's daughter in Thunderball. *Fleming visited Aristotle Onassis – who owned the casino – there in 1958, and it featured as one of the 'Thrilling Cities'.*

capital of the world: an entrepôt for diamonds pilfered from Sierra Leone, arms from Arabia, drugs from Turkey, gold from Aleppo. Another perfect place for Bond, perhaps. But there was something about Arab countries that Fleming never liked. In *Thrilling Cities* he dismissed the whole region, right through to India, as 'the thieving areas of the world'. This attitude might have had something to do with his experience in Kuwait.

In 1960 Fleming was approached by the Kuwait Oil Company to write 30,000 words on that rapidly developing country, a boom state thanks to the recent exploitation of its vast oil reserves. Ian started out with romantic notions of the lands of Aladdin peopled by the sons of Sinbad, combined with some exciting facts he had dug up. 'A million tons of sand from Arabia are blown every year into the Arabian Gulf,' he noted enthusiastically. 'Even birds shelter behind sheep and bushes from the sun.' But when he arrived he was sorely disappointed by the dusty reality that awaited him:

> The desert was featureless and drab. The view from a camel is only just different – there are small features – a tiny hill, an expanse of dunes, a single tree, occasionally a bird or lizard, snake, scorpion. But my impression from reading and seeing was one broadly speaking of a dirty, very dry and dull

> piece of the world, with tough, hungry and thirsty people in tattered fancy dress cooking whole sheep over burning camel dung, wolfing down as much as I eat in a week and then belching to express appreciation.

'All right,' he added somewhat churlishly:

> so there was the solitude and the stars and the beauty of sunrise and sunset. But I know these things, and the companionship of nature. I would far rather share them with really excellent people on top of the Swiss Alps. Oh – the stars would be just as bright, the food just as simple, and the conversation would be about something more interesting than weather, water and the price of dates – the standard chit-chat of the Bedu.

He left the country frustrated. 'Which is better,' he asked himself, 'romantic myth or dull truth?' 'State of Excitement', as he ironically called his manuscript, was never published, and for copyright reasons never will be.

Given his dislike of Kuwait and the Middle East, it is curious that Istanbul made it into the list of glamorous Bond locations. Fleming went to that city in 1956 to attend a 'spectacularly dull' Interpol conference, and then witnessed a spectacular riot which, in his view, was 'the worst insurrection in the history of modern Turkey'. The great city that was once Constantinople fell far short of his expectations. 'There is no romance in the town itself', he scribbled, 'except the dramatic accident of its geography and the occasional whiff of sharp spices from its bazaars. The shops are full of brummagem junk, or a single piece of machinery, or one bicycle.' He found the Turks themselves equally downtrodden. 'They loathe their ancestors and their monuments are grimy with neglect and disdain. They move secretly but with one accord, and if you wish to read them and their intentions you must read them like animals or birds, by small signs and portents.' This was not encouraging. But then a relieved Fleming met Nazim Kalkavan, who offered to show him around.

Oxford-educated, with 'a warm dry handclasp' – a vital sign of a

THE JOURNEYS OF JAMES

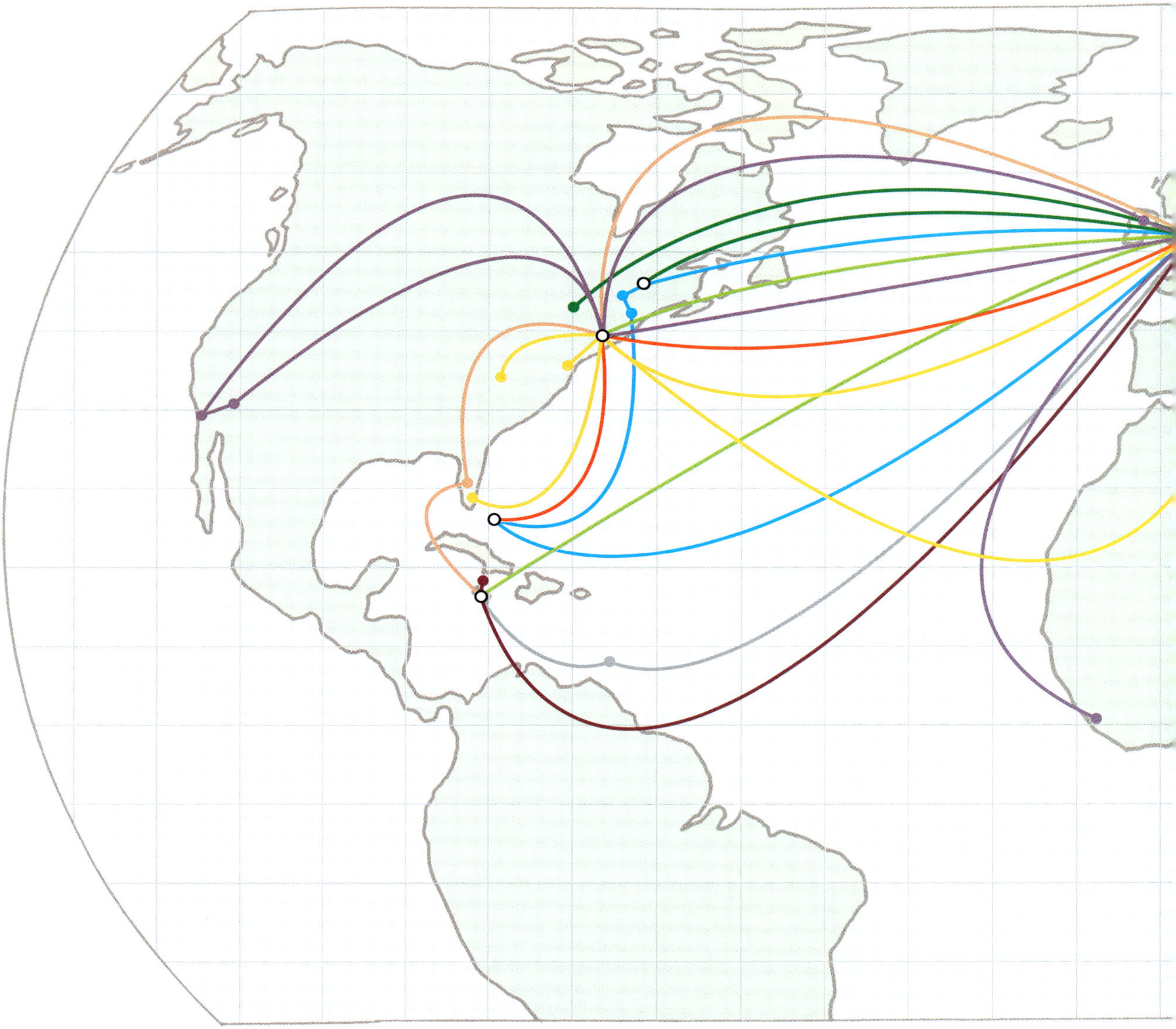

CASINO ROYALE
Royale-les-Eaux, north-east France

LIVE AND LET DIE
London – New York – Florida – Kingston, Jamaica

MOONRAKER
London and Kent

DIAMONDS ARE FOREVER
London – Ireland – New York – Saratoga Springs – Las Vegas – Los Angeles – New York – London – Freetown, Sierra Leone

FROM RUSSIA WITH LOVE
London – Rome – Athens – Istanbul – Belgrade – Trieste – Dijon – Paris

DR NO
London – Jamaica – Crab Key

GOLDFINGER
Miami – New York – London – Kent – Northern France – Geneva – New York – Kentucky – New York – Washington, DC – North Atlantic

BOND

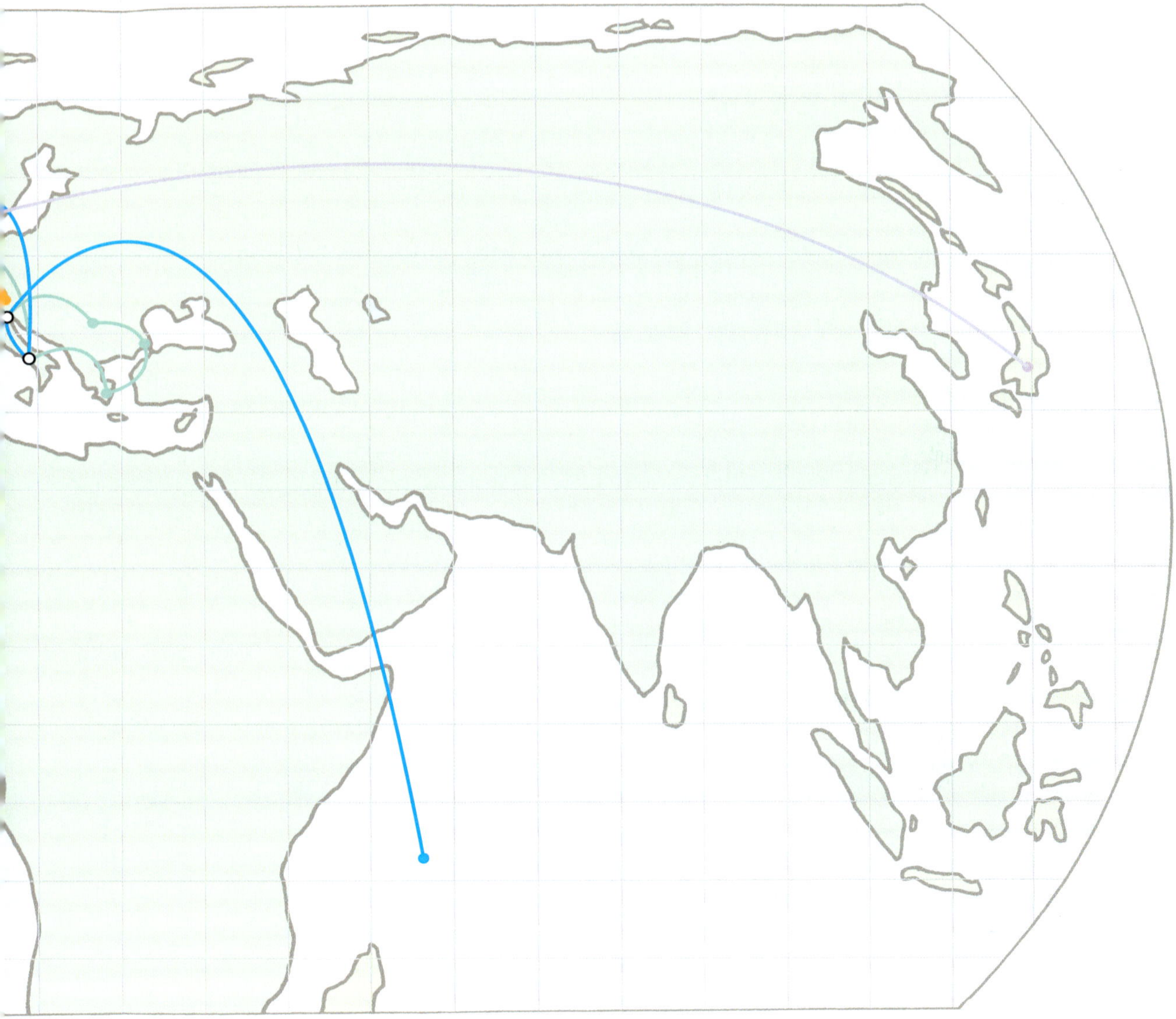

FOR YOUR EYES ONLY
Paris – London – Montreal – Ottawa – Vermont – Bahamas – London – Rome – Venice – Seychelles

THUNDERBALL
London – Sussex – London – New York – Bahamas

THE SPY WHO LOVED ME
Adirondack Mountains – Windsor – London – Montreal

ON HER MAJESTY'S SECRET SERVICE
Royale-les-Eaux – London – Davos – Zurich – London – Marseille – Strasbourg – Davos – Zurich – Munich

YOU ONLY LIVE TWICE
London and Japan

OCTOPUSSY AND THE LIVING DAYLIGHTS
Kingston – London – New York – London – Berlin

THE MAN WITH THE GOLDEN GUN
London – Trinidad (via Central America) – Jamaica

good man in Fleming's (and Bond's) estimation – Kalkavan had a noisy, infectious appetite for good food and beautiful women. Over the next few days Fleming began to see Istanbul through Kalkavan's eyes, and discovered there was far more to this place than just advertising hoardings and dirty mosques. Kalkavan told him about Russian spies who used the ancient sewers as passageways, and Gypsies who still carried vendettas to the death. For five lire they would do a naked belly dance, and for ten lire, Kalvakan assured him, they would stage a fight between two women. 'This starts for the spectator, but ends by a chance blow, when they tear off their blouses and go for each other's faces and breasts.' It was all fascinating, and found its way into *From Russia with Love* – as did Kalkavan himself, who became Darko Kerim, James Bond's great-hearted ally. 'Bond thought he had never seen so much vitality and warmth in a human face,' wrote Fleming. 'It was like being close to the sun.'

Pan Books published Fleming's Thrilling Cities *accounts with all the panache that they brought to the novels, and the links to 007's 'life and times' were never played down.*

The file on Hong Kong teems with colour and detail (opposite). *Fleming adored its 'modern comfort in a theatrically Oriental setting', but in Fleming's stories Bond never actually went there.*

If James Bond isn't fastening his lapstrap en route to some distant location, then in Fleming's mind he is usually doing the next best thing: driving his Bentley on to the small airferry at Lydd, bound for Le Touquet on the other side of the English Channel. Fleming had been a great patron of the airferry ever since the 1930s, when he would hop over for the weekend on a gambling spree with his cronies, or set off in the general direction of the Alps with a few days to kill. 'Driving a fast car abroad is one of my keenest pleasures,' he wrote – 'the eight o'clock departure with some distant luncheon stop as target . . . the kilometres flicking by like pages in a book.' In seven James Bond stories 007 is driving fast through England or France, being tailed, or on the tail of a villain. The Loire valley was Fleming's personal stamping ground, and he luxuriates in all the detailed advice he can pass on, through Bond, to the reader/traveller.

The Loire turns out to be James Bond's favourite river, but beware the local fish: 'Loire fish are inclined to be muddy.' Instead, Bond would recommend a sole meunière – even as far inland as Orléans. Don't stay in Orléans itself, a priest- and myth-ridden place interested only in taking your money; far better to stay outside the town on the banks of the Loire

– at the Auberge de la Montespan perhaps – and eat the excellent 'quenelles de brochet'. On no account patronize the gaudy Breton Auberge on the south bank of the river, which is full of mock antiques and bears the legend above the fireplace 'ICY DOULCE FRANCE'. Alternatively, if you can't make it that far, Bond can recommend 'that farmhouse with the wonderful food between Montreuil and Etaples', and then on to the less explored little towns 'like Beaugency, for instance'. Fleming can't even resist giving a word or two of warning to the aspirant Bond motorist: beware 'the dangerous crossroads where Le Touquet's quiet N38 meets the oily turbulence of the major N1'. The reader could make a mental note to watch that turning next time, or try another route.

When in France, Bond follows Fleming's own well-trodden paths almost exactly. But as the series continued, Fleming discovered that he needed to have new adventures to sustain the Bond fantasy, for France and Jamaica were becoming all too familiar. A perfect opportunity came in 1959, after his seventh novel, *Goldfinger*, was published; Leonard Russell, the features editor of the *Sunday Times*, asked Ian to make a five-week trip around the world, visiting the most exciting cities it had to offer. Russell suggested that Ian could write this up into a series of articles entitled 'Thrilling Cities', and then publish them as a book. At first Fleming demurred: he was, he admitted, the world's worst sightseer, and he had no interest in art galleries, museums or any of the standard tourist fare. 'We don't want that sort of thing from you,' replied Russell. 'In your James Bond books, even if people can't put up with James Bond and those fancy heroines of yours, they seem to like the exotic backgrounds. Surely you want to pick up some material for your stories? It's a wonderful opportunity.' Indeed it was, as Fleming did want to go around the world, preferably at someone else's expense. What he found excited him and depressed him in equal measure, and provoked a fundamental change in the world of 007.

Fleming's first stop was Hong Kong, where he was lucky enough to find another enthusiastic guide in the Kalkavan mode: Richard Hughes, the larger-than-life Australian correspondent of the *Sunday Times*. Hughes, the model for Dikko Henderson in *You Only Live Twice*, was a vast, irrepressible Hemingway type of hero, who seemed to have the inside track on everything from drug gangs to spies. As a result, Fleming adored Hong Kong: it was 'the most vivid and exciting city I have ever seen'. Macao, the

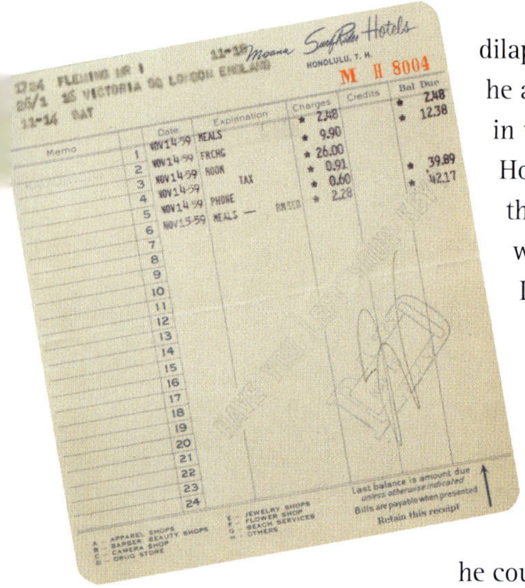

dilapidated Portuguese colony next door, was equally stimulating; there he and Hughes played Foo-tan (a board game Fleming had read about in the adventures of Fu Manchu) and visited the nine-storey 'Central Hotel', the highest and possibly largest brothel in the world. Fleming then met the legendary Dr Lobo, the gold smuggler, 'whose name is whispered with awe throughout the East'. Somewhat predictably, Lobo was nothing like Arno Goldfinger: he was a small, slight man resembling a dentist, who lived in a kind of 'tropical Wimbledon'. This disappointment did not dampen Ian's new-found enthusiasm for all things eastern. The streets were clean, and the people were good-looking and polite. Most of all he admired 'the discretion of the Orient, its desire to please, compared with the blatancy of the me-first-you-nowhere that awaited across the Pacific'. As far as he could see, 'East and West meet only in their love of whisky.'

His appetite whetted, Ian flew on to Tokyo with Hughes in tow, and found his initial reservations about being in the country of a former 'bad enemy' instantly overcome. He stayed at an authentic Japanese inn, had a massage from a Brigitte Bardot lookalike named 'Kissy' (he later changed her name to 'Baby'), composed haiku with geishas, and drank gallons of sake. Like James Bond in the first half of *You Only Live Twice*, Fleming was both confused and charmed by the customs of this utterly different culture. 'In the East,' he wrote approvingly, 'sex is a delightful pastime totally unconnected with sin – a much lighter, airier affair than in the West.'

Hawaii and Chicago were further stops on the 1960 Thrilling Cities *tour. The Ambassador Hotel was to be the scene of Robert Kennedy's assassination eight years later.*

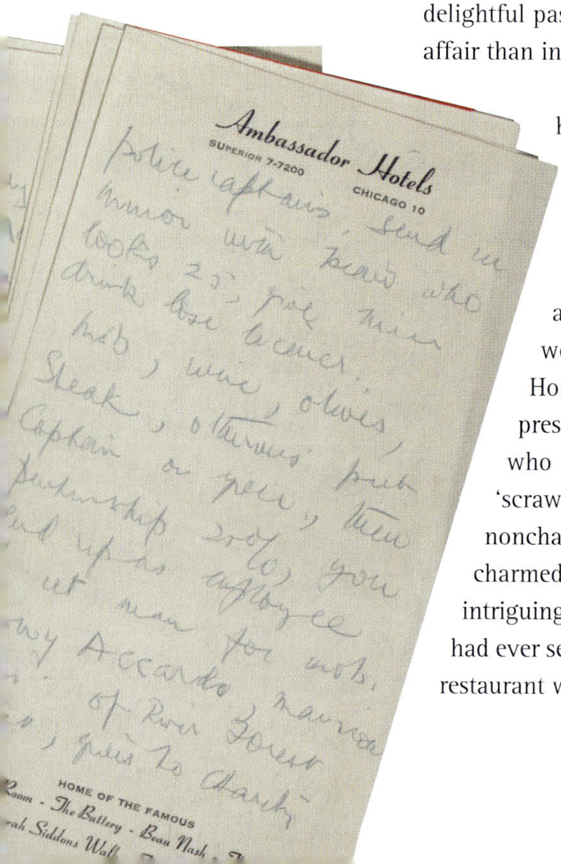

Fleming left Tokyo for Hawaii on Friday the 13th, which he took to be a bad omen, and so it proved to be when 2,000 miles out into the Pacific Ocean one engine of his DC-6 caught fire. Ian was truly grateful for the tiny island of Wake, where the plane put in an emergency landing. Here he met a man who quarantined parrots en route to America and spent his long, solitary hours teaching the birds dirty words to shock their new owners. When Ian finally arrived in Honolulu he found it physically beautiful, but marred by the presence of great hordes of unsightly American pensioners, who spoiled the beaches with their huge blue-veined thighs, 'scrawny necks and sagging bosoms garlanded with leis'. The nonchalant beachbum surfers intimidated, the monkey in the zoo charmed, and Ian took a certain relish in seeking out a restaurant intriguingly named M's Smoke House. Who was M? he asked; no one had ever seen him. It fitted perfectly. 'Sly old devil!' Unfortunately the restaurant was closed.

From there Fleming continued on to Los Angeles, where the policemen impressed him and the movie moguls did not, then Las Vegas, which he had visited before in the company of Ernie Cuneo when researching *Diamonds are Forever*. The airport welcomed visitors with a machine that administered a small shot of pure oxygen through a rubber mouthpiece (Bond tries this out in *Diamonds are Forever*), and to his delight Fleming won so much on the slot machines that his leg was anchored to the floor with all the loose change that accumulated in his pocket. He left the strip $100 dollars up, slipped three stolen ashtrays into his suitcase, and flew on to Chicago. In contrast to the desert gambling town, it was icily cold and full of ghosts. It was also the only place where he decided to visit an art gallery, and he was pleasantly surprised to find Cézannes, Gaugins and Picassos that surpassed anything in Paris. He also insisted on being taken to the garage that was the site of the St Valentine's Day massacre, and to Silver Frolics to watch the hottest striptease in town. 'It was', he declared, 'a display of positively exquisite boredom.'

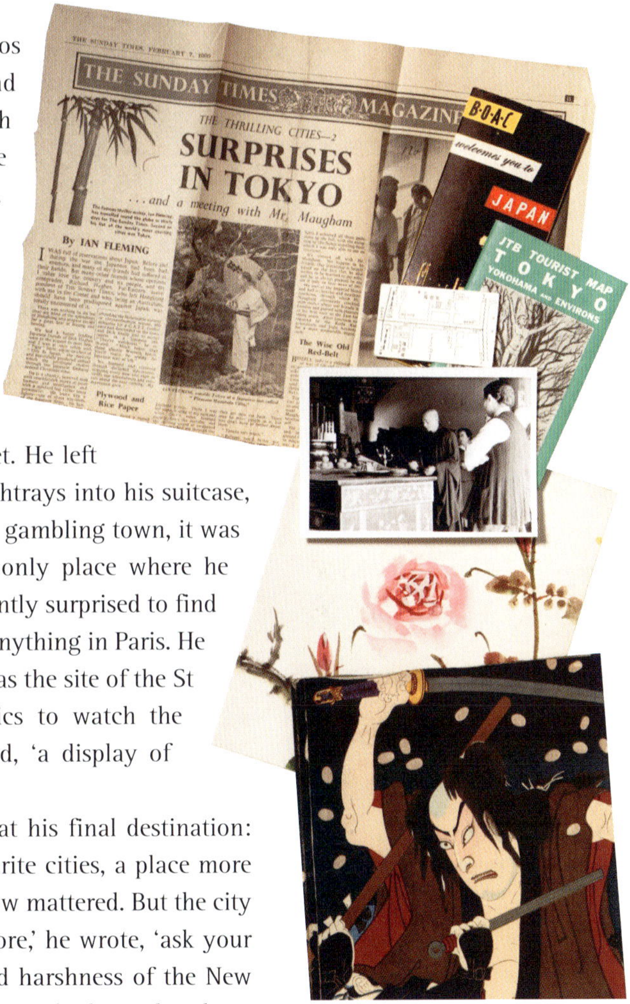

Bond's visit to Tokyo is well documented in You Only Live Twice. *Artefacts from Fleming's trip in 1960 include a flower painting made for him by a geisha* (centre).

A month after setting off, Fleming arrived at his final destination: New York. This had long been one of his favourite cities, a place more than any other where his old traveller's know-how mattered. But the city now failed to impress. 'Go into the first drugstore,' he wrote, 'ask your way from a passer-by, and the indifference and harshness of the New Yorker cuts the old affection for the city out of your body as sharply as a surgeon's knife.' Ian's disaffection for this once-great city was so strong that when the American edition of *Thrilling Cities* was published, his American publisher asked him to tone it down. He didn't, but by way of consolation added the little-known short story '007 in New York', which is certainly less bilious but touched by the same air of bruised nostalgia. In it James Bond travels to Manhattan to warn a secret-service agent that her boyfriend is a member of the KGB. 007 also finds that the St Regis isn't what it was; the best restaurants have been captured by a new breed of 'expense account aristocracy' (which, if Bond paused to consider, is precisely what he is); and, worst of all, Solange, his New York girlfriend – appropriately employed in the indoor-games department of Abercrombie's – won't stop gargling with TCP. Nevertheless, 'New York does have everything', and this story details James Bond's sole recorded shopping expedition, in which Fleming's 'inside intelligence' informs the

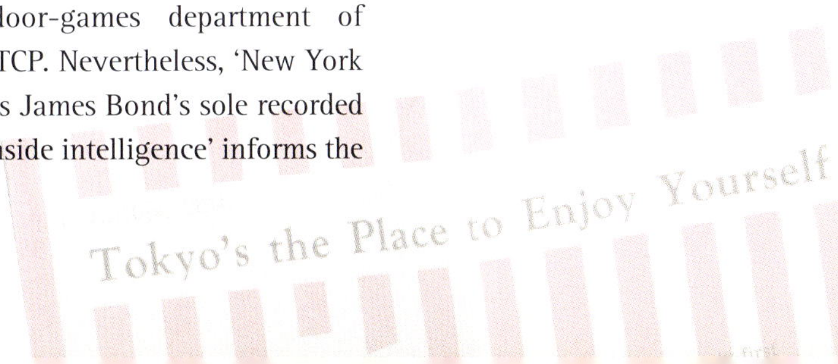

reader where to buy 'half a dozen incomparable Owens toothbrushes' and a particular brand of French golf sock.

Having recovered from this exhausting circum-navigation, the following summer Fleming set off at the wheel of his Thunderbird on a tour of the thrilling cities of Europe. He loved Hamburg – particularly the guiltless sex of the legalized brothels – found Berlin sinister, was charmed by splendidly frivolous Austrians and their incompetent efforts to extract his money in Vienna, met Charlie Chaplin in Geneva, and thought Monte Carlo had become rather seedy. At the end of it all he was able to volunteer some reasonably well-informed opinions on the state of the world, and his conclusion was strikingly simple: 'Go East, young man.' Fleming could not recall meeting a single Briton between Hong Kong and New York (though he did not stop in Australia or New Zealand), and, as he saw it, the Americans had entirely taken over that corner of the globe. 'Baseball, amusement arcades, hot dogs, hideously large bosoms, neon lighting,' spits Tiger Tanaka, the head of the Japanese secret service, in *You Only Live Twice* –'these are part of our payment for defeat in battle.' As far as Fleming was concerned, this trend could be reversed (and by implication British influence re-established) only if 'the spirit of adventure which opened the Orient to us can be rekindled and our youth can heave itself off its featherbed and stream out and off across the world again'. And, anyway, cricket is 'a much more difficult and skilful game than football'.

Fleming's quirky, unusual travel book proved a fascinating snapshot of the world in 1960. 'Dear old Ian,' wrote Leonard Russell, his editor: 'part sensational journalist, part die-hard old club man, part ruthless revolutionary.' Another friend described Fleming's articles as 'the perfect guide for the armchair fornicator'. Either way, the *Thrilling Cities* adventure had enabled Ian to see for himself the British Empire's rapid retreat from the lands of pine and palm, and there was no denying that the world had changed. 'Nowadays', says Milton Krest, the villain of the short story 'The Hildebrand Rarity', written soon after Ian's return, 'there were only three powers – America, Russia and China. That was the big poker game and no other country had either the chips or the cards to come into it. Occasionally some pleasant little country . . . like England would be lent some money so that they could take a hand with the grown-ups. But that was just being polite like one sometimes had to be – to a chum in one's club who'd gone broke.'

This sentiment, designed to rile Bond (which it does), was more or less Ian's own, and, even though he didn't like the situation, he somewhat grudgingly realized that from now on the only way to retain James Bond's credibility on the world stage was to remove him from the Cold War altogether. From 1960 onward, a little over halfway through the Bond canon, 007 no longer single-handedly takes on the might of the Soviet Union. Instead, he tussles with minor villains or else is locked in gladiatorial combat with SPECTRE – and finally Blofeld himself. In this way, Fleming made sure that Bond, M, Churchill, the Queen, and Great Britain would for ever be on the winning side, whatever the true state of the world.

Fleming kept mementoes from various airlines, journeys by plane then being a relatively novel experience.

THE SPY WHO LOVED ME

1962

by Ian Fleming wit
Vivienne Mitchell

First line

I was running away.

Story

The Spy Who Loved Me is an oddity in the Fleming canon. It is not a secret-service story and it is told from a female perspective, in the first person, by the Bond girl Vivienne Michel (her surname was changed to Mitchell in the fictional co-author credit that Fleming gave her for that book). Vivienne begins by narrating the backstory of her sexual awakening, first with Derek, an Etonian schoolboy on his way to Oxford, and then with Kurt, her German boss. Both encounters leave Viv disillusioned and depressed by men. Here Fleming allows himself more licence than usual, and the fire of Viv's passion goes further than his descriptions of sex in any other book. Eventually Viv returns to Canada (her birthplace), where she buys a Vespa and sets out on a road trip down the east coast to Florida. She does not get far before arriving at the Dreamy Pines Motor Court in New York State, a motel that is about to shut up for the winter. The manager offers her a temporary job for the last few days of the season, and leaves her to shut up the motel on closing day. That evening Sluggsy and Horror turn up – two lunatic gangsters who claim to be from the 'insurance company', but actually have come to burn the motel down. It doesn't take them long to start knocking Viv about and promising hideous tortures to follow. At the beginning of Chapter 10, two-thirds of the way through the novel, there is a knock at the door and another gangster turns up, who turns out to be James Bond asking for a room for the night. Bond promises to help the beleaguered Viv, and lures the thugs into thinking they have shot him as he lies sleeping in his cabin. Sluggsy and Horror proceed to torch the motel, Bond rescues Viv, and a furious gun battle begins in which Bond makes a number of uncharacteristic mistakes. Eventually the villains crash their car into the lake, and with that Vivienne and Bond retire to bed. But Sluggsy is still alive, and makes a last macabre appearance at their window. Just as he attempts to kill them for a third time, Bond draws his weapon from beneath his pillow and fires first. In the morning 007 is gone, leaving Vivienne to be lectured by the Canadian police chief about the pitfalls of falling for dangerous men. But it is too late: James Bond has cast his spell.

Last line

A secret agent? I didn't care what he did. A number? I had already forgotten it. I knew exactly who he was and what he was. And everything, every smallest detail, would be written on my heart forever.

Inspirations

The first section, describing Vivienne's sexual awakening with an Etonian boy named Derek (Fleming later removed the references to his old school), is drawn directly from Fleming's own teenage years and his stolen afternoons around Cookham when he was supposed to be at Sandhurst. He admitted to a friend that, unlike his heroine, he had lost his virginity in a box at the back of the Royalty Kinema in Windsor. (Viv would have done too, had the manager not burst in on her and Derek.) The Dreamy Pines Motor Court was also inspired by a real place, a motel in the Adirondacks in upstate New York that Fleming drove past on his way to stay with his friend Ivar Bryce at Black Hollow Farm. Despite using the unfamiliar female voice of Viv, Fleming claimed that this exercise in ventriloquism was the easiest book he ever wrote. It was also the shortest – which was probably just as well, given its reception.

What the readers said

'Just one thing – you oughtna done it'

'This book does not belong in a public library any more than a packet of garbage does'

'It was a great disappointment to me that James Bond did not put in an appearance until near the end. My only consolation is that I have enjoyed your previous works so much that I shall overlook this abortion'

'Now look here Fleming, this catering to fifth-form eroticism must stop. Do you hear?'

What the critics said

'Oh Dear Oh Dear Oh Dear! And to think of the books Mr Fleming once wrote!' – *Daily Telegraph*

'His ability to invent a plot has deserted him almost entirely, and he has had to substitute for a fast-moving story the sorry misadventures of an upper-class tramp, told in dreary detail' – *Glasgow Herald*

'As if Mickey Spillane had tried to gatecrash his way into the Romantic Novelists' Association' – John Fletcher, *The Times*

What Fleming said

In the wake of the backlash from both fans and reviewers, Fleming wrote an extraordinary letter to Michael Howard, his editor at Jonathan Cape, explaining why he had written the book:

I had become increasingly surprised to find that my thrillers, which were designed for an adult audience, were being read in schools, and that young people were making a hero out of James Bond . . . So it crossed my mind to write a cautionary tale about Bond, to put the record straight in the minds particularly of younger readers.

It was impossible to do this in my usual narrative style and I therefore invented the fiction of a heroine through whom I could examine Bond from the other end of the gun barrel, so to speak. This I did by telling the story in her own words of her upbringing and lovelife, which consisted of two incidents, both of which were of a strongly cautionary nature.

The trouble she then got into with the gangsters was of the normal American thriller variety . . . And just to remove some further 'heroism' from Bond, he is depicted as making a considerable hash of his subsequent fight with the gangsters. After the love scene with the heroine which Bond breaks off in a most cursory fashion, there follows a long homily from the chief detective warning the heroine, and the readers, that Bond himself is in fact no better than the gangsters. And on that note the book closes.

I haven't bothered to explain my reasons for writing this book before and I only do so now because the experiment has obviously gone very much awry, and I am in general being criticized for doing almost the exact opposite of what I intended.

TO MY READERS:
I found what follows lying on my desk one morning. As you will see, it appears to be the first-person story of a young woman, evidently beautiful and not unskilled in the arts of love. According to her story, she appears to have been involved, both perilously and romantically, with the same James Bond whose secret-service exploits I myself have written from time to time. With the manuscript was a note signed 'Vivienne Michel' assuring me that what she had written was 'purest truth and from the depths of her heart.' I was interested in this view of James Bond, through the wrong end of the telescope, so to speak, and, after obtaining official clearance for certain minor infringements of the Official Secrets Act, I have much pleasure in sponsoring its publication.
IAN FLEMING

The handwritten title of the Cape edition signalled a departure from the 'stencil' style of previous Chopping covers (see page 231). The title page was also a first, in co-crediting Vivienne Mitchell, the alter ego of the female protagonist and narrator of the story. Much of the action centres on the Dreamy Pines Motor Court motel.

AN INVENTED SECRET SERVICE

Punching Above its Weight

James Bond's secret service – 'Universal Export' as it is known – is another of Fleming's clever cocktails of fact and fantasy. The recipe included a large measure of his most beloved British institution, the wartime Royal Navy, laced with what he knew of the real SIS, the Secret Intelligence Service, and his own idiosyncratic notions of what that service should be like. Bond's secret service had to be an invention: the real business of spying, as Fleming knew, reeked of cynicism and opportunism, and was coloured a thousand shades of grey. As he told a reader in 1958, 'The trouble is that it is much more fun to think up fantastic situations and mix Bond up in them. The ordinary spy world is, in fact, a very drab one and, while a great book waits to be written about it, I am not the one to write it.' Nevertheless, he always claimed that everything he wrote had a precedent in truth, and this is also true of his invented secret service.

When it came to spying, Fleming was an outsider. He had never been a paid-up member of an intelligence service during peacetime, though he did have an acute appreciation of the SIS, which during the 1950s was in a state of transition. The old-fashioned enthusiastic amateurism of the wartime service was finally giving way to a more modern, professional organization. Technology was at the heart of this revolution: in 1956 the Americans began testing their U-2 spy plane, a reconnaissance aircraft that flew on the edge of space and was able to bring back detailed information on Russian targets. Fleming realized that the U-2s, and the spy satellites which would follow them, were rapidly turning his beloved world of spy versus spy into a rusting heap. Their intelligence was 'more voluminous and more accurate than could have been obtained by a

The Cuban Missile Crisis, the 1962 face-off between the USA and the USSR, epitomized the climate of paranoia that reigned during the Cold War. America disliked having Cuba on its doorstep but outside its orbit, and was suspicious of the close links between Castro and Khrushchev.

million ground spies – if one could have got them in there and out again, which one couldn't'.

Nevertheless, the white heat of modern spy technology never dampened Ian's romantic enthusiasm for the second oldest profession in the world. The great game of spying had been played 'ever since the man from the opposition crept under the tent flap in the desert', he wrote in 1962, 'and listened to the plans of the enemy tribal chiefs and then, with luck, ran all night with the news to where the camp fires of his own side were burning away in the hills. It has gone on like that all through human history, and it is like the most exciting of all human adventure stories – the single man, in the darkness, facing death alone for the sake of the great mass of his own countrymen.' For Fleming, this is the heart of the matter. Spying is a solitary, dangerous business in which the spy is expendable, and he knows it. That is why he is paid the danger money; that is why he is afraid of what the guards will do to his genitals if he is caught. 'And believe me,' wrote Fleming knowingly, 'it is those things the professional spy thinks of far more than death itself.'

Given that he had no personal experience of the SIS, it is unsurprising that Fleming should have looked to the wartime Department of Naval Intelligence for inspiration, and the language of the navy saturates the Bond books. The sky is invariably 'gunmetal' or battleship grey;

Strangways – the head of the SIS station in Jamaica – has 'a black patch over the right eye and the sort of aquiline good looks you associate with the bridge of a destroyer'. 'Crash dive,' whispers Mary Ann Russell in 'From a View to a Kill', and Bond knows immediately what this means: this submariner's term has become secret-service slang for very bad news indeed. The navy was also responsible for the prefix 007. 'When I was at the Admiralty during the war,' Fleming told an interviewer, 'all the top secret signals had the double-O prefix. Although this was later changed for security reasons, it stuck in my mind and I decided to borrow it for Bond to make his job more interesting and provide him with a licence to kill.' 0070 had a particular significance. It was the German diplomatic code used to send the 'Zimmermann telegram' from Berlin to the German ambassador in Washington during the First World War. The Department of Naval Intelligence's great feat in cracking this code brought the United States into the war on the British side (there was a brief moment when it seemed the Americans might be potential enemies), and it was celebrated ever afterwards by the use of the double-O prefix on top-secret naval documents.

M

The head of the British Secret Intelligence Service was, and still is, known as 'C'. In the 1950s this was a taboo subject, so as an in-joke Fleming's 'M' might refer to Colonel Sir Stewart Menzies, the head of the SIS during the Second World War. M was the letter by which Colin Gubbins was known as head of the French section of SOE and Fleming also called his mother 'Mie' – or M.

Not surprisingly, as the Bond cult has grown there has been considerable speculation that Fleming was being economical with the truth over his famous 007. This is based on his own love of a practical joke and the ardent fan's natural desire to find layers of meaning where there are none. 007, it has been pointed out, has a much older origin: John Dee, the astrologer alchemist and spy at the court of Elizabeth I, used to prefix all his secret documents for the Queen with 007, the two zeros representing a pair of eyes, indicating that they were for her eyes only. The Duke of Marlborough used a 00 code when communicating with his spies during the War of the Spanish Succession (1701–14), and the zipcode of the Georgetown area of Washington, D.C., where many CIA agents live, is 20007. .007 is also the name of a locomotive that Kipling wrote a story about in 1898. And of course the number seven has any number of special connotations, be they sins, virtues, hills of Rome, etc. The truth is that Fleming knew a good-sounding number when he saw one, and, having seen it on the top of

MISS MONEYPENNY

M's secretary. Named after a character in The Sett, *an unfinished novel by Peter Fleming. Possibly inspired by Miss Pettigrew, the real secretary of Stewart Menzies of the SIS. In the first draft of* Casino Royale *she was Miss Pettavel ('Petty').*

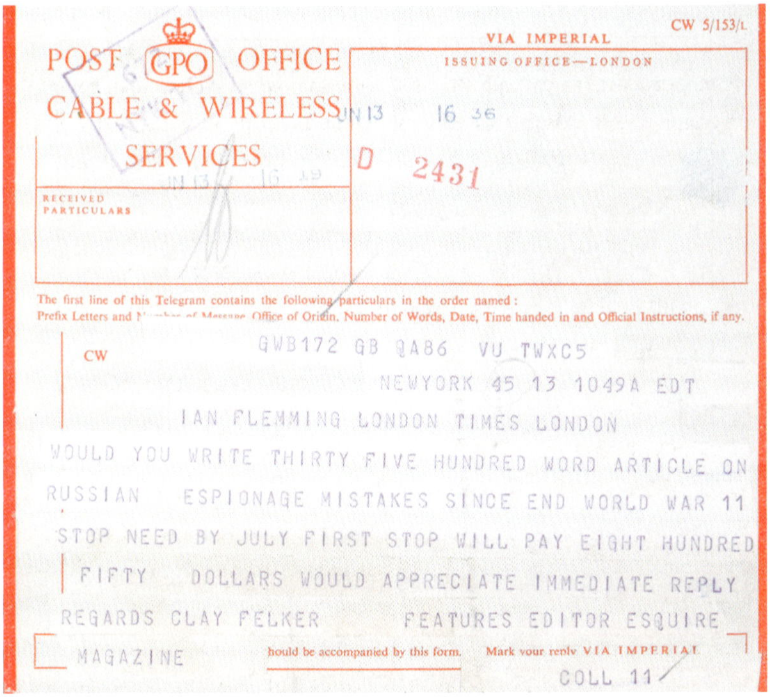

CW 5/153/L
VIA IMPERIAL
POST GPO OFFICE
CABLE & WIRELESS
SERVICES
ISSUING OFFICE—LONDON
JN 13 16 36
D 2431
RECEIVED PARTICULARS
The first line of this Telegram contains the following particulars in the order named:
Prefix Letters and Number of Message, Office of Origin, Number of Words, Date, Time handed in and Official Instructions, if any.
CW
GWB172 GB QA86 VU TWXC5
NEWYORK 45 13 1049A EDT
IAN FLEMMING LONDON TIMES LONDON
WOULD YOU WRITE THIRTY FIVE HUNDRED WORD ARTICLE ON
RUSSIAN ESPIONAGE MISTAKES SINCE END WORLD WAR 11
STOP NEED BY JULY FIRST STOP WILL PAY EIGHT HUNDRED
FIFTY DOLLARS WOULD APPRECIATE IMMEDIATE REPLY
REGARDS CLAY FELKER FEATURES EDITOR ESQUIRE
MAGAZINE
...hould be accompanied by this form. Mark your reply VIA IMPERIAL
COLL 11

Fleming's special status as bestselling novelist and supposed 'insider' in the world of intelligence made him much in demand as a commentator on related matters of the day.

secret Admiralty communiqués, the likelihood is that he decided to use it, somehow, in the novel that he would one day get around to writing.

At the head of Fleming's fictional service is M, Admiral Sir Miles Messervy, a man who gave up the prospect of becoming the Fifth Sea Lord to become the head of the secret service. With his 'keen sailor's face' and 'damnably clear eyes' he appears at first to be a glamorized version of Admiral Sir John Godfrey, Fleming's boss as Director of Naval Intelligence during the war. Godfrey, like M, had piercing blue eyes and an irascible manner, and he inspired utter devotion in Fleming. In the world of James Bond, M is held in similar esteem: he stands third in line behind the Queen and Churchill, and in the more far-flung SIS stations such as Istanbul, M is God. As a sailor, M 'thinks the language of battleships', keeps his tobacco in a sliced-off fourteen-pound shell base, and lives in a house named Quarterdeck, which is awash with naval bric-a-brac. Added to this bellicose naval exterior is a manner that is hardly endearing. Kingsley Amis noted that 'His demeanour or voice is described as abrupt, angry (three times), brutal, cold (seven times), curt, dry (five), frosty (two), gruff (seven), hard (three), impatient (seven), irritable (two), moody, severe, sharp (two), short (four), sour (two), stern and testy (five).'

It is just as well that Commander Bond – another ex-navy man –

knows how to handle the old monster; in his obituary notice M credits 007 with possessing 'what almost amounted to "The Nelson Touch" in moments of the highest emergency'. Though interviews with M were not quite that, as the favourite son Bond is almost always able to put up with his testy boss, whose 'cold voice he loved and obeyed'. He even agrees to do M's dirty work – such as cheating at cards (*Moonraker*) and assassinating the villains who have murdered his friends ('For Your Eyes Only'). Many defenders of Bond considered this last assignment irresponsible and morally corrupt, which Fleming never denied, and John Godfrey was quick to distance himself from this aspect of the character he had inspired. 'James Bond got out of hand and became ridiculous,' he wrote in a note after Fleming's death.

> Similarly he turned me into that unsavoury character, M. With a little care M could have become an adequate and interesting head of the Secret Service . . . M might have taken his place amongst the Victorian eccentrics, but could not exist among my contemporaries of the mid-twentieth century and he had no business to authorize murder and acts of major sabotage. Ian wanted people to take M seriously and questioned me closely about his notional age and career. The end result did not convince or thrill.

Godfrey may have disliked Fleming's cantankerous creation, but if he found the Victorian eccentric unbelievable in a modern secret service he was forgetting the formidable 'Colonel Z', Claude Dansey, head of the Z Organization. Z was an amateur spy ring made up mostly of journalists and businessmen. Before the war it provided the SIS with intelligence it could not afford to gather itself, and when hostilities began Dansey became Stewart Menzies' deputy. Dansey, who had been a spy ever since the relief of Mafeking (during the Boer War), chose to distrust just about everyone he met and everything he read, and his direct, pungent wit ensured that agents often left his office after a briefing with tears in their eyes. 'The only truly terrifying man in the SIS,' thought Malcolm Muggeridge, 'the only real professional.' To Hugh Trevor-Roper, who was exactly the type of university-educated agent that Dansey held in ill-concealed contempt, Colonel Z was 'an utter shit, corrupt, incompetent, but with a certain low cunning'. Dansey, like Fleming, was an habitué of White's and Boodle's, and perhaps it was here that Fleming met him, if not through Conrad O'Brien-ffrench, the Z spy whom Fleming had encountered in Kitzbühel before the war.

LOELIA PONSONBY

Bond's secretary. 'Loelia' was the name of Ann Fleming's friend Loelia, Duchess of Westminster.

Alongside John Godfrey and Claude Dansey, Fleming had another, fictional, model for his head of the secret service: the shifty 'R', who occupies the same post in Somerset Maugham's *Ashenden* stories. These thinly fictionalized accounts of the author's own experiences as a spy during the First World War were so truthful that Winston Churchill forced Maugham to destroy fourteen of them (sixteen survived), as in his view they contravened the Official Secrets Act. Ashenden is Maugham himself, a detached observer in this grey world, who tolerates human weakness and accepts it – in total contrast to R, who is utterly unscrupulous, takes no risks, trusts no one, and regards everyone as expendable. Maugham condemns this self-serving, immoral type of man, which he presumably encountered himself. 'Though ready enough to profit by the activities of obscure agents of whom they had never heard, they shut their eyes to the dirty work so that they could put their clean hands on their hearts and congratulate themselves that they had never done anything that was unbecoming to men of honour.' This describes R, but it could just as well be M. R even spoke like him:

> 'He's known as the Hairless Mexican.'
> 'Why?'
> 'Because he's hairless and because he's a Mexican.'

If R was a fictional model for M, Claude Dansey his real-life counterpart, and John Godfrey was what he looked like, Fleming discovered that he was rather good at playing the role himself. When Gary Powers, the American pilot of a U-2 spy plane, was shot down by the Russians in Soviet airspace in 1962, Fleming wrote a polemic for the *Sunday Times* on how his fictional M (and therefore himself) would have reacted to the crisis had Powers been one of his agents. M would deny all knowledge, and claim that the pilot was delusional and had hijacked the U-2 himself. As a spy, Gary Powers should be treated as one and thrown to the dogs. '"He was expendable," he barked. "Expend him!"'

Having created his naval superstructure, Fleming welded on elements of the real secret service that he knew of through his friends in the intelligence world. During the 1950s the SIS was still a highly secretive, introspective organization that officially did not exist. The public was

THE HEAD OF THE JAMAICA STATION

This secret-service post had three incumbents, all of whom Ian Fleming named after men he knew: Charles da Silva, the first (in Casino Royale*), was based on the real-life Charles de Costa, who had a business in Kingston. Then came John Fox Strangways – an old-Etonian friend – who was murdered at the beginning of* Dr No, *along with his faithful secretary Una Trueblood, the name of Fleming's secretary at the* Sunday Times. *They were replaced by Commander Ross, head of the Jamaica station in* The Man with the Golden Gun, *named after Ian's friend Alan Ross, editor of the* London Magazine.

expected to believe that spies were diplomats working for the Foreign Office, and politicians were not allowed to ask questions about the SIS or its activities. As an outsider, Fleming had nothing to reveal, but he did count many agents among his friends, including Nick Elliott, a high-ranking SIS officer, and the traitor Kim Philby. In James Bond's obituary at the end of *You Only Live Twice*, Fleming even jokes about his hero's tenuous relationship with the real world of espionage: 'If the quality of these books, or their degree of veracity, had been any higher, the author would have certainly been prosecuted under the Official Secrets Act. It is a measure of the disdain in which these fictions are held at the Ministry, that action has not yet – I emphasize the qualification – been taken against the author and publisher of these high-flown and romanticized caricatures of episodes in the career of an outstanding public servant.' This was true, and over the course of fourteen books Fleming never once incurred the wrath of the censor.

FELIX LEITER

Bond's CIA companion. 'Felix' was Ivar Bryce's second name, and Tommy Leiter was a mutual American friend.

The elements of the real SIS that Fleming appropriated were principally the props of the wartime service. The SIS was then based at Broadway Buildings, opposite St James's Park tube station, and was similar in design to Fleming's austere Regent's Park creation. 'Universal Export' was another insider joke, as this was one of a number of covers that wartime SOE agents used when requisitioning valuable items. The real plaque on the wall beside the door at Broadway read 'Minimax Fire Extinguisher Company', later changed to the equally misleading 'Government Communications Department'. The lobby was also deceptive, staffed by two ordinary-looking concierges who did not attempt to apprehend anyone coming in to shelter from the rain. C's office, a deeply carpeted room on the fourth floor, was approached by its own secret staircase, which led into an anteroom flanked by two secretaries. There was a green light outside the door, which flicked to red when C was not to

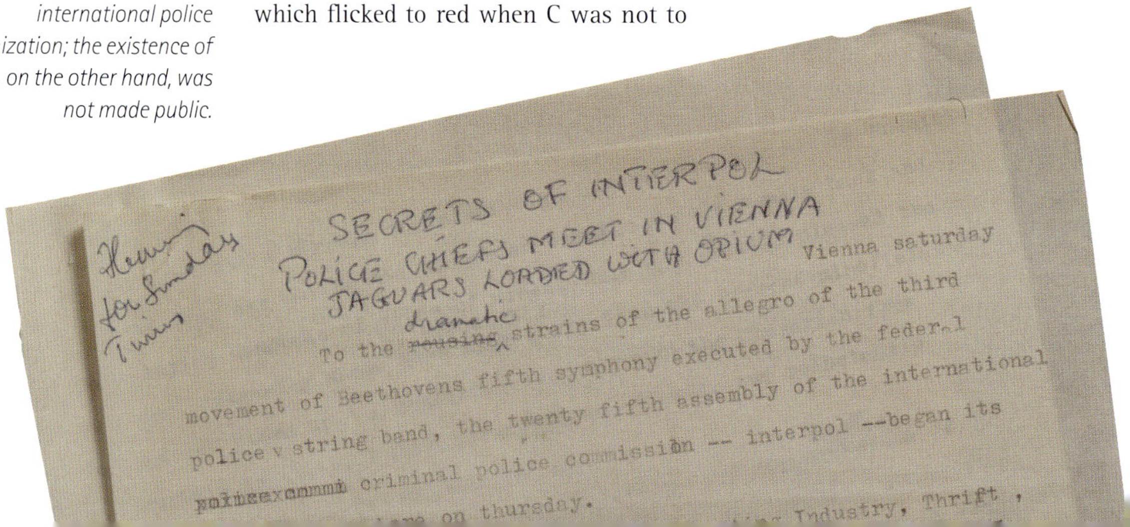
SECRETS OF INTERPOL
POLICE CHIEFS MEET IN VIENNA
JAGUARS LOADED WITH OPIUM

Vienna saturday

To the ~~rousing~~ dramatic strains of the allegro of the third movement of Beethovens fifth symphony executed by the federal police string band, the twenty fifth assembly of the international ~~policexcommi~~ criminal police commission -- interpol --began its ... on thursday.

... Industry, Thrift ,

This article is filed with material from 1955–6. Interpol was a known international police organization; the existence of SIS, on the other hand, was not made public.

be disturbed. Like M, C sat behind a huge Admiralty desk, brought in by the first incumbent of the post, Sir Mansfield Cumming, and he was entitled to use his own green ink, which denoted that anything written in it was from him alone.

The SIS did have stations around the world, where officers used a variety of covers: in *Dr No*, for instance, the local agent is referred to as the 'Passport Control Officer', a real cover used by the SIS ever since the First World War. Fleming was able to use this cover with impunity only because it had been recently discarded in favour of 'Visa Officer'. These foreign agents – in Fleming's world, men like Darko Kerim – made up the small army of semi-professionals who supplied intelligence and supported a much smaller nucleus of men and women employed to spy full-time. In *Dr No* Fleming stated that there were only 2,000 of these agents worldwide, who earned approximately £1,500 a year. These figures were either so wide of the mark or so inoffensive that they provoked no reaction from the government. However, a contemporary insider confirmed that men and women 'enter the service because the lure of excitement means more to them than money, or because patriotic motives drive harder than a desire for monetary gain'. So Bond, the patriot, was not as fictional as he might appear. And this was not the only aspect of his portrayal that contained a grain of truth.

QUARREL

Dr No

This fisherman working for the secret service was based on Aubyn Cousins, a Jamaican fisherman with striking light-grey eyes and a name that confirmed his descent from the captain of a nineteenth-century schooner. He and Fleming would go out in a boat and attempt to lasso sharks.

TIGER TANAKA

You Only Live Twice

Head of the Japanese secret service. Inspired by Tiger Saito, the editor of the magazine This is Japan *and Ian Fleming's guide around that country.*

In Fleming's fictional secret service, James Bond belongs to the most elite section, the double O, staffed by the handful of men who have earned a licence to kill. This sounds like a fantasy, yet in the ten years following the end of the Second World War real SIS agents did, it seems, have a licence to kill. Qualification is needed here, as the evidence is patchy – primarily because the SIS (meaning MI5 and MI6) has never had to submit any documents to the Public Record Office. All that is known of its activities comes either from heavily censored memoirs of former agents or from controversial autobiographies published against the government's wishes, such as Peter Wright's *Spycatcher*, published in Australia in 1985. Though agents probably did not go around with Berettas in their waistbands and knives hidden in their shoe heels, there is evidence that the SIS did carry out assassinations. These were undertaken not by a 00 section, but by a variety of deniable agencies – the SPA (the Special Political Action group), the SAS, or a third party hired to do a 'wet job'.

In October 1949 armed teams of British agents landed on the shores of Albania, intending to use covert action to detach the country from Soviet orbit. The KGB had already received a tip-off that they were coming, courtesy of the duplicitous SIS agent Kim Philby, and the agents were consequently rounded up, imprisoned and then, in 1954, ignominiously paraded before the world's press in a show trial organized by Enver Hoxha, the Albanian dictator. This foreign adventure was followed in 1956 by another, code-named Operation Straggle, in which the SIS attempted to bolster Britain's declining influence in the Middle East by engineering a coup in Syria. Agents were to be sent in to stir up the Syrian border tribes as a prelude to a full-scale invasion from Iraq, and integral to this plan was the assassination of Gamal Abdel Nasser, the Egyptian president. Anthony Eden, the British prime minister, was obsessed with the 'contrived death' of the Egyptian president, as were several other countries. The French had already attempted to shoot him and failed, and the Israelis had persuaded a Greek waiter to put poison in his coffee, which hadn't worked either. At Eden's request, MI6 tried a few underhand attempts of its own. Having failed in a straightforward assassination attempt using a German mercenary, it then asked the head of Q-branch operations, Major Frank Quinn, to inject a lethal poison into a box of Egyptian Kropje chocolates, which were a particular favourite of Nasser's. Quinn had to take considerable pains to conceal the tiny pinpricks of his needles in the base of each chocolate, and he was concerned about the ethics of enticing innocent people to eat his lethal concoctions. MI6 assured him that such an accident would not happen. However, the British never managed to deliver the poisoned chocolates to their destination, and Nasser was never assassinated by the SIS, or by anyone else.

DIKKO HENDERSON

You Only Live Twice

British station agent in Tokyo. Based on the Australian Richard Hughes, the buccaneering Far East correspondent of the Sunday Times *in Hong Kong.*

NICK NICHOLSON

The Man with the Golden Gun

CIA agent. Named after the secretary of the Royal St George's Golf Club.

The logic behind these adventures, if there was one, was the growing recognition during the Cold War that the Soviets had no scruples, and therefore if the West was to compete it must behave likewise. In America at least, this became a deliberate policy from 1948 onwards. 'It is now clear that we are facing an implacable enemy whose avowed objective is world domination by whatever means and whatever cost,' claimed an American intelligence report produced by ex-president Herbert Hoover. 'There are no rules in such a game. Hitherto acceptable norms of human conduct do not apply . . . concepts of fair play must be reconsidered . . . we must learn to subvert, sabotage and destroy our enemies by more clever, more sophisticated and more effective measures than those used against us.' Of course, this refers only to the CIA, but from the scanty evidence available it seems that a similar attitude had permeated the British secret service. For the most part, the public knew nothing of all this skulduggery, which lay hidden below the waterline of the espionage 'iceberg', as Fleming called it. But every so often these adventures did reach the press, and one instance was the strange tale of Buster Crabb.

Buster Crabb was an ageing, unfit frogman with a heart condition, whose glowing wartime record convinced the SIS that he was the man for a particularly delicate assignment. In 1956 the Soviet president Nikita Khrushchev arrived in England aboard the Russian warship *Ordzhonikidze* on a good-will mission. While the ship lay at anchor in Portsmouth harbour, Crabb was asked by Fleming's friend Nick Elliott to make a covert inspection of the hull, as Naval Intelligence hoped it might be fitted with a device code-named Agouti, which had the effect of silencing the propeller. Crabb made two dives. On the first he realized he was not carrying enough weight; on the second he disappeared altogether. Initially it was thought he might have defected, but six weeks later his headless corpse was washed up on a beach further down the coast. This discovery excited all sorts of wild conspiracy theories – Crabb must have been killed by an underwater sentry or, worse, beheaded by the Russians – and Khrushchev made a public complaint about Crabb's misguided exploit. Anthony Eden, who had expressly forbidden any *Boy's Own* adventures by the SIS during the Soviet visit, was then forced to make a humiliating statement to the House of Commons, and Crabb's cat, so to speak, was let out of the bag.

COLOMBO
'Risico'

'Toad of Toad Hall in Technicolour' was not an agent but an ally – named after Giocchino Colombo, the noted Ferrari engine designer who created the supercharged Ferrari 125 in 1947. Its V12 engine powered many 'Colombo' Ferrari road cars of the 1950s and '60s, including the 250 GTE 2+2, which Ian much admired.

This misadventure undoubtedly inspired the scene in *Thunderball* (1961) in which James Bond sets off to make a nocturnal examination of the hull of the *Disco Volante*, which he suspects contains a secret hatch below the waterline to accommodate a mini-submarine. Here Fleming adds his own twist to the Buster Crabb mystery: in his story, Bond does encounter an underwater sentry, and they fight, but it is the sentry who dies – not by having his head sliced off, but by being eaten by a barracuda.

Fleming may have been faithful to the exploits of the SIS during the Cold War, and he was right to suggest that James Bond was far closer to reality than most people imagined: the bizarre incidents of the Cold War *were* far stranger than most people imagined. But in one area he did his best to ignore that reality.

On 25 May 1951 Guy Burgess and Donald Maclean defected to Moscow. These men, both of whom had been to public school and Cambridge, and recruited into the secret service via the standard old-boy channels, were not considered the sort to betray their country: their background and class should have ensured that they would never indulge in that sort of thing. But both had, though over the years they had cleverly managed to distance themselves from their adolescent Communist sympathies. The eventual likelihood that they had been Soviet agents since the 1930s was aggravated by the sensitive positions they held at the time of their defection. Maclean was then head of the American desk at the Foreign Office, and Burgess until two weeks before

Guy Burgess, Donald Maclean and Kim Philby (shown from left to right) *were part of the notorious 'Cambridge spy ring', and their imminent exposure as agents resulted in their defections to Moscow. The Burgess and Maclean scandal preceded the publication of* Casino Royale; *Philby evaded detection until 1964.*

had been second secretary at the British embassy in Washington. To make matters worse, they had been unmasked not by their own service but by the CIA, and, as their dramatic disappearance indicated, they had evidently been tipped off that they were about to be exposed. Clearly there was a third spy in MI6. The press speculated that the 'third man' was Kim Philby - whom Ian knew - but they had no idea that there was even a fourth man - the art historian Anthony Blunt. Blunt had known Burgess and Maclean since their days at Cambridge during the 1930s, and he continued to spy for the KGB. He did not confess until April 1964 (by which time he was Surveyor of the Queen's Pictures) – and then only on the understanding that he would be offered a lifetime's immunity.

Fleming was fascinated by the defection of Burgess and Maclean. These were men like him, like James Bond, but whose moral unscrupulousness enabled them to betray their country. *Casino Royale*, written in 1952, contains a rare moment of doubt in which Bond wonders whether he is on the right side. 'This country-right-or-wrong business is getting a little out-of-date,' he says. 'Today we are fighting Communism. Okay. If I'd been alive fifty years ago, the brand of Conservatism we have today would have been damn near called Communism and we should have been told to go and fight that. History is moving pretty quickly these days and the heroes and villains keep on changing parts.' This is the closest James Bond ever comes to articulating the ambiguities of his job. Thereafter he is always playing St George in search of a dragon, and the secret service he represents is the finest in the Western world.

To the real CIA the opposite was the case. The defections of Burgess and Maclean only confirmed Washington's deep-held mistrust of the British ruling class and the belief that the British secret service itself was a barrel of rotten apples. The discovery of the 'atom spies' Klaus Fuchs and Alan Nunn May in 1950 was the first cause for alarm. These men, both scientists with Communist backgrounds, had been working on the American nuclear programme and passing on secrets to the Russians for years, undetected by MI5, even though the Americans had alerted the

Bond, the Russians reason, and you will do damage to the entire Western alliance.

The idea of 007 somehow carrying the fate of the world on his shoulders sounds like the most fantastical part of Fleming's imaginary secret service. This, surely, is where fact gives way to fairy tale. But, as ever with Bond, even this wild idea had some basis in truth. Once again Fleming looked back to the war, this time to Richard Sorge – 'the man I regard as the most formidable spy in history'. Sorge was one of a rare breed: born to a German father and a Russian mother, he became a Communist who worked for the Nazis but spied for Stalin. Sorge spent the war in the press department of the German embassy in Tokyo, where this 'brilliant, luxury-loving German' built up an extensive spy ring that stretched right up to the Japanese emperor Hirohito. His high-level contacts enabled him to supply the Soviet leader with several crucial pieces of intelligence. The first of these was the time and date of Operation Barbarossa – the German invasion of Russia on 6 August 1941. Stalin chose to ignore this, as he ignored similar warnings from several other sources – wrongly, as it turned out, illustrating that intelligence alone can never change the course of history: action is always required.

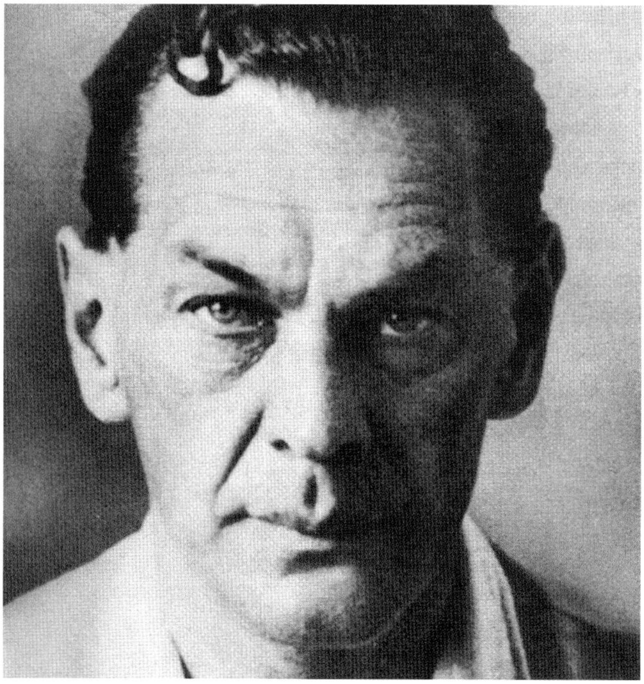

Richard Sorge, seen here in a clipping from the files, was one of Fleming's acknowledged inspirations, and Ian accorded him the highest praise for his achievements as a spy.

The second piece of information, which became more significant because Stalin decided to act upon it, was Sorge's assurance that Japan had no designs on Russia. Sorge had discovered through his sources close to the Emperor that the Japanese intended to push their empire not east, but south and west, towards America. This intelligence allowed Stalin to release the twenty divisions stationed in Siberia, awaiting a Japanese attack, and press them into the defence of Moscow, which was about to be encircled by the German army. It was a move that proved crucial to the fate of the Russian capital, and arguably had an impact on the eventual outcome of the war.

Fleming never met the remarkable Richard Sorge; Sorge's spy ring was exposed in October 1941, and thereafter he was incarcerated, tortured by the Tokkō (the Japanese secret police), and executed in 1944. When Fleming visited Tokyo in 1959 he persuaded his friend Richard Hughes, who had known Sorge, to take him to 'Ketels', the lively and sinister Bierkeller where Sorge had extracted his secrets from the Nazis. He found it had been transformed into a rather drab restaurant, where diners ate along to Pat Boone records. But this could not dampen Ian's enthusiasm for Sorge, 'the most formidable spy in history' – a real example, if any were needed, that an individual spy could shape world events. Just like his own secret agent, James Bond.

1963

The title was taken from a little-known nineteenth-century sailing novel seen by Fleming's friend Nicholas Henderson on a stall in the Portobello Road.

First line

It was one of those Septembers when it seemed that the summer would never end.

Story

On Her Majesty's Secret Service is a complex novel, involving two plots and the second appearance of Bond's enemy from *Thunderball*, Ernst Blofeld. After the flaying Fleming received at the hands of his critics and readers for *The Spy Who Loved Me*, on this next outing he opted to stay on firmer ground, and this novel is widely regarded as one of his best.

The story opens on the beach at Royale-les-Eaux, where Bond is spying on Tracy di Vicenzo, a wild society girl who is attempting to commit suicide. In this she fails. Bond is then surprised to find himself kidnapped and brought before her father, Marc-Ange Draco, the head of the Union Corse, the French mafia. Draco does not want to kill Bond. On the contrary, he wants to pay him a million pounds to marry his daughter (Tracy had slept with Bond the night before), in the hope that he might calm her down. 007 refuses to do this, but he does agree to continue seeing Tracy if Draco can tell him where Blofeld can be found. Bond has spent the last year (since the *Thunderball* novel) on a fruitless trail around the globe, and is on the point of handing in his resignation. It turns out that Blofeld is trying to prove that he is one Comte Balthazar de Bleuville, and has contacted the College of Arms to authenticate his claim. Bond follows this lead, and disguised as Sir Hilary Bray he makes his way to Piz Gloria, Blofeld's alpine hideaway in Switzerland. This extraordinary place is part hotel, part research station, where Blofeld is apparently investigating allergies in the company of his awful secretary, Irma Bunt. Equally intriguing are Blofeld's ten beautiful patients – strapping young girls from different parts of England, whom Blofeld is attempting to cure of their allergies by brainwashing them as they sleep. After several days Blofeld becomes suspicious of Sir Hilary, and Bond escapes on skis, pursued at first by Blofeld's men, then by an avalanche. Bond finds his way to a Christmas fair in the village below, where Tracy suddenly appears to rescue him. A little later – in Zurich Airport – Bond suddenly proposes. Tracy, surprised, accepts. Once back in England Bond reports to M, and it is decided that Blofeld is going to attempt to use biological warfare against Britain, and that his brainwashed girls are to be the unwitting carriers of the viruses. Together with Draco and a team of Union Corse hit men, Bond returns to Piz Gloria by helicopter, and in the battle that follows they blow it up. Blofeld escapes down a bobsleigh run with Bond in hot pursuit, but manages to throw a grenade into the path of 007's sled, sending him careering off down the mountain. Unscathed, Bond still manages to attend his wedding to Tracy on New Year's Day in Munich. As they drive away on honeymoon, a red Maserati tails them, and soon afterwards it pulls level and fires a short burst at Mr and Mrs James Bond. Their car spins to a halt, and when Bond comes around he realizes that Tracy is dead. The assassins, Blofeld and Irma Bunt, have got away.

Last line

The young patrolman took a last scared look at the motionless couple, hurried over to his motor cycle, picked up the hand-microphone, and began talking urgently to the rescue headquarters.

Inspirations

As with golf and gambling, it was inevitable that at some point Ian would draw upon his love of the Alps and use them as a backdrop for a book. Fleming had skied enthusiastically ever since the 1920s, and as a younger, fitter man he had also been a keen mountaineer. Many of these adventures took place at Kitzbühel, including the memorable occasion when he was pursued and then engulfed by an avalanche, which directly inspired James Bond's own escapade in this book.

Ernst Blofeld's Piz Gloria was based upon the Schloss Mittersill, a sporting club in the Austrian Alps that during the 1930s was a playground for European aristocrats and rich Americans. In 1940 the Nazis closed the club down and adapted it to a more sinister purpose: it became the centre for pseudo-scientific studies into the intrinsic inferiority of the Asiatic races, and its beautiful rooms were used to house thousands of skulls from China, India and Tibet. The Schloss Mittersill reverted to an alpine sports club in 1953, and in this book Ian managed to plug both the restaurant and Ursula Andress, 'that beautiful girl with the long fair hair at the big table', whom he had recently met during the filming of *Dr No* in 1962.

The College of Arms was another closed world which, like the diamond trade, Ian enjoyed prising open. His guide to this arcane institution was Robin Mirlees, who held the title of Rouge Dragon (which Ian changed to Sable Basilisk); it was he who researched the family histories of Blofeld and Bond. Ian was delighted to discover that the coat of arms for the Bonds of Peckham bore the legend 'The world is not enough', which could have been designed for James Bond himself.

What the readers said

'Frankly, I'm getting a little worried about Bond. Is he losing his grip? Is it a case of fair wear and tear? Is age taking its toll?'

'Dear Ian Fleming, Quite exceptionally for an author, your profile photograph in today's *Daily Express* reveals you as the type of man that could experience and imagine the thrillers mentioned in your article. The picture also reveals – in spite of the rugged planes of your face – a kindliness and a self-analytical diffidence which does you credit, and keeps your books human, if tough.'

What the critics said

'Solid Fleming' – *Herald Tribune*

'James Bond is what every man would like to be, and what every woman would like between her sheets' – *Sunday Times*

'You can't argue with success . . . but they just aren't writing bad books like they used to' – *New York Times*

'We all know it's formula fiction, don't we? But that doesn't keep us from getting a fine surge of adrenalin in our veins from this novel' – Miles A. Smith, *AP Books and the Arts*

'I'm not so sure *On Her Majesty's Secret Service* is the best to date, [but] certainly I would place it in the first three – which makes it very good indeed' – Gillian Croll, *Books of the Month*

'He's getting a little older. He's starting to look like his middle-aged creator. The time was, in *Goldfinger*, when he could convert a life-long lesbian to heterosexuality in a paragraph or two, but now the lady yields only after he makes good her 40 million-franc gambling debt. Not quite old Bond, that . . . Fleming's new book will not disappoint his millions of fans – as did his last one, *The Spy Who Loved Me*' – *Washington Post*

'Fleming at his urbanely murderous best, a notable chapter in the saga of James Bond' – *Houston Chronicle*

An official-looking stamp spelled out the book title on Richard Chopping's hardback cover. Fleming's knowledge of Europe's ski resorts gave authenticity to the mountain setting.

STRANGER THAN FICTION

The Real Cold War

When Fleming sat down to write *Casino Royale* under warm Jamaican skies in February 1952, the Cold War had reached freezing point. The Iron Curtain – Churchill's phrase for the broken line of fences and watchtowers separated by minefields – divided Europe in two, from the Baltic to the Mediterranean. To the east were Poland, East Germany, Bulgaria, Romania, Yugoslavia and Albania – all Communist countries, satellite states of the Soviet Union, standing in opposition to the capitalist West. This strict geographical division was somewhat muddied by France, whose deep Communist sympathies made it a safe haven for Soviet organizations not tolerated anywhere else. The focal point of divided Europe was Berlin, a city patrolled by Americans and Russians alike, and not yet carved in half by a wall.

The atomic threat hung heavily over the times in which Fleming wrote.

Elsewhere in the world, China, North Vietnam, Taiwan and Burma were all behind the so-called 'Bamboo Curtain', another Communist edifice. American GIs were fighting costly battles against Communists in North Korea, and the British army was hunting down Communist terrorists in the jungles of Malaya. The world was ideologically divided, and, though peace prevailed in Europe, hundreds of thousands of NATO troops were stationed in West Germany fully prepared for the 'Hot War' (the opposite of Cold War), the imminent invasion by the USSR.

Lurking beneath all these divisions was the

shadow of the atomic bomb. In 1952 Britain became a nuclear power. In the same year the Americans achieved a thermonuclear breakthrough that made it possible to manufacture a hydrogen bomb small enough to fit into the nose-cone of a rocket. As it was widely believed that the Soviets had the same technology, the US set about developing this invention as fast as possible, and throughout the 1950s first Atlas then Titan missiles were launched from Cape Canaveral, Florida. The awesome power of these weapons, triggered by the touch of a button thousands of miles from their targets, preyed on the public's mind, and Ian Fleming was shrewd enough to exploit the terrifying 'what if?' scenario that one day these powerful missiles might be launched in anger – or, worse, that they might somehow find their way into unscrupulous hands. *Moonraker*, *Dr No* and *Thunderball* all have villains who in one way or another intend to use these weapons of mass destruction to satisfy their own megalomaniac ends. *Thunderball* was particularly prescient, as its plot revolved around Blofeld's threat to bomb Miami using stolen nuclear weapons – a scenario that two years later, in 1963, came uncomfortably close to reality when the Americans spotted Russian nuclear weapons in Castro's Cuba, sparking off the Cuban Missile Crisis. By this time America's nuclear arsenal contained 25,000 weapons, and the Soviets' about half that number. Given the scale of this nuclear arms race, and the seeming willingness of the two superpowers to push each other to the very brink of destruction, most informed opinion believed that it was impossible for the twentieth century to end without a third world war.

Ian Fleming may not have liked this prospect, but he certainly had no political motivation to do anything about it. His natural inclination was to let the people with 'big brains' worry about this sort of thing, and his phlegmatic view about the fate of the planet is best illustrated in a Negro spiritual he liked so much that he reproduced it in his Atticus column in the *Sunday Times*.

Don'tcha worry, honey chile.
Don'tcha cry no more,
It's jest a li'l ole atom bomb
In a li'l ole lim'ted war.

It's jest a bitsy warhead, chile,
On a li'l old tactical shell,
And al it'll do is blow us-all
To a li'l ole lim'ted hell.

Far more engrossing than mankind's possible global destruction was the Cold War that was being fought in secret, by spies. Ian's old-boy network of Naval Intelligence offered him certain opportunities unavailable to other writers, and one of these was the chance to debrief Colonel Grigori Tokaty-Tokaev from the MVD (KGB), who had 'come over' in 1948. Tokaty-Tokaev gave him a very precise description of 13 Sretenka Street, Moscow, a building whose second floor formed the headquarters of SMERSH, the Soviet organization with the principal task of killing spies both at home and abroad. SMERSH is a conjunction of two Russian words, *Smyert Shpionam*, meaning roughly 'Death to Spies', and the organization was officially disbanded in 1946, to be replaced by the MVD – the Ministry of Internal Affairs. Fleming deliberately chose to retain the obsolete name, in the hope that the public wouldn't know any different, and he then added details about the organization that the defecting MVD colonel had described.

According to Tokaty-Tokaev, the building itself was imposing. It had a wide gated entrance patrolled by two armed guards, who stood on either side of a vast iron double door, and pedestrians would cross to the other side of the street and avert their eyes rather than walk directly in front of it. Upstairs on the second floor was a large conference room, with wide windows, a 'colourful Caucasian carpet of the finest quality' on the floor, and two large tables covered in red velvet. There were four telephones in the room, one of which, marked V.Ch. (standing for *Vysoko-Chastotny*, or high-frequency), was connected to the most secret exchange in

Mr Ross Napier's photograph of the Moscow building that Fleming claimed (wrongly, it turned out) was the headquarters of SMERSH.

the country and used by only the highest-ranking officials. Needless to say, as soon as the receiver was lifted all calls were recorded. Fleming faithfully reproduced these details in *From Russia with Love*, and so confident was he in Colonel Tokaty-Tokaev's account that in an author's note on the flyleaf he confirmed that all the details of SMERSH were factually correct, including the address. 'SMERSH . . . exists', he wrote, 'and remains today the most secret department of the Soviet government.'

This had an encouraging effect on readers and reviewers, who praised Fleming for all the documentary elements he had woven into the usual fantastic Bond adventure. They particularly enjoyed the first eighty-odd pages, which revolve around the SMERSH headquarters. One especially zealous fan, Mr W. Ross Napier, actually went to Moscow, to 13 Sretenka Street, but he was rather surprised by what he found. On the ground floor were two small shops, one selling mushrooms, the other meat, quite indistinguishable from thousands of others in Moscow. Several housewives carrying miserable string bags bustled in and out with their shopping. On the second and third floors shabby curtains hung across the windows, and the roof sprouted TV aerials. Was this really the headquarters of one of the most feared secret organizations in the world? Mr Napier sent a photograph of the unprepossessing building to Fleming, who was more than a little taken aback. 'It is quite clear, from your photograph, that no such building as I described could have existed at no. 13,' he replied, guiltily. 'This upsets me very much . . . All I can plead in view of your evidence, is that I was not being *intentionally* misleading.' So Colonel Tokaty-Tokaev had the last laugh. But he was right about SMERSH, which really had existed, even if by the time of James Bond it had changed its name.

SMERSH was born out of the Special Division – *Chastny Otdyel* – of Cheka, the Russian secret service. This included a section for terror and diversion, first formed during the 'Red Terror' in 1918–20, directly after the Russian Revolution. At that time the 'executive branch', as it was known, was literally an executioner's office, charged with organizing the pursuit and murder of White Russians and other enemies of Communism both in the Soviet Union and beyond. To this end Avanposts were set up – special centres for training agents and spying. In these Avanposts mobile terror squads would be living under assumed names, awaiting orders to prosecute their business. During the 1920s and '30s literally thousands of unsolved murders, disappearances and kidnappings were carried out by these travelling executioners. From 1926, the man in charge of Cheka was Vyacheslav Rudolfovich Menzhinsky, described by

Lenin as 'my decadent neurotic'. His office, in a little three-storey house in Kaljayev Place that served as the unlikely headquarters of Soviet intelligence, resembled the salon of a wealthy aesthete. There were pieces of oriental art and rugs scattered about, and a large window gave on to a fine view of a park and the onion domes of the Kremlin. Menzhinsky was a cultivated and corpulent man, who regularly received guests to his office reclining on a divan strewn with Chinese silks. His great project, he claimed, was to bring culture to the proletariat, but at such speed that bloodshed was unavoidable. With a flourishing hand he translated Persian poems from Arabic into Russian, and he used the same fountain pen to sign the death warrants of his own agents and thousands of others. Menzhinsky was precisely the kind of highly cultured despot who appealed to Fleming's sense of the macabre, and inspired his Bond villains.

As a Pole, Menzhinsky eventually fell foul of Stalin and disappeared in the same way that many of his own victims had done – he was poisoned by his own deputy in 1934. Meanwhile, the Soviet-funded assassins continued to prosper. Leon Trotsky was famously murdered by a Spaniard with an ice pick; Ignace Reiss, the resident director of the KGB in France, was gunned down in the street; Professor Camillo Berneri, an anarchist leader in Barcelona, was shot and mutilated in his own home. Berneri was accounted for by George Mink, a former taxi driver from Philadelphia, who became one of SMERSH's most dangerous hit men. Mink – described as 'a short, strongly built, dapper young man, with a small cruel mouth, greenish brown eyes and irregular teeth' – had joined the Communist Party in 1926, and swiftly became an organizer of the Marine Workers' Union, which had strong links with the Soviets. From there he graduated to SMERSH, and by 1935 he had disposed of half a dozen double agents and prominent anti-Communists in Europe and America, each time stalking his victim under cover of an alias and then disappearing hours after the deed was done.

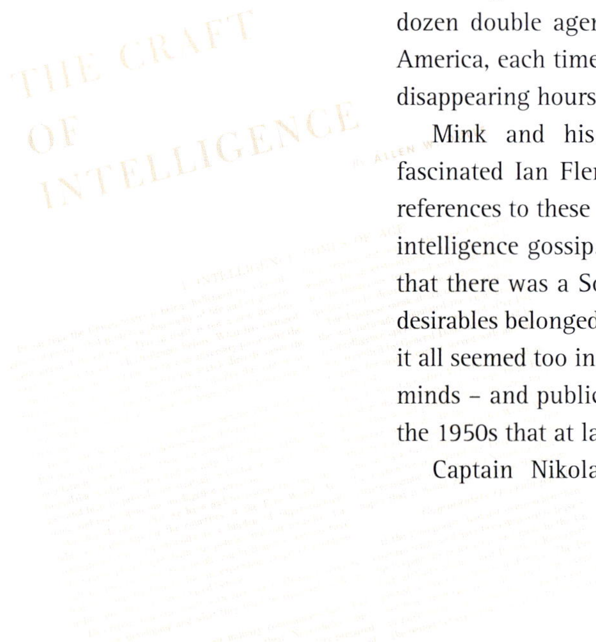

Mink and his fellow Soviet-sponsored executioners had long fascinated Ian Fleming. Throughout his notebooks there are undated references to these cases, which he had either read about or picked up as intelligence gossip. To the more cynical minds in Fleet Street, the idea that there was a Soviet agency charged with the assassination of non-desirables belonged to the pages of fiction or the flickering movie screen: it all seemed too incredible to be true. What began to change journalists' minds – and public opinion – was a series of high-profile defections in the 1950s that at last added substance to this chimera.

Captain Nikolai Khokhlov was the first travelling executioner employed by SMERSH to defect to the West, in February 1954. He bore more than a passing resemblance to the fictional James Bond, and his testimony lifted the lid on a furtive, treacherous world that might have been described by Fleming himself. Khokhlov had originally intended to become an actor, but having been declared not fit enough to serve in the defence of Moscow he was taken up by SMERSH in 1943. Here he proved himself a ruthless killer, executing among others Wilhelm Kube, the Nazi gauleiter of Minsk. After the war he stayed behind in Romania under a new identity, and continued to work for the MVD until he was ordered to Frankfurt to murder an anti-Communist Russian, Georgi Okolovich. Okolovich was the spiritual head of the 'Society of National Unity', which spread anti-Communist propaganda through the ranks of the Red Army. His work proved so disruptive that he was declared 'the most dangerous enemy of the Soviet regime', and his execution order was signed by President Khruschev himself. For Operation Rhine, as it was known, Khokhlov enlisted two other assassins training at the SMERSH school at Karlshorst in East Berlin. All three men were flown back to Moscow, where the two East Germans received further instruction in driving cars, judo and close-quarters pistol shooting – all skills that Fleming made sure James Bond excelled in. Khokhlov was then briefed on the White Russian organization in Frankfurt by a high-ranking female official, Major Tamara Nicolayeva Ivanova, who was one of the few women inside the Soviet intelligence machine to achieve high rank. Khokhlov described her as an 'overworked, nervous spinster'. Could she be a real-life inspiration for the frog-like Rosa Klebb, the lesbian boss of SMERSH in *From Russia with Love*? Possibly, since Cold War reality and James Bond fantasy are both so strange that fact and fiction often become confused. Fleming only added to this muddle by including real people, such as General Grubozaboyschikov, in his invented world of SMERSH.

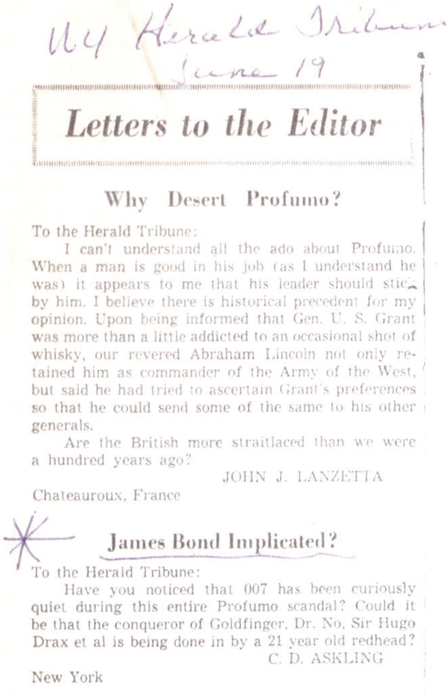
NY Herald Tribune June 19

Letters to the Editor

Why Desert Profumo?

To the Herald Tribune:
I can't understand all the ado about Profumo. When a man is good in his job (as I understand he was) it appears to me that his leader should stick by him. I believe there is historical precedent for my opinion. Upon being informed that Gen. U. S. Grant was more than a little addicted to an occasional shot of whisky, our revered Abraham Lincoln not only retained him as commander of the Army of the West, but said he had tried to ascertain Grant's preferences so that he could send some of the same to his other generals.
Are the British more straitlaced than we were a hundred years ago?
JOHN J. LANZETTA
Chateauroux, France

James Bond Implicated?

To the Herald Tribune:
Have you noticed that 007 has been curiously quiet during this entire Profumo scandal? Could it be that the conqueror of Goldfinger, Dr. No, Sir Hugo Drax et al is being done in by a 21 year old redhead?
C. D. ASKLING
New York

Bond fiction and post-war fact intersect in some of the most curious ways, as recorded in Fleming's own clippings. Allen Dulles, Washington's real-life spy chief, was an avowed 007 fan. And when the sex-and-spying Profumo scandal erupted in 1963 it was only a matter of time before readers drew parallels with their hero's exploits.

Having been fully briefed and trained, Khokhlov and his assistants were then issued with a brand-new toy: an electric gun disguised as a cigarette case. This gadget fired lead bullets containing potassium cyanide, which caused almost instantaneous death on entering the bloodstream. This pistol was yet another real Cold War device that inspired Fleming; he even mentions it in *From Russia with Love*, when Red Grant, the chief SMERSH executioner, pins Bond down with its successor, a ten-shot electric gun concealed in a copy of *War and Peace*.

On the evening of 18 February 1954 Khokhlov entered Okolovich's flat, but, instead of killing him, he told his intended victim that he was defecting. The reason, he claimed, was that his wife had found out that he was an assassin and would have nothing more to do with him if he liquidated Okolovich. So they had made a pact: Khokhlov must warn Okolovich rather than kill him, regardless of the grave consequences this might have for her and their small son. The Americans found this story incredible, as Khokhlov was the first member of SMERSH ever to defect to the West. For six weeks he was extensively debriefed by Western intelligence agencies, and his testimony provided a unique insight into the vast Soviet spy machine and the murky world of its licensed assassins, the Soviet James Bonds. But this information came at a price: three months later Khokhlov's wife, Yanni, and their son were arrested by the KGB and never heard of again.

Once Khokhlov had started talking, he would not stop. Under the pen name E. H. Cookridge, Edward Spiro, a spy and wartime intelligence officer, gave a detailed description of the global organization that Khokhlov had described in his highly readable book *The Soviet Spy Net*, published a year after the assassin had defected. This provided the first glimpse of the real world of Soviet intelligence ever published in the West, and Fleming owned a copy. He may well have known Spiro in Fleet Street (Spiro worked for the *Daily Telegraph*), and he used this book as the background source for most of his Cold War novels.

One of the more colourful characters of the era was Tom Driberg, the maverick left-wing journalist and politician. Here he picks Fleming up on his knowledge of dental care.

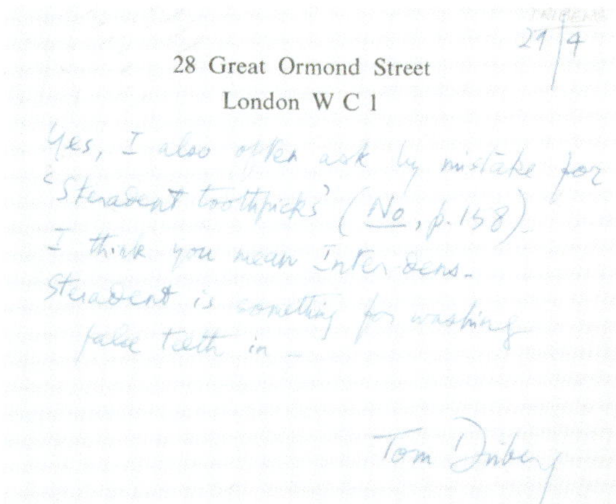
21/4

28 Great Ormond Street
London W C 1

Yes, I also often ask by mistake for 'Steradent toothpicks' (No, p. 158).
I think you mean Inter-dens.
Steradent is something for washing false teeth in –

Tom Driberg

Cookridge claimed that the scale of the Soviet intelligence operation was immense, with a 250,000-strong army of agents, fifth columnists and spies, all working directly or indirectly for Moscow. In addition, there were a further 750,000 informers supplying information. This worldwide web stretched from the Philippines to Sweden. In France for instance, where Soviet penetration was particularly successful, Cookridge said that 200 Soviet networks had been identified and more than 20,000 agents were known to be at large. French counter-intelligence had discovered that virtually all French defence secrets had been betrayed, the police and the unions had been infiltrated to the highest level. In the event of a future war, the Communists 'could provide alternative government administration and an alternative army without difficulty'. The French government had been understandably reticent about publicizing these facts, being only too aware that revealing just how porous its system was would certainly deter the Americans and British from sharing their own nuclear secrets. Fleming copied down these figures into his notebook, alongside Cookridge's more contentious claim that there were '1,000 Soviet agents currently at large in England'. SMERSH executioners in England? Impossible, surely. Cookridge cited seven unsolved murders in Britain in 1954 alone in which the victims were Poles, Lithuanians, Czechs or Ukrainians who had sought asylum. In every country he described similar disappearances, unsolved crimes and mysterious murders, and laid the blame at the KGB's door. It was a compelling argument for Cold War paranoia: they knew who you were, they knew where you lived, and worse, they probably had a file on you as well.

The cornerstone of this vast organization was the Central Index of the Intelligence Bureau, housed in a vast edifice at the corner of Mokhovaya Ulitsa and Vozdvizhenka Ulitsa in Moscow. Here was filed the name of every man and woman who had ever been, or been suspected of being, a spy, an informant, a Communist, an anti-Communist or a member of a foreign intelligence service. The Index was housed in a hundred rooms, each secured by electric doors, and had a permanent staff of 250. It contained literally millions of yellow-backed *zapiska* (files) on every individual in the world who at one time or another was of interest to Soviet intelligence. These mini-biographies included details of appearance, family ties, drinking habits, sexual habits, gossip – anything that might prove useful to the KGB in any future operation. Some files would have 'NASH' written on them, meaning 'Ours' – the individual had been converted to the cause. Fleming enjoyed the irony of an English surname being used in this way, and used 'Nash' as the name the SMERSH executioner Red Grant assumes when he poses as an English agent in *From Russia with Love*. James Bond, 007, has his own fictional *zapiska*, and it must have intrigued the former wartime assistant to the Director of Naval Intelligence that somewhere in this labyrinth must have been another, real, *zapiska* that bore the title 'Ian Lancaster Fleming'.

Another incredible aspect of the Soviet spy organization was its methods for passing on information. While the Central Index was the greatest repository of spy information in the world, agents on the ground indulged in the kind of cloak-and-dagger stuff more associated with schoolboy comics. In cinemas, Soviet agents really did hand each other cartons of chocolates that contained tiny microfilms hidden in the wrapping. One Scandinavian network arranged hairpins in

Profiles of Ian began to appear regularly in the press, and he made a point of collecting these clippings. The CIA supported Allen Dulles's own career as a writer, and the two men lunched on the very day of Profumo's resignation speech. Ian later dubbed Dulles 'Agent 008', and gave Bond his book to read in The Man with the Golden Gun.

various patterns on a wire fence to write messages to each other. According to Khokhlov, the entire network was paranoid: spies spied on other spies, and informants were paid to watch each other, and bug each other too. The organization was so mistrustful that it did not even send coded letters by post, preferring furtive meetings on park benches in cities all over the world.

Occasionally the West discovered some of these schemes. In 1952, during the height of the Cold War, a remote-bugging device was found hidden inside the great seal in the American ambassador's office in Moscow. This was a battery-operated, remote transmitter/receiver that was far superior to anything in the West at the time. Another ingenious bug had been found in the shoe of a US diplomat working in Bucharest. He had sent his shoes to be repaired, and when they returned a transmitter had been implanted into one of the heels – invisible except for a tiny hole in the side, that allowed the diplomat's chambermaid (an agent) to stick a pin through to turn the device on and off. This device had been discovered; thousands more were not. During the 1950s it was standard practice for every businessman or diplomat working behind the Iron Curtain to be bugged, tailed, eavesdropped on and occasionally even drugged by the KGB. At night in certain hotel rooms in Moscow, and on certain sleeping cars on trains, concealed ducts would introduce vapours designed to send the occupant into an unbroken sleep, allowing agents to make a thorough inspection of his bags and anything else. No wonder that Fleming has James Bond endlessly fussing over whether his room has been searched or not. 007 takes care to leave strands of his own hair in the lock of his suitcase, so that he can see if it has been disturbed; he places his razor and toothbrush at a particular angle; he measures the distance between his shoes. Bond, like any real Cold War secret agent, cannot be too careful. But in one respect he remains dangerously, unrealistically, cavalier.

In *From Russia with Love* Bond comes back to his dark hotel room in Istanbul to find a beautiful woman in his bed. Tatiana – who looks a bit like Greta Garbo – is wearing nothing but stockings and a black ribbon round her neck, and of course Bond, being Bond, cannot resist. High above, behind a false mirror on the wall over the bed, two SMERSH agents sweat as they record on film the 'passionate arabesques' of the writhing bodies below. Bond has been entrapped, in exactly the same way as scores of others were during the height of the Cold War, from ambassadors down to the lowliest clerks. John Vassall was one of the latter: a homosexual who worked in Ian Fleming's old Department of Naval Intelligence, he had been 'caught' on film with a Russian lover while working in Moscow in 1950. The KGB blackmailed him into becoming a spy, and over the next few years Vassall provided it with photographs of thousands of classified documents, including blueprints of radar systems and anti-submarine devices, which he had taken using a secret camera supplied by the Russians. Vassall was eventually exposed – ironically, by another Soviet defector – in 1962.

The former SMERSH agent Nikolai Khokhlov also confirmed that the MVD had its own equivalent of Q branch, specializing in disguises, forged foreign documents and unlikely gizmos. Before 1953 it had even had its own laboratory, a notorious place named 'The Chamber', whose sole purpose was to invent poisons for which there was no known antidote – and which left no trace – so that victims appeared to die of natural causes. The Chamber contained so many deadly poisons that even the lab technicians were afraid to walk around it. Ironically enough, this paranoid organization used one of these toxins to silence the very man who had revealed The Chamber's existence. Khokhlov, whose defection had caused so much anger and confusion, began speaking publicly around the world about the Soviet repressive regime. The KGB then began a smear campaign against him, claiming that both he and Okolovich were Nazi war criminals out to save each other's skins. Khokhlov should have known that this was a warning, but he ignored it, and thereafter he became a marked man. In September 1957, while attending a conference in Frankfurt, he suddenly collapsed, and within hours he was in the clutches of a mysterious and violent disease. Tufts of his hair began falling out, blood seeped through the pores of his skin, and his whole body was covered in blue-black swellings and brown streaks. Khokhlov's white corpuscles were decaying, his blood turning to plasma. An American toxicologist later diagnosed that he had been poisoned by thallium, a rare toxic metal that had been exposed to extreme atomic radiation. Somehow particles of this substance had been slipped into one of his meals at the

Such was the public outcry at Bond's 'death' at the end of From Russia with Love *that Fleming was forced to issue a 'Letter to Anxious Readers'. They were reassured that 007 had survived, and he would soon return to confront* Dr No.

29th April, 1957.

Dear Sir,

The Late James Bond.

As a result of Mr. John Raymond's poignant but premature obituary notice of Commander James Bond, R.N.V.S.R., there has been a flood of anxious enquiry.

May I therefore, as Commander Bond's official biographer, ask you to publish the following bulletin which, according to a delicate but sure source, was recently placed on the canteen notice board of the headquarters of the Secret Service near Regent's Park:

"After a period of anxiety the condition of No. 007 shows definite improvement.

It has been confirmed that 007 was suffering from severe Fugu poisoning (a particularly virulent member of the curare group obtained from the sex glands of Japanese Globe fish). This diagnosis, for which the Research Department of the School of Tropical Medicine was responsible, has determined a course of treatment which is proving successful.

No further bulletins will be issued.

(Signed) Sir James Molony,
Department of Neurology,
St. Mary's Hospital,
London, W.2. "

In view of the above I am hoping that, despite the cautionary note sounded by Mr. Raymond and subject, of course, to the Official Secrets Act, further biographical material on James Bond will in due course be available to the public.

Yours faithfully,

The Editor,
New Statesman and Nation,
10, Great Turnstile,
High Holborn,
W.C.1.

mumbled an apology and hurried across the road to hail a taxi. Hours later Markov fell dangerously ill, and he told doctors what had happened. His death was swift. The post-mortem revealed a tiny metal ball, 0.6 mm in diameter, lodged inside his right thigh. This ball contained two holes, each 0.2 mm across, that almost certainly contained ricin, a deadly toxin that has no antidote. The ball had been fired into Markov's leg by a gas-powered device hidden in the bottom of the umbrella. It is ironic that we think of this as a Bond-like incident, when in fact Soviet intelligence agents needed no lessons from James Bond in skulduggery; Fleming filched his ideas from them. What *is* intriguing is how much the fictional character of James Bond actually influenced the real Cold War.

Certainly the official Soviet press thought he did – though not so much in deed as in thought. 'James Bond', wrote Yuri Zhukov in *Pravda* in September 1965, 'lives in a nightmarish world where laws are written at the point of a gun, where coercion and rape [are] considered valour and murder is a funny trick.' The writer objected to the cartoonish Soviet agents and the relentless assassination of 'Russians, Reds, and Yellows' – in fact the killing of anyone Fleming himself felt like killing. Bond was painted as the white archangel of the West 'who sets out to destroy the impure races', and as such was responsible for the kind of thinking that sent US Marines to Vietnam. Zhukov was either ignorant of or chose to ignore the similarities between James Bond and real agents like Stashinsky, who had a genuine licence to kill.

Elsewhere in the Eastern Bloc, 007 inspired not only contempt but imitation. Andrei Gulyashki was another Communist writer who disliked the racist overtones of the James Bond books, and as a Bulgarian he took deep offence at Bulgars being portrayed as oafish hit men employed by the Russians to do their dirty work (as in *Casino Royale* and *From Russia with Love*). In 1966 he wrote the story 'Zakhov Mission', in which the heroic proletarian Bulgarian Avakoum Zakhov takes on an agent of an unnamed Western power, named 07, but, curiously, fails to kill him. This story, widely touted as the Communist answer to James Bond, was even serialized in *Komsomolskaya Pravda*, the paper of the Communist youth league.

Perhaps the most successful Eastern-Bloc answer to Bond was created by Arto Tuovinen, a young Finnish author who had translated Fleming's works into his mother tongue during the 1960s. His hero was one Boris Stolinsky, a Soviet super-spy, a fast-living misfit with a weakness for vodka and a pathological dislike for both Lenin and Buddha. Stolinsky's great enemy is none other than Martin Bormann, Hitler's henchman, who was rumoured to still be alive and in hiding. Bormann's secret organization, Das Reich, threatens to destroy the northern hemisphere if Germany is not united, and over the course of two books secret agent Stolinsky doggedly pursues this elusive enemy. Unfortunately Tuovinen died in 1968, aged thirty-five, and Boris Stolinsky never really became established as a Bond of the Eastern Bloc.

While the Soviets had nothing but contempt for 007, whom they saw as a fascistic, murdering rapist who simply defended the rights of the property-owning class (incidentally, a view also held by the *New Statesman* and several other British publications), James Bond was regarded somewhat differently in America, the home of his most famous fan. In March 1961 *Time-Life* magazine ran an article about the newly elected John F. Kennedy's voracious literary habits. Consuming '1,200 words a minute', the President devoured all kinds of reading matter, including James Bond, and he named *From Russia with Love* as number nine in his top ten books of all time. This admission – which was apparently true, and not merely a White House publicity-machine invention – fitted well with the image Americans had of their dynamic new president and his beautiful wife, and it was a great fillip for Ian Fleming, who milked the connection and made sure that from then on signed copies of his latest hardback were sent direct to the White House.

John F. Kennedy invited Fleming to dinner at his Georgetown house the year before he became president. After reading Casino Royale *he became hooked on the Bond adventures. In some ways he was not unlike 007 himself – good-looking, sexually voracious, and with an acute sense of his own mortality.*

Fleming had actually met Jack Kennedy a year earlier, in March 1960, when he was staying in Washington with a mutual friend and found himself invited by the Kennedys to dinner. The talk that evening was all of Fidel Castro and his Communist rebels who, having seized Cuba the previous year, had now signed an exclusive deal to sell their sugar crop to Russia. Ian, feeling that a contribution was required, made a suggestion not dissimilar to those he had dreamed up during his days in wartime intelligence. Castro should not be taken too seriously, he said; it was much better to make a fool of him. Why not drop leaflets telling Cubans that beards were dangerous, as they trapped particles of radioactive dust and this led to impotence? Fleming was, as usual, not being entirely serious, and Kennedy was amused, but another dinner guest listened intently. John Bross, a veteran CIA agent, reported Fleming's suggestion to his chief,

Allen Dulles, the following day, and it transpired that this was exactly the kind of idea the CIA was genuinely considering. Later it did attempt to put powder in Castro's shoes to make his beard fall out. At that time Dulles was planning the CIA's ill-conceived attempt to oust Castro in what became known as the Bay of Pigs fiasco, and when that failed Kennedy sacked him. The ex-CIA chief then embarked on a fledgling literary career which brought him into contact with Ian Fleming, who basked in his association with this high-profile intelligence supremo. It is not known whether their friendship led to a more formal contact with the Central Intelligence Agency, but Fleming always liked to boast that he had 'the strong indictment of the CIA', and James Bond's influence can certainly be detected in the agency's further dealings with the Cuban dictator.

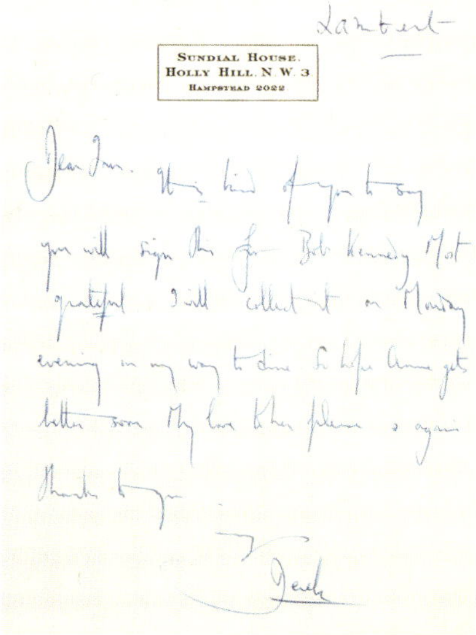
Lambert

SUNDIAL HOUSE.
HOLLY HILL. N. W. 3
HAMPSTEAD 2022

Dear Ian. Very kind of you to say you will sign this for Bob Kennedy. Most grateful. I will collect it on Monday evening on my way to dine. So hope Anne gets better soon. My love to her please & again thanks to you.

Yrs
Jack

This note from Jack Lambert indicates that JFK was not the only Kennedy keen on Bond.

After the public humiliation of the Bay of Pigs, 'getting even with Castro' became one of the CIA's overriding obsessions. His very presence a mere seventy miles off the American coast was infuriating, and 'The Inspector General's Report on Plots to Assassinate Fidel Castro', released in 1993, catalogues some of the more outlandish attempts to get rid of him. At first the CIA contemplated assassination by a surreptitious injection of shellfish toxin. Scientists at Porton Down, the British secret-service development establishment, were very adept at working with this particular poison and had long co-operated with their American counterparts in this field; they may well have assisted in this plan, and their work probably inspired the 'death' of Bond at the end of *From Russia with Love*. The CIA, however, did not have recourse to Rosa Klebb and her spiked boots to administer the poison, so it gave up the idea and reverted to a more straightforward drive-by shooting – the classic 'gangland whack'. This failed too, so it was back to poisoning, and a box of Castro's favourite cigars was contaminated with botulinum toxin, which certainly would have killed him within hours had a way been found to deliver them.

Then the CIA decided to exploit the Cuban leader's passion for scuba diving. At first Desmond Fitzgerald, the CIA's special-affairs chief, had the idea of filling a large, innocent-looking conch shell with high explosives and delivering it via midget submarine to one of Castro's favourite diving haunts. It would be left on the ocean floor and primed to detonate as soon as it was disturbed. This Bond-like scheme was thwarted by nature: there was no indigenous shell in the Caribbean either large enough or unique enough to be suitable for the purpose, and besides the US midget submarines had too short an operating range for such a mission.

A far more viable proposition, and one that the CIA actually undertook, was the gift of a poisoned skin-diving suit. The inside was carefully dusted with 'a fungus that would produce a disabling and chronic skin disease (Madura foot)' and, just to make sure, the breathing apparatus was also infected by a tubercle bacillus. Fortunately for Castro the CIA never had a chance to present the Cuban leader with its gift, as he had already accepted a diving suit from James Donovan, a New York attorney who was brokering secret peace talks between Castro and Kennedy. This confusion caused some anger, and it suggests that Kennedy had no knowledge of the CIA's more fanciful assassination plans, even though he certainly wanted to 'sanction' Castro. For his part, Ian Fleming never shared the agency's loathing of the Cuban dictator. In fact James Bond has some sympathy with Castro's rebels, and it is with great reluctance that he sabotages the Cuban arms-smuggling operation at the beginning of the 1960 short story 'Quantum of Solace'.

In 1962 a *New York Herald* reporter asked Fleming if the CIA had got any James Bond gadgets to work, and he was being either evasive or quite candid when he said that they hadn't. Ian didn't mention any exploding shells or poisoned cigars, but he confirmed that the CIA had experimented with a 'Homer' device similar to that which 007 used to track Goldfinger's Rolls-Royce through France. One might assume that Ian's insider knowledge of some secret dossier or a Soviet assassin's testimony had inspired this device, but it turned out he had stolen the idea from a far less confidential source – a comic entitled *How to be a Detective.*

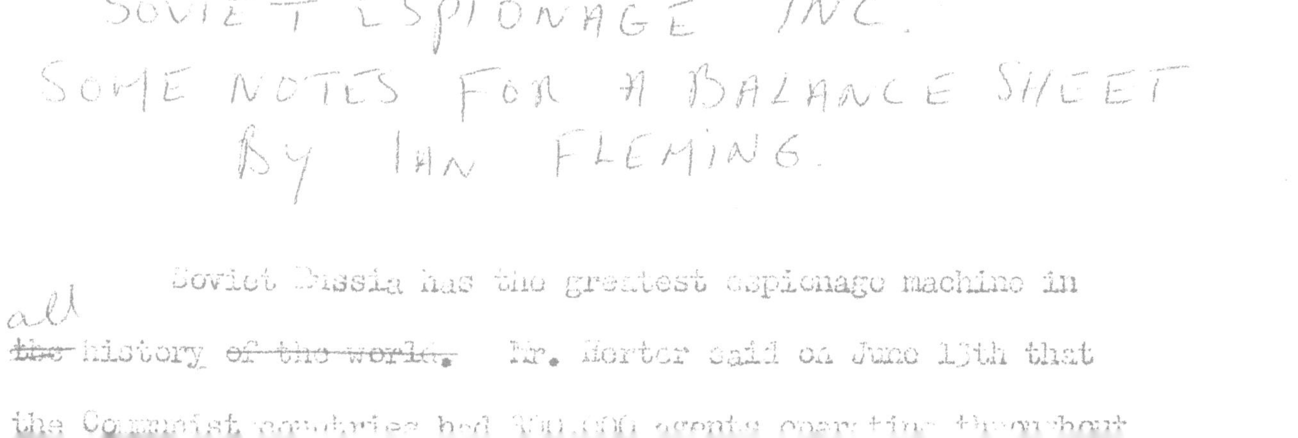

SOVIET ESPIONAGE INC.
SOME NOTES FOR A BALANCE SHEET
BY IAN FLEMING.

Soviet Russia has the greatest espionage machine in all ~~the~~ history ~~of the world.~~ Mr. Herter said on June 13th that the Communist countries had [illegible] agents operating throughout

The article written for Esquire *(see page 191) in which Fleming attempted to provide some context for Cold War spying activities.*

YOU ONLY LIVE TWICE 196

First line

The geisha called 'Trembling Leaf', on her knees beside James Bond, leant forward from the waist and kissed him chastely on the right cheek.

Story

This is the twelfth James Bond book, and the last that Fleming managed to complete before his death in 1964. The mood is dark and claustrophobic, far closer to *Casino Royale* than any of the other books, and this is where Bond finally comes to grips with his arch-nemesis Ernst Blofeld. The beginning finds Bond depressed and withdrawn following the death of his bride, Tracy. Given his mental state, M revokes Bond's licence to kill and promotes him to the diplomatic section with a new number – 7777. Bond's task is to go to Japan and to persuade Tiger Tanaka, the head of the Japanese intelligence service, to share information from its new cipher machine, MAGIC 44, which has broken the Soviet codes. Tiger is reluctant, but after a month of Bond's coaxing he agrees, on condition that Bond performs a service for Japan. On the volcanic island of Kyushu a mysterious westerner named Dr Shatterhand has recently purchased a castle, and on the terraces below he has laid out a garden stocked only with poisonous plants and carnivorous fish. This macabre place has begun to attract suicides, and the Prime Minister himself wants to be rid of both Shatterhand and his burgeoning cult of death. If Bond can find his way into the castle and assassinate Shatterhand, MAGIC 44 will be at the disposal of the British secret service.

To achieve this, Bond is sent to stay with the Ama people on the neighbouring island of Kuro, simple fishermen whose daughters dive naked to the sea floor to collect awabi shells. Bond lodges with Kissy Suzuki, a strikingly tall, beautiful girl who was plucked from this idyll to make a Hollywood movie, but became disenchanted with life in America and returned to the island. Assisted by Kissy, Bond swims the narrow straits over to Shatterhand's castle, scales the wall, picks his way through the poison garden, and finds a way into the castle, only to fall into an oubliette and be captured.

Dr Shatterhand – who is, of course, Ernst Blofeld in disguise – takes Bond to the Question Room and straps him to a throne astride a geyser that spews out boiling mud every fifteen minutes. Bond narrowly avoids this horrific death, and in a final epic duel he strangles Blofeld. He then closes down the geyser, and the castle explodes. He escapes by clinging to the mooring rope of a helium weather balloon, but is barely over the sea when a bullet glances his temple and he falls unconscious into the water, only to be rescued by Kissy. When Bond comes around he has total amnesia. He has no idea who he is or where he is. Kissy hides him from the prying world for almost a year, keeping him as her common-law husband, and eventually she becomes pregnant. Now that the world thinks Bond is dead, M writes his obituary in *The Times*, and it is only the word 'Vladivostock' in a newspaper that finally jogs Bonds memory of his former life. Reluctantly Kissy gives Bond some money and sends him on his way to that city.

Last lines

But then, of course, he didn't know that his name was James Bond. And, compared with the blazing significance to him of that single Russian word [Vladivostock] on the scrap of paper, his life on Kuro, his love for Kissy Suzuki, were, in Tiger's phrase, as of little account as sparrows' tears.

Inspirations

Ever since 1954 Fleming had kept a notebook of ideas and plots for his novels, which he diligently updated twice a year. He drew upon several of these ideas here, including notes about poisonous gardens and the Japanese tendency to suicide. To these he added a much older creation: Dr Shatterhand, the Wagnerian villain in a horned helmet and chainmail, is a direct descendant of Graf Schlick, the Gothic monster that the youthful Fleming had dreamed up around Phyllis Bottome's dinner table in Kitzbühel thirty-five years earlier.

Fleming had already put these ideas into a rough order by the time he came to visit Japan in 1962. He had been enchanted by the Far East on his *Thrilling Cities* world tour three years earlier, and this time he returned with a specific itinerary in mind. Once again Fleming was accompanied by his Australian friend Richard Hughes and by the Japanese journalist Tiger Saito, who became the characters Dikko Henderson and Tiger Tanaka, the Australian secret-service chief and the former kamikaze pilot reprieved by Hiroshima. The three men proceeded to travel the length and breadth of Japan on every form of transport available. They drank sake and turtle blood, ate Kobe beef and raw lobster, and visited Mikmitos island, where girls dive for pearls. 'You must touch to get the precise texture of wet feminine skin,' Fleming insisted, as he caressed a young diver's shoulder. Every evening before dinner Ian retired for a few hours to note down all this travelogue material, and Bond's airy fascination with odd eastern customs such as barging women off trains was entirely Fleming's own. 'First lesson, Bondo-san! Do not make way for women. Push them, trample them down. Women have no priority in this country. You may be polite to very old men, but to no one else. Is that understood?'

'Yes, master,' said Bond sarcastically.

What the readers said

'At times it is as difficult to stop reading as if one had accidentally walked off a cliff'

What the critics said

'England's best export, a spice of adventure, a dash of patriotism, laced with sex, sadism, and expense account know-how' – *Sunday Times*

'Reactionary, sentimental, square, the Bond-image flails its way through the middle-brow masses, a relaxation to the great, a stimulus to the humble, the only common denominator between Kennedy and Oswald' – Cyril Connolly, *Sunday Times*

'I notice that Ian Fleming has taken a hint from films of his books and is now inclined to send himself up. I am not at all sure that he is wise' – *The Spectator*

'He is still in a class by himself' – *Belfast Telegraph*

'Though Mr Fleming's macabre imagination is as interesting as ever, some of the old snap seems to be gone' – *The Times*

'We want a Stendhal or a Conrad of the Spy Age, even if that means ditching James, now that he's a big boy' – Peter Duval Smith, *Financial Times*

'The characteristic which makes Fleming appear so silly also helps to make him popular: his moral simplicity. When we read James Bond we know whose side we are on, why we are on that side, and why we are certain to win. In the real world this is no longer possible' – Robert Fulford, *Macleans* magazine (Toronto)

'*You Only Live Twice* has a decidedly perfunctory air. Bond can only manage to sleep with his Japanese girl with the aid of colour pornography. His drinking seems somehow desperate, and the horrors are too absurd to horrify . . . it's all rather a muddle, and scarcely in the tradition of Secret Service fiction. Perhaps the earlier novels are better. If so, I shall never know, having no intention of reading any of them' – Malcolm Muggeridge, *Esquire*

The lettering for Richard Chopping's You Only Live Twice *jacket features the title in English and Japanese. On his first visit to Tokyo, for* Thrilling Cities *in 1960, Fleming collected copious material.*

BEGINNING AT THE END

Movies, Spoofs and the Legacy

It had always been Ian Fleming's intention that James Bond should end up on screen. Though he knew nothing about the film business and had few contacts in the showbiz world, he would use his annual trips to America en route to Goldeneye to meet with agents and try to drum up some interest in making a film or television series about his alter ego, 007. At first he had some success. When *Casino Royale* came out several companies expressed interest in the television rights, and they were eventually sold to CBS for $1,000 in 1954. The book had just been published in America in paperback, under the title *Too Hot to Handle*, and that autumn it was adapted for the small screen as a one-hour teleplay, broadcast live as part of the weekly thriller series *Climax!*. In it, special agent 'Jimmy' Bond was Americanized and the violence was toned down: instead of having his testicles thrashed with a carpet-beater, 007 has his toenails pulled out in a bath, and Vesper Lynd, the double-agent Bond girl, does not commit suicide. Apart from Le Chiffre, who was played with reptilian cunning by Peter Lorre, this film remains an unloved curiosity in the world of Bondology.

In England there were also encouraging signs. Fleming managed to arouse Sir Alexander Korda's interest in *Live and Let Die*. 'I really could not put it down until I had finished it,' wrote Korda. 'Then I gave it to my wife to read about midnight and she could not go to sleep until she had finished the whole book.' The flamboyant Hungarian-born producer then promised he would show it to Carol Reed and David Lean for their suggestions, but he added a note of caution: 'The best stories for films are always the stories that are written specially for films.' This was very convenient for Ian, as he told Korda that his next book, *Moonraker*, was 'an expansion of a film story that I have had since the war – a straight thriller with particularly English but also general appeal, set in London and on the white cliffs of Dover, and involving the destruction of London by a super V-2, allowing for some wonderful film settings in the old metropolis idiom'. As soon as the proofs were ready Korda received a copy, having assured Ian that he was looking to make the definitive British secret-service film. Unfortunately, it was not to be *Moonraker*.

Throughout the 1950s Ian received sporadic approaches from other movie moguls prowling around the James Bond series, and though he liked the can-do attitude of most Americans, he found the huckstering required to do business in Hollywood tiresome. 'As all foreign authors know,' he wrote in *Thrilling Cities* in 1959, 'Hollywood likes to have first bite at anyone who is "new" and even moderately successful.' He described one of these first-bite lunches he had had with one nameless producer:

> I was treated to the whole smart rag-bag of show-biz pressure-talk in between Eggs Benedict and those eighty percent proof dry martinis that anaesthetize the uvula. 'We gotta see which way the cookie crumbles, Iarn.' (There are only first name terms in Hollywood) . . . 'As we say, "If you want to throw snow on a stove, don't bellyache if it melts." . . . Of course you want to make money. Who doesn't? But they say around here, "A Jew worries how much money he's going to lose, an Englishman how much he'll make, and the American how much *you'll* make." Now, at our studios, we want everyone to make money. How would it be if . . .' And so it went on, a mixture of hollow bonhomie combined with ultra sharp horse-trading.

Ian did have one minor success in this world in 1958, when he was commissioned by CBS to write a thirteen-part television series about James Bond. For this he came up with seven new stories, and then cannibalized sections of novels he had already written to make up the number. He got as far as writing the treatments for the episodes before uncharacteristically pulling out of the project. Always acutely aware of how difficult it was to come up with a decent plot, Ian was relieved to be able to reuse most of the new ideas, in one form or another, in later books. An interesting offshoot of this aborted project was the note he sent to its American producer, describing how he thought the British secret service, and

Although Fleming discussed the film rights for his novels from an early point in Bond's history, it wasn't until 1962 that Harry Saltzman and Cubby Broccoli's Dr No *was released.*

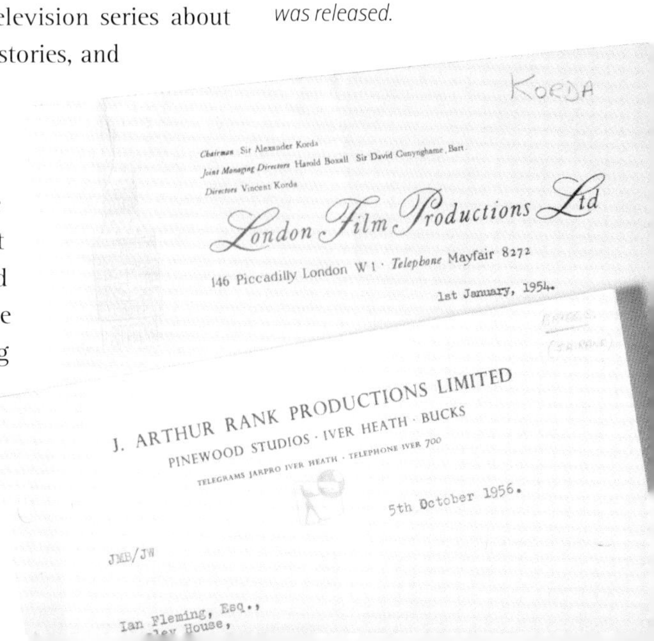
KORDA

Chairman Sir Alexander Korda
Joint Managing Directors Harold Boxall Sir David Cunynghame, Bart
Directors Vincent Korda

London Film Productions Ltd

146 Piccadilly London W1 · Telephone Mayfair 8272

1st January, 1954.

J. ARTHUR RANK PRODUCTIONS LIMITED
PINEWOOD STUDIOS · IVER HEATH · BUCKS
TELEGRAMS JARPRO IVER HEATH · TELEPHONE IVER 700

5th October 1956.

JMB/JW

Ian Fleming, Esq.,

James Bond, should be played. There should be no 'stage Englishness . . . no bowler hats, no monocles, bobbies or other Limey gimmicks', he said. 'In real life, the secret service is a tough, modern organization very far removed from the cheery, tea-drinking myth usually attached to Scotland Yard.' James Bond should be hard and fatalistic, and make no attempt to endear himself to the audience, who should dislike him 'until they get to know him and then they will appreciate that he is their idea of an efficient agent'. This tough, gritty approach, without fantasy, is the polar opposite to what the film-makers eventually decided for the James Bond movies.

In the same year, 1958, Fleming began planning a Bond film of his own. Just as *Moonraker* had begun as a film idea and was turned into a book, the story of *Thunderball* is similar, but with the added complication that the original idea was not entirely Ian's own. Initially he had thrashed around an idea for the film with Ivar Bryce and Ernie Cuneo, old friends who often provided sounding boards for Bond novels in their early stages. Through Bryce Fleming then met Kevin McClory, a fledgling director whose first film, *The Boy and the Bridge* – a whimsical tale of a runaway who lives in Tower Bridge – Bryce had financed. McClory suggested that he himself should take the film idea further, and together with a screenwriter, Jack Whittingham, worked on various treatments until it became an 'underwater adventure story' starring James Bond and set in the Bahamas. As the costs of the project mounted Fleming lost interest, and McClory eventually found that he was unable to raise any finance for the film. So Ian, who was always reluctant to let a good idea lie idle, decided to use the aborted project as the basis for his next novel, *Thunderball*. McClory and Whittingham then objected, claiming that the book was based on their ideas, and in March 1961 petitioned the High Court to issue an injunction to prevent the novel's publication. In this they failed, but a court case loomed; 'they say it's going to take as long as two weeks', moaned Ian. In fact the legal action dragged on and on; although Ian settled his part of it in 1963, the wrangling over the ownership of *Thunderball* was not definitively concluded until 1998, thirty-seven years later. According to Ian's friends, the stress of this whole episode effectively shortened his life.

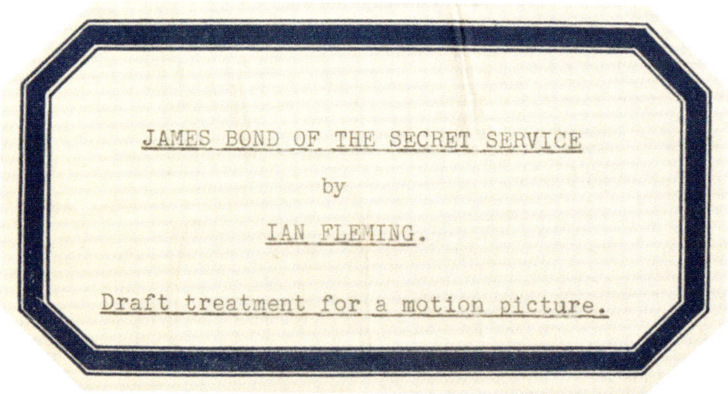
JAMES BOND OF THE SECRET SERVICE

by

IAN FLEMING.

Draft treatment for a motion picture.

As the *Thunderball* case dragged on, the real screen career of 007 began. One of the producers circling around James Bond was Harry Saltzman, a Canadian who, in 1961, bought an option on all the novels except *Casino Royale* (rights to which were still owned by CBS). With the option but no financial backing, Saltzman went into partnership with Cubby Broccoli, an American producer and Bond fan, and together they managed to raise $900,000 from United Artists, set up their own production company at Pinewood Studios, named Eon (which stood for 'Everything or Nothing'), and chose *Dr No*, the most visual of the early books, to adapt as the first Bond film. Fleming would have nothing to do with writing the scripts, which suited him, but he would be paid $100,000 per film and receive a generous 5 per cent of the producers' profits.

Saltzman and Broccoli were undoubtedly a very persuasive pair, but United Artists were encouraged to make their considerable investment by the enormous success of Alfred Hitchcock's *North by Northwest* (1959), which was a kind of James Bond film without James Bond. This glossy spy thriller starred Cary Grant as the suave, suited hero who travels across America in pursuit of a gang of Cold War villains. There were beautiful sets, beautiful food, a beautiful blonde (Eva Marie Saint) and spectacular scenes such as the famous sequence where Cary Grant is chased by a crop-duster aeroplane. The plot was full of unexpected twists, and the audiences loved it – including Ian Fleming, who was a huge admirer of Hitchcock. The only aspect he objected to was the bemused humour with which Cary Grant played the leading role. Thrillers, he felt, should be serious affairs, as was evident from his books. The success of *North by Northwest* proved to United Artists that spy stories – for so long the preserve of B-movies – could now work as big, glossy, mainstream features. The producers of *Dr No* would soon find this out for themselves.

For the casting of Bond, Ian initially suggested his friend David Niven. When it was pointed out that Niven was too old he suggested the young Roger Moore, who was starring as The Saint on television. This idea was also mooted, and finally Ian met Saltzman's number-one choice for lunch at the Savoy. Sean Connery was a thirty-year-old Shakespearean actor who had once been a navy boxing champion, and Fleming was initially full of doubts that this working-class Scotsman would be able to play his well-heeled hero. However, having met him, and having been assured by a female companion that Connery definitely had 'it', Ian was convinced. The fate of James Bond now lay in Connery's hands.

In March 1961 the filming of *Dr No* began in Jamaica. Though Ian had little to do with it, he did stroll down to the set at Rolling River with

Ann, accompanied by the poet Stephen Spender and the critic Peter Quennell. They arrived just as director Terence Young was shooting the now famous scene where Ursula Andress emerges from the sea in a bikini, watched admiringly by Bond hiding in the bushes. Young screamed to the four uninvited guests to get down, which they did, immediately – and thirty minutes later Young was surprised to find James Bond's creator and the two other distinguished literary gents still lying spreadeagled on the sand. Film-making was a 'riot', according to Ian; he loved it, and was predictably fascinated by all the technical paraphernalia of film-making. Two years later he paid a visit to Istanbul to watch the filming of *From Russia with Love*, and a highlight of that trip was a belly dancer who twirled so close to him that her quivering flanks flicked the ash off his Morland Special.

When *Dr No* premiered in London on 5 October 1962 it caused a stir, not least because the timing of its release could not have been more propitious. Two weeks later the Cuban Missile Crisis reached its climax, and Russia and the United States were involved in a face off that might well have escalated into a third World War. As nuclear weapons on a Caribbean island were making front-page news, a film about a megalomaniac who was redirecting US nuclear test missiles from his own Caribbean lair could not have been more apt. Richard Maibaum, the scriptwriter, stuck reasonably close to the novel, though he acknowledged that there was an 'untransferable quality' in Fleming's writing. While Ian's vivid descriptions of colours, sounds and smells created an acute sense of place on the page, on screen these amounted to nothing more than a pretty picture. And his particular knack of describing the precise sensations of driving fast cars and eating delicious food did not translate particularly well either. Instead, the film-makers went for visual spectacle, creating incredible sets for Dr No's mink-lined prison – now on board a ship – and beefing up the technological wizardry of the gadgets.

Maibaum's greatest alteration to the character of James Bond was to give him some self-consciously awful one-liners that are entirely absent from the books. These lightened the tone

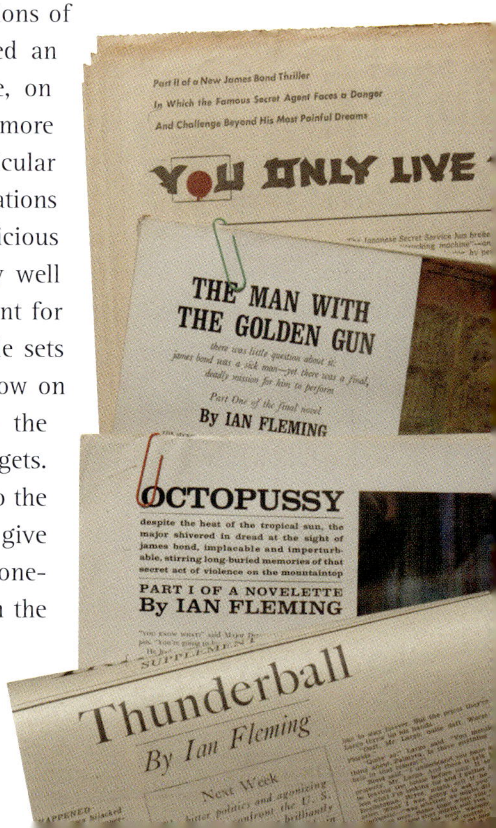

As the novels were published they were serialized in major newspapers and magazines throughout the world, often with specially commissioned artwork.

and set the style for all the later Bond films, and at the time this injection of humour was seen as a daringly modern solution to the problem of steering the sex and violence of James Bond's adventure past the censor. Whether by accident or design, the ploy worked. But *Dr No* was not all jokes. The film contains the only scene in the entire Bond canon where 007 really behaves like the licensed killer of Fleming's books. In it he allows the assassin, Professor Dent (a character not in the novel), to enter his room and, thinking 007 is lying in bed, fire six shots into the pile of pillows that Bond has arranged under the sheets. Once Dent has had his six, Bond appears out of the shadows and after a few perfunctory questions, shoots him in cold blood. He even delivers a superfluous *coup de grâce* into Dent's back as he lies dead on the floor. This kind of hard-nosed behaviour is never repeated.

Fleming was always very polite about *Dr No* and its successor, *From Russia with Love*, the premiere of which he attended in October 1963. Both films had cashed in on the best-seller status of the novels, and their popularity ensured that the paperbacks did brisk business: in 1960 Bond was selling at a rate of 6,000 paperback copies a week; by 1964 the figure was over 112,000. In fact between 1960 and 1964 Fleming's earnings increased tenfold, the Bond cult had become a global phenomenon, and the amounts of money involved were now so vast that they had become almost abstract.

Ian Fleming looked on all of this with an air of intrigued detachment. He had little believed, twelve years earlier, when he let down the jalousies in his room at Goldeneye and began to hammer out the odd, airless dream world of *Casino Royale*, that one day these daydreams would become a global phenomenon. And now he too had become a legend. Once he had written – not entirely seriously – that his ideal existence would be to be the absolute ruler of a country where everyone was crazy about him. 'Imagine yourself waking up', he wrote, 'and instantly the radio would announce to a breathless country "He's awake." Bulletins would follow: "He's shaving." "He's dressing." "He's breakfasting." "He's reading the papers in the garden." Finally at 10.30, "He's ordered the car!" and at 11 o'clock I'd pass out through the gates tossing medals to deliriously happy hundreds of thousands. I'd like that. And so would they.'

Evidence that Bond really had crossed the line between fiction and reality: a get-well card from Bedford Public Library, sent in the wake of From Russia with Love.

Now he had fame he wasn't so sure. 'Ashes, old boy – just ashes,' as he told a friend. 'You've no idea how bored one gets with the whole silly business.' But one surprise consolation of celebrity was that Ian finally came face to face with the real James Bond. The American ornithologist whose name Fleming had borrowed from the spine of *Birds of the West Indies* was visiting Jamaica and invited himself to lunch. Fleming was flattered, and he found Mr and Mrs James Bond 'a charming couple who are amused by the whole joke'.

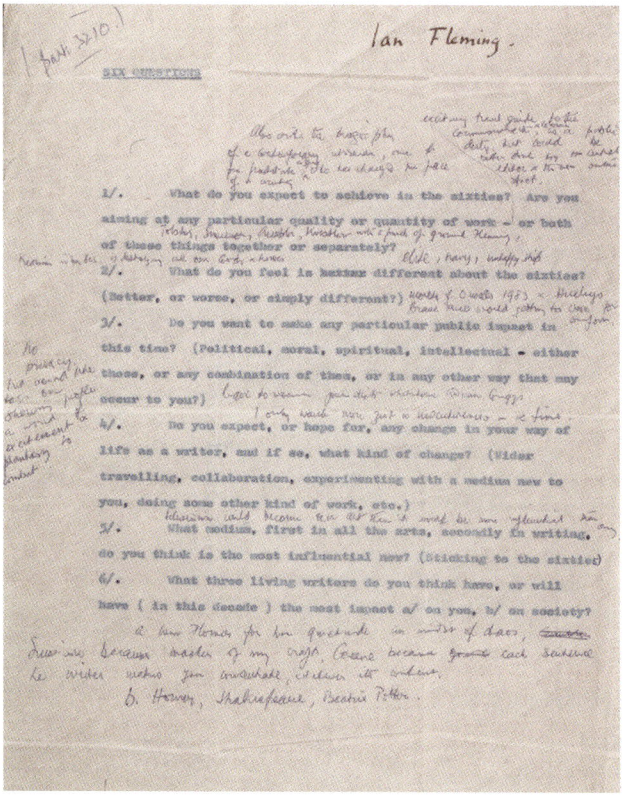
Ian Fleming.

SIX QUESTIONS

1/. What do you expect to achieve in the sixties? Are you aiming at any particular quality or quantity of work – or both of these things together or separately?

2/. What do you feel is better different about the sixties? (Better, or worse, or simply different?)

3/. Do you want to make any particular public impact in this time? (Political, moral, spiritual, intellectual – either these, or any combination of them, or in any other way that may occur to you?)

4/. Do you expect, or hope for, any change in your way of life as a writer, and if so, what kind of change? (Wider travelling, collaboration, experimenting with a medium new to you, doing some other kind of work, etc.)

5/. What medium, first in all the arts, secondly in writing, do you think is the most influential now? (Sticking to the sixties)

6/. What three living writers do you think have, or will have (in this decade) the most impact a/ on you, b/ on society?

b. Homer, Shakespeare, Beatrix Potter.

Fleming faced what was to be the last decade of his life with equanimity, as this written interview shows.

Another, more predictable, consequence of 007's burgeoning fame was the number of James Bond satires that began to appear written in Fleming's own eminently imitable style. *Alligator, by I*n Fl*m*ng* (1962), was a full-length novel produced by two enterprising students at Harvard University, that reworked many Bond scenes from the books and was so close to the original that its humour value was lost. A stranger, and possibly more apt, parody of James Bond was written by Fleming's friend Cyril Connolly, who had long been an advocate of Bond among the twittering London intelligentsia. He read his satirical short story 'Bond Strikes Camp' to Ian and Ann in the autumn of 1962, apparently hoping that its salacious content would irk Fleming, who remained impassive throughout, 'like a whale being nibbled by a little fish'. What Fleming had listened to was Connolly's attempt to give voice to the quietly held view, which very occasionally surfaced in the newspapers, that James Bond, with all his fussiness over food and cars and clothes, was actually quite camp – even gay, despite his strong views on that 'herd of unhappy sexual misfits' which chimed so closely with Fleming's own.

In 'Bond Strikes Camp', published in April 1963, soon after *On Her Majesty's Secret Service*, James Bond's mission is to go in drag to a transvestite nightclub above The Kitchener pub in Fulham and ensnare a monosyllabic Russian general. After the usual routine – the file from M, the visit to the armourer – plus a leg waxing, an extremely grumpy James Bond arrives at the club in a cocktail dress. There he meets an odd-looking character calling himself Gerda Blond, who turns out to be

Loelia Ponsonby – Bond's secretary – dressed as a man. Refusing her attempts to get him on to the dance floor, 007 finally catches the eye of the Russian general, who invites him back to his flat. As Bond wonders quite how far he is expected to go in the line of duty, the Russian leaps on him and in the tussle that follows his disguise falls off and Bond recognizes that the general is none other than M himself.

In retrospect Fleming rather liked Connolly's schoolboyish satire, and after it was published he cabled his friend to express the 'intoxicating pleasure' of being pilloried by him on the same weekend that the *Sunday Times* claimed that 'James Bond is what every man would like to be, and what every woman would like between her sheets.'

Fleming was right to accept parody as a form of flattery, and on one occasion he was not above having a go at it himself. When Lord Beaverbrook abruptly dropped the long-running cartoon of James Bond in the *Daily Express*, Fleming promptly set to work on a short story satirizing the press baron, entitled 'The Shameful Dream'. This remained unfinished – it was suppressed during his lifetime, and never will be published – but in it Fleming attempted to add a few extra eggs to his own rich omelette. The story begins with the newspaper editor 'Caffery Bone' leaving the office: 'The fat leather cushions hissed their resentment at the contact with the shiny seat of his trousers and hissed again as he leant back while the chauffeur tucked the mutation mink round his knees. The door of the Rolls closed with a rich double click and with a sigh from the engine and a well-mannered efflatus from the bulb horn the car nosed with battleship grace away from the station approaches . . .'

International editions of the Bond stories proliferated, each with its own distinctive packaging. This is the window of the Doubleday bookshop on New York's 52nd Street, featuring a display created to launch The Spy Who Loved Me.

These literary jousting matches proved to be some of the rare highlights in the frustrating final chapter of Ian Fleming's life. Ever since a heart attack in 1961 Ian had not been well, but against his doctor's advice he persisted in smoking and drinking far more than was good for him. 'I've always had one foot not wanting to leave the cradle, and the other in a hurry to get to the grave, which has made for an uncomfortable existence,' he had written in a notebook. Fleming was determined to live his life as he wanted, without restrictions, whatever the consequences. But gradually his enveloping heart disease meant less diving on his beloved reef at Goldeneye, less golf, and less scrambled egg. If those closest to him had had their way, it would also have meant less Bond too, as the mental energy Ian used to be able to summon up to write the books at full speed from beginning to end was now dearly bought. 'It's painful watching him create another Bond – I honestly don't how he can keep doing it,' wrote Ann in 1963. 'To start with, the writing was a sort of holiday for him. Then about four years ago it began to be a bit of a grind. A sweat, something he had to go on with, something he had to keep doing.' Fleming was all too aware of this drudgery. 'What was easy at 40 is very difficult at 50,' he admitted. 'I used to believe – sufficiently – in Bonds & Blonds & Bombs. Now the keys creak as I type and I fear the zest may have gone. Part of the trouble is having a wife and child. They knock the ruthlessness out of one. I shall definitely kill off Bond with my next book.'

But, for whatever reason, Fleming never could bring himself to kill off Bond forever. 'I can't afford to now,' he told a journalist in 1964, well aware that by then, more than ever, he could. In January of that year Fleming went to Jamaica for the last time and, despite the 'iron crab' now tightening its grip on his heart, he somehow dragged up enough energy to produce the first draft of *The Man with the Golden Gun*. He found the process so exhausting that he was able to write for only an hour a day, and he returned to England not at all sure that this first draft was up to his required standard. Determined that he should finish with a 'rich bang rather than a poor whimper', he resolved to perfect the manuscript over the course of the summer. But by now time was against him.

Soon after Easter 1964 Ian went out to play a round of golf at Huntercombe in the pouring rain, which left him with a cold. Two weeks later this had developed into pleurisy. After a short spell in hospital he found himself convalescing at the Dudley Hotel in Hove, where, in a curious symmetry, he found himself once again close to his mother. The redoubtable Mrs Val, by now very old and frail herself, was convalescing at a hotel nearby in Brighton. After decades of spurning convention she had finally settled in Monte Carlo and embarked on a long relationship with the octogenarian peer Lord Winchester. It was, she maintained, 'as pure as the Easter lily'. Winchester died in 1962, and Mrs Val had returned to England to live out her last years. On 26 July Ian's mother suffered a massive stroke and died, and less than a month later, on 12 August 1964, Fleming suffered a second heart attack and died himself. He was only fifty-six.

Though his death had been long predicted, it still shocked everyone who knew him. At least it had been quick, which was some consolation, as Ian had always hated infirmity in others and in himself, and he would have made a very bad old man. 'There was nothing really ahead of him,' wrote his brother Peter, 'so I suppose one must feel that it was, in that repulsive phrase, "for the best".'

What was ahead of him was the 'great splurge' of Bond sales that Fleming had long predicted. He had already sold 40 million books, and when the film of *Goldfinger* came out later that year it followed *Dr No* and *From Russia with Love* in breaking all box-office records. In 1965 alone 27 million Bond novels were sold in eighteen different languages. James Bond was now a worldwide concern, and the merchandising was as staggering as it was endless. James Bond items included, in alphabetical order, anoraks, bedspreads, belts, chewing gum, cummerbunds, doll's houses, hats, kites, knickers, leather goods, lingerie, a 007 room at the London Hilton, pipes, pyjamas, skirts, slacks, socks, tiepins, toiletries, towels, toys, wallpaper, watches and whistles. In the midst of all this Bondmania, in 1964, Fleming's children's story, *Chitty Chitty Bang Bang*, was published, followed by *The Man with the Golden Gun* in 1965. This final novel received polite and rather sad reviews, recognizing that the book had effectively been left half-finished, and as such did not represent Fleming on the top of his game.

Octopussy, a collection of short stories, appeared in 1966, and after that the Fleming estate decided to sanction a 'continuation Bond' to ward off the growing number of Bond imitators around the world. The novelist Kingsley Amis, a long-time fan of James Bond, wrote the first of these in 1968, under the pseudonym of Robert Markham. Though *Colonel Sun* contained all the usual Bond elements, Fleming's distinctive, laconic prose style was missing. The experiment was repeated thirteen years later when British thriller writer John Gardner attempted to step into Fleming's shoes; he was to produce fourteen more continuation novels. When Gardner stepped down the long-time Bondologist Raymond Benson came forward and wrote six more. It is fair to say that none of these efforts comes anywhere close to the standard of the original Fleming novels – nor could they, as Fleming's original voice, which after his death the critics continued to savage or applaud, was unique. He had many imitators and no heirs, and to this day his novels remain as escapist, thrilling and entertaining as ever.

THE MAN *with the* GOLDEN GUN

1965

First line

The Secret Service holds much that is kept secret even from very senior officers in the organization.

Story

The Man with the Golden Gun was painful for Fleming to write, and it shows. He managed to complete the first draft months before his death, and the manuscript was then polished by Kingsley Amis and others before it was finally published posthumously in 1965. The story is weak and the characters are sketchy – the villain and the girl being particularly unconvincing. Apart from a couple of scenes, *The Man with the Golden Gun* is what it is, an unfinished muddle, but it begins well. Bond returns to London from Vladivostock, having been brainwashed by the Russians, and his first act is to attempt to assassinate M with a poison-spraying pistol. M's quick reactions save him, and Bond is sent off for six months' 'de-brainwashing' before being presented with one more assignment. He is let loose on the trail of Francisco 'Pistols' Scaramanga, a freelance hit man controlled by the KGB, who has used his gold-plated Colt .45 to assassinate countless secret-service personnel in the Caribbean. Posing as 'Mark Hazard', a security man, Bond meets Scaramanga in Jamaica, and is immediately recognized as a fellow traveller and hired as a personal bodyguard. That weekend an assorted collection of hoods arrive at Scaramanga's half-built hotel, and Bond discovers that this crew are planning to sabotage Jamaica's bauxite industry, smuggle drugs to America, and set fire to the sugar-cane fields to bolster Castro's sugar business.

Listening to their conference through the closed door, Bond realizes that they are on to him too, and that Scaramanga has already planned a particularly unpleasant death. In the final section the party boards a light railway for a trip through the swamps and Bond is tricked into believing that Mary Goodnight of the Jamaican station is tied to the tracks ahead. A gun battle ensues, and Bond, Scaramanga and Felix Leiter (who has been hiding on the train) manage to jump clear before the engine hits the 'girl' – a dummy – and explodes, plunging into the swamp. Bond follows Scaramanga's trail of blood to a clearing, and finally manages to kill him, but not before he has been wounded by one of Scaramanga's poison bullets. Bond convalesces in the arms of Mary Goodnight, and learns from M that he has just been awarded a knighthood for his services to his country. Of course he refuses it.

Last line

At the same time, he knew, deep down, that love from Mary Goodnight, or from any other woman, was not enough for him. It would be like taking 'a room with a view'. For James Bond, the same view would always pall.

Inspirations

For Bond's final outing he is back in familiar territory – Jamaica – which is described in Fleming's usual bright, snappy style. There are also many devices that Fleming reuses in this book, such as the light railway, which he had associated with danger ever since he crashed his car into a train outside Munich as a student. He had already used this device in *Diamonds are Forever*, and he repeats it here. The scene of the villains' conference is very similar to that in *Goldfinger*, as indeed are the odd assortment of crooks. What is new is the influence of the films (*Dr No* and *From Russia with Love* had both come out), and there are far more gadgets in this than in previous novels. The poison-spray gun was a real assassin's tool as used by Bogdan Stashinsky, a Soviet agent who killed two men with it before defecting to the West in 1960. Fleming appropriated the device and its use precisely. Alongside this real Cold War gadget are a number of Fleming's own inventions, ranging from the hi-tech remotely triggered 'Fluoroscope' that takes a surreptitious X-ray of Bond as he walks down a corridor in the secret service, to a classic spy trick lifted straight from a comic, where Bond cuts two eyeholes in his newspaper so he can observe what is going on behind it.

What the critics said

'Surprisingly quiet' – *York Evening Press*

'James Bond should have had a better exit. Sadly, [*The Man with the Golden Gun*] . . . ends not with a bang but a whimper. The world will be a vastly more lacklustre and complicated place with 007 gone' – *Newsweek*

'Action too often stagnates: Bond's amorous sideplay is stilted, and the "epilogue", in which 007 recovers M's approval, is wearisomely anticlimactic' – *Illustrated London News*

'Bond and Fleming were fun. They entertained, sometimes mildly, often grandly – but always consistently. Life will be less interesting without them' – Associated Press

'For those who like to escape to Bondsville, the old boom-town hasn't changed a scrap' – *The Listener*

'Perhaps Ian Fleming was very tired when he wrote it. Perhaps – his publishers don't tell us – he left it unrevised. The fact remains that this posthumous Bond is a sadly substandard job' – *Observer*

'The latest brush to be thrown on one of the damnedest wildfires of all time – the James Bond Industry . . . A gory, glittering saga . . . the James Bond spirit soars on' – *New York Times*

'Bond has gone out like a lamb; even the girls are below par, while the villain seems like a refugee from a seedy Western. But we'll miss our James' – *Books and Bookmen*

'James Bond is a phenomenon of the Sixties and will probably endure until a more sophisticated generation forgets him' – *Hartford Conneticut Times*

'*The Man with the Golden Gun* is undeniably slight, but, like everything Fleming wrote, intensely readable . . . In a sense, Fleming's job was finished. He had irrevocably transformed the genre in which he worked: and, unlike so many intellectuals who toy with the thriller, he had done so from exactly the right point of view . . . Deliberately he produced fairy stories for worldly adults, and made them as glossy and sensually appealing as he could . . . In highbrow novels sex and violence are treated gloomily: in Fleming's stories they are presented cheerfully and with frank enjoyment. This is what the leftists hate, just as they hate fox-hunting, not because it gives pain to foxes but because it gives pleasure to humans' – Anthony Lejeune, *National Review*

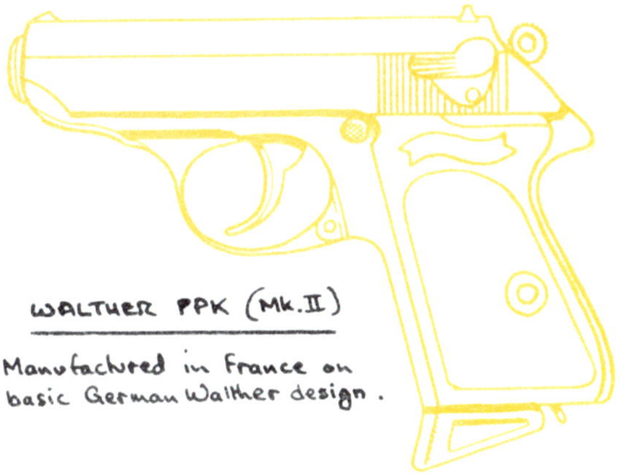

In a break with his 'series', Chopping spelled out the title for Cape's hardback vertically rather than horizontally, but the title page was styled more conventionally. Bond arms himself with a Walther PPK for his encounter with Scaramanga.

FLEMING AND THE CRITICS

'I think a writer should not put on a top hat when he sits down at his typewriter. He mustn't make the mistake of thinking that literature has to be literary.'
– Ian Fleming in a letter to one of his editors

IAN FLEMING

has also written

From Russia, With Love

'Ian Fleming is the most exciting new writer of thrillers to appear since the war, and the phenomenal success of his first four books suggests that a great many other people agree . . . he combines the more sensational features of American gangster fiction with a high degree of literacy and genuine sophistication ; then he presents his whole sleek creation with a cosmopolitan flourish.' TABLET

Diamonds are Forever

'James Bond is one of the most cunningly synthesized heroes in crime-fiction. He combines the tough-tender glamour of the sado-masochistic, Casanovesque private eye with the connoisseurship of a member—perhaps a rather new one — of White's, laces this already heady mixture with a shot of the Buchanish Imperialist spirit, and adds a tiny pinch of ground Ashenden . . . Mr. Fleming's method is worth noting, and recommending.' OBSERVER

Moonraker

'Sheer good writing and skilful development. The game, its setting and the way Mr. Fleming leads up to it make me a convinced admirer of Bond—and of Mr. Fleming.' OXFORD MAIL

'"Astonish me!" the addict may challenge ; Mr. Fleming can knock him sideways.' SCOTSMAN

Live and Let Die

'The second adventure of his Secret Service agent fully maintains the promise of his first book . . . containing passages which for sheer excitement have not been surpassed by any modern writer in this kind.'
THE TIMES LITERARY SUPPLEMENT

'Speed . . . Tremendous zest . . . communicated excitement. Brrh! How wincingly well Mr. Fleming writes.' SUNDAY TIMES

Casino Royale

'Here is the best new thriller-writer since Ambler.' SUNDAY TIMES
'Exciting and extremely civilized.' THE TIMES LITERARY SUPPLEMENT
'A first-rate thriller.' MANCHESTER GUARDIAN
'Supersonic John Buchan.' LISTENER

Ian Fleming had a very peculiar relationship with his critics. Being well connected with various newspaper proprietors, Fleming was never shy about personally promoting his books, and wherever possible he tried to secure himself favourable notices. For the most part this charm offensive was successful, and the first five Bond novels were all well received by reviewers, who, while enjoying the idiosyncratic cocktail of James Bond, were not quite sure whether they should be taking it all seriously or not. Yet, despite Ian's efforts both on the page and off it, book sales remained distinctly average. The situation was worse in America, where both *Casino Royale* and *Live and Let Die* had failed to impress.

Then in 1958 everything began to change and, broadly speaking, the British public's wholesale discovery of James Bond coincided with the critics falling distinctly out of love with 007. When Ian came back from Jamaica in March 1958 with the manuscript of *Goldfinger*, his seventh novel, in his battered case, he eagerly awaited reviews of *Dr No*, which was about to be published. He could not have expected what lay in store. 'Sex, snobbery and sadism,' trumpeted Paul Johnson in the *New Statesman*. Johnson believed *Dr No* contained three basic ingredients, 'all unhealthy, all thoroughly English – the sadism of the schoolboy bully, the mechanical two-dimensional sex-longings of a frustrated adolescent, and the crude, snob-cravings of a suburban adult'. In short, it was the nastiest book he had ever read. Other reviewers commented in the same vein, particularly Bernard Bergonzi in *Twentieth Century*, who deplored the 'strongly marked streak of voyeurism and sado-masochism' in Fleming's books and 'the total lack of any ethical frame of reference'. Suddenly the knives were out for James Bond, and the secret agent was now somehow part of the downward spiral of morality in society – possibly even responsible for it.

Fleming did attempt to defend his creation – 'a squeak from the butterfly before any more big wheels roll down upon it' – but he was not a man who enjoyed being taken to task, and he did not want to be held in some way responsible for Britain's moral decline. There was nothing he could do about *Goldfinger*, which he had already written, but his next offerings did attempt to depart from the formula: *For Your Eyes Only* was a collection of short stories, and a novel later, in *The Spy Who Loved Me*, he tried to write a Bond story from the Bond girl's point of view. Ironically, neither of these experiments was critically or commercially successful, as by 1960 the public had acquired their own taste for James Bond, and what they wanted was more of the same.

As the critics sunk their talons into 007, Ian might have expected to count on the steadfast support of Ann. But Ian's wife had never been a Bond fan. 'I don't like sadism and I thought it sadistic,' she said of *Casino Royale*, and when he offered to dedicate the book to her she refused, saying that 'surely one doesn't dedicate books of this sort to people'. 007 was good for keeping Ian happy and busy, and provided a useful antidote to his natural melancholia, but Ann never pretended that James Bond thrillers were the sort of books she read, or that Evelyn Waugh and her other highbrow friends read either. 'Ann gives me absolute hell about the stuff I write,' Ian once told a friend. 'She says "Ian you're capable of doing something really fine." She doesn't understand, you see, that I've extended my talent, such as it is, to the limit. With these James Bond things I've found my niche.'

There is no doubt that Fleming had to endure a degree of light-hearted banter about Bond at home, which he accepted with good grace. And there is also no doubt that Ann's lukewarm response hurt Ian, whose ego was far less robust than it seemed. Behind his bluff exterior Fleming was a man of remarkably low self-esteem, and he craved the approval of the critics, even if he disliked them. 'I'm not in the Shakespeare stakes,' he declared. 'My books are straight pillow-book fantasies of the bang-bang kiss-kiss variety.' Nevertheless, Fleming was a bibliophile who collected books and admired writers; he may have bought himself a Thunderbird – the boy racer's choice – but in the same year he also purchased a collection of Dylan Thomas's original manuscripts (*Under Milk Wood* was published the same year as *Live and Let Die*). Noël Coward was frustrated on his friend's behalf. 'His observation is extraordinary and his talent for description vivid,' he wrote. 'I wish he would try a non-thriller for a change; I would so love him to triumph over the sneers of Annie's intellectual friends.' Coward also predicted, with great prescience, that the combination of fairy-tale stories and Fleming's vivid writing style would ensure that the Bond books would go on being read 'long after the Quennells and Connollys have disappeared'.

Noël Coward correctly identified Fleming as something of a maverick on the literary scene. Critics often found the books 'maddeningly readable', and recognized that Fleming was an 'uncommonly fine writer', but they were equally aware that the stories themselves were predictable and incredible. 'Comic book thrillers in U prose' was how one reviewer described them. 'U prose' referred to Nancy Mitford's 1954 essay 'The English Aristocracy', which provoked a national debate about class and snobbery. In this she declared that class was defined by language as much as by anything else, and provided a list of words that illustrated this effect. 'Looking glass', 'bike' and 'napkin' were all 'U' (or upper-class) words, whereas 'mirror', 'cycle' and 'serviette' were all 'non-U'. James Bond, the well-dressed, well-fed, well-written hero of the kind of books that were known as 'penny dreadfuls', was a curious hybrid that straddled this divide. Certainly at the time, Bond had no equivalents. Alongside *Live and Let Die* and *From Russia with Love* were published British thrillers called *Spinsters in Peril* or *Alibi Innings*, about skulduggery at a village cricket match. Raymond Chandler, who was a friend of Fleming's, also recognized that James Bond had unique qualities. From an American perspective, 'Ian Fleming is probably the most forceful and driving writer of what I suppose must still be called thrillers in England.' He admired Fleming's departure from conventional mandarin English, his 'daring' sense of place and 'acute sense of pace'. Chandler might have also added that Fleming was unique in having such an acute interest in 'things'.

No other contemporary author so shamelessly indulged in what today would be called product placement. This habit always raised the hackles of the critics, as they felt that to mention names of real products was somehow vulgar. Bond smoked Morland cigarettes and drank Old Grand-Dad bourbon – details that turned him from a serious secret agent into 'an ad-man's mannequin' from 'the wardrobe school of writing'. This sort of thing may not have been in good taste, but Fleming knew that his readers liked to feel 'in the know', and if that involved snobbery then so be it. He wanted to be 'in the know' too. Today books that adopt this style are loosely known as 'sex and shopping' novels, and Ian Fleming can rightly be regarded as an early pioneer of this genre, an accidental by-product of his own curiosity with things. The critics may not have liked it, but in this Fleming was uniquely in step with the times, as *Playboy* acknowledged in 1963: 'His hard-paced, sexy thrillers with their hard- paced, sexy hero James Bond, their photographic sense of place, their mixture of culinary details, current events and fantasy, are precisely, uncannily suited to the mood of the sixties.'

While the critics continued to wrestle with James Bond, unable to decide whether Fleming was writing bad novels very well or good novels that were bad for the soul, the public began to read the adventures of 007 in their millions. When, in 1961, Jack Kennedy named *From Russia with Love* as one of his favourite books of all time, this seal of approval had an extraordinary effect on the sales of James Bond in America. By the end of that year Fleming became the biggest-selling thriller writer in the States, and from this date onward 007 burst out of his chrysalis from cult hero to global phenomenon. By 1964, the *News of the World* regarded the secret agent as a 'national institution . . . as typical of the age as Beatlemania, juvenile deliquency or teenagers in boots'. Fleming even joked that he had become 'the fifth Beatle'. 'I'm still puzzled as to why and how it happened,' he said. 'But so far I have written twelve best-selling thrillers that have been translated into twenty-three languages. My contribution to the export drive is simply staggering. I suppose it's equivalent to the earning power of a small boot factory.' If the numbers prove anything, then Ian Fleming had had the last word.

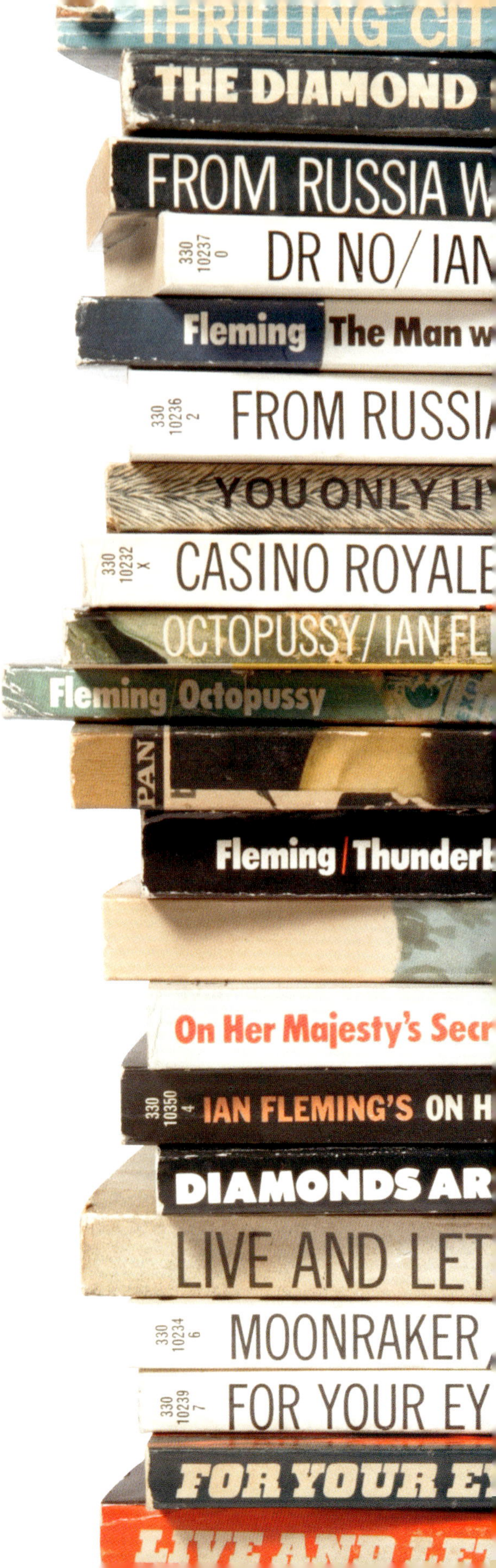

OCTOPUSSY AND THE LIVING DAYLIGHTS

1966

This is a posthumous collection of short stories, in which only 'Octopussy' and 'The Living Daylights' are the main attractions. 'Property of a Lady' was commissioned by Sotheby's to sit in its annual journal, *The Ivory Hammer*, and is really an excursion into the drama of the auction room. '007 in New York' (originally entitled 'Reflections in a Carey Cadillac') is simply Bond's rumination on the fall from grace of that great city, written in 1963. It is remarkable in two respects: first, it contains the only instance in the entire series of Bond going shopping (he buys razors, toothbrushes and French golf socks); second, it contains his recipe for scrambled eggs, cribbed from May Maxwell, Ivar Bryce's Scottish housekeeper.

OCTOPUSSY

Named after a coracle that Blanche Blackwell had given him after a stay at Goldeneye.

First line

'You know what?' said Major Dexter Smythe to the octopus. 'You're going to have a real treat today if you can manage it.'

Story

Written before *You Only Live Twice*, this unusual short story is another in the manner of 'Quantum of Solace', where Bond is merely the catalyst for a tale of deceit. Major Dexter Smythe is an indolent, overweight ex-commando officer living on the north coast of Jamaica, who spends his days paddling around the reef and feeding his 'pet' octopus, 'Octopussy'. His quiet existence is disturbed by the arrival of Bond, who has some awkward questions to ask about an Austrian ski instructor named Hannes Oberhauser, who disappeared during the later stages of the war. At that time Smythe was working for the Miscellaneous Objectives Bureau (MOB), looking for hidden caches of Nazi gold. Bond's careful cross-examination prompts Smythe to admit that he had known the Austrian. Smythe had employed Oberhauser to lead him up to the Franzikaner Halt, a refuge on the mountain above Kitzbühel, where he knew that a hoard of Nazi gold was buried. Once there, Smythe murdered Oberhauser, stole the large block of gold, and hid it in Jamaica, where he has been living off the proceeds ever since. When the truth emerges, Bond gives Smythe ten minutes to consider his options, adding that he has a personal interest in the story as Oberhauser had been a father figure to him during his teenage years and had taught him to ski. Out on the reef, Smythe decides not to submit to the inevitable ignominy of a court martial and allows himself to be stung by a scorpion fish, Octopussy's favourite food. He dies as the octopus begins to eat him.

Last lines

It is only from the notes of Dr Greaves, who performed the autopsy, that it has been possible to construct some kind of postscript to the bizarre and pathetic end of a once valuable officer of the secret service.

Inspirations

Though James Bond is peripheral to this tale, Fleming is on home ground here, as the story concerns tropical fish, the wartime exploits of commandos, and the mountains of Kitzbühel. Hidden Nazi gold was a popular subject at the time, and, as a man for ever interested in treasure hunting, Ian commissioned an article for the *Sunday Times* from his friend Anthony Terry (a former intelligence commando himself) on the Nazi gold that was being recovered from Lake Toplitz. The character of Dexter Smythe is so well drawn that he sounds like a neighbour or friend, which he may well have been, as there were plenty like him in Jamaica – men who discovered they could get by on very little in that tropical hideaway.

Fleming had met a number of them in the Seychelles too – 'pencil-thin Colonels' living off £500 a year with their dusky girlfriends in tow.

THE LIVING DAYLIGHTS

Original title: *Trigger Finger*

First line

James Bond lay at the five-hundred yard firing point of the famous Century range at Bisley.

Story

In this taut tale, Bond – the best marksman in the service – is given the unenviable task of assassinating an assassin. He is sent to West Berlin, and there he holes up in a flat overlooking the no man's land that separates the Eastern and Western sectors of the city. At the appointed hour, in the early evening, a British agent is going to attempt the dangerous crossing from East to West, and the British have been tipped off that a top Russian marksman, nicknamed Trigger, will attempt to kill him. Opposite Bond is a tall, faceless building where it is presumed that Trigger will hide. Bond spends three anxious days in the flat with Captain Sender, a staff man calculated to irritate Bond ('over-crammed and under-loved'). Each afternoon Bond watches a procession of musicians entering the building opposite, and he idly fantasizes about the beautiful blonde girl carrying a cello case. On the third evening the British agent at last decides to makes his run, and Bond spots the barrel of a rifle appear out of an upstairs windows of the building opposite. Behind it is an unmistakable lock of blonde hair – the assassin is the cello girl. Bond uses his .308 Winchester to deliberately hit the gun and not the girl, which irritates Sender, who accuses him of missing intentionally. Bond could not care less.

Last lines

James Bond said wearily, 'Okay. With any luck it'll cost me my Double-O number. But tell Head of Station not to worry. That girl won't do any more sniping. Probably lost her left hand. Certainly broke her nerve for that kind of work. Scared the living daylights out of her. In my book, that was enough. Let's go.'

Inspirations

This story was written in two weeks at the end of September 1961, before *On Her Majesty's Secret Service*. It may well have been inspired by Pat Reid's famous wartime escape from Colditz castle, where the escapers had to run across an open courtyard between two sentries and used an orchestra to cover their movements. Reid had described this in *The Colditz Story*, and the man who conducted the orchestra, Douglas Bader, had played golf with Ian on a number of occasions.

Fleming had visited Berlin in May 1960 as part of the European leg of his *Thrilling Cities* tour, and he stayed a few days with Anthony Terry. Terry, a sometime spy himself, had introduced him to another, and Ian was fascinated to learn that the Allies had dug a secret tunnel beneath no man's land from which they had tapped into the Soviet telephone exchange. Armed with these memories and a map, Fleming placed Bond's hideout at 40a Wilhelmstrasse, a house barred to civilians that directly overlooked Checkpoint Charlie. He also discovered that Russian women were particularly good at rifle shooting – at the last world championship they had come first, second and third.

The golden-haired cello girl, Trigger, is recognizably Amaryllis Fleming, Ian's ebullient younger half-sister, who was a concert cellist and had hair 'that shone like molten gold'. 'But', as Bond comments, 'why in hell did she have to choose the cello? There was something almost indecent in the idea of that bulbous, ungainly instrument splayed between her thighs. Of course Suggia had managed to look elegant, as did that girl Amaryllis somebody. But they should invent a way for women to play the damned thing side-saddle.'

What the critics said

'I am not surprised that Fleming preferred to write novels. James Bond, unlike Sherlock Holmes, does not fit snugly into the short story length: there is something grandiose and intercontinental about his adventures that requires elbow room and such examples of the form as we have tend to be eccentric or muted. These are no exception' – Philip Larkin, *The Spectator*

'Slight and predictable, and usual sex and violence yield to a plausible use of ballistics and marine biology' – *Times Literary Supplement*

Chopping's still life of a fly-encrusted shell and a fish marked the end of the Fleming books, but his artwork also appears on the hardback of John Gardner's Licence Renewed. *The backdrop to 'Octopussy' is the Caribbean that Fleming knew so well.*

ACKNOWLEDGEMENTS

I would like to acknowledge the following for permission to quote from copyright material: John Pearson, for the material he collected for his book *The Life of Ian Fleming*; Fionn Morgan, for letters from her mother Ann Fleming's estate; the estate of Ivar Bryce; the estate of Kingsley Amis; the National Maritime Museum for material from John Godfrey's papers; the Public Record Office.

Quotations are taken from *Colonel Z* by David Fisher and Anthony Read (pages 192-3), *Ashenden* by W. Somerset Maugham (page 193), *Plots and Paranoia* by Brian Porter (page 194) and *Clubland Heroes* by Richard Usborne (page 48). All other sources cited are drawn from the archive of Ian Fleming Publications.

The making of this book would not have been possible without the tireless help of Fleur Gooch, Zoe Watkins and Corinne Turner, who opened up the treasure chest and helped me navigate through its contents. My understanding of Ian Fleming has been increased immeasurably by his nieces Kate Grimond and Lucy Fleming, whose memories of Ian and their father, Peter, have proved invaluable. I would also like to thank Gordon Wise and Cathy Benwell at John Murray, Simon Trewin, Gavin and Charlotte Stewart, Chloe for her endurance and loveliness, and L., I. and E for their patience.

In addition the publisher would like to thank Louise Bowden of Allied Domecq, the Bahamas National Trust, Fred Brard of Bloody Mary for the picture of Harry's Bar in Paris, Bob Davenport, Robert Ellis of the Aston Martin Heritage Trust and Tim Roche of the Aston Martin Owners Club, Andrew Gailey and Nick Baker of Eton College, Alexander Gilkes of Krug, Duff Hart-Davis for permission to reproduce the letters of William Plomer, the Boothroyd estate for permission to reproduce the letters of Geoffrey Boothroyd, Mark Harvey of Moët Hennessy UK for the Dom Pérignon image, Louisa Hollins of Financial Dynamics for the Frank Cooper's image, Bruce Hunter of David Higham Associates, Kate Jones, Michael Korda, Mike Levett, Ivan Mulcahy and Charlie Viney of Mulcahy & Viney, Ian Paten, Sam Peffer, Stephen Pearlman of Japan Airlines, Anthony Tedeschi of the Lilly Library (Indiana University), Ian Thurgood of Wilkin & Sons, Elizabeth Vaughan of Pol Roger and Simon Winder.

Finally, Ian Fleming Publications Ltd/Ian Fleming Will Trust would like to thank Dr Jane Potter for all her work on the Ian Fleming archive.

BIBLIOGRAPHY

(Place of publication is London unless specified)

BOOKS BY IAN FLEMING: FICTION

Casino Royale, 1953; *Live and Let Die*, 1954; *Moonraker*, 1955; *Diamonds Are Forever*, 1956; *From Russia with Love*, 1957; *Dr No*, 1958; *Goldfinger*, 1959; *For Your Eyes Only*, 1960; *Thunderball*, 1961; *The Spy Who Loved Me*, 1962; *On Her Majesty's Secret Service*, 1963; *You Only Live Twice*, 1964; *Chitty Chitty Bang Bang*, 1964; *The Man with the Golden Gun*, 1965; *Octopussy and The Living Daylights*, 1966

BOOKS BY IAN FLEMING: NON-FICTION

The Diamond Smugglers, 1957; *Thrilling Cities*, 1963

OTHER BOOKS

Amis, Kingsley, *The James Bond Dossier*, Jonathan Cape, 1965

Amory, Mark (ed.), *The Letters of Ann Fleming*, Harvill Press, 1985

Andrew, Christopher, *Secret Service*, Heinemann, 1985

Atkins, John, *The British Spy Novel*, John Calder Publications Ltd, 1984

Barron, John, *KGB*, Hodder & Stoughton, 1974

Barrow, Andrew, *Gossip 1920–1970*, Hamish Hamilton, 1978

Bennett, Tony, and Woollacott, Janet, *Bond and Beyond: The Political Career of a Popular Hero*, Macmillan, 1987

Benson, Raymond, *The James Bond Bedside Companion*, Boxtree, 1988

Black, Jeremy, *The Politics of James Bond: From Fleming's Novels to the Big Screen*, Greenwood Press, Connecticut, 2001

Bryce, Ivar, *You Only Live Once*, Weidenfeld & Nicolson, 1975

Buchan, John, *The Thirty-Nine Steps*, Hodder & Stoughton, 1915

— *Greenmantle*, Hodder & Stoughton, 1916

— *Mr Standfast*, Hodder & Stoughton, 1919

Buono, Oreste del, and Eco, Umberto (eds), trans. R. A. Downie, *The Bond Affair*, MacDonald & Company, 1966

Calvocoressi, Peter, *The British Experience, 1945–75*, The Bodley Head, 1978

Cannadine, David, *In Churchill's Shadow: Confronting the Past in Modern Britain*, Allen Lane, 2002

Chapman, James, *Licence to Thrill: A Cultural History of the James Bond Films*, I.B. Tauris Publishers, 1999

Cookridge, E. H., *The Secrets of the British Secret Service*, Sampson Low, 1947

— *The Soviet Spy Net*, Fredrick Muller Ltd, 1955

— *Inside SOE: The Story of Special Operations in Western Europe 1940–5*, Arthur Barker, 1966

Cork, John, and Scivally, Bruce, *Bond: The Legacy*, Boxtree, 2002

Dalzel-Job, Patrick, *Arctic Snow to Dust of Normandy*, Leo Cooper, Barnsley, 2002

Dewar, Hugo, *Assassins at Large*, Wingate, 1951

Dorril, Stephen, *MI6: Fifty Years of Special Operations*, Fourth Estate, 2000

Elliott, Nicholas, *Never Judge a Man by his Umbrella*, Michael Russell, 1991

Fisher, Clive, *Cyril Connolly: A Nostalgic Life*, Picador, 1995

Fisher, David, and Read, Anthony, *Colonel Z: The Life and Times of a Master of Spies*, Hodder & Stoughton, 1984

Fitzgerald, F. Scott, *The Crack-up*, Penguin, 1947

Fleming, Peter, *Brazilian Adventure*, Jonathan Cape, 1933

— *One's Company: A Journey to China*, Jonathan Cape, 1934

— *The Flying Visit*, Jonathan Cape, 1940

— *The Sixth Column: A Singular Tale of Our Times*, Rupert Hart-Davis, 1951

— *Invasion 1940*, Rupert Hart-Davis, 1957

Fryer, Peter, *Mrs Grundy: Studies in English Prudery*, Dobson Books, 1963

Giblin, Gary, *James Bond's London*, Daleon Enterprises, New Jersey, 2001

Green, Timothy, *The Smugglers*, Michael Joseph, 1969

Greene, Graham, and Greene, Hugh, *The Spy's Bedside Book*, Rupert Hart-Davis, 1957

Hart-Davis, Duff, *Peter Fleming: A Biography*, Jonathan Cape, 1974

Knightley, Phillip, *The Second Oldest Profession: Spies and Spying in the Twentieth Century*, Pimlico, 2003

Lenart, Judith (sel.), *Yours Ever, Ian Fleming: Letters To and From Antony Terry*, Printhouse Nelson Ltd, New Zealand, 1994

Lycett, Andrew, *Ian Fleming*, Weidenfeld & Nicolson, 1995

McCormick, Donald, *17F: The Life of Ian Fleming*, Peter Owen, 1993

McKnight, Gerald, and Lesberg, Sandy, *The Secret War of Charles Fraser-Smith*, Michael Joseph, 1981

McLachlan, Donald, *Room 39: Naval Intelligence in Action 1939–45*, Weidenfeld & Nicolson, 1968

Maclean, Fitzroy, *Eastern Approaches*, Jonathan Cape, 1949

Marwick, Arthur, *British Society since 1945* (3rd edn), Penguin, 1996

Maugham, W. Somerset, *Ashenden*, Ayer Company Publishers, 1928

Meyers, Jeffery, *Somerset Maugham: A Life*, Alfred A. Knopf, New York, 2004

Minshall, Merlin, *Guilt-Edged*, Bachman & Turner, 1975
O'Brien-ffrench, Conrad, *Delicate Mission: Autobiography of a Secret Agent*, Skilton & Shaw, 1979
Pearson, John, *The Life of Ian Fleming*, Jonathan Cape, 1966
Popov, Dusko, *Spy/Counter Spy*, Weidenfeld & Nicolson, 1974
Porter, Bernard, *Plots and Paranoia*, Routledge, 1989
Quennell, Peter, *Wanton Chase: An Autobiography*, William Collins, 1980
Sapper, *The Final Count*, Hodder & Stoughton, 1926
— *Bulldog Drummond: His Four Rounds with Carl Peterson*, Hodder & Stoughton, 1929
Schellenberg, Walter, *The Gestapo Handbook*, St Ermin's Press, 2000
Space Weapons: A Handbook of Military Astronautics, Thames & Hudson, 1959
Stafford, David, *Camp X*, Viking, 1987
Usborne, Richard, *Clubland Heroes* (rev. edn), Barrie & Jenkins, 1975
Waldron, Tom, and Gleeson, James, *The Frogmen*, Evans Brothers, 1950
Wall, Robert, *Airliners*, Quarto, 1980
Welcome, John, *Cheating at Cards: The Cases in Court*, Faber and Faber, 1963
West, Nigel, *The Friends: Britain's Post-War Secret Service Intelligence Operations*, Weidenfeld & Nicolson, 1988
— *Counterfeit Spies*, St Ermin's Press, 1998
— (ed.), *The Faber Book of Espionage*, Faber and Faber, 1993
Winder, Simon (ed.), *My Name's Bond*, Allen Lane, 2000
Worswick, G., and Ady, P., *The British Economy in the 1950s*, Clarendon Press, Oxford, 1962
Wright, Peter, *Spycatcher: The Candid Autobiography of a Senior Intelligence Officer*, Heinemann Australia, Melbourne, 1987

PICTURE CREDITS

Original photography on pages 1, 14, 20, 21, 22, 23, 24, 25, 27, 39, 41, 42, 43, 45, 47, 52, 54, 56, 57, 62, 66, 75, 76, 78, 81, 82, 84, 85, 86, 87, 88, 91, 92, 93, 94, 95, 96, 97, 100, 101, 102–3, 104, 105, 106–7, 108, 109, 110, 114, 115, 118, 121, 123, 124, 125, 127, 128, 129, 130, 132, 133, 136, 140, 141, 144, 145, 146, 152, 153, 156, 157, 158, 159, 161, 163, 165, 166, 167, 168, 169, 170, 171, 172, 173, 176, 177, 178, 179, 180, 181, 183, 184, 187, 191, 194, 201, 204, 205, 206, 207, 208, 211, 212, 213, 217, 220, 221, 222, 223, 225, 226, 228, 229, 230, 231, 235, 236, 239, 240 by Derek Askem, © John Murray Publishers Ltd 2005.

Images on pages ii–iii, vi–1, 5, 6, 7, 8, 9, 11, 13, 14, 20, 21, 22, 23, 24, 25, 27, 35, 39, 40, 41, 42, 43, 45, 47, 51, 52, 54, 56, 57, 58, 62, 66, 67, 68, 75, 76, 78, 81, 82, 84, 85, 86, 87, 88, 89, 91, 92, 93, 94, 95, 96, 97, 100, 101, 102, 103, 104, 105, 106–7, 108, 109, 110, 111, 114, 115, 118, 120, 121, 123, 124, 125, 127, 128, 128–9, 130, 132, 133, 136, 138–9, 140, 141, 142, 144, 145, 146, 149, 152, 153, 154, 156, 157, 158, 159, 160, 161, 163, 164, 165, 166, 167, 168, 169, 170–1, 172, 173, 176, 177, 178, 179, 180, 181, 183, 184, 186, 187, 191, 194, 201, 202, 203, 204, 205, 206, 207, 208, 210, 211, 212, 213, 215, 217, 220, 221, 222, 223, 225, 226, 228, 229, 230, 231, 234, 235, 236, 239, 240, 248–9 courtesy Ian Fleming Publications Ltd.

The following credits also apply: The Advertising Archives 64, 83, 147, 150, 151; The Aston Martin Heritage Trust 155; Aston Martin Owners Club 156 (bottom); British Airways plc 170, 180–1; British Columbia Government Travel Bureau 14; Jonathan Cape 42, 56, 84, 110, 132, 142, 146, 186, 204, 234, 236; Jonathan Cape/Richard Chopping 96, 128, 164, 186, 204, 222, 240; map artwork by Martin Collins 72–3, 174–5; Conjay 163; Frank Cooper's Limited 89; Driberg Literary Estate, reproduced by kind permission of David Higham Associates 212; *Esquire* 191; Gordon Freund 184; courtesy of Harry's New-York-Bar Paris 61; letters reproduced by kind permission of Duff Hart-Davis 62, 106–7; CORBIS 219; Bettmann/CORBIS 119, 198 (left), 199; Hulton-Deutsch Collection/CORBIS 49, 198 (right); Marvin Koner/CORBIS 71; John Springer Collection/CORBIS 55; Crown Copyright 36, 37; The Provost and Fellows of Eton College 10, 12; Fergus Fleming 6, 13; Floris 66; Getty Images 189; Loomis Dean, Time Life Pictures/Getty Images 60; Kate Grimond 7, 8, 9, 11, 51; Lockheed 57; Hong Kong Tourist Association 145, 177; Japan Airlines 171, 181; John Jarrell, Inc. 153; Krug 90; Las Vegas News Bureau 169; Lightweight 163; The Lilly Library, Indiana University, Bloomington, Indiana 135; Macmillan Publishing Company, New York 52, 111; Publicité Societé Bains de Mer de Monte Carlo 82, 86, 133, 172; Miller Brewing Company 92; John Murray (Publishers) 69, 240–1; W. Ross Napier 208; Pan Books 75, 85, 100, 114, 176, 201, 239; courtesy John Pearson 15, 17, 19, 30, 134; Sam Peffer 43, 81, 118, 136, 140, 203; Queensland Government Tourist Bureau 130; Champagne Pol Roger 90; Samsonite 152; Shannon Free Airport 171; Smith & Wesson 163; with the kind permission of Sir Peter Smithers 35; Society for the Protection of Flamingos in the Bahamas 183; *Sunday Times* 45, 102, 169, 173; Swiss National Tourist Office 205; *The Times*, London 28; *Trade News* 47; Triumph 156 (top); Wilkin & Sons Limited, Tiptree 88; Graham M. Woodard 161, 235.

INDEX

IF refers to Ian Fleming and JB to 'James Bond'. Page numbers in *italics* refer to captions and illustrations. Fictional characters and places are shown in quotation marks e.g. 'Bond, James'; 'Crab Key'.

Från sluss

Catharina Grünbaum (text)
Tommy Grünbaum (foto)

till sluss

på franska kanaler

prisma

Omslagsbild: Fontenoy-le-Château vid Canal des Vosges i Alsace.

Prisma
Besöksadress: Tryckerigatan 4
Box 2052
103 12 Stockholm

www.prismabok.se

Prisma ingår i
Norstedts Förlagsgrupp AB,
grundad 1823

Formgivning: Tommy Grünbaum
Foto: Tommy Grünbaum
Kartor: Bertil Tillander
Teckningar: Håkan Ljung

Tryckt av Scangraphic, Polen 2009
Prepress: Fälth & Hässler, Värnamo
ISBN 978-91-518-5010-8

Förord

”Från sluss till sluss” är en till dels osannfärdig titel, och det ska läsaren vara glad för. Vi har under våra färder höjt eller sänkt oss genom mer än tusen slussar, men vi tänker inte beskriva dem alla eller ens vägen mellan dem. ”Från sluss till sluss” är ingen kanalhandbok. Den är heller ingen färdbeskrivning. Den kan snarast betecknas som en intrycksbok. Vår avsikt är inte att meddela något av omedelbar nytta. Däremot försöker vi ge någon sorts svar på den fråga som ofta ställs oss: ”Hur är det att glida omkring på kanalerna där nere?”

Sedan vi lämnade vår brygga i Mälaren sommaren 2004 har vi rört oss hit och dit i Tyskland, Holland, Belgien och Frankrike. Vi har gått vissa sträckor flera gånger, besökt somliga platser vid flera tillfällen, återupplivat bekantskapen med slussvakter och hamnkaptener (oftast till glädje, någon sällsynt gång till förargelse), haft besök av gamla vänner och fått nya i det odefinierade nätverk som utgörs av kanalfarare som möts, skils och möts igen. Dessutom har vi under tiden ersatt vår första ”Vanadis” med vår nuvarande ”Vanadis”. Att få någon ordning på berättandet är alltså nästan ogörligt.

För att inte gapa över för mycket låter vi intrycken från Tyskland, Holland och Belgien anstå. Vi börjar nästan direkt i Frankrike, ett land som utmed sina vattenleder för det mesta gör skäl för benämningen ”det ljuva”.

Catharina och Tommy Grünbaum

INNEHÅLL

Kanalliv

Slussvakten låter vänta på sig. Vi har förtöjt "Vanadis" i skuggan vid kanalbanken och slagit upp en flaska cider. Slusstiderna brukar hållas, annat kan inte sägas, men det finns mycket som kan hända i kanalsystemet – en trädgren i en slussport, för lite vatten längre bort eller något som bara är slussvaktens hemlighet. Bakom oss ligger för ovanlighetens skull en svensk segelbåt med masten surrad på däck. Ägaren är otålig. Med oss motorbåtsmänniskor befattar han sig inte, men hans två gastar, lägre i ordningen ombord, dristar sig till att tala med sina landsmän.

Om vi också är på väg ner till Medelhavet? Nej, faktiskt inte. Vi har heller inte tagit oss ner till det inre av Frankrike på nitton raska dygn. Fem år har vi haft på oss för att komma just hit.

I ärlighetens namn är vi också ibland lockade av blått fräsande vatten, fläktande vindar, vita kuststäder och vida horisonter. Men något håller oss kvar på gröna kanaler och floder i ett landskap som utvecklingen gått förbi, ensliga trakter med fågelsång i gryningen och grodor i natten och kor som kommer ner till vattnet för att dricka.

Och så alla dessa slussar.

Nu knattrar äntligen en uråldrig moped in framför slusshuset så att sanden ryker och hönsen sprätter åt sidan. Slusshunden vaknar och sträcker sömnigt på sig.

Jag går i land för att ta hand om ena porthalvan, som man gör i handvevade slussar.

Slussvakten tar av sig hjälmen och låter blicken glida över båtarna. En ryckning i mustaschen – jag tycker mig ana ett litet förslaget leende.

– Här har ni det bra, *hein?* Lugnt och skönt, inte behöva fara runt i hettan. Får ta vara på ögonblicken.

Ack, denna franska fräckhet förklädd till älskvärdhet!

Ta vara på ögonblicken, eller snarare sekunderna, är också seglarens avsikt. Han nosar oss i häcken fram till nästa sluss. Hundra till har han framför sig innan han når sina drömmars Medelhav. Men hur mycket han än försöker vakta på sekunderna kommer han att gå miste om ögonblicken.

Slussen är stängd, slussvakten någon annanstans. VNF, den franska kanalorganisationen, skapade ingen brådska.

Södermanlands skärgård, älskat hemmavatten.

Farväl till hemmavattnen

Många båtar har vi haft. Några vill vi glömma, men desto fler minns vi med värme och rent av lite saknad: skärgårdskryssaren ”Bimbi III”, ett läckande spjut som seglade om allt, den rara kostern ”Lucidor” som gjorde tvärtom, spetsgattern ”Sjöstorken” byggd 1938 av Kynzell i Borgå – hon red ut en storm på väg till Gotland, Sveakryssaren ”Syrsan”. De har burit oss runt den lummiga Mälaren, de har sträckt utmed Sveriges kuster och över till Ålands och Åbolands levande skärgårdar, till Danmarks trevna hamnar, till det kulinghärjade norska Sörlandet.

Flera gånger tog vi vägen genom Göta kanal, vars pastorala behag fick oss att överväga fler färder på inre vattenvägar. En dag hade vi tagit ner seglen för sista gången och börjat en ny sorts sommarliv, på en motorbåt.

Vi har upplevt Strömsholms kanal med Bergslagens järnbruk och blånande höjder, den älskliga Kinda kanals kulturlandskap med lövskog och herresäten, Dalslands vildmarkskanal med raggiga skogar och klara sjöar och till sist den norska Telemarks kanal, där man ser upp mot den snöfläckade Hardangervidda.

Hur kan man avstå från vattendrag som slingrar mellan björkhagar och enebackar och röda gårdar och doftande gulmåra? Hur kan man lämna skärgårdar med friskt vatten och öppna horisonter och vikar med dopping och skrak? Hur klarar själen sig utan långa ljusa nätter där skymning möter gryning?

Det kan vara så enkelt som att man en dag tycker att skärgårdsöarna är sig bra lika med slätsida åt söder och stötsida åt norr och däremellan en fuktig sänka med mygg, med för många båtar i läviken och för mycket grillos från flintastekar och tillräckligt med marodörer som i trettio larmande knop klyver ejderfamiljerna.

Och alla de där resorna som man vill göra nere på kontinenten – varför inte göra dem på egen köl? När man nu har en.

Vattenvägarna – ett kretslopp

Frankrike har ett nät av kanaler och floder, tillsammans mer än 800 mil. Det räcker i åratal för en kanalälskare, kanske en hel livstid.

Många sträckor är en förening av flod och kanal. Man färdas på floden för att emellanåt ledas in i en liten kanalstump med en sluss medan floden strömmar förbi intill och kastar sig utför en anlagd fördämning, en *barrage.* Sedan bär det av ut på floden igen. På andra sträckor går man på en grävd kanal som då och då förenar sig med den flod som förser den med vatten, som Canal du Nivernais, som ständigt möter och lämnar den flödande Yonne.

Att gå på kanaler är ett sätt att leva. Man färdas långsamt, annat är inte möjligt. Man har sitt hem med sig. Seglare må med förakt se på fritidsbåtarnas blomsterlådor, kryddodlingar, cyklar, tvättstreck och sällskapshundar. Men det är inte segelfartygen som är "Vanadis" förebild här nere utan pråmarna. Sådana som bebos av familjer utstrålar både trivsel och äventyr där de dunkar fram. Trivsel med prydliga spetsgardiner och blomkrukor och barnhage med plaskdamm på fördäck och matos från byssan. Äventyr med avlägsna hamnar som mål – Dunkerque, Nijmegen, Basel, Lyon ...

De pråmfarare, *bateliers,* vi har kommit i samtal med när vi gjort sällskap från sluss till sluss berättar enstämmigt om slitet, om osäkerheten med att få laster, om ensamheten när man alltid befinner sig i rörelse, men också om friheten, om samarbetet ombord där hustrun lika ofta och lika skickligt som mannen styr båten i och ur slussarna, om gemenskapen pråmfolk emellan och om tjusningen med de på en gång lugna och ständigt omväxlande vattenvägarna. De kan inte tänka sig ett annat sätt att leva. Är man född i en pråmsläkt – och det är de flesta – går man helst inte i land vid pensioneringen. Man bygger om lastrummet till bostad och stannar på vattnet.

Även för oss som färdas för nöjes skull är kanalfarandet en livsstil. Målet är oviktigt. Färden är meningen. De franska kanalerna och floderna vindlar genom ljuvliga landskap – vinberg, odlingar, betesmarker, slätter, kullar, åsar, skog, dalgångar. Man vet aldrig vad som ska dyka upp bakom nästa krök – ett slott, en sluss, en vit tjur i strandkanten. Städerna är mestadels av behaglig storlek med medeltida kyrkor och torg med kaféer och restauranger. Vill man undvika en stad som verkar trist är det bara att passera, och strax är man ute på landet igen. Inga stora fula förstäder, inga avfarter att köra fel på.

Städerna är för övrigt få. Den bebyggelse man möter mest är små grå byar, bondgårdar och beblomstrade slusshus.

Vi är många som har givit oss hän åt livet på vattenvägarna, men inte så många att det någonsin blir trångt (utom på Canal du Midi under sommarsäsongen). Här mitt i Frankrike möter man emellanåt den frid som övergår allt förstånd, och det är också det enda man möter när man i det dunkelrosa kvällsljuset har slagit ner sina förtöjningsspikar i kanalbankens gräs.

Vi vet att det finns ett annat Frankrike. Ett land med inre motsättningar, ett land med såväl rikedom som svåra sociala förhållanden, ett land där protester övergår i upplopp, ett land där bilar sticks i brand.

Vi behöver inte utrusta oss med skygglappar för att undvika det. Floderna och kanalerna ser till att vi passerar vid sidan om, inte bara i rummet utan även i tiden.

Men det Frankrike vi färdas i är heller inte turisternas. Vi dimper ner i en fransk vardag och blir bemötta som människor som råkar ha vägarna förbi. Nästan alltid med civiliserad artighet, ofta därtill med stor vänlighet och hjälpsamhet, även på de beryktade postkontoren.

Vad vi har upptäckt under våra kanalår är också att vi mer permanenta nöjesfarare är medlemmar i en oorganiserad men högst verklig gemenskap där man möts, vidarebefordrar upplysningar från slussvakter och om slussvakter, varnar och tipsar, rapporterar om gemensamma bekanta, byter kartor, delar med sig av medikamenter, skänker bort eller tar emot tomma gastuber som blivit opåfyllbara när man gått över en nationsgräns, hjälps åt med att försöka laga varandras motorer, elsystem, bogpropellrar och toalettpumpar samt äter och dricker tillsammans, ombord eller på restaurang.

Beklagligtvis är det sällsynt att fransmän ägnar sin lediga tid åt båtliv på innanvatten. Somliga hyr ett flytetyg en vecka och slussar under stor kalabalik och är inte tilltalbara. De få franska fritidsbåtar man ser förtöjda vid kajer och i småbåtshamnar verkar ofta övergivna och är ännu oftare gravt missköttа. Fransmän reser på sin semester till kusten eller till någon av de forna kolonierna eller stannar helt enkelt hemma i trädgården och odlar sin kål. Bland de båtfarare vi kommit att knyta vänskapliga band med – britter, amerikaner, tyskar, skandinaver och holländare som på egen köl glider runt i det stora kretsloppet och möts, skils och möts igen – där saknar vi fransmännen. Det är ändå deras land vi färdas i.

Frankrike har mer än 800 mil kanaler och farbara floder. Många sträckor används i dag sparsamt av yrkestrafiken. Ofta går lederna genom trakter som turisten sällan kommer till. ("Vanadis" färder är dragna med rött.)

Våra färder i Frankrike

Att ge namn åt en båt

Fartyg bär nog alla namnet "Freja", även om det står "Albertina" eller "Gefle" eller "Nordensköld" på namnbrädan.

Freja är den nordiska mytologins Afrodite, skön och åtrådd. Hon har makt över liv och död och kärlek och är kunnig i svartkonst. Hennes namn betyder 'härskarinna'.

Rätt opraktiskt vore det dock om alla skepp verkligen kallades "Freja". De som heter det är redan många nog. Men gudinnan har ett binamn. Hon är av vanernas släkt, den som fanns före asarna men som kom att förenas med dessa. Tor, Oden och Frigg är hårdföra asar. Vanerna var fruktbarhetsgudar: Njord, härskare över hav och vind, Frej och Freja hans barn, båda ägnade en intensiv dyrkan. Freja är en dis, ett kvinnligt skyddsväsen. Hon är vanernas dis: Vanadis.

"Vanadis" var också namnet på en ångfregatt – och som det brukar påpekas ett av den svenska flottans vackraste fartyg. Berömd är hennes världsomsegling i början av 1880-talet, en givande vetenskaplig expedition. Men det är inte för detta som vi gav vår motorbåt det stolta namnet. Under åren 1784–1878 var den lilla karibiska ön Saint-Barthélemy svensk koloni, och "Vanadis" anlöpte tre gånger huvudstaden Gustavia, som till minne därav har en *Place Vanadis,* Vanadisplatsen. Kaptenlöjtnant och sekond var vid ett av dessa tillfällen, enligt uppgifter i släktannalerna, en förfader på Skepparns möderne.

Vad kunde passa bättre? Det överträffade namnet på min faders barndomshem i Kneippbaden i Norrköping, Villa Snöfrid. Viktor Rydbergs goda huldremö förvanskad till "Snofrid" vore heller inte lika tilltalande på franska kanaler.

Men ack, släktuppgifterna visade sig onöjaktigt hopkomna! Förfadern hade alls icke seglat till Saint-Barth med "Vanadis" utan med korvetten "Najaden"! Han hade befarit de sju haven ombord på örlogsbriggen "Väntalite", handelsfartyget "Aelespont", korvetten "Gefle", fullriggaren "af Chapman", fregatten "Eugenie", briggen "Nordensköld", linjeskeppet "Stockholm" och avslutat sin bana med att som fartygschef på ångkorvetten "Orädd" i svår storm föra över Karl XV och kronprins Oscar till ryttartävlingar i England, för vilket han honorerades med en kunglig hederssabel. Men "Vanadis" hade gjort sina seglingar förfadern förutan.

Emellertid hade vår båt redan hunnit registreras under namnet "Vanadis". Vi slapp träffa det omöjliga valet mellan "Eugenie", "Orädd" och de andra. Och, som Tegnér säger: "Yvs ej av fädrens ära! En var har dock blott sin." Våra färder med "Vanadis" kommer inte att, i motsats till förfaderns bedrifter, rendera oss vare sig hederslegion, hederssablar eller andra nådevedermälen. De är i sig själva belöning nog.

Ångfregatten "Vanadis", vår stolta förebild. Målning av Jakob Hägg. (Statens Maritima Museer)

På jakt efter den rätta

”Vanadis” är nu inte en båt utan två. Men eftersom de har färdats på delvis samma sträckor, legat i samma hamnar och mött samma hamnvakter och båtbekanta sammansmälter de till en.

Båda är vita, båda har plats för oss två och därtill två gäster under enkla förhållanden. Men vår första ”Vanadis”, en Saga 32:a, trivdes aldrig riktigt på de lugna vattendragen. Hon var byggd i Bergen och gjord för rejäla tag, med en stark motor och en djup sittbrunn i aktern. Fick hon rida över fräsande sjöar visade hon vad hon gick för. Men som husbåt på kanaler, med en ständig ström av gäster som klämde ner sig i stickkojerna med huvudet mot toaletten, blev hon liten och instängd.

Vi beslöt att ge henne ett bättre liv. Men hur mycket bättre hade vi aldrig kunnat föreställa oss. Efter att ha tillbringat kvällar och nätter med att översätta såväl marina facktermer som floskler till engelska och tyska lade vi ut henne på nätet.

Den förste som hörde av sig var en man från Färöarna. Efter ett par telefonsamtal var allting klart. ”Vanadis” skulle hamna i Høyvík utanför Torshavn, i det klaraste saltvatten med bandtång under kölen. Hennes sittbrunn skulle glittra av intorkade fiskfjäll. Stormfåglar och tretåig mås, inte duvor och kråkor, skulle skita på hennes kapell.

Medan ”Vanadis” ovetande om sin framtid sov i sitt vinterkvarter på Blanquarts varv i Saint-Jean-de-Losne där Canal de Bourgogne förenar sig med Saône hade vi börjat söka den ersättare som vore bättre ägnad för kanallivet. En stålbåt av traditionell holländsk modell var vad vi var ute efter.

Svenskar betraktar ofta båtar av stål med misstänksamhet. Men för långsamma färder på floder och kanaler är ett stort deplacement snarast en fördel. Båten går stadigt framåt och bryr sig inte om vindkast och den ligger still i slussarnas virvlar. När värmen stiger över trettio grader håller skrovet vattentemperaturen som är lägre, och nätterna blir inte svåruthärdliga. Och man får mycket utrymme för pengarna.

Vad vi sökte var heller inte bara ett transportmedel. Vi sökte ett hem där vi kunde vistas månader i sträck.

I Friesland ligger varv och försäljningsställen i varenda kanalkrök. Vi bilade dit i början av februari.

Något plattare än detta marskland finns inte, och vid denna årstid är det mest insvept i dimma. Vi färdades på småvägar där ibland en dunge och ett högt halmtak på en bondgård lösgjorde sig i diset för att försvinna igen. Så nästa dunge, nästa halmtak, mer dimma. Vi passerade ruggiga får, körde över någon liten van Goghsk klaffbro, *ophaalbrug*, där signalerna lös med fast rött sken som speglade sig i isen – och vem skulle begära broöppning nu? Så anade vi en kvarn, en ny bondgård, ännu en kanal.

Och vi tittade på båtar. För stora, för små, för rostiga, för dyra, för stolligt inredda. En barbar från Norden finner handfat bredvid varje koj och dynor i ljusbeige alcantara mest besvärande. Porslinselefanter, tygblommor, buddhastatyetter, ljusstakar och annat som ofelbart skulle fara i durken vid mötet med första pråm kunde vi bortse från, men hur vräker man undan ett

Friesland i februari. Skutor och tjalkar i isens grepp.

tungt ovalt glasbord vilande på en gjutjärnsdelfin när man ska ner i motorrummet?

I fiskebyn Zoutkamp begrundade vi något som var befriat från alla bisarrerier. Men så var det också bara ett skrov med det mesta av inredningen tillfälligt urröjd. Ett renoveringsobjekt. Inget att förälska sig i. Vi fortsatte vårt irrande i diset, tittade på fler rosthögar alternativt lyxobjekt, for över Afsluitdijk, den tre mil långa barriären mellan IJsselmeer och havet, till Den Helder i själva Holland, bara för att finna ytterligare ett hopplöst fall. Vi suckade och körde ut till en fyr och betraktade strandskatorna som spetade bland tångruskorna.

"Bunden är båtlös man", säger man på Färöarna, och där satt vi och hade släppt "Vanadis" ifrån oss just dit.

I skymningen for vi tillbaka över dammvallen och ut på de frisiska småvägarna mot Zoutkamp.

Förhandla med hund

Hos de stora båtmäklarna hade vi alltid blivit artigt mottagna och bjudna på kaffe medan de unga trevliga och affärsmässiga försäljarna noga lyssnat på oss och försökt hitta något passande. Nu var vi tillbaka på det mindre varvet. Det halvfärdiga skrovet hade under vår återfärd börjat ta gestalt inför våra ögon.

Varvsägaren verkade denna gång emellertid mest besvärad av vårt intresse. En annan och mer köpstark spekulant från Tyskland var på ingång.

Vi slog oss ändå ner i kontorsrummet. Knappt hade vi satt oss för att börja någon sorts förhandling förrän hans stora gulbruna racka hoppade upp på en ledig stol. Därifrån följde han spänt samtalet.

När vi kom in på en besvärande detalj började han bryskt att skälla, om och om igen. Det var uppenbart att vi skulle komma av oss.

Över varvsägarens kärva ansikte drog ett nästan omärkligt leende och han betraktade oss oavvänt. Vid nästa försök till förmån från vår sida tog hunden till en ny variant: han körde nosen i vädret och började yla.

När vi sedan gick över till mindre viktiga omständigheter lade han ner huvudet på sätet och blundade.

Så nalkades vi priset. När vi lagt fram vårt förslag blev det först tyst.

Sedan gled hunden ner från stolen och gick ut mot dörren där han satte i gång med att kräkas, högljutt och hulkande. Därpå följde en stunds slafsande. Ägaren teg med blicken ut över det frusna Reitdiep.

När hunden åter var på plats i stolen bröt husse tystnaden och sa att vi borde bestämma oss raskt. Det kunde vi förstås inte.

Här insåg jycken att all tid från och med nu var förspilld tid. Han började stormskälla. Han gormade och levde så det ekade och slutade inte förrän vi hade tagit i hand och skrikit adjö. Då hoppade han upp på bordet, sträckte upp framtassen mot husses bringa och lade huvudet på sned. De båda såg varandra djupt i ögonen.

Bra jobbat?

Bra jobbat.

Men skulle en hund få sätta oss på plats?

När vi lämnade Nederländerna var stålskrovet vårt. Det skulle vara en färdig båt till första maj.

Adjö gamla "Vanadis"

En grinig aprildag när den svenska naturen såg ut som wellpapp med rester av smutsig snö i vecken reste vi ner för att rusta vår gamla "Vanadis" i Saint-Jean-de-Losne.

När vi kom ner från Vogesernas gråkalla skogshöjder slog doften av nyutslagen grönska emot oss. Solen gassade på Blanquarts varvsplan, rödhaken sjöng och kärlekskranka grodor knorrade i småbåtshamnen. Vi åt våra luncher i skuggan under skrovet och svalkade oss med den torra franska cidern. Varannan dag ringde den sympatiske färingen och frågade hur arbetet fortskred, småpratade om livet och vädret där ute i Atlanten, nämnde gemensamma bekanta och berättade om förväntningarna. Tonen i samtalen blev alltmer familjär, men med varje samtal blev därför också vårt arbete med att leverera "Vanadis" i bästa skick alltmer krävande. Vårt namn skulle inte vara vanfrejdat på Färöarna. Vi slet i vårkvällarna tills göken tystnade.

Pråmhamnen i Saint-Jean-de-Losne. Vi vårrustade i kvällarna tills mörkret föll och göken tystnade.

Så en dag släppte vi vaxtrasorna och stängde burken med bottenfärg. En enorm dansk lastbil rullade in på varvsområdet för att ta "Vanadis" till Hanstholm på Jyllands västkust. Vi placerade ut en flaska champagne och ett antal småflaskor med svenska snapsar i hennes stuvfack och klappade hennes stäv. Farväl kära vän, som under åtta år fört oss runt Skandinaviens kuster och ända hit ner och alltid varit att lita på!

Där stod vi på den tomma varvsplatsen. Bara några stöttor och färgpytsar var kvar.

Så sade vi adjö till Blanquarts och satte oss i bilen för att köra upp till Friesland och den nya "Vanadis". Om aftonen i en by i Bourgogne, med bitterdofter från vita fågelbärsträd och slån och med honungsstråk från gullvivsängarna ringde mobilen:

– Nu lastas hon på "Norröna"!

Nu skulle hon alltså ombord på lastfartyget som går rutten Danmark–Färöarna–Shetlandsöarna–Island–Norge och stäva över den vresiga Nordsjön.

Nästa kväll kom nya underrättelser:

– Nu ligger hon i vattnet i Torshavn. Och vi är så lyckliga!

"Vanadis" i Torshavn, tänk, vid kajen med handelshusen och där bakom den näpnaste av domkyrkor med sitt klara lilla klockspel.

Vi skulle få fler rapporter till det vårliga Frankrike.

– Nu har vi varit ute i tjugo sekundmeter. Hon går så flott i sjö!

Det visste vi, men det var gott att höra.

– Nu har det snöat två decimeter, men värmen fungerar.

Ack, "Vanadis"! Vår allra första natt ombord, på småländska Sommen, då var det frost på däcket. Det klarade du bättre än trettiofem graders hetta på Meuse. Lev väl i de norröna vattnen, ditt rätta element!

Torshavn på Färöarna. Ny hemmahamn för gamla "Vanadis".

Vår nya "Vanadis"

Zoutkamp är en rar ort vid Reitdiep, där vattenvägen från Groningen vidgar sig. I ena änden ligger en nybyggd länga med olikfärgade husgavlar som ser ut som Bryggen i Bergen. Där finns Postmas palingrokerij där man handlar palingar, de läckraste små rökta ålar, som stoppas i specialtillverkade långa ålpåsar. Utanför ligger fiskebåtarna med sina nät på tork i vackra bukter. I andra änden av byn ligger slussen ut mot Lauwersmeer och bakom den reser sig masterna från en rad ståtliga segelskutor. Utmed kajen finner man ett par restauranger och världens minsta fiskerimuseum. På bron över slussen dundrar oavbrutet Heiploegs lastbilar med *garnalen,* de små holländska räkorna, men annars råder här ett stort lugn.

Hit återkom vi i slutet av april för att ta nya "Vanadis" i besittning.

Det var med blandade förväntningar. Jag hade under vintern ringt till kapellmakaren för att på egen bekostnad komplettera med ett soltält, mer än nödvändigt när det är trettiofem grader i inlandet. Det måste vara ljust.

– Inga problem, sa kapellmakaren, men ringde tio minuter senare tillbaka med svansen mellan benen.

– Det ska vara mörkblått som kapellet, varvet går inte med på något annat.

Jag anade att den som i gengäld hade hög svansföring var varvshunden. Soltaket blev mörkblått. I julihettan kan man välja mellan att bli kokt under det eller stekt utanför.

Nya "Vanadis" var dock stiligare än vi hade föreställt oss henne, och hennes inre var hemtrevligt – en gästhytt i fören, vår hytt i aktern och däremel-

Vår nya "Vanadis" är en modern holländsk stålbåt, 12 meter lång och 3,8 meter bred. Här just sjösatt, vid bryggan i Zoutkamp.

lan salong och pentry. Mycket trä, rustik gulaktig ek. Klädseln var dessvärre original och storblommig. För all del, man kunde välta ut en tomatsallad i soffan eller till och med bli sjösjuk i den utan att det skulle synas.

Men det fattades en hel del på detaljplanet, och det skulle ta sin tid innan vi kunde lämna vår kajplats.

Varvsägaren hade vid det laget överflyttat sitt intresse på de brevduvor han höll i ett duvslag i varvsbyggnaden, när han inte lastade dem i stora burar i sin bil för att fara i väg till någon duvtävling ett par mil därifrån.

– Hur får man dem att flyga tillbaka? undrade vi.

Han log knipslugt.

– Somliga ägare lockar sina fåglar med mat. Jag använder *vrouwentjes,* små duvdamer.

Med oss var han annars färdig och överlät enskildheterna på sin underlydande, den gladlynte herr L, som från oförutsägbara ställen på varvsområdet under många "ha, ha" rotade fram sådant som fattades – beslag, linor, fendrar, hållare, samt inför Koninginnedagen, som firas med allmän flaggning, en liten flaggstång.

Medan nya "Vanadis" långsamt gick mot sin fullbordan låg vi vid kajen under duvslaget. Var sjunde minut ungefär gick ett ryck genom fågelflocken, som smattrande lyfte och gjorde ett varv över vattnet. Vi väntade med att sätta upp det mörkblå kapellet.

Resan börjar

Från belgiska gränsen till Paris

Skepparparet under fransk flagg.

Från Holland och Belgien når man Paris via floden *Schelde,* som på franskspråkig mark byter namn till *Escaut.* Man kommer in norr om staden Valenciennes.

Vid Cambrai går den kanaliserade floden över i *Canal de Saint-Quentin,* som följs av *Canal latéral à l'Oise,* med floden Oise slingrande bredvid. Vid Compiègne tar själva *Oise* vid, för att vid Conflans-Sainte-Honorine kasta sig ut i Seine. Därifrån styr man österut, uppför *Seine* och till Paris.

Till en början färdas man genom Picardie och Frankrikes gamla gruvdistrikt med slitna orter och nya eller nedlagda fabriker, men landskapet är sett från vattenlederna behagligt med grönska, sädesfält och betodlingar, lövskog och fågelträsk, och det blir alltmer intagande ju längre söderut man kommer. Katedraler och andra kulturbyggnader finns i bland annat Cambrai, Saint-Quentin, Noyons och Compiègne.

Canal de Saint-Quentin, som stod färdig 1810 sedan kejsar Napoleon drivit på det nästan hundraåriga bygget, var länge förbindelselänken mellan Seinebäckenet och de nordliga hamnarna. Fram till 1965, då den stora Canal du Nord kom till, var kanalen landets mest trafikerade, och här transporterades kol, stål, olja, jordbruksprodukter och annan bulklast.

Pråmtrafiken är emellanåt livlig men inte besvärande. Den fem kilometer långa tunneln *Grand-Souterrain* vid Bony kan dock verka avskräckande, av skäl som kommer att omtalas.

"Afton, o hur skön" – men friden är falsk.

Till Frankrike genom bakdörren

Glada känslors uppvaknande vid ankomsten till Frankrike, det var vad vi väntade oss när vi nalkades gränsen. Bakom oss hade vi en färd från Zoutkamp och Friesland över Amsterdam, Gouda, Dordrecht, Middelburg, Vlissingen och slutligen Gent, där vi hämtat upp vännerna Birgitta och Unn, "Väninnorna", av vilka den ena nu ivrigt såg fram mot fransk blodkorv och franska ostar, den andra mot ännu fler katedraler än vad Gent och Tournai har att erbjuda. Vi hade lämnat Flanderns kolupplag och fabriker och fröjdats åt att efter en lång färd i total platthet se de första lövklädda kullarna höja sig. Floden Schelde hade bytt till den franska formen Escaut.

Men ju närmare gränsen vi kom, desto obehagligare blev vår vattenväg. En annan mentalitet än den som råder på Seine och Yonne och kanalerna söderut tycktes prägla de här gamla industriområdena. Vi fann oss glida fram i ett grått avloppsdike mellan oljiga plastflaskor, kladdiga påsar, blöjor och kondomer. I en krök drev en avsliten dockarm av barnstorlek hjälplöst och groteskt runt i en virvel.

Någonstans tvärsöver detta dike i videsnåren gick alltså gränsen. Vi hann aldrig lägga märke till den för vi överraskades av ett bump i båten, ungefär som när man med en bil glider över en asfaltlimpa. Sedan liksom tappade "Vanadis" sugen, rörde sig knappt framåt och lydde inte roder. Makterna, som inte försummar ett tillfälle, framkallade strax en mötande pråm som fyllde synfältet. Den höll god fart och visade inga tecken på att vilja hålla åt sidan. Vi strök varandra så att fendrarna gnisslade. Vattnet sögs undan och blottade en strandlinje med skarpa stenar som lätt kunde riva upp "Vanadis" botten.

I två och en halv knop och med hjälp av bogpropellern manövrerade vi mot Fresnes, den första franska slussen. Strax innan vidgades med ens kanalen till en sjö, från vars andra sida Canal de Pommeroeul à Condé försvann bland buskagen åt nordost. Vilken befrielse efter det smala diket!

Det skogomkransade vattnet vilade i solnedgångsglans och dess yta pryddes av svanar i hundratal. Besättningen utbröt i ett "Afton, o hur skön!". Vi siktade in oss på en tilläggsponton ett stycke före slussen för att där undersöka vår belägenhet. Sämre platser kunde man tänka sig.

Så snart vi förtöjt började sjön visa ett annat ansikte. Vattnet var mer än skogsromantiskt mörkt, det var kompakt svart och fetaktigt. Gasbubblor steg upp ur det och det stank. Bland den övriga soptunneskiten i strandkanten såg vi det uppsvullna kadavret av ett får med benen i vädret.

Men ner i det var nödvändigt.

Skepparn iklädde sig våtdräkt och dykarmask och försvann under ytan med kniv i hand. Därmed var han som uppslukad. Bara ett tilltagande bubbel från ävjan avslöjade att han rörde sig där någonstans. När han kom upp underkastades han omedelbar totalsanering, såväl yttre, med tvål, schampo och halva vattenförrådet, som inre, med en dubbel whisky.

Vad hade han funnit? Han hade trevat sig fram till propellern och i blindo skurit bort någonting som inte skulle vara där. Jag stack ner båtshaken på måfå och fiskade upp ett dyigt trasbylte, kvarlevorna av en kavaj med benknappar som blivit gågröna under sin tid i bottenslammet. Hade en strandvaskare gripit om propelleraxeln?

Vi undvek att titta i ärmarna.

Sedan gjorde vi oss klara för slussning – vi kunde hinna bort från denna plats om slussvakten var välvillig.

Men vi stod fast i dyn. Vattnet hade sjunkit under våra förehavanden. Svanarna där ute simmade inte längre, de stod på botten, och nu kändes de ondskefulla i sin falska skönhet på den svarta spegeln i den ödsliga skymningen. Så stirrade med ens de dubbla röda ljussignalerna från slussen mot oss och visade att den stängts för natten. Nu fanns bara vi och svanarna.

Eller vad de nu var.

Vi undvek att titta i ärmarna.

Fria men fångna

I morgonstunden vaknade jag av en gungning i båten. Förbi oss gick pråmen ”Liberté” och med den följde utslussningsvattnet. ”Frihet”! Vi var flott. Svanarna flöt igen. En trädgårdssångare porlade i strandvidet. Väninnorna dukade till frukost i solen på akterdäck.

Jag klättrade i land och tog mig bland doftande vitklöver fram till slusskontoret.

Fresnes har som gränssluss en rätt stor byggnad. Ingen människa syntes till, men utanför stod en bil med barnstol. Det bådade gott – man vet aldrig vilken slussvaktstyp som väntar – så jag gick upp för spiraltrappan och fann en yngre man med en kopp kaffe och en ostbaguette vid en övervakningsskärm.

– Stör jag i frukosten? frågade jag.

– Ingen fara, Madame. Varmed kan jag stå till tjänst?

Skönt, rätt sort. Stå till tjänst med? Att låta vår färd gå vidare, förstås.

– Men ni vet väl att slussen i Trith-Saint-Léger längre upp är avstängd för reparation en vecka?

Det visste vi inte. Vår färd söderut var alltså tillfälligt stoppad. Men Canal de Pommeroeul på andra sidan sjön? Kunde man göra en sväng åt nordost?

Slussvakten log milt. Den kanalen hade grundat upp och flutit ut och dess mynning bildade just den ödsliga sjön.

Men floden Scarpe då, vars utlopp vi passerat? På den kunde man enligt kortet komma in på Canal du Nord längre västerut.

Scarpe var ett sorgligt kapitel, lika igensandad den. Men båda skulle kanske rensas och öppnas om ett par år!

Goda nyheter. Men till dess?

– Varför inte gå upp och göra sig några glada dagar i Valenciennes, strax före den havererade slussen? Jag släpper igenom er när jag har fått i mig kaffet.

Så fick det bli.

”Liberté”, vår befriare.

Husflit ombord

I ett landskap som mest består av skrotupplag – olika högar med storskrot och småskrot och rundskrot och blockskrot som stora kranar med grepar plockar och lyfter och släpper lite förstrött – i ett sådant går man inte gärna i land på stärkande promenader. Har man å andra sidan gott om tid att fördriva eftersom man ändå kommer att bli låst framför en avstängd sluss tar man det lugnt.

Medan "Vanadis" mellan skrot och vide gled fram mot Valenciennes ägnade sig besättningens kvinnliga del åt handarbete.

Min goda faster Malla hade i slutet på femtiotalet (tämligen billigt förmodar jag) kommit över en försvarlig hög tallrikar från Svenska Amerika Liniens ståtliga passagerarfartyg "Gripsholm", som väl efter denna åderlåtning aldrig hämtade sig. År 1975 såldes hon nämligen och uppträdde här och där under olika täcknamn, för att 2001 sluta som skrot – dock inte riktigt, för på vägen till upphuggningen i Indien passade hon på att gå till botten utanför Sydafrikas kust, en stilfull handling.

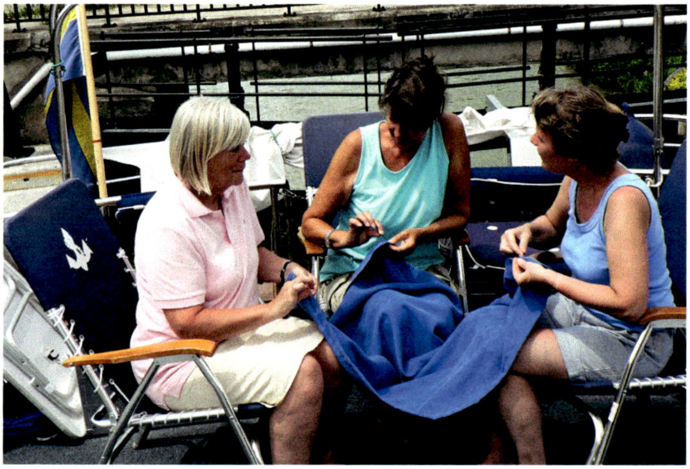

Vi kände oss som drottning Mathildas hovdamer där vi satt och sömmade.

Ja, Sverige har ju stolta skepp på böljorna de blå
och "Gripsholm" lär ju vara numro ett.
Vår kronprins Gustaf Adolf for till Staterna därpå
att skåda vad han aldrig hade sett,

skaldade Evert Taube 1928, och ett fartyg som lär vara numro ett kan ju inte finna sig i vilka skändligheter som helst.

Tallrikarna från Gustavsbergs porslinsfabrik har en gul och en blå kantrand på var sin sida om en krans med spröda grå blomblad (eller kanske torra flugvingar, också förtjusande) och är avsedda att ätas på ombord på svensk båt i främmande farvatten. Efter ett halvt sekel i en sörmländsk sommarstuga har de nu kommit rätt. Ståndsmässigt känns det också att kunna säga: "Vi dukar på Gripsholmsservisen."

Men ett nobelt porslin (om än enkelt) kräver en rättvisande omgivning, i det här fallet en bordsduk. I Tournai hade vi inhandlat ett tygstycke av en angenäm blå kulör, och nu grep vi väninnor oss an med att sittande på akterdäcket tillsammans fålla var sin sida. Vi kände oss, lutade över arbetet, som drottning Mathildas hovdamer sömmande på Bayeuxtapeten.

Uppenbarligen slog denna yttring av kvinnlig handarbetsiver an på skrotmännen i land, för under ett par kilometer följdes vi på stranden av ett litet lok som tutade ivrigt tills dess färd ändades av ett par stoppklossar, varvid de båda förarna hoppade ut med lunchpaket och vinflaskor och visslade och vinkade tills vi förlorade varandra ur sikte i en krök.

Den blå duken blev utomordentlig, ja, så skön att vi inte nändes ta den i bruk. Till middagens rödbetor dukade vi på ett kasserat badlakan, ganska trevligt det med.

Gustavsbergs "Svedese", skapad för svenskhet till sjöss.

Valenciennes, staden med snöret

Valenciennes, påstås det, går tillbaka på *Val en Cygnes,* 'Svandalen', ett namn som förklaras med att en prinsessa en gång räddat livet på en svan här och därefter uppfört ett litet palä vid stranden av Escaut. Sedan fortsatte merovingerna utvecklingen.

Som språkvetare ställde sig Väninnorna och jag oss mer än skeptiska till denna etymologi, och efter natten i Svansjön även till förklaringssägnen om den svanvänliga prinsessan.

Dagens Valenciennes är inte just något som lockar turister. Det skulle i så fall vara själva turistbyrån, inhyst i det så kallade spanska huset, ett av de få riktigt gamla, eftersom staden härjats i omgångar genom belägringar och beskjutningar och religionskrig – staden var under 1500-talet kalvinskt protestantisk – revolutioner och Napoleonkrig, första världskriget och andra, med en förödande brand till följd av ett bombanfall 1940. Men turistbyrån är trevlig och sköttes när vi kom av en kunnig och tillmötesgående ung dam.

– Är ni inspärrade i stan? utbrast hon. Vilken tur ni har!

För inte bara krig och bränder har satt sin prägel på staden. En gång kallades den "Nordens Aten" på grund av de konstprodukter som framställdes här: porslin och vida berömda knypplade spetsar, vad nu sådana artiklar har med det antika Hellas att göra. Rokokomålaren Watteau var en stadens son, liksom 1800-talsskulptören Carpeaux, båda företrädda på stadens pampiga och besökvärda konstmuseum. På 1700-talet började man bryta kol i trakten, och Valenciennes blev centrum för både stål- och textilindustrin i norra Frankrike. Escaut kanaliserades för pråmtrafik till textilstaden Cambrai lite längre söderut.

På 1970-talet kom den stora industrikrisen med nedläggningen av stål och kol och mycket annat, och Valenciennes blev allt mer luggslitet. Men under de senaste åren har staden börjat resa sig. Toyota har uppfört en sammansättningsfabrik, folk börjar få jobb, universitet och en rad andra högre skolor blomstrar, och mellan de vittrande husfasaderna löper en nyanlagd spårvägslinje på blänkande skenor med gräsmatta på sidorna, till en kostnad av det exakta beloppet av

"Spårvagnar är stadens möbler." Valenciennes ultramoderna trick framför den ståtliga gamla järnvägsstationen.

242,75 miljoner euro. När vi kom var det fortfarande en vecka kvar till invigningen, men det övningskördes för glatta livet, och hela tiden hördes glada pinglanden följda av hesa pustanden från pneumatiska dörrar som öppnades och stängdes.

Spårtrafik är en kulturmarkör för en stad. "Spårvagnar är stadens möbler", var ett av de sista yttrandena jag hörde från min far som låg och mindes de gula vagnarna i sin barndoms Norrköping.

Mindre universitetsstäder är alltid trevliga, vare sig de heter Valenciennes, Dijon eller Umeå. Det finns gott om kaféer med unga människor, det samtalas oavbrutet, det annonseras om utställningar, föredrag och besök, gatorna lever om kvällarna. Och att Valenciennes är en stad som tror på sig i all sin nedgångenhet var inte att ta fel på.

Men nedgången är den än så länge. Katedralsugna väninnan Unn fick hålla till godo med kyrkan Vår fru av det heliga snöret, *Notre-Dame du Saint Cordon,* uppförd på 1870-talet och redan efter hundra år farlig att stå intill. Högt uppe på den sotiga ytterfasaden sprängde rötter från flogbjörkar och annan vegetation in sig bakom stenar och utsmyckningar som verkade kunna lossna när som helst. Snöret i fråga fanns att beskåda i händerna på altarets madonna. Den heliga jungfrun hade under ett pestangrepp år 1008 dragit det runt staden och på så sätt räddat dem som hamnade innanför.

Hur sympatisk staden Valenciennes och dess 40 000 själar än föreföll oss såg vi fram mot öppnandet av slussen i Trith. Väninnorna hade efter besöket hos snörmadonnan avrest från den stiliga men bedagade stationen för att på hemvägen avverka några fullstjärniga katedraler – Laon, Amiens, Beauvais. Själva hade vi fördrivit dagarna på konstmuseet med dess imponerande samling av flamländsk konst – däribland ett par väggstora Rubens med mycket muskler och fläsk och välgödda putti skuttande runt med Kristi törnekrona och spikar, och vi hade företagit cykelutflykter i ett landskap som andades övergivenhet, förbi nedlagda fabriker, utmed järnvägsspår med murknande och ogräsövervuxna syllar och vidare till tigande byar med fallfärdiga hus och gropiga gator,

Madonnan ringade med sitt snöre in den pesthotade staden och räddade dem som hamnade innanför. I dag har hon en vida spridd fanklubb.

byar där man känner sig som en inträngling när man tar en öl bland ortsbefolkningen och barhunden reser ragg.

Vår kajplats, om än rätt trevlig med doftande klöver och rölleka i gräset, började kännas allt trängre. Kanalen fylldes hela tiden på med pråmar som av den strejkande slussen hejdats på sin väg mot Saint-Quentin och Dunkerque och nu låg i dubbla led och brummade med sina motorer och generatorer. Det senare var vi i och för sig tacksamma för, det hade räddat oss från strömlöshet.

När budet kom att slussen var i ordning blev det rörelse och uppbrottsstämning. Vi hämtade in vår elledning från den hygglige pråmgrannen och tackade med en flaska vin. Kanalvattnet började piskas av väldiga propellrar, tjocka trossar kastades loss och halades hem och den ena pénichen efter den andra lade ut under rop och muller och tutanden i moln av grå rök. Vi insåg att vi borde ge dem ett dygns försprång. "Vanadis" sögs oroväckande fram och tillbaka när de gick förbi och vi ställde oss så tungt vi kunde på våra förtöjningsspikar som ville slita sig i den luckra jorden.

Så med ens var hamnen tom och tyst.

Lugnet varade ett par timmar. Sedan kom den första omgången pråmar söderifrån och forsade förbi oss, samtidigt som en ny ström av pråmar från norr passerade. Vi slog i alla spikar vi hade och lade spring åt alla håll. "Vanadis" slet och ryckte i tamparna, vi stod ihärdigt på spikarna. Ett stilla regn föll och det blev tidigt mörkt.

Nästa dag var det midsommarafton därhemma.

En midsommarafton

Gasten och Kockan är vår urbesättning. De har varit med ombord sedan början av 1970-talet. Gasten och Skepparn har seglat många år tillsammans och haft sin egen mathållning. Annars är det Kockan som brukar ta över köket så snart hon svept välkomstdrinken. Så är det bäst för oss alla, för hon kan trolla i pentryt och dessutom blir hon hungrig fortast av oss, något som kan vända hennes ljusa lynne till inåtvändhet och fåmäldhet. Men det går över efter första tuggan.

Nu var det midsommarafton, och vi strök i väntan på denna besättning runt på Valenciennes järnvägsstation medan en mörkklädd väktare med något hotfullt dobermannsaktigt i svart munkorg och annat läder med många nitar höll oss under bevakning, båda som uppstigna ur underjorden.

Att åka tåg i Belgien är inte särskilt dyrt. Att komma på rätt tåg är marigare. Gasten och Kockan färdades från flygplatsen i Bryssel kors och tvärs genom de gamla gruvdistrikten, tangerade franska gränsen helt nära Valenciennes, tuffade sedan till sin häpnad baklänges och passerade gränsen längre bort, fortsatte till Maubeuge, passerade återigen gränsen, kort sagt irrade ett antal timmar på det belgiska järnvägsnätet innan de fann ett tåg som tog sig över till Valenciennes. Nöjet var å andra sidan så gott som gratis. Vi tog del av det genom talrika sms.

Till sist dök de faktiskt upp och vi passerade de vaktande avgrundsandarna utan att bli hejdade och stod sedan lättade ute på den lindblomsdoftande stationsplanen.

– Ska vi handla lite lax och försöka få tag i färskpotatis? föreslog jag. Det är ju i alla fall midsommarafton.

Det var Kockan bestämt emot. Nu kunde vi ju kunna slippa den och vad därtill hör, var hennes åsikt. Chèvren och rödbetorna lockade mera. Och vem var egentligen köksansvarig?

Så avgick vi från Valenciennes, slussade i den nylagade slussen i Trith och kom till flodskälet Estrun där vattenvägen delar sig. Åt höger övergår den i Canal de la Sensée mot Lille och Dunkerque för *le grand gabarit,* de breda grabbarna, det stora tonnaget. Åt vänster fortsätter den som den riktiga floden Escaut, som slingrar i väg i grönskan med jordbrukslandskap bakom buskagen. Vi slingrade med i sol och berusande fläderdoft och fågelsång.

Staden Cambrai har en trevlig gästhamn med vist ordnade platser för både metare och båtfolk så att de slipper kivas, och båtarna som låg där var rena kanalreklamen: välhållna småpråmar i smakfulla färger, en liten glad tysk hamnbogserare, en engelsk *narrow boat.* Här fick vi för första gången höra talas om den legendariske Ted Johnson som fixar all teknik som kan tänkas krångla ombord, var man än befinner sig i landet. Han har ett kartotek över alla kända pråmars motorer och deras ingående delar. Alla erfarna kanalfarare bär telefonnumret till Ted Johnson närmast hjärtat. Vi anade att även vi skulle komma att behöva det; vårt kylskåp hade börjat visa svaghetstecken. Skepparn, med ett vakande öga på elåtgången, slog ständigt ner

Stilla eftermiddag vid kajen i Cambrai.
Båtar och metare i sällsynt sämja.

CEDEO
Saaz
CAFE DE LA MARINE
Goldenberg
CAFE DE
LA MARINE
PLOVER
HAMBLE

Den engelska vedettbåten från andra världskriget är i dag hem åt en ryskättad dam med varmt hjärta.

på alla som öppnade det och möttes i gengäld av hot om inställda måltider.

Vi behövde också vatten och gick in bakom en gammal vedettbåt i trä, från vilken en äldre dam, och jag menar *dame*, i prydliga marinblå byxor och hårnät, anvisade oss sin vattenslang, var så goda!

Båten, som var hennes hem, var brittisk och hade under andra världskriget använts för att ta ombord nedskjutna piloter, döda och sårade. Damen och hennes man hade köpt den för fyrtio år sedan, när de slutat segla sin älskade yawl som alltför mycket inkräktat på hans doktorerande.

– Vad skulle vi göra? Hans professor, Madame Joliot-Curie varnade honom: Attention! sa hon – hon älskade också segling, så hon visste – attention, ni blir aldrig färdig om ni ger er seglandet i våld!

Här stod man med en dam vars man arbetat för Irène Joliot-Curie, dotter till Marie Curie, båda Nobelpristagare i kemi.

Nu var damen änka, men livet var ändå underbart. Hon hann i ett svep där allt tillmättes samma vikt berätta om sin förra katt som hembragt en koltrastunge och lagt den i hennes händer, varefter hon fött upp fågeln till evig tacksamhet, ty den sjöng varje år i trädet intill, om sin *grand-père*, som varit marinarkitekt hos tsaren och hals över huvud fått fly till Frankrike vid ryska revolutionen, om sin duva som hjälpt henne att plocka bort vissna begonieblad efter att ha iakttagit sin matte, om sin nya vita kisse som gärna kojade i andra båtar – bäst att vi såg efter innan vi avgick.

Hon ursäktade sig gång på gång för att hon uppehöll oss med sitt prat. Jag kunde bara beklaga att vi inte kunde stanna och lyssna till mycket mer, men på planen mitt emot förbereddes en kommunal grillfest, och bara testkörningen av ljudanläggningen lät ana det värsta. Det skulle ändå inte gå att höra vad någon människa sade.

Vi lämnade sålunda denna varmhjärtade och otidsenliga ryssättling och slussade vidare till Cantigneul ute på landsbygden, en ängsmark inramad av lövskog, några fridsamt betande kor, en slussvaktarbostad med klängrosor och välansade lök- och potatisland, en bro där en ardennerhäst leddes över, klopperiklopp, med ett mycket litet barn på ryggen. Fåglarna flöjtade i den rosa kvällningen och Gasten tog till hustruns häpnad ur packningen fram en burk matjessill och en liten flaska Östgöta sädes.

– Det är i alla fall midsommarafton, sa han.

Gräslök och dill från "Vanadis" egna odlingar till midsommaraftonens lilla sillburk.

Sånger från underjorden

På Canal du Nord går yrkestrafiken med hiskeliga och hänsynslösa pråmar som alla borde heta ”Namnlös Fasa”, det är vad vi fått ut av våra samtal med andra fritidsbåtsbesättningar som en gång valt denna kanal men aldrig mer.

Alternativet är att gå Canal de Saint-Quentin genom den 5 680 meter långa tunneln i Bony. I den får man inte använda sin motor; man släpas i en konvoj efter en elektrisk dragbåt som tar ström från två ledningar i tunneltaket, såsom en trådbuss, medan den gnager sig fram på en kätting, såsom en linfärja.

Vi hade mött dem som hellre sade sig sälja båten där den låg än att på nytt gå genom tunneln.

Vi valde tunneln.

Två gånger om dygnet får man chansen att dras igenom. På vår väg söderut kom vi i kapp ett sällskap om tre utrangerade holländska patrullbåtar, rikligt försedda med grillar och trädgårdsmöbler och framförda av välnärda medelålders par. På deras fråga om vi hade för avsikt att gå igenom tunneln samma dag svarade Skepparn undvikande. Han ville först se hur de betedde sig i en sluss. Det sade han dock inte.

När vi betraktade deras slussande insåg jag hur skönt det måste vara att ha en knölig båt som man kan bångla i med utan att behöva bekymra sig. För bekymra sig var det sista de gjorde. Patrullbåtarna törnade i slussväggarna och i varandra under klonk och skrammel och ”hoppsan!”. Vi var glada över att vi inte rymdes samtidigt.

I den regndisiga eftermiddagen förtöjde vi sedan längs dragvägen i ett djupt schakt med snårskog och ogräs på vallarna. Framför oss gapade den mörka tunnelmynningen.

Patrullbåtarna hade avgått, och i stället kom nu den ena pråmen efter den andra för att invänta morgondagens passage och så småningom också den vackra kuttern ”Calypso” med ett trivsamt holländskt par och lilla ”Festina lente” med ett annat trivsamt holländskt par. I schaktet fanns intet att se eller göra, så vi fördrev tiden med att traska upp till byn där allt utom skolan var stängt. Skoldagen hade just slutat, och det var rart att se ungarna skutta ut, men deras hämtande föräldrar betraktade oss fyra främlingar med blickar som vore vi presumtiva barnarövare. Vi tog inte illa upp, föräldrarnas vaksamhet var förmodligen befogad. Det finns knappast något mer hjärtskärande än att läsa anslagen med efterlysningar av alla försvunna barn, på snabbköpens informationstavlor, på posten, på järnvägsstationerna.

I kanalhandböckerna utlovas grundliga instruktioner från bogserarpersonalen inför tunnelpassagen. Vi hade förberett oss med två trettio meter långa linor som skulle kopplas i kryss till den framförvarande båtens häck. Men dagen grydde utan att någon

Helvetestunneln i Bony. I drygt en halvmil rycktes och knycktes vi på släp efter pråmarna.

ansvarig visade sig. Framför oss hade vi en pråm med en ung familj, och fadern lade våra linor på sina rejäla akterpollare medan modern stolt visade upp sitt sprattlande knyte. Än kan man räkna med återväxt bland *les bateliers,* pråmfolket, skrattade hon.

Och så med ens bar det av. Vi hann knappt få syn på den elektriska dragbåten innan den försvann in i tunneln med släpet av fyra pråmar, så "Vanadis" och efter oss "Calypso" och "Festina lente". Vår plats i mitten var inte avundsvärd. Bakom pråmarna bildades virvlar som sög fören från den ena sidan till den andra, och bakifrån ryckte de andra i häcken. Vi hade fällt ner lanternbågen för att inte komma åt dragbåtens elledningar i taket, men ibland var vi obehagligt nära ändå. Gasten och Kockan hade fullt sjå med att se till att fendrarna inte matades upp och Skepparn försökte parera slängarna med bogpropellern, men den som parerade mest var jag vid förlinorna, och det var tungt. Oavbrutet ljöd Skepparns "Släck babord!", "Spänn babord!", och jag släckte och spände i mörkret i två och en halv timme medan strålkastaren gled över den fuktiga tunnelväggens tiometersskyltar som passerade så långsamt, så oändligt långsamt.

Men när det kändes som mörkast och oändligast hörde vi bakom oss något som lät som en madrigal. Det var skepparen på "Festina lente" som sjöng. Det ljöd klart och märkligt under valvet. När han slutat svarade vi med "Här är gudagott att vara" i stämmor för att uttrycka stundens känsla. Ett ögonblick av tystnad följde där vi bara hörde vattnets skvalp mot

Innan den elektriska bogserbåten togs i bruk drogs pråmarna av hästar eller åsnor som tillbringade sin ledighet i dessa stall.

väggarna. Sedan tog bogpropellerns skärande klagan och Skepparns kommandorop vid igen.

När en kilometer var kvar startade den första pråmen sin motor och fyllde tunneln med avgaser. Jag slokade halvkvävd på fördäcket när vi kom ut. Men o, att möta ljuset, att uppleva att fågelsång och grönska fanns även här på andra sidan! Vi såg bort från härvorna av ledningar och järnskrot på den hopfallna kajen och från rucklen som en gång hyst de ömkansvärda små hästar som ombord på bogseraren dragit runt kättingspelet, före ångans och elektricitetens tid. Linorna kastades tillbaka på däcket, pråmarna satte fart och vi vinkade farväl åt den unga familjen. Vi var fria!

Vem bryr sig om förbud?

"Attention, vipères!" står det på en skylt intill den lilla grusvägen ovanför kanalbanken, "Se upp för huggormar!".

Vi undrar om det bara är ett sätt att hålla kvällsvandrare borta från huset ett stycke längre fram eller om vägrenen faktiskt är särdeles ormrik. Ser upp gör vi hur som helst. Skylten är strikt och auktoritativ, inget hemkludd.

Vid somliga slussar möter man en uppsättning tecken som visar alla fasor som kan drabba den oförsiktige: räddningslöst fall från kajkanten, en avhuggen hand med en blodpöl. Texten förklarar: Risk för stympning!

På ett svajigt och rostigt trådstängsel intill ett vanvårdat slusshus sitter en påkostad plåt i vit och blå emalj och upplyser att det är strängt förbjudet att luta cyklar mot sagda stängsel. Men vem skulle alls komma på tanken?

I skyltarnas Frankrike får vi emellanåt anledning att begrunda det kända stycket ur den internationella fördomskatalogen: "I Storbritannien är allt tillåtet utom det som är förbjudet, i Tyskland är allt förbjudet utom det som är tillåtet, i Ryssland är allt förbjudet, även det som är tillåtet, i Frankrike är allt tillåtet, även det som är förbjudet."

En kväll vid förtöjningsdags möter vi ett anslag med ett oprecist men uppfordrande *Interdit,* rätt och slätt.

Vad det är man inte får göra får vi alltså inte veta, men det spelar ju ingen roll, eftersom även det förbjudna påstås vara tillåtet.

Vi lägger till under skylten.

Varning för sluss. Lemlästning, blod och handlöst fall väntar.

Förbjudet i största allmänhet.

Det levs gott av litet

Slusskurerna på Canal de Saint-Quentin har drag av sommarveranda.

Canal de Saint-Quentin är planerad som en industrikanal, och det låter inte roligt. Men denna vattenväg har sitt behag. Den vindlar genom ett småtrevligt landskap med gröna buskage runt dragvägen, och i luckorna skymtar gula sädesfält och gröna lökodlingar, fågelkärr och beteshagar.

Här i Picardie håller luften en milt blåaktig grundton som ger grönskan ett lätt gråskimmer. Det är som att färdas i en tavla av Camille Corot. Slussbyggnaderna är målade i rött och bär upp en överdel i smårutigt glas, luftigt elegant.

Pråmtrafiken är livlig men inte hetsig och pråmarna är av det mindre formatet. Här och där lägger de till vid små lasthamnar för att hämta säd från de fält man passerar. Slussarna har två kamrar bredvid varandra för att klara trafiken, och på nästan varje ställe var den ena under upprustning. Det satsas med andra ord på pråmtransporter, vilket gör en glad. Kanaler som numera bara befars av fritidsbåtar och en och annan hotellpråm är visserligen lugnare men inte lika levande. Framför allt kan de få en att känna sig som det man inte vill vara, nämligen turist. På en pråmtrafikerad kanal är det yrkestrafikens livsvillkor som råder. Själv är man deltagare och iakttagare men inte föremål och förutsättning för verksamheten.

Vi hälsade på slussbyggarna som alltid tycktes uppdelade på två lag: ett som borrade öronbedövande och ett som åt lunch. Själva slussarna är automatiserade och vi tryckte på knappar och drog i blå stänger. För det mesta fungerade det, slussportarna öppnades och stängdes, vattnet tappades ur.

Canal de Saint-Quentin, som en målning av Corot.

Staden Saint-Quentin var inte lika tilltalande. Det grävdes och revs och såg stökigt ut. Vi vinkades in i gästhamnen där vi fick skrika till hamnvakten för att överrösta larmet från motorleden intill. Kockan och jag trotsade trafiken och cyklade på en tröstlös, gropig och lappad Avenue Victor Hugo mellan bilverkstäder och förfallna bostadshus till en affär för att få ihop till middagen. Det sägs att staden har bättre att bjuda närmare Stora torget och höjden där katedralen reser sig över röran, men vi lämnade ändå hamnen och gled vidare ett stycke på kanalen och fann strax en krök med lantlig frid där vi slog ner våra spikar i gräskanten. Pråmarna "Abyss" och "Cornelia" drog ner farten när de gick förbi och besättningarna vinkade vänligt – vi hade låtit dem gå före i slussarna tidigare på dagen. Nu hade de lastat vete och låg djupare.

Fågelsång i kvällssolen, små sällskap cyklade, joggade eller stavgick på dragvägen på andra sidan. Metarna metade. Vardagsnöjen och trevnad. Det levs gott av litet, och uppe på akterdäck levde vi ännu bättre eftersom Kockan dök upp från pentryt med kycklingfiléer i dragonsås till den butelj med hyfsat rödvin som vi redan hade gått lös på.

Slussvakter och VNF-are

Till Saint-Quentin cyklade vi tillbaka för att skaffa vår *vignette*, det tillstånd som behövs för att man ska få vistas på Frankrikes vattenvägar. Här har den franska kanalorganisationen VNF, *Voies navigables de France,* ett av sina kontor. Den summa man betalar för att i månader gå igenom så många hundra slussar man önskar och orkar är ytterst modest om man jämför med priset för till exempel Göta kanal.

VNF är en prydnad för Frankrike. Visst kan man ibland undra över att kännedomen om kanaler och broar och vattenstånd och allmän framkomlighet ofta verkar ytterst lokal; vill man veta något om vad som händer längre bort får man själv kontakta ombudet på plats. Men varhelst man inträder på något av VNF:s kontor blir man mottagen som en länge väntad kär gäst. ”Vanadis” registreras som om hon vore en kanalernas drottning, man önskas *bon voyage*, och sedan tycks alla man möter vara varskodda om hennes ankomst.

– Båtens namn? Ah, la ”Vanadis”!

Någon form av underrättelseverksamhet måtte ändå pågå.

Så har vi slussvakterna. Av dem finns i detta land tre huvudtyper. De hyggliga, som tycker att det är trevligt att hjälpa båtfarare upp och ner i livet och säger ”Det ordnar sig, Madame” när man letar efter pollare som inte finns och lägger fast på något som man inte får lägga fast på och som tackar för att man tar hand om ena porthalvan. Under slussningen utbyter man synpunkter på vädret, vattentillgången, kanalpolitiken, euron eller bästa sättet att torka skjortor:

– Med kragen neråt, Madame!

Man klappar slusshunden och man inhandlar grönsaker, blaskigt vin, traktens oöverträffade honung och ägg från gäss som drar en i skosnörena.

Så finns de likgiltiga, som öppnar och stänger och sedan går sin väg under slussningen och återvänder när det är dags att släppa ut en, inget mer.

Sällsynta, men i gengäld oförglömliga, är de som under sitt slussvaktarliv tycks ha byggt upp en hätskhet mot båtfarare och VNF och hela tillvaron och som ger luft åt den redan när man lägger sin hand på veven till slussporten:

– Jag har inte bett er att lägga er i mitt arbete!

Männen i de små vita bilarna är allestädes närvarande.

"Åt andra hållet, Monsieur!"

De flesta är av den hyggliga sorten som bidrar till kanalfarandets trevnad. Men de bemannade slussarna har blivit allt färre. På många sträckor är systemet automatiserat, och de blomsterprydda vakthusen bebos av folk som intet har med kanalen att göra. Man får själv med en fjärrkontroll öppna de gistna slussportarna, och man skulle kunna gå hela dagar utan att träffa en människa om det inte vore så att man kan lita på att det fiffiga systemet krånglar. I stället för slussvakter tillkallar man då VNF-personal, som far omkring i små vita bilar.

Om man inte hela tiden bleve så vänligt bemött skulle man nog förnimma en besvärande känsla av att vara under uppsikt. Männen i de små vita bilarna är aldrig längre bort än en halvtimme. Det är något av Richelieus spioner över dem.

Inte heller verkar det som om arbetet har blivit mindre sedan man avskaffade slussvakterna.

Visst fungerar det nya systemet med självslussning, men bara *en principe*, säger VNF-arna. Det förekommer hela tiden incidenter. Klantskallar trycker på fel knapp så att hela maskineriet går i baklås, det fastnar saker i slussportarna, och när det blir åska, *orage*, slås allt elektriskt ut.

Och orage blir det minsann i sommarhettan.

Männen i de vita bilarna är oavlåtligt älskvärda. De beklagar om man fått vänta.

– Jag vågade inte köra fortare, *les gendarmes* är så nitiska.

De säger att det inte gör ett skvatt att man har ångrat sig och vill stanna en stund och luncha i skuggan framför en sluss som man börjat öppna:

– Ingen fara, Madame, det tar vi hand om.

Men de säljer inga gåsägg.

I Frankrike samsas ålderdomlig och modern teknik. Med ett klick på fjärrkontrollen ska dessa gistna portar öppnas.

Om konsten att slussa

Är det svårt att slussa? är en fråga vi ofta får. Många har hört talas om Göta kanal som skilsmässodiket.

I jämförelse med Göta kanals breda slussar som rymmer många båtar och där det ges goda tillfällen till kollisioner och panik, med Strömsholms kanals djupa schakt med hög fallhöjd på vattnet och med Dalslands kanals skrovliga slussväggar är slussarna nere i Europa om inte en barnlek så dock betydligt lättare.

En förutsättning är ändå att man känner sin båt och vet hur den uppför sig. "Vanadis" med sina tolv ton lägger sig ofta exemplariskt stilla intill kajen.

På de mindre kanalerna för pråmar med det så kallade Freycenetmåttet 38,5 x 5,20 meter är slussarna för det mesta låga, bara 2,5 till 4 meter. De ligger ofta tätt, så man får snart rutin.

De stora ledernas jättekamrar håller 200 meters längd och upp till 20 och 30 meters djup, och man känner sig ganska liten bakom en väldig pråmhäck och rent av som en flugprick när man tittar upp mot kontrolltornet, varifrån ett osynligt högre väsen genom en högtalare manar en att lägga fast. Man förtöjer vid en pollare som glider med när vattnet stiger eller sjunker, och sedan går det hela utomordentligt lugnt till.

Men vad innebär det då att slussa?

En sluss har till uppgift att lyfta eller sänka en båt

på en vattenväg med höjdskillnader.

Själva slussen är en vattenkammare med portar i vardera änden. Om man nu är på väg uppåt, *montant*, måste slussens övre portar vara stängda mot vattnet ovanför medan de nedre portarna står öppna. Man kör in och förtöjer vid kajkanten, som ofta befinner sig ovanför ens huvud. Någon i besättningen har antingen cyklat eller gått i förväg för att ta emot linorna och lägga dem runt pollarna i kajen. Om icke återstår att från däck kasta sig på en ofta slemmig järnstege i murverket och klättra upp för att ta emot linorna nerifrån. Vid de slussar som är bemannade kan man i sådana lägen få hjälp av slussvakten, *l'éclusier* eller *l'éclusière* och slippa stegklättrandet, såvida inte han eller hon trycker i sin kur för att det regnar eller befinner sig i ett meningsutbyte med någon tredje person, vilket kräver händernas odelade medverkan.

Franska slussar är individer, vilket betyder att man inte kan förutse att pollare och förtöjningsringar befinner sig på samma ställe från en sluss till nästa. Om de ens finns. Varje sluss blir därför en överraskning, vilket emellanåt höjer temperaturen ombord.

När båten är förtöjd stänger den ilandvarande slussportarna bakom båten genom att antingen veva på en vev, *une manivelle*, eller vandra runt med en lång spak. Båten befinner sig nu i ett kar, slusskammaren, *le sas*. Därefter går medhjälparen till de övre portarna. På passagen över dem, den så kallade portvandringen, sitter de vevar med vilka man öppnar dammluckorna, *les vannes,* så att vattnet forsar in i slusskammaren. Det kan ske ganska häftigt, så det gäller för den som är ombord att följa med och hala in på linorna. Nu höjs båten undan för undan till kanalens övre nivå, och från att ha stirrat in i en vägg ser man först pollare och ofta nosen på en nyfiken slussvaktarhund, sedan ett slusshus och ett nytt landskap som man inte sett där nerifrån. När vattenytan står lika högt i slusskammare och kanal och virvlarna har lagt sig öppnar man de övre portarna och fortsätter sin färd ut på *le bief*, vattnet mellan två slussar i en kanal.

Att slussa neråt, *en avalant*, är som att ligga i ett väldigt badkar som töms. Det är lugnare men inte lika spännande att sjunka.

På många sträckor har slussarna automatiserats. Man förses med en fjärrkontroll som öppnar portarna när man nalkas, och väl inne i slussen drar man upp en blå stång varvid hela processen går i gång utan att

Behändig normalsluss med Freycinetlängden 38,5 meter.

Jättesluss på 200 meter. Den gula pollaren i slussväggen glider med, 23 meter ner.

man behöver göra någonting. Utom möjligen ringa numret till närmsta VNF-kontor för att systemet har gått i baklås.

Tanken på slussandet är vad som avskräcker mången som annars har lust på kanalliv. I Capestang på Canal du Midi mötte vi Sue och George, som lämnat sitt liv i England för en häftig förälskelse: den hundraåriga, vackert inredda holländska pråmen "Vertrouwen". Sue hade med mod och energi gått in för att lära sig manövrera den lilla pärlan, och den tillit som uttrycks i fartygets namn verkade vara på väg att etablera sig. Med slussning hade de dock inte vågat äventyra den än. De ville helst ha hjälp av erfaret folk, och sådant fann de i båtgrannarna Malcolm och Lucie på narrowboaten "Body & Soul", där även vi var ombord.

Debuten skulle ske i Canal de la Robine mot Narbonne, sex små slussar nedåt i all stillhet. När vi förtöjt i den första automatiserade slussen och tryckt på dess knappar upptäckte vi långt bakom oss i kanalen en hyrbåt som i alldeles för hög fart försökte hinna fram innan portarna stängdes. Men förgäves, och bäst så, för "Body & Soul" och "Vertrouwen" fyllde väl slusskammaren, och under denna första pedagogiska övning var det inte läge att pressa in ännu en båt. Hyrbåtens förare, en tysk husfader, gav högljutt uttryck åt sin irritation, vilken mycket upplivade Malcolm, som levererade en rad brittiska lustigheter. De var dock helt bortkastade på Sue, som stirrade stelt framför sig medan vattnet började sjunka.

– Det gick ju galant, sa vi till henne, när det hela var överståndet, men Sue var knappt nåbar, vare sig för uppmuntran eller för råd. "Vertrouwens" styrhytt var i dubbelt avseende en glaskupa.

Nästa sluss var djupare, nästan sex meter. För Sue var den uppenbarligen en avgrund, ja, själva nedgången till helvetet. Vi kunde förnimma hennes panikkänslor även genom glasrutorna. Hon genomförde manövrerna med vitnade knogar och fick faktiskt "Vertrouwen" fint på plats. Båtarna sänkte sig lugnt, portarna öppnades och "Body & Soul" som låg främst gled ut.

Jag stod på akterdäcket och såg "Vertrouwens" förkomma efter – och hur i nästa ögonblick portarnas käftar långsamt men ohejdbart började sluta sig igen. Vi höll alla andan i väntan på kraschen och gnisslet av plåt, men "Vertrouwen" drog sig tillbaka och portarna slöts tyst.

Skepparn hade omedelbart tagit ett tigersprång i land och störtat upp till slussen, där han fann två förvånade små tyska flickor med cyklar vid knappstolpen. Den hetsige fadern i hyrbåten hade sänt

Gasten iakttar författarens klättring. En slemmig stege är ibland den enda möjligheten att nå pollarna i en obemannad sluss.

Den vackra bopråmen "Vertrouwen" lyckligt befriad efter en skräckstund i slussens tortyrkammare .

dem i förväg, och de hade ambitiöst tryckt på allt som gick att trycka på och lyckats sätta i gång en ny slussningsprocedur. Sue hade dessbättre haft sinnesnärvaro nog att kasta sig på backreglaget, och nu fick "Vertrouwen" med besättning uppleva vad ingen av oss andra med mer än tusen slussar bakom oss varit med om, nämligen att hjälplös som en plastanka i ett badkar under påfyllning slussa baklänges, uppåt och utan förtöjningar.

– Värre än så här kommer ni aldrig att få det, lugnade Skepparn när han så småningom fått upp ett par linor och slusskammaren fyllts och vattnet stillats. Men smärtsammare än skråmorna var smäleken när de bakre portarna öppnades och tysken gled in. Nu fick "Vertrouwen" under den förnyade nedstigningen finna sig i att dela utrymmet med sin vedersakare.

– *Don't mention the war!* gastade den oförbätterlige Malcolm till George när de båda båtarna så småningom kom ut. Flickorna, som nu med cyklar tagits ombord, tittade frågande på sin fader.

Knappkalabaliken hade emellertid per automatik tillkallat en liten vit bil med en VNF-are, som raskt fått förloppet klart för sig. Tysken, som fräst om oss på kanalsträckan och låg och tryckte med nosen mot nästa slussport, blev myndigt tillbakaflyttad, och "Body & Soul" och "Vertrouwen" bjöds att triumfatoriskt glida in, varefter portarna skoningslöst stängdes.

– *Zo, ze Britannia rules ze vaves!* ropade tysken med bittert hån.

– *Auf weejnersnitsl, sauerkraut!* tjoade Malcolm hjärtlöst och förvandlade slussningen till ett stycke brittisk krigsparodi. Sådant kan vara lite orättvist, men inte denna gång.

En historielektion

Från utläggningen om slussandets vedermödor återvänder vi nu till vår färd. Från Canal de Saint-Quentin fortsatte vi in på den behagliga Canal latéral à l'Oise, som går intill den gröna och virvlande floden Oise. Där denna kanal slutligen förenar sig med Canal du Nord med sina framforsande stora pråmar ligger på en udde orten Pont l'Évêque. Eftersom vi drog oss för att lämna det smala vattendragets frid och för att få ett litet uppskov lade vi till. Staden, eller snarare byn, hyser en stor hall för byggmaterial som är rest över resterna av ett litet hus som med hela sin gamla tegelfasad med dörrar och fönster och utsmyckningar i smidesjärn har blivit kvar inne i halvdunklet bland rörlängder och isolermattor.

Middagsvila präglade orten, och när vi tittade in i den märkliga hallbyggnaden cyklade innehavaren ut med ett vänligt "Återkommer!". Vi fortsatte vår väg och kom så småningom till serveringen "Au Confluan", trevligt anlagd vid kanalernas sammanflöde, och när vi slagit oss ner på terrassen för dagens första öl fick vi se att ställets andra gäst var just mannen från byggmagasinet.

Georges Clemenceau (t.v.) vid freds-förhandlingarna 1919.

Jaså, det lilla huset där inne? Den märkliga interiören, den ville han inte ändra på, det var så mycket här som hade lagts i grus under de båda världskrigen, men om vi nu var intresserade av orten kunde han ge oss en historielektion från romartiden till i dag.

Vi insåg att det kunde ta tid och beställde för säkerhets skull dagens rätt av restauranginnehaverskan i chockrosa, från läppstiftet till kilklacksskorna. När allt var i sin ordning inledde mannen sin undervisning, och nu följde på en välformulerad franska i lagom takt en strukturerad framställning med både stora linjer och belysande detaljer. Här paraderade den långhårige merovingern Klodvig, kejsar Karl den store, Hugo Capet – en svag typ men stamfar för alla franska kungar ... Kände vi till Barbara Tuchmans "I en fjärran spegel"? Bra, borgen Coucy, utgångspunkten för hennes väldiga rundmålning över 1300-talet, låg inte långt härifrån. Åt andra hållet låg Noyon, biskopssäte sedan 500-talet. Hängde vi med? *Alors*, låt oss fortsätta. Medeltid, reformation, revolution, 1870, vårt sekel ... Clemenceau, "Tigern", konseljpresident och journalist, inledde under första världskriget alla tal och artiklar med "Tyskarna är i Noyon!", som för att hamra in det i fransmännens hjärtan. Slaget vid Somme 1916 pågick under fyra månader på kullarna på andra sidan; Canal du Nord hade använts som skyttegrav. Arton gånger hade Oise-kanalen tagits och återtagits. Döda och sårade på båda sidor uppgick till en miljon, nästan hälften av dem britter. Nästa vecka

Frid råder i Pont l' Éveque. Under första världskriget erövrades orten arton gånger. På udden till höger ligger serveringen där vi blev historieundervisade.

skulle man för övrigt högtidlighålla 90-årsminnet.

Vi lyssnade till denne byggmaterialsmagasinsinnehavare som kunde ha gjort sig i vilket kunskapsprogram som helst. Han svepte med armen ut mot det grönskimrande landskapet som begravt så mycken tröstlöshet och så många fasor. Den fruktade Canal du Nord glittrade i solen, en och annan pråm gled förbi i sakta mak. Mera öl kom på borden.

Den lilla restaurangen, som enligt skylten också tillhandahöll kolonialvaror och gas och dessutom var spelombud, var ett av de få hus som klarat sig när tyskarna blåste ur staden. Tjugosju ton dynamit hade gått åt när Ludendorff satt sig i sinnet att spränga ett historiskt torn ett stycke därifrån. Huset hade stått pall under bombardemangen tack vare en präktig järnbalk i taket. Vi gick in och beskådade balken och den övriga inredningen: hyllor med ärtburkar och pastisflaskor och en uppstoppad räv. Mairen, kommunordföranden, körde förbi i bil och vinkade. Vi tog vid uppbrottet i hand, som man gör, först den chockrosa värdinnan och sedan folkbildaren.

– Visste ni, sa han, att reformatorn Calvin lärde sig simma i Oise här intill?

Älskliga Oise och stränga Seine

Floden Oise är inbegreppet av franskt behag. Efter Pont l'Éveque är det stopp för de största pråmarna, och kanalfararen möter i stället metare i små gröna ekor och roddare från de otaliga roddarklubbarna. Vi fick ideligen dra ner vår redan låga fart för att inte bringa de insektsliknande farkosterna med sina utriggade åror i obalans. De är läckert målade, som leksaker. Grönt, svart och vitt. Fernissad mahogny, rött och vitt. Vitt, grönt och gult. Vi kände oss som i en Renoirmålning bland dessa sorglösa unga män och kvinnor som hojtade till varandra över vattnet.

Vattnet strömmade mellan lövklädda stränder som skiftade i alla gröna och grågröna toner. Grågrönast var silverpilarna med skimrande blad i den lätta junivinden. Ur snåren kvittrade, sissade och drillade oupphörligt rödstjärtar, bofinkar, lövsångare, trädgårdssångare och andra arter som ligger utanför vårt ornitologiska kunnande.

När man svänger runt hörnet i Conflans-Sainte-Honorine ändrar landskapet karaktär. Här möter Oise den breda Seine på dess väg ut mot kusten. Och vid kajerna i Conflans – konfluenten, eller åmötet,

Överallt roddare i insektsliknande farkoster.

I Conflans-Sainte-Honorine vid Seine ligger pråmarna på lätten i väntan på uppdrag. När de sedan är lastade ser man relingen bara som ett streck ovanför vattenytan.

Den heliga Honorine, vars kvarlevor fördes hit undan vikingarnas härjningar i Normandie, har blivit båtfolkets skyddshelgon. Till hennes grav vallfärdar man än i dag. Pråmskepparens liv kan vara kärvt, och det skadar inte med stöd från ovan.

som det hette på äldre svenska – ligger pråmar i täta led. De är lastade med säd, grus, ståltråd i enorma glänsande rullar, skrot och konstgödsel, eller också ligger de på lätten i väntan på uppdrag eller reparation eller på att byta ägare.

Så var vi alltså ute på Seine, Paris kuttrande och sjungande käresta, som det heter i chansonen. Här kändes floden ingalunda ljuv och smeksam, snarare lite ödslig, ja, rent av sträng. Vi svängde babord, mot Paris, för att få höra henne kuttra.

På egen köl i Paris

Det är avgjort roligare att komma till Paris på egen köl än att ta sig från en flygplats genom förstäderna. Seine väster om staden går genom ett grönt och egendomligt övergivet landskap, men när man får en hastig skymt av Eiffeltornet tycker man sig nästan framme, för att strax föras bort igen där floden gör en stor bukt. Rätt som det är glimtar Sacré-Cœurs himmelsmaräng till och lika fort är den försvunnen när den nyckfulla Seine gör en ny slinga. Så här håller man på. Ömsom glider man förbi flotta villor, ömsom förbi bopråmar i skilda stadier av präktighet och förfall. I Boulogne-Billancourt och mitt emot på l'Île Seguin ligger de sorgliga resterna av Renault-fabrikerna, en gång centrum för fransk arbetarhistoria med sina strejker och protesthandlingar. Nu är bara den stora portalen kvar, vittrad även den.

När man på vattnet passerar genom det futuristiska La Défense, under väldiga väggar av mörkt glas som tycks luta sig över ens litenhet, tycker man sig åter nära Paris hjärta, bara två metrostationer från Triumf-

Seine-nymfer på Pont Alexandre III bär upp Paris vapen: skeppet som gungar men inte sjunker.

Notre Dame, Paris hjärta, reser sig ljus och mild över de stränga kajerna.

bågen – och så förs man ännu en gång obevekligt bort. Men så står hon där, frihetsstatyn på Svanön mitt i floden, till formatet långt mindre än kopian i New York, och hon säger att nu, nu är ni på allvar på väg in i staden.

Så kommer då äntligen hela Eiffeltornet, detta sanslösa exempel på mekanoteknik, ett fruntimmer vars vida kjol övergår i en hals som bara fortsätter och blir allt smalare tills den kröns av en liten huvudknopp. Man kan inte annat än älska det, för det är så på en gång vanvettigt och perfekt. Vi drar ner farten och så skålar vi för damen och för Gustave Eiffel som inspirerat till de svenska järnfyrar som kallas heidenstammare.

Framför oss ligger nu Pont Alexandre III, en excess i förgyllda örnar och sprittande flodnymfer, och sedan följer Grand Palais med sitt växthustak i glas, Nationalförsamlingens klassicistiska pelarrad, den förgyllda toppen på obelisken på Place de la Concorde, Institut de Frances palats med kupolen i svart och guld, Louvren som aldrig tar slut, Musée d'Orsay, i dag fullt av impressionister men förut järnvägsstation som ett lok lyckades köra igenom så att det hängde ut över Seine, bouqinisternas gröna lådor, paren som pussas nere på kajerna. Blicken vandrar oupphörligt från den högra stranden till den vänstra och tillbaka men fastnar när vi når själva hjärtpunkten, Notre Dame, honungsgul i grönskan. Man kan inte tro det – här är turistböckernas alla godbitar på ett bräde. Det hjälper inte hur många gånger man har sett allt förut, från eget däck är det något annat. Hej "Vanadis", nu är du i Paris!

När man har passerat hela härligheten girar man babord och kallar upp slussvakten på VHF:en, "Hallå, hallå, svenska lustfartyget 'Vanadis' önskar slussa", och när det röda ljuset växlar till grönt går man in i en muggig och förfallen slusskammare med slemmiga väggar och skräp överallt medan metron skramlar öronbedövande ovanför ens huvud, och sedan glider man in i Arsenalen, Paris gästhamn intill Place de la Bastille. Här får man sin lugna kajplats under höga vallar, undan svallet från pråmar och sightseeingbåtar ute på Seine, här har man nu sitt eget hem, mitt i stan.

Mitt i Paris finns en skyddad hamn – Arsenalen vid Place de la Bastille. Frihetens genius med civilisationens fackla glimmar på toppen av kolonnen.

La Défense

Som grottvarelser kom vi upp ur metrons underjord till ljus och rymd och slogs nästan till marken vid anblicken av ett överjordiskt väsen som välvde sig högt över oss med benen på jorden medan kroppen försvann i skyarna.

Vi befann oss vid foten av *Grande Arche,* den av president Mitterrand beställda över hundra meter höga triumfbågen i skinande vit marmor. Vid sidorna reste sig dess drabanter, företagens höghus med mörka glasfasader som speglade sig i varandra.

I La Défense, Paris downtown, fast utanför stan, gäller inte människans mått. De kontorsanställda, män och kvinnor som i kostym och vit skjorta ilade över den ödsliga stenläggningen, blev små mörka kryp.

Mitt i alltihop arbetade en jättelik byggkran. Kontrasten mellan de stela blanka husväggarna och den levande kranen som sträckte sig hit och dit, styrd av en vildlockig förare i blåställ, fick oss att ta fram kameran.

– Jaså, man blir fotomodell, sa blåstället och stängde av och kom fram till oss. Har ni sett något så idiotiskt som det här? Knappt har man fått upp en byggnad förrän den måste repareras. Glasfasaderna ramlar ner, betongen håller inte, så är det hela tiden. Området är en katastrof!

– Låt inte oss störa i arbetet, sa vi.

– Ingen fara, jag ska ha lunch om en stund. Varifrån kommer ni? Sverige? Ah, mycket natur, det behöver man. Här får man inget syre, det går inte att andas.

Om det är någonstans i Paris som det finns syre borde det vara här där vinden snor runt skraporna och sikten är fri ända ner till den gamla triumfbågen vid Étoile. Men vi förstod vad han menade.

– Om två månader går jag i pension. Då far jag hem till Normandie och metar. Där kan man andas.

Makten strävar efter allt högre boningar. De andra drömmer om ett metspö vid en grön kanalbank.

"Här kan man inte andas. Jag far hem till Normandie och metar."

Den ståtliga ingången till hundkyrkogården i Asnières.

I döda hundars sällskap

På vår babordssida i Arsenalen låg en tämligen begagnad liten paddbåt av den sort som uthyrningsföretagen tillhandahåller för kanalfärder. Den var hem för en mörkhårig kvinna och hennes fem katter och bar namnet "Je chants dans la pluie" – det vill säga "I'm singing in the rain". Det regnade inte en droppe medan vi låg där, så vi fick aldrig höra någon sång. I stället klagade damen på att den stora grå Don Juan inte var snäll mot henne och Don Juan svarade med att gräva ner klorna i hennes magra skuldra när hon lyfte upp honom.

– Han tycker att jag har för många katter, sa hon insiktsfullt.

Don Juan granskade oss med gröna ögon och följde sedan med över till "Vanadis". Mattan på akterdäck var underbar att klösa i. När han misshandlat den färdigt sträckte han ut sig under en däcksstol. Han stannade ombord under hela vår sejour i Paris. Och visst verkade "Vanadis" mer komplett med ett skeppsdjur.

På styrbordssidan låg en båt med ett par från Australien. De hade inga katter och heller ingen hund, i motsats till de flesta gästbåtarna från England och Tyskland och Holland. Båten hade de köpt i Europa, och att ta med sig hund från andra sidan jordklotet låter sig inte göras så lätt. Men utan hund var livet halvt, tyckte de, så de brukade snylta på andras:

– *You have to get your daily doggy-fix.*

Vi insåg att det var vad vi hade hållit på med hela tiden utan att ha ett namn på företeelsen. Katter, liksom åsnor och getter, kan för övrigt i goda fall gälla för hundar.

En dag anlände vännen Helen. Vi brukar tillsammans genomströva begravningsplatser där sådana erbjuds, både hemma i Stockholm och på annat håll. Nu hade Skepparn och jag redan avverkat både Cimetière de Montparnasse och Père Lachaise, men ännu återstod ett besök hos sanktbernhardshunden Barry, filmstjärnan Rin-Tin-Tin och andra vovvar av betydelse för mänskligheten.

Vi tre skramlade därför tvärsigenom stan med metron till förstaden Asnières, traskade ett stycke och befann oss sedan vid den ståtliga ingången till *Cimetière des chiens,* hundkyrkogården från 1899. Men ack, de höga smidda järngrindarna var låsta!

– Det är alltid stängt på måndagar, upplyste ett par parkarbetare som klippte en häck intill.

Naturligtvis. Det finns en fransk lag om att allt man ska besöka är stängt just den dag man är där, och den sviker aldrig. Men så lätt tänkte vi inte ge oss.

– Finns det någon vakthund? undrade Helen.

– Ingen levande i alla fall, grinade parkskötarna, lycka till!

Vi såg oss omkring, och när det var någorlunda folkfritt klättrade vi över stängslet och gled raskt in bakom monumentet över Barry som räddade fyrtio personer i Alpernas snöoväder. Den fyrtioförsta slog ihjäl honom i tron att han var en björn.

Sedan fortsatte vi in i en värld av sorg, tillgivenhet och tacksamhet, känslor som här är starka och ogrumlade av alla de förbehåll som kan förekomma människor emellan. Under gravvårdar med porträtt, hundkojor av sten, en skål med älskade tennisbollar, ja, till och med ett cementträd att lyfta benet mot vilar Minou och Frou-Frou och Kiki och Ulysse och Brother Bill och alla de andra, och guldinskrifterna säger på prosa och på vers att de hänsovna älsklingarna varit trognare än någon människa.

– *Got your doggy-fix?* undrade de australiska båtgrannarna när vi kom tillbaka. Vi försäkrade att på Cimetière des chiens får man värsta hundkicken. Särskilt om man plankar in.

Prinsessan Lobanofs älsklingar i evig väntan.

Under Paris broar.

När det inre arbetet på "Vanadis" var överstökat hade vi redan hunnit ut till Ful-Paris.

Stinkande sorti

Seine gick hög och skvalpig när "Vanadis" kom ut ur slussen från gästhamnen Arsenalen vid Bastiljen. Det blåste varmt men rejält, och turistbåtarna, *les bateaux-mouches,* körde som vanligt hårt och gav svall, liksom pråmarna som öser rätt igenom staden på väg från ett sandtag till ett annat. Skepparn hade fullt upp med att stå vid rodret, men Helen och jag satt på fördäck och tog in Paris hela härlighet. Nu skulle vi lämna staden och fortsätta söderut, men inte utan att först ha gått upp och skålat för Eiffeltornet.

Egentligen ville man skåla oavbrutet för kyrkor och paläer och broar. Paris är nytvättat och nyförgyllt, oanständigt vräkigt och alldeles hänförande från vattnet. Notre-Dame flöt på Seine, ljus och lätt och utan gotisk skräck, och till och med den gamla stränga stenbron Pont Neuf kändes vänlig. Pont Alexandre III:s guld och gjutjärn glimmade i solen och de sprittande mörkhyade flodnymferna hängde åter med tårna över "Vanadis".

Och sen var vi framme vid Eiffeltornet och höjde våra glas. I samma ögonblick ljöd ett nödrop från Skepparn:

– Muggen svämmar över! Ta hand om den!

En vecka i hamn hade blivit för mycket, och vi hade inte räknat med sjögång på floden. Jag kastade mig ner i "Vanadis" inre och började tömma tanken och övergick sedan till att sanera toalettutrymmet. När den avgrundslika stanken äntligen var avlägsnad och golvet desinficerat och jag kom upp låg det praktfulla Paris i fjärran. Vi var redan ute bland förstädernas fabriker och lastkajer.

Var det vi som genom detta kom att sätta punkt för president Chiracs karriär? Han hade lovat att göra Seine badbar. Ännu en politisk motgång, och det var vårt fel!

Utflyktsmål vid Seine för stadsleda parisare.

Seine och Yonne

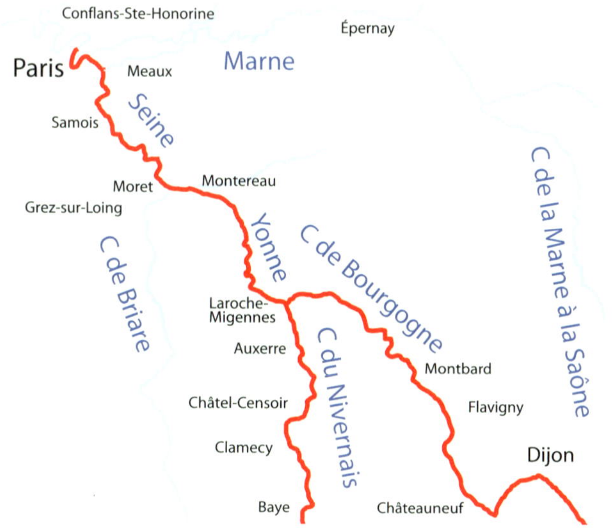

Från Paris färdas man mot sydost på den breda *Seine,* som efter huvudstadens industriområden kantas av *guinguetter,* utvärdshus, och lyxvillor utmed de grönskande stränderna – färre dock än man kunde förvänta sig. Fransmännen verkar inte bry sig särskilt mycket om de natursköna lägena intill kanaler och vattendrag.

I Saint-Mammès, där pråmarna trängs i långa rader, kan man vika av ett kort stycke ner på floden *Loing* och besöka den förtjusande staden Moret och därifrån fortsätta söderut på *Canal de Briare.* Annars går man vidare på Seine till Montereau, där floden möter *Yonne.*

Seine är en återvändsflod medan Yonne leder vidare, på denna sträcka genom ett trivsamt jordbrukslandskap mellan småstäder och byar som Sens, Villeneuve och Joigny. Pråmarna gör floden levande och trafiken är måttlig. Yonne är badbar, vilket man välkomnar när det är hett.

I Laroche-Migennes är det slut på pråmtrafiken. Här väljer man om man vill ta in på *Canal de Bourgogne* eller fortsätta mot Auxerre och *Canal du Nivernais,* båda kanalerna med fortsättning mot Saône och Rhône och Medelhavet.

En välgörerska

Det drog sig mot kväll, slussvakten hade stängt och vinkat adjö, och här låg vi på Seine, mitt i ingenstans utan bröd.

Den människointresserade damen som nu bebodde slussvaktarstugan vaggade ner för att se på oss.

– Boulangeriet, dit är det långt, men ni kan få lite bröd av mig så har ni till i morgon bitti. Jag har alltid lite i reserv åt båtfolk.

Vi förstod att det var en förevändning för en pratstund för en som bodde mitt i ingenstans.

– Kommer ni från Paris? fortsatte hon medan hennes lilla golvmopp till vovve snusade på oss. Besökte ni några fina ställen där?

Vi klappade golvmoppen och nämnde hundkyrkogården i Asnières.

– Å den, suckade hon, den har jag sett ett helt program om i teve, jag grät hela tiden, som jag grät!

Golvmoppen lyssnade uppmärksamt.

Lite längre bort började metarna packa ihop sina don.

– Får de något? undrade vi.

– O, jadå, sa hon. Det är förbjudet att bada, men fisken är utmärkt.

Vi tog farväl och lämnade en chokladkaka i utbyte mot brödet som var segt och nog hade varit det ett bra tag. Aftonen sänkte sig över det icke badbara vattnet, en fisk fördes förbi av det lätta strömdraget med den vita buken i vädret.

I Djangos Samois

Samois-sur-Seine är en by som klättrar uppför flodbrinken. Vi lade till vid restaurangkajen och lät oss förföras av en terrin på pilgrimsmusslor följd av anklår i apelsinsås.

Men det var inte därför vi var där. I eftermiddagshettan, när allt vilade, stretade vi upp till kyrkogården för att besöka gitarristen Django Reinhardts grav.

Vi hittade den så småningom – den var inte märkvärdigare än andra gravar – och vi betraktade porträtten på Django och hans söner och den lilla raden av plektrum som beundrare lagt på den blanka stenen.

Som vi stod där uppenbarade sig en äldre man på en tävlingsscykel som han lutade mot kyrkogårdsmuren. Han ställde sig intill oss och betraktade, han också.

– Han var den störste, sa Skepparn och nickade mot bilden av Django.

– Jag talade med honom när jag var barn, sa mannen. Min far hade roddbåtsuthyrning här. Django kom ofta, han tyckte om att meta.

De fem sista åren av sitt liv bodde Django Reinhardt här i Samois, en fast punkt efter ett liv i husvagn. År 1953 gick han bort, sörjd av byborna vilkas ära han försvarat genom att vara med och spöa grannstaden Fontainebleau i biljard.

– Välkomna till Django-festivalen i juni, sa mannen. Nu ska jag besöka min släkt.

Han krånglade av sig sina cykelhandskar och tryckte våra händer till farväl med en hand som kanske mött Djangos och gick vidare mot nästa grav.

Frankrike hade besegrat Portugal i fotbolls-VM och levde i fotbollsyra. Vi hade upplevt semifinalen i Paris i något som liknade upploppsstämning med skrän och explosioner och avstängda infarter.

Nu låg vi kvar i Samois för att se finalmatchen mot Italien på restaurangen vid torget.

Samois är en städad liten ort, och den publik som började strömma mot rummet med teven var segervisst uppsluppen men inte mer än vad som ryms inom gränserna för gott uppförande.

Flickorna skrattade och studsade runt i kjol, t-tröja och scarf i trikolorens färger, gossarna i baren tappade oavbrutet upp öl, matchen kunde man följa genom susningarna och ropen även om man i den fullpackade lokalen inte kom åt att se teven. Men det brölades inte och ingen var berusad.

Så kom då det fatala ögonblick när nationalhelgonet Zinedine Zidane, allas Zizou, skallade en mot-

Vid restaurangkajen i Samois övergav vi strax de egna kastrullerna.

spelare och blev utvisad. Frankrike hade förlorat. *On a perdu!* – suckarna spreds ut till dem som trängdes utanför.

Sedan blev det tyst. Publiken gled ut i kvällsmörkret och försvann i bilar och på mopeder. När vi hade avslutat våra öl och vandrade ner genom gränderna mot Seine var Samois en tom stad under en ödslig fullmåne.

Nästa morgon gick vi upp till kaféet vid torget och slog oss ner med några dagstidningar. Det var ingen hejd på fördömandena av den skändlige italienare som sades att genom rasistiska tillmälen ha bringat Zizou att tappa fattningen. Men Frankrike var ovedersägligen slaget.

Var det en tillfällighet eller var det planerat att det i en av de större tidningarna skulle stå en resonerande artikel om att den franska självtilliten, för att inte säga självtillräckligheten, var i avtagande, om inte bland politikerna så desto mer hos fransmännen i gemen? Det hade gjorts undersökningar som visade att många fransmän långt ifrån törs hävda den officiella föreställningen att de lever i världens främsta kulturnation och heller inte finner det förvånande eller ens förfärande att franska språket förlorar terräng ute i världen.

Frankrikes *gloire* är inte som förr, och särskilt inte denna avslagna morgon efter VM-förlusten. Männen vid kaféborden rökte håglöst, knäppte uppgivet av askan med tummen och ryckte på axlarna. Tonen var dämpad.

Men i detta land finns också ett vardagsliv som inte bekymrar sig så mycket om *la gloire.* Vi bytte till lokaltidningen och fann under rubriken *Un repas mémorable,* "En minnesvärd måltid", en notis om ett sällskap som efter ett restaurangbesök i en närbelägen stad däckats av magsjuka. Bland småannonserna mötte vi en vädjan om ett nytt hem för Rox, en strävhårig foxterrierblandning: "Mycket lätt att rengöra, viss benägenhet att rymma under jaktsäsongen." En ättling till rackan Arthur, *fox à poil dur* som Maurice Chevalier sjöng om, *woah, woah, woah?*

Vår granne vid Seinestranden var pråmen "Veneranda", den vördnadsvärda, från 1899. Den beboddes av ett par som arbetade i Paris. Mannen gav sig varje morgon i väg på motorcykel, för med den tog man sig förbi alla köer, upplyste han. Vi fick låna ström medan vi låg där, och när vi lämnade tillbaka sladden tillsammans med en flaska vin blev vi ombordbjudna.

En murad tegeltrappa som sinnrikt också rymde en öppen spis – ägaren var arkitekt – ledde ner till ett lite

Vår båtgranne hade inrett sitt hem med häpnadsväckande detaljer.

rörigt och mycket charmfullt vardagsrum med böcker och konstföremål och möbler som gjorts av tillvaratagna ting. På pianot stod ett nothäfte med Chopin. Från taket hängde fullastade bokhyllor i kedjor. Vi drack kaffe på matvråns omsnickrade tågkupésoffor av trä (3:e klass) och såg genom ventilerna Seine glida förbi. Den vördnadsvärdas ägare lyfte upp ett stycke av golvet och visade på vedförrådet i kölsvinet. Allt var mycket praktiskt och uttänkt, men praktiskast var den stora blomsterlådan med bladväxter på golvet utmed väggen. Insatsen var av zink som tål vattenskvättar, ytterhöljet av trä. Vår värd log när vi sa att vi nog visste vad vi såg: en likkista som halverats på längden.

– Det var en bekant som hade fått den över. Och av locket har jag gjort hyllorna som hänger i taket.

Ännu gör vi oss tankar om varför man får en likkista över.

En pråmfamilj

Att det verkligen är Seine som rinner genom Paris kan nog diskuteras. Vid Montereau sju mil öster om huvudstaden förenar sig Seine och Yonne och gör gemensam sak, men det är Yonne som är den både längre och bredare floden. Ingen parisare skulle dock gå med på att det är något annat än Seine som är stadens käresta.

Vi lämnade Seine vid Montereau och tog in på Yonne för att göra en obehaglig upptäckt: slussväggarna lutade, och det tål bara pråmar. Ingen flytbrygga fanns för mindre båtar att lägga till vid.

– Sluta tjafsa, snäste slussvakten, som inte var någon prydnad för VNF. Ska ni igenom får ni gå nu. Jag väntar en båt uppifrån. Ni kan ligga utan förtöjning mitt i.

– Då tar ni det *doucement*, krävde jag, och han tog det faktiskt lugnt.

Men man är ganska hjälplös i strömvirvlarna, och vi insåg att så här kunde vi inte fortsätta. Vid nästa sluss väntade vi på en pråm i vår riktning. Än finns det lite trafik på Yonne.

Så småningom dök det upp en och vi frågade artigt om vi fick gå med och förtöja utmed dess långsida, med hänvisning till de besvärliga slussväggarna.

– De är Napoleons fel! ropade pråmfrun när hon lade fast våra linor på ”Vidis” mäktiga pollare.

Slussarna här, som så många andra, kom till på Napoleon I:s initiativ. De lutande väggarna är ett otyg.

”Vidi” var på väg för att hämta en last med säd. Familjen bestod av man och hustru som delade på jobbet, Caesar fyra år och den obligatoriska vaktschäfern. Det fanns en tonårig dotter också, som gick i en särskild skola för pråmungdomar men som dök upp

Patrick och Gina Amand på ”Vidi” – arbetsplats och hem.

vid lov och större helger. Alla pråmar har en bil på däck för att man ska kunna hämta och lämna familjemedlemmar och göra ärenden. Både Monsieur och Madame var av pråmfamilj – hon var till och med född ombord – annars skulle man nog inte klara den här sortens liv, ansåg de. Å andra sidan kunde de inte tänka sig något annat. Med återväxten – ja, man fick se. Småpråmarnas tid var inte helt förbi, men de flesta unga som stannade kvar i yrket valde *le grand gabarit,* de stora lastfartygen på Rhône och Rhen.

Dottern hade en gång prövat att gå i en vanlig skola och vantrivts nästan till sammanbrott. Kamraterna var inga kamrater – småelaka och svikliga. Det var skillnad på båtfolk och landfolk. Pråmfamiljerna håller reda på varandra och hjälper varandra i en på en gång slitsam och fri tillvaro. I skolor som inrättats särskilt för pråmbarn fanns denna sammanhållning, och i sådan skulle snart unge Caesar sättas.

Detta självständiga barn hade så liten han var krävt att få låta håret växa så att det kunde bäras i två flätor från hjässan till axlarna.

– Han får själv ta mötet med skolan, sa hans mor. Om han har kvar sina flätor då och klarar av det är det en personlig seger. Om inte är det väl också en lärdom.

I två dagar skulle vi färdas tillsammans, prata om kanallivet när vi låg sida vid sida i slussarna och vänslas med den keliga schäfern i land om kvällen, när han inte tumlade runt i gräset med Caesar. Men kom man med så mycket som en hand in på ”Vidis” territorium under slussningen kom han störtande med gurgel och rest ragg och utan att bry sig om att däckets solstekta järnplåtar måste ha bränt under trampdynorna.

Strax före Sens hade ”Vidi” sin silo, och med några eleganta manövrer styrdes alla hennes ton in till kaj. Vi fortsatte vidare.

Pénichen ”Vidi” är en typisk representant för pråmarna av den mindre storleken med Freycinetmått. För det mesta fraktar hon spannmål i det inre av Frankrike.

Varför blir fransmän så arga?

En het dag cyklar vi från Moret längs Canal du Loing till Grez-sur-Loing för att ta oss en titt på den ort där en svensk konstnärskoloni med Carl Larsson och August Strindberg och en hel rad andra höll till på 1880-talet. Hôtel Chevillon, där de bodde, ägs i dag av en svensk stiftelse.

Naturligtvis är huset stängt, enligt den osvikliga lagen om att allt man uppsöker i Frankrike i princip är öppet utom just när man är där. Värdfolket är bortrest över dagen. Vi är svimfärdiga av hunger och törst och tar oss till den enda restaurangen på det lilla torget. Den är också stängd, eftersom det är onsdag. Vi strosar ändå en stund i trädgården på andra sidan Rue Carl Larsson och tycker oss känna igen en del motiv, och då får jag med ens se att inkörsporten öppnas och att någon sorts trädgårdsmästarvehikel kör in. Jag

Hôtel Chevillon i Grez med den trädgård ur vilken vi blev utdrivna. Författaren Robert Louis Stevenson, också utsatt för dåligt franskt humör, bodde på andra våningen.

rusar dit samtidigt som en småskoleklass på tipspromenad med sin unga lärarinna traskar in på gården.

Vi har allesammans gått för långt. Från redskapsvagnen störtar en ung man med hästsvans och isande blå blick.

– Ut, ryter han, ut med detsamma!

Lärarinnan försöker vänligt fråga något, jag försöker hinna få en glimt innanför byggnadens franska dörrar, men trädgårdsskötaren är inte till att tala med.

– *Out, out, out!* gormar han.

Jag protesterar:

– Detta ställe är svensk egendom, jag tänker sända en note till ert lands ambassad om ert uppförande.

– Skiter jag i, *out*! fortsätter han och går hotfullt mot oss, och ögonblicket efteråt står jag och skolklassen på Carl Larssons gata medan barnen med sina små papper i handen låter skräckslagna blickar vandra mellan mig och fröken. Säkert var trädgårdsmannen i sin rätt när han avvisade oss, men sättet! Och varför skrek han *out,* på engelska? Jag minns när vi i England en gång kört in på förbjudet område och en vakt kom emot oss med ett älskvärt ”Oh, sir, oh, madam, här är så gyttjigt, jag tror ni skulle behöva gummistövlar om ni hade tänkt kliva ut bilen”.

Robert Louis Stevenson, som paddlade på Oise 1876, möttes av samma franska avgrundsvrede när han stigit in i ett franskt värdshuskök och hövligt – ”alltför hövligt” skriver han, dristat sig till att fråga om det ginge att få middag. ”En ohygglig naturkatastrof ägde rum i värdinnans ansikte. Hon rusade emot oss och stampade med foten i golvet. – Ut med er, ut genom dörren, skrek hon. *Sortez! Sortez! Sortez par la porte!*”

– Visst är det skillnad, säger Lucie som vi möter i den engelska kanalbåten ”Body & Soul”. Lucie är halvt engelska, halvt fransyska.

– Sånt händer bara här. Själv kom jag en gång och ledde in min cykel på en tom skolgård för att fråga den enda person som fanns i sikte om vägen, och då fick någon sorts vaktmästare långt borta syn på mig och rusade till och skrek och hotade med rektor och polis och giljotin om jag inte omedelbart avlägsnade mig och mitt livsfarliga fordon. Han var inte heller att komma till tals med.

Men varför blir somliga fransmän så tvärarga? Arv eller miljö?

Lucie tror att en del av befolkningen hyser en ilske-gen.

– Mina syskonbarn har en sådan, de är magra och nerviga och röker oavbrutet och är konstant argsinta och far ut för ingenting.

Lucie själv är inte mager och nervig.

Men redan nästa kväll råkar vi ut för en liten undersätsig typ med ilske-genen. Vi har lagt oss vid en nyanlagd väntkaj med fina pollare alldeles före en sluss. Den har stängt för kvällen, men vi vill ändå förtöja så långt bak som möjligt eftersom vi annars kommer att ligga i vägen när pråmarna börjar gå i morgonväkten. Framför oss ligger en liten fritidsbåt, ännu mer i vägen, och akter om oss har en metare installerat sig med en massa spön.

Skepparn upplyser honom om att vi till natten måste backa till hans plats. Det är inget problem, får vi veta, om halvannan timme högst ska han ge sig av, och vi säger att bra, vi äter middag så länge.

När vi har ätit i två och en halv timme och det börjar mörkna säger jag glatt:

– Nu, min herre, är det dags att flytta!

Men då finns det plötsligt inte längre något samförstånd. Den lilla tjockisen rör sig inte alls, i stället kastar han sina metrevar över ”Vanadis”. Vi börjar backa henne ändå, och då gastar han att han har betalat för sin metarplats, han tänker inte vika! Vi behåller kontenansen och påpekar att vi å vår sida har betalat för att gå på kanaler och att dessutom såväl metare som fritidsbåtar i första hand måste underordna sig yrkestrafiken. För resten står det ”Réservé” på en skylt på kajen, och det betyder reserverat för uppåtslussande. Men det finns gott om plats att meta för om oss i stället, vi ska bara flytta den ensamma lilla fritidsbåten också, och sedan, var så god.

Metaren blir nu mörkröd i den djupa skymningen och skriker att den båten är inte vår, rör vi den gör vi oss skyldiga till egenmäktigt förfarande, oerhört!

– *Calmez-vous,* lugna er, säger Skepparn, och jag tar ett djupt andetag, för denna fras vet jag är som att tända en stubin. Det slår aldrig fel. Först ser det ut som om metaren håller på att arbeta upp en apoplexi. Ådrorna sväller på halsen och runt tinningarna. Sedan kommer urladdningen. Han sliter ner sina spön så fort och så hårdhänt att vi tror att de ska gå av, han trampar i håvar och hinkar och hopfällbara stolar och burkar med bete, det är som på film, och sedan rafsar han ihop alltsammans medan han häver ur sig okvädinsord om utlänningar som inte ens kan tala ordentlig franska och borde utvisas ur landet, deporteras!

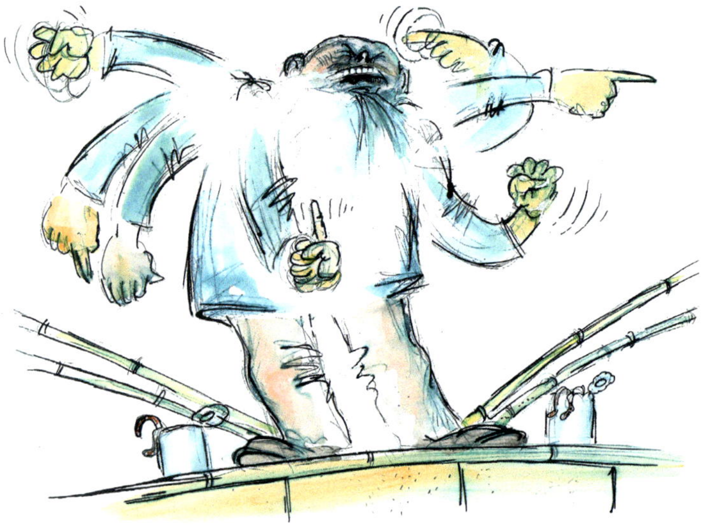

– ”Vanadis”, jag lägger det namnet på minnet! Ni kommer att få problem, jag är *huissier de France!* är hans avskedsord innan han smäller igen bildörren och drar i väg så gruset sprutar.

En huissier är en sorts fjärdingsman, ett farligt F minsann. Vi kalmerar oss själva med ett glas vin på akterdäck.

Medan vi sitter där kommer ett livat sällskap som visar sig rå om den lilla tvålkoppen som vi har flyttat.

– Har ni förtöjt om oss, o, så bra, stort tack! ropar de och försvinner under kapellet.

I gryningen kommer den första pråmen. Hade vi legat kvar hade vi blivit intryckta i kajen. När vi sedan går i land för att kasta loss ser vi baksidan på skylten med ”Réservé”. Där står det: ”Plats för två metspön 25 meter åt vänster, för sex metspön 50 meter åt höger.”

Åt vänster ligger vi. Åt höger, strax akter om oss, ligger en pråm vid speciella pråmstolpar. Den skulle ha haft spöna långt in över lastluckan om metaren hållit på sin rätt.

Men kajen och pollarna och pråmplatsen kan väl inte ha anlagts för metare?

Att fråga slussvakten hur det här går ihop är ingen idé. Vi vet svaret: en axelryckning och det vanliga *Vous êtes en France, Madame!*

Svar på tal

Efter vårt möte med den koleriske *huissiern* undrade vi om han sänt sin bannbulla över "Vanadis" längs kanalen. Men trollet syntes inte till, i träden hördes fågeldrill. Slussvakterna var vänligt likgiltiga eller bara likgiltiga.

Annars är det inte tillrådligt att råka i krakel med slussfolk och i all synnerhet inte att dra ner brallorna på dem. Har man otur sköter de nästa sluss och kanske tio till, och det kan räcka med att de underrättar en kollega om hur man ska behandlas.

Ibland är det dock svårt att lägga band på sig. En gång väntade vi en halv förmiddag, och till slut började vi genomföra slussningen själva. I det läget dök det upp en gnom på en skrällande Velo-Solex, rufsig och bakfull och oförskämd. Han gormade utan ände och ville stoppa den inledda processen. Ombordvarande vännen Lars, som inte talar franska, klargjorde på tydlig svenska vilka plikter som ålåg den försumlige, allt medan han med sin längre och kraftigare kroppshydda drev honom tillbaka från slussvandringen bort till hans moped så att han kunde dra i väg och öppna nästa sluss, illa kvickt!

Det svenska språket bet.

Den behagliga vakterskan i den tredje slussen beklagade oss livligt, kollegan var ökänd, en skam för kanalen och för hela Bourgogne!

Är man försedd med en bottenlös självtillit kan man också göra som den småländske företagare i bekantskapskretsen, som när han vid en gränskö till Italien fann att en nyrik spoling i en öppen sportbil trängt sig före lugnt gick ut och lyfte av honom hans dyra solglasögon, tog hans näsa i ett fast grepp mellan sina småländska pek- och långfingrar och vred om tills det knakade, varefter han satte tillbaka brillorna på den häpne drullen och återvände till sin Saab. Allt utan att yttra ett ord; småländska kunde ha äventyrat proceduren.

Som skandinav är man annars van vid konfliktlösning genom förhandling, men här verkar det ibland som om någon lösning inte alls är eftersträvansvärd; tvärtom gäller det att ta tillfället i akt att få arbeta upp en rejäl adrenalingenomströmning, en sorts katharsis, som får sin fulländning om den kan drivas därhän att en tinningåder brister.

För ett svenskt kynne tar det emellertid ofta emot att bemöta sådant raseri – eller bara grinighet och snorkighet – med kallt stål. Förhandlingsbenägenhet kan man väl tycka är ett civiliserat drag, även om det innebär att konflikter sopas under mattan och får rummet att lukta ovädrat. Att svara med samma mynt tar också på ens svenska själskrafter. Men motstånd är i hårda lägen det enda som hjälper. Behärskning tolkas bara som undergivenhet, och sedan blir man behandlad som mespropp och ärelös.

Hundarna i Moret

Moret-sur-Loing är måleriskt så det räcker och blir över. Det har konstnärerna upptäckt sedan länge. Den älsklige impressionisten Alfred Sisley råkar dessutom vara en stadens son och dyker upp i sommarens ljud- och ljusspel.

Men Moret är också hundarnas paradis, och för hundarna betyder medeltida stadsportar och sirade fasader och kvarnbyggnader där Loing delar sig, åter flyter samman, bryts och faller i glittrande kaskader ingenting. För dem är det strandpromenaden och deltaområdet framför den gamla stadsbron som är härligheten. Där kan man simma och plaska och dyka efter stenar i det solglnistrande vattnet medan änderna lojt makar sig undan.

Alla Morets hundar går promenad utmed stranden, flera gånger om dagen, och den som vill hoppar i medan hussar och mattar stannar för att konversera.

Vi hade koll på dem från akterdäcket. Där var vorstehn som vadade hela vägen, där var labradoren som outtröttligt plumsade i efter en pinne som en lika outtröttlig husse kastade om och om igen, där var mormor med vargen – en snipögd gammal schäfer med något rött i munnen, en boll, en röd luva? Där var små luddiga saker som heter sådant som Minou. Ingen gick i koppel.

Det gjorde heller inte golden retrievern Kim, han hade sitt släpande efter sig, och så fort hans matte närmade sig skuttade han undan, gång efter annan.

– Oh, la, la! ropade hon, så här gör han alltid, *alltid,* han är hopplös!

Kim hade fått vittring på vattnet och var på väg ner. Matten var på gränsen till sammanbrott.

– Vattnet är fruktansvärt smutsigt! Och han kan inte simma! Oh, la, la!

Andra hundägare upprepade ”Han kan inte simma!” och brast i skratt. Är det någon hund som kan simma är det retrievern. Men de försökte i alla fall hejda rymlingen, som emellertid anade oråd och kastade sig åt sidan, vildare ju mer folk viftade med armarna och försökte ställa sig i vägen. Jag hade just gått i land, och när han skubbade förbi mig låtsades jag inte se honom och sedan trampade jag på kopplet.

Spelet var över. Kim och jag utbytte blickar och hans sa att jag var en förrädare. Matten tog Kim i upptuktelse med koppeltampen, sedan tackade hon tusen gånger och sa att så här gör han *bara* med mig, *aldrig* när han går med Monsieur!

Förlåt mig Kim, men till priset av din förlorade frihet har du förhoppningsvis nu också fått ditt sista rapp. Jag försökte få matten att förstå att om hon någonsin skulle få hunden att återvända skulle det vara med beröm och inte med straff. Till Kim sa jag att jag var övertygad om att han kunde simma.

Moret-sur-Loing, återgivet av Alfred Sisley. Vattnet är grunt och klart. Hundarna älskar det lika mycket som målarna. (Musée d'Orsay, Paris.)

Kandisocker, likörer och marmelader i butiken i nunnornas forna fabrik.

Nunnegodis

Sisleys målningar från Moret är ljuvligt skimrande. Men den bild som sprids vida är ingen reproduktion av hans tavlor utan den blåa stadssilhuett som pryder burkarna med ”Le Sucre d'Orge”. Det är ett gyllengult kandisocker kokat på sädesslaget korn. Det har tillverkats här på orten sedan 1634, och de som framställde det var nunnor. Receptet var förstås hemligt. Nunnegodiset var favorit hos Ludvig XIV och hans hov och verksamheten blomstrade. Men när franska revolutionen svepte fram upplöstes klostret, och länge trodde man att tillverkningshemligheten gått om intet. Men som i alla goda historier skulle det förlorade lyckligen komma igen. Receptet hade bevarats hos en av de skingrade systrarna som strax innan hon dog hann anförtro det åt en from väninna. I Moret skulle klostersystrar åter samlas kring kandisockret, och på 1800-talet var sötsakerna en stor produkt som inbragte så pass mycket att nunnorna kunde driva både krigssjukhus och åldringsvård.

När den sista skröpliga nunnan kastade in handduken 1970 överlät hon det hemliga receptet på den familj som nu i andra generationen driver tillverkningen. Innehavaren har även inrättat ett litet museum, och på en video får man se den hantverksmässiga framställningen av småkarameller och avlånga stänger. Hans arbetsamma svägerska svarar för ihällningen av karamellerna i vackra burkar och för inslagningen av stängerna med stämpeln ”Religieuses de Moret” i prasslande cellofan.

Vi träffar henne i butiken i det hus där nunnorna tidigare drev sin verksamhet, och medan vi väljer bland burkar i olika storlekar och små flaskor med likör som gjorts på det märkvärdiga kornsockret och rader med sylter och marmelader och inläggningar berättar hon om arbetet. De ålderstigna maskinerna som vi sett på videon pluttar ut karamellerna i olika format, men allt annat görs för hand.

– Och det tar hårt att vrida runt cellofanet tusentals gånger, säger hon och skakar på handlederna. Vi underhandlar med några ingenjörer som ska utveckla en sockerstångsinslagningsmaskin. De håller just på och funderar på hur man ska få till den rätta knixen.

Karamellerna som tillverkats i snart 400 år.

CARL LARSSON
1883

Konstnärerna i Grez

I Grez-sur-Loing hade vi strövat bland trädgårdsmurar och vatten och brovalv som inte ändrats sedan Carl Larsson målade av dem i slutet på 1800-talet. Hôtel Chevillon, konstnärskolonins hemvist som varit stängt för oss och där vi blivit så bryskt avvisade, ville vi se också inuti. Det har rests ur ett tillstånd av elände av en grupp besjälade göteborgare, bland dem grosshandlaren Erik Malmsten som också tillhandahöll pengarna, och hundra år efter sin första storhetstid invigdes det på nytt. Nu kan konstnärer, författare och musiker tillbringa några stipendiemånader här.

Efter ett telefonsamtal hälsades vi välkomna till ett besök. Vi cyklade återigen den vänliga dragvägen från Moret utmed Canal du Loing, där en och annan yrkespråm gled fram med hund och tvätt och kryddodling på däck, som de alltid har sett ut.

Hôtel Chevillon vilade tyst i middagshettan. Intendenten Madame Bernadette Plissart tog hjärtligt emot oss och visade runt i kök och matsal och bibliotek. Över allt fanns målningar och teckningar av svenska konstnärer.

– Alla som bott här måste lämna något, berättade hon. Många av alstren var kärleksförklaringar till henne, husets ande. Biblioteket var fullt av böcker som skänkts av gästande författare. Alla har varit där.

Men var det alltid så här fridfullt? Vi försökte föreställa oss livet på den tiden då Carl Larsson och hans Karin och Strindberg, Oscar Björck, Georg Pauli, Heidenstam, Zorn och Liljefors ständigt umgicks och åt och drack, sjöng och spelade, diskuterade och bråkade, då byns övriga pensioner hyste konstnärer från England och Amerika och Japan och då det måste ha stått stafflier överallt framför dessa friluftsmålare i färd med att erövra det franska ljuset. Och det var här vår kanotpaddlande föregångare Robert Louis Stevenson mötte sin Fanny. Ett par rum på övervåningen är reserverade för skotska kulturarbetare.

– Folk håller på med sitt, sa Bernadette. De har kommit hit för att få arbetsro.

Nu dök det upp en svensk målare som villigt visade oss bostadsrum och ateljéer. Kanske anses det att konstnärer arbetar bäst under knapphetens kalla stjärna, men i förhållande till sällskapsvåningen och trädgården som sluttar ner mot Loing var gästrummen nedslående i sin torftighet. Ett stort svenskt möbelföretag skulle utan att förblöda kunna skapa både trevnad och svenskhet i denna byggnad vid gatan med det förpliktande namnet *Rue Carl Larsson.*

I Grez-sur-Loing studerade utländska målare det franska ljuset. "Motiv från Grez" av Carl Larsson. (Nationalmuseum, Stockholm)

Den lönlösa brådskan

Ibland får vi frågan ”Hur långt kommer man på en dag?”.

För att ge en uppfattning om proportionerna brukar vi nämna att det tog oss en månad från Paris till Nevers. Tågresan tillbaka gick på två timmar.

Den högsta tillåtna hastigheten på kanalerna brukar vara sex kilometer i timmen. En normal slussning tar omkring tjugo minuter.

Vet man hur många timmar man kan gå under en dag och hur många slussar man har framför sig är det ju bara att räkna.

När man har gjort det bör man sedan glömma alltihop.

Meningen med att färdas på vattenvägarna är just att vara på dem, att lägga till där det faller en in, att ta ett dopp om man befinner sig på en flod, att prata med slussfolk, andra båtägare, åsnor, att vänta tills bageriet har öppnat.

Långsamheten är en del av meningen. Man hinner uppleva förskjutningarna i perspektivet där man glider fram, den nya utblicken när man kommit upp ur en slusskammare, dofterna av vatten, av koskit, fläder, hö.

Att spika datum för olika destinationer är att med berått mod förbereda ett nervsammanbrott. Man behöver visserligen inte utgå från att man ska bli liggande i månader mellan två slussar, men vi har hört om folk som blivit fast resten av säsongen när torkan har satt stopp för verksamheten.

Planerade reparationer av slussar och kanalsträckor tillkännages långt i förväg av VNF. Men verkligheten är oberäknelig. Slussportar hakar upp sig. Broar går i baklås eller blir rammade och faller ner och blockerar farleden halvårsvis. Pråmar sätter sig på tvären. Slussvakter har gett sig i väg till grannbyn ”men är tillbaka när som helst”. Vid ett tillfälle stoppades en kanal under en hel eftermiddag för att en törstig tjur fallit i. (Det olyckliga djuret baxades så småningom upp med plankor, rep och en traktor och blev förstasidesstoff i lokaltidningen.)

Ens eget fartyg kan råka ut för haverier av skilda slag – motor, generator, pumpar, värmare, toalettsystem … Propellrar blir odugliga efter möten med stenar, flytande stockar eller ikastade kundvagnar.

(Om ni fastnar i en sådan, ring inte efter en reparatör, rådde en erfaren båtgranne. Gå upp till brandkåren, *les pompiers*, med en kasse med öl. De blir bara glada åt att få komma ifrån med jobb av det här slaget.)

Man kan bli liggande på en ort i väntan på reservdelar som dessutom är fel när de äntligen kommer, eller bara på att ett *bricolage*, ett byggvaruhus, ska öppna (stängt måndagar, tisdagar eller vilken dag som helst, men alltid just den när man är där).

Fransmännen iakttar stressade utlänningar med roat lugn. Varför sådant väsen? Ni har ju kommit till Frankrike för att vara i Frankrike. Saknar ni något? Vin? Bröd? Inte det? Ja, men då så.

Bopråmen ”France” har lämnat sin kajplats i stan och semestrar på Saône med metspön, parabol, tvätt och hundar.

FRANCE

Pierre-Paul Zivy, kanalens räddare, står staty med en hel sluss på sina fingrar av plåt.

Canal du Nivernais

Canal du Nivernais börjar i Auxerre och följer först Yonnes dalgång för att sedan klättra upp för den bergsrygg som delar Seinebäckenet från Loirebäckenet. Väl uppe vid Baye slingrar den sig åter ner, till Decize vid Loire.

Kanalen anlades i slutet av 1700-talet som en flottningsled för timmer från Morvans skogar – i Paris var behovet av trä och ved omättligt. Senare byggdes den om för godstransporter på mindre pråmar.

Vid mitten av 1900-talet var den hopplöst föråldrad och oekonomisk och lades ner. Förfallet började. Räddningen blev en man vid namn Pierre-Paul Zivy, som insåg dess skönhetsvärden och som med entusiasm och hårt arbete lyckades få myndigheterna att sätta kanalen i stånd för fritidsbåtsfarare, som inte nog kan tacka honom för det. En liten märklig staty av honom där han håller en modell av en sluss med inneliggande båt finns att beskåda i Baye på kanalens höjdpunkt.

Canal du Nivernais är nog den ljuvligaste av Frankrikes alla vackra vattenleder. De etthundratio slussarna gör också att man hinner ta den till sig, steg för steg.

Om hörnet låg en katedral

Till Auxerre kom vi norrifrån genom flodgrönskan, och utan förvarning hade vi katedralen på nosen. Den var en uppenbarelse.

Auxerre slarvar man inte förbi. Längs med vattnet finns ett gammalt kvarter som har bebotts av båtfolk, och längre upp vandrar man mellan korsvirke, kyrkor och ett präktigt stadsur med sol och måne. Här och där finns lustiga statyer i målat trä över stadens döttrar och söner.

Katedralen Saint-Étienne är mäktig och ljus med enastående glasmålningar. Äldst och märkvärdigast är ändå kyrkan som rests över Saint Germains grav. Helgonet som givit namn åt så många franska orter vilar alltså här i en krypta med merovingiska kapitäl och bleknade målningar på väggarna.

Ofta känns det som om tiden mellan antiken och medeltiden förlorar sig i ett töcken, men när man här läste informationstexterna på väggen trädde med all tydlighet Germanus emot en, en flitigt arbetande och resande person: född 378 här i Auxerre av förnäm romersk familj, studier i juridik i Rom, biskop i Auxerre, till England för att komma till rätta med där rådande irrläror, död 448 i Ravenna och i en mäktig procession återförd till födelsestaden.

Han verkade inte längre bort än vilken 1900-talsmänniska som helst.

På den inre anslutande klostergården skulle det bli tangoafton och det surrade av svartklätt hästsvansfolk

Auxerre reser sig över Yonnes vatten.

som byggde podium och testade ljudet. Om detta var ett vanhelgande så var det ändå ett övergående tilltag; Napoleon gjorde ett mer bestående sådant genom att 1812 låta riva en god del av kyrkan för att bygga ett invalidsjukhus intill.

Men hur sevärt Auxerre än var och hur än chablisvinerna lockade kändes vår belägenhet i hamnen i den just utbrutna värmeböljan inte tilltalande. Solen var ett bart huggande svärd, skugga skänktes ingenstans. Vi gav oss därför så småningom av och in på Canal du Nivernais.

Den börjar här och den började bra, med en rar studentska som steg ut ur en slussvaktarhytt som såg ut som ett hönshus, och vi öppnade den lilla slussen med gemensamma krafter. På denna kanal finns ingen elektronik, bara mekanik.

Snart började det bli dags att söka nattplats. Fortfarande var det tryckande hett, men vid Angy där man från kanalen tillfälligtvis går ut i Yonne siktade vi en småbåtshamn vid sidan av leden, och vi såg också hur vattnet strömmade över en solbelyst sandbottnen med friskt grönt sjögräs. Det såg lovande ut, kanske skulle vi finna svalka.

Men först skulle vi gå på grund.

Den lockande bottnen av sand och musselskal kom väldigt fort väldigt nära, och "Vanadis" hejdade sin framfart och snurrade runt ett kvarts varv i strömmen. Där stod vi. Med motorkraft kom vi ingen vart, och för övrigt ville vi inte förstöra propellern. Den unge slussvakten vid kanalens fortsättning en bit bort avbröt sitt vevande och iakttog oss. Tennisklubben intill upphörde med sitt servande och iakttog oss. Skepparn hoppade i med plankan som ligger utanpå fendrarna och försökte stående på botten baxa oss loss. "Vanadis" snurrade ytterligare ett kvarts varv men stod lika stadigt.

– Ett rep, giv oss ett rep! ropade tennisklubben, som nu växt i storlek och ställt upp sig på stranden, där den med halande åtbörder visade hur det skulle gå till.

"La belle éclusière" – den vackra slussvakterskan. Slussvaktarsysslan är ett omtyckt sommarjobb för studenter.

– Ingen hjälp! kommenderade Skepparn bistert.

Vi hade läst skräckhistorier om båtägare som i obetydliga knipor blivit undsatta av företagsamma personer vilka sedan i rätten tillerkänts tio procent av båtens värde.

– Fira ner ankaret!

Jag gjorde som befallt och han vadade ut med ankaret i famnen och försvann med det under vattnet. Tennisklubben, som nu fått ytterligare tillökning av kvinnor och barn och blivit en hel folkhop, skrek av förskräckelse.

Men inte heller ankaret hjälpte. Jag tog hem på spelet så att kättingen var spänd som en bågsträng, men ”Vanadis” var orubblig. Från tennisklubben hördes yttranden som ”Så sorgligt”, ”En så vacker båt!”, och vi uppskattade deras goda förstånd när det gällde ”Vanadis” linjer men inte antydningarna att hon vore dömd att bli vrak.

Ett par metare i en liten sportbåt kom förbi, och nu tog vi risken och langade över en lina. Och med ankare, planka och ett ryck var ”Vanadis” loss. Tennisklubben hurrade. Jag störtade ner efter en flaska vin och höll upp den.

– Släng den bara, det ordnar sig, hojtade metarna, och jag slängde och sen ägnade sig Skepparn och den ene av dem åt en stunds frustande dykning innan flaskan äntligen återfanns och togs om hand av sin nye ägare. Tennisklubben visste inte till sig av jubel och viftade med skärmmössor och racketar.

Den hygglige unge slussvakten som stannat kvar för att släppa igenom oss fastän klockan var över åtta sa att det inte var långt till byn Vaux där det fanns en utmärkt tilläggsplats. Vi följde hans råd, men jag saknade det strömmande vattnet över de ljusa musselskalen och avundades Skepparn som ofrivilligt fått svalka sig så lång stund.

Svalkande vatten, men alltför grunt.

Hetta

Värmen som stegrats under vår färd på Yonne hade nu blivit en fuktig hetta som fick det att flimra för ögonen. I den instängda kanalen badar man inte gärna, och vi såg ibland kvalfyllt floden passera vid sidan av oss med långa breda gnistrande fall, men ouppnåelig. När vi väntade på slussning måste vi finna ett träd att förtöja under, annars skulle vi förgås.

Under en kastanj delade vi en stund skuggan med en motorcyklist som skalade av sig det ena svarta plagget efter det andra. Fram trädde ett sympatiskt ansikte. Dess innehavare hade noterat vår skandinaviska flagga och frågade oss om vår färd, något som ytterst sällan händer oss i Frankrike. Själv var han på väg till Alperna för att finna svalka, berättade han, men hans fru fann motorcyklar obehagliga och hade tagit tåget. Jag sade att vi har en son som har *une moto,* och att jag var nervös för det, och han svarade att han också hade en son med motorcykel och att han – och nu väntade jag mig att han skulle säga att det är ingen fara, men det gjorde han inte alls – att han också var nervös för sin sons motorcykelåkande. Vi skildes i ett flyktigt mötes djupa samförstånd.

Lyckligtvis förenar sig Canal du Nivernais ganska ofta med Yonne, och då kunde vi låta ”Vanadis”

Inte en fläkt på den stilla kanalen.

driva ett stycke medan vi simmade intill i strömmen. Svalkan när vattnet steg upp över halspulsådern förde en tillbaka till livet.

I Bailly finns en gästkaj av det goda skälet att det en bit upp i backen ligger en *cave* där det framställs en förträfflig crémant de Bourgogne, ett lätt mousserande vitt vin. Är man inte stadd vid kassa för champagne är denna crémant ett utmärkt synonympreparat. Själva vingrottan är ett nedlagt underjordiskt kalkstensbrott med konstant temperatur, väl lämpat för tillverkning och lagring av det härliga bubblet. Och inte mindre lämpat för farande på gränsen till värmeslag. Vi tog oss flämtande upp för backen, betraktade floddalen djupt under oss och kullarna i värmediset där bortom och vacklade in i det svala mörkret.

Hur svårt det är att föreställa sig temperaturer! De fjorton grader som en marsdag vid en solig vägg i Sverige kan kännas som sommar var här som is, oändligt uppfriskande i början men så småningom alltför kyliga. Vi återvände ut i ljusflimret som nu slog emot oss som ur en ugn. Kartongen med tolv flaskor fick oss att knäa.

Till kvällen uppsteg väldiga blålila moln medan den låga solen förvandlade halmen på fälten till guld. Vi gick ut och lade oss på svaj och väntade på det förlösande åskvädret. Men förgäves, det drog förbi och visade sig sedan bara som tysta avlägsna kornblixtar i den kvalmiga natten.

Man färdas inte genom ett landskap utan att uppfylla vissa förväntningar som det ställer på en. Lämnar man en märkvärdighet obeaktad kan man drabbas av både ånger och skam. Vi hade den omtalade vinbyn Ivrance framför oss.

När vi nästa dag skulle besöka den hade hettan arbetat upp sig till trettionio grader. Ivrance ligger inte vid floden, men på cykelavstånd. Varma dagar kan en tur med lite fartvind mot ansiktet vara att föredra framför stillaliggande i vindlös skugga. Och vägen såg rak ut på kartan.

Det var den också, men den ledde uppför. Genom ett landskap med vinodlingar och gröna bergssidor, små åkerlappar, vindlande vita stigar och doft av grönska och säd. Men uppför. Vi stannade var hundrade meter. Varje klunk ur vattenflaskorna omvandlades omedelbart till svidande salta droppar från hårfästet ner i ögonen.

Till slut mötte oss ett gytter av röda tegeltak i grönskan, ett soldallrande Pissarromotiv: Ivrance. Stora gatan låg tyst och folktom. De lövkransade vinhusen med erbjudanden om avsmakning, *dégustation,* fick vänta. En kall öl i dunklet på baren lockade desto mer. I teven malde det ständigt pågående Tour de France.

Öl i nästan fyrtio grader – vi borde ha räknat ut att det skulle sätta stopp för all vidare verksamhet. När det pärlat färdigt på våra pannor besteg vi med slaka ben cyklarna och lät oss bara rulla ner igen, alltför fort genom det ljuva landskapet men med vinden fläktande genom hår och kläder. I snabbköpet i hamnbyn köpte vi sedan i blindo ett par flaskor av det berömda Ivrancevinet. Det fick smaka hur det ville. Det ville så där lagom.

När nästa vinby dök upp sa vi torrt: Låt den ligga.

Slusshäxan

En av dessa heta kvällar kommer vår vän Översättaren ombord. Vi dricker kall cider och sänker oss i Yonne och prisar traktens skönhet. Först i morgon ska vi slussa.

Översättaren har tillbringat långa sejourer i Frankrike ända sedan studentupproret 1968. Hans franska är en hyllning till landet och hans översättargärning så enastående att han är fullbehängd av höga utmärkelser från regeringar och vittra sällskap. I denna värme har man dock så lite på sig som det bara går inom anständighetens gränser – shorts och solhatt. Men Översättaren behöver inga synliga dekorationer för att bli väl bemött. Det räcker med att han öppnar munnen. Hans intagande väsen och hans språkbehandling kan få den arrogantaste parisare att uppträda ämabelt.

Men han har ännu inte mött slusshäxan.

När vi nästa morgon går in i dagens första sluss hälsar jag som vanligt på slussvakten, ”Bonjour, Madame”, samtidigt som jag gör mig redo att stänga porthalvan bakom oss, som brukligt är – man delar på jobbet. Svaret är ett skarpt:

– Låt bli det där! Jag har inte bett om er hjälp!

Översättaren ser förvånad ut.

– *Avancez!* Lägg er längst fram i slussen! kommenderar hon vidare. Jag väntar två båtar till!

Det lär bli trångt, och vi är aldrig hågade att ligga

Ne touchez pas!
Statlig egendom!

Efter Honoré Daumier

långt fram när vattnet släpps på, men i denna hetta måste man ta vara på vattnet, det händer att kanaler torrläggs, så vi avancerar för att ge plats.

Där finns inget att lägga fast vid, varken pollare eller järnpinnar, så vi lägger förlinan runt den upprättstående vevanordningen som hör till slussmekaniken. Det får man egentligen inte, det vet vi. Men att man egentligen inte får göra något brukar i Frankrike inte vara något hinder för att göra det. Men här är det absolut förbjudet! *Absolument!* Statlig egendom! Gör omedelbart loss! Omedelbart!

– Hur har ni tänkt er det hela, Madame? frågar Skepparn.

– Håll linan i handen, snäser häxan.

Det är en löjlig tanke. "Vanadis" väger tolv ton och det är fråga om uppslussning.

– Jag har skött den här slussen i trettio år, det är jag som är auktoritet här, ni ska inte försöka lära mig, fortsätter hon.

– Och jag har slussat i trettiofem år i mer än tusen slussar, säger Skepparn, betalar ni skadorna?

– Det är inte mitt problem att ni har en så tung båt. Nu fräser häxan. Ta bort linan!

– Då ska jag be att få gå ur slussen, säger Skepparn och gör sig redo att backa.

Men de väntade båtarna är redan på väg in, två illa medfarna flytetyg från ett hyrföretag.

Häxan inser att intet är att göra och vänder ryggen till. Trettio års slussande med ideliga kontroverser på grund av den felande pollaren tycks i hennes själ ha skapat ett outsläckligt agg till båtfarare. Att be kanalbolaget att sätta dit någon sorts förtöjningsanordning skulle väl beröva henne grunden för denna ihärdigt närda känsla.

Så öppnar hon luckorna. Hyrbåtarna dunsar hit och dit och får ytterligare några skråmor och en uppsliten avbärarlist.

Översättaren är olycklig. Han vill ha fred på kanalen. Han vill gjuta olja, om inte på kanalvattnet så på slussväkterskans kokande sinne. I denna avsikt nalkas han henne och frågar artigt avledande hur många slussar det månne kan vara kvar till järnvägsstationen i Mailly. Han ska nämligen därifrån med tåg återvända till sin parkerade bil.

Men här hjälper inte den utsöktaste franska och den mildaste ton.

– Därom vet jag intet, svarar häxan högdraget. Ni har väl en kanalkarta, ni som vet allt och särskilt hur man förtöjer.

Översättaren bleknar under solsvedan och lommar ombord.

– Är det så här det är på kanalerna, undrar han, hur står ni ut?

– Det piggar upp, grinar Skepparn. Du skulle ha frågat henne om honungen hon sålde var lika bitter som hon själv när du ändå var i konversationstagen.

Vi styr mot nästa sluss. Översättaren är skärrad, här är det Frankrike han aldrig mött. Men vi tas emot av en vän ung man som arrangerar båtföljet på bästa sätt. Vi får ligga längst bak, väl förtöjda. Alla hjälps åt med slussportarna. Alla beklagar och fördömer högljutt slusshäxans uppträdande. Den unge slussängeln ser till att alla mår bra. Vi får tillsammans en sorts upprättelse efter den skymf som drabbat oss alla. Översättaren återfår tron på mänskligheten.

När vi går ur slussen tackar jag ynglingen och tillägger att fru Solstråle i slussen innan visst inte hade någon bra dag.

Han svarar:

– Det är min mor.

Översättarens avsked

Det är dags för Översättaren att bryta upp och fara vidare. Hettan ligger stadigt på trettioåtta grader, och vi har glidit ner i Yonne varje gång kanalen ansluter till floden, men det är en kortvarig vederkvickelse. Nu måste vi också lämna skuggan under soltältet och ge oss ut under den obarmhärtiga himlen.

Jag följer Översättaren till den lilla anhalten utanför byn, en betongkur vid ett spikrakt järnvägsspår som försvinner i grönskimret långt långt borta. Vi sätter oss inne i kurens skugga och känner hur det tillrar under våra solhattar, från pannan, utmed nacken, längs ryggen. Landskapet utanför nästan upplöses i ljuset. Det är som författaren Ryszard Kapuściński beskrivning av kölden i Sibirien, fast tvärtom. När det är som kallast där, berättar en liten flicka, blir det liksom hål i luften med konturer efter människorna. När hon går till skolan kan hon se vem som har gått före henne. Jag undrar om man kan se hål efter människor även i hetta, och vi låter blicken glida över omgivningen, men där finns inte en levande varelse, bara soldaller och stillhet.

I stället berättar Översättaren om hur han den gångna vintern rest med Kapuściński till Kiruna och där till bådas förtjusning nedsänkts i gruvans mörker för att sedan stiga upp i en gnistrande vinterdag.

Men varken Kapuściński eller Översättarens beskrivningar av kyla förmår framkalla någon svalka. Och så småningom lösgör sig en liten punkt långt bort där spåren löper samman, den närmar sig och växer och när den är framme är den en fullkomligt nedklottrad rälsbuss som stannar här mitt i ensligheten. Vi är för svettiga för att omfamna varandra till farväl, men vi är ändå så fyllda av glädje över mötet att det inte spelar någon roll.

Så stiger Översättaren ombord med sin lilla gröna kappsäck som medfört en flaska Gammal Norrlands och Dagens Nyheter. Rälsbussen slamrar i väg på spåret som är lika spikrakt åt andra hållet. Den skapar inget hål i hettan, den blir bara ett par suddiga gula och lila fläckar i flimret, som på en impressionistmålning.

Och sedan kom "Vivante"

Canal du Nivernais är oupphörligt intagande. Efter Mailly-le-Château på en höjd i en krök går den ut i Yonne, och där öppnar sig en ängsmark med klippor vid sidan och betande kor. Här ville vi stanna.

Vi badade, åt och förvånades över att vi så länge fått vara ensamma i denna ljuvlighet när den strax fläktes upp av skräll och skrammel. En pråmför dök upp i kanalens mynning bakom oss. "Vivante" med en stor amerikansk flagga passerade och försvann. Åter hördes högsommarens enstaka flöjtande fåglar och några försynta råmanden från fänaden som kommit ner för att dricka.

När vi så småningom lämnat friden och gled fram till nästa sluss låg "Vivante" där.

– Hon är en njutning för ögat, om än inte för örat, gastade jag till hennes skeppare när jag tog emot linorna och lade fast. "Vivante" är en liten skönhet från 1911, svart med gula och röda dekorationer, ett rundat akterdäck med gulvitrandig markis och prydliga blomkrukor på taket. Men motorn är en helvetesmaskin.

"Vivante" och "Vanadis" fyllde alldeles lagom en

sluss, och vi fortsatte tillsammans till kvällshamnen i Châlet-Censoir. Hettan vek inte, och nu hade den blivit åsktung och tryckande. Vi drack ett glas vitt med Jerry och Barbara, ett par av de många amerikaner som vill upptäcka det Europa som de känner att de kommer från.

– Fast jag är ju en enkel flicka från en mjölkfarm i Australien, sa Barbara. Men katolik!

– Och jag är jude, sa Jerry.

Vi undrade hur det fungerade.

– Inte alls, och alldeles utmärkt, sa Jerry.

Sedan erbjöd de oss en fortsättning på kvällen med isdryck och luftkonditionering till en västernvideo i "Vivantes" salong. Vi tog tacksamt emot. Vi hade kunnat se vad som helst, bara vi fick svalka. Luftkonditioneringen visade sig dock vara ur funktion, men en stark känsla av trivsel och avspändhet bredde ändå ut sig när Barbara lade sig på golvet för att komma till rätta med sin rygg, med benen rakt upp och båtens uråldriga argsinta katta på magen. Där somnade hon medan vi andra följde en oändlig gunfight som utspelades i smattrande hällregn alltmedan onda och goda slirade runt i leran mellan stall och saloon. Ljudarbetet var mycket övertygande; det lät därnere i dunklet som om det verkligen brutit ut ett oväder över oss, och när vi sedan steg upp i den heta natten med cikadornas knirk och den belysta kyrkan på sin höjd ovanför kanalen kändes det mer overkligt än filmen.

Detta var det första mötet med "Vivante". Under den månad som vi skulle tillbringa på Canal du Nivernais skulle stjärnbaneret fläkta "Vanadis" nos i många slussar. Skepparn och Jerry skulle ägna den larmande motorn och andra tekniska problembärare åtskilliga stunder. Den allestädes och ingenstädes närvarande Ted Johnson, vars namn nämnts oss av båtfolk ända sedan Cambrai i norra Frankrike, skulle gemensamt eftersökas för "Vivantes" motor och vårt alltmer sackande kylskåp. Barbara skulle bjuda på god och närande mat, kryddad från odlingarna på däck.

Söndagsstiltje

I Châlet-Censoir skulle vi hämta upp vännerna Helen och Ann-Margret som från skilda håll var på väg till denna lilla by. Vi fördrev eftermiddagen i skuggan under en markis på kaféet vid torget, *la place,* med affären på vänster hand och rådhuset, *la mairie*, och krigsmonumentet på höger. Så ser många torg ut här i landet. Nu rådde fullkomlig söndagsstiltje. *Mille villes et villages tranquilles* malde i mitt huvud, en uttalsramsa från skoltiden, 'tusen stilla städer och byar'. Det är en god beskrivning av den franska landsbygden.

Men så började det röra på sig. Först trippade barnkören som vi lyssnat till genom kyrkans öppna portal nedför backen, fördelades mellan pussande släktingar och skingrades. Sedan ljöd kloppret av hovar, och två präktiga arbetshästar med ett par unga grabbar på ryggen svängde in på torget. Ryttarna band djuren vid räcket under träden utanför rådhuset och slog sig ner vid ett kafébord. Ut kom servitören med öl och sedan med ett par hinkar vatten. En lång stund hördes bara sparvtjipp i hettan och vattendropp från mularna. Så bröts lugnet av en traktor med ett hiskeligt och vacklande halmsläp. Skramlet från järn och hjul mot stenläggningen var öronbedövande och fick hästarna att rygga och gnägga och sparvarna att fladdra i väg.

När samtalen vid borden kunde återupptas strömmade det in en svärm av törstiga söndagscyklister.

I Frankrike är alla sådana Tour de France-wannabeer. I Frankrike cyklar man inte för att man har ett ärende. Man cyklar för själva cyklandet. Ingen trampar upprätt med fyrkantiga packväskor som i Holland, där halva livet tycks framlevas på cykel, eller sansat med en korg på styrstången, som i Sverige – länder där man hoppar på cykeln som man går och står.

Fransmän ger sig inte ut utan tröja i banlon med flammande mönster, specialbyxor, specialskor, specialglasögon, specialhandskar och hjälm. Fransmän är starkt lagda för utrustning. Om hjälmen vore påbjuden av säkerhetsskäl, som i Sverige, skulle den inte sitta på varje cyklists hjässa. Men här är den en smart sportartikel som anses minska luftmotståndet.

Franska cyklister ligger med sina tjugoen växlar som remmar på vägarna och susar med svällande vador förbi en i uppförsbackarna. Och de cyklar i klubbar, inte familjevis. Man ska inte låta sig förvillas av att dessa sportutövare kan höras upphäva glada rop sinsemellan. Själva cyklandet är blodigt allvar.

Inför cykelklubbens invasion gav sparvarna upp för gott och de bålda ryttarna fortsatte sin solstekta ritt. Själva släntrade vi till den minimala stationen där rälsbussen stannade och släppte av våra vänner, de enda avstigande.

På söndagarna svärmar cyklisterna. Låt inte lura er av den glada uppsynen. Cykling är blodigt allvar.

Byfest med hemkört

Nu var vi på mitten av Canal du Nivernais, mitt i Frankrike, mitt i ingenting tycktes det ibland. Vi gled genom ett omväxlande men sovande landskap. Ibland gick vi utmed en vägg av kritklippor, ibland intill sluttningar med buskvegetation, ibland genom förtorkade betesmarker med nötboskap dåsande i skuggan under träden, någon åker, och så gårdarna, medeltida fort med murar och torn och inkörsportar. Fackelblomster med ljusa fjärilar, blåskimrande jungfrusländor, blomflugor, ömsom stilla på svirrande vingar, ömsom med hastiga ryck. Något enstaka flöjtande fågelrop. Himlen nästan vit. Inte en människa.

Kvarnborna höll oss under uppsikt.

Om eftermiddagen lade vi till i den trevliga småstaden Clamecy som hyser ett museum för kanalen. Vi kom den veckodag då museet hade stängt – vad hade vi väntat. Skepparn tog sig i stället på nytt an "Vivantes" motor, som enligt Jerry förhärjats av en mekaniker i Auxerre. Den väntade Ted Johnson dök inte upp, och Helen och Ann-Margret förstod att de skulle få leva med de ständiga påminnelserna om att man inte fick gå i det snart kollapsande kylskåpet. "Hur ska det då bli någon mat?" morrade de, men ägnade sig lättade över det uteblivna museibesöket åt att med stor omsorg inhandla en färdig lammstek och några flaskor bourgogne.

Efter Clamecy försvann den svalkande Yonne i en däld. När vi om aftonen stötte på floden igen vid en gammal kvarn i Asnois hade den smalnat av till en kristallklar ström, mycket grund, och väl var det, för om man inte förankrade sig i botten skulle man ryckas med. Vi blaskade oss i hettan iakttagna av kvarnens inbyggare, några getter, som stack ut sina smala halsar genom dörrar och fönstergluggar.

Vi hade lagt till vid någon sorts utflyktsplats med grillar och stenbord, och när vi i skymningen satt på akterdäcket dök byborna upp i bil och i traktor och till fots, fullastade med korgar och kylväskor. Det stod inte länge på förrän ett par upprymda farbröder nalkades oss med glas med *ratafia* – en dryck som här i Bourgogne består av druvmust spetsad med marc och inte alls tokig.

Stämningen steg, och nu ansåg festarna att det var

Hälften bondgård, hälften borg. Inget har ändrats sedan medeltiden.

bättre att vi deltog än att vi blev störda. Vi var inte svårbjudna, och snart satt vi inklämda på långbänkarna. Våra värdar blev mer än förtjusta när det visade sig att vi kunde stämma in i en del av sångerna, så repertoaren började anpassas efter vad vi kände till. Några av fruarna tyckte så småningom, inte utan skäl, att festen började få slagsida åt vårt håll och började surmulet plocka ihop måltidsresterna medan karlarna tuppade sig och skämtade och korkade upp den ena flaskan efter den andra av vad de kallade champagne, hemgjord i byn.

Vi började bli oroliga för att det skulle sägas om "Vanadis" att hon skapat tvedräkt i Asnois, men till all lycka kunde festen avslutas innan någon riktig misstämning hann uppstå: makterna sände ett kort, efterlängtat regn, vi blev omkramade även av damerna och försågs med en flaska av "champagnen" till minne av de glada asnoiserna.

Den drycken var det första som gjorde sig påmint dagen efter.

Kroppsarbete och skönanderi

Ann-Margret och Helen hade funnit sig till rätta på ”Vanadis”. Ann-Margret cyklar gärna och långt och vevar oförtrutet på allt som går att veva på. Hon är född för tidigt och har därför risig motorik, säger hon, men det hindrar inte hennes framfart. Fast det är på fritiden. Till yrket är hon professor i psykologi.

Ann-Margret slänger sig utan att tveka på cykeln, kliver genom ramen, faller och skrapar sig blodig och blå, säger ”Äsch”, torkar av sig och trampar vidare.

Helen, som gör svensk litteratur känd i utlandet, är av spädare konstitution och avstår helst från att blanda sig i kanalfarandets riskmoment. I gengäld har hon ett skarpt öga för vad som tilldrar sig och därtill en utomordentlig näsa för delikatesser och var de kan införskaffas.

Båda är mycket livgivande ombord.

Efter festplatsen följde en sträcka med ett antal små vippbroar av järn, basculer, med fullkomligt livsfarliga vevanordningar. De ser ut som ritade av Eiffel. I normalläget ska de vara nedfällda. De borde stå uppfällda eftersom båtarna på kanalen är långt fler än de enstaka traktorer som tar vägen över dem för att nå någon åkerlapp på andra sidan. Men det var bara att veva på, upp och ner, och hoppas att mekaniken och vi själva skulle hålla så att vi inte fick ett skenande handtag under hakan och en brakande bro över båten. Ann-Margret och jag slet som Fenja och Menja vid Grottekvarnen och klarade lyckligen allt utan slirande stoppar och klämda fingrar. "Vivante" hade tacksamt slagit följe med "Vanadis" och gled förbi medan vi höll andan vid de uppresta mekanokonstruktionerna.

Canal du Nivernais är helt och hållet handmanövrerad. De bofasta slussvakterna är få. Verksamheten sköts mestadels av unga glada studenter. Det är inget dåligt sommarjobb: heldagspass med en timmes lunch halva månaden, ledigt andra halvan och dessutom gott om tid att läsa kurslitteratur under ett parasoll i väntan på de fåtaliga båtarna, allt till en absolut hyfsad lön.

På ett ställe hade den unga väkterskan sin pojkvän på besök. De kuttrade som duvor i den lilla hytten när vi kom och kunde knappt slita sig från varandra. När vattnet släppts på återgick de till sin tête-à-tête. Amor blinkade åt oss att inte störa, så vi öppnade själva och gick ur slussen utan att de märkte det.

Vi brukar fråga de unga slussvakterna vad de studerar och det blir ofta inledningen till trevliga samtal. I dessa trakter läste de medicin, arkeologi, juridik, engelska och bokföring i Dijon eller teknik, dans, teater och design i Clermont-Ferrand. Nöjet att gissa vad de håller på med har utvecklats till en sport i människokunskap.

I en sluss satt uppflugna på portverket två förandligade ynglingar, den ene med halmhatt och fin mörk skäggväxt i det bleka ansiktet, den andre med hästsvans, båda inbegripna i ett högt svävande meningsutbyte. Det stycke trivial verklighet som "Vanadis" utgjorde förmådde inte störa dem. När vi uppmärksammade dem på vår närvaro bar de sig så

Upphöjt Samtal – viktigare än slussvaktarsysslan. "Parisstudenter", teckning av signaturen Gavarni 1841.

bortkommet åt vid vevar och spakar att vi tre, psykologen, litteraturvetaren och språkvårdaren, tog över hela slussandet.

– Filosofi, väste Ann-Margret om den bleksiktige.

– Vid Sorbonne, väste Helen tillbaka.

– Filosofi vid Sorbonne, svarade ynglingen upphöjt när vi frågade. Och hästsvansen var cineast, det hade vi också kunnat gissa.

När vi några dagar senare kom i fatt "Vivante" berättade vi om vår lilla frågesport.

– Vi har också frågat dem, varenda en, sa Barbara.

Slussvakterna måste ha trott att det står i "Instruktioner för kanalfarare".

Två gästmatroser

Vi hade långsamt slussat oss upp utmed *les collines du Nivernais,* det massiv som skiljer Seine och Yonne från Loire, och nu återstod en sista uppförsbacke med sexton slussar i tät följd. Den riktiga Yonne hade allt smalare stuckit i väg österut, och bredvid oss löpte nu ett tillflöde, en iskall kvillrande silverbäck i en skogsravin.

Vår slussvakterska som följt oss den sista sträckan var en vacker och livsfrisk kvinna med virvlande hår och ett muntert skratt. Som medhjälpare hade hon sina söner i tio-tolvårsåldern. Pojkarna blev omåttligt stolta när vi med rätta berömde dem för att de identifierat vår svenska flagga, och de hade tusen frågor om oss och vår färd. Varifrån kom vi? Kunde man gå på havet med båten? Vad var Vanadis för ett namn? Varför låg det en stor kniv på däck? (För att skära av linor i katastroffall.) Hur många kunde man vara ombord?

"Så här gör man fast." Slusspojkarna var idel vetgirighet.

Smart fråga. Åtminstone ytterligare två personer denna eftermiddag. Vi erbjöd dem att följa med på däck till nästa sluss. Deras mor protesterade milt – pojkarna fick inte verka påflugna. Vi försäkrade att nöjet var på vår sida, och ett nöje var det verkligen. Florian och Malou hade aldrig varit ombord på en båt, men nu tog de tillfället i akt och lärde sig i en handvändning halvslag och pålstek och uppkransning av linor. De gjorde fast och vevade och snärtade loss tampar och låg i, och i väntestunderna studerade vi kartor och samtalade med stort allvar om avstånd och havssjö och skolundervisning och slussarbete. Dessa pojkar från lilla Châtillon någon mil bort visste verkligen att skicka sig. Naturligtvis var det inte tal om att mönstra av, de följde med till dagens sista sluss. Jag letade fram två av de blå matroströjorna med namnet "Vanadis" i vitt tryck, storlek small. De räckte dem ändå nästan till knäna.

Sedan tog vi farväl under fullvuxna handskakningar och ömsesidiga löften om julkort (och det blev också av), och pojkarna började sin barfotavandring tillbaka.

Nu var vi uppe på höjdpunkten och skulle över åsen, genom en smal kanal med ett par tunnlar, så smal att den är enkelriktad. Vi lade oss i Port Brulé vid "Vivante" och väntade, och från den vinlövsklädda vaktbostaden kom pensionerade slussvakten Jean-Jaques med spanieln Macaron över på öl respektive vatten.

Själva luften var grön.

Landskapet under oss började skymma. Framför oss låg en ogenomtränglig lövskog. I bladverket tändes klarsignalen.

Det var trångt mellan bergväggarna, och grönt. Ljusa ormbunkar klängde i skrevorna, murgrönan täckte alla ytor och högt där uppe möttes trädkronorna där ljuset silades ner. Vattnet var grönt, själva luften var grön. Ingen sa något, vi andades knappt. Plötsligt svävade ett valv ovanför oss – en bro, en akvedukt? Den såg ut att vara på väg någonstans, ut ur lummigheten på ena sidan och in bland trädstammarna på den andra, men vart? Hur kunde det alls finnas ett landskap utanför vår gröna tunnel?

Och så öppnades allt mot stora vidder, en väldig solnedgångshimmel i guld och violett, en låg skogshorisont långt borta och framför oss vatten, vatten. Den stora Étang de Vaux. Vi kände oss som på världens tak.

Utmed stenkajen låg småbåtar och bopråmar, bekanta och obekanta, som om de alltid legat där i kvällssolen. Engelsmännen på pråmen "De goude Verwachting" som vi mött av och till lyfte ett glas och ropade:

– *Life is hell, isn't it!*

Från det prydliga gästrummet hos Muriel och Bruno blickar man ut mot trädgård, grönska och kanal.

Den polske rörmokaren – det är ju jag!

Nästa morgon avreste Ann-Margret och Helen i en taxi som förde dem till tåget i Nevers. Vi tog "Vanadis" in till slipen på servicestället intill, "Aqua Fluvial", och försökte baxa upp hennes för ovanför vattenytan. Bogpropellern hade nämligen lagt av, och utan den var slussandet rätt äventyrligt. Skepparn blev lätt stingslig, eller högkoncentrerad, som han själv uttryckte det.

"Vanadis" läge var nu så labilt att vi inte ville bo och äta ombord, och vi hade tur: här i Baye fanns rum med mat, och vi välkomnades till bådadera av värdfolket Muriel och Bruno. Middagen skulle snart vara färdig.

Vi åt tillsammans. Nästan allt kom från trädgården: ägg, grönsaker, kompotter. Sedan visade Muriel och Bruno stolta upp huset. När de köpte det för en del år sedan var det ett stenröse med ett ruttet utedass och svinstia. Av denna ruin hade de skapat ett trivsamt och smakfullt hem med en stor öppen spis och kraftiga bjälkar i taket. Den ena var original, den andra fejk och dolde elegant hela ledningsdragningen. Bruno hade uträttat allt med egna händer.

– Och debatten i år som handlar om att fransmän inte arbetar, sa vi, det heter ju att det är den polske rörmokaren som gör jobben.

– Men den polske rörmokaren, *c'est moi!* utropade Bruno. Jag är utbildad till rörmokare! Min far och mor var polacker. Polska är min familjs språk.

Bruno växte upp i Lilles koldistrikt dit hans föräldrar utvandrat från Polens gruvor. I Frankrike fortsatte de med samma sak som hemma, men Bruno hade gjort en enda arbetsdag i kolgruvan. När han kom upp hade han bestämt sig. Alla faderns arbetskamrater hade dött eller skulle dö i förtid med förstörda lungor. Det skulle inte få hända honom.

Muriel, lite yngre än sin man, kom från stadsdelen la Villette i Paris. Visst kunde det vara rörigt på 70–80-talet i detta blandade område, sa hon, men det var fredligt. På 90-talet kom en ny invandringsvåg, och då blev stämningen hätsk. Hos många unga män mötte man en ny sorts aggressivitet. Hade man en bil, om aldrig så oansenlig, blev man stämplad som rik, och bilen kunde när som helst vara demolerad eller bränd.

De bestämde sig för att börja ett annat liv, här ute på rena bondvischan.

Var det inte svårt att komma in i gemenskapen i en sådan här liten by?

– Inte alls, sa Muriel, det kom flera inflyttare, och utan oss nykomlingar skulle det inte finnas något här.

Att få gäster under sommaren kan ju inte vara så svårt, när folk som trängt ihop sig i hyrbåtar har tröttnat på att sova på matbordet varje natt och när cyklister och metare och jolleseglare dras till dammarnas stora friluftsområde. Men vad gör man under vinterhalvåret?

– Ni skulle se hur det är här när jaktlagen från Tyskland kommer, sa Bruno. Alla gevären ligger upplagda i rad på matbordet, jag står i baren, jägarna sjunger och tjoar. Folk betalar två hundra euro om dygnet för att få häcka på någons markplätt och vara bakfulla och frysa och vänta på ett vildsvin eller rådjur, och det anses ändå billigt, somliga betalar upp till sex hundra!

Vi sov i ett av de prydliga gästrummen och vaknade av dunkanden i väggarna och musettemusik från radion. Det trallades och visslades till. Bruno var uppe och byggde om det gamla vagnslidret till bostadsrum.

– Han sjunger alltid när han arbetar, sa Muriel lyckligt och dukade fram en överdådig frukost med marmelader på gröna tomater, druvor och körsbär. Här bytte man frukter grannarna emellan, det var praktiskt och stärkte samhörigheten.

Vi återvände till "Vanadis" med en liten burk hemgjord kvittengelé.

"We crashed!"

"Mellan varje sluss finns en bief, glöm inte det" var Ann-Margrets avskedsord till oss.

Le bief är det fria vattnet mellan två slussar, och hennes sentens var avsedd att lända oss till tröst när slussandet började bli besvärligt utan bogpropeller. Vi hade fått låta "Vanadis" glida ner igen utan att ha lyckats få propellern över vattenytan, och nu hade vi inte bara de återstående trettiofem slussarna av kanalens etthundratio framför oss utan kanske också Canal du Centre och Saône innan vi till hösten skulle vara uppe på land i Saint-Jean-de-Losne. Och vårt goda skepp väger i alla fall tolv ton, minst.

Men vi gick igenom en rad vackert beblomstrade slussar utan missöden. Vi visste att det skulle finnas ett par låga broar – men det var faktiskt bara en enda som kunde hindra vår färd, som en VNF-are så uppmuntrande hade påpekat när vi undrat om vi skulle våga anträda kanalen. Och då kunde man möjligtvis förhandla med slussvakterna om att sänka vattnet i biefen, om man inte hade för djup köl förstås.

När vi kom till den låga bron såg det hopplöst ut. Vi monterade ner allt som gick att ta ner, även vindrutorna, och gled så långsamt det gick in under valvet. Det blåste en hård och besvärande vind akterifrån. Med omkring fem centimeter till godo på sidorna borde vi ändå klara det, men så fick ett vindkast "Vanadis" att ställa sig på sniskan. Det var nu vi skulle ha behövt bogpropellern.

"Porten kallas trång och vägen heter smal."
Och den låga stensättningen är en fasa.

Under brons ena fäste stack det också ut en liten otäck skrovlig stenkaj, för åsnor och dragare. Vi hade garderat med fendrar ända ner till vattenytan, men vi måste ta det försiktigt så att de inte rullades undan. Med händerna mot brovalvets tak lyckades vi trots allt vrida "Vanadis" rätt och var redan till hälften ute när olyckan till slussvakt uppmärksammade vårt predikament och kom rusande till undsättning.

Innan vi hunnit skrika "Låt bli!" hade han beskäftigt tagit tag i linan till en fender, ryckt upp den och dragit "Vanadis" igenom. Skrapet från stenarna mot "Vanadis" nylackerade skrov skar igenom vind och motorljud.

Jag såg att topplocket höll på att flyga av Skepparn och vädjade till honom att lägga band på sig. Att fara ut mot slussvakten var ingen idé. Skadan kunde inte göras ogjord och dessutom hade mannen makten över vattnet i slussen framför oss. Men vi var inte glada när vi strax därefter lade till i gästhamnen i Panneçot. Vi förstod också att "Vivante" måste varnas, och Skepparn kastade sig på cykeln och ilade tillbaka men kom, ack, ett ögonblick, blott ett ögonblick för sent!

– *We crashed,* sa Jerry tonlöst. Det var en överflödig kommentar.

"Vivantes" vackra styrhytt och aktersalong med slipade rutor låg i en hög av trä- och glassplitter, och över alltihopa slokade den gulrandiga markisen. Flaggstången i fören, som fungerat som höjdvarnare, var knäckt. När den tagit i och Jerry slagit full back hade det kommit en vindstöt mot häcken, och en pråm utan styrfart glider hjälplös som ett stekfat på vattnet.

Jerry och Barbara var lamslagna. Med bistånd av engelsmännen från "De goude Verwachting" förtöjde vi "Vivante" och Skepparn inledde en röjningsaktion. Själv gav jag mig ut för att ta reda på var i regionen det kunde finnas ett glasmästeri och fick veta att det fanns ett just här i Panneçot. I denna gudsförgätna by! En försynens skickelse eller ett orsakssamband? Jag

Brödpuddingen granskas efter katastrofen. Inget glassplitter.

fick mina misstankar när jag cyklade runt och frågade ortsborna var *l'atélier du vitrier* låg.

– Jaså, det var bron i Anizy! Den är ökänd. Vattnet var förstås för högt i biefen. Tur att vi har en glasmästare här!

Så småningom hittade jag glasmannen som kom ner och inspekterade förödelsen. Det visade sig att trävirket fått sina skråmor men kunde fogas samman. Glas kunde skaffas och sättas i redan nästa dag. Utan slipade kanter visserligen, men det var ändå över förväntan.

Barbara hade bjudit oss på middag ombord. Nu protesterade vi – hon hade sannerligen annat att tänka på.

– Men jag har redan gjort den, sa hon med ynklig röst och balanserade upp en jättelik ångande gryta från pråmens inre. Vi borstade av dynorna i den tak- och vägglösa aktersalongen och åt härlig purjolökssoppa och amerikansk brödpudding som var mycket god och utan glassplitter. Rätt mycket vin gick det åt också.

Har ni det så här?

– Har ni det så här hela tiden? undrade en lektör som under arbetets gång fått ta del av några avsnitt av denna bok

Yttrandet kändes bekant. Så småningom kom associationen. ”Herregud, har vi verkligen haft det så trevligt!” utbrister Mona Schildt när maken Göran Schildt läser högt ur dagboken för ”Önskeresan”, deras färd med ketchen ”Daphne” från Skandinavien till Medelhavet genom Frankrike år 1948.

Naturligtvis har vi det inte ”så här” hela tiden. Förvisso har vi varit med om allt vi beskriver, inget är påhittat. Men allt berättande är i grunden osannfärdigt. Allt hade kunnat skildras på ett annat sätt, från ett annat håll. Och liksom minnena från ens förflutna liv framträder som belysta bilder i en stor väv som mestadels ligger i dunkel så är episoderna från kanaltillvaron framsorterade från en oupphörlig färd på gröna vatten kantade av busksnår eller oändliga platanalléer eller betesmarker, från sluss till sluss med öppning, förtöjning, stängning, påsläpp eller utsläpp, öppning och nytt grönt vatten om fören.

Det finns dagar när man är inregnad och brödet är slut och dragvägen igenväxt med brännässlor och bageriet nedlagt när man äntligen tagit sig fram till den lilla grå byn. Det finns dygn när man ligger vid en trist kaj i en trist stad och väntar på en reservdel som ska komma med posten men som inte kommer, alltmedan man släpar hem mat från någon gigantisk köplada flera kilometer bort på andra sidan av en härva av motorleder och sedan ägnar resten av tiden åt att underhålla båten och tvätta fendrar, dagar då en diskussion om spindlars rätt att vistas ombord är den intellektuella prestationen.

– Se dem som biomassa, inte som enskilda individer, säger Skepparn och sjasar dem över relingen.

– Biomassa kan du vara själv, säger jag.

Det finns stunder när man undrar vad det är man håller på med – denna oändligt långsamma men ständiga förflyttning. Man är en gäst och främling, blott en afton stannar man, och även om man försöker göra sig underrättad om platsen kommer man inte nära. Aldrig träder man på jord som känner igen en, jord som man just därför kommit att älska.

Det finns såriga gryningar när man vaknar med Heidenstams dikt om Gunnar på Lidarände på väg i landsflykt, raderna där brodern Kolskägg talar:

> Av människor det mer än nog skall finnas
> vart skeppet styrs av ödets tärningskast.
> Det är ej dem, som du var natt skall minnas,
> det är den mark, där du har vuxit fast,
> det är den vik där du som gosse badat,
> och myrarna, på vilkas falska dy
> du het med spjut i solnedgången vadat,
> och timmerväggens lukt och flöjelns gny
> – – –
> Det är den hund, som du gav värn och vård
> och räckte hälften av din svarta kaka.
> Och ingen jordens kungadryck skall smaka
> som brunnens vatten på din faders gård.

Vad gör jag här? Hur kunde jag släppa det ärvda sommarstället vid Sörmlandskusten? Inte för att jag vandrat het med spjut, men de mulbetade saltängarna i kvällssolen med tofsvipa och horsgök ropar i mig så det skär, och även om brunnens vatten mest smakat järnfilspån var det dock vattnet på min faders gård.

Ack, tvenne själar bo i detta bröst. Vilken av dem är starkast, den bofasta, bunden till den torva jag tror mig förtrogen med, eller den vandrande, nomadiska?

Fackelblomster med vita fjärilar på en kanalbank försätter mig tillbaka till klippskrevorna vid den vik där jag badat alla somrar fram till nu. Doften från en ensam valeriana bär bud om högsommaren som går in över Östersjöns stränder. Ingen här nere skulle förstå den saknad som väcks.

Jag ringer till min syster som övertagit min del av stället. Jag vill bara höra sådant jag tål att höra.

– Vi har algblomning, säger hon. Grannen tjafsar om väghållningen och huset är så ruckligt att det borde göras om från grunden. Och förresten skulle ni bara bli rastlösa av att hållas här och uggla.

Så vi färdas vidare, ständigt vidare, lockade av vad som kan finnas bortom nästa krök. Kanske möts vi där av en himmelssträvande katedral, kanske av en förfallen kvarnbyggnad bebodd av välsinnade getter. Intryck ges hela tiden. Det gäller bara att fånga dem, avgränsa dem, ge dem en form, klä dem i ord. Har vi det "så här"?

Javisst, så här och på en massa andra sätt.

PATISSERIE
charolais
du centre
DISTRIBUTEUR AGRÉÉ
Charolais
label Rouge
PRESSE
BANETTE
CHARCUTERIE
TRALE
Boulangerie Patisserie
Pharmacie
ICI TRAVAUX
PHOTO

Canal latéral à la Loire, Canal du Centre

Canal latéral à la Loire börjar i Briare och slutar i Digoin, där den går i en akvedukt över floden Loire som den följt långa sträckor och som man ser där den buktar sig i en dalgång nedanför kanalbanken. Vår färd började i Nevers och gick genom ett fördrömt jordbrukslandskap med Morvans höjder i bakgrunden.

Vid Digoin vidtar *Canal du Centre*, som förtjänar ett mer attraktivt namn. Till en början går den genom några mindre industriorter där det mesta är nedlagt, för att fortsätta ner mot Bourgognes vinsluttningar med slott och småstäder, ett område man inte bör hasta igenom om man har den minsta känsla för njutning. Sedan leds man ut på den vida Saône.

Än lever kvartersbutikerna. Lördag i Decize.

Okänd tingest i Nevers

Nevers tronar på en hög bank ovanför den sköna men lynniga Loire. Nu i augusti frusade floden behagligt över bottenstenarna och bildade små gnistrande fall här och där, men hon kan stiga, och vallarna runt staden har sina skäl. Den högsta byggnaden är, som sig bör i en kultiverad stad, katedralen.

”Vanadis” roder hade börjat kärva och krävde smörjning. Till det behöver man en fettspruta.

Detta instrument som finns att köpa på varje bensinstation i Sverige visade sig här vara ett nästan okänt begrepp. Vi började vid en mack.

Une pompe à graisse? Beklagar, men försök i järnhandeln!

Vi uppsökte järnhandeln i en annan del av staden. Ack nej, men prova i verkstan intill!

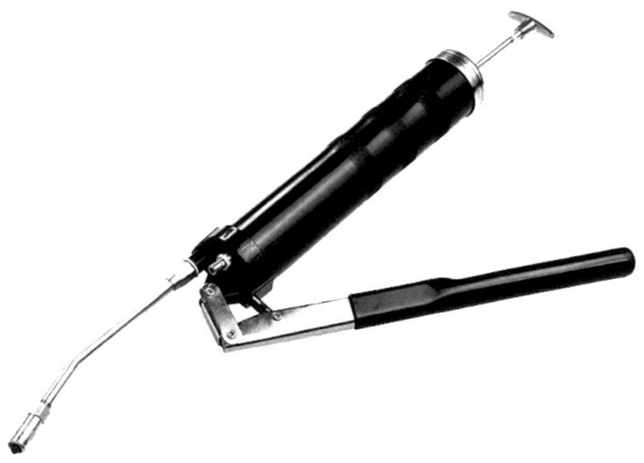

I verkstaden var det tomt, både på folk och på fettsprutor, men i halvdunklet på kontoret utspelades just en fransk version av ”Macken”. Innehavaren talade i telefon med någon som uppenbarligen ville ha sin bil. Vi lyssnade till tretton ”Nästa vecka” i olika tonlägen åtföljt av himlanden med ögonen och axelryckningar och ”Tror ni inte vi arbetar!” och ”Det är ju semester” och ”Ab-so-lut omöjligt!”. Vi gled ut under det fjortonde *La semaine prochaine!* – det skulle säkert bli fler. Sedan drog vi genom den ena butiken efter den andra, varje gång med en rekommendation till nästa. Av badrumskranar och gasolgrillar och konstgjorda brasor måste behovet vara omättligt men av fettsprutor obefintligt. Inte ens den stora lagerbutiken med biltillbehör ville kännas vid denna artikel, vilket förklarar ett och annat när det gäller motorunderhåll.

Tillbaka i hamnen beklagade vi oss för den engelske ägaren av bopråmen ”Torsk”. *A grease pump?* Naturligtvis, låna min, jag har flera.

Bristen på fettsprutor ska dock inte fördunkla intrycket av Nevers. Gatorna är branta, husen vackra om än nedgångna, med burspråk och gotiska detaljer och med slitna gas- och elledningar kors och tvärs på ytterväggarna.

Katedralen Saint-Cyr-Sainte-Julitte är utvändigt prydd med de mest fantastiska *gargouilles*, vattenkastare: harpyor, bockar, hundar, grisar. Intill ligger hertigpalatset från medeltid och renässans och från terrassen framför har man en betagande utsikt över den skimrande Loire.

Om kvällen skiftade staden gestalt och blev mörk och mystisk med stängda fönsterluckor och tomma gränder. Framför hertigpalatset lekte ett ensamt ungt par med en boll, deras skuggor flög som stora andeväsen över fasaden. Bortom terrassens balustrad stod fullmånen och göt sitt silver i flodens svarta virvlande vatten.

Åsnor och åsninnor

När man från Belgien går in i Frankrike byter man förstås gästflagg, men man tar också ner den speciella lilla röda fyrkantiga duk med en vit fyrkant i mitten som obevekligen krävs av de belgiska myndigheterna om man ska befara landets vattenvägar, såvida man inte släpas fram på dessa av en åsna.

Flaggan visar alltså att man inte är åsnedragen utan går för egen maskin och därför utgör en trafikfara.

Hur gärna färdades man dock inte i sällskap med åsnor, dessa tåliga och vänliga djur. Kanalmuseerna, som finns lite här och där, visar bilder på pråmar med små hytter på däck ur vilka det sticker fram huvuden på åsnor som för tillfället har ledigt.

Denna flagg är obligatorisk i Belgien såframt båten inte är dragen av en häst eller åsna.

I England, berättade frun på den engelska pråmen "Torsk", kan man erbjuda sig att ta hand om åsnor som det är synd om, årbräckta varelser som trippat med folk på ryggen på badorternas stränder men som ingen vill ha längre. Hon funderade på en pråmåsna sedan den gamla skeppshunden befordrats till härligheten.

Vi har inte ens skeppshund och saknar ofta en sådan, men ibland väcks hos oss en häftig önskan att medföra en åsna på "Vanadis".

Den skulle förstås heta Modestine, efter Robert Louis Stevensons intagande packdjur som man möter i hans skildring "Resa med en åsna i Cevennerna". Långt före författaren själv blir man fäst vid den egensinniga lilla medvandrerskan, och ens ögon tåras när de till sist skils åt och han säljer henne vidare.

Dessbättre håller folk på landet gärna åsnor, till ingen nytta vad vi kan se, men oss till glädje. Vi tar varje tillfälle som ges att rafsa lite i en dammig hårrem och känna små puffar av en sammetsmule.

En dag hade vi företagit oss en längre utflykt på cykel, vållad av att vi glömt en nippel på en vattenkran i en by vi lämnat bakom oss. Utan koppling till vattenslangen står man sig slätt, och nipplar hittar man inte överallt. Rustade med en lätt proviant bestående av vattenflaskor och äpplen gav vi oss av, men äpplena skulle inte bli långvariga. En åsnefamilj bakom ett ståltrådsstängsel, pappa, mamma, storasyster och lillasyster, vände sina långa öron och milda ögon mot oss, och strax var vi redo att avstå våra äpplen, som benosades och åts upp.

Förr i världen var dragåsnan en medlem av besättningen.

Dessa oskyldiga frukter visade sig ha en oväntad verkan. Åsnehingsten blev tvärpilsk och gav sig på familjens moder, som verkade säga att hon hade huvudvärk och inte var upplagd. Men han var det, och han gav sig inte. Så när hon värjde sig och sparkade bakut överföll han i stället familjens unga flicka. Åsnemön försvarade tappert sin dygd, och en vild jakt började runt inhägnaden. Det var mycket obehagligt och vi kunde inget göra. Men när han lyckats få ett stadigt bett i manen och gjorde sig redo att bestiga henne kastade hon sig med förtvivlans mod mot elstängslet, trängde sig mellan trådarna, rullade runt, kom på fötter och skenade i väg över ett oändligt betfält. Hon stannade inte förrän hon hejdades av en kyrkogårdsmur i fjärran.

"Djur är män", sa vi, som just har fått rapporter om feministdebatten hemmavid. Men det minskade ändå inte vår svaghet för åsnor. För övrigt var alltsammans kanske vårt fel som tillhandahållit ett oanat afrodisiakum.

En morgon strax intill slussen i Abron på Canal latéral à la Loire väcktes vi av en bastant och raggig hund som ville ombord. Han fick en frukostskorpa och blev nöjd. Vi gjorde sällskap till slussen för att begära öppning, och där hälsades vi av en liten vit kisse. Vi sa till den sympatiske slussvakten att han verkade tycka om djur.

– Ni med? Då ska ni se Socquette.

Socquette var ett två månaders åsneföl, ett enda litet grått ludd med rund mage och svarta öron och silkesnos och de pyttigaste hovar man kan se, små ebenholtsbitar. Hennes stolta moder var också en förtjusande bekantskap.

Nu uppenbarade sig slussvaktens hustru med dottern Liza, sju månader, oavbrutet skrattande med två risgryn i underkäken. Storebror Tristan, tre år, var redan i småbarnsskolan. Småpratet fortsatte, och snart satt vi med en kopp kaffe i det trevliga slussvaktarhuset, ett av de få permanent bebodda. Det unga paret trivdes bra fastän de egentligen inte var från trakten utan från Vichy, där hennes far hade en gård med köttdjur.

– Så vi har alltid bra kött, det är bara en halvmil till slaktaren och djuren hinner inte bli särskilt stressade. Det är aldrig långt till ett slakteri i den här delen av landet.

Här satt vi från Sverige som tycker oss ha så mycket att lära EU-länderna om djurhållning. I Sverige fraktas djur i trånga och plågsamma transporter mil efter mil till centralslakterier.

– Kan ni tänka er, sa slussvakten, Socquette kommer på omslaget till en tysk båttidning.

Det kunde vi tänka oss. Det var svårt att slita sig från denna lilla ljuvlighet som snusade på oss med den minsta av mular allt medan dess moder betraktade oss med milda blickar. Deras ägare påminde om den rara gycklarfamiljen i ”Det sjunde inseglet”. Vi lämnade dem, varma om hjärtat.

Sammetsmular, ebenholtshovar och ett milt sinnelag.

Det tysta Frankrike

Efter Nevers var det dags att vända stäven mot hemmahamnen St-Jean-de-Losne. Dit skulle vi ta oss via Canal latéral à la Loire, Canal du Centre och sedan norrut på Saône.

Även Canal latéral à la Loire går igenom fransk landsbygd, oändligt tilltalande för ögat, bara betesmarker och kullar och själva Loire slingrande i sin fåra nedanför oss. September hade infallit med värmebölja. Vi lade till för lunch vid byn Coulanges och begrundade en tavla med uppgifter om vad byn ville erbjuda behövande båtfarare: rörmokare, tryckeri, likkistfabrik, allt med adress och telefonnummer.

Vi slog upp en flaska cider – för allt annat var det för varmt – och lyssnade till ett klämkäckt radioprogram, förmodligen inspelat i våras, som talade om hur skönt det var nu med höstens krispiga luft och sprakande färger och fallande kastanjer. Vi stängde av. Här var det röda tak mot milt sommarblå himmel och den renaste grönska. Den lilla bykyrkan slog några skramliga timslag. Sedan absolut stillhet. Cidern räckte för att knäcka oss. Vi somnade på däck i värmen.

I nästa sluss fick vi vänta. En bruksbåt var på väg, en riktig pråm! Slussvakten var nästan ivrig. Och hade man sett, här på denna sömniga kanal kom péniche n ”Hélène” med några krokiga trädstammar som last.

De flesta slussvaktarhusen här är faktiskt bebodda och välskötta.

– För ett par år sedan var vi rädda att kanalen skulle läggas ner, sa slussvakten, men både stat och kommun anser att den är bra för regionen. Än tänker vi inte förtvivla. Fast det är mycket prat och lite pengar.

Till kvällen hamnade vi intill en liten lantegendom. Uppenbarligen fanns där en levnadsglad hund som rände omkring, för i stillheten utbröt något som närmast liknade Per Olssons bonnagård med mö mö här och gnägg gnägg där och mä mä och bä bä och kackel och kuckeliku och skrammel från kullvälta plåtkärl och en arg röst som gång på gång ropade *Viens ici!*, kom hit!

Men inte bara den lantliga friden (som så småningom återvände när rackan tycktes infångad) övergår allt förstånd utan också den lantliga ekonomin. Var fanns alla de där bönderna som åtnjuter det omdiskuterade jordbruksstödet och som har makt att låta landet gå i stå när de blir misslynta? Och var fanns traktorerna, med vilka de blockerar vägarna fast det vore bättre att de använde dem i jordbruket, som någon har sagt? Ibland fick man känslan att de vita hjordarna av charolaisdjur betade som en gång i lustgården, utan mänsklig inblandning.

Vattendelaren

Efter en ståtlig akvedukt som leder över Loire och in till Digoin tar Canal du Centre vid. Digoin är känd för sin porslinstillverkning, *poterie,* men av tillverkningen av finporslin lyckades vi inget se. Pottor däremot, eller snarare toalettstolar fanns desto fler att skåda i ett väldigt lager utmed kanalen. Slussarna bär beteckningen Océan, och det är väl inte det första man tänker på här i det innersta av landet med Morvans skogiga massiv på håll. Men det påminner en om att man ännu färdas i Atlantbäckenet där Loire hundra mil lång banar sig västerut ut till kusten och kastar sig i havet vid Saint-Nazaire.

Vid Océan 1 hade vi tagit oss upp till kanalens höjdpunkt, 301 meter över havet. Vi gled fram till nästa sluss, Méditerranée 1. Här börjar Medelhavssidan. Man sänker sig ner mot Saône som rinner ut i Rhône som till slut mynnar i azurböljorna.

Vattendelaren var här, denna oansenliga höjd i glesbygden.

Den första slussvaktarstugan hyste ett informationskontor och några rum med kanalattiraljer från förr. Om ett par dagar skulle här uppföras ett litet spektakel om slussvakter och tvätterskor, och lyckliga amatörskådespelare var i full färd med att släpa in gamla kärror och bykkar och träskor. Det skulle bli hur kul som helst, *très rigolo,* sade den glada informationsflickan. Men om vi nu inte kunde vänta så länge borde vi i alla fall besöka den gamla museipråmen som visade hur kanalfolket levde förr. Den skulle vara bemannad just i morgon.

Här i Écuisses har man tillverkat glaserat tegel, och vi fortsatte ett par slussar ner utmed arbetarbostäder-

Frankrike är ett land för artister på alla nivåer. Slusshuset på höjden mellan Loire och Saône.

na med tak och dekorer i rött, grönt och svart, förbi kooperativet med kastanjeblad i majolika på väggen och fram till själva den gamla fabriken. Allt här var utsmyckat med färger och ornament, och invånarna bör nog ha varit stolta över att varenda byggnad ansetts värd något extra. Så länge det nu varade.

Morgondagen inföll med ett strilande regn som fick tegeltaken att blänka. I väntan på att museipråmen skulle öppna strosade vi runt i byn. Beklämning präglar nedlagda industriorter. Förhoppningarna är släckta, rösterna har tystnat, tågen stannar inte vid stationen.

Tystnat hade också ringklockan till museipråmen. Skylten bedyrade att denna dag och denna tid hölls den sista visningen för säsongen, men vakten hade uppenbarligen funnit för gott att låta detta höstens första regn inleda vintervilan. Även informationsstugan var tillbommad. Vi var inte särskilt överraskade. *Nous sommes en France,* det räckte som förklaring.

Det glaserade teglet var en gång orten Écuisses stolthet. Nu är fabriken nedlagd.

Tillbommat och övergivet. Allt är förbi.

En landsortskyrka

Vad allt har inte detta land blivit utsatt för och än mer utsatt sig självt för. Krig, uppror, religionsförföljelser, revolutioner. Överallt ser man vittnesbörd om uppgång och fall, om makt och vanmakt. På den sovande landsbygden möter man gång efter annan slott i vanhävd, somliga obebodda, andra med en flygel eller en våning där en spetsgardin för ett fönster avslöjar en mänsklig invånare medan svartkråkor och fladdermöss har lagt beslag på murkrön och torn.

Man ser kloster som skövlats av 1700-talets revolutionärer för att sedan omvandlas till fabriker, och i stad efter stad står katedralerna med helgonprydda portaler där alla huvuden är avslagna. För fromma människor måste det ha varit svårt att se de heliga tingen förnekas och krossas, hur förhatlig överheten än må ha tett sig. Bakom en halmlada stötte vi på en minimal 1100-talskyrka omgiven av nässlor och svinmålla. Den vandaliserades på de styrandes order och användes sedan som fodermagasin. Nu hade någon ändå försökt återge den lite av dess värdighet. På det vittrande altaret stod ett litet valhänt tilltäljt krucifix. Svalor flög ut och in i den tysta kvällningen.

I Saint-Bérain vid Canal du Centre uppsökte vi byns vackra romanska kapell, kalt, mörkt och fuktigt inuti. Dess enda prydnad var en medfaren gipskopia av Michelangelos "Pietà". På den sörjande Jesu moder saknades huvudet. Ett verk av en bildstormare, eller var det bara tidens tand som bitit till? Någon påhittig person hade emellertid kommit på råd: huvudlösheten doldes av en jättebukett med plastblommor.

Åt detta kunde vi le, men på kyrkogården snördes våra hjärtan samman vid graven över bröderna Philippe, arkebuserade av tyskarna 1944. Demarkationslinjen gick inte långt härifrån.

De unga bröderna Philippe, arkebuserade 1944.

Varenda by i Frankrike har ett monument med namnen på sina fallna söner, så ofattbart många och ofta så hjärtskärande unga. Vi har läst åtskilliga gripande minnesord över dem som fallit och över dem som förts bort. Men efter Pierre tjugotvå år och Michel arton står inga ord, och inga ord behövs. De ser en rakt i ögonen, levande genom åren som gått. Blicken är öppen och tillitsfull. Kanske var de rädda men säkert ännu mer stolta över att få vara med de äldre i motståndsrörelsen, *La Résistance.*

Frihetens instrument

Det heter att en båt är frihetens instrument. Hur mycket frihet man har på en yta från för till akter, dag ut och dag in, kan väl diskuteras. Det är nu inte den sortens frihet seglaren avser när båten lämnar hamn och kursen sätts mot synranden. Men denna frihet å andra sidan, att styra vart man vill, den har man inte på en kanal som obevekligt leder dit kanalen vill och där slussar och slussvakter avgör om man kan fortsätta eller inte.

Frihetens instrument är i själva verket cykeln. Man har den ombord utan större besvär, man tar sig med den miltals från kanalen till platser man annars inte skulle komma till, man befar trevliga vägar och stigar som inte är avsedda för bilar, man stannar var man vill och utbyter tankar med folk man möter, man kan ta ett glas till middagen på restaurang och man kan transportera matvaror från affärer som inte ligger där båten ligger. I städerna slipper man grubbla över buss- och spårvagnslinjer och man har inga problem med parkering.

Och framför allt kan man rulla fram på dragvägen utmed kanalen för att förbereda nästa sluss eller öppna en bro eller bara för att känna vinden mot ansiktet en het dag, stanna och plocka smultron, studera en växt, prata med en häst eller en metarehund – cykla för cyklandets skull. Drar man på en smula och lägger sig före båten kan man på en enslig kanal finna sig mitt i en natur utan motorljud, med bara fågelsång och insektssurr. När den vita fören sedan dyker upp i kröken trampar man vidare.

Utmed många vattenleder underhålls alltså de forna dragvägarna där dragdjur och människor släpade fram de motorlösa pråmarna. På vissa sträckor har de uppgraderats till asfalterade cykelvägar, men de flesta består av två sandiga spår med en grässträng i mitten, och de enda bilar man riskerar att möta är VNF:s på väg till eller från en sluss.

Många kanaler har dragvägar som är cyklistens fröjd.

Vinslottet i Santenay med bourgognskt mönstrat tak. Här möter man de stora vinerna

Bland de stora bourgognerna

Om man vill färdas genom Bourgognes vinodlingar ska man inte välja Canal de Bourgogne, namnet till trots. Denna kanal går genom betesmarker och skog och är en fröjd för ögat, men vinlös. När man äntligen nalkas Côte d'Or och druvorna befinner man sig på den intryckslösa jordbruksslätten söder om Dijon.

Vingårdar, vinbyar och vinslott finner man utmed Canal du Centre.

Vi kom norrifrån och slussade ner genom floden Dheunes dalgång. När man nalkas Santenay upphör de pastorala sluttningarna och i stället vidtar ett landskap som ser ut som om någon gått med en kratta genom grönskan: rader av vinstockar. Snart dök det upp skyltar med erbjudanden om provsmakning och försäljning. Vi kände att vinbergen väntade oss, förtöjde och cyklade i den ljumma septemberkvällen upp på småvägar genom odlingarna där daggiga blå klasar lyste i lövverket. Pinot noir. Lotterna har namn som Morgonstjärnan och Middagsbacken och Aftonsol, beroende på åt vilket håll de vetter, och alla ger de olika karaktär åt druvorna.

Vi stretade uppåt tills vi nådde kritklippor och barrskog och björnbärssnår. Björnbären var mogna och saftiga, en doft av mynta och backtimjan steg från de torra renarna, den låga solen göt guld över hela härligheten och sköt blixtar i det bourgognska mönstrade taket av glaserat tegel på slottet från Filip den djärves tid nere i dalen.

Sedan rullade vi neråt, hit och dit, glatt morsade på av vingårdsmän på väg hem från arbetet i små skramlande traktorer, genom stilla beblomstrade byar med en vinkällare i varje hörn. I det välmående Cheilly-les Marenges med slingrande gator och hus i honungsgul kalksten lockade både caver och vinlövskransade matställen. Vem kan stå emot?

Rully, Mercurey, Bouzeron – namn som lyser emot en i beskrivningarna av de stora bourgognerna finns faktiskt i geografin. Naturligtvis tror man inte annat, men det är ändå något med att möta verkligheten bakom namnet. Vi hade tidigare haft lyckan att råka på några flaskor förnämlig vit Rully, och nu anslog vi nästa dag åt att makligt i solskenet cykla upp till slottet Rully och ner till byn, där vinpatronerna lever bakom praktfulla smidesgrindar som inhägnar gårdsplaner med väldiga ekfat. Här fanns rika tillfällen till *dégustation* och inköp, men våra möjligheter begränsades av cykelväskorna, förmodligen en god försynens ordning.

Under återstoden av kanalfärden ner mot Saône hade vi slottet med sina sagoaktiga runda torn som följeslagare i häcken. Det dök upp i olika vinklar allteftersom kanalen vindlade, för att bli allt mindre och till slut försvinna för gott.

Ut på Saône!

September överöste oss inte bara med milt solsken utan också med regn så hällande att det tog emot att driva ut slussvakterna i det. Det mesta av vevandet stod jag alltså för själv medan de hukade i hytten, och vid dagens slut kunde jag pytsa ut några liter ur gummistövlarna. Vattnet steg över kanalens bräddar och ibland hade vi känslan av att "Vanadis" skulle glida över kajkanter och slussportar.

När vi några dagar senare försiktigt stack ut nosen under den sista slussens port som är konstruerad som en giljotinbila mötte vi Saône, bred och strömmande med vita gäss. Regnet hade fördrivits och strändernas popplar och silverpilar vajade och slet i blåsten.

Till höger glänste kyrktorn och broar i staden Chalon, till vänster sågs master – en gästhamn? Vi styrde dit men hänvisades av en hamnvakt till staden. Här låg privata segelbåtar, och riktiga sådana, inte bara jollar. Men var seglade man? undrade vi. Åjo, från broarna till nästa sluss var det sex sju kilometer, det var inte fy skam!

Vi tänkte på Mälaren som stockholmska båtägare inte gitter ligga i för att den inte hyser fritt vatten. För seglarna på Saône skulle Björkfjärden vara ett hav.

La Saône är en vacker men oberäknelig dam. Hon kan fatta humör och bli strid och bångstyrig men lugna sig lika fort. Kajerna utmed Chalon är höga och flytbryggorna i gästhamnen glider på stolpar med ett spelrum på upp till sju meter. Regnandet hade satt fart på strömmen, och vi tog oss med viss förskräckelse in till en bryggplats medan grästuvor, plankor, stubbar, en stock med en äventyrslysten vattensköldpadda och till sist ett helt träd med uppslitna rötter virvlade förbi pirnocken. En kollision där rodret får en smäll är det sista man önskar sig i en virvlande flod.

Chalon-sur-Saône är en trevlig gammal handelsstad. Är man intresserad av fotografihistoria kan man besöka museet över mannen med det oförlikneliga

Chalon-sur-Saône. Aftonglans över hamn och stad.

namnet Nicéphore Niépce, född i staden 1765 och den som tog den första fotografiska bilden, 1826 – Daguerre skulle sedan samarbeta med honom. Annars kan man nöja sig med att äta gott eller bara avnjuta ett glas vit Montagny på det sluttande torget vid katedralen, ett trivsamt gaturum med bleknade korsvirkesgavlar. Inget är dockskåpssött i de här delarna av Frankrike.

En soppa vi vill glömma

Nu var vi på väg mot Saint-Jean-de-Losne. Saône hade stillat sig. Vi ankrade för kvällen i en bukt medan väldiga molnhimlar tornade upp sig över stränder och betesmarker. Ett par outtröttliga metare hade gjort fast sin båt vid ett strömdrivet träd som fastnat i ett sjömärke. Till sist såg vi bara deras svarta silhuetter mot solnedgången. I farleden gled stora lastpråmar förbi natten igenom med glimmande lanternor. Floden är en av de stora trafikådrorna. Efter kanalernas småskalighet där vi passat in som i ett Märklinlandskap kändes "Vanadis" med ens mycket liten.

Verdun-sur-le-Doubs, ej att förväxla med slagfältens Verdun vid Meuse, ligger uppflugET på en höjd där floden Doubs rinner ut i Saône. Den lilla staden lockar med ett brödmuseum och så den mångomtalade attraktionen *pôchouse,* en soppa som sägs ha uppfunnits på 1500-talet av traktens fiskarbefolkning och som består av bitar av gädda, abborre, sutare och ål i en redning av smör, mjöl, vin och persilja. Rätten har till och med ett eget brödraskap, *Confrérie des Chevaliers de la Pôchouse,* med inte mindre än 3 500 medlemmar som värnar om traditionen.

Oss väntar ingen framtid som soppriddare. Vi valde från matsedeln den rustikare varianten med skinn och ben kvar och tillbringade halva måltiden med att försöka pilla loss köttet. Sådant är överkomligt, även om skeden är ett trubbigt verktyg. Beklagligare var den dysmak som häftade vid fiskarna, som heller inte blev roligare av den stabbiga mjölsupa i vilken de ändat sina dagar. Vi tänkte med vemod på den Loire-gös som serverats oss i Nevers. För att inte tala om den stuvade lake som får oss att försonas med januari därhemma.

La pôchouse – en fiskrätt i vars ridderskap vi aldrig blir upptagna.

Verdun är mer slitet än vad som framgår av handböckernas entusiastiska beskrivningar men har ett enkelt behag med sina hus och fönsterluckor i olika bleka färger och väcker avgjort sympati. Vi blev överallt bemötta med stor vänlighet, men det som fick oss att verkligen ta staden till vårt hjärta var en scen i ett litet snabbköp. Kassörskan hade uppenbarligen inte någon barnvakt åt sin sexårige son som därför bistod henne i kassan och tog emot och knappade in varorna, hela tiden djupt koncentrerad. En av kvarterets åldringar kom instultande med käpp och hörapparat. Han hälsades av alla som en kär vän och fick en stund bre ut sig om sina krämpor: "Aaaah! Det är inte lätt! Doktorn sa ...", och när han fått sin dos av uppmärksamhet och medkänsla gengäldade han med att berömma barnet, som under tiden hunnit lära sig flera nya varor. Alla instämde. Gossen var stolt, modern var stolt, och jag hoppas att ingen myndighet rycker ut och bedömer insatsen som barnarbete. Hur mycket mera av självtillit och ansvar skulle inte denna lilla person få med sig ut i livet än de barn som tvingas förslösa sina unga dagar med att knåpa ihop meningslösa pärlplattor på ett larmande och underbemannat dagis.

En eftermiddag under en orolig oktoberhimmel hade vi nått slutet för årets långa färd. Saint-Jean-de-Losne låg framför oss med sin mäktiga stenbro över Saône. Vi vek av till vänster och slussade in på Canal de Bourgogne som strax vidgar sig i en bassäng med pråmar och småbåtar om varandra. Här ligger de två varv som alla kanalfarare känner till: Blanquart och H2O. Vi har valt Blanquart, och vi har varit nöjda med vårt val.

Höstdimmorna hade börjat ligga kvar allt längre på dagarna. Det var dags att bryta upp. "Vanadis" var i goda händer när hon lyfts ur vattnet och pallats under på varvsplanen. Men att skiljas är ändå att dö en smula.

Verdun-sur-le-Doubs, omflutet av Doubs och Saône som ibland stiger högt upp på murarna. Slitet och sympatiskt och hemvist för en dessvärre oförglömlig soppa.

Hamnbassängen i Saint-Usage med den sista slussen på Canal de Bourgogne.

Saint-Jean-de-Losne, vår vinterhamn

"Här etablissemangen Joël Blanquart." "Vanadis" vintervarv.

Lika vemodigt som det är att lämna Saint-Jean-de-Losne i oktober, lika förväntansfullt är det första mötet när man återvänder om våren. Hur mår "Vanadis"? Vilka båtgrannar har kommit? Vilka nya ska man lära känna? Har David Blanquart byggt ut varvet eller hittat på något nytt? Ska den vackra Nathalie stå bakom disken i butiken och hålla ordning på verksamheten?

Saint-Jean-de-Losne ligger strategiskt där den smala Canal de Bourgogne förenar sig med den mäktiga Saône. Egentligen består den lilla staden av tre delar. Till Saint-Usage hör kanalbassängen och Blanquarts varv och Atélier Fluvial med torrdockan där pråmarna bottenbehandlas. Hit hör också den stora gästhamnen, la Gare d'Eau, med två snårövervuxna öar i mitten där näktergalarna sjunger ostörda, med båtföretaget H2O:s bryggor och Crown Blues Lines hyrbåtar. Saint-Jean är själva staden med affärer och kanalmuseum och kyrkan med tak av glaserat tegel i bourgognskt sicksackmönster. Losne ligger på andra sidan den mäktiga stenbron över Sâone.

En gång var staden Frankrikes största inhamn för pråmar i yrkestrafik. I dag gläds man här åt de många vackra pénicher som byggts om till flytande och flyttbara bostäder, men man har också rika tillfällen att beklaga de rosthögar som ställt sig på botten, bortom all hjälp, för att invänta evigheten. På Canal de Bourgogne och upp till Dijon går det fortfarande någon gång in en lastpråm med senapsfrö. Frankrike har inte tillräckligt av den varan för de berömda senapsfabrikanterna, berättar man på kanalmuseet, så fröna hämtas från Kanada till Antwerpen, där de lastas om för att gå Meuse–Reims–Marne–Saône och in på den stilla kanalen. Men ute på den breda Sâone är trafiken rätt livlig.

Annars är det fritidsbåtarna, ombyggda pråmar som småbåtar, som dominerar bassängerna. Somliga båtägare övervintrar faktiskt, inte sällan infrusna i isen. De flesta är britter, men det finns också en och annan skandinav. Tiden fördriver de med att dricka whisky hos varandra.

Somliga stannar frivilligt, andra för att de ingenstans har att ta vägen. Det förekommer att folk har sålt sitt hus eller sin våning för att förverkliga sin kanaldröm, och när de sedan efter ett antal år börjar känna av gikt och podager upptäcker de att bostadspriserna där hemma har rusat i väg medan värdet på båten inte alls har följt med.

Men när våren sveper in med ljumma vindar och bitterdofter från vitblommande fruktträd, med rödhake och rödstjärt och gök och långa solnedgångskvällar då Sâone oupphörligt skiftar färg och grodorna knorrar i vattenbrynet nätterna igenom, då anländer också de andra båtägarna från världens alla hörn.

Man lär sig snart att inte döma efter vare sig båt eller utseende. De två pensionärer som såg ut som ett

Mytomspunna Meuse

Till Frankrike kan man komma på flera vägar. Floden Meuse är en. När man lämnat Belgiens sorgliga nedlagda industriområden och passerat Dinant reser sig ett nytt landskap framför en. Det är som att omslutas av Wagners ouvertur till "Rhenguldet". En mäktig grön åder buktar sig mellan höga ogenomträngliga lövskogsklädda bergssidor. Man färdas långsamt i strömmens ständigt upprepade tre toner och man anar floddöttrarnas skratt och plask runt skrovet. Här är det ren och högstämd natur och världen är fortfarande på oskuldsstadiet. Än har inte det olycksbringande guldet grumlat gudars och människors sinnen.

Har man upplevt Meuse kan man avstå från Rhen med riddarborgar och Lorelei, städer och motorleder och en båttrafik som på en vattenvägarnas autobahn.

Men Meuses legender är andra än Nibelungarnas. Här handlar det om de fyra bröderna Aymon, som alla flydde undan Karl den stores vrede på den magiska hästen Bayard, sedan brodern Renault som dålig förlorare slagit ihjäl kungens brorson med ett schackbräde. I ett väldigt språng över floden slog hästen i en klippa med bakhoven, och än i dag ser man klyftan i kammen. Nu övar dödsföraktande bergsklättrare på stupen.

Meuse flyter majestätiskt fram. Då och då leds man in på en kanaliserad stump, går igenom en sluss med ett vattenfall vid sidan och famnas sedan igen av floden.

Så småningom blir Meuse mer fransk med lägre stränder, med byar och vägar, med metare och hägrar i strandbuskagen. Och när man kommit ända ner till Sedan är man i en riktig stad.

Mattfabriken i Sedan

Sedan är en stad som det är lite synd om. En gång har den varit vacker och är det på sitt sätt ännu, men nedgången och lite i bakvatten känns det som. Mycket stryk har staden tagit, inte minst under 1870 års krig mot Preussen, och Napoleon III fick kapitulera här efter ett anfall mot staden. Det blev slutet för andra kejsardömet. Tyskarna på sin kant jublade och gjorde Sedandagen till helgdag. Ända fram till 1919 blev Sedan årligen påmint om nederlaget.

Det var också över Sedan som tyskarna under andra världskriget bröt in i Frankrike efter att ha gått över Belgien för att ta sig förbi Maginotlinjen.

Tycker man om Norrköping är det lätt att tycka om Sedan. Liksom Norrköping är Sedan en gammal textilstad. Vatten flyter genom den, med breda fall och broar. Liksom Norrköping var Sedan en fristad för judar och även för protestanter. Och liksom Norrköping har Sedan förlorat sin industri. Här finns sorgliga butiker med totalutförsäljning, och gatorna är knaggliga och gropiga. Men det finns en värme i de många medfarna husens guldiga sandsten och i invånarnas blomsterdekorationer och i all den vardaglighet som råder.

Sedans stolthet är den jättelika borgen på en höjd, och där kan man ta del av stadens historia genom seklerna men framför allt söka svalka i de fuktiga gångarna. Det gör man gärna när det är trettiofem grader och mer.

Brandkåren klarade hettan på annat sätt. Vi såg en utryckningsbil köra ner till kajen där brandsoldaterna, *les pompiers,* mest yngre män och kvinnor, kopplade stora flodsprutan i vattnet och satte i gång med att blöta ner varandra under skratt och skrik. Vad annat är att göra när uniformen är svart och heltäckande?

Hettan och fukten hade väckt myggen till liv, så vi behövde ett myggnät, och här i Sedan hittade vi verkligen en butik med sådant material som metervara. Det var en järnhandel, ett *quincaillerie,* som skulle läggas ner. Butiken såg ut som ordet quincaillerie låter, en massa skramliga saker i en enda röra. Allt var nedsatt till hälften. I kassan satt en uppgiven dam och rökte. Men hon ensam kunde inte ha åstadkommit den inpyrdhet som vilade över lokalen.

Nedgången men vänlig, det intrycket får man av staden Sedan.

Vi plockade på oss allt möjligt som kunde vara bra att ha, inklusive myggnätet, och betalade nästan ingenting. Sedan cyklade vi ut till en konstgjord insjö vid stadsgränsen. Vi blandade oss med ungdomar som möttes här efter skoldagen. De bar sig åt som ungdomar gör: pratade, stilade, provocerade varandra och flängde omkring men bad franskt artigt om ursäkt när de råkade kliva på våra handdukar.

Det var osannolikt ljuvligt att driva på rygg i vattnet i denna hetta, och det var trivsamt att ingå i det sedanska vardagsfritidslivet.

På kvällen börjar vi arrangera myggnätet över "Vanadis" öppningar. Det luktade rök och nedlagd järnaffär så att vi nästan inte kunde sova.

En textilfabrik fanns dock kvar i staden, och den var dessutom markerad som sevärdhet. Där vävde man de berömda Sedanmattorna. Nästa dag cyklade vi dit, inträdde genom en oansenlig dörr, togs vänligt emot och fördes mot en ringa avgift genom en blekrosa pärlspontad gång in i mottagningsrummet.

Lokalen såg ut att vara från förra sekelskiftet. På tegelväggarna – ursprungligt råa, inte designade – hängde präktiga ullmattor i de härligaste mönster, de flesta orientaliska. Även på golvet låg dessa dyrbarheter, att beträdas av vilka skor som helst. På en vägg fanns en informationstavla och på den ett buckligt foto som visade president de Gaulle och presidentskan Jacqueline Kennedy tillsammans – de hade båda köpt just mattor från den berömda Sedanfabriken.

Men det kan knappast ha varit här på platsen de gjort sitt val. Skruffigare miljö fick man leta efter. I ett hörn vilade ensam ett vrak till besökssoffa med ett urblekt blommigt tyg och sitsen direkt på golvet. Mitt i rummet stod ett bord som kunde ha varit utrangerat från Myrorna och fyra skamfilade kaféstolar av olika modell. På detta bord låg några bräckta pärmar där exempel på mattmönstren låg instoppade i halkiga och grådaskiga plastfickor. Vi bläddrade lite. Damen som tagit emot oss ursäktade sig med att hon skulle gå på lunch, men vi fick gärna stanna. Från fabrikslokalen intill hördes bara duvokurr och sparvekvitter.

Vi hoppade till när friden bröts av ett plötsligt brak och slammer som fick allt löst att skallra och duvorna att lyfta.

Det var vävmästaren själv som gjort ett inslag i den stora vävstolen, den enda som tycktes vara i gång.

Han vinkade in oss i byggnaden, varsågoda att gå runt!

Överallt stod gamla rostiga vävstolar, igenbeckade av ludd, några med uppsatta vävar som påbörjats och övergivits. Vi klev runt bland maskindelar och lådor med de komplicerade, en gång så revolutionerande

Den berömda mattfabriken i blomman av sin ungdom på slutet av 1800-talet. Här tillverkades de berömda tapis de Sedan *med en typ av jacquardväveri, den tidens hålkortsteknik.*

mönsterkorten, genom vilka alla de trådar löper som styr inslaget – det fanns kvar kort från starten 1878, och de kunde fortfarande användas. I andra lådor låg ullgarnet från Nya Zeeland, ljuvligt att känna på. Vi rotade i boxar med gamla bobiner av bakelit. Spindelväv fastnade på kläder och ansikte. Duvorna och sparvarna flög ut och in genom det trasiga taket, dammet bildade strimmor i ljuset som föll in genom hålen.

Stillhet rådde en god stund, sedan kom nästa brak med lite slamrande efterskalv från vävmästarens maskin. En femtonårig lärling med en cigarett betraktade verksamheten där han stod under en skylt med *Défense de fumer.* Intill satt en ung flicka och sydde mattkanter på en liten handvevad maskin.

Hörnen var värst, sa hon, dem måste man sy för hand, och det var hårt för fingrarna.

Båda ungdomarna gillade jobbet, men de hade inte mycket hopp om det för framtiden.

Här gjordes mattor för kungahus och ambassader och till och med för Vatikanen, men beställningarna blev allt färre. Vi undrade hur det hela alls gick ihop. Utbildningen för att åstadkomma en god matta tog ändå sju år hade vi läst, och kvadratmeterpriset var 700 euro.

Vävmästaren såg på oss med sorgsna bruna ögon.

– Man får försöka hålla i gång.

Vi ville inte fråga hur det var på vintern i den oeldade hallen med hål i taket. Det vore att ifrågasätta verksamheten. Men nog verkade den dödsdömd.

Vad vi inte visste var att det just hade bildats en förening, där både den lokala sparkassan och kulturministeriet ingick, för att rädda det anrika företaget. *Les Tapis Point de Sedan* var en nationalklenod, och något måste göras.

Vad vi än mindre visste var att även detta stolta projekt skulle gå om intet.

När vi kom att passera Sedan något år senare var dörren till fabriken stängd med evighetens lås. Vi ringde de telefonnummer som stod på skylten och fick bara hänvisningston.

– De slog igen för en månad sedan, sa flickan på turistbyrån. *Mais c'est pour toujours.* För alltid.

På vägen tillbaka från den sorgsne vävmästaren tog vi ett varv förbi quincailleriet. Nu var priserna hälften av hälften. Vi inhandlade en rejäl slägga av den uppgivet rökande damen. Den skulle framdeles visa sig oumbärlig, särskilt för islagning av förtöjningsspikar. Men den luktar alltjämt nedlagd järnhandel, hur det nu är möjligt.

En tapis de Sedan, *ej mer beställningsbar.*

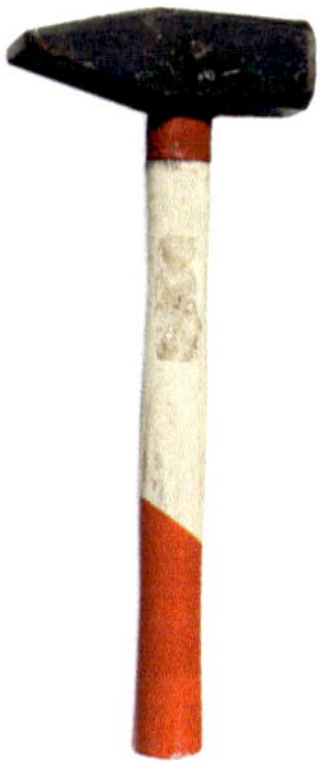

Ett läkarbesök

Till Sedan hade jag medfört en hosta som inte var till att ha ombord. Jag hade övertagit den av sonen som besökt oss på vår färd genom Holland, och under de tre följande veckorna gjorde den sig hemmastadd i mina lungor. Jag skrällde *de profundis* och pep däremellan och väste som en brusten bälg.

Hamnkapten i gästhamnen gav mig en läkaradress. Jag ringde.

– *Chez docteur X?*

– *Oui.*

Det var tydligen doktorn själv som svarade. Jag redogjorde för mitt fall.

– *À deux heures.*

Jag kunde inte avgöra om korthuggenheten var professionell eller tvärtom men tog för säkerhets skull en sväng förbi adressen – ett patricierhus i ljus sandsten. Det verkade lugnande.

Klockan två ringde jag på och togs emot av en mager man i en fladdrig och snedtvättad dieselgrön t-tröja. Två tänder saknades i underkäken. Han lade en slapp hand i min, hostade ticsaktigt och bad mig stiga in.

Mottagningsrummet befann sig i ett skick som motsvarade innehavaren. På hyllor och golv låg kartonger och travar av tidningar, papper, kvitton, gamla skor, ett trasigt paraply. Besöksstolen i svart galon hade stora hål där skumgummit trängde ut mellan tejpremsor. Längst bort i dunklet fanns en undersökningsbrits med ett solkigt skynke och en hushållspappersrulle. Jag hoppades att jag skulle få stanna i besöksstolen.

Doktorn ticshostade och rafsade i röran på det överbelamrade skrivbordet och grävde under pappers-

”Mina herrar, jag har vigt hela min livsgärning åt hälsovården.”
Teckning av Gustave Doré

högarna fram ett stetoskop och en blodtrycksmanschett. Det konstaterades att jag behövde ett antal medikamenter, och doktorn röjde med armbågen plats för att skriva ut recept. Jag påpekade att jag en tid känt mig allmänt darrig och att jag hade blivit tillrådd att ta ett insulinprov.

Här bleknade den redan bleke doktorn och for ut i en lång jämmer om hur orimligt dyrt det var att ta blodprov och hur svårt – själv kunde han inte göra det. Jag hade heller aldrig låtit honom komma i närheten med en kanyl, men jag undrade om det inte fanns någon inrättning för sådant i staden. Jo, det funnes en, men att anlita den skulle som sagt vara ohyggligt kostsamt, och att över huvud taget hitta den var ingenting för en främling att ge sig in på, vägen dit var omöjlig att beskriva, vägen till apoteket likaså.

Det var ingen ände på hur komplicerat allt var.

Jag betalade tjugo euro, lättad över att undersökningen inte varit noggrannare och att min lekamen lämnats i stort sett utan beröring.

Är det något man hittar i en fransk stad är det apotek. Det finns ett i varje kvarter. Det första i min väg var svalkande luftkonditionerat i den trettiofemgradiga värmen. Där hade jag kunnat stanna länge, men till slut var min påse med antibiotika och en massa annat godis färdig och överlämnades med ett ”God bättring, Madame, och behöver ni ett laboratorium för blodprovstagning så ligger det vägg i vägg”.

Där fick jag genast tid nästa morgon, proffsigt och propert. Jag tog i en bankomat ut en försvarlig summa för att klara min lyxundersökning. Om aftonen kunde jag hämta resultatet, flera sidor med en massa siffror som en vänlig medicinare kommenterade.

– Lite risigt, men ni har ju en rejäl luftvägsinfektion, annars inget alarmerande. Ni kan äta och dricka precis som vanligt. Njut av livet, Madame! Trevlig kanalfärd! Det blir fjorton euro i kassan.

Andansvar

Vid Pont-a-Bar vek vi in på Canal des Ardennes, ännu en av dessa smala franska kanaler som letar sig genom en glesbefolkad landsbygd. Allra älskligast är den vid den långa trappa på tjugosju slussar som i mjuka bågar klättrar ner mellan kullarna, Ardennernas utlöpare. Det tar en halv dag, men man önskar att man fick stanna längre och ge sig ut och upp på stigarna bland beteshagarna, där det faktiskt står en och annan ardennerhäst och dåsar under ett träd.

Men här har man en medföljande slussvaktare och blir jagad vidare, om än i behaglig takt.

Vår man ägnade lika mycket tid åt hungrande änder som åt slussandet och stannade då och då för att utspisa någon andfamilj med resterna av morgonens baguetter som han förvarade i sin mopedväska. När en liten tuss till unge hade förirrat sig in i en slusskammare slog han av maskineriet och sjasade ut den vilsekomne och lovade att sörja för att den återförenades med sin moder.

Men när jag sa att det är förträffligt att de franska vattenmyndigheterna tar sig an små andungar blev han svart i ögonen. Det var sannerligen inte VNF utan han, *moi personellement, Madame!* som utövade detta ansvar.

Änderna på hans sträcka levde ett tryggt liv.

Vitkorven från Rethel

Urbesättningen Gasten och Kockan hade kommit ombord, och i den mindre staden Rethel lade vi till för att Skepparn och Gasten skulle få möjlighet att besöka ett militärmuseum. Det låg inte alldeles nästgårds och de fick cykla ett par mil uppför de ardenniska höjderna i tjugonio graders hetta för att beskåda motorcyklar, kulsprutor, tält och kartor från både första och andra världskriget, som gick hårt fram i dessa trakter.

Kockan och jag besökte kyrkan och fick oss en öl på en servering med ett vildsvin på skylten.

Vildsvinet, *le sanglier*, är Ardennernas karaktärsdjur, och från vårt bord på trottoaren betraktade vi fina hotellet "Au sanglier des Ardennes". Själva Rethels karaktärsobjekt är annars dess vita korv på fågel, fläsk och mjölk, *boudin blanc,* som det görs mycket väsen av och som vi hade tänkt prova, men slakteributiken som framställer märkvärdigheten var förstås stängd eftersom det var tisdag.

Rethel for mycket illa under krigen och många hus är slitna och ruffiga. Nere vid kajen där vi låg finns en duschanläggning för gästande båtar, men den används mest av stadsbor som saknar sanitära bekvämligheter hemma. Här samlades nu på eftermiddagen också en grupp skolflickor runt utomhushandfaten. De rökte och pratade och blaskade sig med vatten i värmen, och de bedyrade att i Rethel händer absolut ingenting. De makade sig åt sidan när en kvinna med en stor väska försvann in i duschen och tystnade under menande blickar när en karl strax därpå följde efter. Vattenplask blandades med kutter bakom den stängda dörren, och långt om länge utträdde han, drog med en manlig gest åt svångremmen och promenerade med självmedvetna steg därifrån. Strax därpå kom hon ut i nya fräschare kläder och skakade sina vilda ångande lockar. Men annars hände verkligen ingenting.

Dagens tilldragelse var att vi fick tag i boudiner i en annan butik – Rethel är ändå den vita korvens vagga, som det står i turistbroschyren. De var mjälla och liksom fluffiga i konsistensen och skämdes inte för sig. Kockan, som förestår köket, hade rynkat på näsan vid mina korvförslag, men nu gjorde jag en palett av lättstekta skivor av vitkorv, gråröa örtkryddad fläskkorv och mörk blodkorv – en koloristisk ögonfröjd och en trevnad för gommen.

Till korvorgien gjorde jag väninnan Birgittas potatissallad med citronskal, enligt följande:

Koka ett önskvärt antal potatisar och strimla skalet av en citron. Pressa saften ur citronen och blanda den med olja till en dressing, sätt till strimlorna. Krydda med salt och peppar. Skär den kokta potatisen i lagom bitar och slå över dressingen medan potatisen fortfarande är ljummen. Blanda i finskuren purjolök eller salladslök och försköna det hela med en näve finhackad persilja.

Öl passar bäst som dryck, och det var vad Skepparn och Gasten krävde när de utmattade återvände från sitt museibesök. Men rödvin går annars till det mesta. Trötta på halvfärdiga viner till överpris nöjde vi oss i dessa trakter med en enkel Côte du Rhône från något köpcenter, inget att bli salig av, men drickbart.

Den rethelska urkorven från det stängda charkuteriet förblev för oss en hemlighet, men å andra sidan hade vi den kvar att drömma om.

Vildsvinet är Ardennernas karaktärsdjur. Barer, bagerier, jaktaffärer, presentbutiker – allt kan ha djuret på sin skylt.

Vårt franska kök

Matlagning har aldrig varit vår force. Å andra sidan behöver man inte sakna god mat i Frankrike. Å tredje sidan kan man inte äta på restaurang varje dag när man ligger ute i månader, om man inte har ett välfyllt konto alternativt den sjusablaste bula till plånbok (det är inte alla ställen i de grå byarna där man tar kort).

Följaktligen äter vi ofta ombord. Skepparn ordnar för det mesta frukosten. Det övriga slipper han, för hans mat är så ofattbart tråkig. Ful blir den också, säger han själv, och det går inte att förneka .

Själv kan jag åstadkomma hyfsade måltider, men jag är ofta så oinspirerad. Dessutom klarar jag inte

Savojkålen ska stekas och bräseras i lite cider, puttra i crème fraîche och till sist strösslas med valnötter (självplock från en höstlig kanalbank).

den grundläggande konsten att få alla ingående delar färdiga på samma gång.

När det går upp för våra båtgrannar att vi saknar grill, ugn, mikro, mixer, ismaskin och kaffebryggare grips de inte sällan av djup medkänsla med oss. Som Skepparn är en hejare på krånglande elektroniksystem uppstår emellertid ofta en form av tjänsteutbyte och naturahushållning. När han har hjälpt förtvivlade otekniker, och de är många, med generatorer och laddning och oxidbeläggning och pumpar och annat som får deras vardag att gå i stå, brukar de tacksamt svara med en ypperlig och trivsam måltid. Mitt bidrag kan bestå i att jag i hällande regn cyklar i förväg och förhandlar med slussvakter och vevar upp slussportar och lägger på linor som räcks ut under ett kapell, och när dagen sedan är över är det ingen gräns för hur gärna man vill se min dränkta gestalt på en välförtjänt kvällsvard inne i värmen.

Som väl är har vi också våra gästande vänner. De blir för det mesta vindögda av lycka vare sig de hamnar i en hiskelig supermarché där hyllorna med korvar och ostar och grönsaker förlorar sig i fjärran eller på en torgmarknad med ännu fler lokala korvar och ostar och därtill oliver, patéer och röror av olika slag. Det händer visserligen att en och annan gårdstillverkad produkt med kraft inverkar på peristaltiken, men läckert är det alltid. Slakteributikerna har priser som får en att tro att djuren har handmatats med utvalt gräs, men å andra sidan smakar det köttet också som om så vore fallet.

Av allt som våra gäster faller för under inköpsturerna tillreder de också de härligaste middagar som för det mesta intas uppe på akterdäck, alltmedan aftonen faller och solen slår sina sista stänk av guld och violett i vattenytan. Värdfolket äter bättre än det förtjänar.

Cykeln, frihetens instrument och alla måltiders yttersta förutsättning.

Våra gäster går i spinn i de franska matbutikerna.

Möte med gotiken

Canal de l'Aisne à la Marne går genom jordbruksbygd med vete, raps och majs. Det är tätt mellan lastageplatsernas silobyggnader. På håll i regndis ser de ut som kyrkor, men så snart man kommer närmre avslöjar de sin nyttobetonade arkitektur, gråa och kantiga.

Att man skulle befinna sig i Champagne finns det inget som tyder på. Inte en vinstock så långt ögat når. Och ändå skulle vi snart vara i Reims, säte för flera av de stora husen: Mumm, Pommery, Veuve Clicquot-Ponsardin …

Till Reims har Frankrikes kungar kommit för att krönas alltsedan merovingern Klodvig år 496 erkände den kristna läran och mottog dopet här i katedralen Notre-Dame. Hit förde Jeanne d'Arc 1429, efter att ha deltagit i befrielsen av Orléans, den blivande Karl VII för att kronan skulle sättas på hans huvud.

Hit kom också vi, men utan flygande fanor och klingande spel. Det ösregnade. Gästhamnen låg omgiven av larmande motorleder på alla sidor. Anblicken av slitna bostadshus och sunkiga snabbmatställen var miserabel, gatan som gick upp i stan avslutades med ännu en grå silo i diset.

Det var katedralen.

När vi sedan stod vid dess fot och böjde huvudena bakåt under paraplykanten greps vi av svindel, blicken sögs uppåt och uppåt över ett knyppelarbete i sten: nischer, statyer, rosettfönster, masverk, utväxter, fialer med krabbor och korsblommor, prydnadsgavlar, strävbågar, gargouiller – vattenkastare i form av fabeldjur och djävlar. Inte en slät yta. Tornen förlorade sig i gråvädret och skapade den känsla av himmelssträvan som är gotikens avsikt och kännemärke. Men mitt i

Katedralen i Reims.

denna måttlöshet möts man av fullkomligt harmoniska och sansade varelser: statyerna som flankerar portalerna. En av dem ler, ängeln som blivit representant för Reims.

Byggnaden har utsatts för en omild behandling under seklerna – brunnit, härjats under franska revolutionen då inte bara aristokratin utan även många av kyrkornas helgonbilder miste huvudet, restaurerats lika hårdhänt, för att till sist skadas ännu värre av tyska granater under första världskriget och få några slängar även under andra. Återuppbyggnaden pågår ännu. Mirakulöst nog har flera av de målade glasfönstren från 1200-talet klarat sig, och i koret har de som gick förlorade ersatts av en rad nya gjorda av Chagall.

"La Nature est un temple où de vivants piliers / laissent parfois sortir de confuses paroles – Naturen är ett tempel där levande pelare ibland låter höra otydliga ord." Charles Baudelaires "Correspondances", symbolismens ingångsdikt, kunde vändas på för att beskriva känslan när man befinner i en gotisk katedral.

Man står i en skog med raka stammar vars grenar växer ut till bågar medan spirorna fortsätter högre och högre, halvvägs till himlen, där kronorna möts och bildar valv. Det mumlar och susar i dem, ourskiljbara ord från böner, textläsning och dämpade guider. Där uppe skimrar ljuset men här nere i undervegetationen råder halvdager. Ibland faller ett sken från ett glasfönster och öppnar en glänta på marken.

Katedralen i Reims har stämning, som alla katedraler, romanska som gotiska. Men i Reims möter man inte bara arkitektur utan även den gotiska människan, som är en individ och inte, som den romanska, en representation. Portalens ängel har ett leende som möjligen är ojordiskt, men kroppen under klädnadens veck är kött och blod, om än av sten.

Många av katedralens statyer blev till grus och spillror, men åtskilliga av dem som överlevde har räddats in i det närliggande biskopspalatset Palais de Tau. Där väntar Adam och Eva, hon ivrig och övertalande tätt intill honom, hans pojkansikte så öppet tvekande, båda så verkliga att man nästan inte nänns störa dem genom ett närgånget betraktande. Man kan bli förtvivlad över att deras fastighetsvärd snart måste vräka dem. Än vet de inte om det. Man vill kunna stoppa historien, inte för sin egen skull och inte ens för mänsklighetens, utan bara för att detta unga par ska få fortsätta att vara unga och oskuldsfulla, som ännu i detta ögonblick.

Hur kom det sig, tänker man sedan där man går bland skulpturerna av bibliska gestalter och andans män och borgare och dårar, att antikens realism kunde försvinna under århundraden för att sedan nästan med ens återuppstå i gotikens så ofta behagfulla men på samma villkor också skoningslösa återgivning av levande personer?

I Palais de Tau höll vi oss kvar till stängningsdags. När vi kom ut föll regnet lika stritt. Lusten att fira ankomsten till Champagne med champagne var inte överväldigande i rusket. Mera lockande var whiskyn från Ardennerna i Fina Vinbutikens fönster, den och läsafton i goda värmen ombord. Vi steg över tröskeln.

Adam och Eva ännu i paradisisk oskuld.
Museet Palais de Tau, Reims.

Vildsvinswhiskyn

I Fina Vinbutiken såldes mest champagne. Kunderna bestod av kostymklädda herrar med fruar i små chica matelasserade jackor. Det provdracks vid små bord och kommenterades med kännarmin.

Anblicken av våra enkla uppenbarelser kunde ha utlöst nedlåtenhet från expeditens sida, men vi bemöttes med korrekt artighet. Om det gick att provsmaka whiskyn? Dessvärre inte, men den var en single malt och smakade som en sådan, framställd av ett litet exklusivt bränneri i Ardennerna. Kunde rekommenderas, naturligtvis, annars skulle den inte säljas här.

Den var inte billig, men nyfikenheten och etiketten med de borstiga vildsvinen, Ardennernas landskapsdjur, fick oss att falla. Vi beredde oss på en kväll i trevnadens tecken medan regnet smattrade mot "Vanadis" tak.

Artigt behandlade hade vi blivit, men fulljugna. Eller också hade expediten aldrig druckit en skotsk single malt. *Gout incomparable,* "en ojämförlig smak", bedyrade etiketten, och det var sannare.

Senare skulle jag finna en nätsajt för udda whiskysorter där jag återfann vår brygd, rejält kommenterad med adjektiv som *exécrable,* vedervärdig, på hembrännarnivå! Testaren hade upphävt ett skri som från vildgalten själv innan han låtit vasken ta emot glasets innehåll.

När vi själva tagit den första klunken beslöt vi att spara flaskan till besökare vi ville bli av med.

Bara hälften kvar.
Våra vänners nyfikenhet
har inte stått att hejda.

Champagne i Champagne

Vi stuvade undan whiskyn och lämnade Reims. Kanalen fortsatte ut på den ensliga landsbygden med poppelplanteringar och majsfält – nya inslag i det gamla Frankrikes kulturlandskap. Men där kanalen gör sig redo att förena sig med Marne och dess kanal dök äntligen vinbergen upp, de som på sina kritsluttningar bär champagnedruvorna och ger dem deras speciella karaktär. I varje by fanns säkert femton vinodlare. Med matbutiker var det desto mer tunnsått, men inte ens champagnefrukostar kan i längden bestå av bara skumpa.

Vi passerade slussen i Dizy, platsen för Simenons deckare "Maigret och pråmdragaren". I dag köar inte de hästdragna släpen framför slussarna, och Café de la Marine med sina bord med brun vaxduk i skänkrummet där Maigret sög på sin eviga pipa och frågade ut båtfolket finns inte mer, men en och annan lastpråm dyker ännu upp.

Från kanalen svängde vi in till Épernay, staden som genomlöps av vad som ibland kallats världens rikaste gata, den stora Avenue de Champagne. Den kantas av de stora firmornas paläer: Moët & Chandon, Pol Roger, Perrier-Jouet, Mercier ...

I berggrunden under staden ligger vinhusens tre hundra miljoner buteljer i ett system av gångar på tillsammans elva mil. Dit får man nedstiga om man går på de arrangerade visningarna.

För en båtfarare är gästhamnen emellertid lika viktig, och den i Épernay var av det slaget som man tar till sitt hjärta. En stor, lite naivistiskt målad skylt visade allt vad den hade att erbjuda: servering, tennisbana, kanotuthyrning ... Som en hel badort intill den smala gröna stumpen av Marne.

Allt detta fanns verkligen, men i så liten skala, och just därför så sympatiskt. Den kväll vi kom bjöd hamnkontoret, *la capitainerie,* alla gästerna på en drink, för den allmänna trevnaden. Det slog väl ut. Folk bekantade sig omedelbart, ingen ville gå, och mer av samma sort beställdes in runt borden. Hamnkapten bleknade – mer än ett glas per person kunde han inte bestå oss med, men en livad holländare viftade avvärjande.

– Jag betalar för alla, jag är rik, sa han som en självklarhet, och alla tog det som en sådan.

Bakom gästhamnen reser sig champagnefirman Castellanes mäktiga torn. Vi ansåg att grannskapet förpliktade oss att välja just märket med det röda krysset på etiketten för det obligatoriska besöket i en *cave.*

Vi började med en vandring i underjorden där små

Gästhamnens skylt utlovar en hel liten badort.

Höljda av damm och mögel vilar de mer än hundraåriga dyrgriparna.

tåg kom rullande i mörkret med sin dyrbara last. Överallt fanns sidogrottor med galler, bakom vilka det vilade staplar av buteljer överlagrade med damm och ädelt mögel. Små krittavlor angav årgångarna: 1875, 1902 … En lämplig miljö för filmer med spänning.

– Jo, här har man spelat in scener i ”Arsène Lupin, gentlemannatjuven”, upplyste guiden.

När vi gått igenom hela den komplicerade framställningsproceduren som skiljer äkta champagne från annat skummande vin och därefter avslutat med provsmakning och inhandling steg vi upp i tornet och mötte värmen och skådade över det böljande landskapet. Vinodlingar så långt ögat nådde. Här framställs bubbel för hela världen.

De mindre vinhusen, eller rättare sagt små familjeföretagen, levererar inte statusflaskor som barbariskt skakas och sprutas över vinnare i motor- eller segeltävlingar. De har sina fasta kunder – vinhandlare, restauranger, privatpersoner – och till en sådan odlare begav vi oss med vännerna Lars och Marianne som anlänt med bil och med en rekommendation.

Sålunda inträffade vi hos familjen Maurice Grumier i Venteuil på en höjd ovanför Marne. Om grottan hos Castellane varit mörk och möglig var det här motsatsen. Man hade kunnat dricka eventuellt spilld dryck direkt från golvet. Vinet jäste i glänsande rostfria cisterner, allt övervakades av mätapparatur. Vi fick en lika grundlig visning som i den anrika caven.

– Visst är det mycket som kan kontrolleras rent tekniskt, medgav Madame Grumier, temperatur, alkoholhalt, syra, men när det kommer till den slutliga kvalitetsbedömningen, då är det erfarenheten hos våra näsor och gommar som avgör.

Att verksamheten var lönande hade vi förstått redan när vi såg huset, stort och välskött med fönsterluckor, smidesjärn, trappstenar och trädgård i oklanderligt skick, som hos alla andra i denna välmående vinby. Men det var mycket hårt arbete och mycket lite ledighet i detta familjeföretag som startats av Monsieurs farfar och nu drevs även av den unge sonen. Framtiden verkade tryggad: en ny liten Grumier hade nyligen sett dagens ljus och flinade tandlöst på ett foto bland flaskorna i provrummet.

Från höjden såg vi på andra sidan Marne en slottsliknande byggnad som skimrade i värmediset: Madame Clicquot-Ponsardins residens, som hon kunde uppföra åt sig efter sina stormande framgångar när hon som ung änka i början av 1800-talet tagit itu med att framställa champagne i industriell skala och gjort den till modedryck i den fina världen i Ryssland och hela Europa.

Be någon att nämna en champagnesort och det blir med stor sannolikhet Gula änkan, efter den välkända gula etiketten.

Men av gula änkor gjordes oss inget behov. Vi föll omedelbart för Grumiers Réserve brut. Våra bilburna vänner fick transportera hem en ordentlig laddning som skulle glädja oss mycket under vintern. Och en låda bar vi ombord för akuta behov när ”Vanadis” gled vidare genom flodgrönskan under vinbergen.

De utsökta druvorna pinot noir och chardonnay får sin karaktär av kritgrunden.

På kanal de Bourgogne ligger slussarna tätt. Handvevade är de också.

Canal de Bourgogne

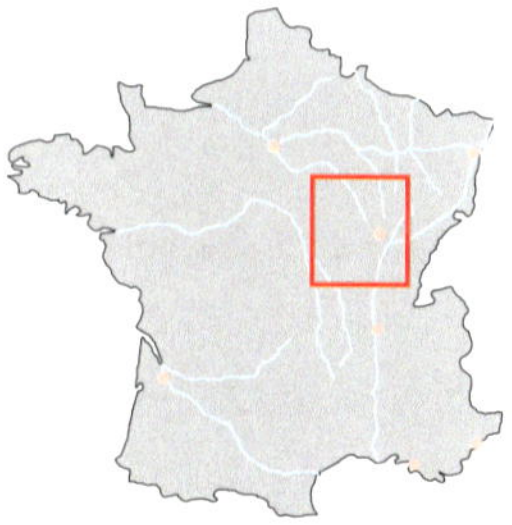

Canal de Bourgogne är ett storslaget projekt: för att förbinda Seine-Yonne med Saône och därmed Atlanten med Medelhavet har man grävt sig igenom ett bergmassiv och anlagt en tre kilometer lång tunnel på nästan fyra hundra meters höjd. Kanalen stod klar 1832, före maskinernas tid, så allt var fråga om kroppsarbete under stora umbäranden. Och hela etthundraåttionio slussar behövdes det för att vin och ved från Bourgogne skulle kunna transporteras till det ständigt glupande Paris.

När kanalen hade sin glansperiod kunde en sluss dagligen passeras av tjugo pråmar i varje riktning. Utmed vattnet levdes ett eget liv med besättningar, dragfolk, slussvaktare, hästskötare och kanalreparatörer. Pråmfolket bytte hos landborna kol, vin och säd mot grönsaker och ägg och det nödvändiga höet till dragdjuren.

Men nu färdas här bara en och annan fritidsbåt. Slussarnas antal avskräcker trots att de är låga och lättmanövrerade och trots att scenerierna där kanalen tar sig fram i floderna Armançons och Ouches dalgångar är en oavbruten njutning. Mestadels färdas man mellan gröna kullar med betesmarker och en och annan liten vinodling till husbehov och ett och annat slott som ögonfröjd, men det finns också sträckor med berg och skog och djupa klyftor där vildsvinen och nötskrikorna är fler än människorna.

Namnet Bourgogne leder tanken till stora viner, men mellan kanalen och vinbergen i Côte d'Or ligger en mäktig och karg högplatå, och efter Dijon går vattenvägen spikrak under poppelrader över en trist slätt med åkermark innan den mynnar ut i Saône.

Under tre septemberveckor skulle vi färdas ensamma nästan hela vägen. Den som vill undvika turistanhopningar går säker på Canal de Bourgogne.

Höstaning i Bourgogne

Var det sensommar eller förhöst här på Canal de Bourgogne? Denna septemberkväll hade vi återförenats med "Vanadis" som väntat på oss i Montbard en hel månad. Vi hade genast förflyttat oss ut i den franska lantligheten och förtöjt intill en kohage. Allt som hördes var bruset från en sluss.

Nästa morgon svävade en lätt dimma över det blanka vattnet. Landskapet var grått, som i en fransk femtiotalsfilm. Åkrarna sov, harvade och dystra, svartkråkor samlades i skränande flockar. Röksvampar stora som kranier glänste i det våta gräset. På andra sidan låg ett fält med överblommade solrosor, en här av dödsänglar med stora mörka ansikten under bleka testar, vissnade bladvingar.

Någon hade passerat, en doft av cigarett dröjde kvar. Var det Jean Gabin?

Vid tiotiden kom ljuset, färgerna återvände, först bleka, sedan allt mer mättade, diset över kullar och betesmarker blev varmare, småfåglar fnattade omkring och åt upp sig inför vintern och högt upp tumlade två glador med kluven stjärt. Gräset glittrade, grönt och frodigt och några knubbiga vita charolaiskvigor kom fram till stängslet och gav oss älskliga blickar under tjocka ljusa ögonfransar. Måtte transporten till slakthuset bli kort.

Vi gick in i slussen. Etthundratrettionio till hade vi framför oss till vinterhamnen i Saint-Jean-de-Losne vid kanalens slut. Slussvakten var en ung studentska. Visst var jobbet var lite ensamt sa hon, men snart började terminen i Dijon. Och än var det inte riktig höst!

Klostret i dalen: Stillhet och vattensorl vid l' Abbaye de Fontenay.

Klostret i dalen

Klostret i källornas dal – namnet är nog för att man ska sätta sig på cykeln och trampa de sex kilometerna från kanalen till l'Abbaye de Fontenay.

När skogsvägen öppnar sig i en glänta ligger det där, ett antal gråa, strama byggnader i fullkomlig ro. Ett cistercienserkloster från 1100-talets början.

Det ser ut som om det legat där helt orört av världens gång. Men klostret har undergått skiftande öden. Efter de medeltida storhetsdagarna då munkarna framlevde sitt liv efter grundaren Bernhard av Clairvaux rigorösa regler skulle det sjunka i andlig förslappning och upplösning, för att slutligen överges under franska revolutionen. Dess räddning från att bli ruin var läget invid det vattendrag som drivit hjul och hammare till den stora smedjan ända sedan grundandet. Ut med religionen och in med samhällsnyttan: klostret byggdes om till pappersfabrik och kom i början av 1800-talet i luftballongstillverkarfamiljen Montgolfiers ägo. Hundra år senare skulle en arvtagare som förstod vad han fått att förvalta lägga ner sin förmögenhet på att återställa klostret i dess ursprungliga skick. Allt som hörde till papperstillverkningen revs, lagerbyggnader, skorstenar, och nu kan besökaren göra sig en föreställning om munkarnas liv i sovsal, skrivsal, trädgård, duvslag och smedja. I dag är klostret ett världsarv.

Kyrkan är allvarlig och utan utsmyckningar som skulle kunna låta tanken förirra sig. I dess norra vägg finns en mindre port som öppnades bara när en klosterbroder skulle föras till den sista vilan. Man förstår dess innebörd: från helgedomens dunkel, strängt som klosterlivet, träder man befriad från det jordiska ut i bländande ljus, grönska och fågelsång och porlet från de klara vatten som givit klostret dess namn: *Fontenay.*

Anis et Chocolat

Säger ortnamnet Flavigny något? Ni har mött det oftare än ni tänkt på det, för det är i Flavigny man tillverkar de vita anispastillerna som säljs i vackra ovala askar i alla välsorterade godisbutiker runt om i världen.

En svag doft av anis var också vad som mötte oss när vi cyklade in genom stadsporten till den mycket lilla och gråa staden på en höjd ovanför kanalen. Vartannat hus här är musealt med medeltida fönstervalv, renässansportar och helgonbilder i nischer. Bakom ett par romanska rundbågar skönjde man ett loft med höbalar. Under stod en gisten CV2:a. Allt var slitet och halvförfallet men kärleksfullt prytt med blommor i krukor.

Minst av allt har man här gjort stor sak av de världskända pastillerna. I sin första variant tillverkades de på 800-talet av munkarna på orten, något man fortsatt med sedan en besökande påve ivrigt uppmanat därtill. Pastillfabriken var stängd för dagen, men vi inhandlade en försvarlig mängd askar i butiken till det lilla hotellet vid torget.

– Är ni svenskar? undrade innehavaren. Då måste jag visa något, om ni har tid.

Och så tog han fram ett par fotoalbum från inspelningen av filmen "Chocolat". Den gjordes här i Flavigny, invånarna var statister och roade sig präktigt med att klä ut sig och skapa sig, och sedan bjöd regissören Lasse Hallström alla medverkande på en hejdundrande middag.

– Hela stan var på benen! Oförglömligt!

Ett kloster och ett kontroversiellt prästseminarium sägs splittra stadens mentalitet, men denna stilla torsdagskväll märktes inget därav. Kanske hade filmens välgörande choklad även i verkligheten lett till allmän försoning där split förut rått.

Ingen av oss var hågad att laga mat ombord, så vi beställde det enklaste på restaurangen intill, bœf bourguignon. Sådan kan vara hur som helst. Men vad som lades för oss var surstek, svart som gammalt blod, mörad så att kniven föll igenom den, lätt syrlig och med en tät sås på rödvin och märg. Vi åt tårögda och förbannade att vi bara tagit in vanligt karaffvin. Även i Bourgogne har sådant oftast smak av vinäger.

På varje bord stod en korg med anispastiller.

Sedan steg fullmånen över medeltidshusen och vi cyklade ut genom stadsporten och rullade hela den slingrande vägen ner genom lövmassorna till den blänkande kanalen där "Vanadis" väntade i tystnaden.

De vita pastilllerna – ett obligatoriskt tillbehör till maten i Flavigny.

Hos gamla galler

Här i Bourgogne rör man sig på gammal gallisk mark, det var uppenbart. Överallt i träden hängde mistlar, den ört som druiderna använde för sina magiska dekokter. Och i den dimmiga morgonens första sluss hälsades vi vänligt av en äldre man med långt grått hår och pampiga slokmustascher, som skapad av Uderzo, tecknaren av Asterix.

Vi befann oss under höjden med byn Alise-Sainte-Reine, den plats som har ansetts som identisk med det Alesia där hövdingen Vercingetorix, från början så framgångsrik i sitt motstånd mot romarna, i en sista strid mot Caesar fick se sig och sin enorma här besegrade år 52 f. Kr. Kejsar Napoleon III lät på 1860-talet uppföra en jättelik bronsstaty över den galliske härföraren. Han blickar nu med mörk uppsyn och väldiga mustascher ner över nejden.

Vår egen milde slussgaller såg ut som Vercingetorix kunde ha sett ut på äldre dagar, om sådana förunnats honom och han inte hade blivit avrättad i Rom efter att ha förevisats och förnedrats i Caesars triumftåg.

Vi frågade inte vår man om han levde på mistelavkok, då skulle han kanske upplösas i morgondimman över kanalen.

Vercingetorix, motståndsmannen, blickar ut över den nejd han förlorade.

Kanalbor

Canal de Bourgogne vindlar genom en landsbygd som avfolkas allt mer. Det är tomt i byarna, butiker och barer har bommat igen. Men utmed kanalen uppstår ständigt möten mellan människor. Halva förmiddagen hade vi hört något som lät som ett gammaldags posthorn runt om i nejden, och ser man på, plötsligt dök en liten gul bil upp. Brevbäraren hälsades hjärtligt av slussvaktarparet, hunden klappades om, något kommenterades.

När jag vid en annan sluss slet med en ovanligt trög slussport stannade en skåpbil med det dagliga brödet.

– Tillåt mig, sa brödmannen, och med tre baguetter under armen och en fimp i mungipan hävde han sig på stången. Klichéfranskare kunde det inte bli.

Förr hade varje sluss här sin egen slussvakt som bodde i det lilla vakthuset och levde med ett visst mått av självhushåll: köksträdgård, fruktträd, bikupor, fjäderfä. Så var det ännu i Braux.

– Madame, ni är välkommen att dela mitt slussvaktarliv, ropade slussvakten när jag vant öppnade porthalvan på min sida. Jag heter Pascal!

– Ett erbjudande svårt att tacka nej till, ropade jag tillbaka över slussen, men jag måste fortsätta.

– Hälsa i alla fall till min svåger som sköter nästa sluss, han heter också Pascal! vinkade Pascal.

Naturligtvis hälsade vi från Pascal till Pascal.

Men mestadels numera betjänar en och samma slussvakt en hel rad slussar. Följaktligen är bara en del av vaktstugorna befolkade. *C'est bien triste.* Inget ser så ödsligt ut som ett hus där den vittrande rappningen faller ner i det som en gång var rabatter men nu bara är snår av nässlor och vissen korsört, där gårdsbrunnens smidesjärn är rostigt och skramligt och där de flagnande fönsterluckorna är stängda mot evigheten.

De hus som har invånare är däremot en fröjd för ögat. Vänliga fönster med trådgardiner och pelargoner. Allt som kan blomsterprydas är prytt. Ur vintunnor, skottkärror och runt avdankade slussattiraljer sprutar, klänger och slingrar pelargoner, krasse, petunior, tagetes och lobelia. Det är färgkaskader som skulle ge en trädgårdsdesigner huvudvärk, och det är underbart.

– Ska dom börja ta hyra, då sticker jag fast jag har jobbat så mycket på det här huset, hotade en arg ung

"Kom och dela mitt slussvaktarliv!"

Prisgivet åt förfall.

slussvakt med hästsvans medan han omsorgsfullt ryckte ogräs ur kajens stenläggning. Röda dahlior prunkade mot hans stängsel som gungade till varje gång hans vrålande pitbull kastade sig mot det. Av slussvakter och slusshundar finns alla slag.

Jo, det talas om att slussvakterna ska börja krävas på hyra, och inte så liten heller. Det innebär att de hellre flyttar någon annanstans.

– De franska lagarna motarbetar varandra, suckade en slusserska som på moped följde oss under en dag.

– Man får inte låta folk bo i hus som inte är i stånd, så i stället för att låta folk inrätta sig som de vill och kan får husen förfalla.

Men själv bodde hon i ett välhållet, och när vi passerade det på vägen fick vi ett efterlängtat uppehåll medan hon stack inom och hängde tvätten i solen.

Ett slussvaktslöst hus hade haft tur. Det lyste med nymålade blåa fönsterluckor, och jag läste ett skandinaviskt namn på brevlådan.

– Ett norskt par, sa slusserskan. De är inte kanalfolk, men mycket trevliga ändå, *très gentils*.

På den här sträckan känner alla varandra.

Châteauneuf – en medeltidsmålning

Tunneln i Pouilly är tre kilometer lång. I början anar man öppningen bara som ett nålstick. Vi tyckte oss i mörkret förnimma suckarna från de engelska krigsfångar som stupat under tvångsarbetet och murats in bakom väggarna, efter vad som berättats oss. Sedan far man som en kork ur en flaska – så kändes det i alla fall – ut i ljuset och ner mot Medelhavsbäckenet, fastän man ännu kommer att ha mäktiga raggiga höjder framför sig. Men just här öppnar sig landskapet, och i Vandenesse tycker man sig som i en av de medeltida kalendertavlorna ”Les très riches heures du Duc de Berry”. Uppe på en höjd ligger slottet Châteauneuf, och falkarna svävar som nyss släppta från falkenerarens hand.

Slottet och byn är alltsammans måleriskt och uthärdligt turistfriande, och vi tittade in hos en konstnär som hade några rätt tilltalande tavlor. När jag tystnade inför priset på en av dem, 2 000 euro, skyndade han sig att understryka att färg minsann inte var gratis, för att inte tala om vilken tid det tog att göra ren penslarna! Så om man såg till timpenningen så …

I slussen nedanför slottet, nr 12, Revin, bebos vaktstugan av Françoise Delabre som gör både tavlor och smycken i olika material. När vi gick den här sträckan en gång i början av 90-talet köpte jag ett par örhängen i det fjäderlättaste trä, matt skimrande i guld och silver. Då hade hon just slagit sig ner i det näpna huset. När vi nu möttes igen föll jag omedelbart för ett par som skiftade i turkos. Men kunde hon leva på sin konst?

Det gick, men det gällde att ta till vara alla kontakter i området. Och det dagliga livet var anspråkslöst. Hon visade på en väldig vedtrave som skulle rädda henne genom vintern.

Kylans andedräkt

Morgnarna hade börjat bli isande, solen fick arbeta sig igenom kölddimman över kanalen. Ibland var det frost i gräset. Landskapet vilade. När en gröngöling slog upp sitt gälla skratt ekade det i den höga luften.

Vi väntade allt längre med frukostarna. Men när solskenet som först tänt trädtopparna på bergssidorna äntligen nådde ner här i floden Ouches trånga ravin steg temperaturen raskt, och till lunch kunde vi äta i sommarvärme på akterdäcket. Lika hastigt kom kylan när solen gick ner. Vi läste och lyssnade på radio i "Vanadis" salong i de långa kvällarna medan fotogenlyktan i akterns ena dävert sände en guldglimt i det svarta vattnet.

På dagarna följdes vi ofta av det vinande ljudet av en sågklinga, och stråk av vedbrand drog genom dalgången. Här i den skogiga delen av Bourgogne lägger man upp rejäla förråd inför den kalla årstiden. Det kan bli både snö och is på trehundra meters höjd.

– Åker ni skridskor på kanalen? frågade jag en slussvakt. Nej, det skulle han aldrig våga! Och förresten var det inte tillåtet. Men han hade cyklat på isen!

– Och vad ska ni göra sedan när kanalen stänger för året? fortsatte jag. Han gjorde en svepande gest mot kanalbanken. Kunde jag inte se att här fanns hur mycket som helst att ta itu med?

– Fälla några träd och sen semester. Som jag har slitit den här säsongen!

Vilse i Dijon

Filip den djärves gravlejon är inte att leka med.

En dag var det slut med grå byar och gröna betesmarker och tysta nätter vid kanalbanken. Vi nalkades Dijons moderna förorter, och sedan befann vi oss i en riktig stad med trafikljud, klockklang och röster.

Nu började en annan sorts tillvaro med museibesök och långa sittningar på serveringarna mitt emot hertigpalatset, *Palais des Ducs de Bourgogne,* dagar med hängande i bokhandlar och senapsbutiker, med strosande på gatorna där folk var i rörelse, inte minst de många studenterna som nu börjat sin termin, somliga efter sommarjobb i slussarna på Canal de Bourgogne och Canal du Nivernais. Kvällsvärmen hade återvänt. Det var inte svårt att trivas i Dijon.

Onda makter drev sitt spel.

Men i Dijon skulle vi också gå vilse.

Vi förstår fortfarande inte hur det kunde gå till. Visst kan man tappa riktningen en mörk kväll i det medeltida gatunätet, men innerstaden är inte stor, och det är inte särskilt långt mellan *le port de plaisance,* gästhamnen, och hertigpalatset.

Det var på tillbakavägen därifrån som kanalen bara försvann. Vi gick och gick och det blev allt närmare midnatt och fullkomligt folktomt, och varje gång vi trodde oss ha vittring på vattnet hamnade vi på någon sorts utfart med skyltar till motorvägar och avlägsna orter. Så mycket kunde bara inte rymmas mellan gamla stan och kanalen.

Det var som i ett datorspel. Framför oss skapades nya områden, först med mörka hyreshus, sedan med tysta villakvarter och till sist någon sorts ödslig halvslum där vi fann det säkrast att inte fråga de skuggor som gled förbi.

Hur länge skulle detta pågå?

Så anade vi långt borta en räddning: en nattöppen

kinesisk matleverantör. Vi övervägde att gå in och beställa något till gästhamnen och sedan springa efter cykelbudet, men de vänliga innehavarna kom oss till hjälp ändå och visade på en karta. Om vi tog oss fram till den stjärnformiga Place Wilson där vi först tappat bort oss och sedan gick rue Transvaal, så skulle allt ordna sig.

Två varv gick vi runt stjärnplatsen och kollade varenda gata som går ut från den. Ingen rue Transvaal. Denna stad tycktes förgjord.

I desperation överföll vi ett ensamt nattvandrande par, och när de hämtat sig erbjöd de sig att visa vägen. Med ens var förhäxningen bruten, ett trevligt samtal tog sin början, och när vi äntligen skymtade "Vanadis" frågade vi om de vill komma ombord på ett glas.

Det ville de gärna. Och nu råkade det hända sig att vi hade lagt in en flaska Castellane i kylen, inköpt vid ett besök hos champagnefirman och dess underjordiska källare i Épernay för flera månader sedan och avsedd att tömmas sista kvällen på årets resa.

Dess pärlor var himmelska i månglittret på akterdäck. Våra skyddsandar Joël och Corinne fick kanske en överdriven uppfattning av svenskars vardagskvällsvanor, men kall, torr skumpa är rätt när man vill fira att man sluppit ur lömska makters grepp.

Efter Dijon gällde det bara att slussa på, trettio gånger på de trettio raka kilometerna över slätten ner mot Saône. Och så låg den där, hamnbassängen i Saint-Jean-de Losne, med varv och kranar och pråmar. Ännu en vinter skulle "Vanadis" tillbringa hos Ets Joël Blanquart, och en gråblek höstdag låg hon upplyft och avrustad på land. Farväl, kära vän, och tack för denna sommars långa färd. När den började var ditt däck rosa av kanalernas kastanjeblom. Nu faller frukterna mot det med små smällar. Sov gott under din presenning.

Canal de la Robine

Mellan Medelhavet och Atlanten går Frankrikes populäraste kanal för fritidsbåtar, *Canal du Midi.* Här glider man fram under platanalléer med vinberg och åter vinberg bakom. I norr har man Montagnes noires, Svarta bergen, i söder kan man i siktigt väder se Pyrenéernas snöklädda massiv. De flesta som hyr båt brukar röra sig på sträckan mellan Béziers och borgstaden Carcassonne.

Vill man undvika trängsel och arroganta båtförare kan man ägna några dagar åt den något mindre frekventerade avstickaren *Canal de la Robine,* som genom en rad slussar tar en ner till Narbonne och fortsätter ut till den genuina fiskehamnen Port-la-Nouvelle. Den sista biten har man vid sidan en enorm grund insjö med klart blått Medelhavsvatten, skild från den grönaktiga kanalen endast av dragvägens smala bank. Men försök inte bada i azurböljorna. Man sjunker till knäna i ävja. Inte ens de flamingor vi såg stod i vattnet, de vilade på ytan.

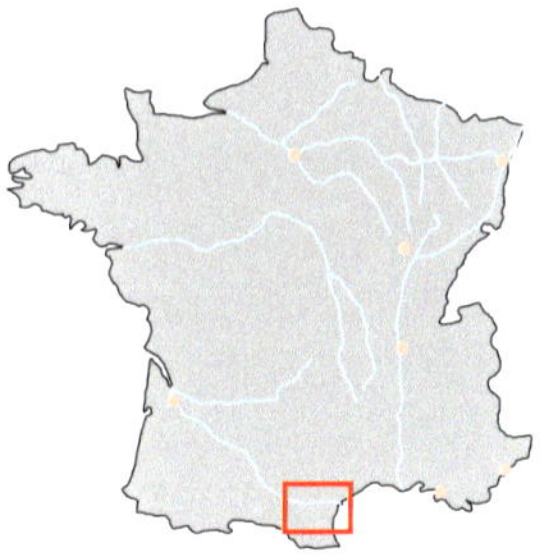

Nästan vid Medelhavet

Har ni inte tänkt på att gå på Canal du Midi? frågar oss folk för vilka en fransk kanal är just denna.

Nej, vi har inte tänkt ta ner "Vanadis" till denna vackra kanal från 1600-talet som under sommarmånaderna drabbas av trafikinfarkt med upp till femtio båtar framför varje sluss, alla grälande med varandra om vem som ska ha företräde, intill rena handgripligheter. Och fyrtio graders värme kan vara mer än nog.

Dessutom har vi redan gått olika sträckor av kanalen i hyrda båtar. Första gången var vid mitten av 1970-talet. Då var nöjesbåtstrafiken beskedlig och vattnet trafikerades ännu av vinpråmar med namn som "Bacchus" och "Dionysos", styrda av kraftfulla svartlockiga damer som också höll ett öga på tvätten som fladdrade på tvättstrecket, pelargonerna i sina krukor, kanariefågeln i sin bur och väl också på grytan på spisen – ofta blandades dieselröken med hetsande matångor där man urskilde lök och vitlök och provensalska örter. Mannen stod vid förtöjningstrossarna, redo att kasta dem i land till slussvakterna. När en sådan pråm skoningslöst kom forsande i en krök kastade sig fritidsbåtarna vettskrämda upp i strandgräset.

I dag finns ingen pråmtrafik och slussarna är automatiserade. Man kan inte längre köpa det languedocska vinet i begagnade tvåliters mineralvattensflaskor för två franc för att finna det odrickbart. Vinet som man inhandlar i vingårdarna har undergått en ofattbar kvalitetsförbättring.

Nej, vi tänkte inte skriva om Canal du Midi och

En smal vägbank skiljer Canal de la Robine från Medelhavsvattnet.

vägen till turistfällan Carcassonne med sina hårt restaurerade murar, om utsikten mot Pyrenéerna som reser sig snöhöljda i fjärran, om de grönskande vingårdarna som omgärdar kanalen. Men så frågade oss Lucie och Malcolm på den breda narrowboaten ”Body & Soul” om vi inte ville komma ner till dem i byn Capestang där de tillbringat vintern och gå med dem och deras små hundar en liten tur på kanalen.

Så en isande grå dag i slutet av mars stod vi på taket till ”Body & Soul” som tuffade fram under platanerna som just höll på att veckla ut sina brungröna löv. Pilträd och buskar visade sin första späda grönska, ginstens gula tussar lyste upp sluttningarna. Vinstockarna i tusental var just beskurna och vred sig knotiga och svarta mot den gula marken – som marterade själar, sa Lucie.

Vi vek av från Canal du Midi in på Canal de la Robine, söderut mot Narbonne och Medelhavet. Sluss för sluss sänkte vi oss ner, och när vi lämnade Narbonne var vi nere på ett slättområde. Solen kom fram,

Marterade själar – beskurna vinstockar i tusental.

värmen steg försiktigt. Vita hästar och svart, långhornad boskap betade längs kanalen. Och plötsligt kände vi nya dofter, av pinjer, av saltvatten, av tång. Om babord, på andra sidan den smala vägbanken, utbredde sig en väldig bläckblå vattenyta, l'Étang d'Ayrolles, en grund invik av Medelhavet. På styrbordssidan reste sig tät vegetation med kärr där det plaskades och tjippades och kuttrades – ett fågelreservat. Här gjorde vi fast för kvällen, fullkomligt ensamma. En liten blå snurrebåt gick ut på étangen för att vittja några nät. Strax slog det ner en flock med skära flamingor intill. Solen försvann i lila skyar som speglade sig i vattnet tills allt flöt samman. Pinjerna ritade svarta silhuetter.

Nästa morgon beslöt Skepparn och Malcolm sig för att ge sig på det elektriska systemet och försvann ner i motorregionen. Lucie och jag tog cyklarna och satte av mot kanalens slutpunkt, Port-la-Nouvelle. Vi fann en äkta fiskehamn med låga hus utmed kajen, båtar, båtar och högar av nät och dessutom den franska kustbevakningens stiliga vita jagare. Lucies kulinariska näsa ledde oss osvikligt till en affär där disken dignade av fisk och skaldjur, och vi trampade tillbaka med tre kilo blåmusslor i en påse med is.

Vi lyckönskade oss till att de som trängdes i slussarna där uppe på Canal du Midi inte kommit på tanken att ge sig hit ner. Hela eftermiddagen satt vi i sol och pinjedoft och skrapade musslor medan vitt vin gnistrade i glasen.

Om aftonen lyfte Lucie en ångande gryta med moules à la marinière av spisen. Hon hade inte sparat på lök, vitlök, persilja och vin. Den kokkonst hon en gång försörjt sig på i England har hon utvecklat till mästerskap i sitt andra hemland.

Så inföll åter en av dessa kvällar som vi upplevt redan i Saint-Jean-de-Losne med prat och lite jazz på Malcolms piano medan torra grenar sprakade i järnkaminen och de små korvarna till hundar, Ted och Spud, snörvlade och småfes i sömnen, utmattade av att skälla på allt som passerat.

En livsform

Det är förunderligt att man i månader kan leva på en så liten yta som den en segelbåt eller en mindre motorbåt erbjuder. Sommartid är man förstås ute så mycket det går, och man inser också att det mesta man har dragit på sig i sin bostad på land är rätt överflödigt. Men ändå är det ett stort steg att ta, det att bestämma sig för att leva ombord året runt. Vi har inte gjort det och tänker inte göra det, men ibland är det lockande.

Vi har mött en rad engelsmän och en del holländare som har installerat sig i mindre pråmar eller narrowboats eller vanliga motorbåtar, människor som har kastat loss från livet där hemma. Och varför sitta i en tråkig bostad i en tråkig förort med tråkiga grannar och tråkig mat i ett uselt klimat när man kan finna både äventyr om sommaren och trygg gemenskap i en hamn om vintern i en trivsam båt där livet är enkelt och ett glas vin räcker för umgänget grannar emellan?

Kanalbåten är ett flytande hem. Året runt.

”Här har jag allt som behövs för ett gott liv.”
Lucie Walker i pentryt på ”Body & Soul”.

– Här nere, säger engelska vinterliggare i Capestang på Canal du Midi, håller vi alla koll på varandra. Om vi vet att någon är ensam eller behöver hjälp så ställer alla upp – någon handlar eller lagar en bit mat, en annan ringer efter doktorn, den som kan det fixar el eller vad det nu kan vara. Hemma kan man ligga död tills man börjar lukta innan någon bryr sig.

Somliga går in för att lära sig franska och sjunger i den lokala kören eller deltar i de organiserade utflykterna. Det tas väl upp av fransmännen. Där britterna sköter hamnverksamheten innebär det också att det blir ordning på den, till glädje även för de få fransmän som har en båt till bostad.

Å andra sidan finns det nerflyttade engelsmän som ser Frankrike som ett nytt kolonialland. De håller sig till sin brittiska gemenskap och fransmännen ser med bekymran hur huspriserna drivs upp och med avsmak på hur engelska sällskap kan flamsa och föra liv på restaurangerna i stället för att andäktigt tillbedja den franska kokkonsten.

För en del är båtboendet en dröm som förverkligas efter många år av jobb och vardagsslit, ett nytt liv som överträffar alla förväntningar.

Lucie och Malcolm Walker har själva planerat sitt flytande hem, kanalbåten ”Body & Soul”. Från akterdäcket kommer man rakt in i köksavdelningen där Lucie skapar läckerheter vid en rejäl gasspis. På väggarna hänger kopparkastruller, köttyxor och vitlöksflätor.

På bilden är Lucie i färd med att skapa en anrättning som även en hopplös matlagare kan klara av. Så här går hon till väga:

Man skivar auberginer och courgetter (zucchini, squash), saltar lite på dem (helst med havssalt), låter dem ligga en stund, bestänker dem med olivolja och steker dem i en grillpanna. En stor gul lök skärs i skivor och får puttra i en kastrull med olivolja och – här kommer klon – en rejäl klick med snigelsmör som finns att köpa i franska kyldiskar. Från kastrullen uppstiger nu en kittlande doft av vitlök och persilja. När löken är lagom glasig tillsätter man mosade tomater – färska eller på burk – lite salt, olika pepparsorter, en timjankvist.

Auberginer och courgetter varvas sedan med lökmojet och drivor av riven emmenthaler i något ugnsfast. Ett tunt lager ost på toppen och lite ströbröd. Alltsammans får puttra i ugnen en stund. Har man som vi på "Vanadis" ingen ugn går det bra med en stor panna.

Bakom ryggen på vår matlagerska tar salongen vid med järnkamin och sittgrupp och Malcolms elpiano. På andra sidan väggen följer badrum och sovrum med egen altan – det vill säga fördäcket.

Under vinterhalvåret ligger de still på någon trevlig plats med andra båtgrannar, när våren kommer kastar de loss.

För andra är båtlivet ett hugskott. Den dag de ändrar sig kan det också visa sig vara ett dyrt sådant. Båtpriserna följer nämligen inte på långt när fastigheternas värdestegring, och de som har sålt sin bostad för att investera i en båt kommer möta en smärtsam överraskning om de ångrar sig. Eller en av dem ångrar sig.

Vi mötte en gång ett äldre holländskt par som kapat alla band för att ge sig ner till Medelhavet och sedan över till Svarta havet i en liten ombyggd pråm. Han var full av entusiasm och visade stolt alla hemgjorda installationer med vatten och värme och köksskåp. Tyska behärskade han och en del franska. Hon däremot talade bara nederländska och bjöd skyggt på kaffe sedan hon lagt sin stickning åt sidan. En minut räckte för att man skulle förstå att hon egentligen ville sitta hemma i ett hus med trådgardiner och trädgård och umgås med barn och barnbarn och grannfruar med samma permanentade frisyr som hon själv. Vintern skulle de tillbringa i Marseille, där hon inte skulle kunna tala med någon. Och sedan skulle de ut på havet i en båt utan köl. "Åk tillbaka", skulle man vilja säga till henne, "utsätt dig inte för detta!" Men vad hade hon att återvända till?

För oss är det långa sommarhalvåret rätt lagom. Vi lever på akterdäck där man kan skrapa potatis eller laga en cykelslang. Regnar det läser vi eller lyssnar på radio i den blå soffan med fotogenlampan på bordet eller arbetar vid datorn på matbordet i dinetten. Vänner kommer och far. "Vanadis" är ett hem, och dock rör hon sig.

Akterdäcket är styrplats, solterrass, matplats, läshörna, tvättstuga och cykelverkstad, allt efter behov.

Floden Doubs gör en slinga genom Besançon och stryker förbi den ståtliga Vauban-kajen, som bär namn efter sin arkitekt.

Canal du Rhône au Rhin, Canal de la Marne au Rhin, Mosel

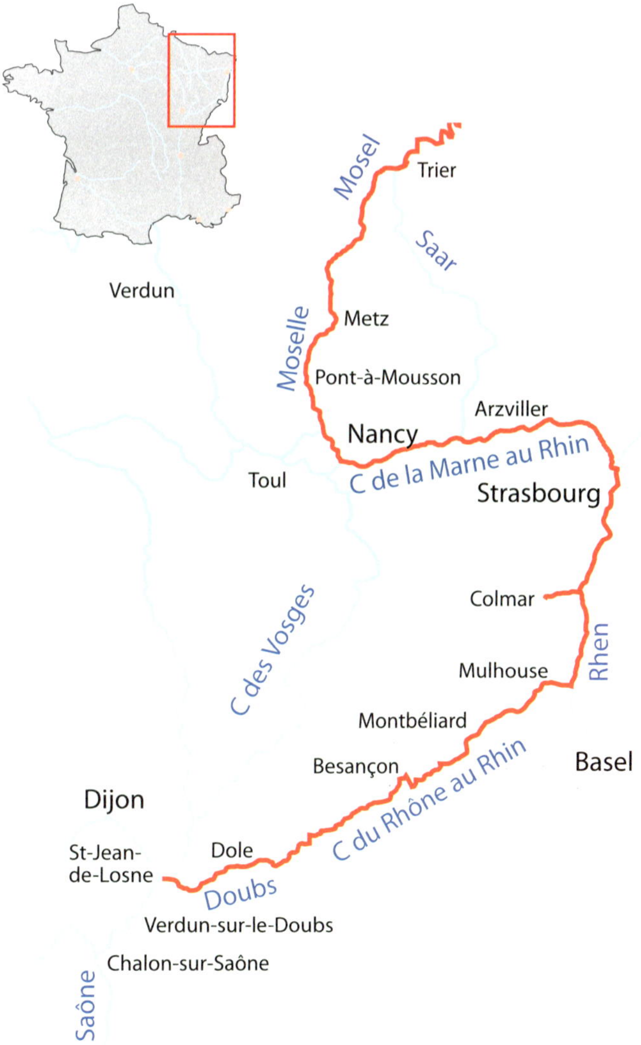

Canal du Rhône au Rhin börjar inte alls på Rhône utan bra mycket längre norrut, på Saône, som den förbinder med Rhen. Genom Juras skogklädda höjder färdas man mestadels på den vindlande floden *Doubs* i ett landskap som är ömsom storslaget, ömsom behagligt. Från bergsängarna hör man pinglorna på de ljusbruna korna som ger mjölken till den härliga comtéosten. Trevliga städer är Dole, Besançon, Montbéliard och Mulhouse. När man hunnit så långt har landskapet öppnat sig och man har på babordssidan Vogeserna som blånar i fjärran och som kommer att följa en länge.

Man slussar ut på den breda kanaliserade *Rhen* som drar i väg med flera knops ström. Vill man trotsa den kan man gå upp till Basel halvannan mil söderut. Stora slussar och stora pråmar. Vi gick medströms och norrut och besökte genom ett par smala avstickare korsvirkesstäderna Colmar och Strasbourg.

Efter Strasbourg följer den pråmfria och storkrika *Canal de la Marne au Rhin,* genom Alsace. Så småningom blir dalgången trång och skogig men vidgar sig när man kommer in i Lorraine.

Efter Nancy svängde vi in på *Moselle* som fortsätter norrut, från Metz och Thionville genom ett flackt landskap med industrier och kärnkraftverk och trafik med stora pråmar, sedan in i det städade Luxemburg och vidare upp till Trier i Tyskland, där floden byter namn till *Mosel* och blir rasande vacker.

Doux Doubs – mer vild än tam

Do, dooo, do dooo, raj raaj raj raaj raj raaaa ... Melodin hade slagit sig ner och förföljt mig alltsedan vi passerat en båt med *"Doux Doubs"*, "Ljuva Doubs", på namnbrädan. Det anspelade väl också på ordet *doudou*, som betyder 'älskling', 'gullunge' – om det nu var båten eller floden som avsågs.

Vi hade lämnat Saint-Jean-de-Losne, gått ett stycke uppför Saône och slussat in på Canal du Rhône au Rhin som drar i väg åt nordost genom Juras skogklädda höjder och mest består av floden Doubs (som alltså uttalas "do:"). Vacker är den så att man kan utbrista i sång, men inte alltid så *doux*, i alla fall inte när vi färdades på den.

Vi hade blivit varnade för vattenbrist, och april hade verkligen varit oroväckande med en torka som fått marken att krackelera i stora sprickor och sänkt vattenmagasinen till augustinivå.

Men i juni kom regnet, och det skulle den sommaren aldrig vara långt borta. Från Juras berg strömmade bäckar och vattendrag och gjorde Doubs livlig och strid. Varje gång kanalen efter en sluss leder ut på floden går man intill en *barrage*, en bred fördämning där vattnet forsar utför i skum och glitter medan man i strömvirvlarna försöker stryka så tätt intill stranden eller kajen som möjligt.

Vi låg med några andra nöjesbåtar vid tilläggsplat-

Vid fördämningarna håller man sig åt sidan så långt det bara går.

Det stod öppet mellan jord och himmel, naturen höll andan.

sen i Ranchot när en VNF-are dök upp och meddelade att kanalen måste stängas av minst något dygn för att inte svämma över. Vi hade att välja mellan att ligga kvar eller att gå ut på floden.

Den enda attraktionen i byn var två sommarstängda bagerier. Vi valde floden. De andra båtfararna skakade på huvudet. När VNF-aren vevat igen stämportarna bakom oss fanns ingen återvändo.

Vi gled ut på det gröna vattnet. Floden vidgade sig, solen bröt igenom, värmen blev ljuvlig. På babordssidan hade vi en mörkgrön bergssida, på styrbordssidan silvriga buskage och där bortom ljusa betesmarker.

– Här, sa Skepparn, är en utmärkt plats att prova ankarspelet.

En god del av våren på Blanquarts varv hade ägnats åt konstruktionen av ett fäste för ett elektriskt ankarspel. Alla omkring oss hade varit förvånade. Ankare på fritidsbåtarna här nere är en prydnad, ingen drömmer om att verkligen använda det och allra minst om att ligga på svaj.

Kättingen rasslade ut och vi fick fäste direkt. ”Vanadis” lade sig som fastgjuten i strömmen. Svarthättan kvintilerade i strandsnåren, barragen bakom oss brusade. Vi tog ett dopp och höll oss fast i en lina med knutar medan strömmen sög runt benen. Vi slog upp en flaska vitt vin. Sedan gjorde vi ingenting. Vi var fullkomligt ensamma så när som på svarthättan.

Eftermiddagen övergick i rosa skymning. Vi låg kvar.

Mitt i natten vaknade jag och kände att vi var iakttagna. Jag tassade upp och stod öga mot öga med en fullmåne som fick allt att glittra, vatten, löv, ankarkätting. Det stod öppet mellan jord och himmel, naturen höll andan i väntan på att mångudinnan skulle hitta sin sovande Endymion i en ångande myrtenlund. Strömmen hade stillat sig, barragen sorlade lågt. Ur buskarna kluckade och flöjtade näktergalarna. Grodorna knorrade kärlekskrankt från näckrosbladen intill land.

Vi slog oss båda tysta ner på däck och blev sittande i den stagnelianska natten.

Till Pasteur!

”Till Pasteur!” lyder maningen till de hyenebitna festdeltagarna i slutet på Falstaff fakirs roman ”Arvingen till Djävulsgrottan”, och under samma fältrop intog vi Dole, efter en lätt kaotisk tilläggning i gästhamnens strömvirvlar. Doubs hade en av sina oregerliga dagar.

Lilla Dole är Louis Pasteurs födelsestad, och i huset med det garveri som tillhörde hans familj har inrättats ett museum där man kan beskåda både dopmössa och laboratorieutrustning och se upplysande videor om det världsomspännande Pasteurinstitutet samt en spelfilm om vetenskapsmannens liv, naturligtvis med den dramatiska episod där han genom vågstycket att prova sitt nya vaccin räddar livet på en vallpojke som bitits av en rabiessmittad hund.

Det stora Pasteurmuseet ligger i Paris, men söker man en anledning att lägga till i Dole, utöver den att strosa upp och ner i de branta gatorna bland gladlynta studenter eller utmed de blomsterprydda kanalerna som en gång försörjt garverierna med vatten, eller att äta på någon av de bättre restaurangerna vid de små vattenfallen, eller att bara ligga insvept i lindblomsdoft vid stadens fot, beskyddad av den höga katedralen ovan de röda hustaken – ja, då är ett besök i Pasteurhuset skäl nog. Om inte annat så för att man får en aning om det svindlande forskningsarbete som ligger bakom det vanliga ordet *pastöriserad,* som man varje dag möter på mjölkförpackningarna.

Aldrig är man så nära det ordets ursprung som när man inhandlar en liter mjölk i Dole.

Louis Pasteur, mikrobiologins fader, är Doles store son.

Guldvinet från Jura

Båtshaken ska enligt den gamla kanalräven Roger Pilkington användas bara för att fiska upp damers ifallna handväskor. Vispar man runt med den i en sluss har man snart kört stången genom en ruta.

Eftersom handväska är obrukligt ombord har vi sällan användning för vår vackra båtshake. Med sin kromade krok och sitt fernissade skaft ligger den mest som en prydnad i sin hållare.

Men när man kommer till ett körsbärsträd intill ett övergivet slusshus är den en välsignelse. De nedersta grenarna är alltid avplockade, men med båtshaken kan man dra högre kvistar till sig och få sig en bunke med mogna bär. Den fullsatta kronan tar starar och björktrastar hand om. En rimlig fördelning av naturens håvor.

Att hitta en lämplig dryck till bären är inget problem i detta land, men härligast har nog varit det *vin jaune* som de ombordkomna Väninnorna, Unn och Birgitta, och jag inhandlade i en supermarché. Vi kom släntrande genom den enorma vinavdelningen när en man med milda mörka ögon och långt grått hår vid en monter fångade in oss och allvarligt frågade om vi kände till vinet i fråga.

Jo, vi hade läst om denna specialitet. Vad var det som egentligen var så märkvärdigt med det?

Nu var vi fast. Ah, det var *très compliqué!* Denna vackra halmgula dryck, Juras guld, görs på druvor som växt på kritgrund i solsken för att sedan lagras på fat i hela sex år och tre månader. Under denna tid får den vätska som avdunstat inte ersättas, och över ytan bildas en tunn hinna av jästsvampar under vilken vinet får utveckla sin karaktär, som har en dragning åt sherry. Och, mina damer, ni kan spara flaskan i två hundra år!

Detta är mitt mycket förenklade sammandrag av den införing vi fick i guldvinets tillverkningshistoria. I mången fransman bor en pedagog och retoriker. Här var en av dem, och vi var dagens kap – tre utländskor till vilka man fick lov att tala väl och tydligt och som lyssnade tacksamt och länge, fångna av de milda ögonen och den utsökta artikulationen, allt medan andra matköpare stressade förbi. Vi å vår sida kände oss utvalda och invigda när vi avtågade med den dyra och sällsamma buteljen.

Vauban – en krigisk fredsbyggare

Den store Vauban, alltid med en plan.

Ständigt denne Vauban. Var man än befinner sig i Frankrike stöter man på någon av hans mer än tre hundra försvarsanläggningar. Det är fästningsmurar och bastioner i stjärnform och torn och täckta gångar och vallgravar och kasematter och magnifika portar. Ludvig XIV befann sig mestadels i krig med sina europeiska grannar, i första hand Spanien, och Vauban var hans idoge fortifikationsmästare, oavbrutet på resa för att anlägga nya befästningar eller modernisera redan befintliga, när han nu inte deltog i fält.

I motsats till sina föregångare, som byggde efter rätt rigida mönster, anpassade Vauban sina anläggningar efter terrängen. Med det arkitektoniska ideal som rådde under 1600-talet gjorde han dem också vackra. ”Det stora seklet” i Frankrike skulle bli stilbildande för byggnadskonst i hela den civiliserade världen, och till de förebilder som spreds hörde också Vaubans konstruktioner.

Sina största framgångar vann Vauban emellertid genom den metod han utarbetade för belägring och erövring av till synes ointagliga värn – med teknik i stället för med dåligt förberedda och utdragna stormningar. Att spara liv ansåg han väsentligt, och han motsatte sig också att man härjade det besegrade Bryssel i Frankrikes krig mot Spanien-Nederländerna. Han gav sig till och med i kast med att utarbeta ett europeiskt fredsprojekt. Alltigenom rationell till sin läggning bekymrade han sig för folkets sundhet och landets välstånd, och orädd och frispråkig föreslog han sin kung ett enhetligt skattesystem som inte gynnade adeln. (Det togs inte väl upp.) Han var på många områden en stor man.

Det är därför med all rätt han står staty uppe på det enorma citadellet som dominerar staden Besançon. Man kunde tycka att det redan före hans förstärkningar måste ha varit omöjligt att inta. När man på Doubs nalkas den över hundra meter höga borgklippan som skjuter ut i floden får man lägga huvudet bakåt för att se ända upp. Men Vauban lyckades 1674 rycka fortet ur spanjorernas händer och satte sedan sin egen prägel på det.

Fredligare är de långa raderna av hus med arkader utmed Quai Vauban, där floden gör en slinga innan

Citadellet i Besançon håller uppsikt över alla som nalkas på Doubs.

man förs in i den skyddade lilla gästhamnen. Själva Besançon är en stad med behagliga mått. Husen är byggda i en gulochblåflammig kalksten från trakten, här och där stöter man på romarlämningar, konstmuseet är välfyllt och staden har därtill ett speciellt museum för tidmätande apparater – Besançon var känt för sina urmakerier. Men framför allt är Besançon en studentstad, med all den livlighet och trevnad som hör en sådan till. När vi gled fram under de stilfulla husräckorna såg vi en flock duvor som samlats runt ett enda av alla de hundratals fönstren. De lyssnade med huvudet på sned till musik som strömmade ut ur det, piano och stråkar. Här ligger stadens musikkonservatorium.

Midsommarångest

Regn, regn, regn. Väninnorna hade rest hem efter att ha berövat det gula vinet möjligheten att bli tvåhundraårigt. Vi hade fortsatt, passerat fabriksbyggnader, industrikajer och ett skrotupplag när vi hejdades av en liten blå lyftbro. Den skulle snart vara öppnad, förklarade de sommarjobbande ungdomarna i hytten, men efter att ha tryckt på alla knappar utan minsta rörelse i bron gav de upp. VNF tillkallades, och vi såg genom den strimmiga rutan hur bromekaniken undersöktes, axlar rycktes på, händer slogs ut, kepsar lyftes av och hår krafsades i.

Inget att göra, man måste skicka efter en speciell liten man. Mekaniken var dränkt, inte underifrån av den överfyllda kanalen, utan uppifrån. Maken till

Regnet blev ett själstillstånd.

regn hade man då aldrig sett. Den lille mannen skulle komma nästa dag, på eftermiddagen.

Schweizaren i båten bakom oss var nära att bryta ihop. Han hade sin hemmahamn några slussar bort, och där stod bilen med vilken han skulle resa hem till ett Viktigt Arbete nästa dag. Men det gick ju inte att lämna båten mitt i kanalen.

Själva kunde vi ligga inregnade här lika väl som någon annanstans.

Det var bara det att det var midsommarafton.

Midsommaren är den grymmaste helgen. Ingen annan högtid skapar sådan ångest. Det är vemodigt att året vänder när sommaren just har börjat. Men värre är alla föreställningar om midsommarfirandets fröjder. Jag har sällan upplevt dessa, men jag har alltid vetat att runt om i Sverige utom just där jag befinner mig dansas det på bryggor och lövade logar till dragspel och fiol, där trallar det muntra lantfolket, där svärmar ungdomar i den ljusa natten och lägger blommor under kudden för att drömma ljuvt, där skrattar barn med krans i håret och hoppar säck, där samlas vänner i glatt lag och intar sill och nubbe tills den rosa gryningen ger återglans i fönsterrutorna.

Själva har vi ofta suttit ensamma på någon kobbe i skärgården eller betraktat krånglande ungar som inte vill dansa "Små grodorna" på någon avslagen festplats där vi inte hört till. På kvällen har vi lagt oss på svaj – man vill ju inte att någon fylltratt ska kräkas på ens däck eller rent av tumla ner på det.

Här på kanalen borde vi vara befriade, inregnade framför en bro i ett land där sommarnatten är mörk och ingen har en aning om vad det är för en dag. Men midsommarafton avskaffar ens svenska själ inte så lätt. Jag dukade i dinettens dunkel med en holländsk konservburk med en fadd sill i någon sorts gräddsås och slog upp ett par snapsglas med Gammal Norrlands och lade på Orsa spelmän.

Det gjorde ont. Sånt ska göra ont.

Och regnet föll. Utanför på kajen rörde sig något gult fram och tillbaka. Det var schweizaren i regnställ som vankade som en äggsjuk höna med mobilen tätt tryckt intill örat.

Nästa dag sveptes regnmolnen undan av en frisk vind, och med den kom den lille mannen. Nu förstod vi varför det var just en liten man som eftersöktes. Han klämde in sig i springan mellan bro och mekanik, grep en handvev, och vips var bron öppnad.

Den krånglande blå bron lät sig till sist öppnas av en liten man – med en större gick det inte.

Mekaniska Mulhouse

Om man vill se hundra ljusblå Bugatti ska man stanna i Mulhouse.

Det ville vi, men vi cyklade fel. En trettonårig yngling på en bmx undsatte oss med ett artigt "Jag har all tid i världen, följ mig!".

Barn har andra kartor än vuxna. Vi körde mot enkelriktat, vi sicksackade på trottoarerna mellan träd, lyktstolpar, hundlortar och förskräckta flanörer för att slippa åka på gatan med dess spårvagnsspår, vi hängde på när han släppte styret i mitten på en bred aveny och vi stannade utmattade när han stolt sladdade in på planen framför bilmuseet.

Naturligtvis bjöd vi med honom in. Men hans cykel saknade lås, så han propsade på att få ställa den i entrén. Det var nu inte tillåtet, den måste stå utanför, men den vackra damen i kassan som insåg vad besöket betydde för skolpojken som stolt visade upp ett par infångade utlänningar lovade att gallskrika om hon såg att någon så mycket som petade på den.

I denna stad, en gång rik på textilfabriker, fanns en stormrik spinneriägare vid namn Fritz Schlumpf. Han kom att bli fullständigt besatt av Bugatti och började samla olika modeller, allt från racerbilar till den typ man brukar se i gangsterfilmer. Samlarvurmen blev en riktig sjuka, och Schlumpf satsade besinningslöst på sina bilar medan det gick utför med hans fabriker. Arbetarna blev förståeligt nog ursinniga när de upptäckte att han i hemlighet använt både pengar och stora lokaler för sina samlingar allt medan de själva gick mot arbetslöshet, och på övligt franskt vis stack de några av bilarna i brand.

Schlumpf rymde landet, staten beslagtog samlingen och gjorde den till nationell egendom. I dag hyser museet över fyra hundra bilar. Inför avdelningen med lyxlimousiner tappar man andan – en crèmefärgad Isotta Fraschini från 30-talet, Charlie Chaplins Rolls-Royce "Silver Ghost" ... Så sköna linjer, så många omsorgsfullt handgjorda delar, så många utsökta detaljer. Det är ingen konst att göra av med en dag där inne, och man blir svårt sugen på att själv få äga åtminstone en enda liten blå Bugatti.

När man sett sig mätt på bilar kan man övergå till tåg. Mulhouses järnvägsmuseum visar uppbyggda miljöer med tåg och åter tåg och puttriga scener från franskt järnvägsliv och olyckor med välta väsande lok. Här finns kejserliga kupéer, de Gaulles presidentvagn och massvis med lokomotiv, från näpna små ångmaskiner till enorma kraftpaket med mycket polerad mässing och blänkande vevaxlar. Man får även se filmsnuttar med Jean Gabin som lokförare i "La bête humaine" och man får se en video med rekordförsöket för TGV, *train à grande vitesse,* 575 kilometer i timmen. Man behöver ingalunda vara tågnörd för att bilda och roa sig här.

Karusellprinsessan

Mest intagande bland alla självgående tingestar i Mulhouse är emellertid karusellen på stora torget. Sådana *manège chevaux de bois,* karuseller med trähästar, är vanliga i Frankrike. Den här från 1900 blankt är ovanligt vacker med landskapsmotiv – vinodlingar, kritklippor, hamnar. Allt är original utom flygplanet ”Le petit Prince” och motorcykeln från 30-talet, barnens favorit.

Karusellen är ett familjeföretag. Unga Sylvie Dureff kör den under sommarhalvåret. Under vintern reparerar pappa den och mamma bättrar på målningen. Inkomsten av verksamheten – tja, *comme çi comme ça* – vi kunde ju själva se att det ofta bara var ett par barn per tur i det halvdana vädret. Och stadens välvilja är också en förutsättning; tillstånd för att ställa upp karusellen måste sökas varje år. Men snart blev det skollov, och då brukade ruljangsen komma i gång!

Sylvie Dureff framför familjens hundraåriga karusell – en av de många som ännu snurrar i Frankrike.

I korsvirkesland

Slusshusen utmed Canal du Rhône au Rhin är alla av samma modell, små präktiga traditionella villor. Men det sista på sträckan är annorlunda. Det är en fräck, rundad grå betongbyggnad, ritad av Le Corbusier. När vi passerat den fördes vi ut på den strömmande Rhen. Vatten och himmel vidgades, det kändes långt mellan stränderna. På denna mäktiga åder dunkar stora pråmar fram mot Antwerpen och Rotterdam och Berlin, och slussarna är enorma containrar, nästan tvåhundra meter långa.

Men slussningarna i dessa jätteanordningar går lugnt till. Man lägger fast vid pollare som följer med när båten stilla sjunker de fjorton meterna ner.

Vi föredrar ändå det mindre formatet och vek därför efter några mil av och slussade in på den trånga stump som leder upp till Colmar.

Colmar är så korsvirkespittoreskt att man skulle kunna bli övermätt, som av schwarzwaldtårta. Och genom stadskärnan går till råga på allt små kanaler. Kvarteren kallas förstås Lilla Venedig. Det finns restauranger överallt där man kan få sitt lystmäte på surkål och korv, riesling och gewürztraminer. Och vilken annan stad har storkar som är gumpbelysta om natten? De växlar värdigt ben där de står i strålkastar-

Colmar – korsvirke och kanaler.

skenet i sitt stora bo på katedralens tak, obekymrade om de sträckta nackarna på torget nedanför.

Men skulle trivseln bli kvävande är det bara att stiga in på museet d'Unterlinden och uppsöka Isenheimaltaret, Matthias Grünewalds korsfästelse-skildring från 1500-talets början, men medeltida till sin karaktär. Jesu lekamen är grönaktig och bestänkt med svartnande blodsdroppar från torterarnas gissel, de öppna läpparna är lila, de genomstungna händerna vrider sig uppåt i plåga. Se smärtornas man! Här finns ingen skönhet, ingen stilla värdighet. Det är en ohygglig död som visas.

Från Colmar är det inte långt till de kända alsassiska vinorterna. Vi tog en cykeltur till Turckheim och fann en näpen by med stadsport och torg och bortom den sluttningar med vin. Innan vi skulle börja vår rundvandring till vinhusen stärkte vi oss med en *tarte brulée* eller *Flammkuchen,* som det också heter i denna tvåspråkiga del av landet, en tunn bakad degplatta med lök och skinkstrimlor som fick oss att aldrig mer vilja se åt någon kläggig pizza.

När det sedan var dags för vininköp hade alla vinhandlare lunchstängt. Men det lokala lilla snabbköpet var öppet, och där köpte vi med kassörskans hjälp så många flaskor Turckheimvin som rymdes i cykelväskorna. Vi erkände inför varandra att vi tyckte att det var skönt att slippa stå och smacka och se sakförståndiga ut och skämmas för att vi inte köpte det dyraste. Och kassörskans omdöme var gott, skulle det visa sig.

Gästhamnen i Colmar är dyr och perfekt välskött. Hamnkaptensparet har lagt ner sin själ på anläggningen. Här finns till och med sopsortering, och vi slet lydigt upp vår ynkliga slaskpåse och delade upp innehållet: en tombutelj hit, två ölburkar dit, en plastförpackning här, en tidning där.

– För vår planet, sa Madame.

Vi är vana vid sopsortering hemifrån. Vi tycker det är bra. Samtidigt hade vi sett tågen och lastbilarna som oavbrutet gick med nytillverkade Peugeotbilar längs vår väg i trakterna av Mulhouse där fabriken ligger, och Skepparn antydde något om proportionerna.

– Man måste börja någonstans, sa Madame, med viss skärpa.

Vem kan säga emot? Och det är sannerligen inte så ofta vi stött på sopsortering.

Slusshuset i Kembs-Niffer. "Ett hus är en bomaskin." Le Corbusier blev förvånad när en ingenjör vid de franska vattenvägarnas kontor i Strasbourg år 1960 ringde upp honom och beställde ett slusshus.

Här en källa rinner

Förr gick det en mindre kanal mellan Colmar och Strasbourg, men den är igenslammad i sin södra del och lär så förbli. För att ta sig mellan städerna måste man åter ut på Rhen som går bred och mäktig med Frankrike till vänster och Tyskland till höger.

På ön med det romantiska namnet Vogelgrün gick vi in i gästhamnen och tankade. Hamnkapten talade ömsom tyska, ömsom franska. Var han tysk eller fransman?

Han var alsassare.

Europa må ha fasta nationsgränser. Men områden som sedan medeltiden genom krig och fredsfördrag hört än hit, än dit är ofta tvåspråkiga och utan stark nationalkänsla. I Alsace är man alsassare. Och även om dagens unga i huvudsak är franskspråkiga lever ännu det tredje språket, den alsassiska dialekten.

Rhen är inte rolig i regn. Gråa vidder, jättelika slussar i betong, framforsande pråmar som man måste upptäcka i tid bakom de vispande vindrutetorkarna. Vid slussen i Rhinau kunde vi åter ta oss in på den mindre kanalen, så smal att trädgrenarna hängde ut över däcket. Och mitt i denna vegetation upphörde regnet med ens, solen bröt fram och lyste genom vattnet som var alldeles klart. Det gröna kanalvattnet döljer annars barmhärtigt vad som är därunder, så när vi nu överraskades av att se botten komma mot oss stannade hjärtat nästan. Men det var djupt nog. Där ljusreflexerna dansade över sanden hade vi nästan två meter under kölen. Här måste en källåder gå fram.

Vi slog av motorn och lät ”Vanadis” försiktigt kila fast sig i strandsnåren. Några nyfikna karpar kom fram och nosade på båten, en gädda stod och lurade mellan stenarna. Vi gled ner i det svala vattnet. Skepparn tog ett varv och kollade roder och propeller. En kungsfiskare pilade som en turkos sidenlapp över vattnet och försvann in i ett hål i strandbrinken.

En timme fick vi i detta undantagstillstånd. Sedan hade vi regnet över oss igen.

Tvättstugor

Varhelst ett vattendrag går fram i Frankrike, det må vara en flod, en kanal, en stilla å, en strömmande bäck, hittar man förr eller senare en *lavoir,* ett tvätthus – en vacker långsträckt byggnad där vattnet leds igenom en stor stenbassäng och ut igen.

I dag står lavoirerna som minnesmärken över en svunnen kvinnokultur. Somliga knäar med instörtade tak och golvet täckt av fjolårslöv, andra har rustats upp och prytts med blommor i hängkrukor. Men inga röster hörs och inga klappträn dunkar. En gång var tvättandet omgivet av ritualer och även hierarkier. Burgnare hushåll överlät sitt begagnade tvättvatten med lut och pottaska och andra kraftfulla ingredienser till sämre bemedlade. Tvätterskan hade en viktig roll i bygemenskapen. Och kvinnokulturen hölls i gång genom mötena i tvätthuset, där det bykta linnet sköljdes. Där pratade man och skvallrade och utbytte erfarenheter.

”Skaffa tvättmaskin ombord”, råder mig ibland båtfarare vi möter. ”Du slipper småtvätta och du slipper vänta på att komma åt en maskin i en gästhamn.”

Nu är det inte bara bristen på plats ombord som får oss att avstå. Just väntan på att komma åt de sällsynta gästhamnsmaskinerna har lett till åtskilliga trevliga samtal och till och med bestående vänskap. Man visar varandra hur apparaterna fungerar, man beskärmar sig över krånglet med dem, man plockar ur föregångarens tvätt, vilket är en hastigt påkommen intimitet som måste hanteras med taktfullhet, man växlar mynt åt varandra, man lånar ut tvättmedel. Vi är alla i samma båt när vi är i tvättstugan, och det kan leda till att vi hamnar i samma båt när vi lämnar den. Ett glas vin går över i gemensam middag, överenskommelser om

Lavoiren är i dag ett byggnadsminne. En gång var den samlingsplats och informationscentral för byns kvinnor.

framtida möten, mejlkontakt ...

Ett sådant tvättmöte har följts av glada kvällar med det holländsk-amerikanska paret Carla och Johan på ”Aqua-Belle”, i Paris och på Oise. Tvättstugan i champagnestaden Épernay ledde till fortsatt färd med Carien och Hans och vovven Taka på bogseraren ”Arend”; senare skulle vi flera gånger övernatta hos dem i Groningen när vi letade efter vår nya ”Vanadis”, och vi skulle ses igen på kanalerna.

Så jag fortsätter att småtvätta, och ”Vanadis” ser med fladdrande plagg på linor mellan dävertar och reling ut som på den gamla pråmtiden. När det sedan blir dags för storbyk kan jag se fram mot ett möte med ännu okända systrar. Kanske blir det bara artighetsprat, kanske blir det något mer. Lavoiren lever, den har bara bytt gestalt.

EU-byggnaden i Strasbourg står mestadels tom. Men varje månad ska 5 000 tjänstemän och 20 ton dokument fraktas hit från Bryssel och tillbaka.

Järnnäven i Strasbourg

Strasbourg trodde vi skulle vara en alldeles för stor stad för att vara trivsam. Vi väntade oss väldiga EU-byggnader, som i Bryssel, och vi såg dem också från kanalen med karavaner av lastbilar utanför. Tjänstemännen ska ju tillbringa fyra dagar varje månad där och alla papper fraktas mellan de två städerna – ett system som är absurt i fråga om tid, kostnad och effektivitet, men tydligen nödvändigt för Frankrikes gloire. Varför inte göra EU-kvarteren i Bryssel till en självständig, icke-belgisk enklav i stället?

Men Strasbourgs innerstad, på gångavstånd från den rara gästhamnen, har en alsassisk stads mänskliga mått och därtill korsvirkeshus, kanaler och broar och så förstås den berömda katedralen. Svältfödda på levande musik efter många dagar i Juras waldeinsamkeit gick vi dit på en orgelkonsert. Själva det väldiga instrumentet hänger som ett grant svalbo utanpå långskeppets innervägg. När kvällens artist Aude Heurtematte gick lös på verket så att valv och pelare tycktes skälva i dånet och bruset var vi ett ögonblick rädda att det skulle lossna och falla ner. Sedan blev vi förvånade när vi fick se organisten på en uppsatt monitor: att en så liten person kunde få så mycket ljud ur pipor och rör. Utanför sjönk solen och fick luften i kyrkorummet att vibrera i blått och rött från glasmålningarna. En stund dallrade hjärtat i toner och basgångar och färger, och världen försvann. Men det märkvärdiga astronomiska uret som kan allt, visa tider, måne, zodiak, paraderande riddare och helgon, hade stått tyst länge nog i sitt mörka hörn. Nu föll det obevekligt in mitt i Buxtehude med plink och plonk och skrammel.

När vi kom ut i kvällsdunklet och blandade oss med turisterna som samlats för att beskåda ett ljusspel på katedralens fasad fick vi se vår organist med ett litet sällskap bana sig väg genom massan. Vi störtade fram för att uttrycka vår förtjusning över den upplevelse hon skänkt oss.

– Ni såg mig? skrattade hon och slöt min hand i sin organistnäve.

Gud bevare mig för att vara klaviatur!

– Det gläder mig att ni uppskattade konserten, fortsatte hon. Men nu ska jag gå och få mig något att dricka!

– Det har ni förtjänat, sa jag och skakade ut mina fingrar.

Orgeln i Strasbourgs katedral, som ett svalbo mellan valven.

Metarlasten

”Om det finns ett franskt nationallyte så är det metarlasten, åt vilken alla kön, åldrar och samhällsklasser verkar hopplöst hemfallna”, skriver Alf Henrikson i sin reseskildring ”Familjebåten”. ”En tidsstudieman skulle bli vansinnig inför de siffror han skulle komma fram till om han försökte räkna ut vad ett kilo snorgärs kunde kosta franska folket i förlorad arbetstid.”

Metarna finns överallt utmed flodstränder och kanalbankar. Somliga mediterar vid ett enkelt spö. Andra riggar upp en hel rad i ställningar och håller sig med mycket kringutrustning som håvar och sumpar och specialburkar för bete och sinnrika stolar att sitta på. Det metas i alla väder. I ösregn ser man bara spöna som sticker ut under väldiga paraplyer.

För det mesta samsas båtfarare och metare. Man drar ner farten för att inte åstadkomma skvalp, och är det trångt lyfter de på stranden upp sina spön en smula. Det vinkas och les. Men somliga typer är förhärdade och gör anspråk på att kanalerna skulle ha anlagts för deras skull och inte för båttrafikens, och de rubbar inte spöna en millimeter, inte ens om dessa sträcker sig över mittfåran. Vi har vid det här laget också förhärdat oss och väjer inte och rycker franskt på axlarna åt invektiven som följer när reven slits av. *Tant pis!* Skyll er själva.

När man däremot cyklar eller promenerar mellan slussarna är mötena konfliktfria och angenäma, man hälsar som god sed är.

– Får ni något?

– Inte i dag, Madame, *ils ne sont pas voraces.*

Voraces, rovlystna! Om snorgärsar och mörtar! Jag ser framför mig glupska käftar, vassa tänder, grymma blickar. Metaren tror att jag har problem med språket, och det har jag ju på sätt och vis. Han förklarar:

– *Ça ne mord pas,* det nappar inte.

Nej, det tycks vara rätt sällan det nappar. Men det är inte därför man metar i Frankrike.

Lorraine – slussar och slagfält

Efter Strasbourg vände vi västerut på den småskaliga Canal de la Marne au Rhin och genom Alsaces skogar och nyskördade åkrar där storkarna stod tätt. Så småningom slöt sig landskapet och blev skogsromantiskt och högt, så pass högt att kanalmyndigheterna på 1960-talet beslöt att ersätta de sjutton slussarna i Arzviller med en lift som på fem minuter lyfter båten 45 meter. Man kör in i en vattenfylld vagga som med hjälp av enorma motvikter tar en allt högre upp. Det är en märklig känsla att på sitt eget däck stiga över björktopparna och se vattnet långt under sig samtidigt som man undan för undan får gårdar och kyrktorn uppe på åsarna i ögonhöjd.

Och så gled vi in i Lorraine. Byar med namn som Xoaxange och Gondrexange ser mindre exotiska ut än de låter, men landskapet var vackert – betesmarker,

åkrar, lövskogsklädda kullar. Och tystnad. Man skulle kunna sälja den om det inte var för lärkorna över fälten och gnisslet från slussportarna.

– Om tredje världskriget bryter ut, stick till Lorraine, här händer allting fem år senare, sa en slussvakt till oss.

Så har det inte alltid varit. Inte så långt öster om vår färd gick Maginotlinjen. I nordväst hade vi Verduns slagfält. När vi om kvällen hade lagt till i Lagarde och handlat vad som fanns att handla i den minsta av butiker vid kajen gjorde vi en sväng genom byn. I dess ena ände låg en fransk krigskyrkogård från första världskriget, i dess andra ände en tysk. Kors vid kors i rader – och ändå vilar här bara en ringa del av de miljoner som stupade. När man ser namninskrifterna här och på de krigsmonument som finns i varenda by, om aldrig så liten, förstår man inte att det över huvud taget fanns några män kvar för striderna i andra världskriget två årtionden senare.

På andra sidan kanalen reste sig i en dunge en minnessten över de fallna i en division av den polska armén i Frankrike som just där i en bajonettattack slog tillbaka tyskarna en juninatt 1940.

Så mycket blod i dessa ängder där korna dåsar under träden.

När man sedan på kanalen möter engelsmän, holländare och tyskar i egna båtar, ett livat och öldrickande franskt fotbollslag i en pråm och polacker och tjecker som äntligen kan resa fritt och hyra båt, alla glatt hälsande på varandra i den gemenskap som slussandets små missöden för oss samman i, då känner man på allvar det storslagna med Europeiska unionen, alla dess brister och besvärligheter till trots.

Med båtliften i Arzviller lyfts ens många ton 45 meter på fem minuter. Man kör in i en vattenfylld vagga som med hjälp av motvikter glider uppför rampen.

Ett av Frankrikes tusentals krigsmonument. I nästan varje by möter man namnen på dess söner som fallit i första och andra världskriget.

De stora fabrikerna i Dombasle framställer salt till både matbord och vägar. Här dyker pråmarna upp igen.

Kanalen är till för fabrikerna

I Dombasle-sur-Meurthe reser sig Solvays sodafabriker och Salines du Midi et de l'Ests saltanläggningar. Här mötte vi de första pråmarna i yrkestrafik på mycket länge, och vi gladdes åt synen. Mil efter mil, sluss efter sluss genom fördrömd landsbygd är förtjusande, men pråmtrafiken är den enda garantin för att kanalerna verkligen ska kunna hållas öppna.

Men den höga blå himlen dolde orosmoln. Visserligen finns det fjorton tusen sätt att använda salt hade vi fått veta, och visserligen ligger sex av Frankrikes tio saltgruvor här i området där floden Meurthe slingrar sig utmed kanalen, men användningen av salt minskar och konkurrensen från utlandet är kännbar.

Vi lade till för natten i Varangéville, intill en bopråm under ett mirabellträd. Kanalbanken kantades av slitna hus, en gång bebodda av pråmfolk och arbetare. På andra sidan i Saint-Nicolas-de-Port strävade katedralens båda torn mot himlen, 85 och 87 meter och landets högsta. Mellan oss gick järnvägen. Vi såg det magnifika byggnadsverket strimlat av elledningar och stolpar och oupphörligen framrusande tåg.

– Här bor vi lugnt och bra, sa bopråmens ägare när han kunde göra sig hörd i en paus mellan två tåg. Jag känner pråmskepparna, varenda en, fortsatte han och vinkade till en som just passerade. Men ni skulle ha sett hur det var här förr! På sextiotalet hade Solvay etthundratjugosju pråmar, och i början av förra seklet låg de så tätt att man kunde gå på dem tvärs över kanalen, man fick öppna en gata när någon skulle ut. I dag är de bara en handfull. En och annan går med kaustiksoda till Arque nära Dunkerque – ni känner väl till det berömda kristallglaset från Arque?

En lång väg med hundratals slussar av Freycinetmått. Hur länge kan det pågå?

Kanalerna i Frankrike kantas inte bara av lövskog, odlingsmark och småstäder. Gång på gång har vi påmints om deras uppgift som transportleder för produkter av skilda slag – tegel, porslin, byggnadsmaterial, stål, kol, spannmål, vin, vegetabilisk olja. Och överallt har vi mötts av nedlagda fabriker, en gång vackra konstruktioner, där rutorna nu är krossade och där taket har störtat in. Vi har gått förbi kvarnar där rännan är tom och en doft av möglig säd kan anas genom den gistna inkörsporten, vi har passerat järnvägsstationer där visarna på stationsuret fallit bort och tiden upphört. Vi har tillbringat nätter i tystnad vid ödsliga lastkajer där ogräset tränger upp ur betongen och pråmnamnen som målats på muren nötts till oläslighet.

Det småskaliga välståndets tid är väl inte helt förbi, men det är inte längre beroende av småkanalerna.

Skönhet i förfallet. Nedlagda fabriker är ingen ovanlig syn längs kanalerna.

Rokoko och art nouveau

”Nancy, en vacker, gammal stad med en ärkebiskop, en fältmarskalk, gott hotell, fältmusik, glass och andra det civiliserade livets lyxartiklar.” Så uttalade sig skotten John MacGregor som på 1860-talet genomkorsade delar av Frankrike och Tyskland i sin kanot ”Rob Roy” och beskrev upplevelserna i sin bok ”En flodfärd i Europa”. Bortsett från de i dag intressanta skildringarna av *wie es gewesen* är boken i mycket en tröttande redogörelse över författarens dagliga sökande efter nattkvarter åt sin kanot och hans belåtenhet med värdshusvärdars och andra lågt stående landvarelsers beundran av hans lilla flytetyg.

Nancy erbjöd varken fältmarskalk eller fältmusik, men väl ett världsarv: *Place Stanislas,* torget som omges av 1700-talspalats, nyss renoverat så att luften skimrade runt den ljusa stenen och allt det förgyllda

Ett av världens vackraste torg. Place Stanislas i Nancy.

smidesjärnet. I dess mitt reser sig statyn över den kulturälskande Stanisław Leszczyński, som en gång med Karl XII:s hjälp blev kung av Polen för att raskt avsättas efter det svenska nederlaget vid Poltava, varefter han tog sin tillflykt till Kristianstad där han tillbringade något år under knappa omständigheter. När han senare skulle komma att bli svärfar till Ludvig XV fick han hertigdömet Lorraine att trösta sig med, och ett litet understöd från Sverige hade han också haft en tid. Den sanslöst vackra platsen har han låtit skapa. Nu satt studenter och turister vid hans fot i solen, och vid en av de plaskande springbrunnarna under en väldig Neptun ägnade sig en clochard åt en omsorgsfull tvagning av sina tår. *Place Stan* har något för envar.

Gästhamnen mitt i staden var livlig med både farande båtar och långliggande bopråmar. Och vid en av bryggorna låg en mörkgrön holländare med avbärarlist av kraftigt rep: ”Risette”, med våra vänner Taco och Jos och deras små hundar, som vi tidigare gått i sällskap med i Holland och som vakat över vår gamla ”Vanadis” när hon tillbringade en vinter på varv hos dem i Hellevoetsluis utanför Rotterdam. Varje gång vi skilts har vi sjungit ”We'll meet again, don't know where, don't know when”. Nu blev det alltså här – de visste att vi var i trakterna och hade inväntat oss.

– Vad ni gör, sa Taco, när de ett par dagar senare kastade loss, missa inte Nancy-skolan.

Nej, vi skulle ägna flera dagar åt stadens samlingar av den *art nouveau,* jugend, som skapats här och finns i sådan myckenhet att vi ett bra tag efteråt betraktade vår fortsatta vattenväg med glaskonstnärerna Daums och Gallés ögon. Näckrosor, ormbunkar, ödlor, svärdsliljor, kaveldun, trollsländor – allt vi såg utmed strandbrinkarna stiliserades i slingor och skimrande överfångseffekter.

En av Gallés mindre vaser, men vår!

Pont-à-Mousson, gatugodsets stamort

Överallt i Frankrike träder man på gatujärn från Pont-à-Mousson.

Fyra olika sorter av det mussipontaineska ölet. Det finns fler.

Bland alla mer eller mindre hemliga sällskap finner man även gatugodsspanarna, de som ägnar sig åt vad som på engelska kallas *drainspotting*. Medlemmar känns igen på att de går med sänkt blick för att kolla in gatubrunnarnas lock, de runda eller fyrkantiga plattor som andra tanklöst träder på. Vackra, ovanliga eller på annat sätt speciella brunnslock från världens alla hörn fotograferas och läggs ut på nätet.

I Sverige kommer gatugodset av segjärn från Tierp och Alvesta eller importeras från Furnes och Ulefoss i Norge.

I Frankrike härstammar så gott som varenda *plaque d'égout* från Pont-à-Mousson. Det gör drainspottandet i detta land mindre omväxlande. I gengäld fylls man av en stark känsla när på egen köl tagit sig till de franska brunnslockens urkälla, Saint-Gobains gjuterier vid stranden av Moselle. Vi kunde överbringa systerliga hälsningar från Ulefoss järnverk vid den smala och skogsdunkla Telemarks kanal, som vi en gång slussat oss uppför.

I Pont-à-Mousson finns också ett bryggeri. Vi förväntade oss alltså att komma till en industriort när vi nalkades den mäktiga stenbron som förbinder stadens delar, men vad som fångade blicken var den ljusa gotiska kyrkan Saint-Martin vid det ena brofästet och där bortom klostret l'Abbaye des Prémontrés, i dag konferenscenter – och vem skulle inte vilja konferera i en sådan miljö? Det är svårt att föreställa sig att stora kvarter låg i grus och aska efter andra världskrigets bombangrepp och efter de förödande striderna då

Pont-à-Mousson vid Moselle. Bron ska passeras under de två gula romberna.

en amerikansk armé under pansargeneralen Patton lyckades undsätta staden.

Vi förtöjde i den skyddade gästhamnen bland några bopråmar och gick upp till Saint-Martin, som i ena väggen har en grotta med en förnämlig Kristi gravläggning: tolv skulpturer i detaljrika 1400-talsdräkter böjer sig mot den döde, och själv står man som betraktare av en sorgescen inom stadens högre borgerskap. I grottans tak svävar små änglar – som vita fladdermöss, sa Skepparn.

Så mycket gravläggning och gatugods krävde något stärkande. Vi släpade ombord ett antal olika flaskor av det mussipontaineska ölet. Jo, invånarna i Pont-à-Mousson kallas *mussipontains*.

Att välja bland dessa buteljer var en svårighet som vi kunde övervinna. Vederkvickta blev vi också.

Försök till farväl

Först nästa vår skulle vi börja vända stäven norrut och hemåt, men nu i september insåg vi att vi inte skulle hinna tillbaka till Saint-Jean-de-Losne för vintern. Ett vänligt tyskt par rekommenderade sin hemmahamn Schweich vid Mosel, norr om Trier, och efter några telefonsamtal ordnades det plats för oss där. Vi fortsatte på Moselle, som floden heter på franska, upp till den trevliga staden Metz, där man firade sensommarens mirabellfest med försäljning av de gula plommonen i allehanda inkarnationer – kompott, likör, marmelad, tårtfyllnad, leksaker. På gatorna mötte man vandrande mirabeller i gul plysch.

Ingen form av mirabell förmådde emellertid hålla oss kvar, och några dagar senare hade vi tagit oss upp till gränsslussen Apache. Nu skulle vi lägga Frankrike bakom oss för gott.

Vemod fyllde våra hjärtan när vi gick vi upp i byn för att ta farväl av landet. Det sista vi skulle se erbjöd också en märklig déjà-vu-upplevelse: den gropiga vägen ner från tyska gränsen, bensinmacken med sina skraltiga pumpar och urblekta affischer, husen med grågröna flagnande fönsterluckor på sned på sina hakar, vedhögarna – en fransk by som vilken som helst, men just denna hade vi bestämt sett förut. När?

För tjugo år sedan hade vi bilat i den tyska Moseldalen på väl underhållna vägar mellan överprydliga korsvirkesstäder. Sonen, sju år, hade förstått att vi var nära franska gränsen och insisterade på att få åka över den. Det var just här, i denna backe ner mot den ruffiga byn, som hans barnaröst hade brutits i förtvivlad besvikelse:

– Är det här Frankrike?

I hans föreställning var Frankrike ett enda stort Versailles.

Mirabellfest i Metz. Lorraines gula plommon dyker upp i skiftande gestalt – som marmelad, likör eller på två ben.

Frankrike har ett sextiotal kärnkraftverk, men i byarna är det veden som står för värmen om vintern.

"Je ne peux pas quitter la France"

Mosel blev allt vackrare medan vi långsamt stävade norrut. Vi gick genom Luxemburg och in i Tyskland, vi passerade Trier och fortsatte en sväng upp till Bernkastel. Nätterna kunde nypa till med kyla men dagarna var varma. Uppe på höjderna började det komma inslag av guld och rost i lövskogen, och nedanför, i de oändliga vinodlingarnas gröna trasmattor med ränder på olika ledder, pågick vinskörden med människor som klängde i branterna med behållare på ryggen. Det låg en doft av vindrank över floddalen.

I de docksöta byarna avlöste vinfesterna varandra med sång och musik och dans på gatorna. Vi drack oavbrutet moselvin av olika tappning, alla härliga, några himmelska. Trevnaden ångade, vi blev överallt hjärtligt mottagna, gästhamnarna var välordnade.

Men det var just det att vi var hänvisade till de fåtaliga gästhamnarna. Ingenstans på denna flod där de jättelika pråmarna drar förbi dygnet runt kunde vi kila in oss i en gammal pil eller slå ner våra spikar i strandbanken eller ens lägga oss framför en sluss på kvällen.

Vi började redan sakna Frankrike. Skulle vi aldrig mer förtöja mitt ute på landsbygden med bara ett par nyfikna vita kor som kvällsunderhållning? Skulle vi aldrig mer vid frukosten på akterdäck hälsas av en lantman på dragvägen med ett galant "God morgon, *M'sieur-dame,* vackert här, inte sant? Jag inbjuder er till en liten promenad i min fårhage innan ni drar vidare". Skulle vi aldrig mer råka i upplivande gräl med en slussvakt eller tvärtom i samförstånd utbyta synpunkter på kanalväsendet eller hönsen medan slussen långsamt fylldes?

Skulle vi aldrig mer röra oss i Saint-Jean-de-Losne i den stora familjen av kanalälskare från världens alla hörn och byta saker och tjänster och avsluta arbetsdagen över ett glas i de ljumma kvällarna? Aldrig vakna av gnisslet från Blanquarts kran när båtgrannar sjösattes eller togs upp och aldrig se hur pråmar kom och gick och slussades i och ur torrdockan? Aldrig mer ankra på en flod med hägrar i strandsnåren och grodknorr och sävsångare, inte kunna ta en simtur före middagen på svaj?

När "Vanadis" gick upp på land i Schweich såg jag Skepparn i ögonen.

– *Je ne peux pas quitter la France.* Jag kan inte lämna Frankrike.

Mot Saint-Jean-de-Losne nästa vår! Gulmåran därhemma får vänta.

Hur gör man?

Kanalfakta

Hur många franska kanaler finns det? Vilka kan man gå på? Vart vänder man sig om man vill gå på dem? Kan man hyra båt? Vilka handböcker behöver man? Måste man kunna tala franska? Och får man se närmare på "Vanadis"?

I det här avsnittet försöker vi svara på några frågor av det här slaget.

En lastpråm av det franska standardmåttet Freycinet på väg nedför Saône – en behaglig flod som i sin norra del erbjuder tilläggsplatser lite varstans utmed stränderna och svalkande bad när sommarvärmen inbjuder till det.

Sedan länge har yrkestrafiken lämnat de mindre kanalerna.
I dag har fritidsbåtarna dessa vattenleder för sig själva.

Små kanaler och stora

Frankrike har näst Ryssland det största nätet av vattenvägar i Europa. För den hågade kanalfararen står mer än 800 mil till buds, från små pittoreska antika system till transportleder för dagens stora pråmar, som kan vara upp till 190 meter långa.

Många sträckor är en förening av flod och kanal. Man färdas på floden för att emellanåt ledas in i en liten kanalstump med en sluss, medan floden strömmar förbi intill och kastar sig utför ett vattenfall. Så är det på Seine, Marne, Meuse, Doubs och Saône. På andra sträckor går man på grävda kanaler som då och då förenar sig med den flod som förser kanalen med vatten, som Canal du Nivernais som ständigt möter och lämnar Yonne.

Redan romarna använde vattenvägarna för att transportera varor – vin, säd, salt. Den första franska kanalen för trafik av någon betydelse kom till under 1600-talet, Riquets Canal du Midi, som i södra Frankrike förbinder Atlanten med Medelhavet. Det bygget var ett ofattbart stort projekt med grävande genom landskapet och anläggande av konstgjorda sjöar som uppifrån höjderna skulle förse kanalen med vatten.

Erfarenheterna därifrån togs till vara och utvecklades när man under 1700-talet drog upp planerna för de kanaler som från Bourgognes skogsområden skulle förse det växande Paris med timmer och ved till eldning. För att nu inte tala om allt vin. Med franska revolutionen kom arbetena av sig. Först i början av 1800-talet stod Canal de Bourgogne och Canal du Nivernais klara. Med sjöar och dammar, med vattenledningar från floder och med tunnlar genom bergen klättrar de flera hundra meter upp genom landskapet för att sedan sänka sig lika mycket.

Under slutet av 1800-talet ökade behovet av transporter, och då insåg man att det var nödvändigt att ge kanaler och slussar enhetliga mått. Industriministern Charles de Freycinet arbetade fram en standard för pråmarna: maximalt 38,5 meter långa, 5,1 meter breda och med ett djupgående på 1,8 meter. Slussarnas djup är vanligtvis mellan 2,5 och 4 meter.

Många äldre kanaler byggdes om efter dessa mått, och enligt fransk logik stämmer de nästan överallt, men bara nästan, vilket förklarar att "Vanadis" med sina 1,1 meters djupgående ibland har fått plöja botten. Då har det bara varit att vänta på att någon någonstans högre upp ska slussa och därmed höja vattennivån en aning.

Annars är det just kanalerna med Freycinetmått som tilltalar fritidsskepparen. Pråmtrafiken är lindrig eller rent av obefintlig och kanalerna går nästan helt och hållet genom natursköna områden. Färdas man i Frankrike behöver man över huvud taget sällan ge sig ut på lederna för det stora tonnaget, *le grand gabarit.* De utgör bara 20 procent av de franska vattenvägarna.

På 1950-talet fick Europa en gemensam standard för de stora lederna. Pråmtrafiken hade blivit gränsöverskridande och behovet av billiga transporter på större fartyg hade bara vuxit. Visserligen har de vattenburna transporterna länge har stått i skuggan av både järnväg och långtradare, men i dag har de stora lederna ökat sin kapacitet och har slussar som är 200 meter långa med plats för pråmar som lastar upp till 11 000 ton. Lyften per sluss kan vara på upp

Europas vattenvägar är inte bara små idylliska kanaler utan också storslagna transportleder som befars av jättepråmar. Här en bjässe på nästan 200 meter på Mosel. Det är samma längd som hos de stora Finlandsbåtarna.

till 20 meter och mer. Transporterna från Atlanthamnarna in mot Centraleuropa sker i dag ofta per båt. På två dygn kan en stor pråm som går dag och natt genom de alltid bemannade slussarna ta sig från Rotterdam till Berlin eller Basel. Det innebär att järnvägen har fått en stark konkurrent.

Planer finns att bygga ut vattenvägarna för större tonnage österut mot Polen och Tjeckien. Rhen och Donau är redan sammanbyggda över floden Main. Man kan nu färdas med större pråmar hela vägen mellan Atlantkusten och Svarta havet. Till 2020 räknar man med att transportvolymen ska vara fördubblad mot i dag.

Ett tungt argument för pråmtransporterna är förstås miljövinsterna.

En större pråm motsvarar 200 till 400 långtradare. En långtradare släpper ut omkring 400 gånger mer avgaser per transporterat ton än en sådan pråm. Den totala miljökostnaden är sex gånger så hög för vägtransporter som för pråmtrafik.

Miljövinsterna med kanaltransporterna har länge varit uppenbara, och varje fransk industriminister har talat vackert om satsningar på att bygga ut kanalnätet. Men, som många slussvaktare fnyser, så är det mycket prat och lite handling.

Framför allt finns det behov av en förbindelse mel-

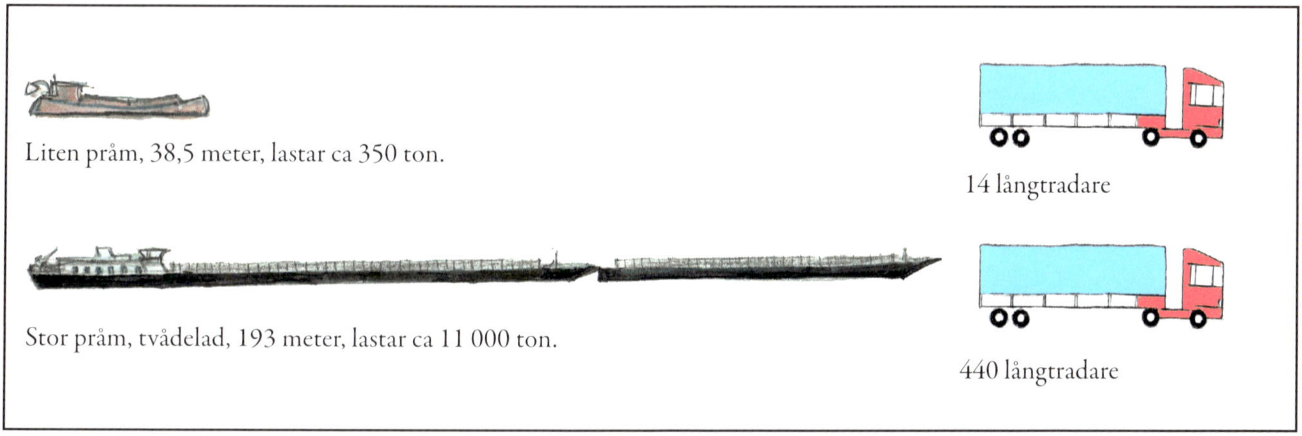

Kanal eller landsväg?

lan Rhen och Saône-Rhône. Canal du Rhône au Rhin som mestadels utgörs av floden Doubs, som slingrar genom Juras sköna berg, duger inte till godstrafik. De gröna i regionen säger ”Rör inte vår natur”, samtidigt som godståg och lastbilar bidrar till klimatförstöringen.

Och visst är det ett dilemma. Mer kreativa miljövänner diskuterar en dragning ett bra stycke därifrån. Det skulle skona floddalen från raka vattenvägar och jätteslussar.

De smala och slusstäta kanalerna, som Canal de Bourgogne, Canal du Nivernais och Canal des Houillères kan inte räkna med någon ny framtid för godstransporter. Vi kanalälskare som färdas där för nöjes skull får vara glada så länge de franska myndigheterna anser det självklart att de ska hållas öppna. En hård satsning på hyrbåtar, gästhamnar med bekvämligheter och restauranger och dessutom på rejäla slussavgifter skulle möjligen kunna driva upp lönsamheten. Men vi som valt kanalfarandet som livsform är tacksamma så länge vi får glida fram på vattenvägar som ligger bortanför turism och kommersialism, vattenvägar som går genom fransk vardag och ibland till och med utanför tiden.

Till Medelhavet kanalvägen

Många båtfarare drömmer om att glida omkring på Europas kanaler. Andra vill nå Medelhavet utan att behöva gå till havs. Från Sverige finns det flera leder att välja på för att nå systemet av vattenvägar, men vanligast är förmodligen att gå in vid Travemünde i Tyskland. Har man segelbåt mastar man av här. Många skickar i dag sin mast med lastbil till Medelhavshamnen för att slippa ha den ombord under slussandet.

Från Travemünde till Port-Saint-Louis nära Marseille är det nästan 200 mil med omkring 150 slussar.

Från Travemünde tar man den trevliga Elbe–Lübeck-kanalen söderut, korsar den breda floden Elbe och går vidare på Elbe Seitenkanal. Den slutar i Mittellandkanal, som är den stora förbindelsen mellan Rhen och Berlin. Man går västerut på denna led som är rätt trafikerad men ändå förvånansvärt vacker och behaglig. Den övergår i Dortmund–Ems-kanalen som mynnar i Rhen.

Här sker ett viktigt vägval. Antingen går man uppför den strida och hårt trafikerade Rhen till Koblenz och viker av på Mosel, något som kräver en kraftig motor eftersom motströmmen på Rhen tidvis kan uppgå till ca 4 knop (ca 7 kilometer i timmen). Eller också följer man Rhen medströms till den beskedligare floden Maas i Holland och går på den söderut över Belgien och in i Frankrike, där den heter Meuse. Den vägen är något längre men äger också stor skönhet och passerar många intressanta städer. En fördel med det senare alternativet är att man därifrån kan ta en sväng över Nederländerna som är ett kanalland av klass.

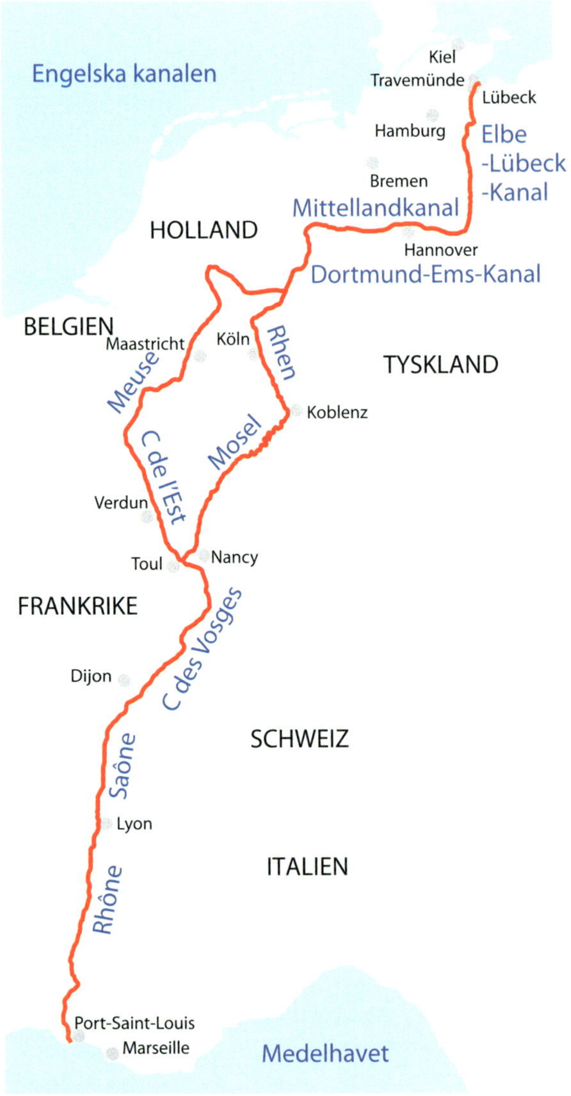

Om man ska direkt ner till Medelhavet går man från Mosel eller Meuse, vilken man nu kommer från, över staden Toul in på Canal de l'Est, även kallad Canal des Vosges, som efter en lövskogsrik och vacker sträckning mynnar i floden Saône, som likaledes är vacker och dessutom badbar och på vilken man i dess norra del kan knyta fast i ett träd för natten.

Saône rinner söderut och flyter samman med Rhône i Lyon. Rhône var förr fruktad för sin vildhet men är numera tämligen tuktad, bland annat genom ett antal jätteslussar. Efter omkring 30 mil på Rhône är man nere i Port-Saint-Louis som brukar vara utgångspunkten för vidare seglingar på Medelhavet. Här finns även flera varv för den som vill lämna sin båt över vintern.

Den som vill göra avstickare in på andra franska vattenvägar har en mängd alternativ att välja mellan, vare sig man kommer från Mosel eller från Meuse. (Karta finns på sidan 17.)

"Vanadis" på Canal des Houillères.

Är man lysten på Paris finns det flera vägar dit, och därifrån kan man ta sig till Saône och Rhône på fem skilda vattenleder, alla med sitt behag, nämligen Canal de Briare, Canal du Nivernais, Canal de Bourgogne, Canal de la Marne à la Saône och Canal de la Marne au Rhin.

Vill man inte gå så långt västerut men ändå se lite mer kan man från Mosel söder om Trier i Tyskland välja den skogsromantiska Saar, som efter en kort industristräcka runt Saarbrücken går över i den franska gamla kolkanalen Canal des Houillères, en ljuvlig led som går genom ett böljande landskap. Den slutar i Canal de la Marne au Rhin, och då kan man välja om man vill gira styrbord och skynda ner på Canal des Vosges eller gira babord och gå över Strasbourg, ett stycke uppför Rhen och sedan Canal du Rhône au Rhin och floden Doubs genom Juras dalgångar för att hamna på Saône.

Det som begränsar farandet – förutom klimatets nycker med för lite vatten eller för mycket, liksom de årliga reparationsarbetena – är den egna båtens mått.

Det maximala djupet i de små kanalerna, bland dem genomfartskanalen Canal des Vosges, brukar anges till 1,8 meter men kan vara mindre. Broarna tillåter 3,50 meters höjd men det stämmer heller inte alltid. På Canal du Nivernais är de på ett par ställen 2,7 meter samtidigt som djupet bara är 1,2 meter. Båtägare med mått som går utanför dessa kan råka ut för hårdhänta överraskningar.

Innan man ger sig i väg är det tillrådligt att kontrollera både det aktuella läget och det väntade med VNF, *Voies navigables de France,* den organisation som ansvarar för Frankrikes vattenvägar. Uppgifter om avstängda sträckor och andra restriktioner finner man under VNF:s hemsida, *www.vnf.fr.* Hos VNF köper man också *la vignette*, tillståndet att befara vattenvägarna. För att få köra egen båt på de europeiska kanalsystemen krävs ett kanalintyg, *certificates of competence.* Denna examen hanteras av Nämnden för båtlivsutbildning, NFB i Stockholm.

Om man vill prova på kanallivet kan man också hyra båt. Uthyrningsföretag finner man på nätet. Bland de större kan nämnas Crown Blue Line, Connoisseur, Locaboat och Navifrance. Ingen form av förarbevis behövs för att köra hyrbåtarna, de är *sans permis,* men någon båtvana bör man ha för att inte drabbas av panik i slussarna – eller skapa sådan hos medslussare.

Till sist en fråga vi får då och då: Behöver man kunna franska för att färdas i Frankrike?

Man klarar sig oftast med engelska, några nyttiga franska fraser och termer samt gester. De slussvaktande studenterna vill dessutom ofta gärna öva sin engelska. Båtuthyrarna har alltid engelskspråkig personal. Båtfarare man möter talar oftast engelska. Men annars är det franska som gäller. Den som någon gång blivit snäst i Paris kan på den franska landsbygden glädja sig åt både uppskattning av och överseende med alla försök att rådbråka språket.

Kartor och handböcker

Från sluss till sluss är ingen handbok som beskriver franska kanaler. Sådana finns det redan flera, och de kartböcker man ändå måste ha för färderna har uppgifter som behövs för kanalfarandet. Ett problem är att vissa fakta blir inaktuella, och många är de tankställen eller mataffärer vi sökt efter som i dag visat sig nedlagda. Även Frankrike förändrar sig.

Två franska kartförlag dominerar kanalmarknaden: *Navicarte* och *Éditions du Breil.* Båda har bra beskrivningar över de olika kanalsträckorna med kartor, uppgifter om djup och brohöjder, slussarnas öppettider och mått, tilläggsplatser, vattenposter, matbutiker och sevärdheter. Texterna är på franska, tyska och engelska.

Vilken serie man väljer är en smaksak, men eftersom de inte riktigt täcker samma områden kan det vara svårt att byta när man en gång börjat med den ena. I valet av sevärdheter är de rätt enstämmiga och även ensidiga; man kan undra om redaktörerna tror att kanalfarare hyser ett omättligt intresse enbart för kyrkobyggnader. Komplettering med en bra turistguide för området, till exempel *Michelins gröna serie,* är således en bra investering. Det tyska förlaget *Edition Maritim* ger ut utmärkta böcker om vissa franska områden, som Moselle och Canal du Midi. För översiktlig planering kan en kanalkarta över Europas kanaler vara bra. En sådan ges ut av *www.euromapping.com* och heter *European Waterways.*

Bibeln i ämnet är *Cruising French Waterways* av Hugh McKnight på förlaget Sheridan House, 4:e upplagan 2005. Denna bjässe på 296 sidor skildrar alla Frankrikes kanaler med uppgifter om längd, antal slussar, tilläggsplatser, historia och sevärdheter.

Ett verk som i detalj beskriver varje kanal- och flodsträcka är *Inland Waterways of France* av David Edwards-May på förlaget Imray. Boken är av intresse om båten går djupt eller är hög eftersom det begränsar framkomligheten. Annars innehåller den väl många detaljer för att vara intressant för en fritidsbesättning.

En handbok med olika kanalsträckors längd och antal slussar är David Jeffersons *Through the French Canals.*

Informativ är Carl Erik Tovås *Handbok för kanalfarare* (2001). På webbplatsen *www.algonet.se/~carlto/* finns utdrag med uppgifter och råd om färdvägar, bestämmelser och annat viktigt för kanalfarandet i Europa.

Trevliga men inaktuella är Roger Pilkingtons olika kanalbeskrivningar. En del av dem hittar man antikvariskt.

Trevlig och innehållsrik är också Ebbe Gustafssons *Det nya båtlivet – följ med på Europas kanaler,* fastän vissa förhållanden har ändrats sedan boken kom ut 1992.

Vill man till sist möta en stämningsbild av pråmlivet från förr rekommenderas George Simenons deckare *Maigret och pråmdragaren* ("Le charretier de La Providence") från 1930.

Kartor och böcker kan köpas hos Nautiska Magasinet i Stockholm eller på internetbokhandeln *www.amazon.com* eller AWN i Tyskland *www.awniemeyer.de.*

Den officiella informationen om de franska kanalernas öppettider, reparationer och dylikt finner man hos *Voies navigables de France: www.vnf.fr.*

VANADIS
GRUNO 32 E Royal

”Vanadis” från för till akter

Den ”Vanadis” vi skaffade oss i Holland är en typisk holländare.

Hon är byggd i stål, vilket är en fördel när hettan slår till. Stål leder både värme och kyla. Vattnet i kanalerna blir aldrig lika varmt som luften, och även om däcket kan bli brännhett på dagen blir nätterna aldrig outhärdliga.

”Vanadis” är 12 meter lång, 3,80 bred, sticker 1,10 djupt och väger 12 ton. Man kunde tro att en så tung båt är besvärlig att hantera vid tilläggningar och andra manövrer. Men vår erfarenhet är än så länge det motsatta. ”Vanadis” rör sig värdigt och låter sig inte så lätt påverkas av strömvirvlar och vindkast.

I det väl tilltagna motorrummet tronar en Ivecodiesel på 120 hästar som kan driva henne upp i 8 knop – en hastighet vi inte behöver på kanaler och floder där vi håller 3, men ändå så låg att vi säkert kommer att förargas när vi en gång ska börja gå utmed Skandinaviens långa kuster. Bränsletankarna rymmer 600 liter, vattentanken 500. Värmesystemet – för det är

Planering i den rymliga salongen. Den stängda dörren leder till akterkajutan. Trappan till höger för upp till akterdäck.

Med dinetten får man två sittutrymmen. Det räcker märkvärdigt bra när behovet av ett eget rum gör sig gällande.

minsann inte alltid trettio grader i luften – går på diesel och ger varmluft.

I det behagliga klimat som ändå oftast råder nere på kontinenten vistas vi så mycket vi kan på det stora akterdäcket. Där finns en styrplats, så Skepparn behöver inte vara förvisad till inomhusvistelse. Akterdäcket ligger högt, lite som på en kogg, och man färdas majestätiskt ovanför kanalbanken med god utsikt över landskapet och inte nere i ett dike. Från akterdäcket går en stege ner till en badbrygga med utedusch.

Fördäcket är också en trevlig plats att sträcka ut sig på, och där fläktar det under gång. Det rymmer också våra oumbärliga cyklar.

Även om "Vanadis" är vårt hem om sommaren har vi inte, som många andra, dragit ombord en mängd blomlådor med pelargoner. Sådant ser mycket tilltalande ut, men vi har försökt att behålla en mer marin karaktär. Ett litet kryddland i krukor har vi i alla fall, och det är en njutning att bryta doftande kvistar av timjan och rosmarin, för att inte tala om dill, *aneth*, som nästan inte går att hitta i Frankrike. (Det klagade redan Karin Larsson på när hon hade hushåll i konstnärskolonin i Grez-sur-Loing på 1880-talet.)

Trappan från akterdäck ner till "Vanadis" inre landar i salongen – ett pretentiöst ord för det trivsamma rum som hyser en långsoffa, ett bord, bokhyllor, radio och ännu en styrplats. Inredningen är i gulaktig ek, sofftyget blått.

En halvtrappa ner från salongen ligger pentryt med en så kallad dinett – en matplats för fyra personer, mot vår första förmodan både praktisk och trevlig när flera vill delta i matlagningen, vare sig det gäller att hacka saker vid bordet eller bara hänga över ett glas vin.

Spisen har vanliga gaslågor. Mikrovågsugnen slängde vi ut – man får vara rädd om elen – och installerade i stället ett skåp för kryddor och andra intressanta burkar som våra gäster inte kunnat motstå under sina inköpsturer.

I fören har gästerna sin hytt med den ena bädden ovanpå den andra, som i en tågkupé. I akterkajutan har vi själva en dubbelkoj. Akterspegeln har en glaslucka, och till morgnarnas nöjen hör att från kojen titta ut över vattnet och se fören på en pråm eller konversera en sothöna som intagit badbryggan. Man har alltid en ny tavla inom fönsterramen.

I en båt som är ett hem har vi förstås också toalett med tank och ett litet duschrum. Men inte tvättmaskin. Vad avsaknaden av en sådan kan leda till berättas om i kapitlet "Tvättstugor".

"Vanadis" är som sig förstår trivsam, men i sina detaljer inte särskilt fiffigt inredd. Som seglare är vi vana vid att varje litet utrymme ombord tagits till vara för stuvning och förvaring. Konstruktören i Zoutkamp såg mer till de yttre linjerna, och de är eleganta, men vi stönar ibland över alla dödutrymmen som hade kunnat utnyttjas. Å andra sidan hindras vi av detta från att dra på oss för mycket. Ändå har vi börjat tappa greppet om vad vi har stuvat undan, och var. "Vanadis" ruvar redan på hemligheter.

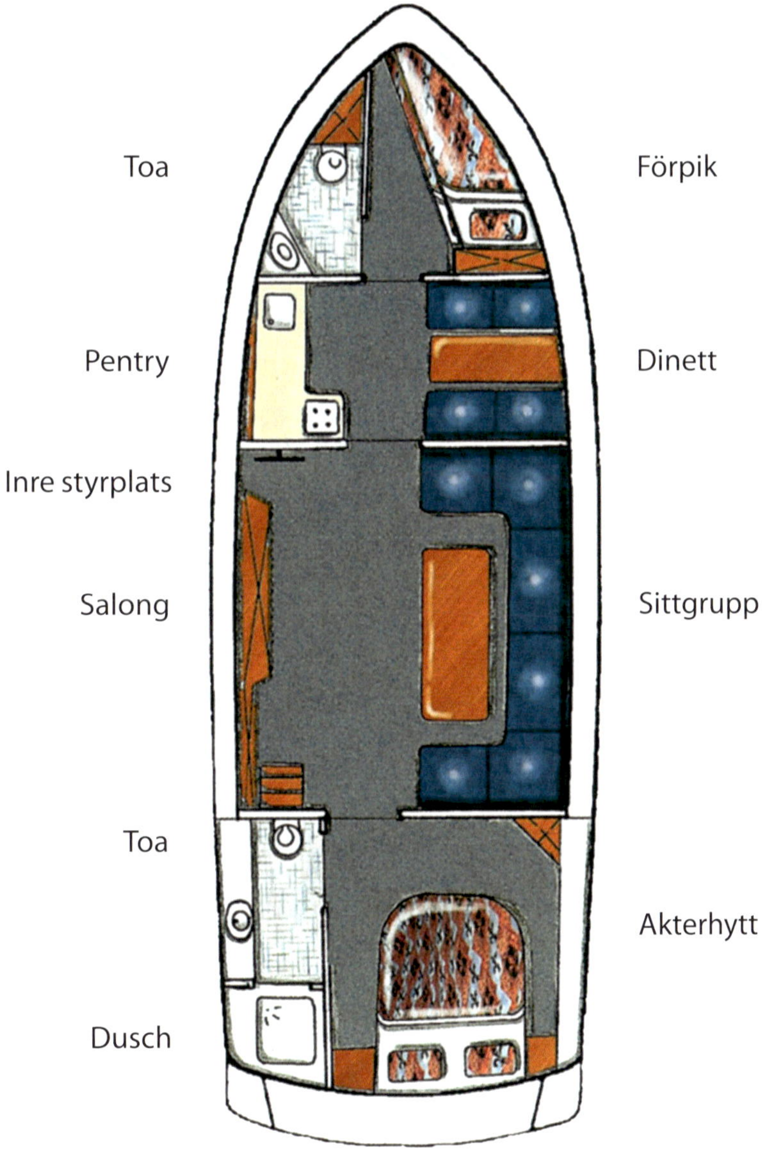
Toa
Förpik
Pentry
Dinett
Inre styrplats
Salong
Sittgrupp
Toa
Akterhytt
Dusch

Pråmen "Charlotte-Anne" på väg på Canal de l'Est-Meuse.

Tacksägelser

Vi avslutar med en sida med tacksägelser till allt och alla som bidragit till att våra färder blivit vad de blivit.

Det första tacket går till Göran Schildt, som med sin ketch ”Daphne” genomfor Frankrike redan 1948. Hans skildring ”Önskeresan” väckte tidigt vår lust att färdas på kanaler. Den boken och hans följande har fått en vid läsekrets att förstå att resor inte bara är en serie händelser och förflyttningar utan än mer möten med människor, kultur och historia.

I dag kan ”Daphne” beskådas i Åbo, där hon utgör en attraktion bland museifartygen. Ombord på ”Vanadis” har vi en korkskruv med handtag av träslaget peroba som vår unge vän båtbyggaren Jonatan Reuter, som medverkat vid restaureringen av ”Daphne”, förfärdigat av ett litet överblivet stycke från hennes bordläggning. Göran Schildt har uttryckt sitt gillande, tillägger vi för säkerhets skull.

VNF, Voies navigables de France, har vår stora erkänsla både för så gott som undantagslöst älskvärt bemötande och för den uthållighet med vilken organisationen bedriver sisyfosarbetet att försöka hålla åldrande kanalbankar och slussar i skick. Måtte ingen tänka tanken att kanalsystemet måste bli ekonomiskt lönsamt på varje sträcka. Vad Frankrike bjuder kanalfararna saknar motstycke i världen.

Slussvakter av alla temperament och sinnelag tackas för de upplevelser de skänkt oss.

Blanquarts varv i Saint-Jean-de-Losne, liksom kapellmakerskan och soffomkläderskan Catherine Rassalle, ska ha ett särskilt tack från ”Vanadis”.

Vi tackar förstås alla goda båtgrannar till lands och kanals. De följeslagare som särskilt nämns i boken är Jos och Taco Mesdag på ”Risette”, Hans Mijnlieff och Carien de Vries på ”Arend”, Malcolm och Lucie Walker på ”Body & Soul” och Barbara och Jerry Kahn på ”Vivante”.

De av våra gästande vänner som förekommer i boken är Bertil Tillander och Annika Eronn (Gasten och Kockan, Urbesättningen) som också medverkat med goda råd vid den tekniska framställningen av boken, Birgitta Lindgren och Unn Hellsten (Väninnorna), Ann-Margret Rydell, Helen Sigeland, Anders Bodegård (Översättaren), vår son Ulf samt Lars och Marianne Sköld som transporterat hem våra champagneflaskor. Vi tackar dem och alla andra här onämnda gäster som förljuvat vår tillvaro ombord.

Till våra vänner räknar vi också Astrid, Saskia, Jetta, Taka, Ted, Spud och övriga vovvar som bidragit till vår dagliga doggy-fix.

Ett särskilt tack riktas till Nils Degerman på Norstedts/Prisma, som oförtröttligt kommit med friska synpunkter på formgivningen.

Sist men framför allt tackar vi alla fransmän som skänkt oss trevliga och givande pratstunder, som vi druckit ett och annat glas med och ofta fått hjälp av i vardagliga situationer. Har man en gång börjat resa i Frankrike är det svårt att lämna landet. Frågan är om vi någonsin kommer att lyckas med det.

Skogsensamhet och fågelsång. Canal des Houillères i Lorraine.